DOLLY IS DEAD

...

THE GARDEN PLOT

Sarah Deane 7 and 8

DUET

DOLLY IS DEAD
...
THE GARDEN PLOT

J. S. Borthwick

FELONY & MAYHEM PRESS • NEW YORK

All the characters and events portrayed in this work are fictitious.

DOLLY IS DEAD/THE GARDEN PLOT
Sarah Deane 7 and 8

PRINTING HISTORY
Dolly Is Dead
First edition (St. Martin's): 1995
The Garden Plot
First edition (St. Martin's): 1997

Felony & Mayhem Duet edition: 2025

Copyright © 1995 and © 1997 by J. S. Borthwick

All rights reserved

ISBN: 978-1-63194-334-8 (paperback)
978-1-63194-335-5 (ebook)

Manufactured in the United States of America

Cataloging-in-Publication information for this book
is available from the Library of Congress.

The icon above says you're holding a copy of a book in the Felony & Mayhem "Traditional" category. We think of these books as classy cozies, with little gunplay or gore but often a fair amount of humor and, usually, an intrepid amateur sleuth. If you enjoy this book, you may well like other "Traditional" titles from Felony & Mayhem Press.

For more about these books, and other Felony & Mayhem titles, or to place an order, please visit our website at

www.FelonyAndMayhem.com

Other "Traditional" titles from
FELONY & MAYHEM

NATHAN ALDYNE
Vermilion
Cobalt
Slate
Canary

J.S. BORTHWICK
The Case of the Hook-Billed Kites/
The Down East Murders
The Student Body/Bodies of Water
Dude on Arrival/The Bridled Groom

JOHN NORMAN HARRIS
The Weird World of Wes Beattie

DANIEL STASHOWER
Elephants in the Distance

CAST OF CHARACTERS

SARAH DEANE — *Bowmouth College teaching fellow, wife of Alex*

ALEX MCKENZIE — *Physician, husband of Sarah*

MRS. ANTHONY DOUGLAS (*Lavinia*) — *Grandmother of Sarah*

MRS. ARTHUR BEAUGARD (*Elena*) — *Matriarch of Great Oaks*

DOLLY BEAUGARD — *Daughter of Mrs. Beaugard, deceased*

MASHA BEAUGARD — *Sister of Dolly*

ALICE BEAUGARD — *Sister of Dolly*

ELIOT BEAUGARD — *Brother of Dolly*

PROFESSOR LENOX COBB — *Brother of Mrs. Beaugard*

JONATHAN EPSTEIN	*Son of Alice and Alan Epstein*
ALAN EPSTEIN	*Former husband of Alice, father of Jonathan*
CAROLINE BEAUGARD	*Wife of Eliot Beaugard*
COLIN BEAUGARD	*Son of Eliot and Caroline*
WEBB GATTLING	*Friend of Alice, cousin of Parson*
PARSON GATTLING	*Cousin of Webb*
GEORGE FITTS	*Sergeant, CID, Maine State Police*
MIKE LAAKA	*Deputy Sheriff Investigator*
KATIE WATERS	*Deputy Sheriff*

This one is for Maddie

Many thanks to ABCDEF Books in Camden for assistance in the matter of auction prices for rare books.

DOLLY IS DEAD

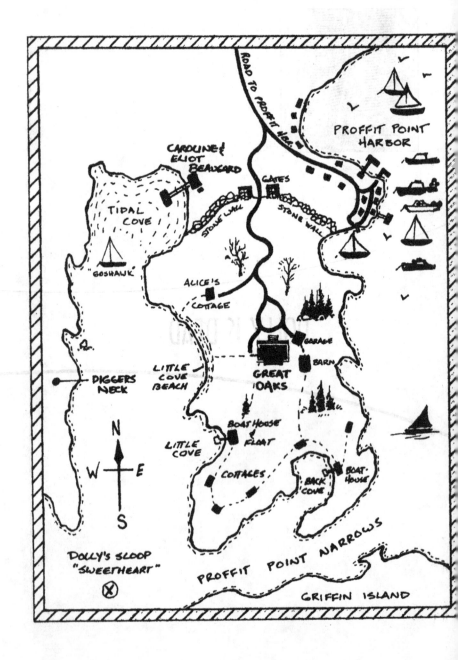

Chapter One

Throw out the Life-Line to danger fraught men,
Sinking in anguish where you've never been,
Winds of temptation and billows of woe,
Will soon hurl them out where the dark waters flow.
Throw out the Life-Line, someone is drifting away,
Throw out the Life-Line, throw out the Life-Line,
Someone is sinking today.
 —Rev. Edward S. Ufford,
  "Throw Out the Life-Line," third verse

THE BODY OF MARSDEN Gattling, pushed by a southwest wind and an incoming tide, rolled onto the seaweed-covered rocks of Little Cove one Thursday afternoon in late September. This untoward arrival on the shores of Proffit Point created among local residents neither surprise nor alarm. In fact, most of the sentiments expressed were those of relief together with an unseemly gladness. When this corpse was followed the next morning—Friday, September thirtieth—by that of his brother, Edward ("Junior") Gattling, the positive feelings animated by the first arrival were reaffirmed.

"Well, that's two of the buggers," announced Tad Bugelski, local harbormaster, as he watched with satisfaction the stuffing of Junior into the black plastic body bag.

"Two down and some to go," said a watching lobsterman.

"Nah," said Tad, who was a short, stocky man with buzz-cut gray hair and the smashed nose of a former boxer. "This'll take the starch out of the Gattlings for a while, anyway. Those two guys should have known better. Probably poaching lobsters, cutting traps loose, or making coke deals. Chugging around in the middle of the night in an open skiff with an old, cranky motor. Found it this morning on a ledge; empty bottle of whiskey rolling around."

"So they went over the side?" suggested the lobsterman.

"Anyone's guess—but the motor was left wide open and it was out of gas. No life jackets aboard. Or on the bodies. Damn fools."

Tad turned to the dark-haired man standing next to him. "So, Alex, death by drowning? No foul-play shit or anything like that?"

Alex McKenzie was the physician and the medical examiner who happened to be on call for Knox County, Maine, which in turn included the small town of Proffit Point and the area surrounded by Little Cove. He now turned back from watching the body-removal operation, and shook his head. "Drowning or hypothermia—or who knows? Wait for the autopsy. It's an unattended and unexplained death. Just like his brother Marsden. Anyway, you'll have the state Police CID boys on your neck for another few days."

"Listen," said Tad. "I can live with the state police and all of the scene-of-the-crime stuff. What I can't live with is some of those goddamn Gattlings. Bad news, half the friggin' tribe." With that, Tad spat on a rock and turned back to watch the loading of the body in the waiting ambulance.

"Bad news" about said it, thought Alex, as he trudged back to his car. The very name left a sour taste in his mouth. The Gattling clan, many of whom were settled like a malignancy across the bay on Diggers Neck, usually did spell bad news right there on the front page of the local *Courier-Gazette*. Bad news—from the eleven-year-old Gattling kid shooting a doe and two bucks out of season, to Grandpa Gattling found after-hours with his hand in the local hardware store till, to Aunt Lou Gattling now in the Knox County jail awaiting trial for vehicular manslaughter.

But this universal opinion about certain Gattlings—that they were usually up to no good—could not possibly apply to Ms. Dolly Beaugard, when three days later, the Monday morning of October third, her body washed onto the very ledge that had played host to the Gattling brothers.

Alex was called from his rounds at Bowmouth College's Mary Starbox Hospital to make his examination while the state police—still busy with the Gattling deaths—confronted the added complication of Dolly.

"Christ Almighty," said Tad, stepping around the yellow scene-of-the-crime tape—still in place from the arrival of the Gattling brothers—to meet Alex. "That's three of them. Family called late last night because Dolly didn't come home. In fact, she hadn't been seen since she took off after the Sunday noon dinner. Then in she comes with the morning high tide. But what in hell was Dolly doing? I'll bet she doesn't even know the Gattlings. Dolly's up for the good citizen award. You know, that church in Camden—St. Paul's something or other—and the hospital, the Girl Scouts. Those bird nuts, the Audubon group."

"I know, I know," said Alex. He took a deep breath, sighed, and then knelt down on the granite ledge to inspect what was left of Dolly Beaugard. One half of his brain—the recording, analytical part—took notes: condition of the sodden body, the greasy strands of seaweed caught around the collar of her blouse, the slight whitening and wrinkling of the exposed skin, the facial and skull abrasions; the other half of his brain reviewed what Tad had just said about Dolly. She was indeed a local legend, one of those indefatigable women who rise bright-eyed and bushy-tailed from their night's repose and go forth into the world to do good. There was hardly an institution in Knox County that had not felt Dolly's helping hand. Or, as some might say, Dolly's iron hand. She was the ultimate volunteer in days when such persons still in healthy middle age had long since vanished into the workaday world.

Dolly couldn't have been in cahoots with any Gattling, Alex told himself—unless she'd been trying to reform one of them. Unlikely, he decided. Dolly stuck to institutions, to group action, wasn't the hands-on type. Dolly's world of good works would never have impinged on the marauding, boozy world of the Gattlings. Then, mentally shaking himself, Alex returned to the business of determining the all-too-obvious fact that Dolly was dead—dead as a mackerel, as Tad had expressed it on the phone.

Alex rose from the ground, pulled off a shred of kelp from his trousers, and pronounced Dolly without life.

"Like Junior and Marsden, drowned?" demanded Tad.

"Wait for the autopsy," said Alex. "Besides, there's injury to the skull. A little bruising, abrasions. She was probably battered around on the rocks, or hit her head falling. Wait and see. Me, I've rounds to finish and a batch of patients lined up for the afternoon."

"Coincidence?" asked Tad. "Junior and Marsden and Dolly don't make three of a kind?"

"What do you think?"

"Never seen the lady around town with those two. Never'd expect to."

"So maybe you've just got three careless people fooling around with boats."

"Could be. Dolly used to take that little centerboard sloop of hers out in any kind of weather, and there were small craft warnings yesterday. Anyway, her boat's gone from its mooring."

"Tad," said Alex, with a certain grim satisfaction. "I'll bet you've just been congratulating yourself that you're in for peace and quiet, what with the summer people's boats being hauled out and half the population left for the winter. Well, forget it. Those Gattlings will set up a yowl from here to the Canadian border, and the Beaugards will probably outyell the Gattlings. Old Mrs. Beaugard is a tiger. Getting feeble now but probably still has a good set of claws. Watch your step, Tad."

"Hey," said a voice from behind the two men. "Tad Bugelski, you're the harbormaster who found the body, right? Hang in here. State police CID needs a statement from you."

"So have a nice day," said Alex, grinning at Tad. He turned, dodged past the police photographer, lifted a piece of yellow tape, ducked under, and made his way for the third time in a week away from a dripping, seaweed-entangled corpse.

About the reactions of the bereaved families, Alex proved only half-right. The predicted howl on the part of the Gattlings was stilled in mid-voice on the discovery of several neatly wrapped and waterproof packages of low-grade cocaine fitted under the engine mount of their large skiff. After these items came to light and after the chief medical examiner in Augusta ruled that death was indeed due to drowning, the Gattling tribe contented itself—for the nonce—with elaborate funeral preparations and the arrangement of floral tributes, real and plastic, at the Diggers Neck Baptist Church.

But Dolly Beaugard was another matter, and her lifeless arrival in Little Cove sent a series of ripples that threatened the tranquility not only of the harbormaster but of the coast guard and the various representatives of the law.

Because it looked like the cause of Dolly's death was still uncertain. Some of the head and facial injuries had occurred before immersion in the ocean, so maybe she was hit by a swinging boom or falling mast. Alex took the phone call from Tad just after his last patient of the day had departed.

"Found Dolly's boat," said Tad.

"Capsized?"

"Yep. Sunk up to the gunwales. Hull and bottom stove in. Coast guard helped raise it this afternoon and the state police have impounded the thing and are going over it. Old lady Beaugard's on the warpath. Says I should have prevented her from going out because of small-craft warnings. But hell, I didn't even see Dolly Sunday. Wind was blowing up to twenty-five knots at least and I was helping Oscar Tabor find his mooring. It'd dragged clear across the cove. I can't nursemaid every wacko who wants to go sailing on a windy day. Besides, Dolly'd never listen to me. Dolly did what Dolly damn well pleased."

Alex gave a weary sigh. "I'm going home now, Tad. But call me if you hear anything else from the forensic people, okay?"

"They won't tell me. A harbormaster isn't on anyone's official list. But you've got connections in high places. You'll probably hear from your pal at the sheriff's department. What's his name?"

"Mike. Mike Laaka."

"Yeah, Mike. So you can keep me posted. And you were right about one thing. I sure am going to be spending the rest of the week dodging Beaugards."

Alex returned home in an exhausted state, driving slowly up the long dirt road that led to the old farmhouse on Sawmill Road. Usually the road through the Camden Hills with the changing autumn colors and the flowering of the roadside asters brought some sort of anodyne after a day's grind. But the afternoon had turned to mist and cold rain and only increased the sense that all was not well with the world.

Once home, Alex flung himself into a kitchen armchair, fended off the attentions of the resident Irish wolfhound, Patsy, and stretched and then slumped back on the cushions. He was really beat. The week had been brutal. The sick had gotten sicker, the healthy had been stricken, and the three bodies that had washed in to Little Cove had certainly complicated an already disturbed week.

Then, hearing the slam of the back door and footsteps, he turned and with a weary wave of the hand acknowledged the arrival of his long-time companion and, since this past summer, his wife. Sarah Douglas Deane. Not Sarah Deane McKenzie because, as Sarah had pointed out, the only reason to yield up your own name to that of your husband in these enlightened days was if the woman's own name was something like Bugsquash or Snakeroot.

Sarah struggled out of her raincoat, put down her briefcase, sank into a neighboring chair, and ran her hands over the damp strands of brown hair that plastered the sides of her face.

"I can't believe it about Dolly," she said. "She was on her way to heaven via good works. As Grandma Douglas would say, 'She trod the path of righteousness.'"

Alex nodded. "So maybe that's it. Righteous people like that often end up in the drink. Or down a deep hole. The world can't stand too much righteousness."

"Oh, come on, Alex. Dolly was a little managing, a little bit of a sergeant major, but who else was going to be on all those committees and boards? Not me. Not you. Not anyone in our family. We're all too damn busy. God, Dolly worked at the hospital, the Scouts, was on the Midcoast Audubon board, and a docent at the Godding Museum of Art. We should be grateful. I'm spending all my time teaching and not more than an hour a month doing anything even vaguely public-spirited."

Here Sarah stood up and reached out a hand for Alex's, squeezed it, then walked over to the woodstove, flipped open the top, and began stuffing small logs into its maw.

Settled back in chairs, drinks in hand (Alex, beer; Sarah, tea), a pleasant glow and warmth emanating from the stove, they reviewed the matter of Dolly Beaugard and the Beaugard family backup team.

"You're right," said Sarah. "The family will make Tad's life miserable. He found the body. He didn't see her take out the boat. He didn't notice it was missing from its mooring until too late. I heard about it during class. In the middle of Intro Lit, this kid says out of nowhere—I'm holding forth about Chaucer, 'The Knight's Tale'—that he'd heard about Dolly from some other kid who lives on the Proffit Point Harbor. That she was covered with seaweed and had a crab fastened to one ear. I mean *yuck*. That wasn't true, was it?"

"There was seaweed here and there," said Alex, "but no crab. Kids like to embellish. But I didn't enjoy the scene, if that's what you mean. It's bad enough when the victims are thugs like Junior and Marsden. But hell, Dolly, we knew Dolly. We knew the family. Not close friends, but they were at our wedding."

Sarah put down her teacup. "Dolly and her whole family were part of the founding summer colony on Proffit Point. But most of the Beaugards live full-time now on the estate—it's called Great Oaks—or nearby. Retired or actually holding jobs."

"And doing good works."

"Dolly doing good works. The rest of the clan isn't quite as community-minded. They have a solid reputation for scrapping with each other, but they always seemed to depend on Dolly. She was the referee. She managed the estate and kept an eye on the cottages, the garden, the boats, the two docks. Took care of her mother's finances. And her mother. Saw that she got to her Shakespeare reading group, her Tuesday bridge, church every Sunday."

Alex nodded. "So with Dolly gone, there may be hell to pay. Cages rattling, toes being stomped on, push turning to shove."

Sarah grimaced and returned to her tea, and for a moment the two sat silent, both imagining the fallout of Dolly Beaugard's arrival on the rocks of Little Cove.

Sarah was a teaching fellow at Bowmouth College, an elderly institution of higher learning fitted into the lower margins of the Camden Hills in midcoast Maine. Not only was she responsible for teaching three introductory classes of English, she was also in thrall to a doctoral program with the possibility of orals on the horizon. These pressures left little time for the civilities of life and even less for any untoward goings-on beyond her own threshold. So now it was with considerable effort that she dragged her thoughts away from the academic world and tried to think about the Beaugards. About Dolly Beaugard. Dolly deceased, washed into Little Cove like any random piece of flotsam. Or jetsam? Could Dolly have been pushed, tripped, encouraged to take a plunge overboard by the flat of a hand pressed into the small of her back? By a foot stuck suddenly in front of her?

"Alex," said Sarah, "it *was* accidental, wasn't it? She was out sailing in too much wind. Or is it possible…" She left the question hanging.

Alex looked over at her, frowning. "Not another word. We've had enough foul play this summer to last the rest of our lives. And don't you go sticking your nose into this business or I'll feed you to the sharks. Or to the Beaugards, which would be worse than sharks."

"But you're already sticking your nose into it."

"Because I'm the medical examiner. I have no choice. But when the results of the autopsy come through, that is that. You, my love, need only to go with me to the funeral. We will send appropriate flowers, write notes, visit the family, and send a donation to the indicated charity."

Sarah looked thoughtful. "Dolly wasn't everyone's all-time favorite. And she was always being held up as an example to me. When I was little, anyway. Grandmother Douglas used to wave Dolly at me like a flag. Dolly did this, Dolly won that. Social Responsibility trophy at school. Camp Spirit three years in a row at Camp Merrilark. And she taught Sunday school while I spent Sundays chasing after a good time."

Alex reached for a section of the morning paper that lay on the table beside his chair. "And I spent my Sundays concentrating on the Red Sox. Listen, let me worry about Dolly because it's my job. You go think about Chaucer."

Sarah relapsed into silence, but the order to put Dolly out of her mind only stimulated thought. Dolly had been the number two child of the family. First came Masha the beautiful. Masha the musical. Seen on posters featuring the Baroquen Recorder Consort. Masha in a white silk blouse holding her instrument and looking disdainfully into middle distance. Cool, contained, auburn-haired Masha built like a Vogue model. Then Dolly. Blonde, stubby Dolly. Vaguely porcine features, always fifteen or so pounds overweight. No student, but a mighty achiever. Or over-achiever? Trying to live down the fact of a fashion-queen, musical older sister? Trying to hold her own through worthy deeds?

And then came Alice. One year older than Sarah herself—Sarah having arrived at thirty this September. In Sarah's class at Miss Morton's Academy—although suspended twice for running away. A childhood friend of Sarah's, but the kind of friend who led Sarah into escapades and briar patches from which only Sarah seemed to suffer feelings of guilt, since Alice positively thrived on the wayward life. Alice: a short-term marriage at eighteen, a college dropout by twenty-one. Another marriage, another divorce. One living child—custody to the father (which father?). Incarcerations to dry out. A brief career as a painter (oils and pastels); a try at writing (a poem published in *The Atlantic*); a period spent as a ski instructor at Sundance; a theater try in Boston; a teacher's aide in Maine. Presently holed up for a period of regrouping at the Great Oaks compound on Little Cove at the end of Proffit Point.

Last—Eliot Beaugard. The pride and joy. The son born after those three daughters. Handsome, stalwart, salty Eliot. Marine insurance, something like that. Married to Caroline, beautiful, sulky Caroline. Husband and wife living in high style outside the Beaugard compound in a "cottage" widely rumored to have at least six bedrooms, ditto bathrooms, a wraparound deck, and an outdoor, heated, saltwater pool.

And now Dolly was gone. Dolly, the good. Dolly, the force that kept the Beaugards from having each other for lunch.

"Is that someone at the door?" Alex reared his head and regarded the kitchen entrance with loathing.

Sarah, recalled from speculation, shuddered. "Can we hide?"

"No. The lights are on, our cars are outside. But we could try total deafness. Hunker down and close your ears."

This proved difficult. First the clang of the doorbell, the rapping of the brass knocker, then a solid thumping of a fist, the kicking of a foot. Then the kitchen door snapped open and the visitor strode over the threshold.

A tall woman, face pale, dark hair wet and tangled, hanging over the collar of her yellow slicker. Blue jeans and rubber boots, mud clinging to the soles.

"Bloody hell, Sarah," said the visitor. "Don't you ever answer your door? Or are you trying to get away from something? Or someone? Well, it won't work because I'm damn well going to see you. Have a nice, old-fashioned session. With you and our friend, the medical examiner. Hi there, Alex. Long time, no see."

Sarah drew a deep breath, raised her head. "Hello, Alice," she said.

Chapter Two

Alex HAULED HIMSELF TO his feet and extended a hand. "Alice. We're so sorry about Dolly. An awful shock. Come on in and sit down. Let me take your coat, you're dripping."

Sarah, too, was now on her feet. "What would you like, Alice? Tea? Cocoa, coffee...or a drink?"

Alice shrugged herself out of her slicker, tossed it into a corner of the room, and threw herself into Alex's vacated chair. "My shrink and I've worked it out so I'm allowed one blessed drink a day. The drink of my choice. One ounce. Period. Got any rum?"

Alex walked over to the kitchen cupboard. "Anything in it?"

"Put anything you want in it. Juice, butter, soda. But make it hot. So it blisters my tongue. I'm cold and wet and chilled through to my spine."

Alex busied himself with bottles and mugs, and Sarah returned to her chair and contented herself with a sympathetic look and a murmur to the effect that she, too, was extremely sorry.

"You're sorry! My God, we're all sorry. Poor old Dolly. The family saint. Listen, I never thought I'd be saying this, but I'd give ten years of a misspent life to see sister Dolly march through the door and suggest that I shape up and make something of myself. Oh shit, why do things like this happen? Why couldn't it have been some slimeball who'd been poaching deer or running for Congress?"

"Here, Alice," said Alex, extending a steaming mug. "Hot buttered rum. The skier's drink. Or the sailor's. And I do have some idea of what Dolly meant to your family."

"Alex McKenzie, you don't have a clue. You don't know a quarter of it. We're a bloody bunch. Contentious as hell. Yap, snap, and bite. Don't deny it, Sarah," as Sarah opened her mouth to protest. A ritual protest.

"We never functioned as a family. Not really. So okay, maybe families never do function, but Dolly made us think that we did. Got us through birthdays. Thanksgiving, Christmas. The only reason we made it through holidays without cutting each other's throats was because of Dolly raving about the sanctity of the family—not that she really *liked* any of us."

Silence. Then Sarah braced her shoulders and said briskly, "Dinner with us, Alice. Just some packaged stuff out of the freezer, but we'd love to have you."

Alice put her face down into the steaming rum, sniffed, took a sip, and looked up. "Okay. If you can stand me that long. Most people can't. I'll try not to rage and thunder about the family."

"Rage all you want," said Alex. "Sarah and I have had our share of family moments. Maybe ours aren't quite as colorful as some, but there have been a few incidents…"

"Like my brother, Tony, trying to marry a jewel smuggler," said Sarah, "and my aunt Julia stealing horses. And Grandmother Douglas being sure if we don't start going to church, we'll all roast in hellfire."

Alice pushed a straggling lock behind an ear and gave a half smile. "Your people aren't even in the same ballpark, but I'm not here to compete. I'm here to say that with Dolly gone, we'll all fall apart at the seams, we'll combust, and maybe that's what somebody had in mind."

"What!" exclaimed Sarah and Alex in exactly the same breath. "You're not serious," added Alex. "I haven't had the autopsy results, but it looks like an accidental death."

Alice put down her mug on the table with a thump. Such a thump that the warm brown fluid splashed over the edge onto the knees of her none too clean blue jeans.

"Alex and Sarah, I'm not here to listen to sympathy and reason. But I say to hell with what it looks like. I say that Dolly was too damn useful to the family. And too damn managing. I say that someone wanted Dolly's finger out of the family pie, out of the family checkbook."

"Have you," said Sarah, carefully sorting her words, "any idea in the least that there is a someone? Have there been threats? Has Dolly any known enemies? I don't mean the sort of people who got steamed because she was a bit of a tyrant on a committee. I mean the real thing."

"No enemies," said Alice. "No threats. Nothing like that. The only people who really seriously grumbled about her were in the family, but they still hung on to her apron strings for all they were worth. It's just something I feel in my bones."

"Dinner," said Sarah. "Let me shove a few boxes in the microwave. Then we can eat and you can tell us about your bones."

The eating of dinner—Stouffer's turkey tetrazzini with salad on the side—allowed Sarah to study her guest and wonder why on earth she and Alex had been singled out for the visit. Although they'd been close when growing up, she hadn't seen much of Alice in recent years, Alice having been entirely too busy with dropping husbands, changing interests, drinking or not drinking, to be bothered with old school friends toiling in the academic world.

Alice didn't look well. A pinched look around the nostrils, fine lines around the mouth, washed-out blue eyes with red rims, a gray whiteness to the skin—at a time when most people still had a summer tan—and a limpness to the mouse brown hair that straggled in separate strands to her shoulders. Well, the red eyes might be due to recent shock, but the other details bespoke poor health. Or rotten habits. Or indifference to life. And Alice wasn't eating much, just moving her fork around her plate. Then Sarah, as she cleared the plates and began dishing out Ben & Jerry's Toffee Crunch, took a good look at Alex as an antidote to Alice. It was a relief. Alex, even though looking like some sort of nineteenth-century felon with a slash of a mouth, determined chin, dark eyes, and a shelf of black hair, and though obviously tired, still seemed like someone in his middle thirties, while Alice resembled a battered specimen closing in on fifty.

Alex, in his turn, glancing from time to time in Alice's direction, found his thoughts turning to the need of a complete workup, blood count, and a liver function test, to health spas, vitamin supplements, outdoor exercise, and the intake of protein and green vegetables. Like Sarah, he compared their guest unfavorably with his spouse and found Sarah, although thin and nervy-looking, still with color across her high cheekbones, a light in her gray eyes, and a shine on her dark short-cropped hair—hair now dried from the rain.

Dinner over, the three settled in the living room, a bare-walled space in the midst of remodeling, with books spilling out of cartons and unhung pictures leaning against the wall.

"But three decent chairs," said Sarah, removing a pile of textbooks and student papers from one and waving Alice to it.

"Now," said Alex, "let's have it. You think Dolly's boat was tipped over on purpose because someone wanted to do her in? Dolly, who, as you said, had no enemies and lived a blameless life."

"Cripes," said Alice. "I know it doesn't make sense. And I know I may be having a knee-jerk reaction because I want

Dolly back. I don't want to be the new Dolly, and I can see my mother considering the possibility. Even sitting there crying over Dolly, she's said things like wasn't it time I settled home for good and began to take on responsibility for the family. For the property. The estate, Grandpa's trust fund. For the dock and the boats and the guest cottages and, of course, her. She's given up driving, you know, because of her eyesight, and she depends on one of us. Though, of course, it was mostly on Dolly. In no time she'll be going on to me about the Prodigal Son...or the prodigal daughter, and I don't want the job or the fatted calf. And neither does Masha or Eliot. Nor Caroline, probably, but she never says much about anything except maybe to complain. Our family zombie."

"Are you trying to say," Sarah said slowly, measuring her words, "that someone might have wanted to get rid of Dolly because none of you wants to fill her shoes and that leaves a vacancy? And some scheming evil person—like a housekeeper or a gardener or a family lawyer—is hovering, waiting to gain her confidence and seize control. Get her to change her will."

"I read gothic novels, too," said Alice, "and the answer is that I love the idea of the evil stranger, but I'm too bloody down-to-earth to believe in one. So I think if anyone's hovering, it's got to be someone in the family. And that leaves me, Masha, Eliot, and Caroline, and, of course, dear old Uncle Lenox. He's retired and moved into the family manse."

"Your uncle Lenox must be quite elderly, then," said Alex. "I can't imagine him rowing out in a dinghy in a twenty-five knot breeze just to tip Dolly over. Or banging her with an oar or a bilge pump."

"Uncle Lenox is a cantankerous bastard in quite good health. Stronger than he looks. All lean sinew and gristle. He gets by in the world by pretending to be Mr. Frail Elderly Scholar. Professor Emeritus. He thinks being a grumbling curmudgeon is fascinating. Listen, I don't trust a single soul in the whole family nest. And to repeat, I just have this feeling in my bones. Dolly's dying has left a void. A big black hole."

Sarah couldn't hold out any longer. "I just don't get it. Why, Alice, have you come to us? If there's anything amiss, well, the state police will be standing there on your doorstep, making your life miserable. It looks like Dolly went out in a big wind and pulled the wrong line or put her foot in a bucket or got hit by the boom. Something happened fast and she went overboard. With or without the boat. No time for a life jacket." Sarah looked up at Alex. "Dolly wasn't wearing a life jacket, was she?"

"No," said Alex. "Not when I saw her."

"We're always glad to see you, Alice," said Sarah. "And if you're feeling rotten about Dolly, well, use us for relief. Friendly shoulders. Anytime. I mean it. But I don't see why—"

Alice broke in. "I'm not here to cry on friendly shoulders. I'm here for help. I know all about you, Sarah Deane. Your grandmother told my mother that you are an expert in sticking your nose in other people's business. That affair at High Hope Farm this summer. People disappearing and being dug up by a horse. I mean you two are well known, you are notorious, you and Alex. How many married couples spend their honeymoon working on a murder that took place at their wedding reception?"

"Spit it out," said Sarah wearily.

"I want both of you to ooze into our family circle. Sympathy visits, condolence calls. Sarah, come for lunch. Better yet, bring your grandmother Douglas over for lunch, and while she and Mother are talking about the decline in morality in today's world, you can soak up ambience. Snuggle up to Masha and ask about her concerts. Pump Eliot and Caroline. They'll ask you over for drinks. Or dinner. They're always looking for new people to admire that great monster of a house they've built on Tidal Cove."

"Alice," said Sarah, her voice taking on a hard edge, "I have just begun my semester's teaching. Three Intro Lit classes. Alex is practicing medicine. Sick people without end. Flu season approaching. He's one of the local medical examiners."

"What Sarah is saying," put in Alex, "is no. We will call on your mother and tell everyone how very sorry we are. I will explain any mysterious medical details that emerge from the autopsy. Both of us will offer comfort and sympathy when needed. But we won't do any oozing into your family circle."

"Hey," said Alice, rising to her feet. "No problem. I didn't think you'd say yes right off the bat. But I'm the youngest daughter, you know. Spoiled, devious. And very persistent. I really like to have my own way, as my two former husbands will be happy to tell you. So I'll give you a little breathing space while we wait for the results of the autopsy. Then, even if it's ruled accidental death, I think I'll zero in and pester you again. Good night and thanks for the rum. I feel more human. Ten percent human, I mean. And for me that's going some."

And Alice, followed by her hosts, marched to the kitchen, snatched up her slicker, bestowed a quick pat to the top of Patsy's head, and made for the kitchen door.

Sarah looked over at Alex, who was glowering at the departing woman. "To repeat Alice's opening remark," she said, "bloody hell."

Chapter Three

TUESDAY, OCTOBER FOURTH, THE day following Alice Beaugard's visit, found Alex at noon cornered in the Mary Starbox Hospital cafeteria by Mike Laaka, deputy investigator of Knox County Sheriff's Department. Mike was a tall Nordic type, fair-haired almost to whiteness, a man more dedicated to the world of the racetrack than to that of law and order. And since Mike was a boyhood friend, there was no need for Alex to waste time on formalities.

Alex found Mike looming large over a pile of plastic trays and eyed him with suspicion. "You're not looking for me, I hope. Maybe your mother's in here for a checkup? Or you've got a splinter in your thumb? Or there's a gang of thieves in the gift shop?"

"Funny," said Mike amiably. He slid a tray from the pile, handed it to Alex, and chose one for himself. "Do you recommend the meat loaf or the Waldorf salad?"

"I don't recommend that you bother me during lunch."

"I'm going to bother you about the autopsy results," said Mike. He chose a villainous-looking piece of lasagne, added a salad, a frosted doughnut, and a dessert dish holding what looked like whipped cotton topped by a cherry.

Alex studied Mike's luncheon selections, shuddered, and went for the vegetable soup and the Waldorf salad.

Settled in a corner, in the middle of Alex's second spoonful of soup, Mike began. "Johnny Cuzak wants to see you. You remember Johnny? Assistant chief medical examiner."

"I know Johnny," said Alex, remembering too clearly his last session with Johnny in a stable bending over a strangled corpse.

"So he wants to see you. In person. Go over first impressions. Your initial exam."

"I made three initial exams. Three bodies, three exams."

"Right now it's about those Gattling brothers. The post mortem details are kinda interesting. Interesting like peculiar."

"Nothing about Dolly Beaugard for now?"

"Wait up. Take the Gattling boys first. Looks like they both had a skinful."

"That empty bottle of whiskey?"

"Yeah, that. And what was in it."

Alex put down his fork carefully. "Not whiskey?"

"Yeah, the booze was there, all right. Or in the blood. Marsden and Junior were drunk as skunks. High alcohol level: point two one. But something was added to the bottle. Like a sedative. The lab's working full steam on it."

"Lethal dose?"

"Of which? The whiskey or the dope? Or the combo because those two items don't make the world's greatest mixers. And lethal? Well, maybe, but that isn't what finished them. Marsden and Junior didn't stay aboard their boat long enough to be killed by the stuff. They went over the side into the drink."

"And drowned?"

"Right. Lungs filled with seawater—plankton and diatoms present. Persistent foam at the nose and mouth. All the signs. So, Alex, you hit that one on the nose."

"But now you've got a complication. Doped whiskey."

"The lab people are going over their boat. Big skiff really. Sixteen-foot job. Some cloth fibers caught on the gunnels. Rips in the guys' jackets. Looks like maybe one of them fell in, the other reached for him and went ass over teakettle reaching out to grab him. Happens a lot. The rescuer dies trying to rescue. But that's all a guess. Wait for the lab."

"But you're not beating the bush for someone who might have reached over with an oar and tipped them in?"

"You mean the someone who spiked the booze with dope and then followed them out of the harbor and waited till they were liquored up and easy marks."

"Something like that," Alex admitted. "Those two guys never won any good-conduct medals, and I'll bet there are plenty of looted cottage owners around or drivers forced off the road by some Gattling or other who might have helped with the project."

"Wait and see. Now you, Alex..."

"We're finished. I'm finished. I'll call the medical examiner later. Now I've got to be at my office by one-thirty."

"Two things. First, go over your report on Marsden and Junior and see if you missed anything. Important since it's not such an easy death-by-drowning verdict as it seemed. Second, the state police are a bit put out by Dolly Beaugard turning up practically on the heels of the Gattlings."

"Coincidence. Dolly wouldn't have been caught dead with—"

"She just was," Mike reminded him.

"Okay, okay," said Alex irritably. He picked up his coffee cup, drained the last mouthful, and rolled his paper napkin into a ball. "What I'm saying is that it looks like Dolly was dumb enough to go sailing in a big wind and didn't wear her life jacket. But I'll bet she wasn't having a secret meeting off some island with Junior and Marsden."

"No bet. I only bet on horses, not dead bodies. But the police are going over her boat now. A life jacket's still aboard."

"The one she wasn't wearing?"

"Her brother, Eliot, said she usually didn't unless a gale-force wind was blowing. But she kept a life jacket handy. Usually hung on a cleat near the mast. Easy to reach."

"And that was in place."

"Tied around a cleat."

"So it wouldn't blow away. Besides, even with a life jacket on, hypothermia would have got her. How about time of death?"

"She must have taken the boat out late Sunday afternoon. Capsized not too long after. Lab puts the time of death between four and six—stomach contents and so forth. Trouble is, no one around Back Cove—that's where Dolly kept the boat—noticed the sloop was off its mooring. Tad Bugelski's being given heat because he wasn't around. The Beaugards themselves didn't think it was odd she didn't turn up Sunday evening. Thought she had some committee meeting. Only called us when she didn't show up later that night. We alerted the coast guard, who it turns out already were trying to track an overturned sailboat after someone called in about sighting it. Anyway, Tad and a couple fishermen went looking around the islands, but as you know, she didn't turn up until Monday A.M."

Alex stood up. "So goodbye, Mike. Call me with any reports, but no more lying in wait at the hospital."

"I have to deal in person sometimes. His high and mighty lordship Sergeant George Fitts of the State Police CID—"

"Okay, okay. We all know George. Inscrutable George with ice in the veins and frost in the mouth. He leaned on you."

"Yeah. You said it. George remembers all the hindrance and help you and Sarah have given to the world of crime, so he wants you to make a sympathy call on the family."

"We're planning to do that anyway."

"And," said Mike, rising in his turn, "see if you can sniff out the slightest odor of Marsden or Junior Gattling in the intimate circles of the Beaugards. Or any Gattling. George went to see Mrs. Beaugard and the rest last night, and they act like it's some name from inner Tibet. To which I say horseshit. The Gattlings are legend around these parts."

"Did Alice deny knowing Gattlings? It doesn't sound like her."

Mike shrugged. "Alice was out last night—over at your place, I hear. But I leave Alice out of the family picture. She's a maverick who once dated Webb Gattling—he's Marsden and Junior's cousin. Maybe that's the connection we're looking for. Alice and Webb had matching motorcycle jackets. Their names in silver studs. Cute. Anyhow, I try not to believe much of what Alice says."

Alex thumped his friend on the back. A heavy and not entirely friendly thump. "Now hear this. If Sarah and I, in the course of our condolence activities, hear anything untoward, we'll pass it along to you. If not, that's that. We're not going to—how did Alice put it?—ooze our way into the Beaugard family circle and open cupboards and cabinet drawers. Or look for bloodstains on the carpet. See you, Mike." And Alex strode off toward the cafeteria door.

"Hey, wait," shouted Mike, loping after him. "Alice? Alice has been asking you to visit? You mean she knows something? Hey!" This as Alex let the cafeteria door swing back in Mike's face so that by the time he had recovered his balance, Alex had disappeared down one of the long corridors of the hospital.

While Alex was beset by the problems of medical practice and irritants from the world of forensics, Sarah was enduring other forms of annoyance.

That morning at seven-thirty, with an eye to making it to her eight o'clock class in good time, her briefcase in one hand, a thermos of tea tucked under an arm, and her handbag slung over her shoulder, the telephone rang. Her grandmother.

Grandmother Douglas, a frail woman of ninety years with a spirit of stainless steel, usually avoided the telephone as an instrument of the devil. She wrote notes or sent messages just as if she lived in the mid-nineteenth century at a time when Alexander Graham Bell was yet in swaddling clothes.

But here she was. On the telephone. Sarah sighed, looked at her watch, and put down her thermos and briefcase.

"Sarah," said her grandmother, in the high-octave tones of the very old, "I have just heard about Dolly Beaugard. So tragic. I need you and your automobile."

"Now, Grandma?" said Sarah, frowning. She had student appointments, an eight-o'clock class, another at ten, one at four.

"This afternoon would be best. Say three o'clock. I must call on Elena Beaugard. And the family. I would have asked Hopkins"—Hopkins was Mrs. Douglas's housekeeper, a stalwart in her eighties—"but she's having something done about her root canal."

"But I have to teach an afternoon class..." Sarah began.

"Yes, I know. But see if you can make arrangements. I want you to drive me there. You know the family and went to school with Alice. It will be most suitable for you to make the visit with me."

"You mean you want me to cancel the class?"

"Yes," said her grandmother firmly. "I do. Sudden death, a tragedy like this, takes precedence over whatever poets and writers you're dealing with—most of them atheists, I believe."

Well, there was no use in tangling with her grandmother over the godlessness of certain literary lions. "It won't be easy, but I'll try, Grandma," Sarah said, looking frantically at the kitchen clock, hoping that it differed from her watch.

"Poor Dolly. What a pillar. I heard that Father Smythe is stricken. Dolly certainly whipped the Sunday school into shape in two weeks after Gloria Merton had that breakdown."

Sarah sighed. "Dolly was remarkable, but I have to go now, Grandma."

"Yes," said her grandmother. "Don't waste time chatting on the telephone. Your whole generation has given up on any other means of communication."

Five minutes late for her eight-o'clock class, Sarah found herself hard put to present Chaucer in an acceptable light to a group of heavy-eyed freshmen who no doubt wished that the computer had not dealt them an early morning class that featured an author who wrote rhymed gibberish about an antique people.

Sarah stumbled through the period and found her own interest in "The Knight's Tale" faltering, so infectious was her students' palpable discontent.

But by her ten-o'clock class, she hit her stride with *Oedipus Rex*—incest being a popular subject with youth—and after lunch made it to the English office and, pleading family problems, successfully wiggled out of teaching her four-o'clock class, which was to have centered on Defoe's *Journal of the Plague Year*.

"I can certainly do without the bubonic plague rounding out the day," she told Arlene, the English secretary.

"You're going to see that Beaugard family?" asked Arlene. "I've been reading all about it in the *Courier-Gazette*. First those two Gattlings—I went to school with Junior, and he deserved everything he got—and then this Dolly Beaugard's body coming right on the very same rock. I mean, whoa, that's suspicious."

"Arlene," said Sarah in an austere voice, "it's just a coincidence. Dolly was sailing and her boat capsized."

Arlene smiled the smile of one whose reading focused on the pages of the *National Enquirer*. "Hey, Sarah, keep me posted, okay?"

"Not okay," said Sarah, stamping out of the office.

The drive from Bowmouth College to Grandmother Douglas's house on Bay View Street in Camden wound through the lower reaches of the Camden Hills, between marshes, ponds, and wooded swales, and served Sarah as a short period of refreshment. It was a shining day, cloudless, filled with early October splendor, each maple outdoing the next in orange, vermilion, and crimson. Above the highway, the rounded hills rose, brown oak, yellow birch, red maple, all mixing with the somber clusters of evergreen, pine, spruce, fir balsam, hemlock, and cedar.

Sarah slowed to a crawl, trying to concentrate on scenery and not her upcoming visit. Then on a sudden impulse she pulled her car, a blue secondhand Subaru, into a small lakeside turnoff, cut the engine, and climbed out of the car. A killing frost had not yet turned everything brown, and the edge of the road was still thick with late purple asters.

Sarah stretched, inhaled, and then made her way slowly down the little stone beach to the water's edge. She looked at her watch. Only one-thirty. Still plenty of time. Grandma Douglas didn't tolerate lateness, but neither did she want an early arrival upsetting her after-lunch nap. On an impulse Sarah knelt down and dipped a hand in the water. It was ice-cold and so clear that she could see her pale fingers like strange polyps, the whole hand like a small sea anemone. And the moment that she had chosen to take her mind away from the upcoming visit to a bereaved household suddenly brought it home. Death by drowning, by taking great gulps of icy water into your lungs, by gasping and choking, and fighting. And losing.

Sarah forced herself to picture the living Dolly. When had she last seen her? Yes, two weeks ago at the hospital. Sarah was in the lobby waiting to meet Alex for a rare lunch together, and Dolly, dressed in the green smock of a volunteer, had stopped by Sarah's chair and smiled down at her—a professional may-I-help-you smile—and asked how Sarah liked married life and how was Alex?

Fair-haired Dolly with her round face, her round chin, that round button nose. Pale blue eyes, invisible eyebrows, hair combed back looking as smooth as yellow satin. A full mouth with perfectly laid on lipstick. Bangle bracelets. The green smock not entirely hiding the plump contours of the body. A woman who would never do anything so messy as allow herself to fall overboard and arrive wrinkled and disordered and seaweed-entangled on a harsh coast to be found by strangers. Hauled above the tide line by strangers. Later, bagged, tabled, sluiced, probed, and eviscerated, her organs weighed and sliced by strangers. Dolly, the fastidious, the take-charge woman—if she existed somewhere as a hovering shade—must now be in a state of humiliation and trembling outrage.

Sarah withdrew her hand, now white and numb, from the water. It looked like a dead thing. She shuddered, then wiped it hastily on the side of her skirt, gave herself a mental shake, and returned to the car.

Sarah's formidable grandmother, supported by the faithful Hopkins—she of the root canal—was standing at the front door of her dark-shingled Queen Anne monster of a house. A house with half the rooms closed, blinds drawn. A house of shadows and worn velvet cushions and threadbare Oriental rugs, of large bronze vases, hat racks, and umbrella stands. Of flocked maroon wallpaper and oil paintings of dismal moors and dank pools. A house that to Sarah's mind was more mausoleum than home, but to her grandmother, an abiding refuge from the relentless stream of time.

Hopkins assisted Mrs. Douglas into the front seat of the car, and Sarah, taking her grandmother's cane, thought it was like settling a large and fragile gray moth into place. Clothes of soft gray material, gray stockings on sticklike legs, a gray shawl of weblike texture enveloping the stalk of her neck. And above the shawl, the small, almost transparent face dominated by the gold-rimmed spectacles and the thin cloud of white hair.

Sarah started the car and drove at a sedate pace down Bay View Street, all the while seeing that her grandmother was looking with disapproval at her red and blue checked skirt.

To forestall the lecture, Sarah pointed out that she was wearing her usual teaching costume. "And besides, no one gets into black anymore, Grandma. Not to make a visit. But I'm not in blue jeans and I'll bet Alice Beaugard will be."

"Alice is not my idea of an example," said her grandmother. "But I've heard she's stopped drinking, so perhaps there is hope."

"I guess Dolly earned her place as the family star," said Sarah, nudging the conversation down a different path. "She was the middle daughter, and don't they say the middle one tries harder? Dolly certainly did. And Masha's a hard act to follow. An older glamour-puss sister. Of course, she's not home much anymore, but when she is, well, who would look at Dolly? And then big hunk brother Eliot and Caroline giving those parties in that big new house. Tents on the lawn, charter boats for excursions."

"Glamour and big new houses," said Mrs. Douglas with scorn, "do not cut ice with honest people. I don't think Eliot and Caroline have been to church since their own wedding. As for Alice, what a record. Married in a hotel by a rabbi and a Unitarian somebody, and the second time in a hole in the wall by a justice of the peace. No wonder she was divorced twice. As for Masha, she only goes into church if she's playing a concert there. Only Dolly and her mother were regular attendants."

And that, thought Sarah, as she turned the car south, sums up the measure of man for Grandma. Unless you go to church—preferably an Episcopal one—you're one of the world's sinners.

"Grandma," said Sarah, picking up speed and clutching the wheel with determination. "I think you should know that Alex and I aren't exactly regular churchgoers. In fact, on Sunday we—"

Her grandmother reached for Sarah's arm and tapped it lightly. "I don't want to know. You are my dear granddaughter and I know that you have a good heart. As for Alex"—here Mrs. Douglas pursed her lips—"I will continue to pray for him."

Sarah pressed her foot more firmly on the accelerator so that by the time the car shot past the general store and made the turn for the Proffit Point Road, the speedometer was nudging fifty-five. Then, anger subsiding, she slowed.

"Tell me about the Beaugards, Grandma," she said. "Mrs. Beaugard. The whole family. Alice said they've always fought among themselves like cats and dogs. But I only visited the family when I was little and haven't seen much of any of them in a long time."

Her grandmother considered for a moment. "Well," she said slowly, "Elena Beaugard—she was a Cobb from Cambridge, although I think her mother came from Europe—Elena was always strong-minded. Difficult. The whole family seemed to go at each other hammer and tongs. Elena's husband, Arthur, usually stayed away out of sight. Spent all his time in his study working on his collections. Nineteenth-century illustrated books. Died at his desk, I am told. A pleasant man when you met him, but that wasn't often. Visiting the family could be exhausting, but I imagine that today they will be properly subdued. Elena's great cross is having a daughter like Alice who drinks and never settles to anything. Picks up husbands and drops them like used clothes."

"But Alice is the brainy one," said Sarah. "At Miss Morton's when she made an effort, she got all A's. Wonderful voice but wouldn't join the choir. Preferred being the class renegade."

"At which she was no doubt successful," said Mrs. Douglas dryly. "But what kind of a mother is she? The father has custody of the son. That's Alan Epstein, the novelist. If you call the sort of things he writes proper fiction. Jonathan is the son and quite spoiled, I hear. Sarah, you are still driving over the speed limit."

Sarah, interested in the Beaugard family life, slowed obediently. "We've said it was hard on Dolly to have Masha and Alice for sisters. But it must have been hard for those two to have a sister like Dolly."

"Nonsense," said her grandmother. "Alice and Masha received all the attention. Masha was a very beautiful child. And gifted. Gifted children usually get more than their share of attention. And Alice was a wilding from the very beginning. What was left for Dolly to do except to be good? To be dutiful."

"At which she was very successful. Saint Dolly."

"I think in the long run Dolly just wanted to be needed. She probably wished for an old-fashioned family with children and a hardworking husband." Here Mrs. Douglas folded her hands in her lap and sighed. "Dolly," she added, "was an extremely boring young woman. Ten minutes spent with Dolly lasted an age. But she did God's work."

Sarah saw ahead the stone pillars marking the entrance of the Great Oaks estate and slowed the Subaru for the road that led to the Beaugard compound and the old family house. And as she did, she thought with astonishment that her ninety-year-old grandmother, who sometimes seemed completely out of the everyday world, might have accurately summed up the Dolly phenomenon. A boring, not very bright woman who wanted attention and found a socially acceptable way of getting it. Whether God had figured in the equation was anyone's guess. But if He had, what was He thinking of to allow His dull but hardworking handmaiden to go sailing in a twenty-five-knot breeze and to capsize her boat and drown?

Chapter Four

WITH DOLLY BEAUGARD IN the forefront of her thoughts, Sarah almost missed the tall, thin figure limping along by the side of the drive. Only her grandmother's cry made her put on the brakes.

"Sarah, look out. I think that's Lenox."

Sarah brought the car to a stop and peered through the windshield. A sticklike man moved haltingly along the margin of the drive, arms flapping like broken wings as if to balance himself.

"He must have hurt himself," said her grandmother. "We'll have to give him a ride. Oh dear. Lenox is such a trial."

Sarah opened the door, undid her safety belt, climbed out, and then turned back to the window to confront her grandmother.

"Alice's uncle Lenox? Lenox who?"

"Elena's older brother. Professor Lenox Cobb. I've heard he is living at Great Oaks now. As of last month."

Of course. *Professor Cobb, I know about you,* thought Sarah with a start. Former scourge of the Bowmouth English Department. Now, thank heaven, retired. She walked on toward the man, who, apparently oblivious of a car stopped behind him, continued his tottering forward progress.

"Professor Cobb," she called. "Are you all right?"

The man stopped in his tracks and gave her a look. "If you had eyes in your head," he snapped, "you could see that I am not all right. I am injured. I have had a serious fall."

"Wouldn't you like a ride, then?" said Sarah, extending an arm. Professor Cobb was swaying like a leaf in the wind. In fact, his whole body had a leaflike quality. An autumn leaf. Brown, wrinkled, and thin to the point of transparency.

"Of course I want a ride. And give me your arm. No, the one on my other side. Use your head, young woman. Can't you see that it's my left ankle that's injured?"

Sarah moved around him and extended her right arm, which was immediately and powerfully gripped above the elbow by a claw of iron. Together they walked slowly toward the waiting Subaru.

"You have a Japanese car, young woman," said Lenox Cobb in a peevish voice. "Aren't American cars good enough for you?"

Sarah fought down an impulse to drop the man in his tracks and explained the need for a four-wheel-drive that was not a truck. And that neither Ford nor Chevrolet had come up with such.

"No excuse," said her companion as they halted by the rear door. This Sarah opened and by a series of awkward maneuvers, managed to seat Lenox Cobb. In place, leaning forward, he strongly reminded Sarah of a large insect, perhaps a praying mantis. Her grandmother a gray moth, and now a mantis.

These analogies caused a sort of choked giggle so that by the time she sat back in the driver's seat, Sarah was fighting for breath.

Fortunately her grandmother and the professor were engaged in greeting each other with a minimum of civility.

"It's you, Lenox," said Mrs. Douglas. "What have you done to yourself?"

"Ah, Lavinia," said Professor Cobb, "is this your Japanese car? I thought better of you. And I have done nothing to myself. I was knocked down. By an unseen force."

"Don't be ridiculous, Lenox. You probably tripped. You aren't wearing your glasses."

Lenox Cobb fumbled at his face. "Why, I had them on when I set out for my walk. I walk every day. Down the driveway to the mailbox and back. We'll have to turn back and search for them."

"No," said Mrs. Douglas. "Not now. I am calling on Elena and the others. Because of Dolly. And this is my granddaughter. Sarah. Sarah McKenzie."

"Sarah Deane," corrected Sarah, thinking, oh Lord, now we'll spend twenty minutes on my name. She accelerated slightly and was able to turn in to the circular drive and park before her grandmother had properly launched into the subject of taking one's husband's name and cleaving wholly unto him.

The business of unloading two breakable elderly persons took some minutes, and it was not until both were settled in the living room of the house in chintz-covered armchairs that Sarah remembered Professor Cobb's complaint.

She turned to him. "You think you were tripped?"

He inclined his head. "Or knocked from behind. Someone in the woods. I went down like a fallen tree. I began to shout and I heard someone running away. Leaves and twigs snapping."

"Could it have been a dog?" Sarah suggested.

Lenox Cobb considered this. "Yes," he said. "It could have been that dreadful animal of Alice's. A dreadful big shaggy thing. No known breed. Completely out of control. It should be tied up."

"Uncle Lenox, are you talking about Willie? He's an absolute sweetheart. You must have annoyed him." Alice was in the room, looking as if she'd been caught in a stiff wind. Scarves, shirts, vests, ties, and belts hung from various parts of her torso, and a ragged pair of blue jeans clung to her lower limbs, which were finished off by a pair of scuffed paddock boots.

Now she walked up to Sarah's grandmother and extended a none-too-clean hand. "So good of you to come, Mrs. Douglas. About Dolly, of course. It's pretty awful, isn't it? Mother will be right along. She's stuck on the telephone with the police. Bunch of ghouls. Want to know if Dolly was depressed. Had ever tried suicide. Honestly, what lamebrains."

Sarah looked up. "Was Dolly depressed?"

Alice threw herself down on the sofa next to Sarah. "Now, don't you start in. Dolly was never depressed. How could she be? She was always doing the right thing. What was depressing was watching Dolly. She depressed me. She depressed Masha and Eliot. And she probably depressed my mother. Only none of us ever dared say so."

Here Lenox broke in. "Well, there's nothing we can do about Dolly. It's all extremely sad and she was the one person who kept this house moving. I, for one, will certainly miss her marmalade muffins. Now, about your dog, Alice. Tie him up or I won't be responsible."

"Uncle Lenox," said Alice, sitting up and fixing him with a look. "If one hair on Willie is—"

But here Elena Beaugard made her presence known by the shuffling of her feet and the tapping of her heavy cane. Eyesight threatened by glaucoma, mobility limited by arthritis, bowed down by grief, she made a slow progress into the room. Lenox subsided and Alice jumped up and guided her mother to a chair, pushed a cushion behind her back, and directed her attention to the arrival of Mrs. Douglas, now settled in an adjacent chair. This produced in Mrs. Beaugard a heavy sigh and a reaching over and laying on of hands on Mrs. Douglas's arm. Who removed them, patted them briefly, and returned them to their owner.

Mrs. Beaugard was built more or less on the lines of Franklin Roosevelt's formidable mother. Dressed in gray knit with amber beads ringing her neck, she was stout, big-breasted, double-chinned, with a beak nose emerging from plump cheeks and her white hair fastened down into a net. As always, she wore silver-rimmed thick-lensed glasses that, together with her heavy eyebrows, accentuated a perpetually severe expression as if she had caught someone engaging in unmentionable activities. Although at seventy-two, she was almost eighteen years younger than Sarah's grandmother, infirmity seemed to have accelerated the aging process so that the difference between the two women did not seem great.

Following in Mrs. Beaugard's train came her oldest daughter, Masha. Masha, auburn hair in a modish chop, eye makeup and dark lipstick perfectly laid on, her slim figure wrapped in an emerald green jumpsuit, was every inch the professional performer. She paused by her mother's chair, extended a hand over to Mrs. Douglas, murmured something in a low voice, and then floated off to a window seat and turned her gaze on the outside world.

Masha was followed by her brother, Eliot, and Eliot's wife, Caroline. Eliot, fair-haired like his sister Dolly, tall, sunburned, looking seaworthy and competent, the epitome, Sarah thought, of the successful businessman. Wife Caroline, staying just behind Eliot's shoulder, reminded her of an expensive doll whose designer had failed to give her a completely human expression. Her lips were parted in a permanent half smile, her blue eyes were open and unblinking, her pale hair was tied back, and her full-skirted rust-colored dress with its white collar had an antique costume look.

Subdued greetings and expressions of sympathy were passed around, and once concluded, Sarah's grandmother and Elena Beaugard settled down for conversation, Alice and Lenox retired to a distant window seat to wrangle in a low key on the subject of untrained dogs, and Eliot and Caroline went to the door to greet an elderly couple who no doubt brought their condolences.

Seeing the Beaugard family well occupied. Sarah was free to study her surroundings and take stock of the bereaved and their visitors.

She had not been inside the old Beaugard "cottage" for years. To picnics, yes, or under a tent for Alice's wedding reception, and for weekend parties having to do with dances and tennis that had taken place on the lawn. Like her grandmother's house, it was a lumbering shingled beast with turrets and bays and protrusions and porches.

The living room was cavern-size and filled with a thicket of furniture—the summer chairs and tables having been augmented by the sale of the family house in Boston and the shipping of the contents to Proffit Point. Now weighty mahogany and dark cherry mixed haphazardly with wicker and pine and faded chintz. But the general effect, although confused, offered comfort and the sort of hominess so common in long-inhabited family houses—even if the families themselves were at swords' point.

And there over the mantel of the great fieldstone fireplace was the large oil study of the four Beaugard children. It must have been painted, Sarah thought, when Alice was about ten. Which would make Dolly, the middle daughter, fourteen, Masha nineteen, and Eliot just about eight. The artist had posed the two oldest girls on a white garden bench, Alice on a cushion at their feet, and next to her, sitting cross-legged, the boy Eliot.

Sarah, curious, got up and walked to the fireplace for a closer look. And as she approached the painting, she was aware of a small shiver running from the nape of her neck and rippling all the way down her backbone. The three girls and the young boy looked so alive. The artist had somehow managed to give a sense of animation and also catch the slightest whisper of friction between the sitters. Masha, auburn hair tied back with a white scarf, wearing a soft summer dress of the palest yellow, kept her chin lifted, her arched nose slightly elevated, her eyes upraised, her feet tucked in next to sister Alice's hand, and her shoulder turned away from Dolly; Dolly, all in white, her yellow hair swept back and held by a blue band, sat with hands folded in the lap of her full skirt. She stared straight ahead, her lips fastened in a careful smile, and somehow the artist had managed, without making her expression in the least unpleasant, to suggest a stubborn and unyielding personality.

Alice was another matter. Sarah imagined that she had been dragged into the portrait sitting by sheer force because the artist had conveyed this resistance. Alice on her cushion had one hand pressed to the ground, as if ready to spring up and away. Like her sisters, Alice wore a floating creamy summer dress, but her sash was untied and one of her party slippers had been pushed off and lay abandoned on the grass. And while Masha looked up and Dolly stared ahead, Alice gazed off to the edge of the picture as if she were searching for an escape route.

Eliot, on the other hand, sitting there with his arms folded across his chest, looked out at the world with a pleased expression. As if he owned the world. Well, he probably did, thought Sarah. The Beaugard world anyway. Eliot, the hoped-for boy born to a mother over forty. Eliot in a sailor suit, short pants, a dark tie, and a lanyard with a whistle. Did boys twenty years ago wear sailor suits even for portraits? Sarah couldn't remember any such costume from her childhood. Her brother, Tony—who was close to Eliot's age—wouldn't have been caught dead in one. But the effect, the sailor suit, the girls in their pale summer dresses, the garden bench, gave the whole a sense of an age long gone by. And it reminded Sarah of something she'd seen before. A painting? Or a photograph of just such a family? She frowned, trying to remember.

"You've seen that old thing before, haven't you?" It was Alice, a cigarette in one hand, a glass of something dark—her daily rum?—in the other.

"I must have," said Sarah. "But I haven't really been in the house for ages. You all look so alive. It's a wonderful picture."

"Well, it scares the shit out of me," said Alice. She brushed a wayward wisp of brown hair out of her eyes and poked it back into the general tangle. "It was done by an artist called Marie-Louise Dauphine. Mother found her in Quebec on some art excursion and hauled her down here to do it. Cost a fortune and we fought like cats all through the sittings. I had to be literally dragged into the scene that first day. And I didn't want to wear a dress, and Masha would sneak her foot over and try and step on my hand, and I'd pinch her ankle and put pebbles into Dolly's shoes. And Eliot would spit at me when no one was looking."

"But the painting scares you?"

"Like I said. I think that Marie-Louise Dauphine was some kind of witch. She used to drink gallons of herbal tea and cackle at us. Mother wanted a sort of period piece, the golden age of childhood. We look positively Edwardian. But Marie-Louise got right inside us, didn't she? Into our skulls. Look at Dolly. You can almost feel her jaw tighten and her hands clench, and yet she's smiling. And Masha as if she was sniffing body odor. Eliot, king of all he surveys. And me, ready to get the hell out of there. I think Marie-Louise got pieces of our souls and didn't give them back. Isn't that what the Indians are afraid of? The Hopis? Or is it the Navajos? Anyway, whenever I look at it, I feel as if someone were walking across my grave. Eliot can't believe he let Mother get him into a sailor suit—I think she had it made for the occasion. Masha says the thing gives her the creeps, and even Dolly said she tried not to look at it. Only Mother thinks it's wonderful. Which I suppose from her point of view it is. Our souls all caught and stuck up there above the mantel for ever and ever, amen."

"Alice, will you help with the tea?" It was Mrs. Beaugard calling across the room.

"Oh Christ," said Alice. "Where's Dolly when we need her? I don't do tea, I just drop cups."

"I'll help," said Sarah, thankful to have employment.

So tea was produced, wheeled in on a trolly by a handsome black-haired woman introduced as the housekeeper, Mrs. Lavender. Cups and waferlike sandwiches were duly distributed and circulated while at the same time decanters, whiskey and sherry, appeared on a side table under the supervision of Eliot.

Eliot, Sarah noticed, was playing the host to a circle of visitors. Sarah caught the repeated name of Dolly, from which she gathered that Eliot was apparently reciting amusing family tales in which Dolly was the featured player—or the featured butt. Why was it, Sarah wondered, sipping her tea, that funereal occasions often turn into slightly-out-of-control cocktail parties where even simple observations take on a hysterical tinge? Where people laugh too loudly, and then look abashed and anxious.

But now Sarah was recalled to her grandmother's side. It was time to go. On their way out the door they were stopped by Masha poised to do the honors. She was sorry not to have properly thanked Mrs. Douglas for coming. So good to see Sarah. All so terribly sad. Dolly, a great loss. Mother is bereft. Dolly drove her everywhere. And what will St. Paul's Sunday school do? Or the Midcoast Audubon. Dolly was the new secretary.

"Of course," added Masha, "I never had her grit. She stuck to projects like a limpet. Got them done."

"Masha," said Eliot, coming up, with Caroline still at his shoulder, "is too damn artistic for everyday grit. Sarah, Mrs. Douglas, come sometime and see our new house. Come for drinks...or"—with a glance at Mrs. Douglas's disapproving face—"or tea. Just say the word." Here Eliot gave his wife a meaningful glance.

Prodded, Caroline bobbed her head. "We'd love to have you visit. Both of you." She spoke with a noticeable lack of energy.

Here Mrs. Douglas broke in and said firmly that she never went out except to church and the dentist and to make sympathy calls, but thank you.

"You, Sarah?" said Eliot. "You and Alex. Hey, we never see you anymore."

You never did see us, Eliot, Sarah told herself, but out loud she murmured about sometime and how nice and then assisted her grandmother out of the room.

To be followed by Lenox Cobb. Limping and with a cane.

"If you will take me to where you found me. I must look for my glasses. They must have fallen off when the dog jumped on me."

"It *was* the dog, then?" asked Sarah, opening the car door and lifting her grandmother almost bodily onto the passenger seat.

"Oh, Alice denies it, but Alice has never told the truth. That great hairy dog of hers counts as much as her entire family."

Sarah, whose Irish wolfhound, Patsy, was one of the loves of her life, confined herself to assisting Lenox into the backseat of the Subaru, trying at the same time not to listen to another fulmination on the subject of Japanese cars.

Sarah drove slowly until Lenox, rapping with his cane, brought the car to a halt. Helped out and put on his feet, the professor limped into the woods that bordered the drive. "Be careful," Sarah called after him, although she was not sure quite what she was warning him about. She had seen Alice's dog asleep in the front hall as they left.

Neither Sarah nor her grandmother spoke for the twelve-mile drive from Proffit Point to the turnoff north on Route One in Thomaston. Sarah wondered whether her grandmother was thinking consoling thoughts about Dolly Beaugard passing through the welcoming gates of heaven, but then, looking sidewise at Mrs. Douglas's rather grim expression, she decided that no, it wasn't heaven on her mind, more likely some of the darker observations in Isaiah and the Psalms—all those verses about grass that is green and groweth up and then withereth and flowers that fadeth.

But when Mrs. Douglas spoke she revealed that she had not been bustling about in the Valley of the Shadow; she had been occupied with more worldly matters.

"Did you know," she began, "that Dolly had taken over most of Elena's affairs?"

"I suppose she had," said Sarah, not much interested.

"And that she had persuaded Elena to give the big house at Great Oaks to the Episcopal Church next year? To St. Paul's-by-the-Sea."

Sarah came alive. "The whole house? The whole estate?"

"No, no. Just the house and about an acre surrounding it. For a retreat. For diocesan workshops."

"Good heavens!" exclaimed Sarah, holding back stronger epithets. "What about the family? Uncle Lenox? He's living there now, isn't he? And Alice? And Alice's son if he ever turns up? And Masha? Eliot and Caroline? They have a boy."

"There are about six guest cottages, quite substantial ones, on the property. Alice is already occupying one of these, and Lenox and Dolly were each to have one. Eliot and Caroline, of course, have that new house on Tidal Cove. But now Dolly will not be here to facilitate the move. However, Elena told me that Father Smythe was quite thrilled."

Sarah made the turn onto the Old County Road, the back route to Camden, and instead of bringing the Subaru up to speed—forty-five miles per hour—she slowed, so interesting was the information.

"You really mean it, Grandma, the whole big family house?"

"As I said. Of course, the plumbing, the electric system, would have had to be redone. The house is quite dilapidated."

Sarah grimaced. "No wonder Dolly's dead. Snatching the house *and* an acre of land from her own family."

"Nonsense. The contents of the house, all those paintings—there's a Monet and a Constable and all those Whistler etchings—were to go to the heirs. And income to maintain the cottages for Alice and Lenox and Dolly. Even after various other bequests, there would have been a great deal of money for all of them. And I presume, although Elena didn't say so, that the heirs would have the rest of the property and the beach and dock to divide among themselves. Proffit Point is an extremely valuable piece of shore land. Really, Sarah, you must not go about saying things like 'no wonder Dolly's dead.' That is irresponsible. You have been involved in entirely too many criminal activities."

Sarah nodded. "I couldn't agree with you more. It's just that I'm surprised."

"I think it was a fine and generous plan. Large properties like Great Oaks need to serve more than a few family members."

"You're a socialist, Grandma," said Sarah, grinning at her.

This remark, her grandmother ignored. She simply shook her head. "But of course, any future estate plans that Dolly may have helped her mother make will be in jeopardy. That family simply lives to squabble. With Dolly gone, the contents of the house, the property, will have to be reapportioned. Elena was quite distressed and said she didn't know who would take over the estate management. Possibly Lenox, although he takes a great deal of pleasure in being contrary. Alice would be hopeless. She would probably try to turn the Great Oaks estate into a wild animal preserve. And Eliot is too interested in his own new house to be any help."

"Which leaves Masha, I suppose. But she's only available between concerts."

"I suppose so," said her grandmother in a distant voice, and Sarah could see that the effort of the visit had taken its toll. Mrs. Douglas's hands were moving about in her lap like captive birds, her eyes were drooping, her head nodding.

"Almost home," said Sarah, turning the car in to Camden's Bay View Street. Then as she drew up by her grandmother's front door, she remembered that Dolly's arrival had followed two other notable deaths. "Grandma," she asked as she held her grandmother upright and began walking her toward the door, "did Mrs. Beaugard mention the two Gattlings? You remember. Those two men who washed up in Little Cove a few days before Dolly's body came in. Did Dolly know any of the Gattling family?"

Mrs. Douglas drew herself up. "Elena mentioned the two Gattling deaths as being the silver lining to the cloud. A Gattling apparently broke into her barn last fall and stole a lawn mower. But the two families have never known each other. Why would they?"

Why indeed? thought Sarah as she turned her grandmother over to the waiting Hopkins, who, by the swollen condition of her left cheek, proved that the root canal had been attended to.

But, she reminded herself, as she headed homeward through the Camden Hills toward Sawmill Road, those Gattlings are all over the place. Two Gattling cousins had a seasonal business hauling floats for summer people and probably casing the empty houses as they did it. Another Gattling manned a Mobil station. A Lola Gattling—Sarah had seen her name tag—worked the checkout counter at the Shop 'N Save supermarket. Probably the Beaugard family, all unaware, had trafficked with Gattlings, had employed them on the estate as anonymous members of a work group, cutting lawns, fixing roofs, dealing with boats and moorings—doing the sort of work needed on any large and unruly piece of property.

With her mind busy considering the possible interfacing of Beaugards and Gattlings, Sarah almost ran full tilt into Alex's Jeep parked smack in front of the house instead of being put away as usual in the old equipment shed that did service as a garage.

She jammed on her brakes and came to a squealing stop.

Alex leaned in the car window. "Good God, you almost wrecked both cars. I was just unloading some shingles. For the shed."

"I was thinking about the Gattlings. Whether they've been mixing it up with the Beaugards. Because I've been doing tea and sympathy over on Proffit Point. With Grandma."

"And I've been doing forensics with Mike Laaka. At lunch and later on the phone. It's just as we thought."

Sarah paused in her climb out of the car. "What is?"

"Marsden and Junior. Death by drowning. With skins full of doped whiskey."

"And Dolly?"

Alex sighed. "Also death by drowning. But complications. Contusions, facial abrasions, a depressed skull fracture, some of which occurred before she drowned. Enough injury to cause at least temporary loss of consciousness. Other injuries are post-mortem from the body hitting rocks and ledges."

"You're saying she got a fractured skull while sailing?"

"Maybe Dolly was banged on the head by the boom swinging around suddenly. Because of the wind that day—squalls and gusts. Or the boat may have gone over on its side in what they call a knockdown. Say Dolly was hit and lost consciousness, then she'd fall down on the floorboards of the boat. The boat would be yawing around, boom banging, sails and sheets all over the place. Water would be coming over the side and she was facedown in it."

"But the boat didn't really sink?"

"No. It's made of wood. It would just fill up with water."

Sarah shook her head. "Could Dolly have fallen overboard before she was hit on the head?"

"Okay, that could have happened. And Dolly might have been hit on the head by the swinging boom while she was trying to hang on to the side of the boat?"

"And lose her hold and go under and drown."

"How it happened is guesswork. As I told Mike, if she hadn't drowned, she would have died from hypothermia because it doesn't take long to die of exposure in the ocean at this time of year."

"I suppose so," said Sarah soberly.

"Drowning," went on Alex, now settling into the role of instructor, "or what we call death by immersion, means that pulmonary circulation due to inhalation of water is compromised, the right heart is distended, and the great veins are filled with dark red blood. The blood is diluted by the inhaling of water, so coagulation is likely to be absent. A mass of foam—water mixed with mucous—often appears coming from the mouth and nose of the victims. All of which happened in the cases of the two Gattling brothers. And with Dolly Beaugard."

Sarah grimaced. "Okay. Okay. Enough already. I've got it. Dolly drowned. The Gattling boys drowned."

"Right. So now it's on to phase two. Or three. Anyway, into how and why. Let's go inside and put our feet up and talk about something else. Like the flu season. It's A-Beijing, this year."

"Wait a minute." Sarah waved at two wooden chairs under an old apple tree by the back porch. "Time out. No more clinical details, no A-Beijing flu. Let's sit down and admire the view. The maple trees are sensational this year."

Alex walked over, and he and Sarah arranged themselves in the chairs. Each looked dutifully at the hillsides, but not more than five minutes was given to the panorama of autumn splendor.

Sarah broke it up. "So what about Dolly's sailboat? Can't the police guess what happened by examining it?"

"Dolly's sailboat," said Alex. "Curious you should ask that. I'm being called as a so-called expert in the matter."

"Her sailboat? You?"

"Me. Old sailor McKenzie. Dolly's boat is a class of wooden sixteen-foot sloops called Weymouth Scooters. Only about thirty or so were ever made, and most of them were sailed out on Weymouth Island—my summer stamping ground. Or sailing waters. A few Scooters—maybe five or six—were built for local people like the Beaugards who lived on the mainland. The sloops are speedy devils, but they never caught on. Centerboard jobs with too much sail and too little weight below. Hard to handle in a stiff wind. My father sold ours after my younger brother, Angus, was dumped. But I learned to sail in the thing. And after one of those Scooters, handling any other boat was easy."

"But Dolly hung on to hers."

"So it seems. But Alice isn't the only one with suspicions. The police want me to go over Dolly's boat because I know what the original boat looked like and perhaps can tell if Dolly's has been tinkered with. Which seems likely because the six Scooters the police have located have been modified to make them seaworthy."

"Why not ask the builder or look at the original designs?"

"Builder is dead, and none of the boatyards can put hands on blueprints. I have a date with Mike Laaka to look at the sloop over at the coast guard station boathouse at six o'clock tomorrow."

"And I can come?"

"You're not invited, but I suppose you can lurk."

"It's what I do best."

"You're telling me. But try and keep a low profile."

"I will crawl around on my hands and knees. I will abase myself. I will kowtow. I will lick boots and polish brass."

"You see," said Alex amiably, "Alice is right. You can't resist sticking your nose into someone else's sleaze."

"Not sleaze," said Sarah. "It's the Beaugards. All of them. There's a sort of horrible fascination about them. Like some sort of bad four-hundred-page novel. And I guess I want to know how it comes out."

"Aha!" said Alex, grinning. "The truth at last. Come on, Miss Marple, it's beer and tea time."

Chapter Five

THE NEXT DAY, WEDNESDAY, October the fifth, at a few minutes after six, Alex, with Sarah a step to the rear, presented themselves at the coast guard station and were led inside a long building housing a number of small boats. There, off to one side, under a bright hanging light, propped up by four metal legs, sat Dolly Beaugard's Weymouth Scooter.

A sad sight, thought Sarah, seeing sails draped over the bow, a tangle of lines hanging over the sides, the tiller cracked, stays loose, the top of the mast broken off. Part of the hull had been splintered, and here and there ragged holes showed. And over the whole, straggled dried strands of seaweed, while an amber sheet of kelp concealed part of the name painted on the stern.

Sarah moved slightly closer, squinted at the letters and made it out. *Sweetheart.* Oh dear. But somehow the befouled name, the seaweed combined with the hunks of gray muck that adhered here and there to the bottom, not only gave the little vessel a dirty and forlorn look, it gave a sober sense of what had happened that blustery day off the Maine coast.

Sarah, mindful of approaching officialdom—a uniformed deputy and Mike Laaka—retreated to watch. It was a slow process. Alex, outfitted in a lab coat, rubber gloves, and covers for his shoes, crept about under and behind the sailboat, then up a short ladder to probe *Sweetheart*'s innards. Sarah, tired of the spectator role, decided to look for another object of interest.

Which she immediately found.

To the rear of the building at a distance from Dolly's boat, propped in the same manner, sat the *Sweetheart*'s twin sister. Only this vessel—named *Zippo*—was clean and shining. White hull, green-painted topside, green boot stripe, red bottom paint. Sarah looked around and saw a familiar face. Sheriff's Deputy Katie Waters—a person with whom she had shared a thoroughly unlawful investigation the past summer.

Katie marched over and Sarah took note of her crisp brown uniform, her trousers with perfect pleats, her Smokey the Bear hat at the correct angle. Katie was short and slightly built with a sharp little triangular face sprinkled with freckles, but she wore such an air of stern professionalism that Sarah realized they were not about to have old-home week about past misdeeds.

To forestall questions, Sarah quickly pointed to the *Zippo*. "What's this one?"

"Are you supposed to be in here?" said Katie warily. Sarah had almost cost Katie her job that past July, and she wanted nothing more to do with the woman.

"Don't worry, Katie. I won't go near Dolly's boat. I came with Alex. He's apparently an expert on Weymouth Scooters. But I thought the police couldn't find one that hadn't been altered. That's why Alex was called in. This looks exactly like Dolly's. Only it's in one piece and cleaner."

Katie melted slightly. Sarah away from the *Sweetheart* could cause no real trouble. "State police just found this half an hour ago on a mooring in Rockport. Family by the name of Baum. Joseph and Melinda Baum. Mr. Baum said he hadn't changed anything, so the police got into gear and trailed it over exactly as is."

The *Zippo* was not propped as high as the *Sweetheart*, since detailed examination of the hull and bottom would not be necessary. And this meant that Sarah could not only walk around the boat but could get a good view of its interior.

It was a tidy thing. Teak floorboards, mahogany seats, brass fittings, halyards, jib, and main sheet all coiled and clean. The sails were bent on, furled, and tied neatly with sail ties. A plastic bucket, a sponge, a boat horn, a bailing scoop, and a small hand pump rested on the floorboards.

"Did Dolly Beaugard's boat have all this stuff in it?" asked Sarah. "The pump and the bucket?"

Katie hesitated and then apparently decided that this information would probably be general knowledge. "Any loose equipment aboard the *Sweetheart* must have floated away when she filled up. Even the floorboards except one. But a life jacket was aboard, tied onto a cleat."

"They say cause of death was drowning," said Sarah.

Katie Waters clamped her mouth shut. "They, whoever *they* are, can say what they want. I don't give out that kind of information. I keep my mouth shut and keep my job."

"I'm sorry I mentioned it, Katie. But Alex told me. He's the medical examiner."

"Alex should keep official information to himself."

"Oh, Katie, lighten up. I'm not going to talk, and by tomorrow the family will know how Dolly died. So will the whole county." Sarah turned back to *Zippo*. "The boat's in perfect condition. The Baum family must not have tipped over much."

"Probably better sailors," said Mike Laaka, coming up behind Katie. "Those Weymouth Scooters are what Alex calls 'tender.' Not 'love me tender,' but mighty touchy in a wind. That's why they're obsolete. Too many people ended in the drink."

"Did Dolly make a habit of capsizing?" asked Sarah.

"We asked around. Seems she had a pretty good record. Went out in stiff winds and came back okay. Once got caught on a ledge at low tide, and this summer her tiller stuck and she drifted into an island, but that's about it."

"So why," said Sarah, still puzzled, "did she get into trouble last Sunday?"

Mike shrugged. "Because there's a first time for everything."

Sarah stood stock-still for a minute, and then, "Mike, is there a telephone around here?"

"Public phone by the town landing. And just who do you want to call? The district attorney?"

Sarah smiled at him. "Just a call to a private family."

"Sarah, butt out, okay?" said Mike.

Sarah lifted her head. "Michael Laaka, I haven't butted in. But something just occurred to me. And I'll be right back."

Sarah kept her word. In less than ten minutes she reentered the boat shed and found Alex, Mike, and Katie standing in the middle of the floor midway between *Zippo* and *Sweetheart*. An argument was in progress about *Sweetheart*'s broken mast.

"Could have snapped in the wind," Mike was saying.

"Doubt it," said Alex. "I've never heard of one snapping off just like that. It probably broke on a ledge after the capsize."

"But if the tip broke off and hit Dolly on the head," said Katie, "then that would account—"

"Unlikely," said Alex. "Because—"

Sarah felt free to interrupt. "Ballast," she announced.

The three turned and stared.

"Ballast," repeated Sarah. "*Zippo* carries ballast. I've just had a friendly chat with Melinda Baum, who said that after their first sail in their Scooter, they decided on ballast. Otherwise she would always be on her ear in the least wind."

"Ballast," repeated Mike. "What kind of ballast? *Zippo* hasn't been modified. That's why it was trailed over."

"It wasn't modified," said Sarah. "It was added to. Lead ballast. A dozen bars of lead laid inside along the centerboard. Keeps her from being knocked down with every gust. Take a look." Here Sarah led the way to *Zippo*, and the four peered into the boat.

"Lift the floorboards," suggested Sarah.

Mike, giving her a look, climbed aboard and pulled up the long segments of teak planking and reached down into the bilge. "Lead," he announced. "Or something like it. Laid two by two."

"And *Sweetheart*?" said Sarah. "Did she carry lead bars?"

Mike stared at her resentfully. "I didn't see any. But if she had, maybe they would have been dumped out when the sloop went over. Or Dolly never carried ballast in the first place."

But Sarah shook her head. "You just said there's no record of Dolly getting in trouble before. Except for two minor incidents. Are you sure? How about coast guard records?"

Mike looked unhappy. "So far coast guard records don't show anything, but we're still at square one. Sarah, I can't believe you just went out and called the Baum family and this all came out. The state police said the Baums swore that their sloop was an original unchanged Scooter."

"So it is," said Sarah. "Only a little weight adjustment."

"One point for the home team," said Alex, who had been listening to the Mike-Sarah exchange with a certain pleasure. It wasn't often that anyone set Mike back on his heels.

"Christ," said Mike unhappily. "Now we'll have to see if *Sweetheart*—what a god-awful name for a boat—carried lead."

"There should be rub-marks, dirt lines," said Alex. "Even with the hull and bottom trashed, you should find some signs of wear from the lead. Paint scrapings, splinters."

"And," put in Sarah, "I don't think *Sweetheart* is such a bad name. It's growing on me. Dolly apparently didn't have a human one, and a pretty little sailboat seems like a fair substitute."

"A human sweetheart," said Katie, speaking after a long silence, "wouldn't have hit her on the head and dumped her into the Atlantic Ocean."

Alex turned on her with a grim expression. "You know better than that, Katie. Human sweethearts can be lethal."

"Never mind," said Sarah. "The question is whether Dolly's boat usually carried lead ballast. And if it did, then why wasn't there a single bar left even after it capsized? With one floorboard still in place, you can't tell me every one of those heavy lead lumps just wiggled loose, floated out, and sunk."

"It's possible," insisted Mike, frowning.

Alex raised his eyebrows.

"Okay, okay, okay," said Mike. "I'll call the Beaugards. I'll call Tad Bugelski. I'll see who helped Dolly rig her boat and launched it for her every year. Who was scheduled to help haul it out. See if *Sweetheart* carried any goddamn ballast. Jesus Christ, we'll take a simple case of drowning and turn it into a suspicious death when we're already run ragged trying to find out what was going on with those drunken doped-up Gattling brothers. It'll keep the state police around everyone's necks until after Christmas."

"Around *your* necks," corrected Sarah. "Not mine, not Alex's neck. We're just vagrants passing through."

"Hell you are," said Mike. "Alex is the medical examiner, and you are very useful because you're intimately acquainted with the whole Beaugard tribe."

"Not intimately," said Sarah with irritation. "Slightly."

"If it isn't intimate now," said Mike, turning to leave, "it will be."

❈ ❈ ❈

"Seriously," asked Alex, as the two, after a pit stop to pick up a pizza, drove back through the Camden Hills and toward Sawmill Road. "How well do you know the Beaugards?"

"I thought I'd told you," said Sarah. "When we spent the summers in Camden with Grandma, I was taken over there to kid birthday parties. And I was in Alice's class for a few years and in the same tent for two years at Camp Merrilark. Then, when I was older—after Alice had more or less deserted the family—there were tennis tournaments, dances at the Proffit

Point Boat Club. Sailboat regattas. I was invited because Mrs. Beaugard knew Grandma and I'd been a friend of Alice's. But I wasn't part of the Proffit Point scene. I always felt like someone's stray cousin being dragged in to fill out a doubles match. Be a crew in a sailing race. I was a fringe person."

"But the Beaugards came to our wedding."

"Grandma insisted."

"And you went to Alice's wedding,"

"The first one. Reception at Great Oaks. Big tent, lawn, music, dancing. And Alice and her husband—Alan Epstein, you know, he writes those sci-fi psycho thrillers that have people turning into reptiles or crows. Well, in the middle of toasts, Alice began a winging argument, Alan got a glass of champagne in the face, and Alice ended up being tossed off the dock in her wedding regalia."

"A sporting affair," observed Alex, slowing for the home turn.

"Memorable, anyway. But the second wedding was family only. A man who owned television stations. I think Alice had a vision of a media career. I don't think the marriage lasted six months. But she's got a son by Alan. Name of Jonathan. Grandma says he's spoiled, but she thinks all children are spoiled."

Alex shook his head. "I'm getting a picture of Alice, all right, and it's giving me a headache. Back to Dolly. Was she the sort to have a death wish? Ever depressed?"

"The police are asking that. The answer seems to be no. Besides, if you were thinking suicide, why would any woman in her right mind take pounds and pounds of lead ballast out of a sailboat, then sail away in a stiff wind in order to capsize and drown? It could have been done with much less effort by simply wading out into the ocean."

"The operative words are 'in her right mind.'"

"Dolly was the most sane female I've ever met. Steady, determined, levelheaded. Dull as dishwater. But sane."

"That's your view."

"It's a correct view. Ask around."

"You know, I might just do that. But it's still most likely to be ruled an accidental death. The ballast business is interesting but not earthshaking. Not yet anyway." Alex swung the car up the dirt drive leading to the farmhouse and then slowed. And swore. "Now, who in hell is that?"

Sarah looked up and ahead. There in the driveway stood an alien vehicle, a small yellow pickup truck. And under the front door light, seated on the steps of the kitchen entrance, leaning against the handrailing, a figure. Female. Long legs crossed on the stoop, the tiny red glow of a cigarette end, and music. The almost eerie sound of a clarinet.

"Mozart," said Sarah in astonishment as Alex brought the car to a halt.

"Who is playing Mozart on our steps?" demanded Alex.

"It's not one player," said Sarah. "It's a quintet. Mozart clarinet quintet. It must be a radio or tape deck But who in God's name?" Then she stepped out of the car and took a step closer. The profile, the cigarette, the careless sprawl of the figure, the sense of clothes in multiple and random layers.

"Oh God, it's Alice."

Then she stopped. "I didn't mean it that way. I'm sorry for her. Even in the middle of her family today she looked so alone. But tonight I wanted to correct papers and crawl into bed."

"Go ahead," said Alex with a weary sigh. "I'm not on call tonight, so I'll do the honors."

Aware that Mozart had ceased in mid-phrase, Alex and Sarah walked toward their guest, who rose to greet them.

"A little night music," she said. "I got sick of waiting and I didn't want to break into the house, so I settled down here with my tape player. Mozart to soothe my savage breast."

"You're feeling savage?" said Alex. "Come on in and help us with a pizza."

"I ate here last night. But okay. And some coffee maybe. I'm being picked up at your house. Hope you don't mind my parking my truck here. I'm meeting someone at your place. I've got two dates." Here Alice rose, crushed her cigarette with her bootheel. "I know you two don't have any common vices like smoking. Anyway, we've had news. Dolly died by drowning."

"Yes," said Alex. "It seems that way." He held the door open and the three trooped in and headed for the kitchen, Alice shrugging off a leather bomber jacket that looked as if it had been through at least two World Wars.

Conversation during the pizza heating and the coffee brewing ranged from the state of Mrs. Beaugard's nerves, the persistence of the police on the subject of Dolly's mental health, to Alice's loathing of Caroline and Eliot's newly built house.

"It's one of those state-of-the art things. You know, pseudo-Victorian Queen Anne shingle on the outside with high-tech goodies inside and every window facing the sea. Which reminds me. You're both invited over. Drinks Friday at six unless that's the day of the funeral. But we can't have the funeral until the police release the body. Mother wants Saint Dolly in a proper casket at the altar. She's choosing hymns and Psalms now. God, I can hear it now." And Alice lifted her head and sang out in a clear and true soprano:

"For all the saints who from their labors rest,
Who Thee by faith before the world confessed,
Thy name, O Je-sus, be for-ev-er blest.
Al-le-lu-ia! Al-le-lu-ia!"

Sarah and Alex stared. It was as if something unearthly had taken possession of the room. Then, after a moment of stunned silence, Alice herself broke the spell. "Think I should join the choir? Okay, Alex, when are the medical people going to let Dolly's body go, because let's get the funeral over. I mean, Christ, so Dolly drowned. What more do they want?"

Alex didn't answer immediately and busied himself with clearing the coffee cups. Somehow he didn't want to let Alice know that the police were also interested in Dolly's head injuries. That every inch of her sailboat was being examined. That it wasn't just a simple case of accidental drowning. Carrying the cups to the sink, he took a sidelong glance at Alice and decided that although she didn't look any better than when he'd seen her yesterday, she didn't seem worse. And somehow she'd managed to have her hair cut, and the improvement was noticeable. Straggle had been replaced by a straight clip, but Alice, like Sarah herself, had the cheekbones and chin to carry a severe look.

But now Alice was explaining why, for the second night in a row, she had invaded their kitchen. "It's not like I'm running away from the family, but the whole scene at Great Oaks gives me hives. Mother wants me to sleep in the house, not in my cottage, because she's trying to turn me into a Dolly replacement. And Uncle Lenox is driving everyone up the wall. He's acting like we're all in his classroom. He's got opinions on everything, and goes on about my dog, Willie, and his blasted glasses. Still lost in the woods. He keeps making little trips to look for them and makes me keep Willie in. He even went out searching last night with a flashlight. New trifocals, he says. What a grouch."

"He did seem a little cranky," Sarah admitted.

"'Cranky' hardly touches it. I think he's gone a little goofy since his fall. But Mother doesn't see it. He's her older brother and she's always had a soft spot for the creep. And I'll bet he's secretly glad Dolly's out of the way because he's been itching to manage Mother's affairs himself and take over Dolly's job at the Midcoast Audubon. Run the Christmas Bird Count thing."

Sarah, who had been about to gather her briefcase full of student papers and retire, paused.

"Christmas Bird Count?"

"You know," said Alice. "Every year around Christmas the whole neighborhood climbs around in snowdrifts in below-zero weather counting chickadees and seagulls. I went along once and it's unbelievable. People arguing about whether they really saw a pink-breasted titmouse or a black-assed woodpecker. Mother loves it, spends the day counting the birds at her feeder, and Uncle Lenox leads a team, and I get the hell out of Proffit Point and do something lowlife like go to a bar or go bowling."

Alex, who had been busy wiping off the counter, looked up. "Actually, I've been asked to help. With you, Sarah. December, Saturday the seventeenth. I'd almost forgotten. Dolly herself left a message last week on my answering machine. Sorry, Alice, you're in the presence of another bird nut."

"Alex is speaking for himself," said Sarah. "I am not a bird nut. I just married one."

"The point is," said Alice, "that Uncle Lenox is in seventh heaven. He hated being organized by Dolly, and now he can run the affair by himself. At least the Proffit Point section of it." Suddenly she came to attention. "Was that a car?"

"Your date?" asked Sarah, going to the window. She peered out into the dark. "No one there. Does whoever it is know the way? Sawmill Road isn't exactly on the main drag."

"Not a real date," said Alice, reaching for her jacket. "More like a business meeting. Husband number one. Alan. He knows the way here because he's renting on this road. He's moving from New Hampshire and teaching at Bowmouth next semester. It's some sort of writer-in-residence deal. Sci-fi stuff is very big. I hope they pay him a bundle. I want Jonathan to have swimming lessons."

"Bowmouth College," said Sarah with feeling, "has never paid anyone a bundle."

"Anyway, Alan has custody. As he should because, as the judge pointed out, I'm a little on the flaky side. But I turn up from time to time to play mother. Jonathan's quite used to the whole setup. Very mature kid. Eleven going on forty. Anyway, what with Alan being in the middle of moving and Jonathan's school situation messed up because of the move, I'm taking him for the school year. Or rather Mother and I are taking him. Co-custodians. The court seems to think that his living at Great Oaks is putting him into a stable environment. Little do they know. So I'm meeting with Alan to go over the details and then have myself a real date."

"Good," said Alex, who was wondering how soon he and Sarah would have the house to themselves.

"We're going to this rock concert thing tonight," said Alice. "I couldn't meet him at home because there would be multiple cat fits and cries of anguish. Mother, Lenox, Masha, and Eliot all keening away. Caroline making little mewing noises."

"Okay," said Sarah. "Who are you going with? The Phantom of the Opera or the Vampire Lestat?"

"He's not a vampire, though Mother would probably much rather he were. It's Webb."

"Webb who?" asked Alex obediently.

"Webb Gattling. I've known him forever. Well, since sixth grade, anyway. And yes, he's one of the famous Gattlings about whom we have all heard so much. Particularly this past weekend. But there's Alan's car now. I won't bring him in. See you, and thanks for the coffee."

Sarah and Alex sat immobile, listening to the car door slam shut, the tires crunch on the gravel, the sound of the motor accelerating, the sound diminishing down the drive. Only then did speech come.

"Gattling!" sputtered Sarah. "Well, wouldn't you know."

"Trust Alice," said Alex. "Mike told me that years ago Alice hung around with Webb Gattling, but he didn't sound as if he thought it was still going on. But here it is. The Gattling connection."

"And it's obvious the Beaugards don't have a clue that this old-time friendship is alive and kicking."

"Maybe not so much ongoing as revived," said Alex. "After all, Alice has been all over the map for the past ten years. Having husbands and a baby and visiting sanitariums."

"And who are we to judge?" said Sarah. "This Webb Gattling may be the greatest guy since Saint Peter. We shouldn't generalize on the basis of knowing that at least some of the local Gattlings belong behind bars. There may be pockets of wonderful Gattlings keeping their heads down and doing an honest day's work."

"Sure," said Alex. "There may be. I just haven't stubbed my toes on any. But I'm open-minded in all things and—"

But here the telephone rang across Alex's sentence and the idea of an honest member of the Gattling clan expired, not to be revived for some time to come.

Sarah answered the phone. Listened, nodded, made a face at Alex, and then said shortly into the receiver, "All right. Yes, he will. I will. Right away."

Alex looked up, glowering. "He will? You will? Right away?"

Sarah sighed. "That's Masha Beaugard. It's Lenox Cobb. He left for a walk around six. Or six-thirty. Into the woods, looking for his glasses. Hasn't come back. It may just be his ankle again. Or he's resting somewhere. They don't want to stir up the police over what may turn out to be nothing."

"They want to stir us up instead?"

"You've got it. We're practically family, says Masha. I love it. We haven't seen them in years except at weddings. Now we're family."

Alex reached for his windbreaker. "I'll go. You correct your papers."

Sarah hesitated, visions of schoolwork finished, hot bath taken, pillow and comforter beckoning, and then shook her head.

"'Whither thou goest, I will go; and where thou lodgest, I will lodge.' Or driveth—as the case may be."

"Hah," said Alex. "Don't put on sanctimonious robes. You are eaten up by an unholy curiosity as to the fate of the egregious Lenox Cobb. Right? You said you wanted to know how the four-hundred-page Beaugard family novel turned out. Well, this is Chapter Two."

"I'm beginning," said Sarah, opening the door, "to see the advantage of sticking to the short story."

Chapter Six

ALEX, A HEAVY FOOT on the accelerator, made it to Proffit Point in record time.

"Really," said Sarah, as he slowed the Jeep at the entrance to the Great Oaks property, "if a moose ever decided to cross in front of us, we'd be raw meat."

But now a light bobbing in the end of the road forced Alex to bring the car to a halt. It was Eliot Beaugard, wearing a blaze orange vest and equipped with a long-handled flashlight.

Alex pulled the Jeep over to the side of the driveway and, together with Sarah and Patsy, made himself known.

"Yo, Alex," shouted Eliot, "you made it." He eyed Patsy. "That dog, does he track?"

"He can try," said Sarah. "He's great at finding porcupines."

"I suppose," said Eliot, "that describes Uncle Lenox. But we can use all the help we can get. That animal of Alice's—Willie—

is hopeless. I've had to take charge of this circus. Mother's home shouting and banging her cane. You'd have thought Lenox was the only thing she had left in life. Me, I think he belongs in a home. He's gone wacko. Senile. Alzheimer's or blocked arteries."

"Where do you want us to start looking?" said Alex shortly. He had no liking for wild speculation on medical matters.

"And if we don't find him in the next hour, don't you think you should call the police?" said Sarah.

"Police," growled Eliot, and Sarah could almost hear Eliot's teeth grinding. "We've had police up to here. Like maggots. Forget the police. We just need a little homemade help. Like you and Alex. People who know us. Hell, this is a perfectly normal thing to happen to an elderly guy whose brains have scrambled themselves. I mean, looking for his glasses at all hours of the night and day. Tying up the entire family. Forcing us to call in strangers..." Here Eliot paused, realizing that two strangers had just been described as friendly homemade help.

"It's all right," said Alex. "Let's get on with it. Where have you looked already?"

Eliot subsided and produced a pad of paper, held up his flashlight, and squinted at it.

"Caroline and our son, Colin—he's nine and pretty sharp—are looking around the beach areas. And I've asked Tad Bugelski to keep a lookout by the harbor. After all, he's not the police. Mother's housekeeper, Vivian Lavender, is checking the house, the flower gardens, and the garage. I've looked in the potting shed and the pool house. Lenox isn't floating in the swimming pool; I turned on the underwater lights."

"And us?" Alex reminded him.

"Try and cover the woods by the gates here—both sides— and I'll case the middle part of the property and snoop around the guest cottages. All but Alice's. Her cottage is on your turf. Wouldn't you know that Alice is out on the town at the one time we could actually use her. I'll tell you this. Dolly could bore you to death arguing, but she wouldn't have let Lenox out of her sight. But hey, you two, we really appreciate you coming out here. And here's a whistle for you. Two blasts if you find the old buzzard."

"And if we don't?" said Sarah.

"Keep looking."

"For an hour. Two at the most. Then the police," said Sarah firmly. "And how about calling in more neighbors? Tad Bugelski could probably line up some of the lobstermen."

"No way," said Eliot, his voice rising. "It's bad enough that the whole county looks at the Beaugards like we're this bunch of weirdos because of Dolly and those Gattling brothers washing in practically on top of each other. No need to make it any worse."

"So let's move it," said Alex, now impatient to be away.

"Right," said Sarah. "I'll take the west side with Alice's cottage and the oceanfront except for the beaches, and you take the woods and the harbor side."

"I don't have two whistles," said Eliot. "You'd better work together."

"No," said Sarah. "I can whistle through my fingers. I do it loud and clear."

"You don't know Sarah," said Alex. "The Lone Eagle of detection. And we've got our own flashlights." And then as Eliot strode off down the road into the dark, "Are you sure, Sarah? Maybe we should stick together."

"Who, me? The Lone Eagle? Not on your life. Besides, Alice's cottage has a porch light on it and not many trees around. It's quite civilized. And Patsy could frighten an army."

But for all her sturdy proclamations of independence, Sarah felt a familiar crawling sensation moving from the nape of her neck down her back. Not because of unknown dangers hiding in the shadows, because indeed her search territory was crossed and recrossed with walking paths and garden benches, and Alice's cottage, just beyond a clump of birch, offered a cleared well-lighted safety zone.

Her unease had more to do with a sense of the nearby ocean. A southwest wind had sprung up; the tide was coming in, splashing softly on the lower rocks of the beach. Sarah could not help having visions of Marsden and Junior Gattling, like unearthly visitors, sodden with seawater, brains numbed with whiskey and drugs, washing in at high tide, followed by Dolly, Dolly turning in the moving waves, her blond hair streaming from her head.

Taking a tighter grip on her flashlight, telling her imagination to cool it, she gave Patsy's leash a tug, pointed the beam at the walking path that branched from the main drive, and, moving the light back and forth, walked forward.

Twenty minutes, six turns, and two paths later, Sarah ended on Alice's front porch. The sparse woods, mostly birch and white pines, had been free of Uncle Lenox—rampant or couchant—and it now occurred to her that if he was as befuddled as Eliot claimed, he might just have wandered into the cottage and gone to sleep.

Sarah fastened Patsy's leash to the porch support and examined the screen door. It was unlocked, as was the front door itself. She stepped into the building, fumbled for the light switch, and was rewarded by a glow from two table lamps and an overhead fixture.

I'm glad Alice isn't roughing it, she told herself. No doubt kerosene lamps were more in the spirit of the simple life, but the electric lights were reassuring and drove away the shadows.

It was a large room in a large cottage—the sort of cottage that many people would consider a house. A brick fireplace flanked by bookshelves filled the back wall. Decrepit wicker and oak chairs and tables did for furniture, and a large Navajo rug stretched down the middle. All in all it was a pleasant space. Except for the junk. Snuffed-out cigarettes overflowed in ashtrays; magazines and newspapers lay scattered about the floor along with a collection of muddy boots and dirty sneakers. Odd articles of clothing hung from chairs; a guitar leaned by a door; a dog leash hung over a lamp. On the walls hung several faded watercolors done by an amateur hand, a print of a Georgia O'Keefe skull, and a poster—a collector's piece, no doubt—of the early Rolling Stones.

But no Uncle Lenox Cobb. Sarah checked the sofa—and behind it—the screened porch off the living room, the kitchen, and then an overflowing curtained alcove that did service as a closet and held no room even for a man built like a praying mantis.

So on to the bedroom. Sarah, feeling now more intruder than searcher, walked across the room to the first of two doors, found the light switch, flipped it, and walked in. Guest room. The bed was made but covered with heaps of blue jeans, jackets, canvas hats, and a pyramid of rolled posters. A folding easel. A small loom strung with a woolly-looking length of something.

But no Uncle Lenox.

Leaving the guest room, bracing for the mess that must be in Alice's own bedroom, Sarah felt her sneakered foot lift with reluctance and looked down. The floor was tacky. She shone her flashlight and found herself looking down at a dark patch of something. Juice? Maple syrup? Blood?

Of course it was blood. She knew it must be even as she pulled her sneaker loose from the spot. She moved her flashlight forward and was rewarded with other spots. Or splatters.

Splatters that led straight into Alice's bedroom.

And now she hesitated, thinking not of Uncle Lenox but of people behind doors. Persons under beds, in closets. Persons curled up ready to spring out from behind bureaus, trunks, desks. Intruders rolled in comforters pretending to be Red Riding Hood's grandmother resting in bed.

And Sarah, for once, was sensible. She turned and ran to the porch, put two fingers between tightened lips, and gave a whistle that cut through the night air like a knife. Then she untied Patsy and retired behind a very large pine tree and waited.

"So I'm a coward," she whispered to Patsy, "but I don't like it in there."

And Patsy, sympathetic to her voice, rose on his haunches, put both paws on her shoulder, and began the reassuring business of washing her chin.

Sarah, hissing, "down, bad dog, stop it," didn't see Alex until he was almost at the cottage's front step. She called out, thinking at the same time, okay, now I've warned whoever it is—if there is someone—that we're here for the taking. Or the shooting or knifing, she added, remembering the dark splotches on the floor.

Alex paused, moved his flashlight, found her, and ran up. Sarah explained in five words, and together, this time with Patsy front and center, they cautiously and silently reentered the cottage. Then Alex, picking up a poker from the fireplace, moved quietly to Alice's bedroom door, paused, gave it a hefty kick, backed up out of sight, and waited.

The door stood wide open. Nothing happened. Two minutes. Five minutes. And then Patsy, pulling against his leash, began a whine that rose to an eerie pitch, a whine that would waken the dead. In case someone was dead.

Sarah came up behind Alex, slipped around him, thrust one arm into the room, and hit the light switch at first try.

The room was empty. The bed mussed, a blue and red comforter falling off one side, a cotton nightgown hanging from a bedpost, the bedside table holding a mix of filled ashtrays, paperbacks, a radio, a box of Kleenex, a jar of face cream.

But on the floor on the far side of the bed, in the narrow space between the wall and the bed—Lenox Cobb.

On his back, staring at them—or at the ceiling; it was hard to tell which. He lay, fitted into the space as if into a coffin, his legs neatly together, toes pointed up, gnarled and veined hands across his chest, head cradled between an overturned wastebasket and a shopping bag. His face was wearing what Sarah first thought was a sort of dark lopsided mask but on closer inspection—she leaning past Alex's shoulder—saw was made of the same viscous material that befouled the floor.

Alex, pausing only for a second, taking in the scene, making sure that any portion of Lenox was not being supported by the bed, grabbed the headboard and, assisted by Sarah, moved it out of the way, then knelt down, ready to begin a preliminary examination.

Meanwhile, Sarah had her hands full with Patsy, who began to show a great interest in the recumbent figure. Finally, pushing the dog into the living room, she returned to hear Lenox asking in a high reedy voice, "What kept you so long?"

"Just lie still, Professor Cobb," said Alex, putting his hand gently on Lenox's shoulder.

"What kept you so long?" repeated Lenox.

"You're all right," said Alex.

"We didn't know where you were," Sarah tried to explain.

"What kept you so long?" said Lenox, his voice rising.

"I'm trying to tell you," said Sarah. "We found you just now at Alice's cottage."

Alex twisted around to Sarah. "Head injury. Loss of immediate memory. Happens a lot after this sort of thing. They repeat and repeat. Hand me my flashlight. Thanks. I'll just check his pupillary responses while you call the ambulance. Proffit Point Rescue Squad. Then go on out and give another of your famous whistles and see if you can raise Eliot."

"Why are you here?" demanded Lenox. "I didn't ask you to come. It's time for bed. Where's Elena? I didn't ask you to come."

"Just lie quietly," said Alex, gently lifting one eyelid and shining the flashlight.

"I didn't ask you to come," said Lenox, now in a fainter voice.

"Yes," said Alex, in a soothing voice. "Easy does it."

"Womoahwamamaaooooo," said Lenox, giving a prolonged groan.

"What's he saying?" said Sarah, returned from the telephone.

"He's leaving us for the moment," said Alex. He ran his fingers lightly over Lenox Cobb's disordered head. "It's not a bad wound. Not a fractured skull as far as I can tell."

At which Lenox gave another groan mixed with an unintelligible mumble that sounded to Sarah's ears like some sort of Eastern dialect. Fortunately, the rescue squad was a speedy outfit, and before long Lenox Cobb had been packaged, loaded onto the ambulance, and whisked into the night, Alex in attendance.

Sarah, after the flurry of activity centering around the ambulance departure, found herself back at Great Oaks' entrance trying to fend off the attentions of Eliot and Masha. She must come back to the house. Mrs. Beaugard wanted to thank her. It would mean so much. Sarah was such an old friend.

Balls, she said to herself. And then aloud, "I have papers to correct for tomorrow's classes. I'll come up for just a minute and then I have to go."

This, of course, was easier said than done. Mrs. Beaugard, in common with the rest of the family, seemed to be under the delusion that Sarah and Alex—"thank heaven for Alex"—were friends and supporters of such long standing that they were ready to shuck their own needs in order to stand by the beleaguered Beaugards. "Just leave Patsy in the front hall. He can make friends with Willie," said Eliot.

Sarah, plied with cider and brownies, found that she was now elevated to the position not only of indispensable family friend but of Alice's special companion. Expected to take over the care and perhaps the feeding of Alice. Ready to hear the plaints of the family on the subject of Alice. And, now, on the subject of poor Lenox, who, in Eliot's words, was obviously wacko.

"Well, it was a head injury," said Sarah. "No wonder he's not entirely sensible."

"He hasn't been very sensible for ages," said Masha. She was sitting on a stool at her mother's feet holding wool in two hands while Mrs. Beaugard made hard work of winding a skein into a ball.

"Jesus, Uncle Lenox's never even been close to sensible," said Eliot. "How did Bowmouth stand him? And now obsessing about his glasses. Why didn't he call his optometrist and have a new pair sent out?"

Mrs. Beaugard paused abruptly in her wool winding. "Leave Jesus out of this, Eliot. He is not responsible for Lenox losing his glasses. But I agree that Lenox hasn't seemed himself lately. And so cross because I haven't turned to him for everything. He's been wanting to take over where my poor Dolly left off. Help me manage my affairs, balance my checkbook, but I really think—"

"Yo, Gran," said a voice from the door. "I'll manage your affairs. I got an A in math last year. And I'm going into pre-algebra now. Hello, Uncle Eliot. Aunt Masha. Old-home week, I guess."

Sarah looked up to see a boy in faded jeans, dirty sneakers, and a black sweatshirt standing in the doorway, a large duffel bag and a book backpack at his feet. The boy was tall and slender, and although his hair was dark, almost black, and he wore steel-rimmed glasses, he was so like Alice—the same sharp face, cheekbones, pointed chin—that she knew at once this must be Jonathan.

"So here I am, Gran," said Jonathan. "I think it's a pretty good time for me to move in because Aunt Dolly's dead and you probably need someone else around. Someone young."

"Jonathan," said Mrs. Beaugard faintly. "Jonathan, I'd forgotten, what with everything. Did your mother, the court...?"

The boy stepped into the room, and Sarah thought that here was a youth absolutely assured. No self-image problems, no inner doubts. He walked across the room as if he owned it, bent over his grandmother, kissed her cheek. "Not to worry, Gran. The court thinks it's okay even though the judge must be out of his tree, what with Aunt Dolly's body floating in on your cove. I mean it isn't exactly a wholesome environment, is it?"

"Jonathan," repeated Mrs. Beaugard, apparently not able to go beyond that one word.

"Listen, Gran, it's okay. My shrink said so and Mom's shrink said go for it. And Dad's happy because he's up to his ears in the Bowmouth College scene. And Mom thought it was a great idea because then she could stay in her own cottage and smoke and play the guitar, and I could stay with you in the big house and fight off intruders and burglars and alien androids."

"Oh, Jonathan!" exclaimed. Mrs. Beaugard, pushing her glasses back on her nose and sitting up straight. "Oh dear, what am I going to do with you? Eliot, did I know Jonathan was coming?"

But here the boy turned, held out a hand to Eliot, shook it, walked toward Masha, gave her a peck on the cheek, and then confronted Sarah.

"I'm Jonathan Epstein. Alice is my mother. I had dinner with her and Dad tonight, and it's all arranged for me to spend the year here with Gran and help out. I'm at Martin Academy over in Rockland, which is private and there's a car pool and that means then I can bat back and forth between parents if I have to. The human yo-yo, that's me. Are you a friend of Aunt Dolly's?"

Sarah stood up, shook his hand, and introduced herself, adding, "I'm just here for a few minutes. I was part of a search party looking for Professor Cobb, who's gone off in the ambulance. He hurt himself in the woods looking for his glasses."

Jonathan subsided in a chair next to his grandmother. "Hey, you mean old Uncle Scrooge is out of it? The only bad thing about coming here for the year was that we can't get along. I've tried, but he just wags his finger at me and calls me 'boy' and goes on as if I'm the sort of scumball who's ruining America."

Mrs. Beaugard reared up. "Jonathan, Uncle Lenox is not Mr. Scrooge. He's just not himself. Unwell."

"He was well enough to chew my head off when he saw me the other day at IGA grocery store in Camden. But I'll try and behave, okay, Gran? And I'm sorry about Aunt Dolly. I mean she wasn't the most fun person in the world, but she took me sailing every summer. When I came for vacation and it was Mother's turn to have me for a while. Or Gran's, because Mother wasn't always around."

Sarah twisted around to face him. "Dolly took you sailing?"

"Yeah," said Jonathan. He reached over to the plate of brownies, helped himself to a square, and took a large bite. Then, mouth full, he nodded, chewed again, and swallowed. "Yeah, Aunt Dolly was my sailing teacher. She wouldn't let anyone on the *Sweetheart* but me. I was the privileged person. I think she thought she was rehabilitating me or something.

Because I was from divorced parents. From a broken home." Jonathan took another bite of his brownie and chomped down.

Sarah gave the conversation a forward push. "She let you sail her boat? By yourself?"

Jonathan gave an heroic swallow, reached for the pitcher of cider, filled a mug, and gulped. Then returned to Sarah. "Nope. Never on my own. Just me and Aunt Dolly out on the wide Atlantic Ocean. She never let anyone touch the *Sweetheart*. Never even put a finger on it. She told me she did all the scraping and painting and stuff in the spring and hauled it out with her own trailer in the fall. She didn't do sports much, so I guess this was kind of her hobby."

"You mean," said Sarah slowly and carefully, "she did all the maintenance herself."

"Yeah," said Jonathan. "Like it was her own baby or something. I mean it was sorta weird calling it *Sweetheart*, but she didn't have any kids or have any men drooling over her—"

"Jonathan, that's enough," said Elena Beaugard.

"Okay, Gran, okay," said the boy. "I'm just answering questions about sailing."

"Did you ever capsize in the *Sweetheart* or have trouble in a big wind?" asked Sarah, trying to keep her tone casual.

Jonathan appeared to consider this. Then he shook his head. "Not real trouble. If the wind got too strong, we'd make for the lee of some island. A couple of times I came about too fast or let her jibe—you know, turn away from the wind, not into it— and the boat flopped around. But no capsize. Aunt Dolly said the *Sweetheart* could handle tough weather." Here Jonathan paused, seeming to follow the implications of what he had just said. "You're sort of saying that it's funny-peculiar that Aunt Dolly flipped over last week in the *Sweetheart*, but I suppose everyone does something dumb every now and then. Even Aunt Dolly."

"That, Jonathan, is enough," broke in Elena Beaugard again.

And Eliot looked at the boy with obvious dislike. "Watch your lip, buddy. Caroline and I don't let Colin speak to his grandmother like that."

But Jonathan only grinned and gave a shrug. "But actually, Uncle Eliot, I don't mean to be rude, but I was talking to Ms. Sarah Deane, not Gran. And Colin's only about nine, isn't he? So he doesn't dare say much."

Sarah, hearing Jonathan skating on the near edge of insolence, turned away and found herself again facing the big fireplace and the portrait of the four Beaugard children. And now it seemed that Dolly, erect and stiff in her white painted dress on her painted garden bench, was looking directly at Sarah with her tight smile, her wide-open blue eyes, her lifted chin. It was as if Dolly were radiating determination and stubborn purpose, and it had the effect of making a hard knot form in the center of Sarah's stomach. It was amazing how some people can be such an active presence even though presumed safely dead and gone. Sarah wrenched her gaze from Dolly's face, swallowed hard, and determined to get home, back to the tedium of her own chores. Confronting the family group again, she realized that Elena Beaugard was addressing Jonathan.

"Your mother"—she said the word with obvious disapproval—"will probably come home late and go right to her cottage. Vivian is there now cleaning up after your uncle Lenox. So you may as well take your things upstairs and unpack. You can have the green room on the north side. You must have some homework and then it will be time for bed. You may kiss me good night."

Jonathan jumped to his feet and leaned over and again brushed his grandmother's cheek. "And I'll say good night to all the nice people and be a good boy and wash my hands and brush my teeth. And hey, Gran, tomorrow I'll take over your business affairs. You can be my social science project." And without more ado, Jonathan walked swiftly to the door, picked up his bookbag, shouldered his bulging duffel bag, and vanished down the hall.

"Christ Almighty," said Eliot. "Does that kid need a crash course in manners. Which he certainly won't learn from Alice." He reached over and patted Mrs. Beaugard's hand. "Poor Mother. A useless big-mouth kid for the winter."

Sarah in her turn prepared for departure, shook hands all round, left the room, and collected Patsy.

Eliot was wrong, she told herself as she opened her car door. Wrong because Jonathan, no matter how rude, had not proved himself useless. In fact, it seemed to her that Jonathan—the chosen sailing companion of Dolly Beaugard—showed great promise as a source of special information.

Chapter Seven

SARAH, ARRIVING HOME WELL after ten o'clock, gave up on the idea of correcting papers and was in bed within the half hour, Patsy snoring by her side. And so soundly asleep were both that Alex's midnight return took place without either moving a muscle.

Thursday morning came too soon. The alarm clock purchased especially for its strident bell came to life at six A.M., and Sarah reached over and slammed a hand down on the control knob.

"Damn," she mumbled. It was her invariable response to the morning summons. Then, rousing slightly, "How's Lenox Cobb? Alive and kicking?"

Alex sat up and ran his hands through his disordered hair. "He's not doing too much kicking, but he's alive. CAT scan normal—consistent with a concussive injury. He doesn't remember the where and how of what happened. Which is what I expected."

"The whole family—well, Masha and Mrs. Beaugard and Eliot—seem to think he's gone completely gaga."

"The family can have a neurology workup if they want. Frankly, he didn't act too differently from a hundred other people with a head injury."

"But the hospital will keep him?"

"For a few days. His regular physician, that's Joe Foxe, has the situation in hand, and I very gladly bowed out." Alex stood up, stretched, and then took hold of one of Sarah's hands. "Rise and shine forth. It's a new day with no rain forecast until tomorrow. So did you escape the hospitality of the Beaugard clan?"

Sarah reached for the comforter and dragged it up to her chin. Then looked at the clock and reluctantly sat up. "No. It was cider, brownies, and Jonathan Epstein. Alice's boy. Mr. Cool. Flip and mouthy. I'd say Eliot wanted to brain him, and with considerable justification. And his grandmother hasn't a clue about what to do with him. Jonathan walked into that living room and spread himself. Says he'll handle Elena Beaugard's business matters as a social studies project, and he may just do that. There's a vacuum in the house, what with everyone doing no more than bemoaning Dolly's disappearance."

"Lenox will be home soon, and taking care of Elena Beaugard's affairs ought to be a permissible activity for him."

"Unless his mind is on a real skid."

"Don't listen to family opinion. Families always think their members have a few loose screws." And Alex disappeared into the bathroom for his shower.

But Sarah, washing and dressing slowly, was perfectly willing to believe that Lenox Cobb was losing his grip. She hadn't taken to him on their first meeting, and the kindest thing to think was that his mind was affected.

But Dolly was another matter. Dolly, that bland fair-haired, dumpy woman, was beginning to haunt her. Perhaps there was more to her than the person of good works. For instance, why would Dolly, the proper pillar of the community, bother about an eleven-year-old smarty-pants like Jonathan? Why was Dolly a solo sailor—except for the dubious and occasional company of Jonathan?

These questions she presented to Alex over his oatmeal and coffee. "Why this penchant for sailing alone?" Sarah complained. "Picnics, tennis, possibly golf, would seem more her style."

"When you live on the seacoast, sailing alone in a small boat isn't an oddball activity," Alex reminded her. "If Dolly had taken up martial arts or skydiving, I might have wondered."

Sarah poured herself a bowl of Grape Nuts—she needed something to crunch down on—and settled opposite Alex. "Dolly dressed like something left over from the fifties, lived this life of service—especially to her mother and the church. In fact, planned for her mother to give the big house to the Episcopal Church for the greater glory of God. Or her mother. Does that all jibe with the fact that not only did she handle her own boat, she put it into the water in the spring and hauled it out on her trailer in the fall? I mean, come on, Alex, that's a hell of a lot of work."

"So maybe she needed a little exercise."

"Hauling boats is miserable grungy work. A sixteen-foot wooden sailboat, with or without lead ballast, is a bitch to float onto a trailer even with a good winch. I know. My brother, Tony, and I had a boat like that we kept at Grandma's, and she made us put it in every summer and haul it out before we went back to school. It's no fun, and to do it by yourself, I mean really. Flats mud and cold water and big high rubber boots and fooling around with trailer axle grease."

"You may have a point. A small point."

"So I'm asking why? Why would Miss Prim and Proper, a woman with money to burn, with all sorts of working hands available, bother with the toil and hazard of dealing with a heavy wooden sailboat? Scraping, painting, and varnishing it in the spring? And ballast. Jonathan said that he and Dolly had never been in trouble sailing the *Sweetheart*. He claimed the boat behaved in all weathers. Just like the *Zippo*. So there *must* have been ballast of some sort. Maybe Dolly put ballast, lumps of lead—something heavy anyway—into the boat in the spring and took it out in the fall."

"That's fairly interesting," said Alex, moving on to his toast and coffee. "But keep your hair on, love, the lab is busy going over *Sweetheart*'s hull looking for ballast evidence."

Sarah frowned. "Maybe Dolly took it out a little while back to get ready for the hauling out. To lighten the boat so it would be easier to maneuver onto the trailer."

"And then had an overwhelming urge to go sailing in a big breeze? And forgot she'd taken out the ballast?"

"Well, why not?" said Sarah defensively. "You know how it is. Summer is gone, winter's closing in, and here's a chance for one last spanking sail. It's like the last ski run of the day, the last season's climb up the mountain trail. You get sentimental and you forget you're tired or it's too cold…"

"Or you've removed a few hundred pounds of lead bars from your boat. Right, sure."

"It's possible," Sarah insisted. "I might forget something like that. Say Dolly tries for that last sail and goes too far out in the cove before she finds out the boat is unstable. And the wind whoops up and she's in trouble."

"Peace," said Alex. "Let the lab churn out its report. Put Dolly out of your head. At least for now. I'll meet you at the hospital at six. Dinner and a movie. I'm not on call."

But the dead woman did not depart from Sarah's head. All through the day Sarah returned to the enigma of Dolly Beaugard. The result of this preoccupation was that her students were allowed to get away with fatuous remarks and crude jokes on the subject of Chaucer's "The Miller's Tale," groans over the stupidity of Oedipus, and even indifference to Defoe's description of the plague.

The trouble, thought Sarah, packing her briefcase after her four-o'clock class, is that I've been given a canned biography of Dolly as the stolid hardworking family saint. But no one has mentioned that Dolly was interested in rehabilitating the young—nor had a fondness for children, let alone a smartass eleven-year-old. Dolly had helped direct the Sunday school, but she didn't teach classes. She hung out at the hospital information desk; she didn't push the gift cart or move patients in wheelchairs. She worked the office side of the Girl Scouts; she didn't hike out with a bunch of squealing girls. Dolly wasn't the hands-on type. Except. Except for mucking about with her boat. And sailing with Jonathan Epstein.

"Damn, damn," said Sarah aloud as she stamped out of the English office and made for the parking lot. What was really annoying about this preoccupation with Dolly was that the woman—from her own memory and from family report—was so bloody boring. If I have to be haunted by someone, she asked herself, why can't it be the ghost of someone interesting? What was Laurence Olivier doing these days? Or Charles Dickens? Or Jane Austen, Charlotte Brontë? Cary Grant and Ingrid Bergman. Mozart, Leonard Bernstein? Mrs. Patrick Campbell, George Eliot, Oscar Wilde, Mrs. Pankhurst. But no, she was stuck with Dolly Beaugard embedded in her brain like some sort of heavy and unearthly burr.

In the parking lot, standing at the gate, she met, like two hovering fates, Alice and Jonathan. Alice in gray sweats and Jonathan in regulation skateboard attire: baggy pants and oversize jacket.

"We're here to see Uncle Lenox," said Alice.

"*She's* here to see him," added Jonathan. "I'm just an extra. Part of Mother's support system. Uncle Lenox hates my guts."

"Jonathan, you don't have to say anything but hello," said Alice. "Listen, Sarah, we need to talk. I called the English office and they said you were coming out this way, so we stayed in ambush."

Sarah sighed and lowered her briefcase. "About Dolly? Or about Uncle Lenox?"

"Both," said Jonathan.

Sarah frowned, looking at the boy who stood almost as tall as his mother, his arms folded, his baseball cap set backwards on his head so that the strap made a line across his forehead.

"It's okay," said Alice. "I've told Jonathan that I think something's weird about Dolly drowning. But I don't know what's weird. And Jonathan's one of the people who really knew Dolly and liked her."

"Because she took me sailing," said Jonathan. "She was captain and I was crew, but sometimes we switched around and I sailed and told her what to do. She was nicer on the boat than she was on land. On land she acted like Uncle Eliot. Like she wanted to put me in a home for dysfunctional kids."

"How do I fit in?" asked Sarah. "Because I haven't the time or energy to do much. I'll go up to the hospital with you, if you want. I was meeting Alex in his office anyway."

"We can walk over," said Alice. "It's just across the campus and I'm on a fitness kick. Aerobics. Webb says I'm flabby."

"You probably are," said Jonathan. "We do sit-ups and run a mile before soccer. You should try it. Anyway, I really do think it's crazy that Aunt Dolly went out sailing and tipped over."

"But you never saw her put in any sort of ballast or take it out," said Sarah, taking care of this neglected question.

Jonathan shook his head. "I was allowed to sail, not fool around with the *Sweetheart*. But I didn't see any ballast, not weights or pipes or blocks or anything. There could have been, but the floorboards were always in place when I went out. Aunt Dolly was super careful. We had this checklist before we cast off. Everything had to be done in order. Like take off the canvas cover, put it away, get out the life jackets, undo the sail stops, untie the rudder, haul up the jib, haul up the mainsail. Check the wind direction. Decide which tack we're going off on. Cast off. Pull in the jib sheet. Fasten it down. Same with the mainsheet. The whole thing like we were in the navy."

"You see," said Alice. "Dolly was organized in her sailing routine just like she was in everything else. No one else in the family is that together. I mean, Eliot runs his marine insurance business, but he has a secretary. And Masha practices her music and knows when her next concert is. But that's about all. Mother thinks she's organized, but she's never done much more than delegate and give orders. Vivian does a lot of the running of household things, but Dolly was the executive. I think Mother was glad that her arthritis and her bad eyesight gave her an excuse to turn it all over to Dolly."

Sarah, wanting to get back to the matter of ballast, turned to Jonathan again. "If Dolly was so careful, didn't she always check before she went sailing to see if the ballast was in place?"

"You mean pull up the floorboards?" asked Jonathan. "Why would she do that? Not if it hadn't been raining like crazy. Even then the canvas cover kept the water out. If there was ballast, like lead blocks or something, they'd stay put. Ballast isn't like sails and lines and stuff that move around or wear out."

"So Dolly never talked about having ballast?"

"Nope, but hey, maybe the *Sweetheart* had a heavier centerboard than the other Scooters. Maybe she had some custom-made centerboard that weighed a ton and kept the *Sweetheart* stable. Or a weight fastened on."

Sarah stared at the boy. Yes, why not add weight to the centerboard? Something permanent. An extra weight at the bottom of the centerboard might have come detached on that last day. Might have broken loose if the boat had scraped a ledge or hit a rock.

"Good point, Jonathan," she said. "We'll have to ask if the *Sweetheart* centerboard exactly matches the one on *Zippo*. Or if there are signs that a weight was added and it broke free."

Jonathan shrugged modestly. "You have to think of all the possibilities, don't you? And you didn't. And I did. But," he added, "you might have later on. Maybe you don't sail that much."

Sarah, knowing that her sailing experience was most often that of an absentminded passenger, nodded agreement.

Jonathan, if she saw much of him, might at a later date require a heavy squashing action, but for the moment he was still a handy source of information.

Alice broke it up. "Move," she said. "We can cut by the library and around to the hospital. Use the stairs. Uncle Lenox is on the fourth floor and the exercise will be good for you, Sarah. You have shadows under your eyes. I think you're out of shape."

Sarah gave her a look. "Have you tried spending the entire day going back and forth from classrooms to offices? Or sitting and correcting papers? It's not a healthy life." To herself she thought, this is Alice Beaugard, relict and waif, Alice who smokes like a chimney and drinks like a fish—or at least she used to and she's telling me about health. Well, I'll show her. "Come on," she said aloud, and strode forth across the parking lot toward a line of trees edging the Bowmouth College Library.

But Alice, remarkably, kept up the pace, her usually pale face flushed, her thin arms and legs in their sweatsuit pumping, and although she was breathing in gasps by the time they reached the hospital, it was a creditable performance. Jonathan, of course, like an overgrown puppy, had circled, jogged, run ahead, and was sitting on the hospital steps waiting when the two women arrived.

"Room 440," directed the woman in the green volunteer smock at the desk. A blonde woman with her hair tied back so reminiscent of the deceased Dolly that Sarah almost gaped. Was Dolly coming back in body as well as by specter?

The three climbed up the stairwell, four flights, their feet echoing in hollow taps on the cement steps. Taking first one corridor, then a turnoff, the party reached a group of huddled nurses, but since the four nurses seemed to be in the midst of some argument, they pushed on and reached Room 440.

Alice, in the lead, gave the half-open door a knock, and then stuck her head around the door. "Uncle Lenox," she said.

But the room was empty.

"In the john," suggested Sarah.

But the lavatory door stood open and was likewise empty.

"Down to X-ray?" said Alice. "Or gone for lab work?"

"Professor Cobb has gone," said an annoyed voice from the doorway, and Sarah looked up to see a nurse in green scrubs. "He signed a release and discharged himself. He said he was going to take a taxi home."

"The lobby," shouted Jonathan. "I'll bet he's down there waiting for the taxi." And without waiting for an answer, the boy ran out of the room and down the hall.

Jonathan opted for the stairs, Sarah and Alice for the elevator, but all three made it to the lobby at the same time. Made it in time to see a sticklike figure wrapped in an oversize trench coat, a crutch under one arm, standing by the lobby entrance.

"Uncle Lenox," called Alice, advancing on him.

The figure turned slowly, and began an unsteady advance upon the trio. Then, "Ah, Alice. It's about time someone in the family appeared. I've waited the entire afternoon and then realized that no one was coming to take me home and I must fend for myself. I've called a taxi. They took me down in a wheelchair because I presume the hospital didn't want to be sued if I fell."

Alice, with Sarah and Jonathan assisting, managed to settle Lenox Cobb in a chair, all the while urging him to return to bed and the tender mercies of the Mary Starbox Memorial Hospital. He looked ghastly, thought Sarah, backing away. Old age, extreme pallor, bruised eyes, and a bandaged head combined to create a picture of a man teetering at death's door.

But Lenox resisted Alice, making his point with a thrust of his crutch into the calf of his niece.

Jonathan, who had been listening to the pleadings of his mother and Sarah, now joined the fray. "Hey, Uncle Lenox, if you don't want to stay and you feel okay, well, why not blow this place? I mean, who wants to be in a hospital like in some sort of animal cage?"

Lenox Cobb regarded his great-nephew with interest. "That, boy, is the first sensible thing I have ever heard you say."

Jonathan grinned. "Thanks, Uncle Lenox. That's a pretty cool coat you've got. It's plenty big, too. I like gigantic clothes."

Lenox looked down at his tentlike trench coat with satisfaction. "The nurses took away all my own clothes. Blood all over them. And no one brought me any clean things."

"We thought you'd be in the hospital for a while," said Alice.

"Don't interrupt, young woman. Except for these dizzy spells, I am perfectly well. But I couldn't leave the hospital in that disgusting hospital nightgown, so I waited until the nurses were all in their station—they spend all their time fussing over charts and ignore the patients—and I went to Room 439 across the way because I have noticed that the occupant was unconscious with oxygen and tubes and an IV drip in his arm. So I slipped into his closet and borrowed his coat. And his shoes." Here Lenox stuck out his thin bare matchstick legs, showing feet encased in a well-polished but obviously outsize pair of oxfords.

"Hey," said Jonathan. "Neat work, Uncle Lenox. You could make it as some sort of international spy."

Lenox didn't answer, but he looked mildly pleased. "Now," he said, "Alice, you must cancel the taxi and then drive me home. There is no use in spending unnecessary money. I will send back the coat and shoes, although it seems unlikely that Room 439 will ever need them again."

"What," said a voice, "is the meaning of this?"

Two physicians. Dr. Joseph Foxe, primary-care physician to Lenox Cobb, and Dr. Alex McKenzie. Both frowning.

"The meaning," said Lenox Cobb, with satisfaction, "is that I am no longer under the care of Mary Starbox Memorial Hospital and its collection of quacks. Alice, after you cancel the taxi, bring your car around to the entrance. Jonathan will stay here and help me into the car when you arrive. I will be leaving shortly. Miss—what is your name?"—this to Sarah—"Thank you for your attentions. I trust I will not be needing your assistance again. Or Dr. McKenzie's. Or that of Dr. Foxe. Good afternoon to you all."

"I have reached the point," said Sarah to Alex that evening over dinner, "of never wanting to see, speak, or interact in any way with a member of the Beaugard family."

"They're a little on the indigestible side," admitted Alex. "But they have amazing resilience. Lenox Cobb certainly surprised me. I thought he'd be down and out for forty-eight hours at least. Joe Foxe is mad as hell. Called out last night from a dinner party forty miles away to deal with the old boy, and then to have him take off like that."

Sarah nodded sympathetically. They were having an early dinner at Miranda's Café in the town of Rockland and planning to take in the movie. After all, as Sarah said, even student papers and unread medical journals could not compete with watching Emma Thompson and Anthony Hopkins go through their paces at the Strand Cinema.

Alex, after attending to the remains of fettuccini Romeo, returned to the question of Lenox Cobb. "I suggested to Joe Foxe, on the basis of what the family said about his being a little goofy lately, that a neurology workup might be in order. Joe said he'd already suggested it to Elena Beaugard, who waffled, so then he'd tried Masha and Eliot. Masha said it sounded expensive and Eliot said what was the use, that Uncle Lenox was obviously disoriented and what could anyone do, anyway, if they found he had some kind of senile dementia. Joe Foxe had suggested that more tests might eliminate a chemical imbalance or some undetected pathology, but Eliot told him to wait. There was plenty of time. In a few days, after he'd rested and recovered, let Lenox come home and settle in and see what happens."

Sarah rolled up her napkin. "And Uncle Lenox beat them all to the punch. So that's that." She pushed her chair back and then hesitated. "Do you think someone—person or persons unknown—banged Lenox on the head? Either when he first lost his glasses in the woods or before I found him in Alice's cottage?"

Alex frowned. "No, I do not. Not the first time, not the second time. My God, the man is elderly. I think he stumbled, lost his glasses, walked into a branch. Second time out when he was hunting for them, I think he did the same. Remember, now he's searching around *without* glasses and he's blind as a bat..."

"And stubborn as a mule," put in Sarah.

"Right. So it was almost dark, and for the second time he walked directly into a tree or a limb. And really clobbered himself. Staggered off, ended up in Alice's cottage, missed the bed and ended up on the floor."

"It does sound plausible," admitted Sarah. "The only reason I can imagine anyone wanting to go after Lenox Cobb is if he happened to be a witness to someone messing around with Dolly's boat. Or just happened to be around when someone was lacing the Gattling whiskey bottle with dope. But if so, well, why not do the job properly? It would be easy to finish an old man out walking by himself. But he was only damaged. And why would anyone bother to do that? Not because he's a cantankerous old curmudgeon. The state of Maine is filled with people exactly like him."

"The proper description of Lenox Cobb," said Alex firmly, "is a man with a self-inflicted injury. An accident. And, to clear your mind of other clutter, Mike Laaka called and said the lab hasn't come up with any signs—yet—of lead ballast on the *Sweetheart*. The centerboard—which is the original one—hasn't had extra lead fastened on. Inboard under the floorboards there are signs of wear, but not severe enough to suggest lead ingots. Only canvas."

"Canvas? How do you mean canvas?"

"Canvas. Heavy cloth. Familiar nautical material. Canvas fibers have been found. Rubbed, worn canvas fibers."

Sarah subsided heavily in her chair. "Canvas. Not weights. And the centerboard hasn't been weighted. Well, damn. But canvas..."—and here Alex could almost see her mental machinery shifting gears—"Maybe, just maybe, Dolly used sandbags. Canvas bags filled with sand. For ballast. What do you think?"

"I think," said Alex, rising and reaching for Sarah's hand, "that we're going to be late for our movie, and since I am deeply in love with Emma Thompson and you are wild for Anthony Hopkins, we had best be off so as not to miss a minute."

"Sandbags," repeated Sarah. "Canvas sandbags. I wonder if they're ever used as ballast."

"They're used to hold in the Mississippi River in flood time," said Alex. "Now, let's move it."

But even the best of movies with greatest of actors cannot deflect a human with a bee in her bonnet, and Sarah emerged from the movie theater shaking her head. "I'm going to write a novel. It's going to be called *The Haunting of Sarah Deane*. I'm bedeviled by Dolly and Uncle Lenox and Alice, and I couldn't keep my mind on a good movie. Let's hope the enchantment wears off before I'm fired from my job."

"Let's just hope that when we make it home, we don't find Alice on our doorstep," said Alex.

They did not find Alice Beaugard on their doorstep; they found Alice Beaugard and Webb Gattling in their kitchen watching a rerun of *Cheers*.

Chapter Eight

"YOUR PATSY IS ONE lousy watchdog," said Alice, reaching over and switching off the television. "I knocked and yelled and then we walked right in. You still don't lock your doors, do you? Anyway, this is Webb. Webb Gattling. One of the notorious Gattling boys."

"For Chrissake, Alice," said Webb Gattling in a deep and, to Sarah's mind, sinister voice as he extended a hand the size of a fielder's mitt.

Webb Gattling was enormous. Long tawny hair, a tawny beard that flowed to his chest, eyebrows that sat like hairy shelves over his pale blue eyes, ruddy skin, and shoulders built for heaving the caber or felling large trees. Sarah, extending her hand gingerly, almost expected him to greet her with a resounding Fe Fi Fo Fum. He was the sort of man, she thought, who brought forth images of animal skins and horned helmets. And Alice reinforced all Sarah's previous ideas of Alice-the-waif, looking like some sort of windblown elf standing next to Webb Gattling.

"Hey, there," boomed Webb, "Sarah. Heard a lot about you. From Alice. She said you and she were always in trouble as kids."

Sarah bit her lip to stop herself from saying that she, Sarah, had been the wimp half of the team, and Alice the real thing.

"I mean," said Webb, "I'm glad Alice had one friend anyway. Some of the things she's told me, hell, it's a wonder anyone around's still speaking to her."

"And this," said Alice, as if presenting a prize horse, "is Alex McKenzie, who married Sarah, and they're both going to find out how Dolly died. Who did her in. This summer he and Sarah were mixed up in some weird murder on a horse farm, so what we've got here is our own undercover investigation unit. I mean, who needs the police and all those pathology creeps? Right, Sarah? Right, Alex?"

"Wrong," said Sarah, as Alex reached out to have his hand crushed by Webb. "You do need the police. And the labs. The whole machine. We aren't the police. We're only…" Here she hesitated and then finished lamely, "Friends of the family."

Alex recovered his hand and tested it for bone damage. Then he confronted Webb. "Sarah's right. We just did some low-level looking around for her aunt Julia. So how about a beer and maybe half an hour of friendly conversation, and then Sarah and I both have some work to do. That okay?"

Alice, worried, looked over at Webb. He nodded. "Okay, a beer. Ale. Whatever you've got. Thanks. And half an hour. We ought to be able to spit it out in fifteen minutes."

Alex paused on his way to the refrigerator for the beer. "You mean something that hasn't been spat already."

"Well, sorta," said Webb. "Nothing new, but maybe…well, something from a kinda different angle."

"What sort of angle?" demanded Sarah, suddenly fearful.

"Like Webb was out in his boat the day Dolly went sailing and he saw her capsize," said Alice. "That sort of angle."

Oh God, Sarah said to herself. Wouldn't you know. The Gattling connection. Not just Alice's old boyfriend but a Gattling on the spot. Trying to pull her thoughts together, she busied herself with a tray, four beer mugs, a piece of cheddar, crackers, and a bowl of nuts. She looked over at Webb, whose size diminished the entire kitchen. What he needs, she thought, are a mead hall and tankards. And meat bones to gnaw on. Fe Fi Fo Fum.

Putting the laden tray down on the kitchen table, she said, "Okay, Webb, you saw Dolly capsize? Or just a boat like Dolly's?"

Webb reached for the green bottle of Heineken, poured it with a practiced hand into the mug, took a slow appreciative sip, then shook his head. "Didn't actually see the boat go over. I was out a ways when I saw it first. It was sailing out past the point and I didn't take a good look. Had other things on my mind. Then I saw it later when it'd gone over, and I came alongside to see if I could help. One of those damfool Weymouth Scooters, those centerboard jobs that flop over if you even breathe on them. Knew Dolly Beaugard had one, but I didn't see the name on the stern because the boat was near sunk to her gunwales. Full of water. And man, I sure hoped it wasn't a Beaugard boat."

"The trouble with Webb," put in Alice, "is that his name is Gattling, and Marsden and Junior had just washed in on the Thursday and Friday before."

"But the Gattlings—" Sarah began, and stopped. She was unable to come up with something positive to say about the Gattlings.

Webb clenched his fist and then slowly relaxed it and took up his mug again and drank long and fiercely. "Okay. Go on. Say it. The Gattlings are the scumballs of the earth. Half of 'em are in prison and the rest should be. Right? Right?"

"I didn't—" Sarah began, and then stopped again. She did and she had.

"Look," said Alex, always the moderator. "Let's forget the Gattling part and tell us what you saw."

"He can't," said Alice. "I mean, he couldn't. Because being a Gattling is why he didn't square with the police before this. Nobody would believe him. They'd have him in maximum security just for saying he was out in his boat the same day Dolly went sailing. You've got to deal with the fact his name is Webb Gattling."

"And I'm not ashamed of it," said Webb, his expression truculent. He again thumped the table, this time so hard that the mugs and bowl of nuts and plate of cheese bounced, and Sarah again thought of giants. Or was it ogres?

"I mean, hell," growled Webb, "Gattlings are all over the place. Gattlings been around since the year one. And sure there are some lousy ones—like Marsden and Junior. And yeah, some of them are kind of wild and some of them like to take a deer out of season. But holy shit, there're some damn good Gattlings like my dad and my kid brother, Davy. And Mom. Or take Captain Jim Gattling. He was my great-grandfather. Good on discipline. Good citizen. Everybody forgets about the decent Gattlings."

Here Webb took a gulp of beer and then went on. "What I'm saying is that because there are a few rotten apples named Gattling isn't a reason for every policeman around to look at the rest of us like we're planning to burn down the town or start a riot."

"Or think you flipped over Dolly Beaugard's sailboat?" said Alex.

"Yeah," said Webb. "And that's what they'd think. So I didn't tell anyone that I was out in the cove that day. Listen, everyone in our whole family is on the hot seat because of Marsden and Junior being dead. And drunk. And their boat loaded with drugs. So the cops think the whole friggin' family's running some kind of a ring, taking little packages of coke around to the islands. And they act like one of us Gattlings got jealous and came out and knocked the boys overboard. Plus the cops are asking the family about what kind of prescription medicine anyone has on hand, so it doesn't take a genius to guess that someone spiked Marsden and Junior's whiskey."

"You see," said Alice impatiently, "Gattling is a local buzzword. Sarah, did you know there are Gattlings at Bowmouth?"

Sarah jerked her head up.

"Don't look so surprised," said Alice. "Sharon Seavy—she was a Gattling—teaches biology or something like that. And Jeff Gattling works maintenance."

"Like he's a janitor," put in Webb. "But he's a good guy." This Webb added because Sarah's expression almost gave away her conviction that here was at least one of the causes of what Bowmouth officials euphemistically called "inventory depletion."

"Back on track," said Alex. "Start when you first saw Dolly's boat. Then when you saw it filled with water."

So Webb, draining his ale, settled back into his narrative. It was a simple story. He was out in his fishing boat—"beaten-up old rig, eighteen foot with a sixty horse"—because he wanted to get away from his family, who were raising holy hell about Marsden and Junior being drowned.

"Gattlings stick together when it's something like this. Two brothers dying, even if they were a couple of real losers. Well, I'd about had it with Aunt Doris and Uncle Lem and their other son, Parson, blubbering about how they were angels in heaven and had been such good loving boys. I mean shit. Those guys weren't going to live to a nice ripe old age. It was just anyone's guess whether they'd be shot in hunting season accidentally on purpose or run off the road in the night. Or be knocked overboard."

"So you took off in your boat to get away," repeated Alex.

"Yeah. To be by myself. Took off around three o'clock, I think. Pretty good wind by the time I went out, so I kept pretty much in the lee of the islands. Didn't see any point in trying to fish, so I didn't put a line down or anything. Just chugged around and then saw this sailboat come out through Proffit Point narrows and didn't pay it much heed. Maybe I noticed it was one of those damn Scooters, but I wasn't thinking about what that meant—that there was too much wind for such a crappy boat. My head was full of Marsden and Junior and the family being in a sweat about them."

Alex put down his beer. "Okay, Webb, wait up. I think we're crazy to be listening to this. You've got to tell the police. Right now. Sarah and I are sympathetic, but we are not the police. Not the proper people. So, okay. Can I call?"

Webb turned on Alice. "You said they wouldn't. You said Sarah Deane was your old buddy. What the hell. I mean fuck it. The police. I'm getting outta here."

Alice looked at Alex. "I thought we could trust you..."

"Webb, keep your shirt on," said Alex. "How about this. Not the state police. Just Mike Laaka. You know Mike, don't you, Alice? And, Webb, you know him, I'll bet? You must be about the same age. Went to school with him, maybe? Rockland High School."

Webb, who up to that moment had been looking more and more like the ogre of Sarah's imagination, subsided slightly. "Yeah," he said. "I knew Mike. We were on the track team. I threw the hammer. Mike did the mile. But he's some kind of detective with the sheriff's office now, so I don't see much of him. Except he came around asking questions when Marsden and Junior washed in."

Sarah, pleased at finding that Webb did indeed throw heavy objects in sporting events, cut a piece of cheese, balanced it on a cracker, and handed it to Webb. Food to soothe the savage.

"So how about it?" persisted Alex. "I can call Mike. He'll only take in what's useful. He's not going to put cuffs on you just because you were out in your boat last Sunday."

Silence. Then Webb, his great shoulders rising in a shrug, nodded. "Okay. If it's Mike. Not that state police guy with the frozen balls. George Fitts."

Alex, losing no time, strode to the telephone, dialed, got Mike on the second ring, and in two short sentences made his point.

"Okay," he announced. "Mike's on his way."

"Alone?" demanded Alice.

"Alone," said Alex, adding, "So put up your feet, have another beer, and keep cool."

"Cool, hell," said Webb in a voice of thunder. "Why should I be cool? Even if it's Mike Laaka, I'm going to have to prove I didn't tip Dolly Beaugard into the drink, that I haven't been selling her coke. That I never had the hots for her, that I never got into her underpants. Or wanted to."

Alice reached across the kitchen table for Webb's hand and pulled it toward her and then folded it around her own small claw. "Webb, take it easy. If you come on like that, Mike's going to think you and Dolly had something going for years. Just tell your story and try not to throttle the guy. Mike's okay."

"Yeah?" said Webb. "How do you know he's okay?"

"Picked me up for operating under the influence," said Alice, "and was kind of nice about the whole thing. Made me walk a straight line, which I couldn't, touch my nose with my finger with my eyes close, which I couldn't, and then did a breath thing."

"So what was nice about that?" demanded Webb.

"He didn't hassle me. Just did his job and drove me home and talked about how he heard me sing at the Lobster Festival when I was a kid. Came to see me once in Augusta when I was supposed to be drying out and getting counseling."

With that conversation ebbed, Sarah replenished the cheese supply, Alex called the hospital about two new admissions, and before long Mike Laaka was at the door.

And Webb Gattling reverted to his ogre mode. Mike's attempts at easy pleasantry were ignored or answered in monosyllabic grunts until finally Alice shouted in exasperation, "For God's sake, Webb, stop acting like an ax murderer and tell Mike what happened."

"And what did?" prompted Mike.

It all came out. Sentence by sentence. Webb looking at the table or off at the fireplace. Never at Mike. How he, Webb, had been out in Davis Cove—out from his own mooring in the Meduncook River—had seen the sailboat go out, how he had lost sight of it, had chugged about around the islands, and then had come across the sailboat wallowing, mast broken, sails down. And no one around.

"You looked?" asked Mike, breaking into the recital.

"Christ Almighty, of course I looked. Cut my motor and put a line around her starboard cleat. Saw a life jacket tied to another cleat. Took my boat hook and lifted up the sails to see if anyone was under there. But the wind had raised such bad chop that the two boats were banging the hell out of each other, so I cast off."

"So you went home?" said Mike.

"No, by God, I didn't. I started looking for Dolly. By then I'd figured it was Dolly Beaugard's boat—the *Sweetheart*. It's the only Scooter in this area. I throttled down to half speed, which with all that wind meant I couldn't maneuver very well, and I went around in big circles and then motored off leeward, but I didn't see anyone floating or trying to swim. Stayed out for almost an hour, but then I was running low on gas, so I headed back into Proffit Point Harbor. Was going to tell Tad Bugelski, but he wasn't around."

"Who *did* you tell?" demanded Mike. "Anyone? The coast guard? The Beaugards? Or did you wait to read about it in the papers?"

"You know," said Webb, "Alice here has been telling me you're a nice guy. I remember you as okay back there in high school, but right now you couldn't prove that by me. You're another hardheaded Finn who thinks he's God Almighty's gift to the Maine coast. You're acting like I'm some sort of an accessory or something."

Mike stiffened, and Alex, who knew his old friend had a temper, waited for the explosion. But Mike held it back, took a deep breath, tapped a pencil on the table. And waited.

And Webb Gattling subsided rumbling.

Finally, after what Sarah considered was a too long and too deadly silence, Mike said softly, "Did you tell *anyone*, Webb?"

Webb looked up, his expression haggard. "No. Not directly. I went into Tad Bugelski's house—the door was open and no one was there. Used his phone to call the coast guard and said I'd found a sailboat half-sunk and I hadn't seen anyone floating around. Then I hung up before they could ask me who was calling. And that's the goddamned truth." Webb stared at Mike defiantly.

"Okay," said Mike. "Better late than never, I suppose. But Jesus, Webb, don't be so hung up on being a Gattling that you can't even function in the real world. You know that I can't just sit on this information. State Police CID is going to have to know. So when did you tell Alice?"

"Next Monday. Noon. Saw her in Rockland. Heard about the body on the local news."

"So both of you have been sitting on this information," said Mike, "since Monday. And tonight is Thursday. And the police have been beating the bush for four days. For anything. Sightings, confirmed or unconfirmed."

"I'm sorry," said Alice in a small voice.

"I'm not," roared Webb. "You know damn well, Mike, that I'd be in custody by now. For Dolly and maybe for Marsden and Junior. Listen, Dolly is dead because she drowned. Her boat went over and she drowned. She wasn't strangled or burned to death or poisoned or hit on the head by a blunt instrument. She fucking drowned."

"How do you know?" said Mike quietly.

"Well, she did, didn't she? Tad Bugelski told me she did. He was around when her body washed into Little Cove."

"Tad Bugelski," said Mike succinctly, "doesn't know the half of it. Dolly drowned, all right. But someone fiddled around with her boat. Just before Alex called, I got the report from the lab. The *Sweetheart* did carry ballast. Lead pigs in canvas covers. Laid fore and aft along the centerboard under the floorboards. But no ballast found when we hauled the boat in Monday."

"So the ballast got loose," said Webb.

"The lab thinks no. They've done some measuring and checking the rub marks, and those lead babies were snugged in like it was a custom fit, probably so they wouldn't move around when the boat heeled. So we're not talking death by mischance. Not anymore. We're talking death through planning and through a lot of hefty removal work and careful preparation. We're talking homicide."

Alice turned first to Sarah, then to Alex, and then swiveled around and looked Mike full in the face.

"So," she said. "What else is new?"

And for a moment Mike turned to stone. He jumped to his feet and stood there staring at Alice, looking, Sarah thought, with his white blond hair, his broad features, and big shoulders, like some Nordic monument. A monument with egg on its face. But Sarah, who knew that since Monday Alice had been muttering about Dolly being murdered, simply rolled her eyes at the ceiling while Alex drummed the table with impatient fingers. But Webb nodded his big shaggy head as if to back up Alice's question.

"I mean," Alice went on, "it's no surprise, is it? Dolly wouldn't have off-loaded the lead ballast and forgotten she'd done it. Dolly remembered everything. She kept lists and made charts and kept books. She could run a small country. She could have organized OPEC or the European Common Market."

"Easy, Alice," said Webb, putting his arm around her—an arm that looked to Sarah like part of a python.

But Alice shook him off and gathered steam. "And she wouldn't commit suicide by dumping the ballast and then going sailing. What a stupid way of killing yourself. Dolly wasn't superbright, she could hardly spell, but she did things straight on. If she wanted to kill herself, she'd read up on it, buy the right kind of poison or the proper kind of gun, and do the thing efficiently. Listen, Dolly was planning to live forever, and get all of Knox County under her thumb. She already had half of it roped and tied. As well as Mother. And the whole bloody Great Oaks estate."

"Okay," said Mike, recovering. He found that he didn't like the investigative initiative being snatched away by the disheveled likes of Alice Beaugard. "Maybe you can come up with some reason for your sister's death. Like Dolly might have made enemies, people that—"

Alice broke in impatiently. "Of course Dolly had enemies. Doesn't everyone? But I don't suppose Dolly's enemies would call themselves that because they were all into doing civic things together with her. Or under her. They probably called themselves coworkers or colleagues or some crap like that. But Dolly had her finger in a lot of pies. She probably drove a whole bunch of people straight up the wall."

"Whoa, wait up there," said Mike. "You can't just throw out wholesale accusations." He fished around in a back pocket and produced a notebook and pencil. "Okay, now. Names. Persons who actually hated Dolly. Were jealous of her. Wanted her jobs or whose toes she stomped on."

Alice frowned and brushed a stray strand of hair from her face. "Well, I'd say never mind about St. Paul's-by-the-Sea because Dolly had talked Mother into giving the Great Oaks family house to the Episcopal diocese. For some sort of retreat or meeting place. Father Smythe started salivating whenever he saw Dolly."

"Stop," called Mike. "You mean Dolly was behind her mother's leaving the house away from the family, giving it to the church?"

"I just told you," said Alice. "Try and listen, will you, Mike? We all knew about it and I heard Mother telling Sarah's grandmother. The point is that even if a lot of people around town might have wanted Dolly to disappear, I think it's someone in the family who got rid of her. Maybe someone who wanted the house."

"But didn't all of you want the house?" asked Mike.

"God no. The cottage is good enough for me, and Eliot and Caroline have that big pile on Tidal Cove. And Masha doesn't like the acoustics and says the damp is ruining her wooden recorders. Fogs them up, So who does that leave?"

"Okay, who?" said Mike, sighing.

"Professor Lenox Cobb, that's who. Dear old Uncle Scrooge. He's moved back into our house and he's settling in like he is going to die in the master bedroom."

Here Sarah came to life. "Your uncle Lenox is older than your mother. Why would your mother die first?"

"Uncle Lenox—even with a bump on his head and half-goofy—is in terrific shape. Oh sure, his balance isn't great, but he's all sinew and gristle and mean as they come. Mean people last forever. Mother has glaucoma and arthritis and diabetes and some sort of cardiac condition. There, you've got my opinion. Last Monday night I asked Sarah and Alex to poke around in the family nest, but now it's pretty damn clear. Uncle Lenox is the guy to nail. Okay, Webb, let's go. You've done your civic duty." And with that Alice reached out for Webb's hand and together they rose from the table. But then Alice turned again to Mike.

"To be fair, I should mention Vivian."

"Who?" said Mike, startled. "You mean the housekeeper?"

"Of course. Vivian Lavender. She's a widow and she's been working for us almost thirty years. When the house goes to the Episcopal Church she might be out in the cold. I don't think they'd keep her on; she's Catholic. I mean, even a nice pension wouldn't make up for Vivian having her own rent-free apartment. So I suppose you'd have to add Vivian to Uncle Lenox as suspects. Maybe they're working together. Except I think that Vivian's a sexy lady, and I doubt if Lenox can perform to satisfaction. I mean, can you picture Lenox bonking Vivian?" Alice grinned up at Webb and then the two started for the door—Alice scurrying to keep up with him.

"Not so fast," called Mike. "Webb, you'll have to sign a deposition. A description of what you saw last Sunday. And, Alice, don't go around accusing people, even a crank like Lenox Cobb. Or Vivian Lavender. Cool it. And you two hang around. Brother George Fitts will want to have a chat with you both."

"The hell," shouted Webb, "he will." And without a backward glance Webb took hold of Alice's shoulder and gave her a push, and with the kitchen floor shaking under his footsteps, they departed.

For a moment, dead silence. Then Mike reached for an unopened bottle of beer, pried open the cap, and drank straight from the top. Then, putting down the bottle, he delivered himself of a weary sigh. "Jeezus, that Alice will be the death of me. Webb, I can take. I understand Webb. Where he's coming from. A decent Gattling in the middle of a bunch of lousy Gattlings. A damn good cabinetmaker from what I've heard. Anyway, I can see why he didn't want to go running to the police."

Alex paused in the act of loading the tray with empty mugs. "You can understand Webb Gattling. Will George Fitts?"

"Of course not. George won't give a damn about Webb's tender sensibilities. He'll put Webb onto his grid and proceed to grind and mince and shake out whatever facts there are to be shaken."

Sarah, who was now delivering the loaded tray to the kitchen sink, stopped. "Never mind George. What do you think about Alice's idea of Lenox as the villain? With or without Vivian Lavender."

"Because of the house going to the church?" asked Mike.

"Yes. It's a fair enough reason. But not only the house, Dolly was managing the whole estate, and as Alice has said, Lenox doesn't like being managed. And I'll bet he didn't much like Dolly."

Mike rose to his feet. "Bullshit, Sarah. Listen, whoever took that ballast out of the *Sweetheart* had to do it in the night. So you and Alice are saying that the old boy found his way down to the beach, maybe with Vivian holding a flashlight, got into a dinghy, rowed out in the dark, climbed aboard a wobbling sailboat, and off-loaded lead bars and rowed back. Dug a hole somewhere..."

"Or dumped them overboard," said Alex.

"And crept back to bed—in that creaky old house where all the floorboards snap and groan—without a soul knowing it. Or without that great shaggy dog Willie barking his head off."

"*The Hound of the Baskervilles*," murmured Sarah. "The dog that didn't bark."

"Come off it. Willie hates Lenox. When we first interviewed the Beaugards, Willie snarled and growled whenever Lenox Cobb came near him. Listen, you're talking about the kind of action that would be tough on a forty-year-old man. This is the guy who walks into tree branches and ends up in the hospital. Here's a suggestion. You and Alice get busy and write the great American seashore mystery and use Lenox Cobb as a murderer. Put in Vivian Lavender while you're at it. They could elope after the murder and escape to Tasmania. Pursued by a robot helicopter. Hey, I've missed my calling. Need a plot? I'm your man. Good night, all, and thanks for the entertainment."

And Mike saluted Sarah with the last gulp of beer and followed Webb and Alice into the night.

With that the telephone rang. And Sarah, rinsing mugs, wrapping cheese, could tell from the sound of Alex's voice and his one-word answers that he didn't like what he was hearing. He put the receiver down and joined her at the sink.

"Tasmania isn't such a bad idea. I'm beginning to think that we're the ones who should escape. Take a Weymouth Scooter with or without ballast, a few clothes, Patsy, and a six-pack of beer and just weigh anchor. Or try the robot helicopter."

"All of which means?"

"That was Elena Beaugard. Her primary-care physician—my friend Joe Foxe—is off to some medical conference in Oslo and she wants me. She doesn't want the doctor he's turned his patients over to because—get this—she doesn't know him. I mean hell, who *knows* their doctor these days? She sounds like she will only go to someone to whom she's been properly introduced."

"Like you."

"Like me. Because—you guessed it—we're almost family. It seems that brother Lenox seems a bit disoriented. More ornery than usual. Or is this her imagination? Or her hearing? Perhaps she needs her hearing checked. Anyway, will I make a house call? Tomorrow afternoon, which is Thursday, which is also my half day off."

"And you said?"

Alex walked to the sink, grabbed a handful of beer mugs, and dumped them into a dishpan of water, breaking only one in the process. "What do you think I said?"

"You said: 'Love to. Certainly. Of course. Happy to oblige. House calls? No problem. Neither rain nor sleet nor gloom of night…'"

"You got it. And she asked if dear Sarah could come and comfort Alice or listen to Masha practice or amuse Jonathan when he got home from school."

Sarah picked up her sheaf of student papers and stuffed them back in her briefcase. "Unfortunately, dear Sarah has a freshman seminar and two meetings and so will not emerge until after five tomorrow afternoon. Much too late for social calls. You, my dearest Alex, are strictly on your own."

Chapter Nine

FRIDAY MORNING, OCTOBER SEVENTH, broke dank and damp, and by nine o'clock a drizzle had begun falling over midcoast Maine. By eleven the drizzle had turned to a determined rain, and large red and yellow maple leaves began to fall and plaster themselves on the ground, turning roads and sidewalks into a patchwork quilt.

This picturesque phenomenon was pointed out by Deputy Katie Waters, sitting in the backseat of Sergeant George Fitts's unmarked state police sedan. Next to the empty driver's seat sat Mike Laaka, who wished that he could have driven Katie to Proffit Point by himself and so be spared the presence of George. However, he and Katie were under orders to join the sergeant in yet another investigatory strike on the Beaugard ménage. This time with a greater sense of urgency since the word "homicide" had reared its head.

"Look at the leaves, Mike," repeated Katie, who was by nature a woman with a sunny disposition. "They're absolutely beautiful. Like someone planned to make a quilt and zoom, along came the rain and down they came."

"You can have the leaves," said Mike morosely. He'd spent the previous hour in the state police barracks getting George's opinion of sheriff's deputy investigators who choose to fly solo, visiting with informants and possible suspects in private houses.

"The trouble with you and George," continued Katie, unabashed, "is that your minds are so loused up with crime that you can't appreciate the beauties of nature."

Mike made a half turn from the front seat. "Listen, Katie Waters, you had better start getting your head together. Plan your approach. George is having you interview Vivian Lavender. He's done one session with her, but he wants another, and he's going to be tied up with Mrs. Beaugard and Masha, and I'm going to be tracking down Eliot and his wife, Caroline, and some of the people who work on the place. You've never met the family, have you? I mean, not face-to-face?"

"I was on the sailboat detail," said Katie. "Crawling around on rocks and getting gunk all over my uniform, ruining my shoes."

"So this is a promotion. You're plainclothes now and you can ruin your own things. You'll be meeting live people. So forget the leaves and what a pretty quilt they'd make."

"I have a theory," persisted Katie. "It's that anyone who sees too much of George Fitts is contaminated and starts acting like him. He needs to find some normal people, but he wouldn't know normal if it bit him. I think he needs a really desperate sex experience. A real kinky session. Like for instance—"

"Shut up, Katie, here he is," growled Mike.

Katie smiled a radiant smile. "Hello, George. All set for a day at the seashore? Should we stop for sandwiches?"

George Fitts gave Katie his wintry smile, nodded at Mike, and slid neatly into the driver's seat. "You can forget about fun at the seashore. But we'll stop for sandwiches. This is going to be an all-day thing. Back to square one." George reached over, turned the ignition, stamped on the accelerator and moved the car onto Route One, turned it south toward the Proffit Point Road.

"How do you mean square one?" said Katie, who was determined not to sit in silence throughout the twelve-mile drive.

"When we first interviewed family members about Dolly Beaugard and talked to the estate workers, the gardener, and to Tad Bugelski, we were thinking it was a drowning accident."

"And," put in Mike, "we were up to our ears with the Gattling brothers washing in, and that one didn't look like an accident."

"Mike is correct," said George. "Dolly Beaugard's death looked like misadventure, but the disappearance of the ballast has changed everything. Now we have to find out who had access to the boat. Find out when Dolly last went sailing in a stiff wind and *didn't* capsize. And work up the Gattling connection. I have an appointment with Webb Gattling late this afternoon and with Alice Beaugard this evening."

"I told Webb that you'd be getting ready to sink your gaff into his backside."

"Thank you, Mike. No wonder I have trouble with interrogations. And, Katie, don't you go trying any of Mike Laaka's tricks. Interviewing material witnesses over beer at a friend's house."

"Webb Gattling," said Mike, as he had said several times to George earlier that morning, "wouldn't have told you the time of day. I went to school with Webb, he knows me. And Alice is a friend of Sarah's, plus Alice is an old girlfriend of Webb's and they seem to have picked up with each other again. George, if you'd been there with your notebook, you would have destroyed the—what's the word?—the camaraderie."

"The last thing you need in a criminal investigation is camaraderie, So I suggest you take—"

"Camaraderie and shove it?" suggested Katie.

George accelerated slightly but otherwise ignored his back-seat passenger. "Forget fellowship. Mike, that's the trouble with you knowing Alex McKenzie and Sarah. Those two are always getting mixed into an investigation, and you encourage them."

"Now, hold it, George," Mike almost shouted. "Hold it. These are small towns. Proffit Point, Diggers Neck, Thomaston, Union, Port Clyde, and the rest. Rural America. Stopovers with one or two gas stations, three churches, and a country store. A grange hall and a fire station. A feed store and a boat dock. Sometimes a Masonic lodge. Or the Elks. Rotary. Every damn soul for miles around knows or is married to or is a cousin of or went to school with every other damn soul. You're from the big bad city, and you still don't get the idea that small-town people and rural folk are so intertwined with each other that you can't mess with one person without messing with forty more. You can't run a big-city-type investigation in the boondocks. You need informality, breakfast in the diner, a drink at a bar. Be grateful to Sarah and Alex. Amateurs like those two—and even that nutcase Alice Beaugard—just happen to know a lot of people. Are related. With those three you've covered the summer colony, the resident's from 'away.' Add Webb and me and Katie here and guys like Tad Bugelski to the stew, and you've got the native, the old-time Mainer connection. The blue-collar opinion."

"Simmer down, Mike," said George. "I get the point."

"I'll bet you don't. What I'm saying is, you need me to have beer with Alice and Webb. You need Alex to help take Lenox into the hospital, and Sarah to make condolence calls with her grandmother. All these people are useful. Besides being friends, they are just goddamn useful."

"Okay, Mike. But after this, let me in on your little visits. I may have information that makes these fellowship gatherings inappropriate. Or dangerous. Sarah Deane is always skating on thin ice. I don't need any more trouble than I've already got on my plate."

"But," protested Mike, "you wanted Sarah to keep an eye out when she visited the Beaugards. You told me to tell her."

"Right. An eye out. By daylight, in a house, with other people around. But not an after-dark search for Lenox Cobb, who may or may not have walked into a branch. So let me know what you're up to. I can make allowances. I am human."

"Couldn't prove it by me," muttered Katie under her breath.

"And I have excellent hearing," continued George smoothly. "And like it or not we three are a team and we're going to work as a team. Got it?"

"Eliot Beaugard," said Mike. "He's the one who orchestrated the Lenox Cobb search. Didn't want the police around because he claimed his family was becoming notorious."

"We will speak to Mr. Eliot Beaugard," said George firmly. "Business executive types can be even more dangerous than well-meaning amateurs. Now, here's the general store. I'll pull in and Mike, you can pick up lunch. I'll have a tuna and a Pepsi."

"Egg salad and a root beer for me," said Katie.

Mike, ducking his head against the rain, went into the store, and Sergeant George Fitts leaned his head back against the car seat and closed his eyes. He had spent a long night dealing with a newly delivered lab report showing that the well-known tranquilizer Valium had been added to the whiskey bottle found in Marsden and Junior Gattling's skiff. Valium was probably in the medicine cabinets of half the citizens of Proffit Point, but one had to start somewhere. He intended to research the Beaugard collection of medications, ease of access to the supply, and get a rundown on the Beaugard prescription history. And look into the fact that the whiskey consumed by the Gattling brothers wasn't your ordinary popular blend but an expensive Canadian whiskey put out by Seagram. Not apparently the choice of Marsden and Junior, who invariably guzzled something cheaper. Here George allowed himself to appear asleep, but behind closed lids visions of whiskeys of all shades and prices passed in a parade before his inner eye.

Sitting in the backseat, Katie Waters had time to contemplate the rear of George Fitts's head and wonder at her recent elevation as an assistant deputy in the investigative arm of the sheriff's department. Until a few months ago, Katie had been detailed to some of the more loathsome and tedious jobs in the uniformed branch. Now she was in plain clothes—slacks and a wool jacket—and assigned to Mike, who worked, often in uncomfortable tandem, with George.

George probably caused, Katie thought, as much discomfort in his coworkers as he did in those he was investigating. What a creep. The top of his head was as bald as a lightbulb, steel-rimmed spectacles glinted around pale blue eyes, and his mouth was like a narrow cut in a rock. Now she stared resentfully at the bristles at the back of George's clipped neck. Even in plain clothes—starched shirt, knife-creased trousers—he looked as if he were in uniform.

But before Katie could formulate any clear thoughts about resigning her job or asking for a transfer, Mike reappeared with a paper bag and a six-pack of Pepsi, George started the car, and they were off. Turning left and on down the Proffit Point Road, the windshield wipers racing back and forth, the wet autumn leaves splattering on the hood, on the road.

The first mile of the drive down the Proffit Point Road toward the Great Oaks estate was slightly enlivened by a broken windshield wiper and the pleasure this event gave Mike Laaka and Katie Waters as they watched George Fitts, standing in puddles by the side of the road, his black raincoat whipping around his legs in the wind-driven rain, struggling with its replacement. This entertainment, however, was replaced by the sound of an approaching vehicle.

Katie had twisted about in her seat. "Hey, here comes an ambulance. Behind us. Do you suppose?"

"You want more bodies? Listen, Proffit Point has more families than just the Beaugard tribe. Besides, it's no emergency. Not speeding. No lights, no sirens."

"By which we deduce," said Katie, "that the ambulance is returning to its place of origin—the fire hall..."

"Wrong," said Mike, "the fire hall is up the hill behind us. The ambulance is on a mission."

"And that means either the ambulance is returning some incapacitated patient from the hospital or…" Katie paused and smiled at Mike. "Or is returning a body to the place of origin. Or is picking up a just-certified dead body to take it to the morgue, and in all cases no need to step on the gas."

Mike smiled. "Head of the class, Katie." He peered again out the rain-washed window. "Poor George, I'll bet he bought the wrong-size wiper… No, he's got it."

With which George Fitts, face and slicker gleaming with wet, climbed back into the car, turned the ignition, and stepped on it. Stepped on it so completely that in five minutes he found himself on the narrow winding Proffit Point Road behind the ambulance, which was going along at a leisurely twenty-five miles an hour.

"Goddamn," said George, who almost never swore.

Katie decided that George needed distraction. "You're stuck behind that thing for a while at least, so tell me about the Beaugards. What are they really like? I've seen the house from the beach, but I've never seen it up close. Or met any of the family. If I'm supposed to interview this Vivian Lavender, I should know something about them."

"The family," said Mike with feeling, "are mostly a bunch of rich loonies. Except for Dolly. She was pretty normal."

"And look," said Katie, "where that got her."

George shook his head. "Thinking of the Beaugard family members as 'rich loonies' is not going to be helpful when you start asking questions. All right, I'll give you a quick briefing. Mike can fill in what he calls the human interest parts. Mrs. Beaugard—her first name, which you will not think of using, is Elena. Summer resident with her husband for forty years, then full-time for the last ten. Husband was a patent lawyer who has a library of illustrated editions. Apparently a valuable collection. Responsible citizen from what I've heard."

"Was a total snob," said Mike. "Went around like he was Boston's gift to Maine. Tennis, golf, hunting with the Union

Valley Hunt Club. Always had a big boat. Last one was a fifty-foot ketch named the *Peregrine* because he was a bird nut. Wife still is. Keeps a bird-feeding station. Anyway, Mr. Beaugard—name was Arthur—kept the boat moored in Little Cove. Both the senior Beaugards pretty much kept to their summer friends, a lot of Massachusetts migrants. Mrs. Beaugard's in her seventies now. Semi-invalid but still plenty bossy."

"Three daughters," continued George. "Masha, she's a musician. Not married. Teaches private students in Boston and hereabouts. Her group gives concerts all over New England, so she's rarely home. Dolly Beaugard, you know about. Next is Alice, age thirty-one, who has been in trouble for driving when intoxicated, for disorderly conduct, for disrupting public meetings, possession of illegal substances—and a number of other things. Two marriages, both ending in divorce. A son, Jonathan, by Alan Epstein, the writer. Custody to the father."

"Like I said, Alice is out in left field," said Mike. "Masha is a cold fish. But you've left out favorite and only son Eliot. Marine insurance business. Has a yacht, the *Goshawk*. Yachts seem to run in the family genes. Does cruising and racing all over the map. Gobs of money. New house. One kid, named Colin. Wife Caroline has this discontented glassy look. Sort of out of focus. I'll bet she's taking something. Or shooting it. I think her elevator doesn't go to the top floor. But she's decorative."

"And that, Katie, is the sort of thing not to listen to. That's Mike at his most dangerous. I have nothing on Mrs. Eliot Beaugard, so wipe that remark right out of your head."

But Mike was squinting through the windshield. "Whoa up. That ambulance isn't turning off. It's heading right for Great Oaks. There it goes, right through the gates. You don't suppose that it really is going to pick up another body? What d'ya bet old Lenox Cobb has self-destructed, which wouldn't be that much of a loss?"

George, slowing down for the entrance, turned his head in the speaker's direction. "Mike Laaka, for once, will you just shut up and wait and see what happens?"

Mike grinned at Katie and reached for a briefcase at his feet and extracted a notebook and a small tape recorder, and in silence the three drove through the splashing rain, the falling leaves, under arching oaks and sentinel white pines until they emerged into the wide circle drive that brought them to the front door.

Well, not quite to the front door. The front door was blocked by the boxy white ambulance with the big orange lettering: PROFFIT POINT RESCUE SQUAD.

George stopped his car on the driveway circle, the better to view the proceedings. He was rewarded presently by a figure on the porch with an umbrella. Who stood and waited while the back doors of the ambulance opened and a small blanketed person with a leg thrust stiffly out was lifted into the arms of the driver and was followed by one of the rescue workers carrying a wheelchair.

Mike, who had been squinting through the windshield, turned to his companions. "My God, I think it's the kid."

"Kid?" said Katie. "What kid?"

"Alice's kid. Jonathan. Right age, right size."

But now George Fitts, like a hound who has sniffed the trail, was out of the car and on his way to the front door, turning at the last minute to shout over his shoulder, "You two, stay put."

"Great," said Katie. "Just great. We sit here and watch the rain and count the leaves, and George has all the fun."

"He may want us to stay in the car in case we have to move fast. Go and get something."

"You don't believe that, do you, Mike?"

Mike sighed. "Nope. I think George sometimes doesn't like to be crowded with lowlife like us. Wants to be big man on campus. Likes deference. Everyone backing up and turning pale when the state police arrives."

"Okay," said Katie. "So we sit here. How about some briefing about this Vivian Lavender? Faithful servant. Loyal and true. All that sort of stuff?"

"She must be faithful because she's been working here for years. Good-looking in a middle-aged way. Tall, dark wavy hair.

Real old-fashioned hair in a bun with hairpins. Probably quite a dish when she was younger. And hey, George is waving."

This was true. George Fitts stood under the portico holding the door open with one hand, and gestured.

"Nothing serious," he said as Katie and Mike joined him in the front hall. "Jonathan Epstein took a bad fall during a school field trip to Little Cove this morning. Broken leg and dislocated shoulder. He'll be out of action for a while. Which I gather is not an entirely bad thing."

"Hello, Sergeant Fitts," said a voice. It was Alice. She extended a hand toward Katie. "Deputy Waters, isn't it? I'm Alice. Alice Beaugard. I don't use any of my married names. I never had them long enough to get used to. So do I call you Deputy or what? I mean, I know I call him Sergeant, and Mike, Mike because I've known him for a while."

"Call me whatever you want, Ms. Beaugard," said Katie, looking with a certain puzzlement at the thin untidy figure before her. Reeking of cigarettes, thin face like a starvation victim, huge eyes with shadows. And clothes directly from a yard sale. "So," she added, trying to sound businesslike, "I'm supposed to see Mrs.—or is it Miss Lavender?"

"She's Mrs.," said Alice. "Married Phil Lavender, but he cut himself up in a chain-saw accident and died, and Vivian went to work for Mother. Been here ever since. But listen, you guys. Now I've got you here in the hall and before Eliot or Mother grabs you, I want you to look into this thing about Jonathan's so-called accident. I've spent the morning at the ER and he's going to be stuck at home for weeks."

"But," said George, looking at his watch, "it was an accident, wasn't it? A school trip. He fell down."

Alice looked over her shoulder, then walked to the door leading into the living room and shut it firmly. "I have doubts," she said in a hoarse whisper. "It was one of those crazy field trips private schools dream up that are supposed to bring everyone together. An early breakfast cookout for the sixth grade. I mean, in this weather, really. With the rain the breakfast had to be indoors in our family boathouse on Little Cove. I mean, heaven forbid Eliot and Caroline should have their house messed up with a bunch of kids. Anyway, Vivian—Mrs. Lavender—arranged to send along the food—bacon, eggs, sausages—as Mother's contribution to all the foolishness. After breakfast the kids and their teacher were going out in Eliot's boat to motor around in the rain talking about navigation or something educational like that. The boat's called the *Goshawk*. All the family use bird names for their boats. Except Dolly, who, of course, had to be different. We've had *Lapwing*, the *Gannet*, the *Peregrine*. I mean talk about totally boring."

"Not an accident, you say," said George, moving the flow back to the mainstream. It was one of his gifts—not letting witnesses float more than a few sentences away from the subject.

"Yes. I mean no. Not an accident. I mean, what do you think? First Dolly and now Jonathan? The point is that someone shoved Jonathan down the gangway. You know, the ramp that goes to the float. It was low tide, so the ramp went almost straight down. Jonathan said he felt a hand on his back. He lost his balance and wham, bang, down he went. Dislocated shoulder and broken leg. Not a bad break, but he's got a cast. They've given him a sedative and he's going to be out of action for a while. I mean, can you picture it? Mother and Lenox *and* Jonathan together in the house. All under the weather. My God."

"Go back, please, Miss Beaugard, to the accident. You say Jonathan felt a hand against his back."

"Yes, and Jonathan doesn't make up things like that."

"How many children were on this field trip?"

"What?"

"It's important to know how many children were trying to go down that ramp. If there was a crowd of them, pushing, shoving, as kids do, well, it's likely it was an accident."

"Oh," said Alice. "Well, I guess that might have happened. But there aren't too many in this sixth grade class. Jonathan's has about twelve kids in it. But guess who else was around."

"Tell me," said George.

"Besides brother Eliot—he was handling the boat—and Vivian, who was picking up the breakfast dishes and leftovers, there was my uncle Lenox. He'd been invited for the cookout. You know, that reach-out-to-the-elderly crap. Jonathan's teacher, Mr. Griffin, apparently had Uncle Lenox at Bowmouth in some Shakespeare class."

"Your point?" prompted George.

"I told Mike last night." Here Alice looked reproachfully at Mike Laaka, who was standing, notebook open, pencil busy, next to a silent and listening Katie Waters. "I told him to watch out for my uncle. That he doesn't want the house to go to the Episcopal Church. That was Dolly's idea. Mike, didn't you tell Sergeant Fitts about what I said? About Uncle Lenox being dangerous?"

"No," said George Fitts. "He didn't. I heard about Webb Gattling sighting the *Sweetheart* but not a word about Lenox Cobb."

"I thought you guys told each other things," said Alice. "Okay, now you know. Uncle Lenox is perfectly capable of leaning over and giving Jonathan just a little push. Uncle Lenox is a loose cannon around here, so you'd better keep an eye on the guy."

George, whose cheek muscles were now in motion, gave Alice a short nod. "Thank you, Miss Beaugard. I will keep an eye on Professor Cobb. And," added George, "I will also keep an eye on Deputy Investigator Laaka, who is another loose cannon."

Chapter Ten

GEORGE FITTS TURNED AGAIN to Alice Beaugard. "We'll want to talk to each of you again—separately—but first I want to meet with the whole family. Please ask your mother where that would be convenient."

"Frankly," said Alice, "Mother would never think any place was convenient if it's the police. The idea of having you here in the front hall just about gives her hives. Nothing personal, but she's one of the old guard who thinks that the only time you should meet a policeman is when you cross the street. But I'll ask her. Do you want Uncle Lenox to sit in? The chief suspect."

"Miss Beaugard," said George, "there is no chief suspect. Maybe there never will be. And yes, if Professor Cobb is feeling up to it, I'd like him there."

"And Vivian?"

"Mrs. Lavender? Certainly."

"How about the gardener and all the little busy gnomes who cut the grass and sweep up leaves? Or my son, Jonathan, who right now is in bed zonked with a sedative?"

"No," said George patiently. "Let Jonathan stay put. As for the rest, we'll get around to them after I have my meeting."

"What meeting? Have I missed something?" The front door stood open and Alex McKenzie walked into the hall. He stopped and took stock of the four persons now grouped in front of a heavy oak seat and mirror affair that sprouted hat racks made from deer antlers. "Hello, Alice. Hi, Mike, George. Katie. All the big guns huddling in the front hall. What's up?"

George Fitts looked at Alex without pleasure. "What are you doing here, Alex?"

"House call. I'm reviving the custom. Beloved Dr. McKenzie making the rounds of his grateful patients."

"I bet," said Mike. "You're here on a private snoop?"

"I don't snoop," said Alex. "And never on my day off. Snooping is Sarah's thing. I'm legitimate. A call from Mrs. Beaugard last night about Lenox Cobb being more than usually fuddled. Or is it her eyesight or hearing?"

"We can combine," said George, taking charge. "Alex, sit in with us while I ask everyone here some general questions. Miss Beaugard, please ask your mother which room we can use."

Alice, shaking her head, opened the living room door and reappeared almost immediately. "The library. Mother doesn't use it much except to check on the bird-feeding station outside the window."

"I'll just go and report to Mrs. Beaugard," said Alex. "I want full credit for a house call."

Mrs. Beaugard, a wool shawl over her shoulders, was fixed in a living room wing chair by a glowing fireplace. She welcomed her substitute physician with slight inclination of the head, giving

Alex the impression that on her social scale, doctors ranked well below the electrician and the plumber.

"I'm worried about my brother, Professor Cobb," she began. "I think he's had one of those invisible strokes. You know, when what someone says is all garbled. But my hearing aid makes this dreadful buzz if I turn it up. And his face seems strange, but I do have glaucoma, so it's just possible I'm not seeing his face clearly. So do you wish to examine him now?"

"I think," said Alex, reaching for Mrs. Beaugard's cane and holding it out to her, "that Sergeant Fitts wants to see everyone. You suggested the library, didn't you?"

"The police have been sent simply to plague me," said Mrs. Beaugard in complaining voice. "With my daughter dead, you'd think there would be a sense about what is fitting. And Jonathan injured. His shoulder *and* his leg. From carelessness, I'm sure. The boy just plunges about, not looking where he's going."

Alex absorbed this new information without comment and contented himself with reaching for Mrs. Beaugard's arm, assisting her to her feet, and placing her cane in her hand. "Let's go into the library together and get it over with," he said.

Together they made slow progress across the room, through a dim passageway, and into a gloomy book-lined chamber. The library.

Being in the room was, Alex thought, as he settled Mrs. Beaugard in an armchair before the unlit fireplace, rather like inhabiting an aquarium. Rain-streaked windows and French doors gave out on an unrelenting dark gray sky and a cluster of dripping evergreens, while the green wallpaper and the glass-fronted bookcases inside reinforced the sense of being under water. Books, in Alex's opinion, usually gave color and warmth to a room, but here glass doors covered with a wire grille obscured row upon row of books concealed in identical green slipcases, and the effect was to reduce the shelves to a uniformly depressing backdrop.

"My husband," said Mrs. Beaugard, looking about her with ill-concealed irritation, "collected illustrated editions. He had special slipcases made to protect them. And to discourage the children."

"The children?" repeated Alex, puzzled.

"Of course. Many of these are children's books. *Robinson Crusoe, Alice in Wonderland, Heidi*. With well-known illustrators. First editions. Many of them signed."

"But off-limits to the children?" said Alex.

"Naturally. Arthur was afraid the children might try and read them. He said children wouldn't appreciate fine illustrations. Children, especially ones like Alice, don't care what they do to a book. Arthur once caught Alice crayoning in a first edition of *The Wizard of Oz*."

"Mrs. B.!" exclaimed a voice, and Alex looked to see themselves confronted by a tall, middle-aged woman. Vivian Lavender, wasn't it? Alex tried to remember what Alice had said about the housekeeper. Something about being Catholic and having a nice apartment in the house. Dressed in red wool, rounded in the right places, she was a handsome woman with an oval face, brown eyes, full lips, ruddy complexion, and dark hair, center-parted and fastened into a knot at the nape of her neck.

"Mrs. B., you're sitting here in the dark. We need more light and a fire. Sergeant Fitts and the two deputies will need to see to take notes. I've been asked to sit in along with the family."

"Vivian," said Elena Beaugard in a testy voice. "The room is fine just as it is. I don't want to settle down here; I want to keep this meeting as short as possible."

"Just a little fire," said Vivian, kneeling on the hearth and reaching for a clutch of kindling poking out of a copper tub. "Think of Professor Cobb. He's been so shaky since his accident. And I like a warm room myself." Here Vivian Lavender smiled up at Mrs. Beaugard and began crumpling up a page of newspaper. "Here they all come. I've started the coffee for later, but I'll make sure the police have theirs in the kitchen."

Mrs. Beaugard nodded approval. "Yes, that will show them that they can't have the run of the place. And two logs will be quite enough."

Vivian settled two birch logs on top of the kindling, produced a match, lit the fire, and smiled with satisfaction.

"There now, Mrs. B. Much cozier. And is this the doctor?" She stood up and stretched out her hand. "Dr. McKenzie. How do you do. We're so glad you could come because there's hardly a physician left who makes house calls. Mrs. B., would it be all right if the doctor took a quick look at Jonathan? After the meeting. He's asleep now, but judging from his color, he may be running a fever."

Alex had begun the ritual protest about other physicians' patients when the library door opened and in trooped the family, Eliot, Alice, and Caroline. Followed by George Fitts, Katie Waters, and Mike Laaka—Katie with a notebook, Mike with his tape recorder.

The group broke apart and settled into the corners of the room, and Alex was again reminded of the aquarium—now a more brightly lit one—in which the fish were turning and twisting and settling into their respective nooks and crannies, under plants, in dusky corners, by the rain-splashed windows. Even the gray and green woven carpet suggested the pebbled bottom of a tank. There was George Fitts, the barracuda, lurking over there in a stiff chair by the bookcase, his face in shadow. Katie Waters, small, wiry, with her short blond curls, a tropical species, undersized but feisty. A butterfly fish perhaps. Mike? Mike might be something playful and porpoiselike. Eliot Beaugard? An expensive and high-class fish, like the Atlantic salmon. And Alice? Something raggedy, perhaps a sculpin or one of the skates. And Caroline...?

"Don't you think so, Alex?" said Mike.

Alex jerked his head up and found a roomful of Beaugards and police staring at him.

"The Weymouth Scooter," prompted Mike. "You know all about them. You had one. That they're unstable."

Alex pulled himself to the surface, seeing the fishlike features of the assembled company fade and take on familiar human characteristics. "Yes," he said, fumbling for words. "The Scooter as it was originally designed flops around in a stiff wind. For Dolly to have sailed without trouble all these years must have meant that she modified her boat—or used extra ballast. Which I gather she did."

This seemed to satisfy the company, and George took over the narration. He seemed to be embarking on a discussion of the hazards of sailing small boats on ocean waters, but as the audience settled back in their corners, eyes shifting, hands twisting, feet tapping, Alex could see that this was one of George's ploys: Given a group of contentious family members, it was a good idea to lull them with recitation, wait until boredom and mild exasperation had set in, then strike. Alex settled back and waited for the strike.

Katie Waters, who was also familiar with George's methods, chose to make the most of the opportunity to check out the interior of one of these old summer "cottages" about which she had heard so much. Her first impression involved the word "shabby." Used. Dilapidated. Leather chairs with slightly gaping seams; a wicker table by the windows in need of fresh paint. And those awful pictures. Dark oils showing sailing ships on greasy waters, hunting prints depicting ducks falling out of the sky or someone holding a dead fox out to openmouthed foxhounds. And, like Alex, Katie thought books normally added a lot to a room. She herself had recently joined a book club and considered the rows of brightly covered jackets gave her little apartment a lot of zip. But these books in their glass prison, with their green slipcases, added to her growing negative view of the Beaugard ambience. Old Boston money might be a great thing, Katie concluded, but if you're not using any of it to cheer up your living space, well, what was the point? The whole room made Katie think about mold.

Mike Laaka, as George wove his way through a description of Proffit Point boating facilities, was repeating the word "snob" to himself. Like Mrs. Beaugard, who acted as if the police had head lice and body odor; like Eliot Beaugard, who referred to small motorboats as "stinkpots" and fiberglass vessels as "Clorox bottles." Like vacant-eyed clotheshorse Caroline or snooty Masha with her recorder group playing that weird music he'd seen on her music stand: gavottes and pavanes and other such stuff. And then Lenox Cobb, an academic snob with the disposition of a wolverine. And the boy Jonathan. Another spoiled kid going to that private school, probably making pottery and weaving blankets. As for Alice—hell, wasn't there always an Alice in every proper family? An Alice to keep the family off balance. What they all needed, Mike thought, was a twelve-hour-a-day job sluicing out fishing boats.

Mike looked up to see that George had given Katie Waters a signal to begin taking notes, which meant it was time for the tape recorder. Mike fished in his briefcase and held it aloft. "Any objections?" he asked.

"I hope not," said George smoothly. "We tape-record these sessions more as a check on ourselves than to intimidate you."

"Yeah," said Alice. "Right. Sure."

"So, okay?" asked Mike, hand on the on button.

Silence. Only a slight shifting of bodies, bottoms on their chairs, a recrossing of arms, a movement of feet.

Then Alice again. She was perched on the lower step of a set of library steps by the bookcase, her arms wrapped around her blue-jeaned legs. "If we object, we're guilty. Of something. Murder, arson, assault, forgery, drowning of Dolly. Right?"

"Alice!" said Mrs. Beaugard. "Let the police get along with whatever they think they're doing."

"Harassment," said Eliot.

"Bunch of dogs!" shouted Lenox Cobb so loudly that everyone, even George Fitts, jumped. "Dogs," he repeated. "The watchdogs bark. Dingdong bell. Hah!" And Lenox subsided with a throaty cackle.

Alex came to. He had been drifting about with his undersea fantasy and had been about to assign Lenox Cobb the role of the spiny spider crab. Now he took a hard look at the man. Color good, no discernible lopsided droop of the facial muscles, voice perhaps a little slurred and hoarse. But what was this business about dingdong bell? Maybe the family was right about Lenox. He was sliding off the deep end. Alex shifted slightly in his seat, the better to keep Lenox Cobb in view.

"Mrs. Beaugard," said George quietly. "We're here to tell you that your daughter's death may not have been accidental, that the ballast her sailboat carried was not in place when the boat was found, and that it's possible the lead was removed sometime prior to Sunday afternoon, October second, when she went sailing."

"She could have forgotten she'd taken it out," said Masha, speaking for the first time. She was wearing a deep green wool skirt and high-necked top and was draped elegantly on a small sofa at the other end of the windows. A green moray eel, decided Alex, looking over at the musical daughter.

"Dolly Beaugard," said George, still in the same low nonthreatening voice, "from all accounts was an organized person. It seems unlikely that she forgot that she'd gone through the tedious job of removing the ballast. Remember, we also know that she took care of every detail of the sailboat's maintenance. So why did she go out in a stiff wind in a boat without ballast? Probable answer: Dolly went sailing that Sunday thinking the ballast was in place. We aren't sure just what happened when the boat foundered, but we must consider her death as a possible homicide." George paused and looked about the room, his usually impassive face wearing an expression that could almost be described as welcoming.

"Mrs. Beaugard," he said, "weren't you concerned about your daughter going out in her small sailboat on a day when the winds were increasing and small-craft warnings had been issued?"

Elena Beaugard came to life. "Sergeant Fitts, I've always been aware of the dangers of sailing, but Dolly would never have listened to me. She went out whenever she pleased."

"So," said George, "you did absolutely nothing to stop her."

"Now, see here, Sergeant Fitts." It was Eliot who rose from his chair by the window and strode across the room to take a protective stance by his mother's chair. "My mother," said Eliot in a threatening voice, "isn't well. Saying something like that is inexcusable. You just cut it out."

"Eliot," snapped Mrs. Beaugard. "I can handle this myself. Sergeant Fitts, I did point out at lunch to Dolly that the wind was coming up, but I knew that she often went out in just such weather and was an experienced sailor. And she always took a life jacket."

"Did you perhaps remind her to check over her boat? The condition of the sails, the tiller. The presence of the ballast?"

"Sergeant Fitts," roared Eliot, "I said cut it out."

But Mrs. Beaugard reached for her cane and snapped it across her son's shins. "Eliot, stop trying to interfere. I've met people like this before. Sergeant, I'll say it again. Dolly never needed to be reminded about safety."

"Did she usually sail on Sunday afternoons?" asked George.

"Yes. After Sunday dinner. We always had a proper Sunday dinner even if only Dolly and I were there to eat it. Vivian and Dolly prepared a meal, usually a roast, so that it would be ready for us after church. Then later she would go for a sail."

"This was generally known? Dolly's Sunday afternoon sail?"

"It was no secret," said Mrs. Beaugard. "Everyone on the point knew Dolly sailed on Sundays. She was so busy with her committees that she often didn't have much time during the week. But her Sunday afternoons were special."

"I see," said George. He turned to Eliot Beaugard. "You're an experienced sailor. Was your sister, Dolly Beaugard, competent in a small boat? Able to go out by herself in all weathers?"

Eliot paused, appeared to be weighing Dolly's qualifications, and then nodded. "I wouldn't say she was an expert. But sure, she was okay in a small boat. Could handle most weather problems that came up. But I guess she really screwed up last Sunday. Misjudged a squall, got knocked overboard by the boom swinging over. Who knows? If the ballast was gone, I'd say she probably took it out herself. But then maybe couldn't resist one last sail before putting the boat in dry dock. It's a god-awful tragedy and my mother's just about had it up to here with the police."

George nodded briefly, then turned again to Elena Beaugard. "She always sailed alone?"

"Except for Jonathan," put in Alice. "Dolly took Jonathan sailing all the time."

"But not on the Sunday of October the second?"

"No," said Mrs. Beaugard. "Jonathan was staying with his father, Mr. Alan Epstein."

"Did Dolly usually haul her boat in by the end of September?"

"About that time," said Mrs. Beaugard. "Because of hurricanes. We always worry about hurricanes in the fall."

George nodded and then directed his attention to Vivian Lavender, who had chosen a particularly uncomfortable-looking straight-backed chair.

"Mrs. Lavender, can you remember the last time Dolly Beaugard went sailing in a strong wind and came home without mishap?"

This question produced the housekeeper's reminder that Sunday afternoon was her half day off. "So I wasn't usually around to see Dolly sail, except perhaps in midsummer when it was warm enough for me to go to the beach. But not in late September."

George threw the question open to the floor and garnered a variety of conflicting answers. Dolly had sailed the Sunday before she drowned and had come in early because there wasn't enough wind (Mrs. Beaugard); Dolly had sailed that previous Sunday but had stayed out almost two hours because there was a good wind (Eliot); Dolly said she cleaned the boathouse that Sunday, so there must have been a dead calm (Masha); Dolly had gone sailing late just the Wednesday before she died, and there had been a ton of wind. It had been windy all week, and Masha was wrong about the previous Sunday—that had been windy, too (Alice).

George then spoke his appreciation for their cooperation and said that now he and the deputies would meet separately with members of the family in various parts of the house. And Deputy Waters with Mrs. Lavender. In the kitchen. He rose, walked to the library door, opened it, and then paused, about to speak.

But Alex beat him to it. On his feet at the same time as George, he glanced at his watch and then, addressing the now rising company, "Anyone know what the weather's going to do? I know it's still pouring cats and dogs, but I had plans for tomorrow and…"

Although perhaps surprised by the sudden question, almost everyone had something to say about the weather. Mrs. Beaugard said Alex should watch the six-o'clock news. It gave the weather. Perhaps tomorrow would be brighter. Masha Beaugard shrugged and said the rain had better stop because it was affecting her wooden recorders—she'd have to start practicing with plastic ones. Eliot proclaimed that the barometer was going up and promised clearing skies by tomorrow night with a wind shift to the southwest, and added for good measure that the high should be in the fifties and that there would be a half moon. Vivian Lavender remarked that she only paid strict attention to the weather just before her day off, and Alice said for heaven's sake, Alex, look out the window and make a guess. That's all those dingbats at the weather bureau do. And Lenox Cobb, who now stood next to his sister and, like her, clutched a cane, said it was stupid to ask a group of people who had no scientific background to make any sort of a prediction. He, Lenox, usually knew what the weather would be because he considered all the variables, including not only air pressure, unstable airstream, cloud formation, whether stratocumulus or nimbostratus or the more dangerous jet stream cirrus, and—

"Thank you, Professor Cobb," said Alex. "I'm no weather scientist, but I'd be glad to have you tell me about your interest. Your sister suggested that since Dr. Foxe is out of town, I take a look at you. See how you're doing after your accident. How about your bedroom in ten minutes or so? Just a short examination."

And Lenox Cobb subsided and began a slow uncertain shuffle out of the room. Pausing at the door, he jerked his head at George Fitts, then jabbed his finger at the waiting Mike

Laaka and Katie Waters. "The police. Bowwow. The watchdogs bark. Bowwow." And departed.

The family filed out and Katie Waters headed for the kitchen after Vivian Lavender. But George and Mike lingered.

"Well, Alex," said George in a none too pleased voice, "you stole my thunder."

"Sorry, George. Couldn't resist it. Thought you might not be getting around to asking."

"It may not mean a thing," George reminded him.

"I know," said Alex. "But anything's worth a try."

"What in God's name are you nattering about?" demanded Mike. "So Lenox Cobb is a frustrated weatherman. So what. In Maine everyone pays attention to the weather."

"Thank you, Mike," said George. "Now catch up with Masha Beaugard and run through her time-and-place schedule for the week before Dolly's death. And ask her what prescription medicines she's taking and if she keeps medications in this house when she's away. As for you, Alex..."

"Time and place with Lenox Cobb?"

"No, that's police business. But you might ask him if he drinks Canadian whiskey."

Alex sighed. "The way he's acting, he'll probably kick me in the teeth for examining him, let alone asking questions."

Mike grinned. "What's that old rhyme? 'I do not like you, Dr. Fell, Why it is, I cannot tell.' Well, I've no trouble telling why I don't like that old fart. Bad-tempered bastard. Watchdogs and bowwow. Jeezus. You'd better commit him, Alex."

"What I'd better do is examine the man and the boy Jonathan. And then get out of here. Salvage an hour of my day off."

And Alex strode out of the room and headed for the stairs.

Chapter Eleven

ALEX, MOUNTING THE STAIRS toward the upper regions of the Great Oaks house, had a reaction something like that of Katie and Mike. But Alex's response to his surroundings was tempered by his familiarity with the genus Maine Summer Cottage. Sarah's grandmother, Mrs. Anthony Douglas, lived in just such a house, but hers was older and gloomier. And indeed his own mother and father had a smaller and livelier version of the same out on Weymouth Island—its interior freshened by white paint and his mother's watercolors. But there was something uncanny about this enormous house, too many contentious generations lurking like dubious ghosts behind the hodgepodge of furniture. Alex trudged upward on the uncarpeted stairs and found his attention attracted by a series of ancient black-and-white framed photographs that rose along the walls. Summer events: The Croquet Party, The Costume

Ball, The Regatta, The Island Picnic, Fourth of July Tennis Tournament. They were like illustrations for an Edith Wharton novel, but Alex doubted that the Beaugard family had ever been as carefree and joyous as these pictures suggested.

"Taking your time, aren't you?" It was Lenox Cobb clinging to the top of the banister.

"Wonderful old pictures," said Alex, reaching the last step.

"What you don't see," said Lenox, pointing his cane at a photograph showing four smiling men in white flannels holding pear-shaped wooden tennis rackets, "is that half the people in these photographs were always ready to kill, shoot, strangle, the other half. Arguments over whose serve it was, which ball was let, who had forgotten the mustard, what boat had not yielded to starboard tack, which family had taken which other families' tennis hour. On and on. Ad nauseam. And now? These police all over our house like hound dogs. I did say dogs, didn't I?"

"Yes, Professor Cobb, you certainly did."

"I'm losing track of what I do say. It's that swipe on the head. The attack on me. I have these blurred periods. And my balance seems off. I can remember a tennis tournament in 1928 and weather details because meteorology is one of my hobbies, but then I blank out completely. Damnation."

"Let's go into your bedroom," said Alex soothingly, "and let me have a look at you."

"But where is Dr. Foxe? He's my regular doctor. He should be here. Although he never seems to want to make house calls."

Alex reminded Professor Cobb of the reason for Dr. Foxe's absence and, after an initial resistance, managed to assist the professor into a cavernous room with a canopy bed.

"Where's your black bag?" complained Lenox, after he had been seated on a wooden chair with claw feet. He pointed to a small green carryall such as fishermen use for their gear.

"Black bags have gone the way of the horse and buggy," said Alex, opening the bag and extracting a stethoscope. "Too many people around looking for black bags with drugs. Now, if you'll let me help you off with your shirt."

And Lenox grumblingly submitted to an examination by rubber hammer, stethoscope, otoscope, and ophthalmoscope. Alex thought as he probed and touched and listened that he himself—a healthy and strong man in his mid-thirties—must seem almost an insult to the elderly professor sitting bare-chested before him. For Lenox Cobb's body had pretty much settled into an assemblage of sinew, gristle, bones, and loose freckled skin. A body closely resembling a plucked and starved turkey.

"Pretty sound," said Alex, closing his bag. "But it might be a good idea to come into the clinic for a neurology workup. Or if you're not too uncomfortable with this blurred sensation you describe, you could wait for Dr. Foxe to come back."

"It's only that I wanted to help Elena get her affairs in order. I'm the only one who understands how this house should be run. Elena depended too much on Dolly. And the Christmas Bird Count needs organizing, but I have trouble concentrating. Even with my new glasses. They don't seem to work as well as the ones I've lost. Alice telephoned in the prescription and she probably left out some information. On purpose."

"You *did* have a concussion," Alex reminded him. "At your age you can't just spring back into action."

"My age, my age. Everyone in this family acts like anyone over sixty is ready for the boneyard. Alice, Eliot, Masha. Bunch of harpies. Waiting for Elena and me to go under. And Dolly wasn't much better, giving our house away. God knows what else Dolly planned. Deeding all of Great Oaks' land to some ladies' auxiliary knitting team or the Bible-thumping crowd over at St. Paul's."

"I didn't know Episcopalians thumped Bibles," said Alex.

"As for me," went on Lenox in a peevish voice, "I'm finished. A relic. Show me a butt of malmsey and I'll jump in. Or retire to Pomfret Castle and talk of graves, of worms, and epitaphs."

"What!" said Alex startled.

"Shakespeare, *Richard the Second*, you muttonhead. Physician, cure thyself. And leave me in peace. And, Dr.... What *is* your name?"

"Alex, Alex McKenzie," said Alex. "And one more suggestion. I don't know if you're much of a drinker, but I'd take it easy with alcohol for now."

"I am a man of the grape," said Lenox Cobb. "Cognac—Courvoisier—and sometimes a dry sherry. I detest other liquors. But I will take your advice and be frugal."

"Splendid, Mr. Cobb."

"It is Professor Cobb."

"Professor Cobb. And now I'm supposed to check on young Jonathan."

"Ah, yes, Jonathan," said Lenox, seizing his cane. Then pausing at a small bookcase, adjusting his glasses, he selected a blue-bound volume. "I'll come with you."

"I think not," said Alex, firmly.

"I think yes. I need to see what's happened to the boy. Out there on the dock with that bunch of young hoodlums from his class. They should have been in school and not having cookouts in the middle of the school week. That's what's wrong with the world. Sixth graders who can't spell their own names out on field trips."

"Which room is Jonathan's?" asked Alex, giving up on the idea of shaking himself loose from Lenox.

"This way," said Lenox, pointing with his cane.

Jonathan was discovered sitting up in bed, one arm in a sling anchored across his chest, the other trying to drag a pair of blue jeans over his leg cast. His mother, Alice, hovered nearby with a dish of melting ice cream.

"He doesn't seem to want to eat anything," she said almost plaintively—quite a different tone from the usual Alice voice.

"Moth-er," said Jonathan. "I'm thirsty, not hungry. Because of the sedative. It dries your mouth. Ice cream will make it worse. How about some ginger ale or a Coke or a nice cold beer?"

"I think," said Alice to the two men, "he's feeling better and he doesn't have a temp. Did you know I can use a thermometer? Took a nurse's aide course once. But I didn't graduate. All right, Jonathan, I'll rustle up something to drink."

Alex introduced himself to the invalid. "I know you've met Sarah. My wife. In this house and at the hospital when Professor Cobb discharged himself."

"Correct," said Lenox, moving closer to the bed. "Now, boy, how do you feel?"

"Hi, Dr. McKenzie, " said Jonathan. "Hello, Uncle Lenox. I feel peculiar. And sorta mad. Like I've really screwed up. I was on the soccer team and now I've blown it. Or someone blew it for me. Gave me a nudge down the dock."

"And no one believes you," said Lenox with satisfaction. "They think you stumbled. My case exactly. I think there's someone out to destroy the Beaugard family. Or the few with brains."

Jonathan nodded agreement and then turned to Alex. "Okay, Dr. McKenzie, Mother said you wanted to look at me. You know what they said in the ER? Distal fibula fracture with slight bone exposure plus a dislocated shoulder. I'm taking antibiotics in case of infection and my shoulder hurts like anything and my leg is beginning to sound off, but I want to get up."

"I've just been telling your uncle to take it easy, so I'll say the same to you, Jonathan. Didn't the doctor at the hospital say to keep your leg up for a couple of days? Normally, after that you'd be able to use crutches, but with your shoulder, it's going to be a wheelchair for a while. Did they give you anything for pain? Yes? Okay, don't be a martyr. Take as directed."

"It's not that I'm sick. I just hurt. And I'm stuck here. With the family."

"Join the club," said Lenox Cobb unexpectedly. "You and I are trapped in the confines of a hostile family. And I can't read. Not more than a few pages because my eyes tire. So I have a proposition for you. You read to me—a book of my choosing—and I will pay you a small stipend for your trouble. You can put it in your college fund."

"More like my Nintendo fund," said Jonathan, managing another grin. "But are you going to make me read Shakespeare and gruesome stuff like that? Or poetry?"

"A compromise," said Lenox, pushing a chair close to the edge of Jonathan's bed. "I choose one book, you choose the next."

"But you'll choose Shakespeare? It's what you taught at Bowmouth, wasn't it?"

"I had the Susan Addinbrook Ransom Chair in Elizabethan Literature. And yes, I dabbled in Shakespeare. Lectured to thickheaded undergraduates for thirty-five years. However, in view of your extreme youth, I will choose from various works. I have brought a volume with me. Something suitable since I assume you prefer a horror story with all the trimmings. We can begin immediately. After this man—Dr. Whatshisname—leaves us alone."

With which Dr. Whatshisname nodded his goodbye and slipped quietly out of the room, hearing from the hall Jonathan's high-pitched boy's voice: "'The "Red Death" had long devastated the country. No pestilence had ever been so fatal, or so hideous. Blood was its Avatar and its seal—the redness and the horror of blood. There were sharp pains, and sudden dizziness, and then profuse bleeding at the pores...'"

Alex descended the stairs, scribbled a quick note for George to the effect that Professor Cobb was not a whiskey drinker, handed it to Katie Waters, who was just emerging from the kitchen, and then headed for the front hall. And ran head-on into Masha Beaugard.

Masha, instead of sliding away after a brief greeting as Alex expected her to do, lingered and indicated distress. Her car was in Camden. Being fixed. Something about the manifold. Was he by any chance going that way? Because didn't he live somewhere in Camden? Near Bowmouth? A lift would be perfectly marvelous.

Alex, who would have given much to drive home in absolute peace, said yes, of course. Just as soon as he'd spoken to Mrs. Beaugard. About her brother.

"Uncle Lenox has gone wacko, hasn't he?" said Masha, reaching for a glossy purple raincoat. "That's what Eliot thinks and Mother's trying not to think. I mean, one minute he's with it and the next he doesn't know his own name."

"I'll be with you in a minute," Alex said, and made for the living room door, where he found Eliot Beaugard standing at the window staring at the dripping landscape while Elena Beaugard, in her accustomed wing chair by the fireplace, confronted George Fitts. George seemed to be winding up proceedings and thanking Mrs. Beaugard for being so helpful.

"I know none of this has been pleasant," George was saying, "but it has to be gotten through. And we do have some news for you. The laboratory is releasing your daughter's body for burial. Sometime this weekend. Perhaps you can let us know if there is a funeral director whom you want to manage things."

Eliot jerked around. "Hell, it's about time. Do you police always hang on to bodies like that? Mother's been worried sick about it. The funeral should have been today."

"Mr. Ouellette of Thomaston always takes care of the family," said Elena in a faint voice. "We can have the funeral Monday. Or Tuesday. Eliot, will you call people? Father Smythe. Put a notice in the paper. Do what's necessary. Oh, Dr. McKenzie. How is Lenox? Is he recovering properly? He seems so confused at times that I thought he might have had a very tiny stroke. And just when I was thinking of letting him help me manage the estate. Take care of some of the accounts. The things Dolly used to do for me. But now I'm afraid he's not up to it."

"Well, not yet," said Alex. "He's in pretty fair shape, but a neurology workup wouldn't be a bad idea. After all, he had that blow on the head. Twice."

"Walking into a tree," put in Eliot. "Wandering around in the dark without his glasses. But hey, Alex, thanks for coming, letting Mother drag you all the way out here. And don't worry about Uncle Lenox. We'll all keep a close eye on the guy. Alice ordered two pairs of spare glasses for him, so we shouldn't have any more searches in the woods. Maybe we'll put an alarm on his belt. The way they do with little kids."

"Not a bad idea," said Alex, saying to himself, not a bad idea in more ways than one.

"And listen, he and Jonathan can buddy up. Couple of invalids and both a pain in the ass—sorry, Mother. I'd say they could neutralize each other."

Here Eliot paused and then patted his mother's shoulder. "Okay, sorry again; I know Uncle Lenox is your special only brother. But sometimes I've had it with him. He spews out so much piss and vinegar that it's hard to stir up much sympathy. And, Alex, don't forget tomorrow. Saturday. You and Sarah. Drinks at our place. Around six. We need to get Mother out of the house. Just a few close neighbors. The family, Masha, and—"

"And Alice," said Alice, coming into the room, followed by Mike Laaka.

"Hell, Alice, you don't need to get out of the house; you're hardly in it. But come along. And bring your current boyfriend if you have one. As long as he's remotely civilized. Not out on parole or spaced out on drugs. A cross-dresser with a size C bra. Nothing to upset Mother here, who isn't exactly New Age. Hey, look out." This as Alice advanced menacingly across the floor. "Just kidding. Okay?"

"Kidding, my foot," said Alice, glowering. "Listen, Eliot..."

And Alex made for the door. And into the front hall, where he collected Masha, who stood sheathed in her raincoat, a handbag over her shoulder, a folding music stand tucked under one arm, and a bulging leather musical instrument case in her hand. "I have a rehearsal after I pick up my car," she explained.

Mike Laaka caught up with the two just as Alex had settled into the driver's seat.

"I'll stop in tonight."

"Why?" demanded Alex, turning the ignition.

"Because I love you," said Mike. "I love Sarah. I love all mankind. And because George says so."

"Get lost," shouted Alex, shifting into first and turning the Jeep toward the drive.

For the first six miles he and his passenger drove in silence, and then when Alex was beginning to feel a relaxation of tension and contemplating which tape would not only soothe him but please a player in a recorder group, Masha came to life.

"It's bizarre," she said. "Or ironic."

"What is?" said Alex. "Dolly's death, the Gattling brothers, or just life?"

"Well, all those, though I suppose everyone expected those two Gattlings to come to a sticky end. I meant Lenox and Jonathan. All poor Mother needs is to have those two underfoot all day, every day. Jonathan with his big mouth and Lenox with his bigger one. Like having a pair of crabs scuttling around."

Alex glanced over at his companion. A beautiful woman. Very white skin, which was odd after the more than usually hot summer, so perhaps she spent most of her time under umbrellas or in rehearsal halls. Her auburn hair was cut straight across her high forehead, hanging straight and short around her head; her arched nose, her wide mouth, her firm little chin, her sleek compact person, all these came together in a way that made Alex think of sophisticated females of the twenties. The Jordon Bakers or Gatsby's Daisy, or better, a Siamese cat. Yes, Masha Beaugard would do very well as a Siamese cat.

"Just like crabs," repeated Masha. "Don't you think?"

"You have a point," said Alex, coming to and wondering where the conversation was going.

"Mother at this time in her life needs peace and calm. Dolly gave her that. Dolly might have seemed a bit much to everyone, and God knows she did drive Eliot and me up the wall twenty times a week. But she took care of Mother."

"Did you mind about the Episcopal Church? Alice told me about your mother's idea of giving Great Oaks to the diocese. Fairly soon, not after she died."

"I don't really mind," said Masha slowly. "I haven't any sentimental attachment to the stuff in the house. But if I'd had a say, I'd have given the house over to a music group. For a permanent music school and summer youth program. Tanglewood north. We've got enough churches around, but not enough music facilities. I'd like to see our recorder consort have a permanent home here. But that's just my interest. I don't think anyone else in the family knows Beethoven from the Beatles. Except maybe Alice. She has a terrific voice and won't sing a note. Sheer orneriness. But that's Alice for you."

"Won't you all inherit all the land around the big house? Along with Lenox. If none of them are interested in keeping the place, you might have your music school after all."

"God knows about Uncle Lenox," said Masha crossly, "but Eliot would be sure to sell off his share. And get big bucks for it because it's shore land and has deep water for moorings. Then he could buy another new boat or add a wing to that house of his. Alice would probably sell out, too, since it's ten to one she'd be in some sort of jam and need cash."

"Dolly didn't have any plans for your mother to dispose of the rest of the property? As far as you know? The Nature Conservancy, for instance?" Alex asked this carefully, having long thought that someone as super-organized as Dolly Beaugard must have considered the future of more than the house. All those cottages, several acres of woods, a sand beach, a pebble beach, and two coves.

Masha was silent. She looked out the window, scowled at the rising mist, the still-falling rain, and then tapped her finger on her knee. Then returned to the window and seemed to take an interest in the scene—Madison's General Store, a sheep farm—and then almost at the Thomaston town line, she nodded.

"You're right. I can't believe that Dolly stopped short at the house. She did everything to the nth degree. She must have had an estate plan for Mother that included disposition of *every* damn thing on the property, down to every acorn in the woods and pebble on the beach. And she probably wrote it all down somewhere. But the police have been suctioning up everything

Dolly owned, and I haven't heard a word about an estate plan. Or Mother's will."

"The police," said Alex with feeling, "are not into sharing. They may be incubating Dolly's Line-a-Day Diary, but they won't be telling you about it. Not yet."

"Because we're all suspects," said Masha bitterly.

"Everyone in Knox County is fair game," Alex pointed out. "This is a homicide. Apparently."

"Because of the lead ballast? Honestly, I think it was exactly like Eliot said. She couldn't resist one more sail and forgot she'd taken out the ballast. Dolly *did* make mistakes. She once gave Mother the wrong medication for some stomach bug and Mother threw up all night. Dolly wouldn't have admitted it, but Vivian found the empty prescription bottle in the wastebasket. Dolly was one of those people who is never wrong, and if she was, she'd cover her tracks like crazy. Okay, Alex, you can let me off at the garage on the next block. Thanks a lot. And listen, Mother likes you. I can tell. And Sarah. See if you can make a suggestion about leaving some property for a music school." Masha paused, the car door open, then shrugged— "Don't listen to me. As Eliot would say, 'just kidding.'"

And Alex pulled the Jeep to the curb, and Masha, clutching bags and music case and music stand, departed.

Sarah was discovered kneeling on the fringe of a patch of rough grass referred to optimistically by the owners as the lawn. Even though the rain had somewhat abated, the ground was sopping. But rain or no rain, Sarah was planting peach trees. Five of them. Alberta peach trees.

"At this time of year?" demanded Alex, examining the tags.

Sarah pushed a mound of peat moss around a slim twiglike trunk, then straightened and wiped a wet and grimy hand across her forehead. "I think it's safe. Spring or fall is okay. But you have to wrap the trunk because of mice. I wanted something to grow and bloom and have fruit. We can make peach pie or *pêche* melba. The trees are a sort of an antidote to *l'affaire* Beaugard." She pushed another handful of peat in place, rose, stamped on the squelching ground, and then gathered up the half-empty bag of peat. "Let's go in and you can tell me about your adventures at Proffit Point."

An hour later, sprawled in chairs, drinks in hand, the two reviewed the day.

"So," said Sarah, "how did the house call turn out? Uncle Lenox has gone gaga or is he being maligned by evil forces within?"

"Uncle Lenox—whose brain does seem a little on the fuzzy side—is being read to by young Jonathan Epstein. Who is also out of action. I think they've found each other and have each decided that they've been pushed into or off something. By the evil forces or visiting aliens. Jonathan has a broken leg—simple fracture apparently—and a dislocated shoulder."

"I suppose they deserve each other."

"Don't knock it. It keeps two potential antipersonnel bombs out of everyone's way. Lenox actually proposed the reading program and will pay Jonathan. The professor's eyes are not up to snuff."

"His brain *and* his eyes?"

"They sometimes go together, those two things. Anyway, I left Jonathan and Lenox and Edgar Allan Poe going at it."

"While George and Mike…"

"Plus Deputy Katie Waters. Busy with more interviews. The family more or less accepts that Dolly is a possible homicide. George asked when Dolly last went sailing safely in a strong wind. A point on which there was much disagreement—short-term memory loss all round. Then I stuck my long nose in and asked a weather question and beat George Fitts to the punch. Here's the question: What's the weather going to do? How would you answer that?"

"You're kidding."

"No, serious."

"Well, I think it'll stop raining. it usually does."

"That's it? Your complete opinion?"

"I'm not planning a garden party tomorrow or a track event, so I don't much care. I mean I'll be glad to have sun, but I can live with rain. Good for the peach trees. So what's this all about?"

"You made the point yourself. You don't much care about the weather because you haven't planned anything that relies on it."

"So?"

"So what if you planned to do in a woman by taking ballast out of her small sailboat? Wouldn't you want to do it when a strong wind was predicted? No point in lifting the lead if there was going to be a long period of dead calm or light breezes."

"And you found out that the Beaugards all go around with barometers, holding their fingers into the wind?"

"Mrs. Beaugard listens to the six-o'clock news; Vivian Lavender checks when her day off is coming up; Eliot knows exactly what the barometer is going to do; Alice told me to look out the window; Masha worries about her recorders; but Professor Emeritus Cobb—get this—is the weather bureau personified. Statistics, the variables, the air pressures, all the appropriate jargon."

"So Eliot and/or Uncle Lenox, cohorts in crime, dumped the lead ballast."

Alex made a low rumbling sound that suggested disgust. Then he stood up and made for the oven, from whence the smell of chicken emanated. "I think the weather idea may be a bust. It would only make sense if everything else was in place. So let's eat before Mike comes to spoil dinner."

"Mike's coming? Tonight? Oh shit. I'm fond of Mike, but…"

"But oh for an evening without him."

"Tell him he has exactly twenty minutes of our precious time and then he's out on his ear."

"Make it fifteen and I'll agree."

Chapter Twelve

At EIGHT-THIRTY A HEAVY hand sounded on the kitchen door.

"Twenty minutes," Sarah announced as she opened the door to Mike Laaka. "And only twenty minutes," she added, as she led Mike into the kitchen, his slicker gleaming from the still moist air. "Alex and I are trying to have these little pockets of normal evening life, and there's no room for you."

But Mike only grinned, patted Patsy, accepted a mug of coffee from Alex, and settled down in one of the overstuffed kitchen armchairs. Then, after a few moments spent in discussion of rain, mist, and drizzle and the question of Hurricane Griffin, now hovering somewhere west of the Azores, Mike got down to business.

"As you know, Alice claims Wednesday afternoon as the last time she saw Dolly out sailing. We didn't really believe her because Alice hardly goes about with a calendar in her head. Or much of anything else. But we've a report from a fishing boat that a boat like Dolly's was out then. And confirmation from the weather gurus that last Sunday afternoon the wind was offshore and blowing east. Or east northeast. Tide turning and flowing out. Which means—"

"Which means," Alex interrupted, "that Dolly would cast off from her mooring in Back Cove and run out through the Proffit Point narrows into open sea with the turning tide, before the wind, not need ballast or a keel—may even have left her centerboard up—and wouldn't have hit trouble until she let down the centerboard, hauled in sail to go off on another tack. Or tried to come about."

"You got it," said Mike. "If wind had come from another direction—say the usual southwest—she would have known right off something was wrong, could have made it back to shore or at least dropped her sails and grabbed a paddle. The *Sweetheart* apparently carried an emergency paddle."

"So," said Sarah, getting into the act, "our weather expert knew in which direction the wind was going to be blowing. Or took a chance on it. That means Lenox Cobb or Eliot Beaugard. Or both working as a team. End of case. Good night, Mike."

"Sarah, Sarah," said Mike, settling back against the pillows and taking a healthy gulp of coffee. "After all we've been through together. Listen, if you get rid of me, you'll only have George infesting your kitchen. What I've come here to say—in part, and this is between us—is that old George is a bit thrown by the Beaugard family. It's not his scene. Not that it's mine, but George is in charge, not me. Like some decayed royal family—old lady Beaugard acting like Queen Victoria; Eliot, the crown prince and their dad, papa Arthur Beaugard, with his illustrated editions, most of them kids' books, for God's sake, because I heard some adult talking about Daddy's first edition of *Peter Rabbit*. I mean, Christ, a grown man collecting books about bunnies."

"Your point?" said Sarah.

"My point? I think our Sergeant George, for once in his life, is almost glad that you're in the mix. He actually said to me he'd like you to hang around with the Beaugards and keep your ears open. Chat about Peter Rabbit. Goldilocks. Socialize with Alice Beaugard. And Webb Gattling."

Sarah sat up straight. "Oh, good Lord, bugger off, Mike. We've done what we could. We haven't much extra time for much more. Not for Alice. Or Webb. We have jobs, remember."

"Actually no real effort is needed on your part. I gather the Beaugards will hang around you. Light up your life. Just don't discourage them. There's this cocktail thing tomorrow night. And Dolly's funeral. You can network like crazy. Mingle."

"All that and Alice and Webb Gattling," said Alex. "You mean Sarah and I can double-date?"

"Go for it. We really need to firm up the Gattling place in all this. Right now Webb and Alice are the only links."

"Are you now saying the Gattling drownings do fit in with Dolly's drowning?" said Sarah.

"It's being thought about. The lab is reexamining the Gattling skiff looking for canvas fibers. Looking around for supplies of Valium. Both Mrs. Beaugard and Caroline—Eliot's wife—have prescriptions for it. Actually, Mrs. Beaugard has about twelve different prescriptions for this and that. And Caroline admits to enough stuff to stock a pharmacy. As for Alice, God knows what she's got stashed somewhere in an old shoe. Everything from hallucinogenic toadstools to castor bean candy bars."

"Alice says she's trying to kick the alcohol habit, so maybe she's trying to stay away from drugs," put in Sarah. "So how about the Gattling family prescription collection?"

"No Valium in Marsden and Junior's immediate family. But the Gattlings have probably ripped off a few drugstores in their day. Let's just say Valium is very available and that some of the Beaugards have a supply."

"Weak, weak," said Sarah. "Won't stand up in court."

"And the whiskey bottle found in the boat. Seagram's V.O. Canadian Whiskey. Not your ordinary rotgut stuff that Junior and Marsden liked to pour down their gullets. So, Sarah and Alex—"

"Oh sure," said Sarah, "we're to go to Eliot and Caroline's cocktail party with a little notepad and an instant camera and check out the liquor supply. See if Canadian whiskey is featured."

"I knew you'd cooperate, Sarah. If we find any tie—even a flimsy one—between the three drownings, then we'll have a—"

"Real mess," said Alex. "Good night, Mike."

The next afternoon—Saturday, exactly ten minutes after six—found Sarah and Alex driving down the Proffit Point Road in the direction of Eliot and Caroline's new and splendid house. Neither passenger, however, was rejoicing at the lifting of the rain and the clearing of the air.

"It's like being taken hostage or something," complained Sarah. "Getting dressed up to come all the way over here to be with people we don't much like. Except Alice. There are moments when it's possible to like Alice. Away from her family, that is. Anyway, we could have gone to the movies and seen Anthony Hopkins and Emma Thompson again. Or rented a video. *Godfather Seven* or *The Return of the Slime*. Something uplifting."

"We have a mission," Alex reminded her. "Case Eliot's liquor inventory. We're looking for Canada's finest. Seagram's V.O."

"Well, I hate whiskey, so I hope they have rum." Sarah paused for a moment and took in the passing scenery. And like Katie Waters before her, she gave herself a minute to marvel at the patterns of colors left on the road by the fallen leaves. "Not exactly Shelley, but the colors are hectic enough."

"Shelley? What's he got to do with anything?"

"It begins 'O wild west Wind, thou breath of Autumn's being' and goes on about dead leaves…'like ghosts from an enchanter fleeing, / Yellow, black, and pale and hectic red. Pestilence-stricken multitudes...' And so forth and so forth."

"In the first place," said Alex, ever practical, "there isn't a whisper of a wild west wind today, and those leaves aren't going anywhere. They're plastered flat. 'Pestilence-stricken multitudes'? Phooey. Shelley should have run into a few real pestilence-stricken people."

"Poetic license," said Sarah. "Shelley's using the leaves to go somewhere else. Never mind poetry. You don't deserve it. What we have to do now is brace for this evening because it isn't really supposed to be a 'cocktail party.' Not with Dolly dead. It's for family distraction and moral support. With drinks on the side."

"To quote Eliot, it's to get 'Mother out of the house,'" said Alex. "We'll do a slow spin around, bare our teeth, press hands and admire the view of Tidal Cove, case the whiskey. And duck out."

"Forget the view, They have a brand-new house. They'll want to show us all over so we can gasp with envy."

The turn in to Eliot Beaugard's drive was marked by one of those mailboxes whose fiberglass sides are impregnated with the likeness of mallard ducks or cardinals—in this case a schooner with all sails set, and beneath, the name E. BEAUGARD in large black print. The chief reason for Sarah and Alex's scrutiny of this everyday object was that, uprooted from its guardian position by the side of the drive, it lay directly in the path of the Jeep.

Alex slammed on the brakes and cut the engine.

"Wild west wind?" said Sarah.

"Wild west people more likely," said Alex, grimacing. He climbed out of the car and hauled the mailbox, its post still attached, to the edge of the drive and propped it on a stone. Then he bent, reached into the open flap, and extracted a rolled newspaper, a copy of *Time*, a copy of *Business Week*, one of *Yachting*, a few catalogs, and several letters.

"Guess no one's been down for the mail today," he said, returning to the car. "I'll do a hand delivery. Looks like a chain saw got it. What is it about mailboxes? They've become a universal target. In hunting season they're shot full of holes, and in the winter they get trashed for the fun of it. You know, why go bowling when you can just crowbar a few mailboxes?"

The drive was not a long one, but it wound left and right through spruce and hemlock, then dipped suddenly and went via a narrow stone bridge over a brook before rising toward the house.

And for the second time, Alex slammed on the brakes. A figure had suddenly risen from beside the bridge, jumped into the road, and held out his arms.

"It's Webb Gattling," said Sarah, frowning at the man standing spread-eagled in front of them. She looked again. Standard Maine rural wear: jeans, black and red checked shirt, black baseball hat. High-laced boots. But the man was too short for Webb. She shook her head. "No, it isn't Webb. It's just a lot like him. Big head and hairy. Like Webb if he'd been shrunk in the wash."

"Damn," said Alex, "we're going to be good and late." But he rolled down his window and poked out his head.

"Help you?"

The man approached the car, making sure he still blocked the drive. "Maybe," he called. "You the police?"

"No," said Alex. "We're not."

"Well, you the Beaugards? Any of them?"

"No," said Alex, "and if you'll please move..."

"Please, can you prove you're not the Beaugards?" said the man, maintaining his position but giving a backward glance over his shoulder that suggested to Sarah he had an adjunct in the vicinity.

"Believe me," said Alex, "we're private citizens making a visit."

The man moved three steps closer, and now Sarah could see that he was at least two heads shorter than Webb, his hair was darker, more brown than blond, and his beard lacked Webb's fullness.

"But you're going to see the Beaugards?" said the man. "So I've got a holy message. From me. And all of us. My whole family. We have our sacred grief, too. Marsden and Junior are gone to glory. Brothers in Christ and now in rapture with Him. Praise the Lord. I'm praying that the Beaugards will tell the police to leave us in peace. Okay, you understand that, my brother?"

"I understand," said Alex, "and now could you please move?"

The man did, but only another step forward so that he almost leaned across the hood of the Jeep. He peered at Alex and then squinted at the windshield toward Sarah. "I've seen you before. Both of you. Around with Mike Laaka. With that state trooper, George Fitts. They are godless folk and I pray for them. Daily I pray for the police, but they are blind to God's perfection."

Here the man became increasingly agitated, almost hopping from foot to foot, his bearded chin quivering. "Go and tell unto the Beaugards that we are innocent of Dolly Beaugard's blood. That Dolly Beaugard was a saint on Earth. And some of us have taken action which I do not condone. But remember Jesus among the money changers. The mailbox shall be a sign unto you."

"The mailbox was your work?" said Alex.

The man shook his head. "I would not lift a hand to do such work. Praise the Lord. But there are those that would. Listen, brother, tell the Beaugards that Parson was praying for them. For the truth to trample out the vintage where the grapes of wrath are stored. Bless you." And the man jumped back down from the bridge—amazingly agile for one of his bulk—and disappeared into the lengthening shadows of a late October afternoon.

"Good grief," said Sarah. "The Troll of Proffit Point. Or the Mad Hermit. Parson. Who on earth is Parson? I mean, it's obvious that he's related to Webb, but is he one of the 'good' Gattlings or one of the bad ones? Or just the craziest. Bitten by the Lord."

"Frankly," said Alex, gunning the Jeep over the bridge and up the hill, "I don't care. Good, bad, crazy. But he's certainly in touch with someone who has a penchant for mailboxes."

"The police must be leaning on the Gattlings and they're feeling the heat. Every available Gattling has probably been worked over about Dolly as well as about Marsden and Junior, and they probably think the Beaugards are pointing accusing fingers."

"So some Gattlings are fighting back with mailboxes, and others are praying," said Alex, as he swung the car up to the house, rounded the circle, and parked behind a sleek dark vehicle with the familiar BMW logo on its butt.

The news of the fallen mailbox and the meeting with Parson Gattling—if that was truly his name—did much to change the tenor of the cocktail gathering. In any event, the gathering Sarah guessed from the subdued murmurs and lack of movement coming from a wide-open living space overlooking the cove, was more dedicated to the details of Dolly's death and upcoming funeral than to anything else.

Alex had no sooner made his report to Eliot, who had opened the door, than Eliot swore loudly, strode into the living room, and made the announcement. "My mailbox. Cut down with a chain saw. Those goddamn Gattlings. Alex and Sarah met one of them at the bridge. Parson. Says he's praying for us but seems to think we're blaming them for Dolly's drowning. That's close to blackmail, so I'm going to telephone the police." And Eliot stamped out of the room.

Leaving Caroline Beaugard to do the honors. Which she did in a disinterested, almost disdainful way, standing, languid hand outstretched. She was wearing a turquoise caftan and her hair fell like honey down her back, but her beauty had an unreal quality as if she were not involved in anything she said or did. She was a real puzzle, Sarah thought. A druggie or into something spiritual? Cosmic awareness. Finding her inner—or outer—self, transcending the mundane world of house and home.

The introductions went forward: the assembled Beaugards—minus Jonathan, but including Professor Lenox Cobb, who must have been dragged protesting to the party. A dark-clad figure, scowling and clutching his cane, he sat hunched on a white and pink flowered sofa. Besides the Beaugards there were several strangers, a couple by the name of Roxford, an intense-looking man whose first name was Helmann. A young woman—Amy—clasping the arm of an older man, Duncan. Plus two middle-aged second cousins of Elena Beaugard with names straight out of Tolstoy: Nicholas and Katerina Smeltovich or something like that.

"Do you want to wait for Eliot to fix your drinks?" asked Caroline. "Or fix them yourselves; everything's there." With this gracious offer, Sarah and Alex walked as directed to a table laden with bottles, lemon slices, orange slices, olives, cherries, seltzer waters, plain waters, and mixers of all sorts.

Alex helped himself to Scotch and water and returned to the other guests while Sarah considered possible choices. It was a full bar, she noticed as she reached for the rum and mixed up a rum and orange juice. Thus equipped, she turned to study the scene. Alex seemed to be engaged with Masha reenacting the confrontation with Parson Gattling. Alice Beaugard was sitting on a bench with one of the Tolstoy cousins, and Caroline floated—there was no other word for it—from guest to guest, pausing only to bestow her vague smile, listen to a few words, and then turn and join another guest.

Then Sarah remembered. The mission. Whiskey. Well, it was a perfect moment for an inventory. She turned and tried to register varieties and types. Dry sherry, Bristol Cream, Dubonnet, a burgundy, Chablis on ice. Then brandy, rum, vodka—all in high-priced bottles. Tanqueray gin. Whiskey and blends. Chivas Regal, Jack Daniel's, and three pricey bottles of Scotch. No Seagram's V.O. But wouldn't any sensible malefactor involved in lacing whiskey with Valium get rid of his supply of Canadian?

Sarah, with regret, placed her glass of rum and orange juice behind the fat bottle of Bristol Cream sherry, and walked over to join Alice and wait for Eliot's return.

It worked as predicted. Eliot, somewhat red in the face, rejoined his guests. "The sheriff's office is sending a deputy right over to check around. See if there's any damage beyond the mailbox. I asked about this Parson Gattling and I got zip. The guy even laughed at me. Parson's probably wanted for something, but do you think those birds would let on?" Here Eliot paused and seemed to remember that this was a festive occasion—or at least semi-festive. And that there were two newly arrived guests. And that one of them stood empty-handed.

"Sarah, where's your drink? Didn't Caroline? Well, never mind. What would you like? Name your poison."

"I don't suppose you have any Canadian whiskey?"

Eliot frowned. "I don't know. You may have caught me on that one. No one in our family drinks it, but then, I should have it on hand. Let's go over and see." And Eliot marched to the long table and began examining bottles. Then he excused himself, left the room, and came back empty-handed. "Sorry, Sarah. Thought there might be some hidden away in the pantry, but I guess we've never had anyone ask for it lately. Caroline," he called over his shoulder. "Next time you're in town, pick up some Canadian whiskey, will you? Sarah, we'll have to have you back some evening for a solo drink. Now, what other kind of whiskey can I interest you in? Or how about a nice Scotch?"

"Actually," said Sarah, repressing her relief, "rum would be fine. In juice if you have it."

Eliot smiled. "That's a switch. Whiskey drinkers don't go for rum. Never mind, I've got the makings." He turned back to the table and began busying himself with bottle, ice, and glass. And returned with Sarah's drink. "You're not alone. Someone else went for orange juice and something and left it behind the sherry. Now, in a proper mystery scene, we would have to check the glass for fingerprints."

"Fortunately," said Sarah, "we're not in a proper mystery. And your house, it's marvelous." Confident of the perfect distraction, she waved a hand at the surrounding walls and expanse of seaward windows.

It worked. Sarah was taken in hand and given the tour. It was all splendid: soaring ceilings, high beams, glass—every window facing the sea—the land walls hung with contemporary tapestries, abstract oils, and glass shelves featuring small ship models.

Returned to the living room, she fortified herself with a handful of mixed nuts from a bowl, and a piece of hard cheese sitting on a small cracker—quite meager pickings, she thought, considering the general upscale ambience. Probably Caroline's choice. On the flowered sofa she found Lenox Cobb had been joined by Alex, and the two men were deep into a detailed discussion of the coming Christmas Bird Count: species seen, species hoped for. The possibility of a king eider, the scarcity of the red-necked grebe. A recent sighting of a number of Bohemian waxwings. It was a subject, in Sarah's opinion, that did not grab. She looked about and settled on a bench next to Alice, who was still occupied listening to one of the Tolstoy cousins, Katerina, describing the experience of putting her life into the hands of Weight Watchers while at the same time editing a book on home cooking.

"I drool all over the manuscript," she was saying.

This did not seem promising, so Sarah shifted her attention to the Roxford couple, who were engaged in a hissing argument on the question of admitting new members to the Proffit Point Tennis Club.

"Fifteen families are too many," hissed the female Roxford. "We don't get enough time on the court as it is."

"But Dolly Beaugard is gone. That leaves a vacancy."

"She never played anyway, and neither do the rest of the Beaugards. Except Eliot. What we need to do is get rid of one of the full-time families..."

Sarah turned back to Alex and Lenox Cobb. Counting birds began to seem more attractive. And Lenox for the first time seemed relatively affable. He was sitting up and vigorously extolling the virtues of a new field telescope.

Lenox, Sarah thought, listening to the professor, might have redeeming qualities after all. And he seemed to be having no speech difficulties of the sort that Alex had described. She had just decided that the visit had lasted long enough and was wondering how to extricate Alex from Professor Cobb's orbit when Eliot Beaugard saved her the trouble.

"It's time for Mother to go home," he announced, and with this there followed a putting down of drinks, a general rising, and a murmuring of thanks. And because of recent events, there was much clasping of hands and meaningful looks of condolence.

Sarah and Alex joined the general exodus, but were stopped at the doorstep by Eliot. "You're both in cahoots with the police, aren't you? Mother knows all about last summer with Sarah's aunt Julia Clancy and that business of the groom murdered by a horse."

"Not by a horse," said Sarah, "a human. And we're not in cahoots with the police. It's just that—"

"I've got you," said Eliot. "I won't say a word. But if you could just find out about this Parson Gattling. He sounds dangerous. As well as cracked in the head."

"Really, you'd better let the police handle it," Sarah began, and then saw Eliot had turned and was staring in the direction of the shore where, in the fire red of the setting sun, the dock, the little dinghies, the moored sailboat, the islands and peninsula beyond, stood out in dark profile like cutout silhouettes.

"Beautiful," said Alex. "These fall sunsets. If you took a picture, no one would believe it."

"I never get tired of sunsets," said Eliot. "Even my old *Goshawk* looks terrific." He waved at the sloop, which sat out on the flat dark waters of the cove as if it had been painted there.

"'A painted ship upon a painted ocean,'" said Sarah, happy to move away from police matters.

"*Rime of the Ancient Mariner*," said Eliot. "But it's a magic boat. You wouldn't believe where I can go in that old thing. Right up in coves and through shallows."

"A centerboard?" asked Alex.

"You've got it. A big centerboard in that baby means I can take her where boats this size with a keel wouldn't think of going. Hell, when I'm cruising I can sneak into little inlets, drop the hook, and have a night's peace while all the other guys are stuck out in a crowded noisy harbor."

"But a retracted centerboard must take a lot of cabin space."

"That's the downside," said Eliot. "And old *Goshawk*'s getting a little creaky." Then he seemed to remember what had brought him outside. He extended his hand to Sarah. "Thanks so much for coming. It means a lot to Mother to have old friends around at a time like this. And don't forget about Parson Gattling, will you? Prior convictions, what he was doing when Dolly drowned."

Alex and Sarah turned and walked in silence to the Jeep. And in silence completed the first ten miles down the Proffit Point Road.

Then Sarah drew a long breath and said, "That meeting with Parson Gattling does give me the shivers. Talk about weird."

"Just your everyday nut with a religious flavor, I'd guess," said Alex. "But I will ask Mike when I see him."

"Oh shit!" said Sarah suddenly. She pointed at her feet.

"Oh shit what?"

"Look there. The mail. Eliot's mail. Caroline's mail. From the mailbox. We forgot to take it in."

"I'm not going to turn around. We're halfway home. We'll get it to them tomorrow."

"What's the penalty for mail theft?"

"Probably years in a federal prison."

"One of those minimum-security ones, I hope. We can learn basic skills, how to run a laundry and play volleyball. Not a Beaugard in sight. It's sounds wonderful."

Alex nodded and, to the great hazard of safe driving, reached over and kissed Sarah on the cheek.

Chapter Thirteen

SUNDAY PROMISED TO BE a day of clear autumnal weather with a surcease of trouble from the direction of Proffit Point.

Sarah and Alex sat lingering over a very late breakfast since Alex was not on call for what was left of the weekend. And Sarah had spent the dawn hours finishing a pile of papers on Defoe.

Both were therefore in an unaccustomed state of mellowness.

Alex yawned and stretched and shoved away the sheets of *The Maine Sunday Telegram* that lay strewn around the breakfast table. "A whole day free. Where will we go? How about a hike? Climb Megunticook. Or something bigger?"

"How about Mount Desert? If we left now, we could drive up Cadillac Mountain and—"

"Hike, not drive. Patsy would enjoy a little muscle flexing, wouldn't you, Patsy?" Alex reached over and ruffled the gray head.

"Anything you say. I've corrected every paper in my possession. And I have Defoe and *A Journal of the Plague Year* to thank for some almost good writing efforts. Bubonic plague seems to turn students on. It's better than the incest in *Oedipus* because that takes place offstage, which is no fun at all. Students want their incest close up and in living color."

"I think," said Alex, "that you're on to something. Lenox Cobb had Jonathan reading 'The Masque of the Red Death,' and according to reports, Jonathan—Mr. Junior Cool—was fairly gripped. You might consider a curriculum of plague literature next year."

Sarah nodded absently, examined her teacup, found it empty, and reached for the teapot. "Well, speaking of plagues, what about Lenox Cobb? He was almost genial last night, sitting there on the sofa with you. Birds seem to be his thing. Or one of his other things. Along with the weather and Shakespeare."

"He wants to manage the south Proffit Point end of the Christmas Bird Count, but I think it's beyond him. He's still on the fragile side and complains of headaches and blurred vision. And he did repeat himself yesterday, got himself tangled into some more quotations from *Richard the Second*. Anyway, I said I'd help out with the count. Along with you. It's the Saturday before Christmas."

"I can't believe you're thinking about anything connected with Christmas. It's October, for heaven's sake. But when the time comes, I'll be your recorder. But I will not count birds."

"Understood. And Lenox is going to have to accept help other than mine. Even help from nephew Eliot, who's apparently an acceptable birder, but a man Lenox cannot stand. As well as the whole high-style profile of Eliot and Caroline's."

"Eliot and Caroline. Oh my God!"

"What?" demanded Alex, alarmed.

"The mail. Their damned mail. Saturday's mail. Eliot and Caroline's. We'll have to deliver it. Right now."

Alex gave a long gusty sigh. "I knew it was too good to be true. A whole day."

Sarah pushed herself away from the breakfast table. "We'll have our day. Only a small slice of it goes to mail delivery. Get your jacket and I'll put Patsy on a leash. He needs fresh air. I think he's been a little under par lately."

"We've all been under par lately," said Alex, standing up and stretching. "Okay, we deliver the mail and take binoculars. Practice for the bird count."

Driving toward Proffit Point, Sarah returned to the subject of plague. "It's not only my students and Jonathan. Pathology, violence, has certainly turned the Beaugards on. They're fairly quivering. And it's not just the very real grief. The whole family's more, well, alert. Ready for action. It's very peculiar."

"Actually," said Alex mildly, "the Beaugards are just catching up to the rest of the world, where peace and calm is what's peculiar. The Beaugards—except for Alice—have always been pretty quiescent. Sheltered, staid, and stolid. Frozen into a past of social propriety. Big houses with gates and protectors. Gardeners and housekeepers and nannies. But after Dolly washed in, they've had a look at the real world."

But Sarah had moved on. She had been holding the heap of Eliot and Caroline's mail on her lap when several envelopes slipped to the floor of the car. In retrieving them, she brought a glossy brochure to the fore.

She turned it over in her hand. A handsome two-masted sailboat photographed against roiled waters with a message in gold: GREETINGS FROM SEAOVER YACHTS. YOUR BROKER FOR THE FINEST SAILING VESSELS AFLOAT. THE SEAOVER 36 SLOOP; THE SEAOVER 40 YAWL; THE SEAOVER 46 CUTTER-RIGGED SLOOP; THE SEAOVER 55 SCHOONER.

"Hey," said Sarah, waving the folder in front of Alex's face. "Do you suppose Eliot's going to dump the faithful *Goshawk*?"

"I don't suppose anything. But I do know you're reading someone else's mail."

"You sound like my grandmother. This is just a brochure. Fair game. Practically public property. There's a catalog from Brooks Brothers and Lands' End. And L.L. Bean. Winter Fun in the Outdoors. And from Orvis. All quite high-toned stuff. As for personal mail, I wouldn't dream of glancing at any."

"I'll bet."

"Well, just turn it over carelessly in my hand."

"Give me those letters," said Alex, reaching over.

"Certainly," said Sarah, pushing the pile back in shape and slipping it onto his lap. "The rest is pretty boring. Bills from the telephone company and cable TV."

The delivery of the mail went without a hitch. Caroline answered the door and accepted the bundle without a word and halfheartedly invited them in for coffee. "Or a Bloody Mary or something. Eliot's out on the *Goshawk*." Caroline pointed in the direction of the cove where the sloop sat at its mooring and a rubber Zodiac raft bobbed at its stern.

Alex and Sarah declined the invitation with thanks, and Alex asked if the sailing season was coming to an end.

"I guess so," said Caroline. "Eliot's going to run her over to Little Cove this afternoon and have her hauled out for the winter. Well"—she hesitated—"thanks for the mail. We wondered. Sorry you won't come in." And she turned and closed the door.

"What's with that woman?" complained Sarah as they started back to their car.

"Be grateful. You didn't want to go in, did you? To help her read her mail."

"Oh, shut up. No, I didn't, but she has as much charm as a doormat. All looks and nothing else. Maybe it's low blood sugar."

"Maybe, my love, she doesn't like us. Doesn't share the Beaugard lust for our friendship. Ever think of that?"

"Actually, she reminded me of a rabbit. A well-dressed irritable rabbit who doesn't want to come out of its hole."

"A pretty expensive hole, that house," said Alex. Then as they reached the Jeep, "Oh hell, Patsy's jumped out. Didn't you close the window?"

"Didn't you?" retorted Sarah.

"Your dog," said Alex, reaching for the leash.

Patsy, excited by low-flying seagulls, making bounding and barking progress around the muddy margins of the cove, was corralled after a forty-minute pursuit.

"Damnation," said Sarah, looking at her spattered trousers. "Wouldn't you know it was almost low tide. And look at Patsy." She looked down at the dog, whose wiry gray hair was thoroughly wet and streaked with dark and inky swaths of flats mud.

"Home," said Alex. "Bath, change, put dog in run, and then we'll have our day. Even if it's midnight, we're going to have our day. Now, put that mutt in the car."

"Irish wolfhound," said Sarah, hauling at the leash.

"Mutt," said Alex, opening the rear door of the Jeep.

The rest of Sunday, the evening that followed, remained in Sarah's mind as a delightful parenthesis. A brief period of tranquility undisturbed by the demands of medicine, academe, or a single member of the Beaugard household. Even Alice, with or without Webb Gattling, failed to turn up at the kitchen door, and the twilight sighting of Parson Gattling holding a placard across the street in Rockland did not upset equanimity.

But then came Monday and the funeral of Dolly Beaugard. And the funeral of Marsden and Junior Gattling—all three bodies having been released to their families the past weekend. As if indeed the circumstance of their deaths, the sharing of the drowning waters, had brought the trio into a sort of synchrony.

The first event took place at two o'clock at the Diggers Neck Baptist Church; the second two hours later at St. Paul's-by-the-Sea in Camden. Thus, it was just possible for a mourner to make the Gattlings' obsequies and then gun it to Camden in time to attend Dolly's event.

Several people managed to pull this off, among them Sergeant George Fitts, Deputy Michael Laaka, and Alice Beaugard—she sitting in the rear with Webb Gattling and holding tightly to his clenched hand.

Alice, meeting Webb around the corner and just out of sight of the church, had a fierce argument with Webb on the subject.

"Webb," she pleaded, "look at me. Wearing a gray skirt and black coat at least a size too big. And this blouse with a ruffed neck. It was Dolly's. I mean, God, I look like something out of *Hamlet*. Just for your family because mine doesn't care if I go in a clown suit. I mean, they expect it of me."

Webb, his beard combed smooth, his hair slicked down, a giant trussed up in a dark suit and tie, looked down at Alice with approval. "You look okay. If you looked the way you usually do, like you're some kind of refugee from what's that place, Bosnia, hey, you'd scare my relatives to death. They're not so damn happy about the Beaugards as it is. Parson's been going around making sermons about the cops and your family. We'll sit in the back. But I'm not ashamed of being with you, so it's time everyone knew it."

"Me, too," said Alice. "I mean, it's time my family knew about you. So if I'm going with you to Junior and Marsden's funeral, then you can come to Dolly's and sit with me."

Webb frowned down at her. "You don't get it, do you? Look, in plain English, your family can always come slumming. Give us the benefit of their presence. Doesn't work in reverse. You're one of the summer people who've sort of moved in full-time. You guys live in houses with names like Great Oaks and go sailing for the fun of it. Or like Dolly, you don't have to earn money, so you can volunteer. Or Masha, playing in a little artsy-crafty group. Don't get me wrong. You know I like music, even her stuff. You took me to a concert, remember. It wasn't so bad. But for a living? I'll bet she couldn't make a living out of playing the recorder without family cash behind her. Or how about you, batting around, letting your family pay your rehab bills?"

Alice, who normally would have been shouting with anger under such an attack, found tears racing down her cheeks. "Hold it," she choked. "Goddamn you, Webb, I'm not like them. Not really."

"Let me finish. First, I love you. Hope you love me. And I don't care who your family is. But be real. To your mother we Gattlings are just lowlife scumballs. And if I go to Dolly's funeral, hell, it'll be as if some kind of Al Capone turned up. Someone who might have tipped Dolly over in that goddamned boat. Or dumped the goddamned ballast. Yeah, I've heard all about that. So I won't go to your funeral. But you'll come to ours. Because even if my family hates Beaugard guts, they don't think the Beaugards killed Marsden and Junior, except for Parson, who has fleas in his brain. So let's get to the church. Me not ashamed of you, you not ashamed of me. Then I'll drive ninety miles an hour and drop you at Dolly's funeral. And tonight we'll go out for dinner and forget what our last names are."

And Alice, her face collapsed into a strange mix of defiance and agreement, allowed Webb to take her arm and bear her off.

George Fitts and Mike Laaka, fortunately, had no problems—psychological or social—with attending the Gattling double funeral. George believed in covering all bases, and this was an event featuring two suspect deaths. Two possible homicides. And in George's experience, it sometimes happened that the murderer was in attendance. Anyway, no harm in keeping an eye out for untoward arrivals. And for once, George was glad to have Mike along. Mike was local and could sort out who was there—like any of the Beaugards, for instance—and then they could research any persons who did not fit into the Gattling mourner profile.

Together the two men left the car, George's green Ford Escort—unmarked but well known by half the county; together they walked up the steps to the church and at the top step split, George to the left, Mike to the right. Each in possession of a memorial program.

If that's what they're called, thought Mike, settling himself in a back pew, far to the right, and opening the double-folded piece of cream paper. Embossed lilies—in silver—on the front. In silver the words IN BLESSED MEMORY OF MARSDEN JOSEPH

GATTLING AND EDWARD "JUNIOR" WILLIAM GATTLING. REST IN PEACE. Opening this up, Mike could see that a number of hymns were interspersed with the service and that interment in the Sunny View Cemetery would follow. But for now the crowd was thickening, streaming down the aisles, looking for space in the pews. Women in floral dresses and dark coats, men whom Mike knew spent their lives wearing jeans, coveralls, and high rubber boots, and now looked, as did Webb Gattling, strangely constrained in suits and ties. Mike knew most of them. Gattlings of all flavors, of course. And there was Tad Bugelski, Proffit Point's harbormaster and finder of the bodies. And the postmaster. And the guys from the Texaco station. And, for God's sake, Alice Beaugard and Webb: Alice in that outfit, dressed like some sort of visiting nurse, and looking as if she'd got something in her throat that wouldn't go down, hanging on to Webb's arm. Was this an announcement? Or an "in your face" appearance by the two of them? Mike twisted his neck sideways and was rewarded with the sight of the two clambering into a rear pew opposite his own. So they weren't going to flaunt themselves and mix it up with the family up front.

Mike now examined the front of the church. Two caskets side by side. Closed. Well, he supposed that even the most skilled cosmetic treatment couldn't restore those two boys to healthy looks. Up front, lecterns, a sort of semicircular painting with Jesus and people wading around in blue water. And a real tub—did Baptists call it a tub? Or an immersion vessel? A font? Never mind, Laaka, pay attention. They're not paying you for guessing about what Baptists duck their members in. Who else?

Mike turned around to face the entrance. One of the cashiers from the Camden National Bank. Was she a Gattling? And that real estate salesmen, what was his name? Levensitter, Tom Levensitter. Was *he* a Gattling? And Digby Reynolds. Well, he went to all the funerals, did Digby. Music, shelter, and sometimes free coffee and food. He'd probably make it to Dolly's, too, if he could find a ride. And, well, would you look at that? Vivian

Lavender. Navy blue with a yellow scarf. Standing there as big as life by the middle door. On enemy territory. A Beaugard spy. Or a second spy if you counted Alice. Mike allowed himself a stare and just then Vivian looked his way. Their eyes met, Mike saw a visible wave of relief move across her face, and before he could think about changing his seat, he was joined.

"Thank heavens," whispered Vivian. "Someone I know."

"You grew up around here," Mike reminded her. "You know as many people as I do. You know the Gattlings."

"Yes, of course I do. But you know, working for Mrs. Beaugard, living at the house. All these years." Here Vivian lowered her voice so that Mike had to lean toward her. "I just don't feel quite right about being here."

"Then why are you?" said Mike.

"Eliot convinced me. Said his mother would have wanted it. Because both Gattling men washed in on Beaugard property. Into Little Cove. Eliot said he felt that some gesture..."

"Why not send flowers?" asked Mike. "Or make a donation?"

"They did that, too. Everything proper."

Mike couldn't resist. "Guilty conscience?" he suggested, and was rewarded by the shock on Vivian's face. But now the Gattling family began filing in and seating themselves one by one in the front row. Large, small, old, young. Giants like Webb and shorties like Parson Gattling who brought up the rear.

Then, in a loud voice from the front of the church: "I am the Resurrection and the life, says the Lord our God. He who believes in me even though he is dead, yet he shall live..."

Mike allowed his attention to wander. Vivian Lavender. In the flesh. Sent by Eliot. Well, according to George's theory, this is significant. The unexpected mourner. Right beside him in her navy blue suit with the stylish yellow scarf knotted about her neck. The housekeeper. Well, Mike had read *Rebecca* as a kid. Seen the thing on video. He knew all about housekeepers. An evil bunch.

Suddenly Mike was aware of a poke in his side and the presentation of a hymnal. "Top of the page," whispered Vivian.

They stood and Mike found himself singing, baritone to Vivian's alto, both very tentative:

"Blessed assurance, Jesus is mine!
O, what a fore-taste of glory divine!"

The service went on. Pastor Bob Bonner promised a place in heaven for Junior and Marsden beside other Gattling loved ones, and the whole thing ended with, in Mike's opinion, a strangely selected hymn that went on about "a fainting, struggling sea-man" and

Some poor sailor, tempest toss'd,
Trying now to make the harbor,
In the darkness may be lost.

Even Vivian seemed to think this an improper ending. "*May* be lost! Didn't they read the papers?" she demanded, collecting her handbag. "Well, I'm off to St. Paul's. Goodness, what a day."

The housekeeper, repeated Mike to himself. But how? And why? Putting Valium into Canadian whiskey and smuggling it aboard the Gattling skiff. Impossible. Or nearly. The Gattling brothers had put out from Diggers Neck across the cove. At night. With packages of cocaine. Even Sarah's overactive imagination couldn't put water skis on Vivian and send her out to meet them midcove. Well, then, how about Alice? Webb's girlfriend. And Webb has a skiff. But why? And what for? Oh hell.

These thoughts he shared with George Fitts on their high-speed trip across Knox County to St. Paul's-by-the-Sea.

"Vivian Lavender's been with the Beaugards for ages," said Mike. "I might be able to talk myself into thinking she had it in for Dolly. You know—jealousy, Dolly managing everything in sight, stepping on Vivian's toes. But why kill the Gattlings? Come on."

"You always want to rush," said George. "I'm making out a time chart for the entire Beaugard and Gattling setup. See if there's any intersecting. People in the wrong space. Don't go leaping into the dark before you have a single fact."

"Okay, okay. But don't you think it's funny about Vivian turning up?"

"I'm paying attention to her being there. And Eliot sending her—if he did. And Alice turning up. I didn't expect that."

"Webb must have a good grip on Alice," said Mike. "Anyway, I think Vivian's a damn handsome fully packed female. I'll bet Dolly wasn't crazy about her. Now, if Vivian had drowned and Dolly—"

"Mike, relax. I'm not forgetting Dolly. I've been asking around. She seems to have not only done good works, but she tossed an enormous amount of money into her various projects. Gifts to the hospital, the church. We've had an auditor going over the estate books, but so far nothing seems to be out of whack. Dolly must have used her trust fund income."

"Saint Dolly," murmured Mike as Camden came into view.

Sarah, after only a token protest, had been pressed into service at the church in the hours before the funeral. While Masha arranged the flowers from the family around the altar, Sarah was handed the job of the "other" flowers. Because although the newspaper notice—rushed into Monday's paper—had said "flowers gratefully declined," there were always those who sent them. These had to be marshaled, their donors noted, in the Beaugard Room of the Parish House—"where the family will receive guests following the service." Beaugard Room? wondered Sarah.

Having no classes on Monday, Sarah simply canceled her student appointments and spent the day at the church figuratively and literally with her sleeves rolled up. Then, as noon approached, she was pressed into arranging tea things, dealing with a caterer's delivery of small cakes and tiny cookies. In this she was assisted by a tall young woman who announced that she was Mary. Mary Dover, the assistant rector of St. Paul's, her office being attested to by Mary's round collar, her black dickey, and the silver cross that hung from her neck.

"Such a loss," said Mary. "Why, we could never have finished the Beaugard Room without Dolly. Never in a hundred years."

"Oh?" said Sarah.

"Well, we had the space, but it was a wreck. More of a storage area really. For Sunday school supplies and blackboards and so forth. But we needed paint and plaster and a decent rug. New beams, tables, chairs, a modern kitchen. And along came Dolly."

"Very generous," murmured Sarah, busy stacking tea saucers.

"That's why it's the Beaugard Room," said Mary. "Of course, Dolly said her mother was behind the donation. But Dolly was the engine. And when we needed a whopping big sum of money all at once, there she was. Well, now, everything looks in order. I'll go and review what I'm going to say. So much about Dolly that was truly inspirational. What an example to all of us."

So, said Sarah to herself. Dolly not only did good works. She funded them. So big deal. The Beaugards have money dripping out of their pockets. But a whole room? Then turning around, "Oh, hi, Alex. Lunch?"

"Just have time. A quick lunch, then back to the hospital."

"Okay, but can you pick up Grandmother Douglas around three-thirty? She can't bear to be late for anything. I have to come back after lunch and deal with all this. Flowers up the yin yang. I'm trying to make the place not look like a gangster's funeral parlor. All those orange and pink gladiolas from the Girl Scouts and the St. Paul's Dorcas Society. Didn't any of them read the notice in the paper?"

"Appropriate, though, gangster's funeral parlor. Whiffs of homicide along with the incense."

"Don't say that to Grandma. She takes funerals seriously. I wonder if they'll sing 'For All the Saints.'"

Eliot Beaugard arrived at three o'clock dressed in somber oxford gray with a navy tie, and confronted Sarah. "Hey, there, great job. How did we ever get along without you?"

How indeed? said Sarah to herself. Aloud, she thanked Eliot and asked if the family had arrived.

"Ready to roll," said Eliot. "Literally, as far as that young squirt Jonathan goes. He's in a wheelchair. Alice is missing, natch. And Vivian is on an errand—well, not of mercy. Say diplomacy. I told Mother that since those Gattlings washed in at Little Cove, we should at least acknowledge them at the funeral. Vivian's gone as the family representative."

"But Vivian..." Sarah objected.

"You're going to say she's not a Beaugard, not one of us," said Eliot. "But Vivian's been with us so long, she *is* one of the family. A damn important part of it. She's local; the Gattlings will accept her." And Eliot, after a quick glance at his watch, made off toward the stairs leading to the church proper.

"You," said Sarah aloud to the tea service, "are full of it." Then to herself she added, no way will Vivian be thought of as a Beaugard substitute. In fact, it'll be damn lucky if she's not considered an insult. And Sarah gave her short hair a quick smoothing, pulled down her sleeves, wrapped herself in her green wool coat, and headed for Dolly Beaugard's last public appearance.

Eliot Beauregard arrived at Hoon't look dressed in somber oxford gray with a navy tie, and comforted Sarah. "Hon, there, great job. How did we ever get along without you?"

"How indeed?" said Sarah to herself. Aloud she thanked Eliot and asked if the family had arrived.

"Ready to roll," said Eliot. "Literally, as far as that young squirt John is concerned. He's in a wheelchair. Alice is missing, natch. And Vivian is on an errand—will and of mercy. So apparently, I told Vivian that since those Cartlings washed up in Little Cove, we should at least acknowledge them at the funeral. Vivian's gone as the family representative."

"But Eliot," Sarah objected.

"You're going to say she's not a Beauregard, not one of us," said Eliot. "But Vivian's been with us so long, she is one of the family. A damn important part of it. She's local, the Cartlings will accept her." And Eliot, after a quick glance at his watch, made off toward the stairs leading to the church proper.

"Yes," said Sarah aloud to the tea service, "and full of it." Then to herself she added, no way will Vivian be thought of as a Beauregard in spite. In fact, it'll be damn lucky if she's not considered an insult. And Sarah gave her short hair a quick smoothing, pulled down her sleeves, wrapped herself in her serge wool coat, and headed for Polly Beauregard's last public appearance.

Chapter Fourteen

RATHER THAN LEAVE THE church and enter by the front steps, Sarah chose to slide in via an anteroom that opened into a side aisle of the nave. The room was one Sarah remembered from other ceremonial occasions as serving as a holding tank for the chief attendants at funerals, weddings, and christenings.

This choice gave Sarah a good look at the Beaugards en masse. Since they were all occupied with each other, she was able, by slowing her steps and angling her head, to take in the main features. Uncle Lenox Cobb, a gray suit, blue striped shirt, a crimson bow tie. Seated. Hands on cane. Glowering into middle distance. Next to him Jonathan. Wheelchair, cast-covered leg stuck out in front of him, left arm strapped across chest. Pale angular boy's face, hair brushed, khaki trousers—one leg slit to accommodate the cast. White shirt. Crimson bow tie. Two red bow ties? Was it a club and Jonathan and Lenox the only members? The Masque—or the tie—of the Red Death?

She checked her watch. Still thirty-five minutes to go. She hesitated and then found a bench behind a potted fern where she could be seen if wanted, but was not obtrusive. No point in rattling around in the church among the empty pews; she'd hang in here for another ten minutes and then see if she could spot Alex and her grandmother coming in. Who else had turned up? Not Alice. Good old unreliable Alice. Where was she? But Masha had made it. Masha in a knit maroon tube thing, turtleneck to ankle, was sitting alone by the window—one of those fake Tudor casements—and studying a piece of music. A leather instrument case stuck out of a large open handbag. Deduction: Masha was part of the service.

And ensconced in a leather chair, the mother. Mrs. Beaugard. Entirely in black. From head to toe. Shoes, stockings, dress, jacket. And hat. With a veil. Black veil. No one wore those anymore, did they? Well, yes they did, because here she was, Elena Beaugard looking exactly like those old photographs of bereaved wives and daughters: Mrs. Woodrow Wilson, Sarah Delano Roosevelt, Queen Mary, the Queen Mum, Queen Elizabeth.

Eliot was leaning over his mother in a consoling posture; Vivian Lavender, the hired family diplomat, hovered on her opposite side. Vivian, to Sarah's eyes, looked rather flushed, and the bun at the back of her neck had let loose a lock of dark hair. That hasty trip from funeral one to funeral two had no doubt taken its toll. But the flush was becoming, and as far as healthy looks went, Mrs. Lavender, along with Eliot, was a clear winner.

Caroline Beaugard provided the real contrast. What was that song—or was it a poem?—something about pale hands, pale lips? Caroline, sitting by herself, had chosen a gray many-layered silk costume, and the general effect was of someone recently brought up from the grave. Or about to descend into it. And the heir apparent, nine-year-old Colin Beaugard, in navy blazer and flannels and navy tie, stood well apart from his mother, intent on some electronic gadget in his hand. A pocket Nintendo, Sarah decided.

And here was Alice. Rushing in, wearing clothes at least a size too big. Kissing her mother and having trouble with the black veil. And judging from her mother's gestures, she was being reprimanded and then forgiven, her hands patted by the black gloves.

And now the organ. A great thundering groan from the partially opened door. "Glorious Things of Thee Are Spoken/ Zion City of Our God." Or if you preferred: *Deutschland, Deutschland, Über Alles.*

Time to go. Sarah slid out from behind her fern, waved at Eliot and his mother, and made for the church.

Right on time. Alex with Grandmother Douglas bent on his arm stood at the rear. Sarah hastened forward and all three made a stately entrance and settled into a middle pew, a choice that prevented Sarah from checking out those who preferred the rear.

After the bowing of heads, however, Sarah sat up and let herself drift. What was it about Gothic-type churches with their vaults, ribs, piers, those stained-glass windows—Mary and Martha, the Loaves and Fishes, the Marriage at Cana? These out-of-world artifacts together with the trappings of the funeral, the groaning organ, the somberly clad people, the flowers, all had a fatal effect on concentration. The more one tried to focus on the virtues of the dear departed, the more the mind darted off into distant byways and dubious side alleys.

At first Sarah made an honest effort to focus. She opened the memorial service folder—cream paper, black print. Prelude, hymns, readings, a Psalm, the homily, another hymn, another Psalm, prayers, the commendation, the blessing. And Dolly's real name: Dorothea. Sarah had forgotten that. Dorothea Sophia Beaugard. Seeing it spelled out that way gave Dolly herself a certain exotic flavor. Where had the Sophia come from? Oh yes, those two cousins at the party. The Russian connection. But Sarah was sure that, in Dolly's case, the stodgy Beaugard DNA had probably tamed any wild impulses from the

Volga and the steppes. And as far as Dolly's death went, nothing exotic about it. Just good old homegrown homicide.

Sarah drifted away again. She found herself reviewing a college course in the history of architecture. What was the crucial development? Oh yes, the stilting of the longitudinal rib. From thence came buttresses and vaults, the pointed arch, the whole bit. At St. Paul's-by-the-Sea, even the secondary spaces and rooms were determinedly Gothic. Even the Beaugard Room with its fan vault.

A fan vault. My God, that must have been expensive. Had Dolly and her mother funded the vaulting as well as the kitchen? Sarah, dimly aware of the opening chords from the organ, stood up, gripping one side of the open hymn book. But instead of joining in with "Lead on O King Eternal," she began taking inventory of the Beaugard Room. Spacious. Approximately eighty by forty. Refinish the floor, panel the walls, which looked like oak. Or oak veneer. Say $4,000, plus or minus. Oriental-type carpet—it couldn't be the real thing, could it? Or perhaps Dolly had rolled up a spare from the Great Oaks attic and presented it. Suitable footing for Beaugard shoes. Put down $5,000 for an imitation, $25,000 for the real thing. Compromise at $10,000. Refectory oak table, at least eight straight chairs with leather seats. Two armchairs. So for furniture—being conservative—three grand. Curtains: lined, plum brocade for six windows: $400. At least.

And the kitchen. Ye gods. Sarah and Alex had finally upgraded their 1930s farmhouse kitchen, and she knew what a kitchen could do to a budget. Wouldn't there be a six-burner institutional stove and megasize sink and fridge?

"Sarah," hissed Alex. "Stand up."

Another hymn. As predicted: "For All the Saints Who from Their Labors Rest." Saint Dolly. Or Saint Dorothea. Was she the martyr beheaded for refusing to be raped? Or was that Sofya or Sophia? Sarah had a poor grip on saints.

Sitting down, Sarah allowed her attention to center for a moment on Masha Beaugard, who now stood by the organist and joined him in "Sleepers Awake." But the Beaugard Room exerted too strong a pull and Sarah returned to her accounting. Let's see. Add those four mullioned windows that matched the rest of the parish house. Plus the handsome etchings of English cathedrals: Ely, Salisbury, Wells, York. Hardly garage-sale stuff. Then the fan vaulting, which might be a fake, not structural. Well, however you sliced it, the total was sneaking up on $100,000.

"Good God!" Sarah said aloud in a shocked voice.

"Sarah," said Alex. He indicated her grandmother with her head bowed. "Our Father Who art in heaven, hallowed be Thy name," he said in a threatening voice.

Sarah adjusted her posture and began reviewing the Beaugard Room, item by item. Maybe more than $100,000.

"Amen," said Alex.

"Amen," said Grandmother Douglas.

"Good God," repeated Sarah, shaking her head. And she'd probably left a lot out. The kitchen utensils, the china, the glasses, for instance. Even if it all came from Wal-Mart, there had to be a lot of it. And that tea service looked new. She glanced up and found Father Smythe looming benevolently over the congregation. "...be gracious unto you. The Lord lift up His countenance upon you and give you peace, both now and evermore. Amen."

"Amen," said Sarah belatedly.

The church crowd surged into the aisles forward, through, and up—to the Beaugard Room—or to the front doors and fresh air.

Mrs. Douglas was collected by the faithful Hopkins, who had sat in the back, and Sarah and Alex edged out of their pew.

"Okay," said Alex. "What's next?"

"The Beaugard Room wherein the family will greet guests. Named for chief benefactors, the Beaugards. Especially Dolly." Here Sarah paused and observed the somberly dressed crowd pressing toward the entrance to the Parish House stairs. "Look," she added, "there's no point in fighting our way into the room until later. Let's go outside for a while and then go back in."

"Sorry, I've got to be back at the hospital. I'll push up and shake hands now and you dribble in later."

This plan agreed to, Sarah joined those retreating to the rear of the church and found herself shortly on the wide stone steps. And almost into the arms of Parson Gattling. A Parson Gattling in a navy blue serge suit and a stack of small cards in one hand.

They stared at each other, both realizing that they'd had an early encounter of a questionable nature.

Sarah, her mouth running ahead of her brain, said, "It's Mr. Gattling. Aren't you at the wrong—I mean, wasn't there another..." She stopped, closed her mouth, and tried to regroup.

Fortunately Parson Gattling was a man with a mission. "I'm here today," he said, "because of getting God's justice done. On all you Beaugards and us. After what was done to Marsden and Junior and Dolly. And I'm praying for Beaugards because they are deep into sin with the Lord. And I am praying for the repose of the sacred soul of Miss Dolly Beaugard. Rest her in peace."

Sarah, vastly annoyed, grabbed at the second sentence. "I'm not a Beaugard. I'm not even related. My name is Sarah Deane, and what do you mean, 'deep into sin with the Lord'? As far as I know, all the Beaugards have done is lose their daughter."

"The Beaugard family has a date with God," said Parson Gattling, in his gravelly voice. "We in the Gattling family do not cry out for vengeance, but vengeance is mine sayeth the Lord God of Israel." Parson hesitated and then extended one of the cards from his pack. "Read and beware," he said. "Forgiveness is divine, but first comes prayerful confession."

Sarah found curiosity overtaking irritation. What was the man talking about? "Explain, please, Mr. Gattling. Who should be confessing? And why? What *are* you talking about?"

"Let those who have done evil come forward," said Parson Gattling. "I'm not saying it's you who should come forward if your name isn't Beaugard. But all of us have sin on our shoulders and have consorted with evil. And I'm here to say that Marsden and Junior have not died in vain." And with that Parson shot his head forward rather like a turtle and gave Sarah a meaningful look. Then he turned and joined two men hurrying down the steps and presented each with his card. Both men, Sarah noticed, seemed too surprised by the offering to refuse, and by the time they came to, Parson had accosted another departing party.

She turned the card over. It looked like a homemade printing job. But the message was simple enough. BEWARE OF FALSE PRIDE IN THOSE WHO ARE NOT NAMED. TRUTH WILL OUT EVEN THOUGH IT IS NOT SOUGHT. IN MEMORIAM: MARSDEN GATTLING, EDWARD "JUNIOR" GATTLING. ALSO MISS DOLLY BEAUGARD. R.I.P.

Oh, for heaven's sake, Sarah said to herself. It's like a very bad thriller. Parson—was that his real name?—sneaking around by wrecked mailboxes and infesting other people's funerals and handing out nasty cards. But since the encounter had rather tainted the hoped-for fresh air, Sarah turned on the steps and headed through the church toward the Beaugard Room. And toward Alice. Find out about this Parson person. But first the proper expression of sympathy to Elena Beaugard.

"A wonderful service," said Sarah, who had hardly heard a word of it.

"Thank you, my dear," said Mrs. Beaugard. For a moment she retained Sarah's hand in a now-ungloved hand. The hat and veil, too, were off and she seemed simply a tired, white-haired woman.

"And Masha," said Sarah. "She plays beautifully."

"I should hope so," said Mrs. Beaugard, sounding a little more like herself. "Five years of college and study in England. It cost a small fortune."

And what, said Sarah to herself, after she had left Mrs. Beaugard, does she think the Beaugard Room cost? But I suppose there are priorities. Musical training is hardly in the same category as a room dedicated to the greater glory of God. Or the greater glory of St. Paul's-by-the-Sea.

Sarah found Alice nibbling on a cookie by a casement window. "The Beaugard Room," she said. It was all she needed to say.

"I am absolutely damned," said Alice. "I didn't have a clue. I mean, I heard Dolly and Mother go on about fitting up some old storage space in the church, but you know I don't hang around at St. Paul's the way they did. Except for weddings and affairs like this. I mean, look at the rug. It's not from Great Oaks, so it must have cost a bundle. Talk about benefactors. You'd think Mother was the Arthur Vining Foundation or the Margaret Milliken Hatch thing on Public Television."

"It's all pretty impressive," Sarah admitted.

"It's pretty scary," said Alice with vehemence. "I wonder if there's any cash left to pay the oil bills this winter."

"Did Dolly have an allowance?" asked Sarah. It was a touchy sort of question since if Dolly was being subsidized, so probably was Alice. And Dolly at least worked for it, what with all the household management and driving her mother to and fro. Alice had been, Sarah was sure, a continuing drain on the family coffers. Masha was no doubt partly self-sustaining, and Eliot completely, but how about Lenox Cobb? Was he maintained by the Beaugard support system?

"We all have allowances from the trust fund Father set up for each of us. Not huge but good enough for food on the table and clothes on our backs. Good enough except for me because I've been kind of a major expense." Alice gave a hollow laugh and pushed her hair off her forehead. Her face was pinched and wan, she licked her lips continually, and her gray skirt and black coat, rumpled from sitting at two funerals, hung unevenly from her thin shoulders.

"Would Dolly's trust allowance have funded the Beaugard Room?" Sarah persisted.

"Are you kidding? No way. Oh, maybe a chair or so. The table. A set of dishes or a coffeemaker. No, this must have come straight from Mother. With Dolly's encouragement. Dolly going on about lay not unto yourself treasures and that sort of stuff."

Sarah nodded and changed the subject, determined not to let Alice disappear until she'd cleared up one more thing. "Parson Gattling. What do you know about him? And is that his real name? Is he some kind of minister or something?"

Alice shrugged. "He's Parson, all right. It's his name. Maybe he thought he had to live up to it. He's a sort of preacher at one of those little churches no one has ever heard of. Like Blood of the Lamb Tabernacle or Evangelical Wonder Church. He's not a bad guy, but he's cracked about religion, and right now he's all riled up about Junior and Marsden. I think it's because of Dolly dying at the same time. He apparently admired Dolly. It's all totally boring. That's what Webb thinks, too. That Parson's not a bad guy, but he's got a few loose screws in his head. I went to the Gattling funeral; did you know that? Parson did a sort of eulogy. You'd have thought they were burying the Archangel Gabriel and his twin brother. And now I'd better see about getting Jonathan and Uncle Lenox home. Or getting them a ride because I should stay here and hold the fort. I mean, I *am* stuck here and then I'm supposed to meet Webb. You don't suppose, I mean, would you…"

Sarah saw the handwriting on the wall. Oh well, what the hell? It was something useful she could do, and it got her out of the now-congested Beaugard Room, heavy with the mixed scent of the massed floral arrangements and industrial-strength coffee.

It was all arranged in a minute. Professor Cobb was detached from an argument with Father Smythe on Shakespeare's use of biblical images, and Jonathan in his wheelchair was relieved of a coffee cup filled with sherry. Together the three made a slow progress down the stairway ramp—St. Paul's was accessible to the handicapped—and with Alice's rather distracted help, the invalids were fitted into Sarah's Subaru.

"The funeral wasn't so bad," said Jonathan, as Sarah turned the car out of the church parking lot. "I mean, it wasn't the greatest way to spend the afternoon, but I was going stir-crazy inside the house stuck in a wheelchair, and besides, I think Aunt Dolly might have liked it. All those readings and the music and the hymns and stuff. She was sort of traditional."

"The Episcopal Church has abandoned the King James version at its peril," said Lenox. "One more nail in the coffin of the literate world."

"You mean all the thees and thous," said Jonathan. "Like Shakespeare?"

"Jonathan, what are you reading now to your uncle?" said Sarah, anxious to move away from a lengthy condemnation of all contemporary society.

"We're finishing up Edgar Allan Poe," said Jonathan. "He's pretty neat. I like 'The Fall of the House of Usher' best so far. It's really creepy, that part about Lady Madeline being buried alive. But next week I can choose the book."

"And what are you going to choose?" asked Sarah.

"Well, Uncle Lenox didn't stick me with Shakespeare right off the bat, so I won't stick him with anything too gruesome. Maybe some sci-fi stuff. But hey, what did you think of the Beaugard Room? It must have cost a million bucks. Or a thousand anyway."

"Far more than a thousand," said Lenox. "I must talk to Elena. I would like to do her books, but my eyes are still a bother. But I think Dolly may have been dipping into capital. I wonder if she had power of attorney."

"No, she didn't," said Jonathan unexpectedly. "I came into the room one day last summer and Aunt Dolly was having an argument with Grandma about it. And Grandma said no. That she wasn't in the grave yet and hadn't lost her mind and it would just cause trouble with her other children."

"Elena never said a truer word," said Lenox sharply. "Power of attorney in Dolly's hands would have ruined the family in the first week. The entire estate would have been given away. Dolly was obsessed with giving."

"Hey," said Jonathan, "you can say that again. And she was really obsessed with sailing."

Which remark caused a blight to fall on the conversation and Sarah drove her passengers home in welcome silence.

Chapter Fifteen

THE FUNERAL SERVICES FOR Marsden and Junior Gattling and for Dolly Beaugard marked for many the end of the first phase of the three Proffit Point drownings. A conclusion of sorts. A resting.

After all, the bodies of the three victims no longer lay in the limbo of the state pathology laboratory but had disappeared—after appropriate graveside obsequies—from sight. Dolly had indicated in a note found in her desk that after cremation she wanted half of her ashes interred (in their receptacle) in the Sunny View Cemetery. This was done with Vivian Lavender, Masha, and Alice in attendance—Mrs. Beaugard and Lenox abstaining. The remainder of the ashes, Dolly had requested sprinkled over the ocean beyond Little Cove, a task that Dolly's brother took care of on a calm October morning. However, since Eliot did not make the effort to tow his rubber Zodiac raft much beyond the tidal zone of his own cove, it seemed likely that every twelve hours at low tide some fragments of Dolly Beaugard might return on the incoming tide to familiar shores.

The Gattling family, on the other hand, opposed cremation on the basis that resurrection seemed more hopeful for a set of bones than for a pile of ashes. Thus twin graves in the same Sunny View Cemetery received the mortal remains of Marsden and Junior, and in a curious twist of fate, ensured that Dolly and the two Gattling brothers would continue their unlikely association.

The other persons concerned in what were now being considered by the constabulary as three possible homicides hiding under the name of "death by misadventure" settled back into their daily lives and attempted to deal with the changes wrought by these events.

Elena Beaugard, driven by housekeeper Vivian Lavender, made a number of trips to see her lawyer, Mr. Snagsby, about altering her will and adjusting the disposal of her estate without a Dolly to advise or to inherit.

Alice continued to see Webb Gattling for evenings of argument and lovemaking. And to hand over her black shaggy dog, Willie, to his care, fearing that Lenox Cobb's dislike of dogs might bring harm to the animal. Also Alice continued to drop in unexpectedly at Alex and Sarah's kitchen to ask about progress in what she referred to as the "cover-up" of Dolly's death.

Masha Beaugard departed for a concert tour of Vermont, intending to return at intervals and certainly for Thanksgiving.

Lenox Cobb, still afflicted with uncertain balance, occasional confusion, blurred vision, and recurring headaches, continued to try and advise his sister on the management of her estate and to listen without undue adverse comment to wheelchair-bound Jonathan Epstein, who, after finishing with Edgar Allan Poe, read his way through *A Hitchhiker's Guide to the Galaxy* (Jonathan's choice), *Macbeth* (Lenox's choice), and *Dune* (Jonathan's).

Eliot Beaugard returned to his office and the world of marine insurance, and at home to the business of hauling out his boats and float for the winter. To these activities he added a number of filial visits to his mother to request that she put the estate management in his hands. This always refused.

Caroline Beaugard was known to consult a psychic in the town of Tenants Harbor on subjects unknown and to sign up at the local community college for a course in computer competence. From which she was dropped due to lack of attendance.

Deputies Mike Laaka and Katie Waters, already burdened by the Gattling-Beaugard investigations, were forced to look into a series of break-ins among the summer cottages not only at Proffit Point but in several nearby coves, inlets, and harbors. In the time left over, the two deputies continued to check out purchasing records of Seagram's whiskey and the filling of Valium prescriptions.

George Fitts, while awaiting the lab report on cloth fibers found in the Gattling skiff, busied himself by seeing to the dragging of Proffit Point Harbor and Little Cove with an eye to finding—or not finding—ballast ingots of lead from Dolly Beaugard's little sloop, the *Sweetheart*. At the same time he instigated the undercover pursuit of the Gattling-Beaugard link through Webb Gattling and Alice.

Parson Gattling continued his confused demand that the Beaugards admit their sinful complicity in the death of his younger brothers, Junior and Marsden, and of Dolly Beaugard, for whom he seemed to entertain a strange admiration. These efforts involved handing out his printed cards on street corners as well as standing, a placard held high, as a reproachful presence at the entrance of Great Oaks. Sometimes, particularly in the evening, Parson could be heard by passersby chanting a sort of dirge or, as some claimed, speaking in tongues.

Vivian Lavender continued in faithful service to Great Oaks and its owner, adding to her many duties the answering of sympathy notes from the beneficiaries of Dolly's volunteer efforts.

Alex McKenzie retreated into the practice of medicine, ready to face the approaching flu season and trying to accept the unwelcome news that Elena Beaugard had decided to retain him, not Dr. Foxe, as the family physician. Periodic house calls on the several ailing members of the household, Mrs. Beaugard reminded him, would be appreciated.

Sarah Douglas Deane returned to her classes, to the serving up of Defoe, Chaucer, and assorted Greek tragedies to her sometimes resistant undergraduate students. And in what remained of her time, to wondering about the cost of the Beaugard Room. And then asking herself whether the Beaugard Room was a lonely phenomenon or were there other rooms? Other bequests or endowments among the institutions Dolly favored with her volunteer activities.

In such a way did the first three weeks of October pass. Two threatened hurricanes went out to sea and so missed the coast of Maine. The deciduous trees came to full glory of red, yellow, gold, and russet, and the humped and rolling blueberry barrens of Hope, Appleton, and Liberty turned crimson and purple. Jugs of cider and bushels of apples and baskets of pumpkins and acorn squash decorated roadsides. The air became keen with the temperature dropping below thirty degrees at night so that sea smoke rose from the still warm ocean coves and ponds.

And then it was over with a driving rain and a wind switch to the northeast, the wind increasing to gale force, the rain becoming opaque. Becoming sleet. Becoming snow.

"Damn," said Sarah, emerging from the warmth of the Bowmouth Library late one Saturday morning and hesitating. Then she retreated from the steps to the doorway and addressed the head librarian, Miss Murdstone, who was struggling into her raincoat. "Snow. I can't believe it. It's only October."

"October twenty-ninth," said Miss Murdstone. "Almost November. But *The Farmer's Almanac* is predicting a mild winter."

"Well, the National Weather Service isn't," said Sarah testily. "And I'm not even finished with summer, let alone fall."

"Weather," said Miss Murdstone, "is a state of mind," and she tied her raincoat belt, lowered her head, and bucked her way into the driving wind.

"The hell it is," said Sarah to no one in particular. She backed up into the library anteroom and considered the options. She had planned to finish wrapping the newly planted fruit trees against the ravages of hungry mice. But not in this storm. So back to work? No, she'd already spent the morning wrestling with conflicts in the midterm exam schedules. To the gym for a workout? No, an intercollegiate basketball game was planned for the day.

And then Dolly Beaugard's name wiggled into her brain. It had, of course, only been temporarily pushed underground. So why not a little expedition to find out what other lucky institutions St. Dolly and her mother had supported? The figure of Dolly in her green volunteer smock rose before her. It seemed to beckon. Sarah returned to the main desk of the library.

"Where," she asked the librarian's aide—an undergraduate who was working on her eye shadow—"could I find a list of bequests? Contributions, that sort of thing, to the Mary Starbox Hospital?"

"Hey," said the aide, "I don't know. Try microfilm. Plug yourself into the scanner. Or go to the hospital library."

But ten minutes in the hospital library brought forth from a publicity pamphlet nothing beyond the fact that the Beaugard family was listed as a "friend" of the building fund. Over $5,000 made you a benefactor, $1,000 a patron, $500 a friend. Alex, Sarah was interested to note, was a "contributor"—in the $100–$200 range.

But she supposed there were other veins to be explored. Other gifts. Weren't people always being urged to contribute to a new X-ray gismo, a new MRI, a neonatal unit? The chapel? With the word "chapel," Sarah found her thumbs pricking. The pious Beaugards, if they gave anything, might be attracted to the hospital chapel. A stained-glass window, a pew perhaps. Sarah left the library and, following hall signs, hurried down the hall in the direction of the emergency room and the pathology lab. And the chapel.

The Beaugard Chapel.

A small polished brass plaque on the door proclaimed it such. And as luck would have it, a man of the cloth—round collar, dark suit—was just leaving.

Sarah buttonholed him. The chapel. How long had it been the Beaugard Chapel?

"Oh," said the man. "About four months. It never had a name before, but then the Beaugards—Miss Dolly and her mother—gave the money for refinishing the pews and the red carpet and those two stained-glass windows. A new font—we do have baptisms here—and an altar cloth. Wonderful additions. The patients, their families, really appreciate our chapel." The man hesitated, apparently thinking that standing here before him was a troubled person.

"You may come in to pray and rest just anytime," he offered. "Or ask for counsel and comfort. Someone of your denomination."

Sarah assured him that she was not in need, would not detain him, just wanted to look around. And the man, looking faintly relieved, departed.

Crimson runner going up the short aisle to the little altar space. Polished oak pews with crimson seat cushions. Kneeling stools also covered. Window on the right: Jesus touching a woman with his hand, she rising from a bed. Window on the left: Jesus and a circle of children, background a flock of lambs.

In Sarah's head, a cash register. The chapel, to be sure, was nothing on the scale of St. Paul's Beaugard Room, but even so, this was a substantial outlay. Add to the Beaugard Room's total and the donation thermometer might be up as high as $120,000.

And what other pricey good works had Dolly and her mother been up to? Sarah reviewed in her head what she knew of Dolly's volunteer record. The Godding Museum of Art, The Farnsworth Museum. Paintings? Special exhibits? How about the Girl Scouts? The Midcoast Audubon Society? Sarah looked at her watch. Ten past twelve. She headed for Alex's hospital office.

A half hour later, Alex returned from rounds and Sarah announced their plans for a wintry Saturday afternoon.

"A wintry afternoon," Alex reminded her, "can happen at home by the fireplace with a good book and beer available."

"It can happen at museums and organizations dedicated to the nurture of youth and the environment," said Sarah.

"Now what?" demanded Alex impatiently.

"One hundred and twenty thousand dollars, give or take a few thousand," said Sarah. And she explained.

"Well," said Alex thoughtfully, "I knew about the Beaugard Chapel; I pass it every day. But I didn't think much about it. Figured Mrs. Beaugard with Dolly pushing her had coughed up some cash. Not remarkable. People with large incomes do it every day. Older people especially. They know they're getting on and think it's time to do some good in the world. Visible good."

"So people can say how wonderful they are—or were?"

"Sure. So what's the excitement?"

"The chapel and the Beaugard Room at the church."

"I still don't get it."

Sarah paused and then shook her head. "It's just that I've had the impression from Alice that money was tight. And Dolly didn't have power of attorney, so even if she wanted to have rooms and plaques all over the state, she couldn't. She had an allowance for household spending plus a modest income from a trust fund. All the children had that, even Eliot, who doesn't need it."

Alex walked over to a coat rack and hung a slicker over his arm, walked over to his office door and held it open.

"Exit please. So your idea of a smashing Saturday afternoon is to prowl around and see how much more cash has been thrown at deserving institutions. Okay, I'll drive around, visit museums and waste time. But consider this. Mrs. Beaugard has no strings on *her* income. Can't you assume that Dolly made the suggestions and Mrs. Beaugard wrote the checks?"

Sarah walked out into the corridor and then turned back to Alex. "I could, but I'm not going to. Mrs. Beaugard's got a reputation as a tightwad. Grandmother Douglas suggested as much. Small donations, not rooms and chapels. Hospital 'friend,' not 'benefactor.' Dolly headed committees, wore smocks, but I've never heard she personally gave out great wads of money."

"How about Eliot? He may be the man behind all this."

"Eliot strikes me as someone only interested in feathering his own beautiful nest."

"Stalemate," said Alex, as they both, shoulders hunched, heads down, dove out into the snow and wind and made for the parking lot.

"Your car or mine?" he shouted.

"Follow me home and then we'll take yours. What we've got to do after hitting the museums and Scouts is to nail George Fitts to his office desk. He's got the Beaugard estate books, but he may not have seen the chapel and the Beaugard Room, and if the estate books don't show the donations and tax deductions, then something's amiss."

"But he won't let us know."

"He'll let Mike know and we'll squeeze it out of Mike."

For once, Sarah's plan moved forward on oiled wheels. The Godding Museum of Art in Rockport sported two large marine oils and a Thomas Eakins labeled as gifts of the Beaugard family. These just acquired and hung within the last six months. The Farnsworth Museum secretary was pleased to acknowledge the acquisition of a Fairfield Porter depiction of a summer sailing scene. Purchased with a donation by the Beaugard family.

The Girl Scouts were less fortunate. Only two camping scholarships for deserving and needy girls. The Midcoast Audubon director, Joe Bartlebury, admitted to the Beaugard funding of a lecture series on native Maine birds. Arranged six months ago.

"Not big bucks," said Sarah as she climbed back into Alex's Jeep after this last visit, "but add it to the chapel and the church room and it's impressive."

"I'm beginning to wonder at the timing," said Alex. "Everything in the last two years."

"Yes, the Beaugard Room was finished last month; the chapel, ditto. I wonder," Sarah went on thoughtfully, "if Dolly had intimations of mortality."

"Or immortality via conspicuous donations. Although," he went on, "Mrs. Beaugard's getting on and she's not well. She'd be the one to be worrying about her life expectancy."

"Let's hit George Fitts. Lay this on him. See if we can make his eyebrows shoot up."

"It would take more than a few hundred thousand dollars to get a rise out of George," said Alex dryly.

This proved the case.

George received Sarah's report in his state police office—a beige space without charm or the distraction of pictures, carpet, or comfortable chairs.

"Interesting," said George, without sounding or looking interested.

"You'll look it all up, won't you?" said Sarah. "I mean, what if there's not a single record of all this giving out?"

"I would be surprised," said George, who was never surprised.

"But if there's nothing," pleaded Sarah, "then wouldn't you think that someone's siphoning off some cash?"

"How?" said George. "As you've said, no one in the family has or had power of attorney."

"Could Dolly have sold off some of her own jewelry?" asked Sarah. "That is, if she had any."

But George shook his head. "We have access to Dolly's safe deposit—because of the possibility of homicide—and no jewelry is missing. She had a diamond bracelet, a sapphire ring, sapphire earrings, and other fairly valuable pieces. It's all being held until the estate is settled. No records of Dolly having sold any."

"You don't suppose Dolly got her mitts on her mother's jewelry?" said Sarah.

"Forget jewelry, Sarah," said. George. "We've checked. Four years ago Mrs. Beaugard divided her jewelry among her three daughters and Eliot—for his wife, Caroline. Mrs.

Beaugard kept only her wedding and engagement ring and a small diamond-set watch."

"And everyone still has the stuff?" demanded Alex.

George smiled his smile—the slight upward bend of thin lips. "Yes. Except Alice. She sold most of it about three years ago and the rest last year. Rumor has it the money funded a new pickup for Webb Gattling."

"But you will go through the estate account books and see if Mrs. Beaugard's been shelling out big hunks. To Dolly or directly to the church and the others," said Sarah, returning to the matter of greatest interest

George inclined his head. "Yes, we will. Thanks for your efforts, both of you. Believe me, the whole investigation is under control. And now, if you'll excuse me…"

The telephone rang. George reached for the receiver, listened, nodded, said yes, no, no, right away. And hung up. Then, without changing the expression on his face—a face that Sarah had long ago decided was made of an exceptionally hard rubber like erasers—George said, addressing Alex, "That was Mike Laaka. He's heading down to Proffit Point. Beaugard place. The entrance. A delivery van driver just called in to the sheriff's office. A body's turned up. Or two bodies. No details."

Alex took a deep breath. "You want me to come?"

"You're one of the medical examiners, aren't you?" said George.

"A body? You mean homicide?" ventured Sarah.

"Homicide?" said George, as if the word were new to him. "At the moment it's an unattended death. Or two. Wait and see."

"At Proffit Point? But who?" persisted Sarah.

George rose, flicked an invisible piece of lint from a sleeve, and reached for his black raincoat hanging on the door hook.

"No ID at this point. Not even a decent description. The driver—he was on an outing with his family—is fairly incoherent. One of the bodies, at least, appears to be male. That's as far as the report goes. Expect that even when we get there, identification is going to be difficult."

"Oh?" said Alex, eyebrows lifted.

"One body disfigured," said George. "Head battered. Sarah, go with Alex and see if you can keep the Beaugard family away from the scene until I get a trooper up to the house. The Beaugards might listen to you since you're such a friend of the family." And George wrenched open the office door and pointed the way out.

Chapter Sixteen

JONATHAN EPSTEIN SLAPPED THE copy of Frank Herbert's *Dune* closed and groaned.

"I've had it," he announced to his uncle, who sat beside his wheelchair.

"You mean the book?" said Lenox. "I thought it was one of your favorites. Favorite books can be read more than once. You have no patience. None of your generation has any patience."

"Cripes," said Jonathan testily. "It's not the book. I still like *Dune*. It's this house. Being trapped. The whole thing sucks."

"Wonderful expression. So defining."

"Well, it does suck. What I'd really like to do is make a video of *Dune*. Do a screenplay, though I guess I'd have trouble with the technology. But now it's your turn to choose a book, and I suppose I'll have to read *Hamlet*. Or one of the others. Or something gruesome like a poetry collection."

"No," said Lenox. "I thought we'd try Stevenson. *Treasure Island.* I haven't read it since I was twelve years old. Although I realize you cannot believe I was ever twelve."

"Nope, I can't," said Jonathan. Despite his obvious discontent, he almost smiled. "I think you were born Professor Lenox Cobb with a copy of *The Complete Works of William Shakespeare* in your mouth. And I haven't read *Treasure Island* because everyone was always saying I should."

"I think you may take to the book. A few murders, some gunfire, swordplay, a bit of madness, alcoholism, a sailing ship, and a treasure map. With fine illustrations by N. C. Wyeth. I assume there's a copy somewhere around."

"Probably," said Jonathan gloomily. "But I don't want to start reading right away. I want to blow this place. I've got a walking cast on so I can put my leg down. If I can manage with one crutch to go to the bathroom, I can make it outside."

"You probably could," said Lenox. "But you shouldn't. Besides, it's snowing and blowing a gale. Also it's getting dark."

For a moment Jonathan hesitated and then looked down at his watch. "It's only quarter of five, and the sun doesn't go down until almost five-thirty."

"What sun?" demanded Lenox. "There's a snowstorm going on. The sun isn't out."

"I don't care," said Jonathan defiantly, "if it's pitch-dark. I want to get out of the house, and you can't stop me."

Lenox looked at the boy without expression. "I wouldn't dream of disturbing myself so far. Go on. Get it out of your system, and if you fall down and fracture your other leg or pull your arm out of its socket, I do not wish to be blamed."

Jonathan paused in the act of hoisting himself out of his wheelchair. "Will you do one thing, Uncle Lenox? Just help me downstairs. Help me balance. It's a little tricky. I tried it yesterday. Please, Uncle Lenox. Then I won't bother you. Honestly. And I'll wear a jacket. And don't let Grandma know. You know she'd go crazy. Mother wouldn't, but Grandma would."

"You want me to be an accomplice, is that the idea?"

"You got it," said Jonathan, grinning. He pulled himself up with his one good arm—his right one—reached for the crutch that lay across his bed, pushed it under his armpit, and stood up. Then, awkwardly, his leg in its cast thumping down on the floor, he hopped and wobbled his way to the bedroom door.

Lenox Cobb followed.

Downstairs at the front hall coat closet, unmolested by Grandmother Beaugard or Housekeeper Lavender, or any other member of the family—Jonathan struggled into a windbreaker, pushed one arm into a sleeve, then fastened it around his neck and buttoned it below his sling—this procedure watched but not assisted by his uncle.

Jonathan hopped to the door, wrenched it open, and for a moment paused as the snow, blowing slantwise, stung him in the face. The moment's hesitation allowed Lenox to jam a knitted hat over the boy's head.

"Be off with you," said Lenox. "And if you cripple yourself for life, I don't want to hear about it."

With which Jonathan swung himself out onto the front porch, reached back, and slammed the massive front door shut. Then, clinging to the rail, he hopped down the three front stairs and disappeared into what strongly resembled a minor blizzard.

In the front hall Lenox Cobb moved to a narrow side window and squinted through the snow-streaked windows into the increasing dusk. For a moment he stayed without moving and then, abruptly, he jerked himself around, reached into the coat closet, grabbed the first garment that came to hand—an ancient black chesterfield topcoat belonging to Elena's dead husband, Arthur—nothing was ever thrown away at Great Oaks—whirled about and snatched a cane from a carved mahogany umbrella stand, and reached for the front doorknob. This he turned, tugged open the door, stumped out, slamming the door behind him.

"Goddamn that boy to hell," shouted Professor Cobb into the snow and wind. And, enveloped in the oversize coat, cane first, he stepped off the front steps and into the storm.

It wasn't easy. Jonathan, after the first rush of exhilaration produced by his escape from the house, began to falter. Began to think seriously of turning back. The wind was sharp as a knife; the snow was blowing straight into his face and down his neck. His crutch and his one good left foot kept slipping in the accumulating little drifts, and he couldn't use two hands for balance. And it was really dark. Almost like night. Besides, hadn't he made his point? Sticking it to them all. Showing Uncle Lenox that he was not just a kid who could be treated like some invalid baby. That he had real guts.

The trouble was, he didn't want to be back in the house. To be almost suffocated in the seventy-four degrees of heat his grandmother dictated for her thermostat setting. Stuffed back there in his wheelchair reading *Treasure Island* to Uncle Lenox. *Treasure Island*, Jonathan was sure, was one of those books adults thought were good for you. Stevenson, yuck. He was the nerd who'd written that *Child's Garden of Verses* which had been dumped on him when he was too old for junk like that. Stuff about "I have a little shadow that goes in and out with me." Total yuck.

And then as Jonathan, stooped over on his one crutch, was hesitating, there came one of those sudden switches in weather for which the state of Maine is so justly infamous. This time, however, uncharacteristically, the switch was toward benevolence. The northeast wind abated, stalled, considered, and then grooved over to the southwest. The snow ceased driving, regrouped, and began to float straight down. Even the dark gray gloom of late afternoon seemed to lighten and the black lines of the oak tree trunks and feathered branches of evergreens became visible.

Jonathan, caught in the middle of turning about, blinked. Stopped, and then, bracing his shoulders, stumped forward down the sloping driveway. Carefully. Mindful of each step, each putting down of the crutch into the white-covered ground.

Where was he going? Nowhere in particular. Just out, out, out. He began to hum to himself, counting his steps, one-two, one-two. Foot-crutch-foot, foot-crutch-foot.

Moving steadily if awkwardly, Jonathan made good progress. The spruce trees along the verge of the drive with their widespread branches acted as a canopy, and the snow was not so heavy on the ground. He kept moving, almost rhythmically now, warmed by his exertions, until he reached the exact halfway point between the house and the big stone entrance pillars. He knew it was the halfway point because the narrow road off to the left led around to his mother's cottage, branching off on a narrow path that descended to the beach below Little Cove. Jonathan knew the beach well. It had a nice stretch of sand and had long been the focal point of children's summer swimming lessons, rowboat and canoe excursions, and family picnics.

So how about the beach? He paused, considered, and rejected. Early bravado had faded; his shoulder was beginning to ache with the strain of the walk; the end of his broken leg, even with a protective sock over the cast, was soaking wet. No, he'd just go on to the entrance gates. The whole driveway from house to the main road was slightly over half a mile long. Both ways added up to a mile. Far enough.

Almost a quarter of a mile to the rear, moving at the pace of an uncertain but angry snail, came Professor Lenox Cobb. Although, unlike Jonathan, his limbs were sound and his arm was not strapped to his chest, he was having a great deal of trouble getting over the ground. He was still suffering vertigo from his concussion, and his vision, always imperfect, was now partially obscured by snow falling onto his glasses. Furthermore, the black chesterfield coat, snatched so hurriedly, was several sizes too large and flapped and blew about his knees and tangled around his legs so that he resembled nothing so much as an ambulatory tent.

When the kindly change of wind came, Lenox, as had Jonathan, came to a halt. He, too, had been thinking of turning back. Let the boy fall down and freeze to death. Ungrateful brat. Loudmouthed unmannerly snip. The sort of personality he had most dreaded turning up in his undergraduate classes. To hell with him. But then the snow began its slower filtering, the trees on either hand became visible, and the professor, with the deep sigh of a martyred man, stuck his cane into the ground and pushed forward.

The last hundred yards of the Great Oaks drive slopes more sharply toward the level of the Proffit Point Road. Standing just before the descent, a viewer has a clear picture not only of the foot of the drive and the top of the stone entrance pillars but of the mailbox, which stands lone sentinel beside the left-hand or beach-side pillar.

But not this afternoon. Even in the increasing dark, Jonathan could see a muffled figure standing in front of the mailbox. Leaning back against it, in fact. A figure holding up a placard like some sort of prophet. Or from one of those sci-fi books that blast people—prophets and monks and witches in medieval dress—into future centuries. Jonathan shivered, with excitement rather than cold because he was now almost too warm, sweating from his efforts. He took off the knitted hat and with his one hand stuffed it in his windbreaker pocket. And then shuffled a little closer, a few yards down the drive. Yes, even with the snow falling, there he was. Parson Gattling.

He was sure it was Parson. I mean, he told himself, who else? Everyone had been talking about Parson since Aunt Dolly's funeral. Parson standing on the steps of St. Paul's handing out printed cards, Parson railing against the sin of the Beaugards and the drowning of his brothers Junior and Marsden as well as Aunt Dolly. Parson hanging around the Great Oaks entrance.

This was better than any sci-fi movie. And now Jonathan could hear him. A sort of chanting, a monotonous rise and fall of a rusty voice. Jonathan couldn't exactly make out what he was saying, just isolated words. Something about God and miserable sinners.

Jonathan had no intention of confronting Parson. Not face-to-face. But he wanted to watch him, listen to him for a little while. Maybe if he was lucky, he'd catch Uncle Eliot or Aunt Caroline coming over to visit and seeing Parson. Talking to him, getting mad at him. Trying to send him away. Uncle Eliot and his grandmother had said that it was time to call the sheriff. Charge Parson with vagrancy or harassment. His own mother had said no, he was harmless, just mixed up. Maybe his mother would come home now and talk to Parson. Or Dr. McKenzie would drive up and stop, because he knew his grandmother wanted to have the doctor make house calls. Or even Aunt Masha might come home from her concert, though she wasn't as likely to make as interesting a scene as Uncle Eliot.

Jonathan really wanted a scene. He'd been bottled up in that house for too long reading about scenes. But here was the real thing. Almost like a video. Or a good action-suspense movie. Jonathan had long since decided his future lay with the movies. To be a director, like Steven Spielberg, that was the ultimate. Now he worked his way to the edge of the drive, then stepped off into the brush, stepped behind an oak tree, and began inching his way—foot-crutch-foot—down the slope. Quiet now, he mustn't alert the enemy. Was Parson the enemy? Or just some sort of alien presence. Jonathan, fresh from the world of *Dune*, was up for an alien. It would be fun to pretend that he, Jonathan, alone of all earthlings, had spotted an intrusion from another galaxy. Perhaps an escapee from the starship *Enterprise*—Jonathan was a faithful *Star Trek* fan.

Now closer, Jonathan could see that Parson—or Parson's clone, the alien—had subsided on a large rock and that his placard on its stick rested like a musket over his shoulder. Well, Jonathan didn't blame him; he must be plenty wet and cold. Unless, of course, he came from a planet that specialized in inner-body heating mechanisms the way the *Dune* people worked their moisture conservation. Jonathan took two steps down and stopped. And shivered.

Actually this was stupid. It was getting pretty dark and now he'd have to go uphill to get back. His shoulder was really hurting and the toes on his broken leg felt like they had turned into little ice cubes. Oh shit. Anyway, Parson wasn't that interesting. In fact, he was totally boring. And forget the crap about aliens. That was for little kids. So Parson was hanging around the Great Oaks mailbox. Big deal. Jonathan planted his crutch in the ground and turned to go. And froze in place.

Something dark, something black, was moving just below him. Like a bent-over man. Or woman. Or something. It was moving and twisting through the bushes and trees, stopping almost every step and twisting around looking. But there was no face. Just a sort of oval shape like a big black olive stuck on top of shoulders. Black arms and legs. Sliding, slipping a little, but hardly making a sound. It was heading for the road. Little by little. And carrying something. Something sort of round and light-colored.

Jonathan planted his crutch deeper into the not-yet-frozen ground. And stood there frowning into the soft falling snow, seeing the black shape getting closer and closer to the road. Closer and closer to the hunched figure of Parson Gattling, who sat on his rock, his placard slung over his shoulder.

Suddenly Jonathan knew what he was seeing. Without knowing it, he let out a strangled yip, lost his balance, and tumbled forward into a tangle of snow-covered leaves and brush. And then lifting his head off the ground, he saw, as if he were watching some sort of old black-and-white horror film, the figure in the black hood raise the light-colored object and bring it down like a hammer, like a splitting maul, on Parson's head.

Heard the dull thud, a sort of gasping breath—perhaps it was his own gasp, perhaps the black figure was gasping—saw the black arms raised again, the object descend, heard a second, softer thud. Saw Parson sway to the left, slip off the rock, and crumple on the ground like a bundle of dirty laundry.

Saw the black figure stand up, turn, and stare directly at him. At the very place of leaves and bush where Jonathan lay prone, legs splayed, crutch fallen under his chin. And then, running lightly, the black thing started toward him up the gravel drive.

And like a well-timed bit of choreography, down the drive stumbled Professor Lenox Cobb, cane raised on high, yelling like someone leading a cavalry charge straight into the firing line of the enemy.

Chapter Seventeen

MIKE LAAKA FOR ONCE in his life wished that George Fitts were there keeping things from going totally haywire. Cool-hand George managing everything. Jeezus, it was like he had to hold down an octopus. Put cuffs on it. Here he was stuck with securing the scene of the crime, nursemaiding all the passengers of the delivery van—FRIENDLY FLORISTS—FLOWERS FOR ALL OCCASIONS. I mean, said Mike to himself, you don't usually have a whole frigging family finding bodies.

As he told Alex later, "Take Jake Marooni, the driver. If he hadn't stopped on the other side of the Great Oaks entrance just because his kid Ben had to pee, then he'd have driven on by and someone else without the whole family in tow could have found that goddamn awful bloody mess by the Beaugard mailbox. I mean, there was a snowstorm going on, but this kid can't wait. And the kid has a modesty fit because his mother and sister are in the van, so he goes way up into the woods to unzip, and then Jake gets impatient and gets out of the car and all hell breaks loose. Jake finds the body, its head mashed like a Halloween pumpkin, the whole mess being lit up by that highway lamp that's right by the entrance. Well, then Ben Marooni comes out of the woods yelling he's seen a covered-up body and a live man's head next to the body and runs crashing down through the woods and back to the entrance gates, and he sees this other body by the mailbox and sees his Dad vomiting. So the kid keeps up yelling and, natch, out of the van comes Mom and little sister Rachel and they see the body and everyone starts carrying on. Like there was a major massacre, which it sure looked like. So I've got to call in for help and guard the body by the mailbox and at the same time see what in hell the kid is yelling about. Has he really found a body and a head, or was he just spooked being in the woods when it's dark? I mean, talk about triple trouble."

Mike, as he went on to explain, decided that it was best to pursue the living—the live head—rather than stand guard over body number one, about which nothing immediately useful could be done. Shouting at the Marooni family to stay put, to stay away from the corpse, to touch nothing and to keep an eye out for the police—they were coming—Mike took off. But in the excitement he hadn't taken his flashlight, and although he heard someone calling, he couldn't find the source of the voice. Particularly as the voice was indistinct, and this was probably because the Marooni family were still crying and shouting up a storm down there at the end of the drive. Mike swore and damned the lot of them.

Stumbling in the dark, cursing himself and the world in general, he turned back, sped slipping and sliding in the snow back down to his car, grabbed his flashlight, yelled at the Maroonis to for God's sake just shut up, and dashed back. Up the drive, into the bushes, half-blinded by the snow that cascaded down from the low spruce tree branches.

And then he found them. Two more bodies, it looked like. Or a burial mound. Two human shapes under...under what? A black tarp? A blanket? Mike swung the flashlight around and discovered two black shoes attached to two legs, one foot in a sneaker, and the other foot covered in a sodden-looking cast. And one head. Rearing itself out from under the black blanket.

Professor Lenox Cobb.

"What took you so long?" demanded Lenox in a hoarse voice, echoing the very words he'd used before when he had been discovered by Sarah behind the bed in Alice's cottage.

"This boy," said Lenox, indicating the lump beside him, "has had a severe shock, and I'm sure he's suffering from exposure."

"I'm okay," came a muffled voice, and the second head rose out of black cover. "It's just I can't stop my teeth from chattering. It's a sort of biochemical thing."

"Hold your tongue, Jonathan," said Lenox, "and keep your head under. Heat escapes from the top of the head. I gave you a hat and you've lost it. Hypothermia is a serious condition. We are both at risk. I'll thank you to call the rescue squad and the police immediately. It's fortunate that I had the sense to bring a coat at least two sizes too large."

"Stay where you are," commanded Mike.

"We have little choice," said Lenox Cobb's head. "Jonathan has broken his crutch and I am completely enervated. As well as," he added severely, "in danger of pneumonia."

But at that moment came the sound of sirens whooping, cars, trucks squealing to a stop, their roof lights whirling. "Hang in there, Professor," Mike yelled. "Help is on its way."

And it was. Help in the form of sheriff and police, uniformed and plainclothes. Help in the form of the ambulance, the Proffit Point Rescue Squad, the scene-of-the crime crew, and all the minions and apparatchiks of the law. And medical examiner Dr. Alex McKenzie. And Beaugard close family friend—she had given up protesting this title—Sarah Deane.

Jonathan Epstein and Professor Cobb, attended by two members of the rescue squad, left in the ambulance, which also carried Katie Waters with notebook and tape recorder ready for statements.

Sarah was escorted by Sheriff's Deputy Riga on a circuitous route through the snow-filled woods and back to the drive—the drive entrance having been surrounded with yellow scene-of-the-crime tape. "What you've gotta try and do, according to Mike," said the deputy, "is you gotta keep the Beaugard family in place. Not have them coming down here and causing trouble. We got everything under control, and we'll send someone up to the house just as soon as a few more of our guys show up. Right now everyone's busy at the scene and looking around. So tell the Beaugards that all their family members are okay, that the old man and the kid are just going to have a little checkup in the ER and probably come home good as new. Okay, you got that?"

Sarah, wishing she were anywhere but on a difficult visit to the Beaugard headquarters, said yes, she'd got that.

"If they ask you what's going on, just say there's been an accident. You don't have to go into it. You don't have to say a body's been found or anything like that. Just an accident. And you don't know who it is, probably no one connected with anyone around Proffit Point. A vagrant, maybe someone from out of state."

Sarah stopped and looked directly at Deputy Riga. "I heard Mike say when the ambulance left that it was Parson Gattling. Mike heard the boy—his name is Jonathan Epstein—say he'd seen him standing by the mailbox."

"Hey," said Deputy Riga, "don't go jumping. No ID yet. The guy's head was stove in, so we'll have to wait for prints. Wallet, contents of his pockets. Dental records."

Sarah, who had been trying not to think of Parson—or anyone—with a "head stove in," grimaced. "I'll try and keep the family at home until you send someone up," she said. "But I can't prevent someone like Alice Beaugard—she's Jonathan's mother—from getting involved. Getting in a car and coming on down to the end of the drive."

"We've called the boy's mother at her cottage and she's not home. Not up at the big house either. We're setting up a roadblock on the main Proffit Point Road and one midway down the Great Oaks driveway. We're counting on total family cooperation."

"Good luck on that," was all Sarah could think of saying, and in silence they crunched their way the distance to the main house.

Sarah was at first received with gratitude. Vivian Lavender opened the door and ushered her into the living room, where Elena Beaugard sat in her commanding wing chair by the fire. Mrs. Beaugard seemed more outraged by her grandson's and brother's absence from the family hearth than by any possible harm they might have suffered.

"Thank heavens, Sarah, you're at least someone we know. I couldn't believe it when another of those dreadful deputies called in to say that Jonathan and my brother were off to the hospital but that they were just fine. Just a little chilled. What on earth did they mean by that? Of course they were chilled. It's been snowing all afternoon. Why were they out by the road? Jonathan's fault, I'm sure. He isn't supposed to leave the house, but then, he is so spoiled and headstrong that he must have taken off and poor Lenox went after him. Lenox is not well enough for that sort of thing. And besides, it's past dinnertime. Vivian has been keeping everything warm."

Sarah, obeying orders, said her piece, adding that the nature of the accident had not been determined, and as far as she knew, it did not involve anyone known by the Beaugards. Which, if the "accident" is Parson Gattling, she said to herself, isn't exactly true. He may not have been "known" by the family, but all the Beaugards were certainly aware of his almost daily appearance with his placard at the foot of the Great Oaks drive.

"An accident?" repeated Elena. "That's what this deputy said. But what kind of an accident? An automobile? A hit-and-run?"

"I don't know," said Sarah truthfully. And again she added to herself, accident, hell. When she had climbed out of the car she had kept her head averted from the bundle by the road, but even if she dodged seeing the bludgeoned skull of the late Parson Gattling, the twisted limbs and blood-soaked clothes had caught the corner of her eye. That was no accident. She swallowed hard and tried to respond to Mrs. Beaugard's invitation to dinner.

"There's plenty of food," said Elena, "because of Jonathan and Lenox not being here, nor Masha. And I never know whether to expect Alice, so we always have too much."

To this less than gracious invitation, Sarah pleaded absence of appetite. The last thing she wanted right now was a plate of food. Parson's death was a much too recent event to allow for anything but nausea.

Fortunately, the quadruple arrivals of Caroline and Eliot and Alice and Masha distracted Elena, so Sarah was spared further urgings.

"What in hell is going on?" demanded Alice. She had stamped into the house, hair plastered against her face, patches of snow clinging to her coat, her heavy boots dark with wet. "I mean," she went on, "there's a bloody great police barricade set up at the gates. Yellow tape and squad cars, the whole nine yards. No one would tell us a thing, and the police made us drive away from the gates and take the harbor road all the way around to Back Cove."

"Yes," said Masha, her pointed nose red with cold. She unwound a long scarf and began stamping her fur-edged boots. "The Back Cove Road," she added, "and it's a mess. We never use it in the winter. We had to ditch our cars by the Back Cove boathouse and walk from there. I've driven from Vermont and they made me leave all my clothes in the car and carry my instrument case."

"Hounded by a deputy sheriff," complained Eliot.

"Did you all come together?" asked Sarah, interested, as the group straggled one by one into the living room. It seemed strange that the entire family through some sort of telepathy had arrived simultaneously at the Great Oaks entrance.

"Hell no," said Alice. "I don't travel in a caravan. But the police had a roadblock. Bunch of other cars stacked up. We had to wait until we were all checked over. Name, address, age, color of eyes, weight, purpose of visit. Whole crock of shit."

"Alice!" said Mrs. Beaugard.

"Okay, Ma, but talk about a waste of time."

"And the taxpayers' money," said Eliot.

Alice turned to her brother. "I know why I'm here. I live on the property. So does Masha when she's free."

"Right now I am," said Masha. "For a few days anyway."

"But why are you here, Eliot?" demanded Alice, asking the very question Sarah wanted answered. "And you, Caroline?" Alice went on. "Is there a party? And I'm not invited? Sarah's here. Why? Not that she needs an invitation, but why would she want to ruin a perfectly good Saturday night eating beans and cold ham?"

Eliot looked slightly offended. "I don't need a reason to turn up at my mother's. But if you must know, I was finishing a shower and drying myself and looked out the window. Saw all those police cars racing down the road, their lights going like blazes. So I got dressed and went out down to the end of our road. Saw the Great Oaks entrance gates looking like a police circus. Came back and dragged Caroline away from the tube."

"I was getting dinner," said Caroline in her dull voice. "I always watch the news then."

"Anyway," said Eliot, "we had a problem even getting out of our driveway. My car—the Explorer—had a flat tire. Happened this noon; I ran over a big nail. That's the problem of a new house. Nails are always coming to the surface. Anyway, it was blocking Caroline's BMW. So we had to do a bit of maneuvering."

"And here you are," said Masha impatiently.

"There's nothing like an accident," said Alice sarcastically, "for bringing families together."

Eliot ignored his sister. "We drove down the road and were caught in the jam with all the cars held up by the roadblock."

"The point is," said Alice, "what the hell happened? Who's hurt? Or dead? Or hit by a car? No one told us anything."

Mrs. Beaugard shook her head. "None of us knows a thing. But at least it's no one in the family. And Jonathan and Lenox will be coming home soon. They're quite all right."

"Christ, what do you mean they're quite all right?" shouted Alice. "Where is Jonathan, anyway?"

This question took some time to answer, and since no one in the living room knew the exact reason why Professor Cobb and his grandson were visiting the emergency room, a certain amount of arguing and general restlessness resulted until Alice called the hospital and was told that the two patients in question were doing fine and would shortly be coming home. A matter of exposure and repair to the boy's leg cast. Thank you for calling.

"They said Deputy Waters—that's Katie Waters—was with them," announced Alice. "Something's going on and we're being jerked around. At least I am."

"No, you're not," said a smooth voice from the doorway. George Fitts slid on little oiled wheels into the living room. "I knocked, but you were all talking. Mrs. Lavender let me in and said to tell you dinner was getting cold, and would Mr. Eliot carve the ham if he's staying?"

Alice ignored the possibility of dinner. "If we're not being jerked around, why does it feel like we are?"

"The police," said George quietly, "have been extremely busy. The accident is a complicated one. Now, if you'll please go in to dinner, I'll prepare to take statements from all of you. And from Jonathan Epstein and Professor Cobb when they arrive. I'll also tell you as much as I can about what's happened. And Dr. McKenzie is coming in and can answer any appropriate medical questions."

At which point Dr. McKenzie, on cue, came in. Looking, to Sarah's eyes, like an accident himself. His face had been raked, probably by branches, and bore several long scratches. His hair, his clothes, were wet and his boots clotted with mud.

He looked down at these apologetically. "I'll take them off," he said.

"You need not bother," said Elena Beaugard. "Everyone else is dirty." It was a true statement. The walk from Back Cove had rendered the Beaugard arrivals unfit for proper living rooms.

"So," said George Fitts, taking charge, "if the members of the family will please go in to their dinner, I will be ready for them when they come out. Dr. McKenzie and I have to go over some ground together. I assume we can use the library again?"

With which, like oversize children, the Beaugard clan trooped out the door, one by one, and headed for the dining room, but the docility lasted only to the hall. Then Sarah heard loud questions, expostulations, and Mrs. Beaugard's thin querulous voice rising above the others. What was that old play, Sarah asked herself, with Tallulah Bankhead? Or Bette Davis? Or both. *The Little Foxes.* That was it. Family members trying to have each other for lunch. Or dinner, as the case may be. Sarah followed the others to the library and confronted George Fitts.

"I am not a nonperson, George. I'm involved. I've been sent up here as a buffer or a placater or something. I've been used. So give. What is going on? That god-awful thing down there on the road which I tried not to see. Was it Parson Gattling?"

George settled himself in a leather lounge chair and opened his ever-ready notebook. "Yes, it was Parson. Massive injuries to the skull. Alex can give you the details later if you want. He said there were depressed fractures to the cranial and occipital areas of the skull."

"I don't want the details," said Sarah. "I can imagine."

"Unconscious immediately," continued George. "Death soon after. Probably not self-inflicted wounds since the damage was to the top and back of the head. From a very quick examination, it looks like the weapon was used more than once. A repeated blow."

"The first one would have done the trick," said Alex. "Another was probably insurance."

"Or temper," said Sarah.

Alex nodded. "Whatever. The weapon? Who knows? I'm not going to second-guess the pathologist, but it looks like our friend the blunt instrument. No sharp indentations, tears, knifelike slashes."

"Poor Parson," said Sarah. "Standing on street corners holding his pathetic sign and chanting about sin and forgiveness and the Beaugards."

"Not just in town, standing at Great Oaks' entrance," Alex reminded her.

"If you were out to get Parson," said George, "a quiet country road in a snowstorm when it's getting dark would be a good choice." He looked up from his notebook. "Parson's death gives us the same problem we had with Marsden and Junior. Is killing Parson part of a 'get the Gattlings' scenario? Or did Parson's public campaign suggesting Beaugard complicity in his brothers' deaths point to some sort of Beaugard-Gattling relationship we don't understand? Also, Parson seemed to admire Dolly. Why? Whether from hearsay or actual knowledge we don't know."

"Well, there's the Alice-and-Webb connection," said Alex.

"I know," said George in an annoyed voice. "I've had them tailed for weeks and nothing has come of it. Even Webb's sighting of Dolly's sailboat isn't that helpful. Why would Webb—Alice's boyfriend—try and kill Dolly? Unless Alice put him up to it. But why would she do that? Is that in character for Alice?"

"You know Alice is a flake," said Sarah. "And she's a little devious. But I don't think she could possibly have pushed Webb into destroying Dolly, no matter how jealous she was of her sister. Alice has been living on the wild side, but it was a sort of self-destructive unfocused wildness. She seems more stable lately—maybe thanks to Webb. And I think she's got a soft heart, plus she really seems to have appreciated Dolly's efforts in taking care of Mrs. Beaugard. All that driving around and taking her to church and bridge and to her reading group."

George nodded. "Well, we'll keep our eyes on Alice and Webb. All we're sure of is that the Gattlings don't accept Alice, and Webb would be an outcast among the Beaugards. The two of them have kept away from both families. Alice keeps her dog, Willie, and her clothes at Webb's cabin. She's living two lives."

"That's nothing new," muttered Sarah. "And as for Parson, I just can't see either Alice or Webb bludgeoning the poor man. Webb's a sort of gentle giant. Paul Bunyan."

"Sarah, don't get stuck in literary types," said Alex. "There are giants and giants. And ogres. But, George, you do have two witnesses to the attack. Professor Cobb and young Jonathan."

"Katie Waters phoned in a report. She rode in the ambulance with them and tried to get some answers. Stubbed her toes right away on the professor. He clammed up and told Jonathan to keep quiet. But I gather Jonathan did see something of the assault on Parson and that Lenox Cobb came screeching in on the scene just when the perpetrator was heading in the boy's direction. And that scared him off."

"The murderer, him?" demanded Sarah.

"Or her," said George. "Except Katie said that she had the impression Jonathan felt he'd seen something strange. Not just the killing, which must have been frightening in itself. But that the attacker looked weird. Jonathan kept referring to 'it.'"

Chapter Eightteen

IN SPITE OF THE family objections—Mrs. Beaugard demanding, Lenox Cobb forbidding, Alice pleading—George descended on Jonathan within twenty minutes of the boy's return to Great Oaks.

"Strike while the iron is hot," George told Alice. "The boy isn't going to forget what he's seen, but he may start elaborating. Or denying. Substituting. Giving in to his imagination. We need answers and it's lucky Jonathan's a bright kid who doesn't seem like the hysterical type. Then I'll follow up with Professor Cobb."

"Not Lenox," Elena said, sounding her cane on the floor. "He isn't well. He gets muddled and has those awful headaches."

"The report is that Professor Cobb was perfectly rational in the ambulance," said George. He paused and looked at his watch. "It's just nine now. Give me and Mike time with Jonathan and then I'll see your brother. And I expect everyone in the house to stay put. Thank you. And you, Alex…" The sergeant looked over to Alex, who stood by the living room entrance hoping to grab Sarah and depart for home. "Alex, stay with Professor Cobb, will you? The library. Out of everyone's way. I don't want him questioned by the family. And, Sarah, you may as well go to the library with Alex. Keep to neutral subjects. Understand?" And George, followed by Mike Laaka, walked into the hall and toward the stairway.

"Thus spake Zarathustra," said Sarah to Alex.

Alex grinned ruefully. "And let no man put asunder. But hell, I thought we'd be able to slide out of here about now."

"No way," said Alice, appearing at their side. "You might as well get used to being Beaugard adjuncts. Miserable with the rest of us. But I hope that Sergeant Fitts doesn't pounce on Jonathan and turn him into a basket case."

"From what I've seen of your son," said Alex, "it'll be the other way round. Kids like Jonathan nowadays cut their teeth on blood and guts. Think of the daily dose on the tube. I'll bet Jonathan doesn't stay tuned to the Disney Channel."

"Jonathan," said Alice defensively, "is quite sensitive. He puts on a good act, but a lot of it is just that. An act."

Curiously enough, Alice Beaugard was on target. About both the sensitivity and the act. And George Fitts was correct in believing that kids allowed their imaginations to take control of facts.

The result was that George had a hard time of it. Jonathan was discovered reclining on his bed, his leg in a fresh fiberglass cast stuck out in front of him, his arm in a clean sling, and a copy of *Doomsday Comics* resting on his stomach. He was wearing cutoff jean shorts and a black T-shirt with the legend in white letters: STOLEN FROM THE MAINE STATE PRISON.

Jonathan's act was a variation of the "what, me worry?" stance; his sensitivity to recent events shown by a repeated licking of his lips and a tremor in his speech. Led through his arrival above the Great Oaks entrance, his distant view of Parson Gattling, hearing Parson chanting his message, the arrival of the attacker, the bludgeoning of Parson, the attacker running toward him, and the appearance of Lenox Cobb, the yield was sparse. George recited and Jonathan said "yes," "no," and "maybe" in appropriate intervals.

Finally George put down his notebook in exasperation and withdrew to the window with Mike Laaka while Jonathan, with an ostentatious yawn, picked up his comic book. "Okay, Mike, you want to try?" asked George. "Because I'm getting nowhere…"

"You need to go at it differently," said Mike, realizing that for George to admit failure was a rare event. "The kid is shook but isn't going to admit it. You need an angle."

"And what angle do you suggest?"

"I don't have an angle, but I know someone who would."

"Oh?" said George suspiciously. "Not his mother?"

"Sarah. She's an English teacher. She's up to her hips with kids every day of the week."

George sighed. "I was hoping not to involve Sarah in this one beyond her help as someone who knows the family. Besides, Sarah teaches college students, not eleven-year-old boys."

"The difference isn't always that great," said Mike. "Listen, trust me. And trust Sarah. She does know kids and she has a younger brother who's over twenty and sometimes acts twelve."

George shrugged, nodded, and Mike went to find Sarah, who, along with Alex, was trying to interest Lenox Cobb in a discussion of the finer points of backgammon. A subject selected by Alex as being almost devoid of emotional content.

"The problem," said Mike as the two climbed the stairs, "is that George wants to start at A and end at Z. He usually takes a witness over the jumps in order, backs 'em up when it's needed, gives a loose rein for a little, then hauls 'em back on track. But no dice with this kid. He's doing George's thing right back at him."

"I'll try," said Sarah. "I have one idea. Jonathan belongs to the media generation, and Alice told me once that his hero is Steven Spielberg. Let me try that angle. It might work. It means beginning as if nothing was real. It didn't really happen."

"That's not going to make George happy. It did happen."

"You two stay in the background," said Sarah. "Don't butt in, and if I strike out, okay, I strike out."

George and Mike retreated to the far reaches of the room by the window, partially out of sight but within earshot.

"Okay if they hang in?" asked Sarah to Jonathan. "I mean, they *are* working on this business. They have to earn their salary."

"No sweat," said Jonathan, turning a page of his comic book, and Sarah could see a space vehicle exploding in a splash of yellow and red fire spots.

"Why do you think I'm here?" asked Sarah, helping herself to the bedside chair usually occupied by Lenox during the reading sessions.

"Oh, the police guys probably think that I'll go all mushy because you're a female and a friend of my mother's," said Jonathan, turning another page showing a two-headed crocodile in orbit.

"If you were making a movie and had a scene with a witness and a detective, how would you handle the interrogation? If the witness wasn't exactly spelling out what happened?"

Jonathan lowered his comic book. Then raised it up again. "I'd hypnotize the witness," he said. "Make him relive it. Like in *Dead Again*."

"That was a pretty neat movie," said Sarah. "So let's say you're the director of a movie. Or a TV show. A horror movie. You want a lot of suspense and action. About a kid with a broken leg who is taking a walk in a snowstorm and happens on a murder."

"You don't like the hypnotizing idea?" said Jonathan.

"Yes, it might work. But you've got to have the boy relive the experience. Show him being put under and at the same time move the boy into the scene. How would you handle that?"

Jonathan, still holding the comic book, frowned. "I suppose I'd do a fade-out. Fade out from the hypnosis scene and gradually make the boy look solid in another setting. A spooky one."

"Like a snowstorm? When it's getting dark?"

"I told Sergeant Fitts everything I know."

"Listen, Jonathan, take yourself out of what happened. Just for a little while. Be the man behind the camera. I've heard you're interested in directing movies. Okay, here's your chance. Who would you cast for the boy? Not Jonathan, but who?"

Jonathan frowned. "Not a kid. Maybe someone like Indiana Jones. Harrison Ford."

"Okay," said Sarah. "Set the scene."

"It's not snowing. It's Africa. And there's a gang of murderous extraterrestrial smugglers around. They smuggle skins of endangered species for their own planet. Which doesn't have solar heat. It has a double cold moon." Jonathan put down his comic book and sat up. "It takes place at a hunting lodge."

Oh brother, said Sarah to herself. I hope George and Mike can keep their shirts on through this. Aloud she said, "Okay, set the scene and roll the camera."

"His name isn't Indiana Jones, it's...it's Roderick Usher. He's a reincarnation. Of the first Roderick Usher."

"Okay," said Sarah.

"He's had this fever and now he's a lot better. The fever is due to gangrene in his foot and he has to use a crutch. And his shoulder is tied up because he was mauled by a Bengal tiger."

"Got it," said Sarah.

"And he's tired of being stuck in the hunting lodge with this old medicine man named...named Edgar Allan Poe. He's another reincarnation. Actually this is the twenty-second century and everyone is a reincarnation. I mean, there's an Abraham Lincoln and a Magic Johnson around. Well, Roderick, he starts down the road in the rain. It's monsoon time. Do they have monsoons in Africa?"

"Go ahead and have one if you want."

"I want this to be accurate."

"Sure they have monsoons," said Sarah recklessly.

"And he goes miles and miles down this dirt road and suddenly he sees down by the mailbox...no, not the mailbox, the road sign pointing to the next village. It's raining hard, but he sees this beggar. The kind of beggar that wears an orange sheet and carries a begging bowl. And the beggar—he's a Buddhist—is singing a mantra. And Roderick Usher listens and all of a sudden..." Jonathan paused and took a deep breath.

"Bring the camera in," suggested Sarah.

"No, bring the sound up. Sort of bushes being mashed down by the wind and background of Elton John. His early stuff. And then the camera picks up this thing like a man. Or a woman. Wearing black. It comes out on the road and it's carrying a round thing and you can't even see its face because it's an alien and doesn't have a face. And it lifts the thing it's carrying..."

And Jonathan subsided. "That's all. The camera scans uphill and picks up the old medicine man, who is totally naked except for lions' teeth around his neck, and he comes screeching down the road, but the alien's gone. He's vaporized. That's the end of the scene. And that's all I'm going to do tonight. I'm hungry. Ask Mother if she can send up some pizza."

"Just one more thing," said Sarah. "The head of the alien. Is it totally absolutely black? No face?"

"Sort of shiny black. Like the rest of him. Because it was raining. He looked like one of those people in books about the Middle Ages. We've been doing the Middle Ages in school. Knights and serfs and varlets and that sort of stuff."

"What sort of Middle Ages person did he look like?" asked Sarah softly.

"Like an executioner," said Jonathan, picking up his comic book. "With the ax. He's called a headsman and he wears this black hood and chops off people's heads when the neck is put on a block of wood. It's called a beheading. So do you think you could ask about the pizza and maybe some ice cream? Chocolate Nut or Toffee Crunch if there's any left."

George and Mike escorted Sarah downstairs.

"It's a ski mask," said Mike. "A perfectly dressed murderer."

"A shiny ski mask?" asked Sarah, "Aren't they usually wool? Something knitted."

"Neoprene or some synthetic," suggested George. "I'm not sure that session was very useful. Aliens and Indiana Jones and Africa."

Sarah turned on him. "George Fitts. You and Mike said you were getting zilch out of Jonathan. Never mind the frills and native village and medicine man stuff. Now you know the man—or woman—was all in black and wore a mask and a hood and carried something round."

"Or something that looked round," said Mike. "George, thank the lady."

"Thank you, Sarah," said George. "I suppose we're a step ahead with that description. But someone all in black isn't much help. Now, please join Alex again in the library and tell Professor Cobb I'll see him in about ten minutes. I want to fill in my notes about Jonathan's scenario."

"I think," said Sarah, "he's got a future in cinema. Watch out, Steven Spielberg."

Arriving in the library, she found that Alex and Lenox Cobb had exhausted the possibilities of backgammon and were arguing about what an eleven-year-old should be reading.

"Shakespeare cannot possibly hurt him," said Lenox. "He's a spoiled boy, but he's not without intelligence. He got through *Macbeth* without trouble. I'm thinking of renting the video. Later on we can try *Julius Caesar*. Then *Hamlet*. After all, he's subjecting me to extraterrestrial mayhem."

"How about the good old classics?" asked Alex. "King Arthur, Jules Verne, or Rider Haggard?"

"*Treasure Island*, I thought. One chapter tonight. It will take his mind off what happened. The business of blind Pew and the Black Spot is quite diverting. There should be a copy around. I can't reach the top shelves here, but I know that Elena had a set of Stevenson somewhere."

"I'll help you look," said Sarah. She looked around the room. One wall was covered in ceiling-to-floor open bookshelves; the other two longer walls, by the glass-fronted cases holding Arthur Beaugard's collection of illustrated books. And there was a library stepladder ready and waiting. At least, looking for *Treasure Island* would distract Uncle Lenox. She began the search, starting low and working up to the top. Stevenson was discovered three rows from the top of the open set of shelves. But no *Treasure Island.*

"I don't think it's a complete set," she called down to Lenox Cobb. "*Treasure Island*'s missing, and so is *David Balfour* and *Kidnapped*. I suppose those were the popular ones and they're floating around somewhere."

"Eliot probably took them off to his house," said Lenox crossly. "He thinks since he's the only son, he's entitled."

"I'll keep looking," said Sarah. "Maybe they're misplaced."

"Never mind," said Lenox, "I can borrow one of the illustrated editions. It's not as if we're going to spill soup on them. I'll make Jonathan wash his hands."

At which juncture George Fitts appeared and summoned his other witness to the murder. Or witness to the post-murder attack on Jonathan. "In the breakfast room," announced George. "I've set up a tape recorder. I didn't use one with Jonathan because I was afraid it would disconcert him, but you as a professional will be quite used to it."

A good touch, thought Sarah. Nothing like appealing to Lenox Cobb's overstuffed sense of pride.

"You can help look," Sarah told Alex, who had settled down comfortably with a dog-eared copy of *Huckleberry Finn*.

Alex smiled up at her. "It's all yours. The exercise will do you good. I've been crawling all over the driveway entrance out in the snow. I need rest."

So Sarah continued the search. Up and down. Leather, cloth, old paperbacks, early Everyman editions; even *Kidnapped* came to light next to *The Scarlet Letter*. It was clear, she thought, that no one in the family had paid much attention to order; the books were stuffed in regardless of author or subject—Gibbon next to *Gulliver's Travels*, which leaned cozily against *Pride and Prejudice*.

"I'll try the illustrated editions," said Sarah. "Besides, I'm dying to look at them. Do you think anyone would mind?"

Alex looked up. "No one in the family seems to be exactly book-oriented," he said. "Just don't drop them."

But Sarah had already advanced on the first glass bookcase. Unlocked. So much for security. Or was it that no one cared? Maybe they weren't all that valuable. But they were certainly dreary with their green cloth slipcases and the uniform black and gold titles giving the names of the books and the illustrators. Like those on the open shelves, these, too, were shelved without regard for author, title, or illustrator. Any proper librarian would have a fit. As expected, the majority were children's books. Sarah ran a finger lightly over the titles. *Peter Pan in Kensington Gardens*—Arthur Rackham; *The Arabian Nights*—Maxfield Parrish; *The Dance of Death*—Albrecht Dürer (an adult title departure); *Wind in the Willows*—Rackham again, and also the same title with E. R. Shepard's illustrations. Sarah would have dearly liked to stop and ruffle through a few volumes, but *Treasure Island* came first. She climbed one step higher and there it was. N. C. Wyeth, the illustrator. The last slipcase at the end of the top shelf, right next to *A Child's Garden of Verses*—Jessie Wilcox Smith.

Sarah climbed to the top of the library steps, reached, and pulled the slipcase toward her. It came, light as a feather.

So light, it almost flew out of her hand. Puzzled, she pulled the two parts of the slipcase apart. Empty. No *Treasure Island*. She scowled at the slipcase halves. Well, someone had beat Lenox to it. A family Stevenson fan. Or the volume had been sold. Traded. Auctioned off. Or...?

Sarah reached toward the middle of the top shelf for the Rackham *Peter Pan*. As light as *Treasure Island*. And as empty.

Then from the top shelf she drew out an *Alice in Wonderland*—Tenniel; a *Don Quixote*—Vièrge illustrations; and a "Night Before Christmas"—W. W. Denslow. All empty slipcases.

"Alex!"

"What now?"

"They're empty. The slipcases. The whole top row. It's a false front. Just for looks."

Alex rose from his chair, joined her, and reached to the end of the second from top row and pulled out Defoe's *Robinson Crusoe*—Cruikshank, the illustrator. Empty.

"What on earth," said Sarah. "The collection is just a sham."

Alex shook his head. "It wasn't a sham ten years ago when Arthur Beaugard was alive. My mother is crazy about Arthur Rackham illustrations, and she went to an auction in Portland and stubbed her toe on Arthur. It was a limited edition, bound in vellum, signed by Rackham. It went for big bucks, too much for Mother, but Arthur outbid everyone. She told me that he was bidding high all day, illustrated books, first editions, signed editions, editions with letters bound in." Alex stepped down and then walked to the center of the bookcase and pulled out *The Story of Miss Moppet*. Beatrice Potter. Not empty. The opened case revealed a small gray book with green lettering and a color paste label. And an envelope filled with a typed file card. This Alex extracted, read, and whistled.

"What's the matter?" demanded Sarah, who stood with an empty case of *The Knave of Hearts*—Maxfield Parrish—in her hand.

Alex read aloud. "'*The Story of Miss Moppet*. London: Frederick Warne and Company, first edition in book form; 1916. Dust wrapper. With letter from Beatrice Potter to a 'young friend.' Purchased at auction, Kennebunkport, 1982. Thirty-five hundred dollars.'" Alex looked up. "And I'm in medicine when I could have been collecting children's books."

He reached again toward the middle of the shelf. Again heft and weight. A copy of *The Nutcracker*, by E. T. A.

Hoffman, Illustrated and signed by Maurice Sendak. Limited edition, 1984. Bought by Arthur Beaugard for a mere $950. Another three books from the center of the bookcase all proved to be filled with the labeled books, with prices going in one case as high as $7,000. But when Alex checked the ends of the top and the bottom shelf, he came up with empties.

"There's a pattern," he said. "The stuff in the middle is good goods. The hard-to-reach books are hollow."

But Sarah was dragging the library steps over to the second of the glass bookcases. Also unlocked. She opened the door and mounted the steps and reached. Top row, last book on left. *Sleeping Beauty*. Illustrator: Edmund Dulac. Hollow.

She climbed down and withdrew *The Tempest* from the front and center. Arthur Rackham. Filled with a large quarto with a vellum back and gold stamping. White dust wrapper with red lettering; 1926. The file card announced, with two exclamation points (was it glee or was it sorrow?) that Arthur Beaugard had bought the Rackham signed book from a Boston bookseller for a mere $2,600.

Sarah put the book down on a small table by the window. "Good grief," she said. "We are in the wrong business. Well, someone's been doing some secret reading. Or borrowing."

"Or dipping into the honey pot," said Alex.

"Or buying large sailboats named *Goshawk*," said Sarah.

"Or helping Webb Gattling purchase motorcycles or buying expensive rosewood recorders. Masha told me good recorders start around three thousand dollars. And she has seven of the things."

Sarah paused, opened *The Tempest*, and contemplated Arthur Rackham's signature. Then she said, "Or just maybe, someone has been furnishing a space called the Beaugard Room."

Chapter Nineteen

FOR A MOMENT ALEX stared at Sarah, and Sarah stared at *The Tempest*. Then, holding the book gingerly, she slid it back in its slipcase and placed it back, front and center on the shelf, and closed the bookcase. And turned to Alex. "Now what?"

"Try and put those books back in order."

"They aren't in order, they're all mixed up. I think I've overdone it looking for *Treasure Island*." Sarah subsided in the leather chair by the fireplace. "What shall we do? Anything? Pretend we weren't snooping?"

"Speak for yourself," said Alex. "I wasn't snooping."

"You're an accessory. But is this anybody's business but Mrs. Beaugard's? For all we know, she may have been selling off books for years. Perfectly legitimately. She's not a collector."

"Or," Alex added, "Arthur Beaugard may have been—what's the museum word?—deacquisitioning. It's not our business, and I doubt if it has anything to do with Dolly being dead or with anyone else being killed. It's one of those messy irrelevant facts."

"Maybe an embarrassing fact. It doesn't look exactly on the up and up. Leaving the filled books front and center and the empty cases on the top shelves and at the end. Keeping up the appearance that the collection is intact."

"Maybe if Mrs. Beaugard's behind it—or her husband sold them off—they didn't want to leave empty shelves. Okay, okay"—as Sarah began shaking her head—"granted, it looks as if someone has been helping themselves."

"And I'm afraid," said Sarah in a disappointed voice, "it wasn't Saint Dolly. She didn't need to pawn books. She had the access to her mother. If George Fitts comes up blank with the estate accounts, we'll have to think again. But for God's sake, it's not as if Mrs. Beaugard doesn't know about the donations. She's been in the Beaugard rooms taking bows, getting credit for Oriental rugs and stained-glass windows. She must have known generally about the cost, though maybe not down to the last penny."

"So you have another candidate with sticky fingers?"

"I'm afraid so. It's Alice. Eliot doesn't need money, and Masha seems to live fairly modestly even if she owns expensive musical instruments. Recorders aren't in the same class as violins and cellos, But Alice's life has been an absolute shambles. All those drying-out sessions and medical events and starting and stopping careers. Doling out cash to Webb from time to time. Selling her own jewelry. Besides, there's Jonathan."

"But Alan Epstein must be paying child support for Jonathan. Even here at Great Oaks. And before that, Alan had the whole expense of the boy. But granted, Alice seems to be the needy one."

At which interesting point Alice Beaugard poked her head in the door. "I'm coming in. I've had it with Eliot and Caroline. They're arguing with the police about whether they heard anything of the so-called accident out on the road. George Fitts keeps saying 'are you sure,' and Eliot says how much can you hear if you're in the shower, and Caroline says she was watching the tube. The police really want to know if Parson was on the Beaugard payroll, but he wasn't on anyone's payroll. Picked up odd jobs but never worked at a steady one."

Sarah made a sudden decision. "Alice, do you know where there's a copy of *Treasure Island*? Your uncle Lenox wanted to start Jonathan off on it. Their reading program."

Alice yawned and wiped her hand across her mouth. She looked exhausted. "I suppose there's one around. Did Uncle Lenox look?"

"He asked me to. No copy on the regular shelves, and the copy from the special collection is missing. Just the slipcase."

Alice threw herself down on the sofa, pulled off her boots, and lay back on tapestry cushions. "So someone's borrowed it."

"Actually," said Sarah, "someone's borrowed a lot of books. I was looking for *Treasure Island* and found out that some of the slipcases are empty."

Alice shifted into a sitting position and eyed Sarah with a certain amount of pleasure. "That's what I mean. Snooping is in your blood. You can't help it. It's like a cat with mice. You have investigative DNA. That's why I asked you to help with Dolly's death. And see what came of it. We all finally know that Dolly was murdered. But now that poor goof Parson has been killed. And now Sarah the Snoop has found empty slipcases."

"You're not surprised?" asked Alex, speaking from an opposite sofa. With the three of them settled by the fireplace, any visitor would have assumed that here was a late Saturday night gathering of friends, a pleasant scene with the light of the flames flickering on the brass andirons, the marble clock ticking sonorously on the mantel, the snow falling soundlessly against the glass windows.

But now a small amount of color crept into Alice's cheeks. "No, I'm not that surprised. I mean, anybody could help themselves, and they probably have. The cases aren't locked. And I know what some of those buggers are worth."

"Oh?" said Sarah encouragingly.

"Well, Dad always said they were valuable. It was no secret, what with all the time he spent going to auctions. The books are just sitting here asking to be lifted. Oh, okay, if you want to know, I did get into the collection. Sort of. Just before Dad died, he gave Jonathan a Christmas present. You know, the first grandchild, and Dad wanted him to have something special. Jonathan was about three. It was a first edition set of the Winnie-the-Pooh books. All four of them. With dust jackets, which I guess makes them more valuable. Signed by A. A. Milne with an extra sketch by E. H. Shepard in the front of each. It was a neat present, but I was totally out of cash and I told myself, what the hell, Jonathan doesn't care if he reads a first edition. So I bought him a brand-new set and sold off the valuable ones. For a nice hunk of cash, believe me. I spent it fast on back rent and a new therapist."

"And that's all?" asked Sarah. "No other books?"

"Once more. I was desperate again. I'd just been divorced and fired from my job and I couldn't keep asking Mother for handouts. So I palmed *Peter Rabbit* and *Jemima Puddle-Duck*, both first editions. I had them hidden in a wastebasket when Dolly came pouncing in. Caught me holding *Tom Kitten*. Quite a scene, so I put *Tom Kitten* back and she promised not to tell Mother. Dolly, our little family watchdog. Except I did have the two Beatrix Potter books, and you wouldn't believe what I got for them. Enough to buy a very good secondhand car. But that's all there is to it."

"Not quite," said Sarah.

"You mean someone else has been lifting books?"

"A lot of the top slipcases and the end ones are empty."

Alice sank back on her cushions and rolled her eyes. "Well, well. I'm not alone. Wish I'd hit the shelves for more while I was at it. Now I suppose it's too late because you and Alex know and you'll probably leak it all to the police."

Sarah shook her head. "We don't think it's any of our business. It isn't as if it has anything to do with Dolly dying. But if you're interested in insurance or tracing the books, you should probably report it."

Alice was silent for a full minute and then a smile spread over her face. "Or I could just ignore the whole thing and finish the job. Siphon off the rest of them, and who's to know? Mother's never given a damn about the collection, Masha is a music-only type, and Eliot reads sailing magazines and spy stories. And Caroline, the only stuff she reads is off-the-wall psychological books."

"What *is* wrong with Caroline?" said Sarah. "It's as if she had a glass door between herself and the world."

"What's wrong with Caroline," said Alice succinctly, "is Eliot. The marriage from hell. Yeah, I know I'm a great one to talk, but those two are impossible together. Eliot's the outdoor action and social party type; Caroline complains and turns her head away from everything. Life with her eyes closed. The thing they had in common is a big new house, but the novelty's wearing off. Of course, there's Colin. He's nine and he's learned to keep his distance from his parents and make his own space. Jonathan likes him, so he couldn't be all bad."

"So who's lifting illustrated books?" said Alex, returning to topic A.

"Anyone," said Alice. "The butcher, the baker, the candlestick maker. Family members or someone who works on the place. Listen, I don't think I'll tell anyone. Not yet. No point in laying any more stress on Mother by going public. She's called a family powwow for tomorrow. Wants to talk about the estate, about Dolly's own plan, she says. Make sure we're all happy with it and know we'll be taken care of. Cottages, trust funds. So bringing up missing books will snarl everything. Eliot will go on about estate valuations and inventories and all that shit."

"Your family will have to know sometime," said Alex.

"Yeah, sure, but I don't think it's going to cause major trauma. Mother might get a little sentimental because the collection was Dad's pride and joy. Though when he was alive, Mother used to bitch about the time and money he spent on the books. All those auctions. Running off to Portland and Boston and New York. To say nothing of L.A., Dallas, London, Rome, and you name it."

At which Vivian Lavender appeared in the door. "Professor Cobb wants to know if you've come up with *Treasure Island*."

Sarah rose, went to the open bookcase, and brought out a volume. "*Kidnapped*. A good substitute."

Vivian disappeared and Sarah turned to Alice. "Mrs. Lavender. Would she…?"

"Have snitched books? It's an idea. She might have. To feather her nest. Or her future nest, since as you know, Mother plans to leave the house to the Episcopal Church, and Vivian's RC, so she'll probably be given the boot. With a nice pension."

"As a matter of fact," said Sarah, "I've seen her coming out of St. Paul's-by-the-Sea when I've dropped Grandma off. Maybe she's switching gears."

Alice raised her eyebrows. "Smart move, smart move. If she really has. I didn't give Vivian enough credit. It's a good way to ensure future employment. And it's just a step sideways, isn't it? Drop the pope and support married priests. But church or no church, Vivian deserves what she can get. All these years of coping with this house and all of us. If she's lifted a few books, I'm not going to start yelling 'stop thief.' After all, I took some, why not Vivian? Or anyone else. It's a wonder we have any left."

"So how about locking the bookcases?" asked Sarah.

"You mean not give the rest of the world equal opportunity? Okay, not a bad idea. And for now our lips are sealed. Too bad I can't tell Jonathan. He'd love it."

"Nix on Jonathan," said Alex. And then seeing the door open and the bald dome of George Fitts appear around the corner, he stood up. "Okay, we're excused, George? Enough is enough."

"Yes," said George. "We've wrapped up interrogations for the night." He turned to face Alice, who was back on her cushions feigning indifference. "I've told your mother we're leaving a team down at the site by the entrance. And I'm putting two men up at your house at access points. Your mother's not happy about it."

"Mother," said Alice, "is probably having kittens. The idea of men to whom she has not been properly introduced lurking in our bushes will drive her bananas."

"Actually women. I should have said women. Female troopers," said George, who had grave reservations about female troopers.

"Even worse," said Alice. "Mother doesn't approve of female troopers. Mother's barely accepted the vote."

"Good night, Alice," said Sarah, pulling herself to her feet. She walked to the door and opened it. "We'll be in touch."

"You can bet your sweet life we will," said Alice. "You, Sarah, and you, Alex, are under contract."

"What's she talking about?" demanded George suspiciously.

"Not a signed contract," said Alice. "A verbal agreement. But binding. Isn't that what the lawyers say? Or call it a moral obligation to deal with whatever accidents, murders, drownings, general attacks, and pails of shit are thrown our way."

"No, you don't," said George to Sarah.

"Right," said Sarah. "No, we don't."

"Good night," said Alex loudly. He strode to Sarah's side and seized her sleeve. Stopped by George.

"You can take the main drive back out; we've put a tarp over the site. And we're doing the post on Parson Gattling at seven A.M. Path lab in Augusta. You'll have to leave by six to make it."

The snow had stopped, the wind had died, and Proffit Point lay under a soft shroud of white.

"So beautiful," Sarah sighed. "The first snow in a quiet woods. It always makes me think of those stories where a snow wizard steps in front of the sleigh, raises a hand, and the prince or the maiden is transported to some iceberg kingdom."

"Instead," said Alex, whose moments of fancy, always somewhat limited, were now completely short-circuited by an intense desire for home and hearth, "we're transported to the land of yellow scene-of-the-crime tape."

"You, Alex," said Sarah with irritation, "could drive anyone to the brink of murder—no, damn it, I didn't mean murder. See what a noxious influence you are. Sometimes I absolutely loathe men of science. Well, this maiden will be transported, but the prince will turn into a block of ice and serve him right. I say the snow is beautiful and I say to hell with the yellow tape."

Alex, now arrived at the entrance, slowed the car to a crawl, and guided by a series of posts and policemen, maneuvered the car out onto the highway and in the direction of home. "Okay, I'm willing to think about the snow," he said. "Now that we're out of Great Oaks. You talk about noxious. That place is super-noxious. And tomorrow, most of the morning anyway, will be blighted by Parson's autopsy."

But Sarah had subsided. "You know," she said, "I think we're both living on at least three levels. At least I am. It's like having a multiple personality disorder. First, there's my everyday life—teaching, feeding the dog, going to see Grandma Douglas, calling my family in Vermont. On another level I'm living in the middle of the Beaugards, tangled into that huge emotional net. We may not have started out as bona fide 'friends of the family,' but we are now. Whether we like it or not. Whether we like *them* or not. After all, some of the Beaugards may have alienated the entire neighborhood, and we're fresh fodder. But I am sorry for them all. Talk about your family stew."

Alex shook his head. "But taken individually, not beyond recall. Mrs. Beaugard marches on, a little damaged but intact. Masha has her musical life, Alice doesn't seem to be drinking, Eliot is obviously in good shape, Caroline doubtful, but Professor Lenox is perking up. Seems sharper, less fuddled. And the Jonathan reading scheme seems to be working out. Good for both of them. Couple of ego types having to make do together. So what's the third part of your personality disorder?"

"That," said Sarah, "is a side of me I like to pretend doesn't exist. It's Sarah the Nosy Parker. Sarah the machine, sifting facts, making comparisons. Collecting trivia, asking questions."

"What questions, for instance?"

"Okay, here's a sample. Why did Alice take only a few of those illustrated books? It could have been a steady source of income at a time she badly needed money. Yes, Dolly caught her at it, but why not try again? And then how about Mrs. Beaugard and this estate-planning business tomorrow? What's she up to? Doesn't sound like a blueprint for family harmony. Think of the trouble things like that cause. At least it does in Agatha Christie novels. And what's with Eliot? Is he really concerned only for his mother's welfare? Wanting to be helpful handling her accounts? And my God, Caroline, what's eating her? Is she a space case or sniffing glue? Or had a recent lobotomy? And Vivian Lavender. The faithful housekeeper. Is that an oxymoron?"

Alex, now frowning at an approaching snowplow, simply made an assenting motion with his head and then, after the plow had added a sheet of snow to the windshield, cursed, flicked on his wipers, and said, "Okay, beloved. You may now return to personality one. The feeding of our dog, the preparation for the bed, the thoughts for the morrow. Sunday. You can correct papers and shuffle about in the snow and I'll be in Augusta viewing—as they say—the remains."

"Parson Gattling," mused Sarah. "Such an oddity. What do you think? A latter-day prophet or just a public nuisance?"

"Something the pathologist won't concern himself with. Just the blunt instrument. Its size, shape, material, weight, height. How delivered. With what force. From which angle. From above or below or from the hip. Backhand, forehand, left hand, right. Or by tooth and claw."

Sarah sighed. "The pathologist's life seems so simple. Just the facts. The gruesome facts."

"The whole goddamn business is gruesome," said Alex with a sudden fervor as he swung the Jeep up the drive and jammed on the brakes. "But here's home and dog and a night's sleep."

"To knit up the raveled sleeve of you know what," said Sarah as she reached for the car door.

"Only it didn't," Alex reminded her. "Try another quote."

Sarah gave him a small smile. "'Oh sleep it is a blessed thing/beloved from pole to pole.'"

"That," said Alex, "only puts me in mind of a dead albatross and a boatload of bodies."

Chapter Twenty

THE NEXT MORNING—IT WAS Sunday—Sarah, although tempted, did not hunt about for a treatise dealing with multiple personality disorders. Instead, she let her thoughts move, albeit uneasily, from the world of academe to the more volatile world of the Beaugards, all the time trying to dampen her overdeveloped bump of curiosity. This last effort naturally proved impossible. The contradictions and crosscurrents, the three drownings and the murder of Parson Gattling, refused neglect. Thus, when Alex came home for lunch after his session at the autopsy table, Sarah demanded information.

"Not a blunt instrument," said Alex, throwing himself full length on the sofa. He was feeling particularly sorry for himself. He had really wanted nothing more of the afternoon than to consider the questionable prospects of the Boston Celtics—now with Larry Bird forever lost to them—and perhaps to start the new Elmore Leonard paperback he'd picked up the day before. But at one o'clock he had come home to five messages from his answering service on the subject of new admissions. And he wasn't supposed to be on call. Someone had blundered, the backup system had faltered.

"What do you mean it wasn't a blunt instrument?" Sarah demanded. Sarah, who had labored wrapping fruit trees, correcting papers, taking Patsy for a run in a road now slick with frozen patches of yesterday's snow, was, in Alex's opinion, not able to leave bad enough alone; he regretted bringing up the subject.

He moved a pillow under his head, pushed Patsy's cold wet nose away from his face, sighed, and then repeated himself. "Not a blunt instrument. Well, not really."

"You mean a sharp instrument?"

"No. Just not a blunt one."

"You're not making any sense."

"Neither did the pathologist, Johnny Cuzak. He seemed to think that whatever did the damage was made of a smooth heavy rounded material because there weren't a lot of bone fragments in the skull, the sort you see when something sharp is used. Like an ax or shovel."

Sarah pulled his ankles to one side and settled herself on the end of the sofa, a cup of tea balanced in one hand. "If it's not a blunt weapon or a sharp one, what are they talking about?"

"They're not. Not talking. Johnny doesn't speculate. Two things seem sure. Two blows on the head. Parson was unconscious immediately. Death shortly after the second blow."

"But smooth and rounded?"

"Or curved. Judging by the wound configurations. Beyond that, it's anyone's guess. Okay, shall I pick up some chicken for tonight on my way home from the hospital?"

"If we keep having chicken," complained Sarah, "we'll both start to cackle. But thanks, yes. We can soak it in something Japanese and add mushrooms. And now I'll probably spend from today until Christmas thinking about things round and hard. Like baseballs or field hockey balls or those giant wrecking balls they knock down buildings with. Or bowling balls." Sarah suddenly stopped. "Bowling balls! Well, why not? Perfectly round, very hard—I've dropped them on my foot—and portable. Just tuck it under your arm and when you want to use it, there are those little finger and thumb holes."

"I suppose," said Alex, "it's a perfect weapon."

"And it could be cleaned easily and put back with a bunch of other balls and rolled down an alley into the pins, accumulate lot of strange fingerprints, and no one the wiser."

Alex looked at her with respect. "You know, Sarah, you have a talent for coming up with oddities. I'll bet George and Johnny haven't even considered bowling balls."

"It's a wild stab. Didn't Jonathan say his executioner figure was clutching something to his stomach? So let's see if we can find out who bowls. Which of the Beaugards. The Gattlings. Vivian Lavender. Whether any bowling alleys are missing balls."

"People have their own bowling balls. They have their names on them, keep them in special bags."

"Whatever," said Sarah impatiently. "But after using the ball as a weapon, it could be put back in the alley, as I said, or it could be deep-sixed anywhere along the coast. But I think the subject is worth a little amateur effort."

Alex picked up *The Boston Globe* Sunday edition from its scattered position on the floor and shook out the sports section. "I'll call George and see if he likes the idea. You, my dearest love, please stay put and wrap fruit trees."

"I've done that. What I need is a little drive into town."

But Alex wasn't listening. He had unfolded the sports section and was deep into the convoluted world of the Celtics.

So Sarah pulled on a jacket, loaded Patsy in the car, and drove directly to The Happy Family Lanes outside of Rockland.

"What d'ya mean you don' wanna bowl?" demanded the stubby hirsute manager whose name just happened to be Eddie

Gattling. This unnerving fact caused in Sarah a brief shiver, but swallowing hard, she persisted.

"I'd like to look at the balls, see if I can lift them. In case I want to take it up. My husband loves to bowl," lied Sarah, "and I'd like to join him. If the ball isn't too heavy."

"Hey, no problem," said Eddie. "Lots of ladies bowl like almost seven days a week. It's a big thing for ladies. They got leagues and auxiliaries and teams. Special shirts embroidered with your name and league colors. Go to Rockland Embroidery. Say Eddie sent you. Manager's my cousin. Ten percent off. Shoes, too. You're gonna need shoes. And listen, we got balls all weights. Kids' balls, too. You name it."

"I have a sore arm, an accident," said Sarah, thinking she might as well go all out in the matter. "I'd need a lightweight ball. Do you know the different weights?"

"Didn't I tell you," said Eddie, "ladies' balls? An easy lift. Or kids' balls. Designer colors. Pink and blue. Sort of marbled like. And finger holes for ladies' fingers. Hey, let's try you out. Come on over here and we'll just see how you do. A pair of shoes, we rent 'em. You can try a few balls. See how it feels. Just don't dump the ball down hard. Let 'er roll. Follow through. Eye on the pins. Watch me once. Footwork is half the game."

Sarah's friendship with Eddie Gattling was cemented twenty minutes later after six gutter balls followed by two strikes and a split. After which Sarah admitted that she expected to bowl not only with her husband but with her close friends Alice Beaugard and Webb Gattling. Well, why not? she told herself. The way things are going, I wouldn't be surprised to find myself bowling or on a high wire or leaving for Fiji with the two of them.

Webb's name produced the desired effect.

"Hey, he's my cousin. On my dad's side. Webb's built like a gorilla. What an arm. Listen, if he wanted, hell, he could clean up bowling. Go on the tour. But that ain't his interest. And that Alice, she's not too bad. Just sorta scatterbrained."

Half an hour later, Sarah, now Eddie Gattling's future protégée—"hey, you got a good eye on you"—left Happy Family

Lanes with the promise to come back with her hotshot bowler husband and maybe Alice and Webb, "to try out that pink ball."

From the bowling alley, Sarah, with Patsy slumbering comfortably in the backseat, took herself to the town of Camden and the AbaCaDaBra Bookshop, a well-known institution dealing in secondhand, out-of-print, and, in a locked room, rare books.

Once in, Sarah ferreted out the manager, Mr. Rafferty, a small man with a goatee and gold-rimmed glasses wearing a striped apron. To him she described herself as an ardent fan of illustrated books. A fan who wanted to start a collection. First editions. Signed editions. Extra illustrated editions. For instance, did they have any Oz books?

"I hope," said Mr. Rafferty severely, "you have some idea of what beginning such a collection will cost?"

"Money," said Sarah, now a slave to untruth, "is no problem. I just don't know quite how to begin. Children's books, I suppose, are the best source."

"They are a good source, but not the only one," said the man. "The Oz books—first editions with dust wrapper intact—have gone out of sight."

"How far out of sight?" asked Sarah.

"We're talking three, four, five thousand dollars," said the man. "*Ozma of Oz*, first edition with a dust jacket, just brought well over four thousand dollars at auction. A second printing. And you're interested no doubt in first printings."

Sarah acknowledged that first printings were of the utmost importance to her. And she did want them signed.

An hour later, Mr. Rafferty had turned quite red with excitement. The locked door of the rare-book room was unlocked and Sarah had been given a full view of the shop's high-priced spread. Very high-priced. Sarah was shocked.

Finally, after much backing and filling and expressions of admiration and wonder, Sarah extricated herself on the excuse of a consultation with her husband, who was also very interested. Alex is so useful, she thought, especially when he isn't around.

Feeling fulfilled, she returned home, dragged Patsy on a second walk up Sawmill Road, and presented Alex with a summary of her day's efforts.

Alex eyed her with annoyance. "I've told George about your bowling ball idea. He said you're to avoid any investigatory visits and not to join a bowling league. Especially don't ask about who bowls where and when. You have his permission to think about other round portable objects. Johnny thinks the thing must have weighed something over ten pounds and been delivered with considerable force from a strong right hand."

"Bowlers," said Sarah, "sometimes have arms like John Henry."

"Or Webb Gattling?" suggested Alex.

"But," said Sarah, changing direction, "you don't have to be a John Henry. Or Webb Gattling. Bowling balls come in all weights. They have lighter women's and kids' models. Pink and blue with a marbled effect. Very fetching."

"George," said Alex, "is now researching alleys and the whole scene. Private bowlers, teams, leagues, collectors of old balls—there are such—but he thanks you for your continued interest."

"My continued interest has also dragged me over to a rare book dealer in Camden. Illustrated editions, eighteenth, nineteenth and early twentieth in good condition, signed, with dust jackets, are big bucks. Enough of them could furnish a chapel or two."

"Why not come to the obvious conclusion? Mrs. Beaugard dipped into the collection. Along with Alice and maybe the rest of the bunch from time to time. But first and foremost, Mrs. Beaugard."

"Encouraged by Saint Dolly, who handled the marketing end. I'll have to see if Mr. Rafferty remembers her. He's my new friend. I'm the customer to whom price is no consideration and who wants to start a collection of illustrated books. First editions, first printings. Dust wrappers. Signed. The very best."

In the days that followed, winter established itself with two more short snowstorms followed by a freeze, a sleet storm, a lengthy thaw, and then a dip by the thermometer into the single digits. With the increasing rawness of the weather in midcoast Maine, the faces of its inhabitants began to assume that look of grim endurance that characterizes the visages of northern peoples from November through the frozen mud season of March. The fact that the *Farmer's Almanac* had predicted a mild and pleasant winter with southern zephyrs did nothing to soften local tempers.

But Sarah hardly noticed that November had tightened its grip; the weather, compared to what was going on in her life and the lives of her dear friends the Beaugards, was simply a damned nuisance. She brought out her quilted coat, oiled the leather of her winter boots, pulled on her knitted hat, and trudged forth from classroom to classroom, from her Grandmother Douglas's to the living room of the Beaugards, and from time to time dropped into a bowling center to admire the variety of balls on sale or for rent, and to a number of secondhand bookshops to inquire about the availability of first editions of illustrated books. And sometimes, when both their schedules permitted—as on a certain mid-November Wednesday—Sarah made it to the hospital cafeteria to meet Alex for lunch and compare notes on things temporal and spiritual.

"Turkey loaf today," said Alex. "And fun in the afternoon. Office hours and another house call to make on Mrs. B. She's complaining of weak spells, feeling a little dizzy. Thinks Jonathan's shoulder isn't much better. Which, of course, it isn't, what with throwing himself on the ground the way he did. He's stuck in his sling for another few weeks or so. And I'm supposed to check up on Uncle Lenox, who seems to be better and brighter."

"That's supposed to be a good sign."

"Son Eliot—this from Mrs. B.—feels it's a bad one. The light before the dark or some such garbage. I think Eliot is dying to stick Lenox in a nursing home and get him out of the family manse. He seems to think his mother defers to brother Lenox and not to him. Eliot isn't used to being number two. But actually, I need to talk to the professor. He's supposed to be putting together this Christmas Bird Count business, but I doubt if he's up to it. I think the whole thing should be turned over to Eliot, who's done it for years as Lenox Cobb's second-in-command. They usually split the Proffit Point territory. Eliot takes the north and Lenox the south."

"You just said Lenox was much better. Let him get on with it. Why trouble trouble? Getting caught between family cross fire."

"Better doesn't mean perfect. He wants to go out in the field and do the actual count with a team. This in December, which usually features blasts of wind and snow. He'd be spending six or seven hours slogging about in it."

"He won't take it kindly if you ground him."

"I'm not going to ground him out of hand. Just suggest that he take it easy. Cover only part of the territory. He'll snarl and I'll change the subject. But the idea will be planted. Anyway, I probably won't make it home until after six."

"And guess who's coming for dinner. Actually, they're bringing the dinner."

"Surprise me. No, don't. It's our new buddies, Webb with his bowling arm and Alice, probably with her monogrammed bowling ball. Okay, who needs a quiet evening?"

"Webb might be helpful, because I'd like to know more about Parson," said Sarah. "Whether he was simply a religious nut, or paranoid, or privy to special information. Did he actually know Dolly, and was he the real link between the two families? I don't think Webb is the link. He seems too straightforward."

"Are you saying Webb is uncomplicated? That uncomplicated doesn't mean trouble? You're thinking in stereotypes, which is something I'm sure you tell your students never to do.

You have this picture of Webb as John Henry, Paul Bunyan, or the Jolly Green Giant. A muscleman unable to do more than bed Alice and lift weights. But not someone—because he's so uncomplicated—who can bash cousin Parson over the head or tote lead sailboat ballast or spike a bottle of whiskey with Valium. Here's what I think. You've taken to Webb Gattling and have a sneaking old-time fondness for Alice, so you'll be damned if they have anything to do with murder."

"That," said Sarah, "is complete hogwash. I'm being completely objective."

"Right, sure," said Alex. But Sarah had picked up her briefcase and was walking rapidly to the door of the cafeteria.

As predicted, Professor Cobb would not hear of any curtailing of his efforts regarding the forthcoming Christmas count. Alex had finished examining Mrs. Beaugard, expressed sympathy for her spells of feeling "weak and dizzy," and suggested a workup at the hospital clinic sometime in December. Following this, Lenox Cobb was tracked down in the library together with Jonathan. The boy was explaining why *Robinson Crusoe* (Lenox's choice) was a really totally lousy book but might make an okay movie. If Jonathan had the job of cinematography and was in charge of the casting, the lighting, the script, and special effects.

But the subject of the Christmas count, once broached, brought vehement response from the professor. "You're in league with Eliot. You think I'm too old and out of my head because of that concussion. Want to put me in restraints and cart me off to a nursing home. Well, I am damned if you're going to. Eliot can work with the north Proffit Point people and stay out of my hair. You, Alex, can help me with the South team. Elena will watch her birdfeeders and keep track of the different species that come there to feed. Jonathan can help her. His eyesight is excellent and it is not beyond his capability to identify a common bird."

"Jonathan," said Jonathan, "doesn't know a bird from a bird nest. So I won't."

"We shall see about that," said Lenox Cobb, with a look at the boy. "Your school wants you to do a biology project while you're stuck here. A bit of ornithology ought to take care of the matter."

"The only good bird is a dead bird," said Jonathan. "I want to dissect a dead bird. All its organs and digestive canals. That'll make a great project."

Lenox wisely ignored this passage, and Alex made one more try. "Professor Cobb, if the day of the count is clear, the sun out and no wind, well, maybe you could go out for a few hours. But if we have a stinker of a nor-easter, something like that, think about staying home and helping with the feeder count."

"That suggestion," said Lenox, "is totally unacceptable."

And Alex let it rest and took his leave.

The evening found Sarah and Alex and their buddies Alice and Webb making an evening of it at Happy Family Lanes. Sarah had suggested it over dessert, and Alice was enthusiastic.

"You mean," said Sarah, "you bowl? You know how?"

"Of course. My father loved to bowl. We had our own alley at Great Oaks, though now it's used for storage. It's out behind the vegetable garden attached to the potting beds. Duckpins, we called them. Or candlepins. My father felt it kept us safe at home. But when we kids were older, had wheels, we'd escape and go and do real bowling in Rockland."

"You were serious about bowling!" Sarah exclaimed.

"Hey, Sarah, I'm not serious about anything," said Alice. "But bowling was sort of a cool thing to do. It wasn't fashionable like tennis or sailing, and Mother always thought the commercial alleys attracted scumbags."

"Scumbags like me," put in Webb, who was polishing off his second piece of squash pie.

"Dolly even had her own ball," said Alice. "She kept it in a blue canvas bag with her monogram. A real Dolly touch. The rest of us just used the balls of the alley."

"Her own ball?" said Sarah.

"Yeah. Her very own. Fitted. Dolly had small stubby fingers and said she had to have her own ball."

"Where is her ball now?" asked Sarah, trying to make the question offhand, careless.

"God knows. Maybe Sergeant Fitts impounded it with the rest of her stuff. Maybe he's a bowler. Actually, I heard that Dolly tried to start a hospital league, but it fell through and she gave up the game. Anyway, even if she did have her own ball, she was always better at candlepins because the ball is smaller. Lighter."

Sarah, who was now gathering coffee cups and stacking them on a tray, paused and absorbed this piece of information. But Alex, who read Sarah's mind, answered the unasked question. "Smaller, lighter, and no finger holes."

"So," said Sarah slowly, "you wouldn't have much control with a ball like that. It would be slippery, wouldn't it?"

"Honestly, Sarah," said Alice. "You kill me. What are you planning to do with it? Go fishing? Juggle it? You just throw the damn thing down the alley at these thin pins. Candlepin bowling in Maine is big. Where've you been all these years? You're culturally deprived, that's what you are."

"Let's get going," said Alex. "We'll bowl for an hour and that's it. I've got a heavy day tomorrow."

And Sarah, wrestling with the idea of two types of bowling balls, simply nodded, promising herself to check up on the world of candlepin bowling at some future date. In the meantime she had neglected Parson Gattling. It had not seemed proper to introduce the subject during dinner. After all, digestion came first, and Parson's death was a singularly bloody event. But now it was time. Sarah made a point of making Alice sit in the front seat of the Jeep with Alex and she plunked herself down in the small space left by Webb's bulk in the rear seat.

"We're still so sorry about Parson," she began. "I never knew him."

"Well, why would you?" said Webb unhelpfully. "Being a Gattling and all that. But listen, no one knew Parson. None of us did. Always was on the weird side. Think it was his name. I mean, if your parents name you Parson, isn't that asking for trouble?"

Alice twisted around from the front seat. "Parson thought he had a sort of mission. To testify. But no one was ever sure what he was testifying about. One minute he was in a lather about the size of lobsters, and the next he was standing on the street corner with signs about gays in the Boy Scouts—or not in the Boy Scouts, I can't remember which, maybe both. And then for a while he went on about God not being dead."

"You got it wrong," said Webb. "God was dead in New York and Boston and California. In Chicago. But he was alive in Texas, Canada, Maine, and parts of Vermont. Maybe in New Hampshire."

"So," said Sarah, "you'd say he ruffled some feathers."

"Ruffled," roared Webb. "He goddamn plucked feathers out by the root. By the handful. Wasn't a family around that hasn't been riled up by Parson some time or other, felt he was kicking their ass. Of course, Parson didn't kick. He sort of mourned and chanted and hung around looking like some kind of hound dog. The Beaugards were his last project. Parson, he got all steamed up when Marsden and Junior washed in at Little Cove. And then with Dolly Beaugard drowning about the same time, well, he added two and two and came up with…"

"Four?" suggested Sarah.

"More like thirteen," said Webb. "None of Parson's ideas added up to much more than making people mad as hornets. I guess it sorta caught up with him, more's the pity. Hey, Alex, watch it, the alley's right there on the left."

And with that summary, Sarah, for the time being, had to be content. Bowling became the feature of the evening, and as time went on, she found her attention more and more centered on bowling balls, the ease with which the fingers slipped into their holes and gripped the ball, the size of Webb Gattling's biceps and forearm, the force with which his ball left his hand and smashed into the pins. And the accuracy and skill with which skinny Alice Beaugard hurled a man's ball down the alley.

Chapter Twenty-One

SARAH, DISTRACTED BY THE picture she had conjured of a black-clad assassin in a ski mask creeping through the woods clutching a bowling ball, had little time to speculate on other aspects of what she thought of as the Beaugard-Gattling stew. Further, the approach of midterm exams at Bowmouth College, the threat of Thanksgiving dinner at Grandmother Douglas's, complete with a number of distant and eccentric relatives, plus the apparent need of Alice and Webb to drop in without notice, all contrived to fill her waking thoughts. In fact, it wasn't until Sarah had picked up her grandmother from her weekly trip to the hairdresser's on the Monday before Thanksgiving that another aspect of the Beaugard saga came to light. An aspect that she, Sarah, had completely forgotten.

Her grandmother, belted and settled in the passenger seat, her fine-spun white hair newly shampooed and fastened into its net, showed signs of not wanting to go immediately home.

"I would love to have a drive," she announced. "That is, if you're not too busy. Somewhere out in the country."

Sarah nodded. Luckily she had nothing going on beyond the usual paper correcting and the ongoing speculation about bowling balls.

But it appeared that there was more than scenery on Mrs. Douglas's mind. The drive was a pretext, and Sarah was amused to find that her stern grandmother was not above a little spate of gossip. The Beaugards. And who else? Sarah said to herself.

"I had tea with Elena Beaugard," began Mrs. Douglas. "Eliot dropped her off on Sunday afternoon for a visit. She is a difficult woman, but I do feel sorry for her. That business of the dreadful Gattling person."

"Which dreadful Gattling person?" asked Sarah. She turned the car in the direction of the Camden Hills. The drive promised to be a lengthy one.

"That man who stood around holding up placards. A name like Preacher or Parson. Elena could talk of nothing else. A murder at her very gates, coming so soon after Dolly's death. Elena is trying to put her life together, which is not easy because Alice is such a worry. She's been seen in the company of some sort of backwoods person. A lumberjack. And then Elena has the boy Jonathan at home all day because of his accident. And Lenox Cobb underfoot."

"But Mrs. Beaugard is coping?" said Sarah.

"She is trying to. She has been seeing her lawyer and is following through on the plans Dolly made with her for the estate. She feels that this will be a memorial to Dolly."

"I'd say the Beaugard Room at St. Paul's-by-the-Sea and the Beaugard Chapel at the hospital and the paintings given to the art galleries add up to quite a clutch of Dolly memorials."

"That remark, Sarah," said her grandmother, "shows a mean spirit. Those are gifts from the whole Beaugard family—although I must say Elena seemed a bit surprised at the extent of the furnishings. The stained-glass windows and the kitchen, the new pews at the hospital. But I suppose Elena's memory isn't quite what it was or Dolly hadn't made the details clear."

"And this estate plan?" prompted Sarah.

"The carrying out of Dolly's plans is to be a memorial to Dolly alone. Sarah, where are you going?"

"I thought I'd drive you up Mount Battle and you can see over Penobscot Bay. The roads are pretty clear and I have four-wheel drive."

This idea deflected the description of Dolly's estate plan, and it wasn't until Mrs. Douglas had viewed from the safety of a heated car the dark waters and darker islands stretching before them, had recited Edna St. Vincent Millay's poem about three tall mountains and a wood, and they had started the drive down the mountain road that Sarah was able to remind her grandmother.

"Quite extensive, the whole plan. Dolly's interests are to be remembered. The barn and cottages and the dock at Little Cove to the Audubon Society for a nature camp. To be shared with the Girl Scouts. And a piece of land and three cottages on Back Cove together with the boathouse for a summer art center."

"And no objections? How about access to the beach? Is the whole shoreline being gobbled up?" demanded Sarah, now seeing the Beaugard heirs barred from the ocean.

"Not gobbled," said Mrs. Douglas. "Given for the public use. In the true spirit of Christian giving. And the family members will retain the use of the Little Cove Beach, which stands below Alice Beaugard's cottage. We had picnics there in the old days when your grandfather and Arthur Beaugard were alive."

Before Mrs. Douglas could lose herself in nostalgia, Sarah brought up the subject of the two docks. "Won't the family need a float and moorings and a place to land a boat?"

"No one in the family has need of anything more than a little skiff that can be pulled up on the beach. No one sailed but Dolly. And besides, I am sure the Audubon people and the Scouts will allow the family to make landings if needed."

"Eliot sails," Sarah reminded her. "That big baby called the *Goshawk*."

"You have not been paying attention, Sarah. You know that Eliot has docking facilities at his own cove."

"Is Vivian Lavender going to be turned out?"

"A pension and the single gift of a large sum at Mrs. Beaugard's death. But, quite heartening, did you know that Mrs. Lavender has been taking instruction?"

"In what?"

"The Anglican Church. From Father Smythe. After much searching, she has brought herself to see a wider truth, a more liberal and kindly way to God. The Episcopal Church. It is an heroic step. Leaving the Roman Catholics. She will be taken into the congregation the Sunday after Thanksgiving. I have met her several times in the fellowship hour after the service. And I pride myself—in a very small way—that I helped her to the light. She was quite disturbed by the idea of a woman priest—an idea to which I myself have hardly become accustomed—but I told her that God moves in mysterious ways His wonders to perform."

"That did it?" said Sarah, surprised. "Women priests for someone who's been a sturdy RC from the word go seems quite a lump to swallow. I mean, talk about indigestion."

"Sarah, instead of making smart remarks, I suggest you concentrate on your driving. If you would spend a portion of the time you devote to unseemly activities in attending church—any reputable church, by which I do not mean congregations that speak in tongues or claim to be saved—you might comprehend what I am saying. Mrs. Lavender is to be commended and her decision celebrated."

And Sarah, her mind too busy with Dolly's estate plan to be annoyed, turned the car and did as her grandmother requested.

That evening, Thanksgiving reared its festive head. A telephone call from Mrs. Douglas's faithful Hopkins brought the news that Sarah's grandmother had had a slight fainting spell; her physician had ordered rest and quiet and the cancellation of the forthcoming dinner. But, added Hopkins, her grandmother was distressed at the thought of Sarah and Alex without a place to go on Thanksgiving and had called Mrs. Beaugard and it was all arranged. They were expected to join the Beaugards in their celebration.

"Oh shit," said Sarah, hanging up the telephone and turning to Alex. "Thanksgiving. Well, shit."

"If the Pilgrims could only hear you. You'd be in stocks for a year. What's the matter?"

Sarah told him, adding, "We can't even use our family. Your mother and father are going to Montreal, and my parents are off in Chicago with Aunt Julia in tow. And Tony…" Here she paused. The idea that her footloose brother would ever be in one place long enough to plan a meal seemed unlikely.

"Forget Tony. You're stuck. Stuck but good."

"*We* are stuck," said Sarah. "Not just me."

"I may be on call on Thanksgiving."

"The hell you are. I've seen your schedule. And don't go offering to take over for some other doctor. Okay, we can stick it out because it might be interesting to see if Mrs. Beaugard's estate plans have rattled any cages, see if it's on the menu."

"The Beaugards certainly won't talk about anything so personal on Thanksgiving. What are we supposed to bring? Cranberry sauce or celery sticks or something major?"

Sarah made a face. "The turkey. We won the jackpot. Twenty-two pounds at least. Don't ever say Mrs. Beaugard is careless about money."

"Nor is she one to talk about it. That estate plan of hers will not be on the table. Believe me."

Driving through a new spate of what weatherpersons call "mixed precipitation," a term that covered a simultaneous fall of ice, sleet, rain, and snow, Sarah and Alex agreed that their

Thanksgiving job was to act as go-betweens to the various Beaugards. But, as Sarah pointed out, since sailing, the church, sickness, divorce, death in any form, and the estate itself were forbidden subjects, they had better stick to neutral subjects like the meaning of Thanksgiving. "I'm in my best Calvin Klein copy dress and shoes that pinch like hell, but I suppose it's in a good cause."

"The cause is to prevent a Thanksgiving Day massacre among the Beaugards—a family in your opinion rivaling the Borgias."

Sarah ignored this remark and confined herself to hoping that the turkey was well done. Here she leaned over the car seat and examined a savory-smelling foil-wrapped object that lay cradled in a laundry basket.

The two began their Thanksgiving visit seated well apart from each other in the vast living room of the Great Oaks house with its forest of chairs and odd tables and stray sofas, its large mantelpiece oil portrait of the four Beaugard children in their antique summer clothes brooding over the gathering.

On later consultation, Sarah and Alex could both testify that Great Oaks' estate plan was indeed the feature of the evening. Mrs. Beaugard's—or rather Dolly's—plan was not only on the table, it was served with drinks and hors d'oeuvres, it appeared with the mushroom soup, it strove for attention with the turkey, the creamed onions, the mashed chestnuts, the glazed carrots, it got equal time with the mince and pumpkin pies, the sorbet, the Stilton and water biscuits, and it lingered over the coffee.

In fact, at the very moment of the guests' arrival there had been not a moment's hesitation before the subject was brought out like a newborn baby for all to admire. A plan apparently viewed with gladness—almost jubilation—on all sides. It was, thought Sarah, sipping gingerly at her sherry—not a favorite drink—as if the prayers of the entire family had been answered. At least this was her initial impression when the buzz and hum about the plan began bubbling up in all corners of the room. And not a single Beaugard was showing any reticence in bringing the subject to the surface.

"Well, it's all settled," said Eliot, seating himself by Sarah, a martini in one hand. "An estate plan that does Dolly proud, which is what Mother wanted."

"Including the Episcopal Church, from what my grandmother said," put in Sarah, abandoning any idea of staying away from the subject. "Your mother told her about it."

"That was all arranged last spring, but the church is only a piece of the action. But now the Audubon and the Scouts and the art community will have a slice."

"All Dolly's favorite projects," observed Sarah.

"Mother's, too. Mother and Dolly were pretty close in their interests. And Mother's none too well, you know. Breathing problems, her eyes, her arthritis. Let's face it, she may not have many more years, and now she can relax knowing that Great Oaks won't be turned into a condo development or a fish factory. In January we'll help her move into one of the estate cottages. All on one floor with a nice view and a room for a nurse if she needs one."

"And her brother, Professor Cobb?"

"A winterized cottage nearby. Perfect. Just close enough, but they won't be on top of each other."

"And you're not worried about Back Cove and Little Cove taken out of family hands? The docks, the floats. Moorings."

Eliot laughed. "Who needs those things? Dolly was the sailor. Oh, sure, I am, too, but I've got my own setup, and if I want to bring the *QE2* into the harbor, I'm sure the Audubon people will let me tie up. No, I'm glad the whole thing's done with and we can get back to normal life. Alice and Masha will have their space, and Vivian is taken care of."

"Jonathan seems to be an emerging sailor. Dolly's student."

"He can go right on with his sailing career. Go to camp and learn properly. Camp will do that spoiled egomaniac good. And he and Colin—that's my boy—can sail together out of our place. Mother's right when she says we can't hold the estate together for every generation to come. And now, do you really want to drink that stuff? Mother's had that sherry for years. Let me get you something else. What were you drinking at our house? Juice with rum, wasn't it, because I was out of Canadian whiskey?"

"Rum, please, if there is any," said Sarah. "I've given up on whiskey. An allergy, I think."

Settled back with a substantial dose of rum in a tall glass while Eliot bustled off to take care of Father Smythe's refill, Sarah found herself joined by Masha. Masha with gold earrings and in a high-necked claret-colored dress that swept the floor. Probably, Sarah decided, the perfect recorder concert costume.

"Hello, Sarah. I've been meaning to come over and say hello, but Father Smythe trapped me. Wants our group to play next Sunday in church. Not giving us much notice. And he's on his third whiskey." Here Masha took a delicate sip from a wineglass. "Anyway, what do you think of our news? Great Oaks is to be the Dolly Beaugard memorial. I hope those organizations can get along without fighting, but it's no skin off our backs if they don't." She seemed suddenly bored with the subject and rose to her feet. "I'd better see what's going on in the kitchen." Then she bent over and lowered her voice. "I can't say that I'm not disappointed that one hunk of land and one cottage couldn't have gone for music. A summer fellowship program with a resident musician. Oh well, I suppose it's good that the dust has settled and we can stop fussing about the place."

And so it went.

Alex found himself the recipient of the same sentiments expressed to Sarah. Eliot had told him that it was all for the best and that he wished he could have been on the ground floor of the planning, but that was Mother for you. Next, Alice perched briefly on the edge of Alex's chair. Her holiday costume resembled an ensemble associated with early Diane Keaton movies: baggy pin-striped trousers and a wide flowered necktie. She, speaking in a hoarse stage whisper, told Alex she was bloody well tired of the whole business and was glad it was down in black and white. All that needed doing was the final drawing up of the plan. Buildings, boundaries, goods and chattels, all that crap. The whole thing should be wrapped up after New Year's. And she, Alice, was happy that the family could get on with what they did best. Normal everyday bickering and in-your-face activities.

Professor Lenox Cobb, in ancient tweeds, stick tapping, moved Alice from her perch, waved her to another part of the room, and planted himself on a straight chair facing Alex. In general he agreed with Alice, although not in the same words. It was high time that Elena made a decision about the estate. She was not in the best of health. The new estate plan wasn't one that he might have made. He, Lenox, might have considered Bowmouth College as a proper recipient of a piece of the land, but then, Elena had never listened to him. If he hadn't had that accident, had been able to function in the period after Dolly's death, things might have been different. But now that the business was decided, well, he for one accepted it. "Now, Alex, I want to discuss the Christmas count with you as I fully expect to take my place in the field. You must bring your telescope. We are always short of telescopes."

The theme of satisfaction expressed during the drink period persisted through the dinner itself—this served from the sideboard since Tad Bugelski's daughter Sharon, brought in to help in the kitchen, could not be asked to serve, and Vivian Lavender had joined the family in the role of a guest. One by one the celebrants settled about a long table made festive with mounded fruit and yellow chrysanthemums. Then over steaming basins of mushroom soup—"Aunt Ethel's Spode," announced Mrs. Beaugard—Father Smythe kicked off with grace. But even the Thanksgiving grace was not immune to the estate settlement fever. Oblique reference was made to the plan so that the general thanks to the Lord was backlighted by the example of Dolly Beaugard as a Christian woman and the generosity of Mrs. Beaugard in the arrangement of her worldly goods. Amen.

Sarah found herself flanked on one side by Father Smythe's hard-of-hearing wife, and on the other by Jonathan. Facing them was Caroline Beaugard—who just as well might have been mute as well as deaf for all the conversation she generated—and Eliot and Caroline's son, Colin, the nine-year-old cousin of Jonathan.

Jonathan, having expressed his opinion of first the mushroom soup, then the creamed onions, and now the mince pie, put down his fork and, leaning over to Sarah, whispered that he thought the whole estate plan sucked. "It just stinks. Where's the dock going to be? On that rinky-dink beach? You can't haul up a sailboat with a keel on that beach."

"You don't have a sailboat with a keel," Sarah reminded him.

"Someday I will. When I'm older. And I'll need a deep-water place to keep it. With a heavy-duty mooring. There's a good holding bottom in Little Cove. Aunt Dolly told me it was."

Here cousin Colin spoke up. His fair hair was brushed back, and just as for the funeral, he had been dressed with attention to his grandmother's approbation: gray flannels, navy blazer, white shirt. But already one end of his button-down collar had come loose and a dribble of mushroom soup showed on a cuff. Normal kid, Sarah told herself.

"You don't need to get a keel boat," said Colin. "You can buy a big centerboard boat like ours and bring it almost into the beach. Or," he added magnanimously, "you can use our dock."

But Jonathan only nodded at his younger cousin and switched subjects. "I know you're an English teacher," he announced to Sarah. "Well, I've been reading these books to Uncle Lenox because his eyes were blurred because of his concussion and my school says it's an okay project if I do something with one of the books. And I wonder can you borrow some video stuff at Bowmouth. I've asked my father—he's Alan Epstein and he's teaching there—but he says he hasn't access to any. Anyway, I'd need a camcorder, one with a zoom and a macro close-up and maybe some lights."

"I guess," said Sarah slowly, "I could borrow some equipment for you. What book are you going to use?"

"That was tough," admitted Jonathan. "First I wanted to do 'The Masque of the Red Death,' but that needs a big cast. And then Uncle Lenox thought maybe the death scene in *Hamlet* with poison and swords, but we haven't read *Hamlet* yet, so I guess it'll be 'The Fall of the House of Usher' because Gran's house will make a neat setting. I can make it look all falling down and grungy without too much trouble. Will you help? We could put it on at Christmas."

"In the true spirit of Yuletide," murmured Sarah.

Jonathan grinned. "Okay, well, maybe it's not like the *Christmas Carol*, but even that had some gruesome parts in it." Here he leaned across the table. "Colin, you can be in my movie. A video really. 'The Fall of the House of Usher.' It's totally gross. You'll like it."

Colin, who had been mashing pumpkin pie with his fork, looked up and smiled. A beautiful angelic smile. Why, thought Sarah, startled, that's how Caroline would look if she would ever smile. Or speak. He's exactly like her.

"Could I?" asked Colin. "Is there a part in it for a kid?"

"We're not talking kids," said Jonathan loftily. "We'll take the men's parts. Like I said, there's a lot of really gross stuff. You can be Roderick Usher, which means acting crazy a lot of the time. I'm the person who tells what's happening. He's called the narrator. And we need Lady Madeline, who gets put in her coffin alive. Maybe my mother will be Madeline."

"You could research the costumes. Have you got illustrations in your book?" said Sarah. And instantly regretted it. Illustrated books were high on the list of subjects to be avoided.

But it was too late. Jonathan's face lit up. "Hey, sure. Grampa's collection. Our copy of Poe doesn't have any pictures, but I'll bet there's a copy in Grampa's library. Uncle Lenox"—calling across the table—"is there a copy of Edgar Allan Poe in

Grampa's collection? Colin and I are going to do a video. For Christmas vacation. In this house. We need to see illustrations to find out about the costumes."

"Just use your imagination about the costumes," said Sarah hastily, but the idea was in motion, and Alice Beaugard now entered into the scheme.

"We always used to have plays over Christmas. There's a whole trunk full of things put away in the attic. Top hats and sword belts, even uniforms."

"I don't want to do plays," said Jonathan. "I want to do a video. Sarah Deane is going to get me a camcorder and some film. We'll film a story by Edgar Allan Poe."

Here Mrs. Beaugard looked up, puzzled. "I don't remember any Christmas stories by Poe."

"Oh, we can put in some Christmas stuff," said Jonathan. "Like we could have a tree set up. And a wreath on the door. And Hanukkah candles because my dad is Jewish. I haven't decided what religion I'm going to be yet. Maybe an atheist."

"As long as you tidy up afterwards," Elena said absently, and returned to her coffee. Dinner was over, the table cleared, and the elders were finishing with coffee and brandy.

"Did Grampa have a copy of Poe in his collection?" persisted Jonathan. "So we can tell about the costumes. And the setting."

"I suppose so," said Mrs. Beaugard. "He had everything under the sun. I never saw the attraction. So many of them children's books. For a grown man... Well, it was his hobby and I tried not to interfere, though Lord knows he spent enough money on the books and those matching slipcases. We'll have to arrange for a sale when it's time to clear out this house." Then Mrs. Beaugard turned to Father Smythe. "That reminds me. I wanted you to have a book as a memory of Dolly and me. And Arthur. Something personal. Perhaps there's an illustrated Bible. A children's Bible."

"Mother," said Masha in a tense voice. "If you're giving out mementos, I'd like to choose a book."

"And," said Eliot, suddenly alert, "I wouldn't mind one of the Wyeth-illustrated ones. *Robin Hood* or *Treasure Island.*"

"*Treasure Island* is gone," announced Jonathan. "Uncle Lenox looked."

"Oh," said Eliot, eyebrows lifted. "Well, I hope nothing else is 'gone.' But *Robin Hood* will do."

Sarah stood up. "I hope you'll forgive us. It's been a wonderful Thanksgiving, but we really have to go. Thank you so much."

And here Alice scooted around the table and grabbed Sarah by the sleeve. "Oh no you don't."

"Oh yes we do," said Sarah, detaching Alice. She smiled at Mrs. Beaugard. "This is a private family thing and I know you'll forgive us. Alex, didn't you have to check in at the hospital?"

"Not that I know of," said Alex at his most aggravating.

"Alex," said Sarah between clenched teeth. "The family will be going into the library. Together with Father Smythe. To look for books. Illustrated books. Just the family."

Alex suddenly jerked his head up and Sarah saw that he had come to. Just in time. They both shook hands all round and made it to the front hall and had the door open when the first cries of outrage from the library fell upon their ears.

Chapter Twenty-Two

THE DRIVE BACK TO Sawmill Road was made hideous by sleet, slick roads, an overturned semi, and sundry cars spinning their wheels in unexpected swerves and turns.

Usually such weather would have turned Sarah tight-lipped and anxious and kept Alex silent as he peered through the snow-splattered windshield. Instead, oblivious to the weather, like escaping culprits, they found themselves prey to an unseemly amusement.

"My God," Sarah exploded, "do you think they'll start throwing empty slipcases at each other?"

"More likely grabbing the ones that still have books in them."

"And accusing each other. Yelling 'you did it.'"

"And Mrs. B. going on about Dolly's memory and her legacy, and then the awful thought will occur to her that husband Arthur…"

"About whom she seems to have had doubts..."

"Yes," agreed Alex, "there are undercurrents. Arthur away at auctions spending all that money on children's books, and he a grown man. And there've been rumors that Arthur wasn't always alone on his trips. After a murder, rumors come bubbling up like sewer gas. I heard from Mike—yesterday, in fact—that sometimes the invaluable Vivian Lavender went along to drive him. Particularly in the last few years. Like his wife, Arthur had eye problems. Look out, hang on." Here Alex made a correction in the direction of the Jeep, which had begun to slip sideways on a patch of ice toward a drainage ditch. Returned to the road, he slowed slightly. "Even four-wheel drive can't handle this stuff. Anyway, it seems that sometimes Vivian Lavender played chauffeur for the old boy."

"Vivian Lavender." Sarah ran the name around her lips. "Well, anything's possible. Or what could happen probably has. Elena Beaugard may have been an inspiring sex figure in her day, but somehow I doubt it. After all, she's Lenox Cobb's sister, and I think the Cobb blood runs cold. And Vivian is what they call 'Junoesque.' But we shouldn't leap to conclusions. Let's just say that the late Arthur Beaugard inspired doubt. At least on the subject of book auctions."

"But Arthur Beaugard was buying books, not selling them, right up until the end. By telephone, if he couldn't make it to sales." Then, as the Jeep slithered its way up the Sawmill Road hill, fishtailed up their drive, and came to rest slightly askew by the kitchen door, "We made it. Home, beautiful home."

"Let's call Mike," said Sarah, as they debarked. "See if George has found any big holes in the Great Oaks account books."

"It's Thanksgiving," Alex reminded her.

"Just try," said Sarah. "It can't hurt. But if Arthur Beaugard didn't filch his own books and Alice only took a few, and Eliot and Masha and Lenox and Vivian are clean..." She didn't finish the sentence but turned and handed Alex the telephone.

Mike was tracked down at his parents' house in Union, and even thanked Alex for calling. "You got me out of a game of Go Fish with six-year-olds."

Alex completed the call in four quick minutes of question and answer, and faced Sarah. "George has been working on it. He thinks the estate books have been cooked and money washing has been going on. Odd hunks of cash coming in. And going out."

Sarah shook her head. "It looks like everyone's been asleep at the switch. We should have guessed, but we were just befuddled by all the folderol about her."

"Saint Dolly."

"Yep. The hospital chapel, the art donations, the Beaugard Room at the Parish House. And Mrs. Beaugard being a little surprised by the extent of *her* generous gift. *Their* gift. Actually, Dolly's gift."

Alex corrected Sarah. "Not Dolly's, Arthur Beaugard's gift."

"To the greater glory of Dolly."

"What did Robert Frost say about the beauty Abishag and boughten friendship? Well, old Dolly may have done one better. Buying sainthood. The fact that she died about thirty years early only means that her reputation is set. Nothing like an untimely death to cement sainthood. And now the entire Great Oaks estate—give or take a few family cottages and the Little Cove Beach—will be the Dolly Beaugard Memorial, all a tribute to a woman who knew the value of books." Sarah was silent for a moment, and then, reluctant to let the subject rest, "What on earth is Mrs. Beaugard going to do when she realizes what her dear Dolly has done?"

But as the days counted down from Thanksgiving to Christmas, it became obvious to all concerned that Mrs. Beaugard did not realize what dear Dolly had done. Would not realize. Would not listen. Would not consider for a minute.

Alice was the first to give warning of the maternal deaf ear.

On the Friday morning following Thanksgiving, Alice, followed by Jonathan—now back on crutches—and his cousin, Colin, burst into the Sawmill Road kitchen. Alice wheeled on the two boys. "Out. Out. Go outside and wait for your ride. What I'm going to say isn't fit for your ears." She turned to Sarah, who was struggling with the trash. "The two boys are spending the day with Alan, thank God. He's picking them up. Lunch, dinner, movies, the whole bit."

With the retreat of the two cousins, Alice sounded off. "You lowlife slimeballs. You and Alex. You just took off and left us with that whole library scene. We almost had another murder—or four murders—on our hands. First I'm accused because I have the honesty to admit that I took a few books, and then Eliot begins stamping around and pulling books off the shelves, and Masha joins in, and pretty soon we're standing there yelling at each other and Mother is collapsing on the sofa and going on about Dolly's legacy and how the books belong to the estate. Then, if you can believe it, Uncle Lenox gets into the act and starts hee-hawing."

"Hee-hawing?" said Sarah.

"Chuckling. Sniggering. Making obscene noises like he was some sort of visiting hyena. And Mother's going on about feeling faint and she needs her pills and her heart won't take it—which it probably won't. And you two rats have left us holding the bag—or the bookshelves."

Sarah drew a string around the neck of a large green trash bag, strangled it with an angry tug and then swung around on Alice. "Now hear this. We didn't leave you holding any bag, we left you holding your own blasted empty bookcases. And they're empty because someone in the house besides you had very sticky fingers. Listen, we did you a favor by getting the hell out of the house."

Alice raised her eyebrows. "This is Sarah Deane, my always calm and cool buddy of school days? This whole thing must be getting to you."

Sarah swung the trash bag over her shoulder and hauled it to the back-door steps, returned, and made a face at Alice. "I've never been calm and cool. It was an act. At school I was scared stiff about some of the messes you got us both into, but I was always boiling over inside. Most of the time I'm your basic wimp. But I thought I should let you know that Alex and I aren't just existing to help the Beaugard family get through each day. I have a life. Alex has a life."

"And I should get a life?" Alice grinned and settled herself at the kitchen table. "Well, I'm on the way to having a life. With Webb maybe. We'll see. Anyway, Sarah, you're involved. It was pretty clear from the yells and screams last night that none of the rest of us has been dipping into rare books, and so you know as well as I do whose sticky fingers must have been turning the books into memorial windows and chapel pews."

Sarah sighed. "Yes, Alex and I think so, too. But what about your mother? Isn't she in shock?"

"We told her and she didn't listen. Eliot was standing there ready to administer oxygen. Masha wanted to call Alex to prescribe a sedative. Vivian ran to get Mother's pills. But Mother, after flopping around and hyperventilating, dug in. Dolly, how could we think it? What sort of monsters were we? Wretched jealous children. Not a word would she hear. And so forth. Total denial."

Sarah went to the counter, examined the coffeepot, and decided that there was enough for one cup of coffee for her uninvited guest. "Okay, Alice, one cup and then I've papers to correct."

"Okay, okay, I know you're a working woman and I'm a fly-by-night. Actually today is shrink day. I'm going to talk about what happens when the family saint has befouled the family shrine and the matriarch won't believe it."

Sarah came over and took the other chair. "Shrinks like denial," she said. "Gives them something to sink their teeth into."

"Mother's the one doing the denying, but she would never be caught at a shrink's. Anyway, the point, according to Eliot, is that we should lock up the bookcases, take inventory, and move on. What's done is done, says Eliot. And Masha, too. But boy, are they burned. Me, too. We've wasted all this energy admiring Dolly, the community angel."

"Go back to Lenox sniggering. Why on earth? You don't suppose he was an accessory?"

"No way. He's only just moved to Great Oaks this fall. Before that, he had his own place near the college and rarely came over. But I'd say from the way he's acting that he isn't all that surprised. Says he always knew Dolly was too good to be true, and now she's proved herself a real Beaugard. Heh-heh-heh."

"And Vivian was shocked?"

"Yes, she went all pale and dithery. I sort of got the notion that she thought that we thought she was the guilty party. You know, the lowly housekeeper augmenting her salary. But when it came clear to all of us—except Mother—that Dolly had been busy, well, Vivian was mighty enthusiastic about the idea."

"And Caroline?"

"That was peculiar. She didn't say a word. Well, Caroline never does say much, and lately she's been imitating someone who's taken a vow of silence. But anyway, she kept quiet through the whole library wingding and then she began to cry. Silently. Just tears coming down like rain. And then sort of gulping. To cut the story short, it seems she was having some sort of breakdown right there in the library in front of everyone, and it ended with Eliot driving her to the hospital. She's been admitted. Psychiatric section. That's why I have Colin. For the weekend. Maybe for longer. Which is okay since he and Jonathan are planning some Poe horror production."

Sarah nodded. "Yes, I promised to try and get some video equipment."

"Uncle Lenox is all for it. In fact, the more horrible everything gets around the house, the more Uncle Lenox seems to like it. He just seems to thrive on all the infighting. And since rescuing Jonathan from Parson's murderer, he's been positively genial. At least for him. Still a sourpuss, but not as bad as before. So now I'll leave you to think about Dolly, who may be frying instead of floating about on celestial clouds."

"I have no intention of thinking about Dolly at all," said Sarah firmly. "I don't plan to mix it up with your family until the Christmas Bird Count—if it's still going to be held."

"Of course it's going to be held, although Uncle Lenox may throttle Eliot before it happens. Two chiefs and no Indians."

"Alex and I plan to be the Indians, and you can come with us."

"Sarah, I would no more spend a December day slogging around in the snow counting feathered things than I would swim nude in the harbor. No, I'll skip that one and make Webb take me bowling. I'm getting my own ball because I'm tired of rental ones. No one, not even the police, seem to know where Dolly's ball's gone. It seems to have disappeared completely." And with this interesting statement, Alice took her leave.

Sarah was given five minutes of peace to collect empty cans and bottles and drag them to the barn for recycling classification. There, Alice's place was filled by the arrival of Mike Laaka. He settled himself on an upturned milk crate and pulled out a notebook. "Time for a little cross-checking, and I don't mean hockey. You and Alex have been sitting on some info. Not sharing like George wanted you to. I had to find out the hard way. Eliot Beaugard called last night saying some of his father's rare books are missing."

Sarah paused in the act of reading the bottom of a plastic bottle. "Okay, I knew that. Alex knew that. Alice did, and Dolly knew that Alice had lifted a few. Alex and I decided it wasn't vital information, that it was internal family stuff."

Mike regarded her in astonishment. "George Fitts would have you in cuffs for that statement. Wasn't vital? God-a-mighty, you didn't guess it might be Dolly? Eliot seems pretty sure. No proof, but he says there's a family consensus on the matter. Except for the old lady, who wants Dolly's halo to stay on her head."

Sarah had moved on to the returnable bottles and was counting. "Three dollars and five cents, ten cents, twenty, twenty-five. Okay, that's one bag full." She turned back to Mike. "Actually, Alex and I were very slow on the uptake. Figured it was probably Alice, maybe the others dipping in when they needed cash."

"George has gone wild with the estate books. Well, wild for George, which means that his machinery is whining faster than usual. Dolly's accounting system reexamined, rare book dealers visited, cash disbursements rechecked, and so far, there's an emerging pattern of cash deposited to a Parish Fund at roughly the same time as an outgo of cash listed for something called the Vicar's Fund. Followed shortly by donations to St. Paul's itself and to the other lucky institutions. None of that seemed significant early on. I mean, Dolly had her hands on all sorts of church funds, altar guilds, the St. Paul's white elephant sale—the Church Breakfast Fund—you name it. Nothing to suggest income from rare books, but that doesn't mean Dolly didn't keep track somehow. She was plenty methodical about everything else."

"So you didn't follow up on any of these church accounts? Go over them with Father Smythe or his secretary?" It was time, she thought, to take the offensive. Take the heat off Alex and herself and show up the police as derelict.

Mike shrugged. "No, that all seemed beyond an investigation into a suspicious drowning."

"Was there anything else in her accounts that struck you—or George—as weird?"

"I suppose," said Mike, "the shrewd amateur is going to nail something that the stupid police missed. Well, you won't. It's boring. Disbursement categories are stuff like household, insurance, employees, withholding taxes, clothing, health, utilities. All the usual, except for donations and charitable gifts, which, as you know, sucked up a lot of cash."

"And income?"

"What you'd expect. Trust funds, dividends, bonds, IRA withdrawals, and interest paid on savings accounts. Normal hefty income sources. Substantial payments from a trust fund, from dividends of stocks, bonds, interest paid on bank accounts. All perfectly normal income sources. Except for this Parish account."

"Does the income from the Parish account match the outgo into any of the other church accounts? The Vicar's Fund, for instance?"

"Nope," said Mike. "No match. The Vicar's Fund got small potatoes. But George is going over the whole thing to see if he can find an in-out match by combining several accounts."

"And what parish?" demanded Sarah.

"St. Paul's, we assume," said Mike. "I mean, that was the family church."

"But why is the parish giving money to the Beaugards?"

"Got me. Maybe a fund Dolly was taking care of. Maybe she acted as a holding tank. After all, she was knee-deep in everything that went on at St. Paul's. George now thinks the church might be into some hanky-panky. A real laundering scheme."

"That's plain crazy," said Sarah. "Churches don't go around doing that. Do they? I mean some of those evangelical TV guys are pretty sharp fund-raisers, but not the boring old Episcopalians."

"George will have St. Paul's down on its knees praying for mercy. If anything fits with Dolly's death or the church has started an off-track betting parlor—which I'd kind of like—George will ferret it out. So okay, we missed the pattern before, but hell, we all had a lot of stuff on our plate. God, three drownings or homicides in one weekend. We all just thought Dolly and Mrs. Beaugard were great benefactors. Mrs. B. didn't throw up her hands in horror when she visited those Beaugard rooms."

"You're right," said Sarah. "That's what fooled everybody. Mrs. Beaugard accepted the thanks and praise and smiled, and everyone thought she was part of the Lady Bountiful team. Well, she was, all right, but she didn't know that her husband's books had funded three quarters of the donations."

"Right," said Mike. "Dolly kept the Great Oaks estate books, so we assumed that Mrs. Beaugard peeked into them to see how her finances were going. Probably signed a bunch of blank checks. Hell, Mrs. B. *trusted* Dolly. She'd probably have noticed if the balance was way out of whack, but it never was. Not for long anyway. Dolly must have sold a load of books—for cash, no paper trail so far—maybe deposited the cash in this Parish Fund, then turned around and made the donation."

"Maybe the Parish Fund was managed by St. Paul's," suggested Sarah. "Maybe they even sold the books for her. Acted as a fence."

"I like it," said Mike. "I like it real well because here's another detail. So far—and of course, it's early—not a single local book dealer remembers anyone vaguely resembling Dolly coming into his shop to wheel and deal with illustrated books. George and his team hit the five or six dealers at home this morning before breakfast and got a solid negative for his trouble."

"So maybe Dolly did it by mail. New York dealers, Boston, Philly. Wherever."

"That involves checks, money orders, credit cards. Documentation, and so far we've got a blank. No, I'm crazy about the idea of St. Paul's as a fence. Beautiful!"

"You'd better keep your mouth shut or a thunder bolt will get you. Anyway, how does this whole book-lifting business change things? Assuming for sure it was Dolly. Besides tarnishing Dolly, what does it tell you about her murder? Was Dolly killed by someone in the family because she was marketing rare books from the estate, books that belonged to all of them?"

"It *is* a motive."

"Oh, come on," said Sarah. "Why not just blow the whistle on her? Exposing Dolly—watching her wriggle in public, disowned by church and hospital and art gallery, drummed out of the Girl Scouts—all that would have been a lot more satisfying to some of her siblings than a complicated sailing murder scheme."

Mike rose from his milk carton, the crossed pattern of the plastic dividers imprinted on his pants. "Yeah, I suppose I agree. Why kill Dolly when public humiliation would have been so satisfying? There's enough money to go round the family twice over. Frankly, this book thing is just another crazy knot in the plot. With or without the church. What I want is the knot that connects Parson and his murder and the Gattling brothers to the Beaugards. And I don't buy Webb Gattling as the link."

"Nothing yet?"

"Nothing solid. The lab has mislaid the samples of cloth fibers found in the Gattling skiff. George was hoping for a match with the canvas covers of the lead bars. Boy, that would be a connection we could cheer about."

"I thought," said Sarah, "that some of the Gattling tribe must have worked for the Beaugards some time or other."

"You're right, they did. Gattlings have been part of labor crews brought in to work on the docks, the floats, the moorings, to trim trees, rake driveways. Do maintenance. The whole county, as you know, is riddled with Gattlings, so it isn't surprising we've dug up some who've been on the Beaugard payroll. Some guys—including Gattling relatives—have confessed to beer given out by Vivian from time to time, but no contact with the family. Eliot apparently had a couple of Gattlings as part of a construction crew when he had his dock put in. Dolly had a crew rebuild the Little Cove boathouse, and Parson Gattling was one of them. No, don't get excited. Even if Parson turned up outside Dolly's funeral, I don't think it means a damn. So far as we can tell, none of the Gattlings or any of the other workers seem to have been on friendly terms with the Beaugards. I mean, why would they, the Beaugards being such snobs? Except for Alice. And Alice," went on Mike with a certain edge to his voice, "has the luxury of playing the free spirit, the sot, the sensitive female—

even the slightly loony one—because there's that nice squishy Beaugard money cushion behind her. Shrinks, private school for the kid, a cottage, home when she wants to come back to it. Sometimes people like Alice plain make me want to puke."

"Ease up, Mike. Alice is just one of those people who never fitted in at home or anywhere else, and now she's found Webb. Someone stable. Going out with Webb, sleeping with him, going bowling and hey, I almost forgot, Alice is buying a new bowling ball."

"So?"

"Bowling ball, bowling ball, bowling ball," shouted Sarah in exasperation as Mike turned to leave. "The weapon. Round, smooth, heavy, absolutely lethal. The perfect weapon. Well, Alice says the police haven't got Dolly's ball, and no one in the family has seen it, so she's buying a new one. So where do you suppose Dolly's ball has rolled to? I'll bet right in Proffit Point Harbor. Or out past Little Cove."

Mike's face took on a quizzical look. "Okay, so the bowling ball is a terrific round weapon, but forensics called in yesterday and they've recovered a micro-size chip of paint embedded in Parson's skull."

"Not a bowling ball chip?"

"They're looking into bowling ball composition, but this is a paint chip. Light tan. Hard paint. Or paint that goes on metal. Or marine paint. Lab tests not finished."

"Metal, marine!" Sarah almost shouted it.

"Metal. Sea hammers, pry bars, sledgehammers, wrecking balls. Marine. Seawater. Ocean. Boats, docks, hulls, masts."

"How about a painted bowling ball?"

"Sarah," said Mike, sighing heavily, "you find us a painted or retouched bowling ball or a seagoing bowling ball or a metal bowling ball, or the murderer's glove that just happened to have a fleck of paint on it. We'll all be as grateful as hell. See you." And Mike turned on his heel and departed.

Chapter Twenty-Three

SARAH WAS LEFT TO her own devices, free to attend to her student papers, to the sorting out of the books for the living room bookshelves. To the hanging of pictures, Alex's mother's watercolors, Grandmother Douglas's murky oil of sheep grazing on a blasted moor, her own favorite prints. Free to call a friend for lunch, to look up, see if Anthony Hopkins and Emma Thompson were showing somewhere. Free to go about a normal humdrum life.

Here Sarah paused in the middle of these pleasant plans, then turned and gave the plastic milk case—lately warmed by the rear of Mike Laaka—a vicious kick. So vicious that it spun across the barn and whacked into the barn door. Damnation. She wasn't free.

No way. Her other life was taking over, swarming over what was known at Bowmouth College as "Thanksgiving break."

Break, hell! The netherworld of Beaugard-Gattling violence had left her free to only contemplate a murder with something other than a bowling ball. Free to consider a church laundering scheme, to contemplate St. Paul's—or its minions—acting as a fence. Maybe the Vicar's Fund was Father Smythe's own special payoff. So much percent for each bookload sold. Like Mike, Sarah now found herself rather attracted to the idea of Father Smythe as the silver-tongued agent who slid about town with laden book bags. Father Smythe with his benevolent smile and soothing words for the bereaved. With his long white hands and his white hair and smooth-shaven face and his round white collar.

If Dolly hadn't unloaded the books in person, was it still possible that she had sold the things out of town? Had George checked to see if Dolly had made trips to the big book cities?

But what did any of this rather fascinating scenario have to do with the three drownings?

"To hell with it," said Sarah aloud. She marched out of the barn and was about to reenter the kitchen when she felt a waft of warmer air. The warm front. The weatherperson had promised a warm front, and by heaven, here it was. Probably the last warm front delivered to the state of Maine until May. Already she could see that the dirty patches of ice along the driveway edge were melting.

Okay, I'm out of here, Sarah announced to herself. Her brain needed a long rest. What she needed was movement. Action. Her bicycle. A plunge down Sawmill Road, a whirl around the campus, maybe lunch with Alex if she could find him free at the hospital. Lift those legs, tote that body, blow some air into her head.

It took only a minute. Mountain bike, bike helmet, windbreaker, gloves, water bottle. Her willing partner, Patsy. Patsy, who needed a break from tame walks over ice and snow and excursions into his dog run.

A sort of reckless excitement took charge, and Sarah screeched out onto the main road, hurtled down Sawmill Road, bounced over the ruts and cracks of an ill-paved secondary road, then crossed into the side campus road like something pursued by furies. Patsy, a giant gray wolflike presence bounding at her side.

But having survived the descent, she came a cropper on the flat. Swerving around the hospital parking lot, she hurtled down the main walking path toward the English office. Fortunately, the campus was emptied of the usual teeming student population and the first hundred yards was clear. The few pedestrians encountered jumped to one side in advance of Sarah's charge.

But at the Malcolm Adam Hall—home of the English Department—a boy flung himself out of the door and raced for the sidewalk and careened into Sarah's path. Dodging the boy, Sarah confronted another figure bent over on his crutches, and this obstacle was too much. She jerked her wheel sharply to the left, the wheel hit a root of a guardian tree, and after a brief airborne flight, she ended headfirst in a clump of decorative barberry bushes.

Extrication was painful, and Patsy's heavy licking of her face made it no easier. Untangled at last, she faced Jonathan Epstein on crutches, Colin Beaugard, the running boy, and their escort, Alan Epstein, former husband of Alice. Sitting up, trickles of blood running from her scratched face, she stared. The Beaugards. Again. Was there no safe space? "I give up," she said as she clambered painfully to her feet.

The immediate result of the encounter was a visit to the English office for washing material and Band-Aids. The end result was lunch at the student cafeteria, Sarah having given up on Alex.

Lunch had a hilarious quality. There is nothing, Sarah reflected, so likely to break ice as the sight of a damaged adult. Both boys had enjoyed Sarah's collapse, and this inclined them to chatter. Alan, preoccupied with his chicken stir-fry, pretty much let the conversation run riot.

After the boys had finished instructing Sarah in the rudiments of doing wheelies, riding without hands, and jumping ditches, the subject turned to the projected video film of "The Fall of the House of Usher." Jonathan seemed torn between working out special effects, such as having Roderick Usher grow fangs and begin to slaver midway, and developing atmosphere through a number of sound effects such as wolf howls, thunder, wailing voices, and Lady Madeline's heavy scratching as she tries to rise from her coffin.

Colin, as the unfortunate Roderick Usher, seemed fixated on everything about the video being perfect, and to this end wanted to put off the final family viewing until midwinter.

He finished the last of his french fries—dipping the last in a pool of ketchup and twirling it expertly and conveying it to his mouth. "It's my dad," he said through a mouthful. "He wants everything sort of professional. I mean, he inspects my bedroom and gives me points. And when he takes me sailing, I have to pass all these dumb tests and tie knots and figure out the course we're sailing like we were in a race or something. Like our new house. Everything had to be the best. Everything had to be perfect. Like we can't have our video look like it was done by a couple of kids."

This idea, Jonathan contested hotly.

"You try to be perfect and you're just sitting around spinning your wheels three years later. I say go for it. Creative stuff can't be made to fit into some sort of stupid rule book."

Here Alan Epstein looked up from his stir-fry. "There speaks a wise man. Listen, Colin, just get on with the project. Don't get hung up on perfect. Nobody's perfect. If I tried to write the perfect novel, I'd never have published anything."

"You just don't know Dad," said Colin. He reached for his mug of root beer and took a gulp. "He's different. Like this new sailboat that's coming. The *Gyrfalcon*. That's a big hawk. He uses bird names. Anyway, he's been yelling on the telephone to the builder and saying there's no point in launching the boat at all if it's going to be second-rate."

Sarah lifted her head. "You're selling the *Goshawk*?"

"Yeah," said Colin. "I liked her a lot, but now that Dad is going in this transatlantic thing next summer and he's the new commodore of the Proffit Point Boat Club, well, he wanted—"

"Let me guess," said Alan. "The best. The perfect boat."

Colin nodded. "Maybe that's why Mom cracked up. I mean, she's been sort of out of it for a while, but she liked the *Goshawk*. And she liked our old house at Great Oaks. It wasn't a real house, just one of the cottages, but it had three bedrooms and a new kitchen and stuff like that. Anyway, we're going to see her this afternoon." He turned to Sarah. "You want to come? She's in the psychiatric part."

"I don't think—" Sarah began, but Alan forestalled her.

"I think Caroline has trouble with conversation. That's what Alice told me. So come along and we'll all keep the ball rolling."

Later, on their way to the hospital with the two boys ahead of them, Sarah wheeling her bike and walking next to Alan, he elaborated. "Caroline's in Never-Never Land. Withdrawal. I think it all got too much for her. The perfect house, the perfect this, the perfect that. She's tried floating along on the surface for a while, but I guess she just decided it was easier to slip under. According to Alice and even allowing for Alice's over- or understatement, Caroline hasn't been with it for ages. Beautiful woman, though. Looks like one of those models photographed in a fog, looking out to sea, wrapped in blowing gauze. Actually, I think she did work as a model for a bit. Never much of a mother. Didn't want a kid at all. Said children put too much pressure on you. But Eliot wanted a child—you know, keep the Beaugard line going, though why, I can't imagine—and Caroline gave in. Colin's probably part of Eliot's picture of the perfect family. But then, Eliot hasn't got much time for him. Lucky he's a self-sufficient kid, but I'm glad to see him hang around with Jonathan. They're close in age. Both very bright."

"Won't Caroline," Sarah said, "think its odd if I turn up?"

"She won't think. Period. Any more than she'd think it odd if Alice's divorced husband turned up. Or Mickey Mouse. Or Phil Donahue. Relax and just talk about anything. Easier on the kids. Two boys can't be expected to keep up the chat with a woman who's inhabiting outer space."

The visit, like all visits to psychiatric facilities and their inmates, had the sense of taking place in a bell jar. But Sarah and Alan kept up a running conversation about weather and about the eccentricities of the Bowmouth English Department and its faculty. It was a subject that got them easily through the forty minutes while all the while Caroline sat in a turquoise vinyl chair, neatly combed and dressed in a pink cotton jumpsuit, thumbing her way through *People* magazine and occasionally directing her gaze to a framed reproduction of Monet's lily pond.

Masha Beaugard met them at the door as they left. She was carrying her recorder instrument case and looked, as usual, faintly exotic in green suede with an orange scarf around her throat.

"Any change?" asked Masha, lingering by the door, and to Alan's negative turn of the head, she nodded. "No, I suppose not. Dr. Shrank—can you believe a shrink called Shrank?—said not to expect any. Well, I'll stay for a while and go through whatever family news I can dredge up. And keep the subject away from murder and Dolly. Sarah, hey, good to see you."

Leaving the hospital, with the two boys well to the rear—Jonathan moving slowly on crutches—Alan and Sarah returned again to the pleasant business of dissecting certain aspects of the English Department, the tyranny of secretaries and the vagaries of students who flip in and out of classes, lose their texts, and respond with great self-pity if reminded of these lapses.

"But," said Alan, "I have this genius kid in one of my classes. He just laps up the stuff. Creative as hell. Working on a sci-fi short story and it's good. Rough, a little overblown, but good. Funny thing, his name is Gattling. Mark Gattling. It's as if no one can get away from the name. They're like hamsters."

"Gattlings have always been around," said Sarah, "but we haven't noticed all that much. Except when one of them is hauled into court. But now with Parson being banged on the head..."

"Jonathan keeps bringing up the Parson business," said Alan. "Made quite an impression. A boy's first murder. He can make hay out of it for years. His first novel, his first TV miniseries, his first film script. And wouldn't you know it, the murderer was in costume. Just like one of his horror comics."

"If you call a ski mask a costume."

"Jonathan calls it an executioner's suit, hood and all. To be serious, he was quite shaken. You know, I had qualms about letting him spend the winter at Great Oaks. Even with Alice on an even keel, all of them—Uncle Lenox, Caroline, Mrs. B.—remind me of the Munsters. Not your average warm and fuzzy family unit."

"Professor Cobb and Jonathan seem to have worked out a relationship," Sarah pointed out. "Reading his way through a list of a boy's Great Books. The book choices took some forbearance on Professor Cobb's part. I think the two are good for each other."

"Yeah, surprise, surprise, because Lenox can be a real grouch. And Mrs. B. when she goes into her royal mother act is tough to take. But you're right, on the whole it's working out. Even Alice seems to be working out. Webb Gattling seems solid—in all senses of the word—from what I've heard. Jonathan thinks he's okay, and that's what seems to matter. After all, I'm up to my eyebrows on this Bowmouth job, so parenting has to take second place for a while. Seeing Jonathan on weekends and during vacation breaks."

Sarah suddenly couldn't resist a question. "What was Dolly like early on? When you married Alice. When you were part of the family."

Alan raised his eyebrows. "Correction. Never part of the family. Adjunct. Barely tolerated. Mrs. B. never wanted any additions to the family tree. Including Caroline, which may be part of Caroline's trouble. It was Eliot who wanted to move off the Great Oaks estate, but Mrs. B. blamed Caroline because Eliot was the beloved and only son. Colin is welcomed—sort of—as carrying the precious Beaugard name, although Mrs. B. hardly gives Caroline credit for birthing the boy. As for me, she never made me feel welcome. She felt I came from a dubious background—my father designed swimming pools on Long Island—and I'm Jewish, not that I work very hard at it. However, I've asked Jonathan about her, and he says she's okay. But if it weren't for his wrecked shoulder and broken leg and Lenox Cobb's reading program, I'd probably yank him out of there and try and find a housekeeper."

"Dolly?" prompted Sarah.

"Oh yeah, Dolly. Look, Dolly and Eliot were the fair-haired children. Literally. Alice was off-the-wall, and Masha learned a long time ago to distance herself. Dolly was queen bee. Dolly was Mrs. B.'s rod and her staff, and now, it appears, her in-house thief."

"No absolute proof that it was Dolly," said Sarah. They had reached the English Department and had stopped at the side door.

"Good God, who else? Must have been Dolly. And if Mrs. B. isn't made to see the light, well, the entire estate is going to be turned into one giant Dolly memorial."

"But," Sarah reminded him, "none of the children seem to mind. Eliot seems happy, Masha only wishes some piece of land had been left for a summer music place, and Alice doesn't seem to care. Only Jonathan was mad. He wanted the dock and the boat facilities."

"Jonathan will survive. Speaking of which, I see the kids are almost on our necks and I promised Burger King and a horror flick."

Sarah extended her hand. "Good to see you, Alan. I really like Jonathan even in his uncouth moments."

"Thanks. He'll shape up, I hope." And with that the two boys presented themselves, and Jonathan announced that Colin had come up with the really neat idea that Roderick Usher should have fits.

"You know, seizures," said Colin. "I can roll my eyes up and hold my breath and I'm good at falling down."

"It's for the audience," Jonathan pointed out. "Part of the story is kind of slow, but if Roderick Usher has a fit right away in the first scene, it makes it more interesting. I mean, the audience will be more sympathetic to Roderick that way."

"I could foam at the mouth," said Colin. "Shaving cream. I could have a little plastic bag ready."

Sarah grimaced. "Awesome. Absolutely awesome." And she turned her bicycle and, followed by Patsy, rode away towards Sawmill Road.

From an investigatory point of view, the post-Thanksgiving week continued a period of relative stagnation, but the next Thursday, December first, brought not only a new snowfall but Mike Laaka with glad tidings. He arrived at the Mary Starbox Hospital in the late afternoon and cornered Alex as he was leaving his office.

"Wait," said Mike, "until you hear this."

"I can wait," said Alex, putting on his parka and fumbling in his pockets for gloves. "I can wait for days."

"This will make your eyes pop out."

"Try me," said Alex, waving good night to his nurse, who was busy dousing the office lights.

"Don't play indifferent with me," said Mike. "That's Sarah's act, and we all know she's panting for information. Anyway, listen to this. Guess who was handling Dolly's rare book scam. Guess who was our middleman, our fence."

"Okay," said Alex, as the two men walked down the corridor, "out with it. You'll feel better."

"Parson Gattling. The mad preacher. Seems he got the goods from Dolly all neatly wrapped and packed in small cartons and took them around to different dealers. Up and down the coast. Apparently Dolly made the arrangements by phone and Parson was the conduit. He delivered the books, picked up the cash, and took it back to Dolly. Anyway, that's how we guess it worked. Then after delivery, Parson got his cut. The Vicar's Fund. Vicar—Parson, get it?"

Alex stopped dead by the doorway. "Are you sure? That's fantastic. Parson! Parson and Dolly. Those two working together."

"Crazy, isn't it? Crazy as this whole case."

"Are you all sure it was Parson?"

"Absolutely. George added a photo of Parson to those we were taking around to book dealers and we had a one hundred percent ID from all of them. It was Parson, all right."

"Good God, how did Dolly ever dream up Parson as her delivery man?"

"Who knows? We found out—and I told you this—that Parson worked on the Back Cove dock when Dolly was having it rebuilt. Or, for all we know, he met Dolly at one of those reach-out-and-touch-someone church affairs. You know, when different churches tie themselves in knots pretending they're all just loving Christians together. But however they met, Dolly probably figured that no one would ever connect the two of them."

"If Dolly hadn't drowned, they wouldn't have," said Alex. "Okay, that's news to take home for dinner."

"One more little tidbit," said Mike. "Several fibers from the Gattling skiff—the lab's located them—match the canvas covers of the lead bars. There you are. Another Gattling connection. And one that probably finished those two beauties. They helped off-load Dolly's boat and got murdered for their trouble. Dead men tell no tales. Now we'll have to sniff out which Beaugard—if it was a Beaugard—or a Vivian Lavender, or persons unknown, hired Marsden and Junior. So how about Parson himself? That's a wild idea, isn't it?"

Alex, the bearer of hot news, was greeted by Sarah that evening with her own brand of news. She was at the kitchen table engaged in sorting through her Christmas card list, adding new names and canceling the undeserving or the deceased—the latter of which included Dolly Beaugard. "You're to call Great Oaks," she announced. "Lenox Cobb has a chest cold. Or a cough. Mrs. Beaugard is worried, and she herself is feeling a little faint."

Alex hurled his parka at the corner of the kitchen and stamped his feet. The recent spell of warm weather was a thing of the past, and along with the new snow had come a sharp-edged cold front. Ten above that night was predicted. "I suppose," he said, "that puts the lid on the professor's taking the field in the Christmas Bird Count. He's too old to take chances with a respiratory problem. But Mrs. Beaugard specializes in feeling faint, particularly when things haven't been going her way."

"You mean Dolly, whose reputation is being muddied by her jealous siblings?"

"Exactly. But now she's got another reason to feel faint. The Gattling connection has really come home to roost." And Alex delivered Mike's news, adding, "I don't know which is scariest, but maybe it's the Parson-Dolly hookup."

"The Vicar's Fund, of course. Dolly didn't have the imagination to think up a better cover name for him. And the Parish Fund. That must refer to money she gave to the church."

Alex objected. "The Parish Fund lists money taken *in*—as into Dolly's account *from* the parish, i.e., the church. And then a few days later a check for cash—a fairly small one—is made out from the Vicar's Fund and the money presumably is given to Parson Gattling. For services rendered. That still suggests complicity on the part of St. Paul's-by-the-Sea. Because the donations Dolly made later to St. Paul's and the hospital, the Scouts and galleries, are listed by name. Perfectly straightforward."

"You're making my head ache," complained Sarah. "I haven't even begun to come to grips with someone hiring Marsden and Junior to unload the ballast from Dolly's boat, and certainly can't deal with St. Paul's sending money to Dolly. Unless, of course, the books traveled from Dolly first to the church and then from the church to Parson. Isn't that the way they launder money?"

"Now you're making my head ache," said Alex. He stood up and reached for his parka. "I'll go over to Great Oaks now before the weather gets any worse. See if I can talk sense into that old coot Lenox Cobb about doing what he's told to do. When I come home I expect you to have a clear explanation of the Parish Fund for me."

And Sarah did.

"No problem," she said after dinner as the two lounged together in front of the living room fire. "Parish Fund doesn't have to mean parish. Nor St. Paul's. There are other parishes."

"Don't be cute. It's been a long day and I'm not up for anything subtle."

"Take Dolly," said Sarah.

"I did. I have. Go on."

"She wasn't supersmart. Highly organized, capable, did good works. Okay? But no student. A lousy speller, said Alice."

"You're close to boring me," said Alex with sigh.

"Not a speller. Parish, for instance. The name meant church to all of us because this whole business is tangled up with the church. But add an extra letter to Parish and what do you have?'

"You're enjoying yourself, aren't you?"

"Yes," said Sarah. "It's these little triumphs that get us through the winter. Parish can turn into Parrish. P-A-R-R-I-S-H. As in Maxfield Parrish. Noted illustrator of books. I called Alice tonight, and she said funny I should ask because Parrish was one of her father's favorite illustrators. He started his collection because he'd had one of Parrish's books as a little boy. Hawthorne's *Wonderbook*, actually."

Alex, now alert, nodded. "So the money Dolly got from selling off chunks of the collection was put in the Parish-Parrish Fund. Like Parson's payment going into the Vicar's Fund."

"You've got it," said Sarah with satisfaction. "And it may not have been a spelling mistake. Using normal spelling is a good disguise. Dolly, as we now know, was plenty devious."

For a moment the two settled back and allowed themselves to enjoy the warmth of the fire, a fire whose glow was made more welcome by the contrast it made to the snow slanting down on the living room windows.

Then Sarah roused herself. "Okay, so Dolly had a bookselling scheme that used Parson Gattling and benefited church, God, and country, but answer me this—"

Alex interrupted. "I know what you're going to say, and the idea will keep you awake."

"What I'm asking," Sarah persisted, "is not only who killed Marsden and Junior for those services rendered, but why are Parson and Dolly dead? Was it something to do with Arthur Beaugard's collection? Is there some maniac book dealer on the loose? So who killed those two? And why?"

Chapter Twenty-Four

THE NEWS OF THE Marsden-Junior role in unloading ballast from the *Sweetheart* did not reach the Beaugard homestead. But the Parson Gattling-Dolly Beaugard alliance leaked out and created a small sensation.

Eliot Beaugard, on being queried by George Fitts about his sister's cofelon, appeared genuinely flabbergasted. "Goddamn," said Eliot. "Nothing can surprise me now. Tell me Dolly ran an underground drug ring or had a job as a hooker and I won't bat an eye. But don't tell Mother."

"I understand," said George, who had already tried Mrs. Beaugard on the subject and had almost been turned from the house because of it.

"Hot spit," said Alice, when reviewing the subject over sandwiches with Sarah at the Bowmouth student cafeteria. Alice was calling on the still-incarcerated Caroline; Sarah was between classes. "I mean, holy somoli, there was more to Dolly than met the eye. Parson Gattling! Prim and proper Dolly with her own fence. But," she added, "what was that crap about the Beaugards being sinful that Parson went on about? Do you think he was mad for Dolly and had decided that one of us did her in?"

Sarah looked up from her apple crumb cake. "Anyone's guess what went on in Parson's head."

"Well, he did show up at Dolly's funeral," Alice reminded her.

True, thought Sarah later as she trudged up the stairs toward her classroom. But Parson hadn't been mourning Dolly, had he? She couldn't remember exactly what he'd said. Maybe he had assisted in her death, the ballast unloading, and was regretting it.

This untoward idea was expressed to Mike Laaka by Masha during one of Mike's continuing interviews with members of the Beaugard clan. "I think Parson did it," she announced. "Killed off Marsden and Junior because of the drug business. Parson wasn't getting his share, so he doped their whiskey. And Dolly wasn't giving him a big enough cut when here he was risking his neck carrying those books around. Maybe he even tried to blackmail her..."

"But then Dolly would have killed *him*," Mike pointed out.

Masha shook off the suggestion. "Say she resisted blackmail and that made him angry, so he just took care of her."

But Jonathan, in Mike's opinion, took the prize for suggestions. He ran into Alex on a chance meeting in the hospital—Mike was there to try and extract a few words from Caroline Beaugard on the subject. "Jonathan's idea takes the cake. As he sees it, his uncle Eliot wants all the Beaugard land so that he can turn it into an international yacht resort facility complete with clubhouse, marine shops, condos, heavy-duty moorings for sixty-foot jobs. Tennis courts, gift shops, lagoons, the works. Club Med in Maine."

"Jonathan thinks big," observed Alex. "Does he have any reason to think Eliot is thinking of constructing a resort?"

"He told me that his uncle might use the resort as cover for a worldwide smuggling center for the sort of microchips that do robot navigation for yachts. That maybe Uncle Eliot was working for the Japanese."

Alex shook his head. "I'd say Jonathan doesn't like Eliot."

"Very true. Jonathan's mad about Back Cove and Little Cove being given away in the estate plan, and he said that Uncle Eliot could stop it if he wanted to, but just because he has his own dock, he's not interested in doing anything."

The visit to Caroline Beaugard bore bitter fruit. She indicated by nods that she was not surprised about the Dolly-Parson tandem, nor at anything that happened. Asked if she had any hunches about who might be the murderer, or murderers, of the two, she spoke for the first time in days. "Why not Eliot? He makes me miserable. Everything I do is wrong. I choose the wrong colors for the rugs and the furniture. I wear the wrong clothes. I haven't any life at all. If it wasn't Eliot, it was probably Alice. She gets away with murder anyway. Why not the real thing?" And Caroline turned away and gazed out the mesh-covered window.

Vivian Lavender expressed herself to George Fitts as troubled on behalf of Mrs. Beaugard. "She needs to believe in Dolly." When reminded that Mrs. Beaugard had not accepted Dolly's guilt, he was told that "deep down she believes and it is destroying her."

"Is Mrs. Beaugard any worse, healthwise?" asked George, meeting Alex, who was making one of his increasingly frequent after-hours house calls at Great Oaks.

"Her heart's a little tricky and caused some shortness of breath, but for the rest, it's the chronic stuff—arthritis, glaucoma. But don't ride roughshod over her, George. And take it easy with Professor Cobb. He's not in the best of health, either. I'm going to take a look at him now."

Lenox was sitting up in a window-side chair wrapped in an ancient dressing gown of Oriental design, a large-print edition of *Timon of Athens* on his lap. He was coughing when

Alex appeared at the door and made a visible effort to quell the spasm. "I am much better," he announced. "I hardly cough at all. It's the smoke coming up from the kitchen. But I still can't read even large print without trouble. But I shall be in shape for the bird count."

"We'll see," said Alex, sitting down and pulling his stethoscope out of his pocket.

During the examination that followed, Lenox reverted to Topic A—the Dolly-Parson phenomenon. "I suspected Dolly from the word go. Beware of people wearing halos, is what I say. Arthur's books were just crying out for someone to snatch them. And they weren't all children's books. Some big items. An Antonio Novelli, Honoré Daumier's *Les Robert Macaire*, and a number of Cruikshanks and Rowlandsons. A William Blake, *Songs of Innocence and Experience*. Of course, I never connected Dolly with books since she was barely literate, but she certainly knew value when she saw it. I think the entire estate plan of Elena's should be scrapped. Now, about the Christmas count. We need at least to equal last year's number of sixty-six species. They saw no owls. We must try to find owls."

Alex returned home to tell Sarah that, judging from what he'd heard around town, all the members of the Beaugard family were equally guilty of murder, everyone knew Dolly was up to something, and Lenox Cobb was in no condition to go out and count birds on December seventeenth.

"Well, I've made up my mind," said Sarah. "It's Vivian Lavender. She did it all. She was Arthur Beaugard's mistress—that's almost a fact since we know she drove him around—and she hated Dolly for taking away her job security. And she's madly in love with..." Here Sarah paused.

"Go on," said Alex, "in love with..."

"Well, it would be too easy to say Eliot and like father, like son. So how about Parson Gattling? They were probably at school together, and as I've said, I think Vivian has warm blood and Parson had that mystical quality. But then he done her wrong and started playing games with Dolly. Answer: Vivian must kill Dolly and Parson. And look ahead to bedding down with Webb. Webb has that shaggy basic strongman quality, which means that Alice had better watch out. Housekeepers know everything that goes on, they're privy to family secrets, and they want wealth and power and sex because they've been denied. Okay, do you buy it?"

"Go to bed and sleep it off," said Alex.

The Midcoast Audubon Society's annual Christmas Bird Count took place as planned on December seventeenth on a crisp sixteen-degree day that followed several days of heavy snowfall. The addition of a brisk north wind meant that the birders went forth to do their counting wrapped and layered, booted and hatted, lugging telescopes, notebooks, and binoculars, looking very much like figures out of a Norse saga.

"Just why are we doing this?" demanded Sarah, struggling into her heavy-duty lined jacket. "It's only six A.M. and dark as pitch and freezing cold. Why not count birds in the spring? There are lots more around then and we'd be comfortable."

"Birds are counted then, too," said Alex, who was folding up his telescope. "It's not a sport, though it started out that way. The point is to see which species are losing ground, which species are holding their own. How many are staying around for the winter."

"More fool they," said Sarah, winding a polar fleece scarf around her neck. "Okay, what's the drill? I'm ready with my trusty pencil; you say 'hark, look, a pink-coated yellow snapper,' I write it down. Right?"

"Right," said Alex. "Now, move it. I'll fill the thermos and take the telescope, you grab the binoculars."

"I'm not going to be sighting anything," said Sarah. "But at least the whole affair is a vacation from the Beaugard machinery."

"Not entirely. I'm going to stop in and make sure Lenox Cobb stays put in the house. I've put Jonathan up to suggesting he read *The Tempest* to his uncle as consolation. The professor did his dissertation on *The Tempest*. Colin will be staying with them, and they can both read and help Mrs. Beaugard watch and count the birds that come to the feeder."

"And then?"

"Then we meet our team—with Eliot as commander in chief at the entrance gates—and go to work."

It fell out as planned. Professor Cobb, in the last stages of his cold, after token grumbling, gave in to Alex, and the assembled bird-watchers climbed into their cars and headed for the frozen wastes and frigid shores of South Proffit Point.

Sarah, standing in the shelter of a group of pines, notebook clutched in a mittened hand, watched the members of the Proffit Point team wade through a snow-filled field trying to verify a reported snowy owl. Because of the cold and the wind, the wearing of ski masks, balaclavas, and face masks was de rigueur, and they looked, she thought, exactly like Jonathan's description of Parson's murderer. Hooded executioners, all of them.

"One snowy owl," announced Eliot with triumph—although with his black coverall and red knitted balaclava, it was hard to tell that it was Eliot. "First snowy owl we've seen in three years. And five juncos, six blue jays, nine chickadees…"

"And a partridge in a pear tree?" suggested Sarah.

But Eliot had no time for levity. He pointed to the scraggly branches of an apple tree. "Look over there. Waxwings, I think. Let's keep an eye out for Bohemians." And he moved off through the snow, binoculars raised.

And here Sarah found herself joined by a slender figure so muffled that again identification as to name or gender was impossible. But the figure, speaking in a high breathless voice through its ski mask, announced she was Sandi—"Sandi with an *i*"—Sandi Ouellette, that her husband was a funeral director, and they had met Sarah at Dolly Beaugard's funeral.

Sarah, extending a hand, thought with resentment, I can't get away from Dolly out here in the middle of a field. But Sandi went on to say she simply didn't know a thing about birds, but her husband had wanted her to help keep score.

"Be my guest," said Sarah, proffering her pencil and pad, but this was refused. "I can't cope with all those weirdo bird names, so I'll just hang out with you for the duration. Okay?"

Sarah said okay, and for the next three hours Sandi dogged her footsteps as the team of birders slogged through drifted snow, slid about on frozen ponds and marshes, and stood on the shore in the teeth of the north wind counting gulls, ducks, loons, and grebes.

"And four great cormorants and at least twenty black guillemots, and one Iceland gull," said Alex, the visible part of his face looking frostbitten but pleased.

"How exciting," squeaked Sandi Ouellette, and Sarah decided that she was being partnered by a Barbie doll.

The day progressed, a watery-looking sun out, the wind softened and shifted slightly to the west so that tears did not come immediately to the birders' pinched faces. This moderation, followed by a sandwich-and-thermos lunch and the sighting of a single fox sparrow and two brown creepers, put the group into a mood that could almost be described as jolly, so that when Eliot suggested they finish the day at Diggers Neck, there were no dissenters even though the area was known for its difficult footing on barren stretches of rock and ledge.

"But we'll do Great Oaks first, won't we?" asked a tall man wearing a red plaid duck-hunting cap with the earflaps pulled down—a man Sarah now recognized as Sandi Ouellette's other half, the undertaker Fred Ouellette.

"Well," said Eliot, collapsing the legs of his telescope, "I thought I might have seen a king eider out past Little Cove yesterday. An adult male. Maybe the female. But I'm not sure. My telescope wasn't set up. But I think it's worth checking out."

This announcement caused an immediate stir and there was a general movement toward the cars.

"What's a king eider?" asked Sarah, catching up to Alex.

"It sounds exciting," piped Sandi, trotting along behind her.

"A king eider," said Alex, slipping into his instructional mode, "is a stubby sea duck with an orange bill shield. The female—"

"I've found it," said Sandi. "In my Peterson. That duck is some weird." "Weird" seemed to be one of Sandi's favorite words.

"The female," said Alex doggedly, "looks almost exactly like the female common eider, but the head is rounder, the bill looks shorter. But if we really see either, it's quite a find."

"Awesome," said Sandi, climbing happily into the front seat beside Alex.

What was awesome, Sarah said to herself, was the numbing cold. Wind or no wind the temperature seemed to be falling. The others, undoubtedly warmed by the possibility of a king eider, seemed immune to such suffering. Suddenly, as the car rounded the circle by the front door of the Great Oaks house and stopped, she decided. "Goodbye," she said. "I give up."

Alex twisted around and eyed her—the only facial expression possible through the slits in his ski mask. "Are you sure? We're going to be hiking out to Little Cove. Maybe pick up some land birds on the way."

"You pick them up," said Sarah. "Me, I'm going in and enjoy central heating and imagine a trip to the Everglades."

"Gosh," said Sandi, "you're going to miss the king eider."

"He's all yours; go to it, Sandi," said Sarah, and she clambered out of the Jeep and walked with determined steps toward the house.

"Come on, Alex, get out of the car," said Sandi, plucking at Alex's sleeve. "The others are getting ahead."

Sarah reached and lifted the front door knocker, waited, then hearing no answering footsteps, turned the knob and the door swung open. Honestly, she thought, the Beaugards are just asking for it. Not only those bookcases but the whole house is unlocked. And the place is loaded, paintings, prints, cupboards full of china and a sideboard heavy with silver.

Once in the front hall, she called softly. Softly, because she didn't want to wake Mrs. Beaugard should she be napping in front of the fire as any sensible person should be on such a day. Then, pulling off her heavy boots at the living room entrance, she poked her head in the door. Empty. Of course. Mrs. B. was in charge of watching the feeder birds, and these could best be seen from the library window. Fine. She, Sarah, would settle in the living room. She looked at her watch. Quarter of three. It would be getting dark soon and the birders would pack it in. But now, just to sit by the fire. Sarah took off her parka and woolen hat and sank into an overstuffed chair, closed her eyes, and let the warmth cover her like a quilt. A down quilt, she murmured. An eiderdown quilt. A king eiderdown quilt. Down, down, down. And Sarah was asleep.

Later she never remembered what had disturbed her. A door closing somewhere, the sound of steps. A car starting up. Whatever it was, she was awake instantly. On her feet. Looking at her watch. Four-fifteen. Almost dark. And the house was so quiet. Had everyone gone to sleep, too? Uncle Lenox and Jonathan and Colin over *The Tempest*. Mrs. Beaugard over her bird feeder. Vivian Lavender over whatever she was doing.

Sarah shook herself and considered. Then, aware of sounds on the stairs, she turned to the door that opened into the hall in time to see Jonathan with his crutch, his left leg still in its walking cast, Colin behind them, and riding herd, Uncle Lenox. All in outdoor clothes. Why? Perhaps to meet the birders and to hear the reports. As the front door closed behind the trio, Sarah decided she could skip hearing the details and all the excitement over the snowy owl and the king eider. She would leave the house by another route, climb into the Jeep, and huddle over the heater until Alex extricated himself from the group.

The library. It had French doors into the garden, and if Mrs. Beaugard was there, she could thank her for warmth and comfort. Sarah pulled on her parka, her hat, retrieved her boots, and walked quickly to the library. She opened the door and was immediately hit by a wall of arctic air. One of the French doors stood partly open, its guardian curtain bellied out in the light wind. And no Mrs. Beaugard, What was left of the fireplace blaze was flickering uncertainly in a bed of ashes; a white mohair shawl lay across a sofa back, a copy of *Gourmet* on the cushion. And on the floor a tablet of paper, its leaves ruffling in the breeze from the door. And oddly enough, in the corner, faceup, a tattered horror comic book, sure sign that Jonathan had made a library visit.

Sarah hesitated, then stuffed her feet into her boots and stepped across the room, intending only to rescue the notebook and close the door. She picked up the tablet, noting as she did that Mrs. Beaugard had faithfully recorded the species of birds seen at her feeder and that blue jays and chickadees led the list. This, she placed on the sofa, but the door was another matter. Part of a small hooked rug had become wedged underneath its bottom edge, and Sarah was forced to bend down and yank it away.

And it was in this position that she saw it. A late afternoon winter tableau set against the snow. For a moment, rather insanely, Breughel's painting of the returning hunters came into her head: the lowering sky, the silhouetted figures against the snow, the black lines of the trees. And then she knew what she was seeing.

Three figures. One standing stock-still, his hands raised against his masked face, the second kneeling down in the snow, reaching out, touching. Touching the third figure. A third figure who showed as a long dark sprawled shape only partially visible to Sarah because it was sunk deep into the drifted snow. Snow that seemed to surround the shape with a comforting enfolding softness.

Then two of the tableau figures moved. The kneeling figure turned into Alex, who let his hand drop, rose, and shook his head at the first figure, who became Eliot Beaugard. Who in turn shook his head slowly as if unbelieving. And then the others, the South Proffit Point bird-watching team, swarmed into the scene.

And Sarah retreated. Backed out of the room and headed for the front hall. Where she intended to go, she could never afterwards explain. Perhaps to join the others gathered outside the library window. Perhaps to telephone the ambulance. Or the police. Or both. Perhaps to find Vivian Lavender. Uncle Lenox.

But the sound of an automobile motor stopped her short, and wrenching open the front door, she peered into the increasing dark and saw a sedan back out from the open garage, turn in a series of jerks around the jumble of parked cars, then move forward and, gathering speed, disappear down the Great Oaks drive.

And Sarah broke into a run, had almost reached the Jeep, when she felt her coat grabbed from the rear. Alice.

"Was that Jonathan?" Alice shouted. "In that car? I just got here and I thought I saw him get in with Uncle Lenox and someone else. Where the hell…"

Sarah gave her a push. "I'm going to find out. Right now. I'm taking the Jeep."

Alice gave a return shove, "And taking me with you. That's my son. That's Jonathan."

"I'm not going to argue," said Sarah. "Get in the car." She reached for the Jeep door. Unlocked. The keys? In the ignition. She climbed into place and Alice threw herself onto the front seat; the Jeep motor rumbled, coughed once, and roared. Sarah cranked the wheels sharply to the right, swung away from the car ahead, and gunned the motor so that the vehicle shot through the snow-drifted driveway like some kind of runaway snowplow.

And hit the main Proffit Point Road just in time to *see* the taillights of the sedan disappear over the hill, heading south.

Chapter Twenty-Five

"I'M AFRAID SHE'S GONE," said Alex, standing up and returning the flashlight to Eliot. "Facedown in the snow like that."

"Oh my God," said Eliot. "My God. Mother. Poor Mother."

"She may have fallen, felt faint, but the signs of asphyxia—being smothered—are pretty clear. The protruding tongue, the eyes. Look, you don't want the details, but take my word."

"Smothered in the snow? Good Christ. But what was she doing out here anyway? In weather like this?"

For answer Alex pointed silently to a partly snow-covered tin. "Bird feed. She may have gone out to fill the bird feeder."

Eliot shook his head. "Oh God," he repeated. "Oh Christ."

"Listen," said Alex. "I'll stay here. You go call the ambulance and then the police."

"Police," exploded Eliot. "Why the police? Jesus, haven't we had enough of the police? Mother fell down. Had one of her dizzy spells. And smothered. Poor old thing." And then he took a step toward the partially snow-covered form. "We can't leave her lying out here. Let's get her in the house."

"We shouldn't move her," said Alex. "But see if you can find something to cover her. To keep the snow off."

"Right away. I'll do that right away," said Eliot, and he turned and headed for the open door of the library.

"Go around," shouted Alex as Eliot grabbed for the door handle. "Footprints, fingerprints."

"Oh goddamn," answered Eliot. "This isn't a crime, it's a... it's a tragedy."

"It was also an unattended death," said Alex. "But right now we have too many attendants." He indicated the dark forms of birders who, shifting uneasily from foot to foot, now stood at the edge of the little garden that held the bird-feeding station. "Take everyone around to the front and let them in the house. And keep them there. Do you hear?" This as Eliot stayed, apparently frozen in place by the library door.

Eliot hesitated, came forward, took another long look at his mother's body, and retreated, calling the birding team to follow.

"Mr. Ouellette," called Alex. "Come over here, please." Then, as the tall lanky undertaker detached himself from the group following Eliot, Alex beckoned him to his side. "I don't want to move the body. Will you stand guard while I make sure Eliot's gotten hold of the police?"

Alex discovered Eliot at the library door, his arms full of a wadded-up blanket apparently yanked from the nearest bed. He grabbed Eliot by the shoulder. "Not through there. Remember what I said about not walking through the area. Go back the way you came. I'll be right out."

Eliot turned, his face angry. "I've called the ambulance and the goddamned police." Suddenly he glared at the floor by the corner of the room. "Look at that. That comic book. Jonathan's been down here in the library." Then, his voice growing increasingly agitated, "That rotten kid. He probably talked Mother into filling the feeder. And didn't stay around to help her. Damn him." And Eliot turned from the room, the hem of a blanket trailing behind him.

Alex left the library, found Tad Bugelski's wife—she was an enthusiastic birder—and stationed her at the library door. "No one in," he ordered. "Not until the police say okay. I'll be outside."

And as had happened so often in the recent past, the police, in the shape of George Fitts, Mike Laaka, Katie Waters, and other law enforcement types, together with the rescue squad and an ambulance, converged on the house at Great Oaks, and the person of Mrs. Arthur Beaugard was immediately subjected to those necessary indignities to which in life she would have vehemently protested.

George Fitts, having herded the members of the birding team into the living room, delegated Mike Laaka to corner Alex. This he did in the front hall.

"What do you think happened?" demanded Mike.

"Let the pathologist do the guessing," said Alex. "She was an elderly woman with multiple health problems including a cardiac condition. And none too steady on her legs. Out there in the snow and wind, well, anything might have happened."

"Perhaps an assist from someone near and dear?" suggested Mike.

But Alex only shrugged and then peered in the direction of the living room. "Where the hell is everyone? I mean the family. Jonathan, Colin, Lenox Cobb. And Vivian. My wife? Eliot's the only family member around."

"Masha's here," said Mike. "She was upstairs taking a nap. We had to bodily prevent her from going out to see her mother." At which point Eliot strode into the hall and announced that he couldn't find Lenox or the two boys upstairs or down. And that he didn't trust his uncle as far as he could throw him, but by God, he was going to find the three of them.

"Hold it," said George Fitts, appearing behind Eliot. "We need statements, and that's going to take time. Perhaps you could ask Mrs. Lavender to make some coffee. I'm going to let all these people call home to say they're delayed here, but I want a deputy to stand by next to them when they call."

"Have you secured the bird feeder area?" asked Mike.

"Yes," said George, "but with the wind blowing the snow around, we haven't much hope of finding anything for now. I've sent for lights, and the lab people will be here any minute."

"You're treating it like a homicide?" asked Mike.

"Use your head, Michael," said George. "Considering the past two months at Great Oaks, wouldn't you take precautions?"

"Aaah," said Mike. "I think that's overkill. I think it's an accidental death. Most of the family was around this afternoon; she was alive at three and then the bird-watchers arrived. They may be a pain in the neck, but homicide isn't their thing. The old lady was pretty tottery. And had lousy eyesight. An accident waiting to happen, right, Alex?"

But Alex was looking again into the living room and now said, with some urgency, "The family may have been around—some of them—but where are they now? And Sarah. She was going to meet me here. Or in my car."

George scowled, turned on his heel, disappeared for the space of ten minutes, and returned with a uniformed trooper. "They've just finished a quick search of the house. The following people seem to be missing. Mrs. Lavender, Professor Cobb, Colin Beaugard, Jonathan Epstein. And Alice Beaugard. Her sister, Masha, saw her drive in at least an hour ago."

"Sarah Deane?" demanded Alex.

The trooper shook his head. "No one has seen Sarah Deane since she left the birding group and entered this house by the front door." And he added, "We went to check with Eliot Beaugard and now we can't find *him*."

Alice peered through the windshield of the Jeep. "I can still see taillights, but I don't know if they're the ones we want. But it doesn't make any sense. They can't drive."

"Who can't drive?" said Sarah, as the Jeep rose up over the second hill of the Proffit Point Road.

"They can't. None of them. I mean, if it's Jonathan and Colin and Uncle Lenox—the three you saw together—they can't. The boys certainly can't, and Uncle Lenox has double vision or blurred eyes. He hasn't driven since his accident. His car's just been sitting in the garage."

"Then they've gotten someone to drive them," said Sarah.

"But who, for God's sake? And why? Why are they tearing around at this time of night? It's still snowing and it's cold enough to freeze the brass balls off a monkey."

"The movies," suggested Sarah. "Lenox is taking them to the movies. Maybe Alan picked them up. Maybe it was all pre-arranged."

"Not likely," said Alice, grumbling. Then she stiffened. "I forgot. What was going on at the house? You started to talk about an accident. Whose accident? One of that birding group?"

Sarah, trying to keep the taillights of the car ahead in view, thought for a second how to tell someone that her mother had been found facedown in the snow and that Alex was shaking his head. And then she told it straight, describing her visit to the library, the open doors, the dark shape under the bird feeder.

"Oh Christ," said Alice. "Mother. Do you think?" And before Sarah could answer, "No, you don't think, do you? She's dead. Frozen to death out there."

"I don't know what happened," said Sarah. "Do you want to turn back? Are you absolutely sure that Jonathan's in that car ahead? Or any car?"

But Alice nodded vehemently. "I'm sure enough. And I can't do anything about Mother. I can't even take it in. But I can do something about Jonathan. And Colin. If it turns out Uncle Lenox and maybe Alan are taking them to the movies, fine. Great. I'll go home. So keep your eye on that car. If they go straight on into town and head toward Rockland, it could be the movies. Or someplace to eat. Only, Alan always drives that old VW Rabbit of his..."

"So what kind of car am I following? I can't tell at this distance."

"Same as Mother's. A Ford Escort. Both dark, hers black—she special-orders black cars. Uncle Lenox has dark blue."

Sarah slowed her car, the Jeep giving a little shimmy on the now snow-packed road. "Car's almost stopped ahead at the Diggers Neck turnoff. It's going right under the streetlight."

"And I see three heads. Three heads. Not four."

"And," said Sarah, through her teeth, "it's turning left. It's not going to town. I'll bet it's headed south, taking the Route One shortcut."

"Get on its tail, close the gap," shouted Alice.

"I can't. I'll end up in a ditch. But they're slowing a bit. At least I can keep up. Alice, are you sure Jonathan doesn't know how to drive? I don't mean 'does he drive,' just does he know *how*? Most kids of his age do. They get a chance to steer, to drive on farm roads, on private driveways."

"Well, as a matter of fact…" began Alice.

"I thought so."

"Just around Great Oaks. From the entrance on. Down to the boathouse, around back to the harbor. Perfectly legal."

"Legal's not the point. The point is that between Lenox Cobb and Jonathan, they can probably drive a car. And for all we know, young Colin probably drives, too."

Colin did drive and rather prided himself on his skill. Sitting next to an obliging adult, he, too, had taken the wheel at Great Oaks and had logged an impressive number of miles over the past two years. However, on this occasion he had been forced into the role of passenger and lookout.

"Watch for anyone following," Professor Cobb had ordered. "Jonathan and I have enough to do to keep the car on the road. And no, Colin, I will not tell you where we are going. There comes a time in life when younger people must trust the wisdom and sense of someone older. So not another word. I think I saw headlights behind us. Watch and let me know if they turn off."

Twenty-five minutes later, as Lenox applied a light braking, Jonathan, squeezed tight against his uncle, hanging on to the wheel for dear life, made the left turn from the town of Waldoboro onto Route One and headed south.

"That car's behind us," announced Colin. "I think it's the same car. Like a Jeep or something."

"If it's a Jeep, I won't worry excessively," said Lenox. "Let me know if you see anyone else on our tail."

"Okay," said Colin. And then, "I'm hungry."

"Contain your hunger," said Lenox. "We'll wait until we find a parking lot with a lot of cars. Then we try a stop."

"A pit stop?" said Jonathan.

"Precisely," said Lenox. "Fast in, fast out."

"And you won't tell us yet where we're going?" repeated Colin.

"I said I wouldn't and I meant it." And Professor Cobb folded his lips and squinted into the driving snow. Besides, he added to himself, at the moment I haven't the faintest idea.

❀ ❀ ❀

At ten-fifteen that evening, Katie Waters watched the last of the Proffit Point South team bird-watchers climb into their cars and one by one drive slowly down the snow-covered drive while at the same time Alex stood by the kitchen telephone. And received the first autopsy report from that long-suffering pathologist, Johnny Cuzak.

"I object," said Johnny, "to bodies on the weekend. It's my youngest kid's birthday and I left my wife with a house full of eight-year-old boys. I'd promised to help."

"Okay, Johnny," said Alex. "We all had other plans today. So what gives? Asphyxiation?"

"Yeah, as far as we can tell. We're lucky because sometimes these buggers don't show external signs."

"Go on," said Alex, wincing at the idea of Mrs. Beaugard being referred to as a "bugger."

"Well, as you noted, the tongue protruded; it was bitten, too. The eyes were prominent and there was evidence of slight bleeding from the nose and ears. Cyanosis of the face and petechial hemorrhages of facial skin and the conjunctive present."

"Any cardiac pathology?"

"Early stages of congestive heart failure, arteries a mess. Possible bruising around neck and shoulders. Maybe as a result of her fall. If she fell. Even if she hadn't suffocated, hypothermia might have got her. Mighty cold tonight."

"Thank you, Johnny," said Alex. He turned to George. "So that's that. Asphyxiation. And now what news about the strays? I'm getting worried. Three cars gone, Mrs. Beaugard's, Professor Cobb's, and my Jeep. Which I assume Sarah has taken for reasons of her own. But I called home and no answer."

"Mmm," said George. "Is it possible there was some prearranged affair? Something they all went to? One of the bird-watchers told me that there's a big dinner after the bird count when all the reports from all the territories covered are given."

"You're right about that," said Alex. "There's always a banquet and then the reports. But no one from this house would go to a banquet with Mrs. Beaugard dead. You can scratch that idea."

"It was a long shot," admitted George. "So we've sent out an all-points. They'll be picked up within the hour. I'd bet on it."

But George lost his bet. The police of all sorts, state, town, deputies, were out in force dealing with the usual road accidents that befoul an icy winter Saturday night. Jackknifed semis, drivers under the influence, speeding teenagers, all took priority over three cars proceeding at legal speed along a heavily traveled route.

"This is a damn funny sort of chase," observed Alice. "Going along at thirty-five miles an hour."

"Fast enough in this weather," said Sarah. "Besides, the Bath Bridge is no place to put on speed. And we're keeping them in sight. They probably don't dare go any faster either. Particularly if either of those two kids is doing part of the driving."

Alice twisted around in her seat. "I'd swear that there's a car hanging in behind us," she said. "A Saab like Eliot's, which means maybe he's following us from Great Oaks. Chasing *us*."

"Listen," said Sarah. "Saabs are all over the place. Relax." But as Sarah said it, the familiar spectral hand crept down her neck and crawled along her spine.

Alice grimaced. "I guess I'm just chronically paranoid. I wish we had Webb in the backseat. For extra insurance. Nobody messes with Webb."

"I'm not expecting a fight," said Sarah. "Just to stop them and find out what crazy thing they think they're up to. I suppose it's possible that your uncle has completely flipped his lid and the boys are egging him on into some horrible adventure. A Stephen King book come to life."

"God, I hope not. No more bodies, please. Oh Jesus, I keep forgetting poor Mother. I hope it was quick. Like being hit by lightning. They say freezing isn't so bad after the first part. Like going to sleep. But you're right that Jonathan and Colin, when they get together, well, they haven't got much of what my shrink calls a reality quotient."

"Hey," said Sarah. "They're turning in. Right toward that shopping mall. Oh brother, we're going to lose them in the parking lot. I'll bet they're going to eat."

"Take a guess. Colin loves McDonald's, but Jonathan goes for Burger King. And there's an Arby's down the line."

"McDonald's is closest. We'll grab a takeout ourselves and then hang out at the exit back onto Route One."

Settled back with two Big Macs and two Cokes to go, Sarah was able to point out a number of Saabs coming, going, and parked. This seemed to reassure Alice, but the more Sarah soothed her companion, the more she felt prickling at the back of her neck.

"There they go," said Alice suddenly, pointing. "Step on it. They beat us to the draw. They came out of Arby's."

"Damn," said Sarah, stamping on the accelerator, and with a surge of power, jammed the Jeep in front of a pickup truck. "Listen, they can't drive all night. They'll pull in somewhere, we can telephone, and we'll be home before midnight."

"You hope," said Alice.

"The point," said Lenox to the two boys, "is never tip your hand. The Jeep is still behind us, but a car that looks familiar has been tailing her. We will hole up in Brunswick and no one will find us. Academic friendships have their uses. We will make a quick turn off Route One and double around and into the back drive of my old friend, Professor Ambrose Hoffstedder. He is fortunately a widower and keeps late hours. I've rescued him several times from reaching foolish conclusions about Christopher Marlowe. Jonathan—pay attention—now I'm giving it some speed. Keep your wheel steady. Good, we turn left, down Pleasant Street, then turn again. Aha, that red light caught them. Now sharp left and left again. Let her skid, no one's on the street. Good boy. There's hope for you yet. No, Colin, you may not steer. Now turn. The garage is open. In we go. Easy does it. I'll get Ambrose to close the garage door, so stay put and I'll roust him out."

And Professor Cobb, lively as a cricket, bounced from the car, left the garage, mounted the back step of a small shingle house, and banged on the door.

The results of these efforts were entirely satisfactory and in a short time the three were bedded down—Lenox in the spare bedroom, the boys on two living room sofas—and a clock set for five A.M. sitting in the middle of the floor.

But the comfort of Lenox Cobb meant the discomfort of Sarah and Alice, who, by taking turns sleeping and waiting, wrapped in coats and a spare blanket—left over from a summer camping trip—kept vigil at an all-night Texaco station on Route One. And the Saab following the Jeep? It passed through the town, turned, returned, turned again, and finally took up a position at the parking lot of a Dexter Shoe Outlet a few miles south beyond Sarah and Alice's watch place near the junction of Route One and I-95.

At shortly after ten-thirty Sarah had taken advantage of a public telephone booth to call Alex at the Beaugards'. "We're okay," she told him. "Alice saw Jonathan in one of the Beaugard cars—I think he's with Professor Cobb and Colin. She was scared and wanted to follow them, and we're in Brunswick now waiting for them to surface. They've gone underground somewhere. And as soon as we catch up with them, we'll make them turn around and come home."

There was a pause at the other end of the wire—Alex conferring with George, no doubt, thought Sarah—and then Alex came back, his voice harsh. "Get back here on the double. George has put out an all-points and Professor Cobb will be picked up as soon as he sticks his nose out. Eliot and Vivian Lavender are missing. His car and Mrs. Beaugard's black Ford are gone. You can draw your own conclusions. Kidnapping, escaping murderer. Murderers. You name it. And Mrs. Beaugard died of suffocation. Face down in the snow. Maybe it was an accidental death. That may—or may not—ease Alice's mind. But what you're doing is plain hazardous. To the two boys, to all of you."

"George Fitts wants us back," Sarah reported to Alice. "And Eliot and Vivian and Lenox Cobb and the boys are 'wanted.' Three cars on the loose. An alert's been issued, so the police will pick them up any time now. And we're to draw our own conclusions."

"You mean pick a card, any card. Has Uncle Lenox stolen the boys for hostages and is making his getaway? Is Eliot absconding with Vivian? Or is he being followed by Vivian? And is Eliot trying to rescue Colin from Uncle Lenox? Or grab Jonathan. Or kill Uncle Lenox. Because Uncle Lenox or Jonathan saw Eliot kill Mother?"

"Except Eliot was bird-watching all day, and Alex says it's possible your mother fell in the snow. An accident."

Alice subsided briefly. Then, "Damn, I won't turn back. If you won't go on, I will. I'll rent a car. Flag them down."

Sarah shook her head. "Did I say I was turning back? No, let's push on. Let's be hung for a sheep, not a lamb."

Alice murmured assent, climbed out of the car, disappeared briefly inside the Texaco station ladies' room, and then clambered into the backseat and curled herself into a sleeping position as Sarah was to take the first watch. "Lucky you had all this bird-watching junk," she said. "Extra hats and jackets. I may take up the sport."

Sarah, after her watch, slept uneasily and then, on her second watch in the early hours of the morning, began to try and fit the puzzle together. Draw your own conclusions, Alex had said.

Okay. Take Lenox Cobb. Had he really been a victim of an attack, as he claimed? An attack to limit his activities and his participation in Mrs. Beaugard's affairs. Or had Lenox just been clumsy and bumped into tree branches? Well, first and foremost, Lenox had saved Jonathan when Parson was killed. So he wasn't guilty of killing Parson. Two: Lenox could have bought Canadian Whiskey and dosed it with Valium—anyone could lay hands on the stuff—but had he ever had contact with Marsden and Junior? Known them well enough to hire them to off-load lead ballast? Verdict: a hung jury. Three—and this was a nasty one: Lenox was at home during the entire day of the bird watch. He was disappointed at not being in the field but was planning—along with his sister, the late Elena Beaugard—to keep an eye on the bird feeder. The reading of *The Tempest* could have taken up only part of the day. Did Lenox resent Elena's estate plan—particularly in the light of Dolly's thievery? Lenox, as reported by Alex, had thought the family was being robbed. Could Lenox have escorted his sister out to the feeder to refill it? Tripped her. And ever so firmly kept her nose down in the snow? Verdict: a possible guilty.

Sarah, her eyes blurred with sleep, shook her head back and forth. The snow had stopped in the night, and except for an occasional car passing, everything on the almost-deserted street seemed to have come to a halt. Then, for something to keep her awake, she began to read, with the help of the streetlights, the signs of the various shops across the way, these being mostly old frame houses converted to commercial use.

Directly across, in pink clapboard: "THE KINDEST CUT OF ALL"—UNISEX HAIRSTYLES. To the left: MAZZINI'S GARAGE: MUFFLERS, FULL BRAKE JOB, RADIATOR REPAIR, ALIGNMENTS, SHOCKS. And beyond in Permabrick and stone: GORDON AND GOSS: CONSTRUCTION, EXCAVATION A SPECIALTY. And to the right: OCEANSIDE SCUBA DIVING. CLASSES, AIR TESTING, WET SUIT RENTAL. And under the lettering, the crude painting of a black-suited figure swimming underwater.

Sarah blinked. Wet suit. Hood, jacket, pants. Shiny when wet. Like a costume from the Middle Ages. Or a sci-fi movie. The hood and mask of a headsman with his ax. An executioner.

Not a ski mask. But why hadn't anyone thought of a wet suit? Because...because no one, not even George Fitts, could imagine a wet suit out in the snowy woods. Away from the water. Away from its natural habitat. But how simple. When it is dark and snowing, row in your rubber raft—your hard-to-see rubber raft—or better, swim, across to the Great Oaks beach, the site of so many jolly family picnics, climb up through the woods clutching your bowling ball—Sarah had not given up on the bowling ball—and brain Parson. Parson, who must have had information from his brothers about doing some sort of job for you. And was calling the wrath of the Lord—and probably the attention of the police—down on your head.

Now go back in time—to the end of September. Hire those two useful thugs Marsden and Junior to off-load lead ballast from the *Sweetheart*. Choose a period in which brisk north winds are predicted for the rest of a week. You're a sailor, you keep a close watch on the weather. Then, knowing that Marsden and Junior are out every late afternoon in their boat, you intercept them, and for a job well done you reward your helpers with a bottle of fine Canadian whiskey. You don't know their brand, but you know they drink like fish. You buy expensive whiskey because you always buy expensive liquor. You like the very best. But you have the sense not to choose a brand you keep at your own house. And you lace the whiskey with a dose of that most available drug Valium.

Later, after Marsden and Junior take off, you, in your handy wet suit, row out in the darkened cove in your Zodiac and assist in the demise of the two bad Gattlings. Or perhaps it's a hands-off operation. You supervise from a safe distance. The two brothers are drunk and zonked and fall overboard. No problem.

Next it's Dolly. Dolly the estate planner. Dolly the sailor. Out for one last sail on her usual Sunday. A Sunday afternoon when there's a big north wind and perhaps many of the fishing boats will stay at their moorings in the harbor. Besides, Sunday is a fisherman's day off, a family day. A good day for unobserved activities. But Dolly for that last sail will go out in her Weymouth Scooter, which can handle a blow because of that extra ballast. You wait for her boat to put out from the harbor, watch it blown like a leaf across the bay. You're in your wet suit waiting out in the bay—or sitting in your rubber raft or just swimming around. Wet suits are buoyant, aren't they? Divers need weight belts to keep themselves under. Anyway, there you are ready to assist the struggling skipper of the capsized *Sweetheart* to drown. The bowling ball perhaps? Or just an oar cracked on the skull. Remember those bruises and abrasions.

And it all made sense. Oh maybe some of the details were mixed up, but God, it made sense.

But why? Why was murder done? For the pleasure of killing in a wet suit? For the well-concealed jealousy of a doer of good works? For the hate of a Dolly Memorial estate plan? Why? Because you have money, house, dock, a new boat on order, the works.

And who—if anyone—pressed Elena Beaugard's nose into the snow? Sarah reviewed the possible candidates. Lenox? Masha? Alice? Vivian Lavender? But not Eliot. He, according to Alex, was fully occupied in directing the search for a king eider.

Back to the drawing board.

Chapter Twenty-Six

IF NOT ELIOT, HOW about Vivian? Could she really be Eliot's ladylove? Certainly the unstable Caroline didn't seem to be much of a deterrent to another relationship. Or was this just an idea born of Sarah's overheated imagination? More important, was Eliot shaken by his mother's death? Really shaken. Could he have put Vivian up to it? A murder team. Sarah had bumped into a recent case in which husband and wife had worked in double harness. I have to call Alex, she told herself. She looked at her watch. Four-thirty. He wasn't on call this weekend, so he'd be at home. She slipped out of the front seat, careful not to disturb the sleeping Alice, and returned to the telephone booth.

Alex answered after one ring. He seemed wide-awake. "Why aren't you back here? Damnation, Sarah. I'm as worried as hell."

"It's Alice. She wants to keep on going. Because of Jonathan. And Colin. And to be honest, so do I. We don't know what Lenox is up to. He's disappeared somewhere inside Brunswick."

"I know," said Alex with a growl. "The police haven't found a trace of his car. They're betting he's holed up with some academic buddy. Now, why don't you turn around, because you're going to complicate the situation beyond belief. Eliot's on the loose and so is Vivian. Separately. Do you want to get brained with a bowling ball? Get back here."

"Actually," said Sarah with asperity, "we're in a good position to catch Lenox on the way out of town. He almost has to go on the interstate."

"Unless he doesn't," said Alex. "Unless he cuts off and takes a secondary road. And tell Alice that Webb Gattling is storming around like a mad bull. Mike and Webb are picking me up in a few minutes. We're coming right down there."

"Listen," said Sarah, "we're going to be sensible. No confrontations. No high-speed chases. And it *is* Alice's son. Eliot's, too, for that matter. Eliot may be chasing after Colin to save him. Anyway, it's Eliot I've called about. I think he's the man who got Parson. Wearing a wet suit, that executioner's hood that Jonathan described, and came into the woods by way of the beach. Swimming or with the Zodiac. But did Eliot seem shocked at his mother's death? Did he seem surprised? Grief-stricken? Or even sad?"

There was a pause on the other end of the line. Then Alex said slowly, almost regretfully, "Well, maybe not surprised. After all, she'd been in fragile health for some time. But yes, I'd say he was extremely upset. Shocked, as you said. He was close to tears. Of course, it could have been put on, but..."

"But you don't think it was?"

"Eliot doesn't strike me as someone who can fake emotions. But you never can tell. One thing I do know. He reacted like crazy after he found Jonathan's comic book in the library. He seemed to think Jonathan might have come in and suggested his grandmother fill the bird feeder, but didn't stay to see she did it safely. And it *is* possible it happened just like that."

"Look," said Sarah. "We're bound to catch up with Lenox sometime, and remember, he may not have chosen those two boys as companions, but as hostages."

"That idea," said Alex dryly, "had occurred to all of us."

Lenox Cobb, Colin, and Jonathan finished a hastily assembled breakfast of cereal, milk, and, for the professor, coffee. And then he shook hands with his friend Professor Hoffstedder and thanked him for hospitality and the loan of his Toyota Lexus.

"It pays to keep up with one's colleagues," remarked Lenox after the boys were belted in place and the remains of a box of doughnuts placed in their laps. "I dislike being found in an expensive Japanese car which is certainly more conspicuous than the Ford, but we have no choice. The denouement approaches, which means that we'll soon have an end to all this folderol. Jonathan, you are dribbling doughnut crumbs. You, too, Colin. You boys have the manners of orangutans. Jonathan, can you use a manual shift?"

"Sure," said Jonathan. "Automatic is no fun. Dad lets me shift for him in the Rabbit. He says it's good practice."

"I'm glad to hear your father has some sense," said Lenox. "None of his novels indicates as much."

"But," asked Jonathan, "where are we going now? I know we're not to ask questions, but is it anything to do with my family?"

"That," said Lenox sharply, "is an understatement. Now, be quiet. Just trust me and pay attention to your driving." And he turned the key, and the car gave an encouraging roar.

Alice and Sarah, having had the foresight to fill the Jeep's gas tank to the brim, caught the Lexus at the pass. It was moving at a sedate pace past the Texaco station at five-fifteen A.M. on the almost deserted stretch of the business section of Brunswick's Route One. "That's him, that's Jonathan," shouted Alice. "And it's Uncle Lenox at the wheel and Jonathan squashed up against him steering. What in hell are they doing in a Lexus? Boy oh boy, is that sinister or what?"

But Sarah had the Jeep in gear. "Your uncle Lenox has switched cars," she muttered. "Clever. But also stupid. Now he's acting like a real criminal."

"He always has," said Alice.

At Dexter Shoe Outlet the watching, waiting Saab driver missed the Lexus leaving Route One and its left turn onto a smaller road. But he recognized Sarah at the wheel of the following Jeep and put his car in motion, apparently unaware of being followed himself by a black Ford Escort identical to that belonging to his mother. Then the parade of four cars, the Lexus, the Jeep, the Saab, and the Escort—each separated by a number of intervening vehicles—continued slowly south on a snow-covered secondary road.

"Where in God's name is Professor Cobb going now?" demanded Sarah, slowing for a red pickup that cut in ahead of her.

"Straight for Freeport, and we're being followed," announced Alice. "It looks like Eliot's car. Really it does. You can't go on pretending that the highway is filled with Saabs."

"Okay, okay, it probably is Eliot," said Sarah. "And maybe Vivian's hiding out in the backseat, except Alex said your mother's car is missing. The black Escort. Eliot and Vivian both disappeared just as the police started taking statements. And they're either tracking us or tracking Professor Cobb. Or both. Or maybe each other. Nothing would surprise me. And I'd guess either Eliot might do something nasty, or he's on a rescue mission. Saving the boys from the mad kidnapping professor."

"This whole thing is totally unreal," said Alice. She looked over at Sarah, her disheveled hair, her crumpled clothes, her red-rimmed eyes. "And you look totally unreal. Awful, like something dragged out of a rat hole."

"I feel like something out of a rat hole," said Sarah. "I've been in these clothes since yesterday morning. And you look like me. We both look like escapees from the dump."

Alice rolled down the window trying to crane her neck to see around the pickup truck. "This is so stupid. Why the hell Freeport? Does Lenox want to buy a canoe at L.L. Bean?"

"You two boys are familiar with canoes and tents?" demanded Lenox Cobb, as they neared the outskirts of the town of Freeport.

"Duh," said Jonathan.

"I don't want lip. It's an important question. Listen, you two, because I intend to frighten you. Seriously frighten you. I am going to give you instructions and you are to follow them exactly. If you do not follow them, I expect that one or both of you may be hurt. Injured. Maimed. Out of action. You understand?"

"Hey, no problem," said Jonathan, for once sounding genuinely alarmed, while Colin echoed, "No problem."

"So concentrate. For once in your heedless self-centered lives, concentrate. We are coming up on L.L. Bean."

"We know Bean's," said Jonathan. "But what's that got to do with why we're here? Listen, I know something happened to Gran because I heard Dr. McKenzie talking to Uncle Eliot. Is that why—"

"Quiet. I have chosen L.L.Bean's because they have such a big reputation that even on a Sunday morning the place will be filled with people. It will not be easy for anyone to find us alone there. But to make sure, I am going to give you directions. A script to follow. Jonathan, you want to work in the film industry. Here's your chance for actual on-location practice."

"I don't get it," said Colin.

"Quiet. Listen to me. We will drive down the main street past L.L. Bean's, turn right toward the side parking lot. After we turn, Jonathan will hand over the steering wheel to me, you will both unbuckle your seat belts. At the entrance to the parking lot I will pause, you will both get out—Jonathan will have to manage without his crutch; he'd be too conspicuous. Colin can take his arm. Then you both must head directly for the entrance, making an attempt to stay with other shoppers. Enter the front door with these people as if you were both members of a group. Once inside, go immediately to the camping section. Be casual. Pretend to be interested in the camping items, and when you see one of the salesmen looking the other way, duck under or behind one of the display canoes set up on the floor. If there is no accessible canoe, find a tent and crawl in. Close the flap. And wait. If after an hour—Jonathan has a watch—I have not returned, stick your head out and make sure that there is no one you recognize about. Check for a salesperson. The staff wear green polo shirts. Go to him or her and say you are lost. L.L. Bean salespeople are trained to be helpful and courteous—good role models for you both. Tell the salesperson you want to stay with a staff member until your father, Professor Lenox Cobb, comes for you."

"You're not our father," objected Colin. "You're too old."

"Colin, close your mouth and listen. Deny any relationship to anyone else. Including anyone from Great Oaks or whose name is Beaugard. Understand? Because if you don't do as I tell you, I will have you flayed, stuffed, and eaten for dinner." Both boys nodded, Jonathan now looking thoroughly unnerved and Colin positively trembling. "All right, Steven Spielberg and Roderick Usher, here's your chance. We make the turn, slowing because there's a car ahead of us. Safety belts off. Now we're coming up to the entrance to the parking lot. Now, out, out," shouted Lenox Cobb, his voice shrill with urgency. "Out, out, out. Get going."

And the two boys scrambled down, hit the pavement at a trot, and as good luck would have it, immediately inserted themselves into a family group of five complete with a baby in a stroller.

Lenox watched until the group disappeared around the corner and then turned in to the main entrance, immediately found a parking slot reserved for the handicapped, pulled in, and turned off the engine. Then, reaching into an inner jacket pocket, produced a small firearm, laid it on the passenger seat within easy reach, and awaited developments.

"It *is* L.L. Bean's," shouted Alice. "I mean it. Way up ahead. They're turning. My God, L.L. Bean. Now I can't see them. You don't suppose they're off on some camping trip? Uncle Lenox may have gone completely off his rocker. Eliot says—"

Sarah cut in. "Listen, I think Eliot is our murderer. I'm sure he killed Parson. Coming across the cove and through the woods. That description of Jonathan's. It's a description of a wet suit."

Alice frowned, but then shook her head. "He couldn't have," she began, but Sarah waved her into silence.

"We'll hit the parking lot and drive around until we spot the Lexus."

"And lead Eliot right to Uncle Lenox and the boys?"

"We'll decoy. If we spot Eliot on our tail, we'll keep going on. We're the ones he's following. Remember, the Saab let the Lexus go right past and didn't get into the act until we pulled out."

But now a minor traffic jam had developed in front of the turn in to the L.L. Bean side parking lot. The access road was one-way and a car coming the wrong direction had slithered on a patch of ice and had stopped athwart the traffic.

Alice twisted in her seat, opened a window, and peered out toward the rear. "I can just see Eliot's head. This is like some stupid Keystone Cop thing in slow motion and now we're just going to sit still in a traffic jam. Eliot is about four cars behind. But you're wrong, Sarah. Eliot can't have killed Parson. Remember, he said he was in the shower and looked out the window and saw the roadblock and the police lights. Caroline was watching the tube, and her car was behind Eliot's, which had a flat tire."

Sarah frowned. It was true. Eliot couldn't have been both in the shower and at the Great Oaks entrance in the space of fifteen or so minutes. Even wearing a wet suit and magic flippers or using a flying boat. Now waiting amid that tangle of cars filled with would-be L.L. Bean customers, she moved her mind back to the entrance to Great Oaks. The distance from Eliot's cove to the Beaugard beach. By water. By land. Walked herself back to Eliot's driveway, remembering the uprooted mailbox, Parson appearing like a troll. Eliot's house. The drinks. Canadian whiskey, the tour of the new house. Remembering Eliot explaining about the architectural wonders of the building. The height of the cathedral ceilings. And the view. Designed so that every window faced the sea. The sea!

"Alice," she said. "Every window of Eliot's house faces the sea."

"Big deal," said Alice. "You have money, you get a view."

"And he couldn't have seen the ambulance and the police from his bathroom window. Because…"

"Every window faces the sea," repeated Alice slowly. And then opening her eyes wide, "Every blasted upscale, thermo, double-glazed custom-made designer window faces the goddamn sea. Jesus Christ, what do you know? He lied. Little brother Eliot lied, and that just about nails his coffin shut. But why? Why in hell did he do it? Parson? Maybe Dolly? The two Gattlings? It's beyond me. But, and this really freaks me out, how could he kill Mother? He was the number one kid. Favorite fair-haired boy. The pride and joy. I'd have sworn that even Eliot, for whatever wild reason, would never have killed Mother. And that he'd be hit hard if she died."

Sarah nodded, "That's what Alex said." And then, "Hey, that car is out of the way. Okay, the parking lot, cruise slowly, and don't stop even if we see the Lexus. God, the place is jammed even at this hour. I hope the boys have the sense to keep their heads down."

"I hope Uncle Lenox isn't holding a gun to those heads," said Alice grimly. "Jonathan has a big mouth. He can be really aggravating. And you know Lenox has this gun. A little stubby thing. Goes on about the right to bear arms, but with his eyes he couldn't hit the broad side of a cow."

"Be quiet, Alice, I've spotted the car," said Sarah, accelerating slightly. "Pulled into a space by the entrance. Gray Lexus. Handicapped parking. Wouldn't you know."

"I see it," said Alice. "But only one head. Looks like Uncle Lenox. So Christ, where are the boys?"

"Maybe they really are keeping their heads down. Look, I'll turn at the end and circle back." But as she said this, a sick chill shook her. No boys in sight. Lenox Cobb, if he *had* suffocated his sister, might have no hesitation about using his little gun on two often obnoxious youngsters. Had he had time to stash them—alive or dead—in the store, under a nearby bush, to be claimed later for disposal? No, that wasn't realistic, but the milk of human kindness was not one of Professor Cobb's distinguishing features.

"There's the Saab. It's turning in," cried Alice. "Now back up, let Eliot see us, and we'll lead him the hell out of here."

But the decoy act was never necessary. Like the sudden appearance of feeding sharks around a clutch of open boats, there erupted from every entrance police cars. They swarmed and surrounded, lights flashing, sirens screaming, loudspeakers blaring. Men in uniform, men in jackets and wool hats, women in uniform, women in plain clothes, were everywhere.

The Jeep was covered almost immediately. "Both of you get out and put your hands on the top of your heads," ordered a harsh voice, and Sarah and Alice climbed out of the car, were assisted in flattening themselves against the side of the Jeep, and subjected to a thorough weapon search. Then ordered into the back of a squad car, where they were locked behind a grille.

"You horse's ass, you've got the wrong people," yelled Alice at the retreating policeman, but his attention was fortunately elsewhere. Both women found by twisting around and looking through the rear window, they could keep the Saab in view. And there was Eliot Beaugard, standing in a patch of icy slush, confronted by uniformed state troopers and because the squad car's front window was open, the two women in the rear could hear the trooper's words.

"Eliot Beaugard, you are wanted for questioning in the death of Mrs. Elena Beaugard. If you wish to come with us or..."

And then, like an extra brought in to fill a small role in the last act, Vivian Lavender appeared. Was walked right onto the scene accompanied by a plainclothes female of impressive size and width. But Vivian looked, as she was marched into view, just as if she had just come from church. Tidy, her dark hair neatly center-parted, its bun pinned and centered on the nape of her neck, her complexion rosy. She stood there next to Eliot, erect in her black wool coat with a red paisley scarf fastened into the collar. So, thought Sarah, she really must have been following Eliot. Or following us. Or Lenox Cobb and the two boys.

The state trooper standing with Eliot addressed himself to Vivian. "Vivian Lavender, you are wanted for questioning in the death of Elena Beaugard on the afternoon of December seventeenth—"

But the sentence was never finished. Eliot jerked around and, with a single smooth motion, raised his fist and brought it down like a sledgehammer on Vivian's skull. And Vivian went down like a kind of malfunctioning doll. Her neck twisted sideways, her knees bent, her shoulders hunched, and she crumpled to the pavement.

So startling was her collapse that the two troopers, the large plainclothes detective, and Sarah and Alice had entirely missed the sight of Professor Cobb leaning out the window of his car and pointing a small pistol at Eliot. All they saw was that Eliot shuddered slightly and then fell heavily, arms outstretched, directly on top of Vivian Lavender in a terrible parody of someone protecting a fallen loved one from the onset of wolves or earthquakes.

Chapter Twenty-Seven

THE HUMDRUM, THE ROUTINE, followed—as it always does—the bizarre. Eliot simultaneously being given emergency first aid and arrested. One policeman rolling Eliot over and applying pressure to the seeping wound in Eliot's groin; another reaching around and applying handcuffs while reciting in a monotonous voice, "You are under arrest for assault with attempt to commit bodily injury. You have a right to remain silent. Everything you say can and will be used against you in a court of law. You have a right to an attorney. If you cannot afford..."

And catercorner from this scene, Lenox Cobb, his thin scarecrow body in its trench coat plastered against the side of the gray Lexus, his hands in cuffs behind his back, was listening to the same recitation. It was, thought Sarah, captive with Alice behind the grille, like some strange atonal musical round with Professor Cobb's Miranda warning following two sentences behind Eliot's. "You are under arrest for attempting to commit bodily injury by the unlawful use of firearms. You have a right to remain silent. Everything you say can and will be used against you…"

And Vivian Lavender, face livid, hair disordered, blood trickling down from one eyebrow, struggling to sit up and being firmly held down by a kneeling policewoman.

From all sides came the forces of law and order barking orders, securing the scene, escorting shoppers returning for their cars into a makeshift corral by the side of the road.

And Sarah and Alice released from their backseat cage. "Hey, sorry about that, you two. Some balls-up with the intercom message about a Jeep that looks like yours. We were looking for a couple of dames heading south after a convenience store robbery in Belfast. A couple of grungy Thelma and Louise types. You two sure fitted the bill, but then this scene blew up and I stuck around to give 'em a hand. Man, what a day."

"You can say that again," snapped Alice. She turned to Sarah. "How do you go about suing people for false arrest or false detention, stuff like that?"

And Sarah, after hours, days, even months of putting up with the general heedlessness of Alice Beaugard, stopped in her tracks. "Goddamn it, Alice, shut up. For God's sake, shut up. Try paying attention to something important. You wanted to find Jonathan and Colin. That's what's important." Here Sarah stamped a foot directly into a puddle and was rewarded with a muddy splash in the face. A result that infuriated her further. "Forget about suing the police and look beyond your own nose. You saw what happened. Eliot whopped Vivian on the head and then your crazy uncle Lenox plugged him. And we've got to find the boys. So let's—"

But the sentence went unfinished. Eliot, now alert, lifted his head from his position on the ground, twisted his neck toward Vivian, and roared. Roared at Vivian, who was being shifted onto a stretcher, roared like some damaged and betrayed beast.

"You killed her," he shouted. "You killed my mother. You bloody bitch, you killed her. I told you not to. I said watch out. I said be careful, take it easy, but you had to kill her. And now she's dead. Do you hear me, she's dead. My mother's dead. I was there. I saw her. Jesus Christ, I saw her."

But Vivian turned her head aside and with a small pink tongue began licking away the blood as it dribbled into the corner of her mouth. And Eliot, yelling incoherently, was loaded into a waiting ambulance, and presently the disappearing wail of the siren was heard as it sped through the streets of Freeport.

"Jeezus!" exclaimed Alice. "What in hell was that all about?"

"Never mind them, not now," said Sarah. "We have to make your stupid uncle tell us where he's put the boys. They're going to be taking him away, too, for God's sake, pulling a gun like that."

But confronting Lenox Cobb wasn't necessary. A uniformed trooper approached the two women. "One of you is Alice Beaugard, right? Okay, your son and his cousin are inside Bean's. Camping section. Mr. Cobb told them to stay put until he came to get them, so we're taking him inside to help flush them out. You're to come with us so we can release the two kids to Miss Beaugard's temporary custody. The old guy's under arrest. And hey, there's a deputy from Knox County and some doctor and another man just turned up asking about you both. All mad as hell. Spitting nails."

Jonathan Epstein, settled into his mother's cottage at Great Oaks, his Portland Pirates cap pulled down on his head, lounged back on the sofa and tried to appear the cool, calm, nonchalant kid of vast experience. Mike Laaka had been given the job of interrogating the boy as well as Colin Beaugard, who waited in the kitchen with Katie Waters. Jonathan's man-of-the-world stance did not fool Mike for a minute; he had three younger brothers.

Mike began offering a wailing and anxious Alice a nearby chair, but her presence was refused by Jonathan. "Yeah, I know I'm a juvenile, but I'll just make Mother nervous. What do I say, something like I waive my rights for parental observation? That sounds good anyway."

Mike grimaced, nodded to Alice, and then addressed himself to Jonathan by expressing regret about the death of his grandmother. Jonathan, who had expected to be plunged into the matter of Lenox Cobb's drive down Route One, was put off balance.

"Gran," he said. "Yeah. I'm sorry. I guess I'm sorry. I mean, I never saw that much of her even if we lived in the same house. She took naps a lot and didn't want to be bothered, and when I was home I was supposed to go and do something else. My homework or help rake leaves. Or find Colin and play with him. She didn't like me all that much. But I'm sorry she's dead. Out in the snow. That's where I saw her lying with Dr. McKenzie and Uncle Eliot looking at her. I don't suppose Gran planned to die out there by the bird feeder."

"I don't suppose she did," said Mike dryly.

Jonathan frowned. "It was an accident, wasn't it?"

"We'll have to wait and see," said Mike.

Jonathan's frown increased. "When people say that, they always mean something bad's happened. Or is going to."

But Mike only shook his head and suggested that Jonathan describe his experience of the chase to the L.L. Bean parking lot that Sunday.

And Jonathan's expression turned to one of mild scorn. "In the first place," he said, echoing his mother's earlier opinion, "that wasn't a chase. A chase is a chase when everyone's car is screeching around corners and just missing people and knocking over fireplugs and the sirens are going. This thing was sort of a stupid slow-motion scene like it was a funeral. Anyway, we were in the front car and Uncle Lenox and I were sort of driving together because of his eyes being lousy, so I guess it would have been dumb for us to go fast because we would have had to coordinate a lot faster. I still don't know why he made us go with him, but I guess it has something to do with Gran being dead. I know she had a bad heart, so maybe she had an attack, but Uncle Lenox wouldn't tell us. He said he was getting us out of the house for our own good. But Uncle Lenox is sort of a nutcase. I mean, he's smart, but he does crazy things every now and then, and wow, does he have a temper."

Asked about the parking lot scene, Jonathan reminded Mike that he and Colin had been inside L.L. Bean's hiding out in a tent. "That was Uncle Lenox's idea, and it was a piece of cake. There was this family from Brazil ahead of us, and they wanted to buy a whole bunch of sleeping bags and backpacks and two-man tents, so they kept the salesman busy. I made Colin get into this big geodesic tent because we cold scrunch in the corner if someone looked in. But after a while it was totally boring."

"Were you worried about your uncle coming back for you? Perhaps doing something dangerous?"

Jonathan considered the question for a minute and then shook his head. "Nah. Not really. In the beginning I was a little scared because he got sort of fierce, and I guess Colin believed him when he said he'd eat us for dinner. But after a while I told Colin, look, this guy is old. I don't think he's about to go and kill us. Even if he's murdered Gran. I mean, he could have killed us without driving all the way to Freeport. There's plenty of room at Great Oaks to have done it. And we drove to this house of a friend of his and he fed us and gave Uncle Lenox his own car. I guess Uncle Lenox was just trying to get us away. Away from whoever killed Parson Gattling or Aunt Dolly. Or even Gran if she was killed by some human and it wasn't a heart attack."

"Okay, Jonathan," said Mike. "You say you think that your uncle was getting you out of the house for your own good and that maybe it had to do with your grandmother. Did he give you any other reason? A reason having to do with your Uncle Eliot? Or any of the other people who were following you?"

But Jonathan shook his head again. "All he said was not to ask questions and to look behind us. When I told him we saw a

Jeep following, he said he wasn't worried about the Jeep. Do you know if he's going to be in jail because of shooting Uncle Eliot?"

"I don't know," said Mike, "if he's going to be held or will be allowed to post bail. But you can go now and I'll have a word with Colin. He'll be staying with you and your mother for a while, until some other arrangement can be made. Or his mother gets out of the hospital."

"That's okay, Colin and I are working on a film script. But is he staying with us because Uncle Eliot is in the hospital?"

"Your uncle Eliot will be detained somewhere for quite a spell," said Mike, closing his notebook and standing up. "Now, scoot to the kitchen and call Colin."

But Jonathan lingered. "It's pretty amazing, isn't it? I mean, the whole thing. Aunt Dolly and Parson and Gran. And the two Gattlings. It's like some sort of massacre but strung out. And there's something even more amazing."

Mike sighed. "Okay, I give up. What's even more amazing?"

"Uncle Lenox. Being able to hit Uncle Eliot in a vital place. At least, one of the policemen said it was vital. In his gut or somewhere. Uncle Lenox can't see across the street even when he's wearing his glasses."

"Thank you, Jonathan."

"I suppose Uncle Lenox was trying to protect Mrs. Lavender so he can plead self-defense or something sort of like it."

"Goodbye, Jonathan."

Jonathan started for the kitchen and then turned. "Or maybe he was trying to shoot Mrs. Lavender and hit Uncle Eliot by mistake. Or he could have been trying to hit the policeman to save both of them and just missed."

"Jonathan Epstein, get out of here," shouted Mike.

The big Great Oaks house had a strange empty feeling, Sarah thought. With its matriarch gone, its resident curmudgeon, Lenox Cobb, detained, Eliot, the son and heir in irons, Vivian

Lavender in custody, and Jonathan at his mother's cottage, the whole house seemed hollow, dusty, as if a fine layer of grit had settled on every surface. The furniture, the curtains, pictures, carpets, it all reminded her of a stage set left in place too long after the curtain had been rung down. And like the empty stage, the house had no meaning or purpose now that the principal players had departed and the script lay in tatters.

They were in the cavernous Great Oaks kitchen, settled around a massive walnut table, George Fitts, Alex, and herself. The kitchen had been chosen as an acceptable meeting space since George's preferred spot, the library, was ringed in yellow tape as an extension of the scene of the crime. Or, Sarah reminded herself, plural, one of the scenes of one of the crimes.

"Eliot?" Sarah asked George. "Was he badly hurt?"

George, ready for questions and interrogation, had spread before him notebooks, tape recorders, a set of pencils, a cup of coffee, and a number of telephones—portable and fixed. Now he looked up from a rough chart of the Great Oaks property.

"Condition stable. He's in the hospital under guard. Later on we'll try for a probable-cause hearing and hope the judge denies bail." He returned to his chart and with one finger circled the Beaugard estate. "A messy case," he declared. "Even arresting Eliot Beaugard."

"Why wasn't that simple?" asked Alex. "He'd hammered Vivian Lavender on the head and then, after he was shot, there he was lying there on the ground shouting at Vivian Lavender, practically announcing he was an accessory to killing his mother."

"First," said George, as if instructing slow members of the sixth grade, "Eliot wasn't under arrest until after he'd assaulted Mrs. Lavender. Before that the only legal thing we could do was to ask him to come in for questioning. But after he hit Mrs. Lavender, he could be put under arrest for assault. Unfortunately, he was shot almost at the moment of his striking her, and this meant he was incapacitated when the trooper gave him the Miranda warning. His lawyer could claim that he was in no condition to understand its meaning. Probably have the statement about his collusion with Mrs. Lavender not allowed as evidence."

"But what about Vivian Lavender? Eliot yelled, called her names. She may not be feeling very supportive about Eliot. If they really were working together all this time."

George brightened—a faint flickering across his impassive face. "We have hopes of Vivian. State's evidence. I hope she can be encouraged in that direction because I think we have her cold for the murder of Mrs. Beaugard. Lab just called and they picked up three of Vivian's hairpins—those old-fashioned long ones she wears—in the snow at the site of the body. And some fair snow-packed footprints next to the body, including an imprint on the back of the victim—we're lucky there hasn't been a thaw." Here George glanced with satisfaction at an inside-outside window thermometer showing an external temperature of fourteen degrees Fahrenheit.

"Mrs. Lavender," he continued, "has a mild concussion from Eliot's blow, but she's obviously angry with him. In fact, the detective with her says she's already made some very useful statements about the nighttime unloading of the ballast from Dolly's boat by Junior and Marsden Gattling, with Eliot supervising while Vivian kept watch at Great Oaks to make sure that the family was occupied. Eliot used his Zodiac raft, the Gattlings used their skiff. We got a search warrant this afternoon, grabbed the raft, and the lab just called to say they've recovered canvas fibers from under the floorboards of the Zodiac. As you know, we've already had matching fibers from the Gattling skiff. It was a joint murder enterprise."

"And one that younger brother Parson must have known about," said Sarah. "Which explains all those crazy biblical threats."

"Don't forget that Parson was Dolly's middleman for the rare book deals," said Alex. "Eliot was guilty—we haven't proved it yet, but it seems likely—not only of doping Marsden and Junior's Canadian whiskey with either Caroline's Valium or

Mrs. Beaugard's—but when Eliot got rid of Dolly, he got rid of Parson's job. His income source. Why wouldn't Parson be sore as hell? His two brothers, his valued employer, all dead because of Eliot. So he goes public threatening, spouting curses. Made certain he'd be next."

"But was Vivian Eliot's mistress?" queried Sarah, who felt that this interesting subject was being neglected. "We guessed she might have been. Alice thought probably."

"Looks like it," said George. "We had been scouting the local motels with no luck, but after we got the search warrant, we've found evidence of their relationship in the loft of his boathouse. It's a comfortable space where he keeps boat cushions, sails, and so forth."

"Don't tell me, more hairpins?" exclaimed Sarah.

"As a matter of fact, yes. Some articles of her clothing, which she identified in the hospital an hour ago."

"But I have real evidence about Parson's death," Sarah announced. "Not just hairpins. I should have thought of it before because I've had a tour of Eliot's house. He lied about Parson Gattling and seeing the police cars at the roadblock." And she told George about the windows that faced only the ocean.

"That," said George, making a hasty note, "is very interesting. We haven't had a chance yet to really go over that house of his. Sarah, I'm glad you caught that. It saves us trouble. There are times when I forgive you for being underfoot."

"How gracious of you, George," said Sarah.

"But I don't thank you for chasing Lenox Cobb. You had Eliot on your tail and Vivian Lavender behind him and Professor Cobb in front. You could have been caught in the middle."

"Alice," said Sarah. "It was her son. We had to go."

"It would have been much safer to leave it to the police."

"George," said Sarah in a dangerous voice. "The police never caught up with anyone until L.L. Bean's. They were too busy with road accidents to concern themselves with murder and a possible kidnapping. So Alice was right to chase her son and Colin. And you know, we did provide a buffer. If Eliot had tried to pass us, we wouldn't have let him."

"And that," said Alex, rousing himself and pushing away an empty coffee cup, "is exactly why I told you to come back. Besides, there was Lenox Cobb packing a gun. It was just plain stupid."

"It was plain right," said Sarah stubbornly. "I'd do it again. But think of Lenox Cobb being armed. Alice apparently knew. What did he use? A pistol from the Civil War?"

"He used a thirty-eight Smith and Wesson Chief's Special Airweight," said George with ill-concealed fury. "Imagine that old goat with his attitude going about armed. It's a wonder he hasn't left a trail of bodies."

"But he didn't," said Sarah. "It was Eliot and his henchwoman, Vivian. But why was Eliot chasing Lenox and the boys? Did he think that Lenox killed his mother?"

"Judging from his remarks before he took off, Eliot may have thought that Jonathan, through carelessness, or possibly Lenox, might have been responsible for her death. He saw Jonathan's comic book in the library and lost his temper. Or, and this is also possible, he may have thought Jonathan, or Lenox, or both, saw Vivian doing her job on his mother and had to find out. Maybe to eliminate them because they were witnesses. But unless Eliot comes clean, we may never know."

"And Vivian, why was she following Eliot?" demanded Alex.

George picked up a notebook. "Statement from Vivian. She followed because she loved him. She actually said so. Used those very words. Like a soap opera. They had a deal. He was going to marry her after he divorced Caroline, which he'd been promising for some time. She seemed to think he was taking off without her and so she went after him. After all, where else could she go?"

Sarah nodded agreement. "Okay, I think I can understand Vivian. In the beginning maybe she was afraid she was just going to lose her job because of Dolly's giveaway estate plan.

That's where the switch to the Episcopalians comes in. But then Eliot began to be an important part of her life, so perhaps she thought as Eliot's wife she was going to be the heiress presumptive of Great Oaks. But Vivian was never calling the shots, was she? Eliot was. But again why? Why get rid of Dolly? And did he knock Lenox down? Or Jonathan? There must be a reason. Some common denominator. Not money. You know it isn't money. But why?"

"And what was Vivian supposed to do to Mrs. Beaugard?" demanded Alex. "If not to kill, her, what? Half-kill her? Maim her? Put her out of action for a while?"

"All we know," said George, "is that Eliot thought killing Mrs. Beaugard was a mistake. Mrs. Lavender has admitted holding her down but says she didn't expect her to die from it."

"What crap," exploded Sarah. "You push an elderly woman with a bad heart down in the snow and don't expect her to die?"

"You know," said Alex slowly, "if we can hang Lenox Cobb's injury and Jonathan's leg and shoulder, and what was supposed to be just an injury to Mrs. Beaugard, all on Eliot, then there is a pattern. After Dolly's death and the Gattling boys were eliminated as witnesses, Lenox was second-in-command. Until he was hurt. And Jonathan is a bright active kid. Maybe it was useful to slow him down. Not kill him, hobble him. And hobble, maim, injure, slow up Mrs. Beaugard. Not kill her. Leave her incapacitated and then guess who takes—"

Sarah looked up. "Hey, Alex, I think you have something, because then Eliot could become the estate manager and scuttle the Dolly memorial plan before it was made final in January. But...but why? In God's name, why?"

George sighed. "As I've said before, I hate motivation. I know it fascinates amateurs and armchair psychologists."

"Like me?" said Sarah.

"Exactly," said George. "The police do much better with cloth fibers and bloodstains. Real evidence. So leave it for now. As I said, it's a messy case. The public expects this neat package: the crime, the evidence, the motive, the verdict, the sentence. Well, multiple-death cases like this can go on for years. We can't prove the injuries to Jonathan and Professor Cobb were anything but accidental. But some sort of end is in sight—if we can persuade Mrs. Lavender to cooperate. Let the lawyers worry about whether Eliot's actions are tied to Dolly Beaugard's estate plan."

Sarah stood up. "Okay, okay. So I'm hung up on motivation. So I'm an amateur. But I'll say it again. Why? Eliot didn't need, want, or care about the estate. He had everything his heart desired, including Vivian nesting in his boathouse. So good night, George. Let's hope we all get through Christmas without bumping into each other. And now I'm going to check on Alice. I lost my temper and yelled at her back there at L.L. Bean's because sometimes Alice sticks in my craw. But her mother's dead and she's looking ragged, so I can show some sympathy and see how Jonathan and Colin are holding up. Poor Colin. His father in jail, his mother in the hospital. Alex, you can join me if you want. But I don't want any more lip about Alice and my little drive to L.L. Bean's."

"Did you ever think, best beloved, that you have a singular talent for driving me as batty as any Lenox Cobb?" asked Alex as they pulled on coats and boots preparing for the drive down to Alice's cottage.

"Looking back," said Sarah, "I can see how crazy that caravan of cars was. Crazy and maybe a little on the dangerous side."

"A little!" exclaimed Alex.

"Mostly from Lenox. If I had known that he carried—what was that thing?—a Smith and Wesson something, well, I would have left more space between us. I wonder if he was really aiming at Eliot."

"All will be revealed," said Alex. "In the meantime…"

"In the meantime I'm going to get a grip on this business. If I can figure out *why*, then I can make sense of Eliot running around in a wet suit, dumping lead, killing Gattlings. But we forgot one person. Masha. Where was she all yesterday afternoon when everyone was looking at birds or reading Shakespeare?"

"Telephoning. Arranging the winter concerts for her group. Talk about detachment. Anyway, George has a log of her phone calls, all long-distance. Twenty or more. Masha is covered."

"As is Eliot, isn't he? For Mrs. Beaugard's death?"

"I think by thumping Vivian on the head at the Bean parking lot, he's established his innocence of that one. Not of planning a milder version of it, which involved Vivian putting his mother out of action. He used the king eider. A duck any bird-watcher would kill—pardon the expression—to see. And he made sure everyone was busy setting up telescopes and scanning the cove, leaving Vivian a free hand without bird-watchers sneaking around."

"Except for one bird-watcher. Me."

"There's one in every crowd."

"And a lot of good I was. Fast asleep in the living room. If I'd stayed awake, I might have saved her."

"Maybe, maybe not. It was probably a quick job. Talking Mrs. Beaugard into going out and filling the feeder. And Vivian probably didn't hesitate; she may have done it with a certain relish. All those years of servitude. Mrs. B. wasn't a user-friendly employer. She was a pretty autocratic woolly-minded old biddy."

"God, what a crew," said Sarah. Then, pointing, "Stop at the top of the hill. Alice's driveway is a devil with snow. We won't find any answers in there, but my conscience will be a little clearer. Alice has a good heart. At least I think she does."

And Sarah, followed by Alex, climbed out of the car and began the slippery descent to Alice's cottage, Sarah little guessing that the answer to at least one of her questions would shortly come from a highly unlikely source.

Chapter Twenty-Eight

JONATHAN AND COLIN WERE discovered on the living room floor surrounded by sheets of paper and cardboard. They hardly looked up, simply announcing that they were working on set designs for their upcoming video. Mike Laaka was in the kitchen with Katie Waters, dealing with cocoa and a frozen pizza. "Alice is in her bedroom, but she said if you and Alex turned up, to send you in. Katie and I are feeding the boys, keeping them busy. They're okay now, but the whole thing will probably hit with a bang tomorrow."

Alice was sitting on the edge of her bed staring bleakly at a framed copy of a Matisse cutout. "I bought that during my art-appreciation period, but now it doesn't do it for me anymore. Things are so fouled up that I even think I'll quit smoking. It's a theory of mine; you know, provide a counterirritant. Besides, I promised Webb. He's coming over tonight. We're going to talk about getting married because then I might get joint custody of Jonathan, and the court might okay temporary custody of Colin."

"Well, that's good news," said Sarah. "But are you getting married just to get custody?"

"No. I really want to stay with that guy. I need something solid and massive to butt my head against. Webb fills the bill. Besides, he seems to want someone flaky and unstable and restless, and I fit that description. Another odd couple abroad in the world. Besides, he wants to keep Willie."

"How about your uncle Lenox?"

"You know what's funny? I found myself offering to take him on. My mouth just opened up and said so. That's if he gets a suspended sentence or is out on bail or something. Webb can handle the old buzzard, and believe it or not, Jonathan likes him. He wants to have Uncle Lenox come to the school and help show this video he and Colin are putting together. 'The Fall of the House of Usher,' only I think it should be 'The Fall of the House of Beaugard.'"

Here Alice gave a short harsh laugh. "The boys will probably get through this whole thing better than I will. Even Masha will handle it because she can go all remote and retire into her music. That's why I need Webb. To walk me through the next few days. And through the rest of my life."

But it was Colin who answered the question that was still buzzing like an angry fly in Sarah's brain.

She returned to the living room and found Alex on the floor with the two boys moving cardboard pieces around on a chart.

"He's helping us see spatial relationships," Colin explained.

"We've decided," said Jonathan, "to do 'The Fall of the House or Usher' in the twenty-third century. Sort of like *Star Trek*. I think the Great Oaks house setting is too boring. We'll have a flying sailboat with all the latest technology. Our ship will be capable of landing on water and going through the stratosphere, and landing on planets in all the galaxies. It'll have a retractable keel."

"Like the *Goshawk*," said Colin. "But not like the new boat."

"The new boat?" said Sarah, puzzled.

"The one my father ordered because he's sailing transatlantic next year. If he's not in jail. He's the new commodore of the Proffit Point Boat Club, so he said he needed a new sailboat."

"Oh yes," said Sarah, remembering. "It had a bird name, too."

"The *Gyrfalcon*," said Colin. "It's fifty-six feet and a special design, but the centerboard doesn't retract like the *Goshawk*. It's got a real keel."

"So," finished Jonathan, "we'll use the *Goshawk* design and make it much bigger. Bigger even than the starship *Enterprise*."

"How about Roderick Usher?" asked Alex, now much amused.

"He'll be Captain Roderick Usher," announced Jonathan. "We'll need a bigger cast, but most of the action will be in the control room and we won't bury Lady Madeline alive in a casket, we'll vaporize her instead and hide her in the instrument panel."

But Sarah's brain had been busy. "Wait up, Colin," she said. "How could your father keep a keel boat like the *Gyrfalcon* at your mooring? There's very little water at low tide in most of the cove. It's even named Tidal Cove."

"Yeah, I know," said Colin, now struggling with two elliptical pieces of cardboard. "These are part of the defense shield systems," he explained.

"So what was he going to do with it?" persisted Sarah.

"The new boat? Moor it somewhere else, I guess."

"Did he mention where he thought of mooring it?" demanded Alex, and Sarah could tell from the tone of his voice that he understood where her question was heading.

"Oh, maybe at Little Cove or at Back Cove. Over at Great Oaks. Back Cove is a good place if a hurricane is coming."

"But if the Great Oaks property is going to be given away—" began Sarah, but Alex nudged her arm.

"I think that's enough," he said quietly. And then to both boys, "Quite an idea bringing Edgar Allan Poe into the twenty-third century. How are you going to end the story?"

"Oh, we've changed Poe's ending," said Jonathan. "Captain Usher goes crazy, but then he has a brain transplant from a sub-alien form and he's okay. It's done with lasers and neural-sensor probes."

"And Lady Madeline is reconstituted," said Colin. "Into an engineering-room ensign. A man. We didn't want any women in central command."

"So much for the women's movement in the twenty-third century," said Sarah as they closed the cottage door behind them.

"But you have your answer to why. Murder done for the greater glory of Eliot Beaugard, commodore of local yacht club and transatlantic blue-water sailor. I suppose it wouldn't be the first time that vanity beat out moneygrubbing as a motive."

"I doubt," said Sarah, "that George will be that interested. It's a minor piece of the puzzle for him. For us it's a biggie. Eliot didn't want the estate or the house or cottages; he wanted two good places to moor the *Gyrfalcon*."

"Deep-water sheltered anchorages. Safe from big blows, complete docking facilities. In an area served by the Proffit Point Boat Club. Those are worth more than all the tea in China, or the cash of all the Beaugards. You know that young squirt Jonathan wasn't so far off base when he suggested that Uncle Eliot wanted the Great Oaks land for an international yacht resort facility."

They reached the Jeep, and Sarah turned to look back in the direction of the Great Oaks house. "Dolly stealing books so she can be called the saint of the year, Eliot murdering left and right to be the yachtsman of the year. Mrs. Beaugard a self-centered domineering old woman. Masha retreating from human contact, Caroline in her own particular deep end. You know, it makes Alice and Lenox Cobb and the two boys seem positively lovable."

With that she climbed into the front seat of the Jeep and slumped back against the headrest, an enormous weariness like a thick blanket coming over her. She closed her eyes and sighed. "I didn't get much sleep in the Jeep last night," she told Alex.

"And properly so," he answered. "They who refuse to listen to caution, reason, good sense, and the advice of a loved one get the rest they richly deserve."

In the days that followed that particularly eventful December Christmas Bird Count, certain movers and shakers in the world of law enforcement saw to it that Eliot Beaugard, after a preliminary hearing, was denied bail, and his case was referred to the county prosecutor's office for presentation to a grand jury. This matter had been facilitated by Vivian Lavender's agreeing to turn state's evidence against Eliot in the hope of a modified sentence—manslaughter perhaps instead of first-degree murder.

Professor Lenox Cobb, after entering a plea of guilty to the possession and unlawful use of firearms, was, as a first offender, nailed with a large fine and released on his own recognizance, burdened only with a year's parole and a suspended sentence. It was observed by all who subsequently met him that although the professor spoke with regret of his departed sister, Elena, and quoted from *The Tempest* the lines about his charms being "all o'erthrown," he was, all in all, remarkably chipper. Particularly lively was the account of his rescue of the two boys from the evil Eliot Beaugard and the daring escape of the trio to the L.L. Bean parking lot, where with great coolness he, Lenox Cobb, professor emeritus of Bowmouth College, disabled Eliot with the timely use of his Smith and Wesson. This rejuvenation of an elderly man puzzled Alice until Sarah suggested to her that recent events had obviously had a highly stimulating effect on her uncle.

The body of Mrs. Arthur Beaugard was, after autopsy and the verdict of homicide by suffocation, released for burial and a small service was held at St. Paul's-by-the-Sea by Father Smythe, who twice mistakenly referred to the deceased as "Dolly." This affair was attended by the remnants of the

Beaugards and by Sarah's grandmother Douglas, who, as Sarah drove her home, remarked in an annoyed voice that Elena had always been troublesome.

Webb and Alice Beaugard were married quietly in a civil ceremony attended by Colin, Jonathan, Professor Cobb, and Alan Epstein, with Alex and Sarah standing by as witnesses. Masha, driving in from Boston, arrived just in time to play a short seventeenth-century pavane on the alto recorder before the exchanging of vows.

Caroline Beaugard showed mild gratification on hearing that her husband's future residence would most probably be limited to the Maine State Prison in Thomaston. However, when offered a trial weekend to her house on Proffit Point and the company of her son, she became sullen, saying she'd never really liked children. But Colin, if he wished, could make short visits to Green Pastures, a newly established psychiatric halfway house.

Colin Beaugard proved himself remarkably resilient to what amounted to the loss of two parents. It was generally thought that this was either because he was a very tough little boy, or, more realistically, because he had always had so little attention and real affection from either father or mother that he did not now feel their absence. Thus, the last heir of the Beaugard name was quite content to move for the moment into his aunt Alice's cottage, where he and Jonathan continued to work on their script and stage mock-up of the newly named "Voyage of the House of Usher," in which latter task they were assisted by Webb Gattling's skill with saw and hammer. Colin was also initiated by Jonathan into the pleasure of receiving double the usual number of gifts through the celebration of Hanukkah with Alan Epstein and Christmas with Alice and Webb.

The first day of January dawned with one of those welcome shifts of weather from ice and zero temperatures to the beginning of a January thaw. On New Year's day the thermometer hit fifty-seven, coats were exchanged for light windbreakers, and the citizens of midcoast Maine went about smiling and lifting their pale faces to the sun. And at exactly noon of January first, the last wrinkle of the Beaugard case was smoothed and made plain.

It happened because Webb Gattling, in his new role as stepfather and stepuncle, suggested a winter picnic on the beach below Alice's cottage. A fire would be built; hot dogs, salad, cake, cocoa, coffee, rugs, and tarps would be brought, and the New Year would be given a proper push toward better days.

Sarah and Alex with Patsy in tow arrived with a hamper of sandwiches and a thermos of hot soup to add to the collection. Masha, on a two-day break from the concert world, brought a sinister-looking chocolate torte, Lenox Cobb was established with a rug, a folding chair, and a pair of binoculars in case some rare species drifted by, Alice and Webb produced a bucket of shrimp, and the two boys bore marshmallows and packages of frankfurters.

The first order of the day was the gathering of firewood. And this effort, if Sarah had not exercised remarkable self-control, might have resulted in the cancellation of the picnic. With Patsy leashed and straining toward Willie, who was tethered at a safe distance from Professor Cobb, Sarah wandered about through the spruce trees and bushes that rimmed the beach, here and there picking up a fallen branch or bundle of twigs. Until, stubbing her toe, she fell flat into a mound of melting snow. As she sat up, reaching to see what had caught her boot, her hand encountered something round. And smooth of edge. She jerked herself upright and reached under the snow. A bowling ball. A bowling ball. The words came banging into her head. Oh God, not a bowling ball. Not *the* bowling ball.

But it wasn't. It was like a ball cut in half with a neck protruding from its center. A neck with a hole in it, and fastened into the hole was a short length of chain, which in turn joined a length of dirty rope, which disappeared into the snow. Sarah probed, dug, and delivered several feet of the line and a cut and frayed end. She stared, ran a finger over the painted surface.

And then seeing Alex walking past on the beach, called softly, but with urgency.

And Alex, the nautical half of the marriage, knelt down in the slush and identified the object. "It's a mushroom anchor. Good for mud bottoms."

"Like the mud bottoms around here?"

"Correct."

"It was under the snow. I tripped over it."

"It's a little one," said Alex, eyeing the anchor. "Useful for small skiffs, prams, dinghies."

"Or rubber Zodiac dinghies owned by someone in a wet suit?"

Alex stared at her and then slowly nodded. "Yes, like that."

"And it would do the same damage as a bowling ball, wouldn't it? Leave the same sort of imprint on somebody's head?"

Alex nodded again, and for a moment they were silent looking at each other. Then Sarah stood up. "Let's not spoil things. Leave it there until after the picnic. Tomorrow is soon enough. Later we can call George. He'll be happy. He likes the sort of evidence that you can measure and weigh."

Sergeant George Fitts managed a mildly pleased expression after he had arrived at Great Oaks and collected the mushroom anchor the next morning. "That was one of the missing pieces," he told Sarah, as he stowed the object in a paper evidence bag. "I never believed in the bowling ball. A bowling ball was too good a weapon. And Eliot Beaugard didn't bowl. But he owned a mushroom anchor, which is missing from his rubber raft. And this one even has his initials painted on the bottom."

"I suppose," said Alex, "that he may have dumped it overboard, and it hit a rock bottom or it didn't set itself properly in the mud, may have dragged and rolled closer to the high-tide line. As an anchor it's a lightweight affair."

"All right, Sarah," said George. "You win. It's obvious to me that even if you aren't actually looking for something, you'll stumble on it anyway. And now I've got to go up to the house for a last look round. The furniture is being moved this afternoon."

"Furniture? What furniture?" said Sarah, startled.

"From the house. I gather some is being sold, some put in storage, and the rest divided between Alice and Lenox. The Episcopal Church takes possession on the fifteenth. The gift of the house didn't depend on Mrs. Beaugard's death; she and Dolly arranged for the transfer last summer."

Sarah never knew why, instead of shaking the dust of Great Oaks from their feet, she and Alex followed George's car up the long winding drive to the house. "I suppose," she told Alex, "it's wanting to see the end of things. Closure. The end of the end. We won't be coming back here. Alice and the boys are moving to Webb's cabin in Diggers Neck, and Lenox has decided to go into some sort of retirement home for cranky academics."

The way to the front door was blocked by an enormous moving van, and a continuous stream of men and articles of furniture moved from the door to the ramp of the van. Alex parked the Jeep and both climbed out to watch. The house already seemed abandoned, shades pulled down in the upstairs rooms, curtainless windows staring from the ground floor. Sarah, standing by Alex, recognized a wicker chair from the living room, the plant table from the library, the fringed lamp that had stood next to Mrs. Beaugard's winged chair.

"I don't even feel a twinge," said Alice, appearing suddenly at Sarah's elbow. "Of course, some things are supposed to go to Eliot, but we'll store his stuff. Or give it to Caroline if she ever comes back into daylight. The church is buying the piano and keeping the dining room table and sideboard. And look, here comes the family." And Alice pointed to the front door, where two men were carrying a large painting. The portrait.

"You're not selling...?" Sarah began, but Alice nodded vehemently. "I don't want it. Masha doesn't. I got word to Eliot in prison, and he doesn't. The two boys aren't interested, so off it goes. It's always given me the fidgets. Good riddance, I say."

And Sarah, Alex, and Alice stood and saw that the painting in its heavy gilt frame had been carefully leaned against the front steps while one of the men approached with a heavy comforter and a roll of tape.

At that moment the sun, which had been hesitating behind a clump of clouds, slid out and shone directly on that painted group of summer children. Stubborn Dolly with her honey-colored hair, Masha staring off into space, Alice looking for an escape, and Eliot in his sailor suit, master of all he surveyed.

And then the comforter swaddled the painting and it was borne away, up the ramp, and fitted between two bed mattresses. And Sarah suddenly remembered.

She turned to Alice and Alex. "I knew that portrait reminded me of something. A photograph I'd seen before in a magazine. In a biography. Except for not being the right number of girls, it's just like one made of the Tsar's family."

"The Tsar?" exclaimed Alice. "What Tsar?"

"Tsar Nicholas. Of Russia. You know, his family when they were at the Summer Palace. The girls in their afternoon frocks. Olga, Tatiana, Marie, and Anastasia. And the little boy, the Tsarevitch, in his sailor suit. The photograph always made me shiver because I knew what was going to happen to them."

Alice was silent and then she blew softly through her lips. "Maybe that's what I always felt. A sense of doom hanging over us. Except," she added with a light smile, "in our case there were one or two survivors."

"What are you doing standing there moping?" said a cracked voice. Professor Cobb. "Why don't you stop gawking at furniture nobody wants and come out to Little Cove. The king eider is back."

"You mean," exclaimed Sarah, "there really *is* a king eider here?"

"Of course," said Professor Cobb crossly. "Eliot found it and took everyone to see it the day of the Christmas count. A very fortunate sighting and a first record for Proffit Point. Eliot has many serious faults, but even Eliot would not claim a bird he had not actually seen."

For my daughter, Margaret, without whose prodding I would never have trudged through a hundred European gardens and to my granddaughter, eight-year-old Louisa, who cheerfully endured although she has now sworn never to look at another flower.

Many thanks to Dr. Daryl Pelletier for suggestions, information, and a supply of periodicals on matters pertaining to the problems and solution of this mystery. To be more specific would be to give it all away. And a grateful nod to Snowshill Manor and to those wonderful gardens at Barnsley House, at Kiftsgate Court, Hidcote Manor Garden, the Cambridge University Botanical Garden, Sissinghurst Garden, Monet's garden at Giverny, and the gardens of the Villa Melzi. In all these nothing untoward took place; only cheerful help and hospitality.

THE GARDEN PLOT

A Gateway to Gardens

Whirlaway Tours and tour director Barbara Baxter are delighted to present a once-in-a-lifetime European tour for the Midcoast Garden Club of Maine. In addition, Lillian Garth, Garden Club president, has arranged for noted horticultural expert Dr. Ellen Trevino of Bowmouth College to travel with us and through informal on-site lectures to join us in celebrating the wonders of the chosen gardens.

SATURDAY, MAY 20, 7 P.M.: "Getting to Know You" dinner at the Surfway Restaurant in Rockport, Maine. Following dinner Barbara Baxter and Dr. Trevino will share with us some of the highlights of our trip.

TUESDAY, JUNE 6, Depart 8:10 P.M. from Boston's Logan Airport on British Airways. Please arrive at the international departure gate at least two hours before departure for passport and baggage check-in.

WEDNESDAY, JUNE 7, 7:35 A.M. Arrive London's Heathrow Airport, meet tour bus and drive to Ibis Hotel for refreshment and rest. Depart for Gloucestershire and the Shearing Inn.

JUNE 7–14: The Shearing Inn, High Roosting, Gloucestershire. A charming old inn will be our base for visiting many famous Cotswold gardens.

THURSDAY, JUNE 15: Depart High Roosting and visit a variety of cottage gardens in the Cambridge countryside. Overnight we are in the heart of Cambridge at Hotel Fatima.

FRIDAY, JUNE 16: To the weald of Kent and the fabled gardens of Sissinghurst created by novelist and poet Vita Sackville-West and her husband, historian and diplomat Harold Nicolson. In Kent we spend the night at the old world Hagglestone Arms in nearby Cranbrook.

SATURDAY, JUNE 17: We take le shuttle to France, meet our bus at Calais, and drive to Vernon to the Hôtel Fontaine in time for dinner.

SUNDAY, JUNE 18: Giverny. A day to enjoy the world of Claude Monet: his house and studio, the *Clos Normand*, the water gardens. In the evening we drive to the outskirts of Paris to a delightful country inn, La Moustache Noire.

MONDAY, JUNE 19–22: Depart 10 A.M. Air France for Milan from Charles de Gaulle Airport and continue by bus to Lake Como and the picturesque town of Bellagio, where we stay at the Hotel Albergo Nuovo. Since ample time is provided for exploring the famous gardens of the Villa Melzi, the Villa Serbelloni, and the Villa Carlotta, we will also be able to visit Bellagio's many museums, shops, and restaurants.

THURSDAY, JUNE 22: Return by bus to Milan, spend the night at the Buonarroti Aeroporto Hotel and depart June 23, British Airways 11:40 A.M. Arriving Heathrow 12:35 P.M. Depart British Airways 3:50 P.M. Arriving Boston 6:10 P.M.

CAST OF CHARACTERS

The Midcoast Garden Club on Tour

EXPERTS, DIRECTORS, AND TOUR LEADERS

BARBARA BAXTER — *Director, Whirlaway Tours*

ELLEN TREVINO — *Professor of Botany, Bowmouth College*

HENRY RUGGLES — *British garden expert*

THE TOUR GROUP

SARAH DEANE — *Teaching Fellow, Bowmouth College, wife of Alex McKenzie*

JULIA CLANCY — *Aunt to Sarah*

EDITH HOPPER — *Sister to Margaret*

MARGARET HOPPER — *Sister to Edith*

DORIS LERMATOV — *Mother to Amy*

AMY LERMATOV — *Fourteen-year-old daughter of Doris*

FRED OUELLETTE	*Undertaker*
SANDI OUELLETTE	*Fred's Wife*
JUSTIN ROSSI	*Lawyer from Boston*
STACY DANIEL	*Publicity Director, Boston bank*
CARTER MCCLURE	*History professor, Bowmouth College*
PORTIA MCCLURE	*Garden enthusiast, wife to Carter*

AND ALSO:

ALEX MCKENZIE	*Physician and husband of Sarah*
GREGORY BAXTER	*Brother of Barbara*
MIKE LAAKA	*Deputy Sheriff Investigator*
GEORGE FITTS	*Sergeant, CID, Maine State Police*

Chapter One

> Lilies will languish; violets look ill;
> Sickly the prim-rose; pale the daffadill;
> That gallant tulip will hang down his head,
> Like to a virgin newly ravished,
> Pansies will weep; and marigolds will wither;
> And keep a fast, and funerall together...
> —"The Sadness of Things,"
> *The Lyrical Poems of Robert Herrick*

LILLIAN GARTH COULDN'T concentrate. Everything was spinning around and there were these blank spots. Had she fallen over her own big feet? That's what her husband, Sam, seemed to think. Lillian did remember it had been the Midcoast Garden Club meeting at her house, and that new member, Sandi Ouellette, had asked a question about root cellars. After that, a gap, something about the stairs and everything going black. Then coming to with her head pounding like hell in the Intensive Care Unit of the Mary Starbox Memorial Hospital. And Sam hanging over the bed rails saying, "For God's sake, Lillian, what possessed you to go down into the cellar without turning on the lights?" Which wasn't very sympathetic of Sam, but she'd tripped down there only two months ago so his reaction wasn't surprising. That time she'd missed the last step and only cracked her elbow.

But now her head was banging away, her leg—the right one—and her ankle—the left one—were both propped up encased in something rigid. Oh, God, she'd really done a job on herself this time.

Or had she? Something at the farthest edge of memory nagged at her, tried to take shape, and then faded. It was a feeling really. The feeling of something solid—something flat and hard, the heel of a hand maybe, hitting against her back. Shoving, that was it, shoving. And driving. Driving her forward into this awful whirling black emptiness. If only, she muttered to herself, I could remember.

But Lillian could not, and because she failed to give shape or definition to this wisp of memory, the hand would be free to push and strike again. And again. And again.

As Miss Austen might have written, it is a truth universally acknowledged that an expensive item offered free of charge will be accepted without thought to whether the item is desired or even useful. Thus, on a morning in late April it happened that one Julia Clancy, doyenne of the local equestrian world, found herself with the opportunity of visiting foreign parts during the month of June without the bother of paying for it.

It happened thus:

Saturday, April third began with what the French describe as a "blow of the telephone." Julia, who disliked telephone calls in general and early morning ones in particular, got stiffly to her feet, reached for her cane—her arthritis was very bad this spring—stumped over to the telephone, and barked hello.

"Julia?" queried the voice.

"Of course, it's Julia," said Julia. "That's who you were calling, wasn't it?"

"Julia," repeated the voice.

"Is that you, Adelaide? Well, I'm very busy in the barn so I can't talk now."

"You're not in the barn, Julia," said Adelaide—Adelaide Dempster, local stalwart of the Midcoast Garden Club. "I called there first and your stableman said you were at the house. Now do listen for once. I have an offer..."

"...I can't refuse? Oh yes I can. If it's your summer garden tour, I'll buy two tickets and not go."

"Wait up," said Adelaide. She was Julia's second cousin and knew her ways and moods. "Not tickets. I mean, yes, it's a ticket—actually two tickets. A real tour. Not just around here. The UK, France, and Italy. The Cotswolds, Sissinghurst, and Giverny. Monet's lilies. And Bellagio. It's on Lake Como."

"I don't want to go away," said Julia in a cross voice. "I want to go down to the barn and check on my horses. It's past seven-thirty and Duffle cast a shoe last night. I've got to call the farrier."

"You must take the tickets. The Whirlaway Tours people have to be guaranteed a certain number of tickets or the whole trip will be canceled. Everything's paid for. I can't go; my back has gone completely flooey, and yesterday Lillian Garth fell down the cellar steps."

"What!"

"An accident. Well, I suppose it must have been an accident because poor Lillian is a little careless. You see, Lillian organized the whole tour and was going to help lead the trip. She's a real powerhouse when it comes to pulling things together..."

"Get on with it," growled Julia.

"Well, Lillian not only nailed another dynamo—Dr. Ellen Trevino (she wrote that book on English cottage gardens)—but she turned up this expert leader from Whirlaway Tours, Barbara Baxter, who's a sort of facilitator. Barbara's been terrific and she's already dug up two people to fill out the numbers. We needed four and you're the other two. A handsome man called Rossi and this other gorgeous blonde female..."

"For God's sake, Adelaide, I don't give a damn about handsome men and gorgeous blondes, so get to the point."

"Well, Lillian got the whole travel group together at her house—tea, coffee, cake, drinks, the whole bit—and Sandi Ouellette, who's a sort of bubblehead—asked about root cellars, and Lillian went to bring up some tubers she's been nursing along, and down she went. Not the first time, either, because it seems she slipped on the same stairs a while back. So, now she's got a concussion along with a broken right leg and a smashed left ankle. Totally out of action. So Barbara Baxter, along with Dr. Trevino, is going to handle the tour. So there you are. Two tickets. Mine and Lillian's. The whole thing on a platter—airfares, hotels, inns, B&Bs, and seats on the bus."

Julia, one of the world's non-gardeners, sat heavily on a kitchen stool and studied the roof of her stable, visible from her kitchen window. "There's so much to do on the farm," she said, but her voice betrayed a rising interest. The idea of going free to England and France and Italy in June had a definite attraction.

Adelaide persisted. "Not only the gardens, which are beautiful even if you know absolutely nothing about flowers, but you could hire a car and sneak off from time to time. Breeding farms, thoroughbreds, warmbloods," said Adelaide, who knew Julia's Achilles' heel.

"But I hardly know a poppy from a peony and my own garden is a mess. Besides, next month is such a busy time. The new foals. The show schedule and the dressage clinic. Riding lesson schedules."

"Julia, be quiet and listen. Your manager, the wonderful Patrick, can handle the farm nicely without you. And you have plenty of other help. Stablemen and those working students you starve to death. Give them all a break and go away."

"I'm on a cane," complained Julia. "My blasted knee hurts like hell."

"So keep your cane. It's an advantage. I'm sixty-three and use a cane all the time. It empowers me. People give way. Get your family doctor—it's Alex McKenzie, isn't it, practically a relative—to plug you into some high-powered anti-inflammatory and go for it. You'll be fine. I'm just sorry I can't make it."

So it was that Julia Clancy dug out her passport, called her niece's husband, Alex, for a prescription, and began thinking of all-purpose washable garments. And a suitable companion. And who else but that selfsame niece, Sarah Douglas Deane, an adjunct on past assorted junkets and visits?

"No," said Sarah when called at her office in the Bowmouth College English Department. "I'll have just finished the spring teaching term and be a wreck. Besides, I wanted to paint the living room. That leaves Alex to do it by himself. Or not do it which is more likely. And what about my dog, Patsy?"

"Patsy can come over to the farm. He loves my setters. And Alex did just fine for years without your help. Besides, I called his office because I want some killer drug for my arthritis. He just got word he has a Lyme Disease conference in Bologna the last week in June. We can be in the tour for the first part of the trip and later meet up with Alex in Italy. But I don't want to spend the whole time crammed in a bus with other people, so we'll hire our own car and duck out from time to time and go off on our own."

"So why not scrub the entire tour? Just fly over with them, then split and do our own thing?"

"Don't be foolish. Free meals at inns and hotels, free admissions to the gardens. Everything's paid for. Besides I thought you were getting into a garden mode. Those new peach trees."

"Eight feeble peach trees do not a garden make."

"Don't be a stick-in-the-mud. I need you."

"Who's this Barbara Baxter person?"

"Tour boss. She'll have to do the whole thing now that Lillian's laid up. And she doesn't have to know much about flowers because there'll be a real expert along. Dr. Ellen Trevino."

"Wait," said Sarah, her voice a shade more enthusiastic. "Did you say Ellen Trevino?"

"Yes, that's the name. I think she teaches at your college. Biology, botany. Something like that. Have you run into her?"

"Run into her?" Sarah exclaimed. "I grew up with her. Next door. In Carlisle. When my family was in its Massachusetts phase. Ellen was sweet but very shy and kept to herself. I was one of her few friends and we've known each other since sandbox days. I'm always amazed when I think about her lecturing, standing up in front of students. In grade school she used to freeze if the teacher so much as looked at her."

"Well, good. A friend on the trip. Besides old Julia."

"I haven't seen much of Ellen, really, for years. She's not a people person. She gives her lectures and goes into hiding. No time for lunch. Every now and then I go out and visit her—she lives way out in the country—and she's nice about it, but I can always tell she's itching to get back to her greenhouse."

"So why has she agreed to lead a group all the way to Europe? Be locked in with a bunch of strangers."

"Oh, I've heard she does that from time to time. Probably needs the money. Bowmouth salaries barely support life."

Julia returned to the matter at hand. "So Ellen Trevino is a plus. And I'm grateful she'll be along because I haven't time to read up on gardens. I'm much too busy with foaling."

Sarah's sigh was audible over the telephone. "And I'm too busy with exams."

"Not the same thing. Foaling is day and night work, very strenuous and quite nerve-racking. All you do is sit at a desk, ask questions, and scratch out answers with a red pencil."

Sarah ignored this thrust. "And I hate flying," she said. "A few hours is bad enough, but crossing the Atlantic wondering if the life jackets really float is my idea of torture."

"They have pills. Alex will prescribe for you. Something to knock you out. Now I've got to go. Work on your French and Italian. Useful phrases like *Aidez-moi* and *Où se trouve* the ladies room? In Italian it's *Dove sono i gabinetti?* And, Sarah, check your passport. Goodbye."

"Aunt Julia, wait," shouted Sarah, but the line was dead.

"Damn that woman," said Sarah aloud.

"So you're going on the garden tour," said her husband, Alex, when he made it home from the hospital that night. He threw himself down in one of the ancient wicker kitchen armchairs and grinned at her. "I know you're going even if you think you aren't. Aunt Julia has spoken."

Sarah looked up from a heap of student papers and rammed her red pencil down on the top sheet, breaking the point. "I am not," she said. "Never. Not on your life."

But somehow time went by, April turned into May and June stood on the horizon, and Sarah found herself, like Julia, checking her passport, taking out an international driver's license, and looking into wrinkle-proof clothing. And filling out the short "getting to know you" biographical questionnaire sent out by the Whirlaway Tours leader, Barbara Baxter—a waste of time in Sarah's opinion since most of the Garden Club members must be entirely too familiar with each other by this time.

But the final annoyance came when the energetic Ms. Baxter sent out announcements of a tour party in a back room of the Surfway Restaurant.

"I don't have time to go to some party," she told her aunt Julia, when informed of the event. "Besides, I'll meet everyone on the plane and on the bus. At lunch and dinner. Why rush it?"

"We'll look like a pair of snobs if we don't go. Barbara Baxter has this idea that if we know each other ahead of time everything will run more smoothly. One happy family on tour."

"Gag. She didn't say that, did she?"

"No, I said it to get a rise out of you. Pick me up at six-thirty."

The tour group appeared to have been made up of a core from the local Midcoast Garden Club plus the two outside enthusiasts—the described handsome male and the gorgeous blonde—both from "away," as the people of Maine refer to those unfortunate enough to have been born beyond its borders. Barbara had waved vaguely in the direction of Massachusetts when introducing the apparently unrelated man and woman. "Both have been on our Whirlaway Tours before and we're so lucky they're free to go."

Sarah glanced around the table as she worked first through a daiquiri, then chicken Kiev and apple crisp. There was her old friend, Ellen Trevino, who, as the honored speaker, sat in the center of the table next to Barbara Baxter. Sarah had waved at her on entering the dining room, but had given up hope of conversation since Ellen, as the evening's ornament, had been from her arrival surrounded by garden enthusiasts.

Most of the club members were everyday types, she decided, the sort of people you could picture down on their knees with a trowel and a hand rake. Julia, of course, didn't fit the profile of persons devoted to slow nurture and silent growth. Her voice was too sharp, her gestures too abrupt. Only when dealing with horses did the patient side of her aunt become manifest; for the general run of humans, Julia had little tolerance. Now, having chugged two pre-dinner whiskeys and gotten into a brisk argument about rotted manure, she was nodding over her coffee while Barbara Baxter made welcoming remarks.

This done, Barbara, armed with a map and a marker board, began drawing lines and triangles, listing dates and indicating inns, hotels, National Trust houses and gardens, periods of rest, and every now and again a stop for shopping and tea.

"And I hope to God the possibility of hard liquor," put in a fellow tour member, Carter McClure. Although many of the others were strangers, Sarah knew Carter by sight from Bowmouth College; he was one of the pashas of the History Department and said by his colleagues to be obsessed with his garden. He and his wife, Portia, were seated almost under Barbara Baxter's elbow, and Sarah found that they made a strange trio. Barbara had a pleasant freckled face, short-cropped sandy curls, and had a sturdy physique that suggested a former college soccer star. She had obviously dressed carefully for the occasion in a patterned navy skirt and a red blouse. Carter, on the other hand, was a tall, lean, hatchet-faced man with gray hair in a porcupine cut who, in contrast to other males present who wore jacket and tie, sported an in-your-face costume of black jacket, black shirt, and faded jeans and Nikes. Next to him sat Portia, a handsome African American woman with sharp eyes, a firm chin. Portia wore an olive dress hung with several chains of colored beads and from time to time laid a firm hand on Carter's arm in an attempt to restrain her husband from offending the entire party.

"I mean," said Carter, "I won't belong to any tour that neglects opportunities for a stiff drink. We'll be stomping around gardens all day, so we'd better not be booked into some goddamn temperance inn. And I'll say right now, forget the shopping."

"Carter," said Portia. "Be quiet."

"Hear, hear," said Julia Clancy, waking up and blinking.

But Barbara Baxter was not one to be derailed by the likes of Carter McClure. She wound up her speech, suggested that they were all kindred souls—and then with an eye on Carter began detailing the greatness of English ale, the friendly pubs, the inns and hotels chosen for the tour. Not to mention the gardens themselves. The treasures of England. This was actually her very first garden tour, but she was doing her homework, boning up. And she certainly looked forward to visiting the cottage gardens of the Cotswolds.

"So exciting," gushed Sandi Ouellette. "I'm going right home and reading up on cottage gardens." She paused. "What is a cottage garden, anyway?"

"An excellent question," said Barbara, "and one of our experts, Dr. Trevino, will be glad to answer." She indicated the thin-faced woman sitting at her right hand.

Dr. Ellen Trevino, after the briefest of hesitations—Sarah was reminded of the shy, withdrawn schoolgirl she had known—stood up and in a low but clear voice began to extol the virtues of the English cottage garden, and as she went from the problems of various soils, peat and sand, and other useful particulate matter to the actual planting and dividing and massing of flowers, Sarah understood that here was a woman in love. In love with what she was doing with her life. And she remembered Ellen as a twelve-year-old running ahead of a small tractor her father was running and snatching blooming flowers out of his path—Ellen shouting, "You're killing them, you're a murderer, you're killing all the flowers."

But then Ellen's father himself was killed in an automobile accident, her mother remarried and moved, and the two girls lost sight of each other. Even so, Sarah through a trick of memory was able to superimpose the thin child Ellen with the fair skin, the taut mouth, the determined small pointed chin, onto the slender adult Ellen with her light brown hair in a braided knot on the back of her head, the chin still assertive, the skin still pale except for the two patches of color on her cheeks—color no doubt brought on by the excitement of lecturing.

And lecturing it was. Ellen was making few allowances for the uninformed likes of Julia and Sarah—or Fred and Sandi Ouellette, for that matter. But as Dr. Trevino's peroration became more and more larded with Latin tags—*Anemone pulsatilla, Campanula lactiflora, Syringa persica laciniata*—Julia slumped in her seat and Sarah found her attention moving away from Ellen to her fellow tour members. This examination was facilitated by a large mirror on a side wall that reflected the party. Sarah found that by twisting slightly in her chair she could account for almost the whole group.

The mirror, she thought, what with the flickering table candles and the angle of the reflection, the deep shadows in the background, turned the table scene into a nineteenth-century period piece. She studied the reflection and then, having received the printout of every member's questionnaire, she decided to amuse herself by trying to fit the answers to the faces reflected in the mirror. First, of course, there was her aunt

Julia, a terrier of a woman, fierce of eye, bristly gray hair on end, linen jacket rumpled. Julia had restricted her response to listing herself as the owner of High Hope Farm, a trainer of horses and riders, and one who knew absolutely nothing about gardens. Sarah, herself, had not been quite so honest. After noting her employment as a lecturer in English at Bowmouth College, she had put herself down as an amateur gardener, one whose special interest was peach trees, but was hoping to put in some peonies and perhaps a rose bush in the near future. Squinting at her own reflection in the mirror, Sarah decided that she was looking a little haunted tonight, what with her end-of-term pallor; her cheekbones prominent; her chin almost as sharp as Ellen's; her gray eyes, somehow exaggerated by the lighting, looking almost black; and her short dark hair standing unnaturally away from her head—static electricity perhaps.

Then there was Carter McClure, now hidden in the mirror by Ellen Trevino. Carter had noted on his information sheet that space did not permit the listing of his many botanical interests and areas of expertise, adding only that propagation of hardy variants of *Viburnum plicatum mariesii* was a new project. Portia McClure, now concealed by Barbara Baxter's torso, had written that she raised King Charles Spaniels and loved herbal gardens, but that her real passion was developing superior compost.

Who was next of the Midcoast members? The resident feather-brain—Sandi Ouellette. Sitting there in a pink dress hung with bracelets, rings, and drippy earrings. A double row of twinkling buttons starting from her scoop neckline, traveling over her perky little breasts and disappearing waistward. Sandi, a person Sarah remembered from a previous encounter as being an enthusiast regardless of the event in progress. Even when the event had turned out to be sudden death, Sandi hadn't lost her friskiness. And her signature on the copied bio sheet showed a little circle over the "i" in her first name and a tiny happy face inside.

Sandi's partner in life was Fred Ouellette, a local undertaker, a tall bony dark-haired man who bore a slight resemblance to Abraham Lincoln. Fred thought Sandi was entrancing and Sandi thought Fred was a scream—this because Fred had a large stock of stories centered on lawyers and doctors in embarrassing situations. Fred himself had listed his profession as "mortician," one interested in the "burial practices of all nations," the good works of the Rotary, and especially in classic floral arrangements. For classic funerals, Sarah wondered. Or was it a joke?

She moved on to contemplation of the two Hoppers. Sisters, Margaret and Edith, who, having married cousins, shared the same last name. They were said to be staunch Garden Club loyalists. White-haired, they wore matching cable-stitch cardigans over their flowered silk dresses and carried Nantucket Lightship baskets. Margaret had declared herself a retired school librarian devoted to her grandchildren and the culture of Siberian Iris. Her sister Edith, retired from the management of a local bookstore, put in time with the Humane Society and enjoyed working in her rock garden. Both wore thick-lensed eyeglasses attached to beaded chains.

Then there were the four tour members seated at the end of the table who gave back interesting blurs of fuzzy heads and moving spoons and cups. Impossible to tell what they really looked like. The two other locals, Doris Lermatov and her daughter, Amy, sat together. Doris wrote that her interest was divided between "going to wonderful places to eat" and raising different varieties of delphiniums. Amy, age fourteen, expressed an interest in British rock bands and in finding a really weird haunted castle.

Sarah moved on to the two outsiders. The man, last name Rossi—showing an indistinct but interesting reflection—looked familiar. The other woman, Stacy, a sort of blond lioness, appeared in the mirror only as a melting of pale blue into cream. But even at the distance she looked as if she had stepped straight from the pages of *Vogue*.

Sarah was about to refresh herself with the personal history of these two when she became aware of a switch of speakers. Ellen Trevino had sat down and Margaret Hopper held the floor. The injured Lillian Garth was the subject. Such a distressing accident. How much she would be missed. Her strong leadership, her enthusiasm for herbaceous borders, all the reading she had done about Vita Sackville-West, Harold Nicolson, and Virginia Woolf and then to miss Sissinghurst. A real shame.

"Sissinghurst's not going away," said Carter McClure. "She can go next year."

Margaret Hopper ignored Carter. "Edith and I think we should send her something from a nursery. From all of us. Something Lillian can plant later. A hardy azalea perhaps."

There was a murmur of "Hear, hear," a vote was passed to send a suitable shrub to Lillian, and the table broke into little conversational groups, leaving Sarah to prod Julia and suggest home. But then Barbara Baxter was on her feet. "No oversized suitcases, and for any of you who are unsteady on your feet"—here she looked pointedly at Julia and then at the Hopper sisters—"let poor Lillian's accident be a warning. Bring appropriate shoes because we will be doing a lot of walking. Remember traveler's checks or credit cards, and meet me at Logan Airport on June sixth at the gates for international departures. British Airways. Flight 214. Two hours ahead of departure time. Your passports must be validated, your luggage ticketed, your seats assigned." And your baggage searched for bombs, Sarah said to herself, feeling a twinge in the bottom of her stomach.

The members of the Midcoast Garden Club and the extras from "away" rose en masse, milled briefly, and then headed for the coat room. Sarah tried vainly to reach Ellen Trevino for at least a few words in honor of old friendships, but Ellen had slipped away from the crowd of admirers and vanished into the night. As she always does, thought Sarah, feeling rather cheated. Privacy was all very well, but really. She picked up her handbag and found herself joined by Sandi Ouellette.

"I just hope I can remember everything. Fred says I'm a real fluff-head when it comes to dates and places. And English names for things. But I'm not such a fluff-head that I'd forget to turn on the cellar lights. I'm very safety conscious."

"That's good," said Sarah absently, hunting ahead for Julia. But Sandi had more to say. "And so is Lillian Garth. She's the one who proposed me for a Garden Club member because we're in the same yoga class, and I'm sure she turned on the cellar stair lights that day. I know because I wanted to go down for her, and she said I was to stay put and she'd go down herself and bring up some roots she was storing, and, besides, she knew where the light switch was. It was on the left side, not the right, because the electrician had made a dumb mistake. So there. I think she fell down because she's careless, not because she couldn't see."

Sarah frowned. "You mean the lights were *on* when she fell?"

"Well," said Sandi, "I went to see her in the hospital and she can't remember what happened, but I say she couldn't have forgotten the lights because she talked about them. But, you know, they were off when we found her. I think a fuse blew or something. Anyway, I'm sorry Lillian can't go because she's a real organizer and knew how to make everyone feel at home."

"And Barbara Baxter doesn't?"

"Oh, of course she does. Barbara's wonderful the way she's taken hold, but, anyway, it's a real shame," concluded Sandi, shaking her blond tangle of hair. And she scurried ahead to catch up with Fred, who stood by the door waiting with Julia Clancy.

Sarah was silent as she drove home with Julia but, as they neared the turn off to High Hope Farm, she could not resist saying, "Sandi Ouellette says Lillian Garth meant to turn on the cellar lights. She actually mentioned it to Sandi."

Julia turned in her seat. "Sarah Douglas Deane, stop that right now. You are asking for trouble. I swear you would stand at the heavenly gates and tell St. Peter that the gates are off their hinges and one of the angels is wearing a false nose. You have a diseased mind."

"Only a curious one," murmured Sarah. "It's sort of a habit."

"Well, go back to literature and stop bringing all those tangled webs and evil plots into our quiet everyday life."

"Your everyday life, my dear aunt," said Sarah firmly, "would choke a horse. And probably has."

"No unnatural harm has ever come to my horses," rejoined Julia.

"No," said Sarah, remembering only too vividly a summer of mayhem at High Hope Farm. "The horses have made out all right. It's the humans who haven't been so lucky."

Chapter Two

IT WAS ALMOST A week later when Sarah managed to catch sight of Ellen Trevino. It was after one o'clock on the last Friday in May and Sarah was heading for the faculty parking lot when she saw Ellen ahead, briefcase in hand, moving purposefully.

"Ellen," she called. "Ellen, wait up." Sarah hastened her steps and caught up with her friend. "Ellen, I'm so glad you're going to be on this garden thing. Maybe you can even teach a horticultural idiot like me a few things."

Ellen came to a stop and smiled. In the days when campus dress—even for faculty members—was casual to the extreme, she seemed to have stepped from a pre-Raphaelite painting with her long brown hair, her pale cream complexion, her long cotton skirt in a dark tapestry pattern, topped by a white ruffed-neck blouse held at the collar by a gold and jade brooch.

"Lunch," said Sarah, on sudden inspiration. "I've just finished the last of my student exams and I'm starving. We'll find some place quiet because I know you don't like crowds."

But Ellen shook her head. "Sarah, I just have too much to do. I'd love to sometime. Anyway, we'll all be having lunch together on this garden trip. I'm almost dreading the whole thing, and for two cents I'd cancel and let Barbara Baxter run it. She seems capable. Three weeks elbow to elbow, toe to toe. And Carter McClure can be such a pain in the neck; even Portia can't keep him civil all the time."

"Then why did you agree to do it?" demanded Sarah. "The money?"

Ellen gave a slight lift of her shoulders. "That, yes. I'm always short of cash and I'm still paying for that new all-season greenhouse I put in last year. Of course, it's a good chance to see English gardens in June. I'd have stuck to England, but the group wants France and Italy. Anyway," she added with more energy, "I'm afraid I've worked out a pretty rigorous schedule. It's not going to be a tourist trip—you know, with side trips to Harrods or Stratford, or going out of the way to eat at fancy restaurants."

"Not even a pub or a village churchyard?"

"At night they can all do what they want. But I think everyone will be tired after hiking around all day. It's to be a focused trip just as Lillian Garth planned it." Here Ellen paused and then brightened. "But I'm glad you found me. I need something to read on the trip. Nothing violent. English and nineteenth century and I've read all Jane Austen. What do you suggest?"

Sarah thought for a moment, discarded the Brontës and Dickens, and then said, "Try Trollope. Any of the novels, but if you haven't read him, start with *The Warden* and *Barchester Towers*."

Ellen gave a little affirmative bob of the head. "Thanks, I'll do that. And now my greenhouse is calling. Time to finish thinning the perennial beds." She hesitated. "But it was nice of you, Sarah, to think of lunch. Only I almost never eat out." And Ellen turned and was lost among the cars in the parking lot.

Sarah watched the slim figure, her dark skirt billowing slightly in a slight gust of wind. So much for old times and gossip with childhood friends, she thought rather sadly. But then she shrugged and headed for her own car. Ellen was just being Ellen, her own private person. Focused on her own special piece of the world and steering carefully clear of the rest of it.

Sarah, at the beginning of the following week, tried once more to touch base with Ellen. Alex, hoping to see the last half of a Red Sox doubleheader, had agreed to drive Julia and his wife to Boston's Logan Airport, and Sarah thought, Why not offer Ellen a ride? If she was short of money she might appreciate the lift.

But when Sarah phoned the offer was declined. "I think I'd rather drive myself," explained Ellen in her quiet voice. "I may stop here and there. Stop at a greenhouse. Look up someone. Or maybe not," she added vaguely. "But, anyway, thanks."

The departure date, Tuesday, June the sixth, came at last. Julia Clancy clutching two small phrase books sat in the back seat of Alex's Jeep and attempted to engage Sarah, in the front passenger seat, in what Julia considered to be essential French and Italian sentences. Alex, acting as chauffeur, let the two women get on with it while he listened to the Red Sox fumble their way through three innings against the Toronto Blue Jays.

"*Je m'appelle Julia,*" said Julia to Sarah. "*Mi chiamo Julia,*" she repeated in Italian. "*Où se trouve le téléphone? Dov'è una cassetta postale, per favore?*"

"For heaven's sake," said Sarah. "Stick to one language. *Je m'appelle Sarah*, and shouldn't you be using '*tu*'? You're my aunt."

"Nitpicking," said Julia. "*Il fait beau aujourd'hui, n'est-ce pas?*"

"*Il fait* lousy," said Sarah. "The sky is dark gray, it's hot as Hades, and it's going to thunder and lightning and rain, which means wind shear and down drafts. And I don't like to fly even in good weather."

"In French," scolded Julia.

"Je n'aime pas les aeroplanes. J'aime seulement le chemin de fer ou l'autobus. Et peut-être a horse—*un cheval."*

"J'aime aussi les chevals," said Julia. "I mean, *les chevaux."*

"Hey," said Alex from the driver's seat. "A double to left field and two runs in. That ties it up. Okay, passengers, New Hampshire border ahead. And," as large raindrops splattered the windshield, "here comes the rain."

Sarah made an effort to put the flight out of her mind. "How is Lillian Garth? You said you'd been to see her this morning. Why? You don't do orthopedic stuff."

"She ran a little fever this morning. We were about to send her off to rehab but she began coughing. She's eaten up with jealousy about you all going off."

"Better not get on to the subject of Lillian," said Julia, "or Sarah will convince you that she was hurled down her cellar stairs by some alien assassin. It's too bad about Lillian, but the loose ends seem to be taken up by this Barbara Baxter. I think she could handle a platoon of teenagers with acute attention deficit disorder. And Ellen Trevino will make a good co-tour leader. She's very knowledgeable," said Julia, who had dozed through most of Ellen's talk. She tapped Sarah on the shoulder. *"Maintenant, je parle francais. Je pense que les jardins d'angleterre sont très beaux, n'est-ce pas?"*

"Certainement," said Sarah, subsiding.

Meanwhile from assorted corners of the state in a variety of vehicles came the members of the Midcoast Garden Club. The Hopper sisters, Margaret and Edith, had chosen to join Sandi and Fred Ouellette in an airport limousine to the Portland Jetport and thence to Boston, and as Alex and his passengers crossed from Maine into New Hampshire, these four were busy discussing the necessaries for transatlantic flight. Margaret and Edith explained that in the interest of comfort they carried inflated pillows that fastened around their necks, and Sandi explained that she had bought an English novel—*The Shell Seekers*—because she wanted to soak up as much atmosphere as possible as this was her absolutely first trip out of the country. To this Fred added that he'd brought a Patricia Cornwell mystery because the author featured the autopsy table, to which Margaret and Edith both exclaimed "Goodness" and then offered the fact that they never traveled without a folding photo album with pictures of their children and grandchildren and Edith's cat, Trixie, and Margaret's little Westie, Rob Roy.

It was generally believed by the Hoppers and the Ouellettes, as well as by the rest of the travelers, that Barbara Baxter would contrive to arrive early at the British Airways Terminal, ready to soothe, explain, and generally manage the departure of her flock, and that Dr. Ellen Trevino would stand at Barbara's right hand and make herself generally useful.

These surmises proved incorrect.

Sarah and Julia were the first of the party to arrive at the international terminal, partly because Julia always fussed about being late, but more importantly because Alex wanted to get to Fenway Park as soon as possible; he just hoped that the rain, which was still falling, wouldn't force a cancellation.

Sarah, in her usual state of knocking nerves, was able only to give her husband a quick kiss and a weak clasp around his neck and assure him that she did love him, even though by encouraging her to fly he was allowing her to die before her time. To which Alex laughed, hugged her, and said he'd see her in Italy in a couple of weeks.

Julia, distracted briefly by having to unearth her passport from a pouch hanging next to her bra, joined briefly in the farewell, and then led Sarah away in search of the other tour members. The international terminal was crowded with early summer travelers and already two lines had formed in the British Airways section—first class and economy.

"Economy, that's us," said Julia cheerfully. "This way. They'll want to see our passports and then they'll take our bags."

"I wish I'd only brought my shoulder bag," said Sarah, looking unhappily at her large canvas suitcase that was refusing to roll smoothly on its little black wheels. Pulling this object and clutching her shoulder bag and overseeing a large leather handbag was proving a chore.

"Well, Barbara did tell us to travel light. Everyone takes too much. I always travel with Tom's army duffel with the shoulder strap. Makes me think Tom is coming along on the trip."

Sarah nodded sympathetically. Irish Tom Clancy was Julia's long dead husband, never too far from Julia's thoughts. Together they had built High Hope Farm, together they had bred, trained, and shown their horses. It had been, Sarah knew, a most happy marriage founded firmly on a jointly held obsession for all things equine. "Uncle Tom," Sarah began, but Julia pointed to a door opening. "It's Fred Ouellette and Sandi. I don't have the energy to talk to Sandi. And Fred talks too much."

"Well, here come Edith and Margaret Hopper," said Sarah. "They're safe. They like to read and they won't rave about the wonders of flight the way Sandi will."

"And there are the McClures," said Julia, craning her neck. "I just hope Portia can keep a clamp on Carter's mouth."

"It's about time Barbara showed up," said Sarah. "All that talk about being early."

But, after a period of group restlessness, Justin Rossi, Stacy Daniel, the two Lermatovs, and Barbara arrived in their midst, Barbera pulling behind her a large wheeled suitcase.

"It's as big as mine," said Sarah. "So much for her advice."

"She probably has it stuffed with guidebooks and garden Cliff Notes," said Julia.

But now Barbara, explaining that their Delta 5:05 flight had been held up, began checking off names. All present and accounted for, she announced cheerily. Except...

Except for Ellen Trevino. Had anyone seen Dr. Trevino? Was she driving to Boston? Or flying? Did anyone know?

Sarah offered the information that she thought Ellen meant to drive, a remark contradicted by Doris Lermatov, who had seen her at the dentist's and thought Ellen mentioned a flight from Augusta. Or perhaps her dentist was the one flying from there. She wasn't sure, but then she hadn't been paying attention.

These remarks set up a buzz that ran round the Garden Club members. Sarah could hear exclamations of concern, surprise, and—from Carter McClure—annoyance. "Trust an academic," he said to the room at large. "They never know what time it is, let alone the day of the week. The Bowmouth Biology Department had Ellen Trevino for a couple of guest lectures and she was late at least once."

"Carter," said Portia, "everyone can hear you, and you're an academic, in case you've forgotten."

Carter drew himself up, his lean face turned into a sardonic smile. "Ah, I am the exception that proves the rule. Admit it, Portia. The Bowmouth faculty is filled with brainless hens and clucking chickens and mindless tomcats, and as for the English Department, they live on another planet entirely." Here Carter raised his eyebrows, looked directly at Sarah, and closed one eye in what looked like a provocative wink.

But before Sarah, who at times agreed with Dr. McClure, could think of how to defend the English Department, Barbara Baxter excused herself saying she was going to find a telephone and try to find out what was holding up Ellen. And she disappeared into the ever increasing swarm of overseas travelers.

Sarah, shuffling along toward the British Airways passport checkpoint, had now reached that state of preflight jitters where her mouth was dry and her palms were wet. Right now she didn't give a damn whether Ellen turned up or vanished for good into the stratosphere. She didn't care whether she lost her suitcase or whether the flight attendants were all vampires. She stuffed her sweaty hands in the pockets of her new camel hair jacket and gave her suitcase a vicious kick that sent it flat on its side, its little black wheels spinning.

At this juncture, Julia, who was usually oblivious to the moods of others, seemed to realize that all was not well with her niece. "For God's sake, take your pill," she ordered. "That's what it's for. Alex said an hour before we take off. It's nearly seven and we take off at eight. And you needn't fret, it's a Boeing 747 and big enough to carry elephants. Get a grip."

Sarah made an attempt to pull herself together. She pointed at Carter McClure, who had managed to insert himself and Portia ahead of the entire Garden Club entourage. "Carter fits the terrorist profile," she said. "That black shirt and the dark glasses. All he needs is a hand grenade."

"Oh, don't even say those words," squeaked someone in back of her. It was Margaret Hopper. "We'll all be arrested or put into some sort of observation lounge. It happened to a friend of mine."

Sarah nodded and moved forward, submitted her passport, surrendered her suitcase, swung her shoulder bag across her neck, gripped her handbag, and followed her aunt into the main terminal. There, surrounded by the hundreds of noisy travelers, college students, families foreign and domestic, women in saris, Sikhs in turbans, Asian tour groups hung about with cameras, Sarah allowed her aunt to administer tea and then prod her forward through the metal detector, into the departure lounge, and on to the embarkation tunnel.

The tunnel, she always thought, was like some sort of mechanical intestine that by means of reverse peristalsis pulled its human fodder through its rectum and thence into the abdomen of the jumbo silver beast. It was a distressing image, and Sarah had never felt so disposable. Inching along, she had just reached that point where the passageway dips down into the plane entrance when Julia plummeted against her, sending her shoulder bag into orbit and knocking her forward and down in front of the welcoming flight attendant. She fell to her knees, turned, and reached for Julia and found Edith Hopper on top of her aunt. And Barbara Baxter athwart Edith and the man called Rossi bent double over a toppled Sandi Ouellette. And Fred

Ouellette convulsed with laughter, hanging on to the beautiful Stacy, who seemed to be on all fours.

It was all like one of those turnpike pileups where one vehicle coming to grief causes a chain reaction. After cries of "I was pushed" and "you tripped me," everyone, no doubt in the crest of excitement, became cheerful. Bags, duffels, magazines, paperbacks, sections of the *Boston Globe* were retrieved, and amid a certain amount of hilarity, the boarders surged forward to be met by the laughing flight attendant who had assisted in the pickup and now welcomed them aboard Flight 214 and pointed out seats and aisles.

"She's got an English accent," exclaimed Sandi Ouellette as she stored her new trench coat overhead. "Now I feel I'm really going somewhere foreign."

"You are," said Julia, sounding exactly like Carter McClure. Then finding that both their seats were in the middle aisle between the McClures on one side and the Hopper sisters on the other, she smiled at Sarah. "We lucked out," she announced, indicating Sandi and Fred settling in down two rows and across the aisle.

"Shhh, they'll hear you," said Sarah.

But Julia was engaged in stowing her possessions, thrusting the airline pillow behind her back, and producing to Sarah's surprise a square of needlepoint canvas on which the sketch of a horse flying over a timber fence could be made out. "I always do needlepoint when I travel. I don't want to feel I'm wasting time."

But Sarah had not heard her aunt. Her head was down and she was rummaging about in her shoulder bag. "I'm looking for my book," she explained. "I thought..." but she never finished her sentence. Instead she held up a pair of black-rimmed sunglasses.

"These aren't mine," she exclaimed.

"You can't have too many sunglasses," said Julia. She was busily unfolding her needlepoint canvas and threading a needle with copper-colored wool.

"I already have a pair. These belong to someone else."

"They'll probably be useful," observed Julia, plunging her threaded needle into a horse's nostril.

"Read my lips," said Sarah. "My glasses are prescription. These are cheap and look like something a dope dealer might wear."

"Or someone with perfect vision who doesn't need to spend a lot of money."

"Well, I don't want them," said Sarah. "I have enough extra junk. But how do you suppose...?"

The question was cut short by the insistent blinking of the seat belt light and the appearance of the no-smoking sign. Then the flight attendants took their seats, buckled up, and the 747's engine rumbled ominously, increased its volume, and the giant plane backed, turned and began its trundle toward the takeoff runway.

Sarah tightened her seat belt, wiped her wet hands again on the cloth of her travel jacket, leaned back, closed her eyes and began a recitation of a long ago learned poem she had commonly used when finding herself aboard a heavier-than-air machine. The poem fortunately went on forever and so could be employed for the entire take-off period. "There are strange things done in the midnight sun," she muttered, "By the men who moil for gold;

The Arctic trails have their secret tales
That would make your blood run cold;
The Northern Lights have seen queer sights,
But the queerest they ever did see
Was the night on the marge of Lake Lebarge
I cremated Sam McGee."

She had just reached that interesting point in the poem where "And before nightfall a corpse was all that was left of Sam McGee," when at exactly three minutes after eight o'clock eastern daylight time British Airways Flight 214 bound for London's Heathrow Airport mounted into the rain-filled air, climbed over Boston Harbor and turned northeast toward the coast of Maine.

"We go right over my house, I think," said Margaret Hopper to Sarah. "All the trouble of us getting to Boston and then we fly right back over where we came from."

"Maine?" said Sarah stupidly.

"Well, yes dear," said Margaret. "Check your map. Then it's on to Newfoundland and Iceland and so forth. What fun!"

"Fun?" said Sarah.

"Fun," repeated Margaret firmly. "At least I hope so because Edith and I are spending every penny we own on this trip. Even if it rains every minute." She pointed to the sunglasses on Sarah's lap. "You won't need those inside the plane. I think they turn the lights down later on."

This observation roused Sarah to greater verbal effort. "The glasses aren't mine. I just found them. In my shoulder bag."

Margaret nodded. "You can't have too many sunglasses, I always say. But you may not need them right away. It's raining in London. That's what the flight attendant told me."

At which point Julia put down her needlepoint. "I knew I'd need something waterproof so I brought my oilskin riding jacket. I can ride for hours in it and be almost dry."

"We're not going to be riding," Sarah reminded her. Again she indicated the glasses. "When we all fell into each other and everyone was grabbing books and magazines someone must have shoved these into my shoulder bag. It doesn't have a zipper, only leather straps and buckles. I should ask around."

But Sarah's plan was put on hold; it was dinnertime. Flight attendants, spruce in their tricolor scarves or ties, passed menus, took orders, delivered trays, and Sarah felt a slight relaxation in tension—the pill kicking in perhaps. Also, she had a fuddled idea that if the plane were in immediate danger of falling from the sky, the serving of dinner might take a backseat.

Unfortunately for post-dinner nerves, that other soother of the anxious—the evening movie—was canceled due to a malfunction of something electronic, leaving Sarah to wonder aloud that if the movie machinery was on the fritz, what about the plane itself?

"Sarah," said Aunt Julia, "shut up. Go around and ask about the sunglasses. It will do you good to move around. Then find your book. I, for one, am going to sew for fifteen minutes and then work out some breeding problems. I'm worried about repeating my Welsh-thoroughbred cross because I'm not getting the bone I wanted."

Sarah found no takers for the sunglasses. The only person interested was Portia McClure, who had forgotten her own, and Sarah presented them to her. Returning to her own seat, teeth brushed, face sluiced, she found her aunt and Margaret Hopper in conversation about perennial borders, her aunt contributing the opinion that the only flowers worth having were those that came up entirely on their own and Margaret shaking her head in disapproval.

"No takers," Sarah announced, "so I gave the glasses to Portia. She'd forgotten hers. And I'll take Aunt Julia's advice and read. I brought *Cranford* because nothing really happens in it."

She reached down into her shoulder bag for the second time and again came up with an alien object. This item proved to be a dark red and black patterned scarf, rather rumpled and knotted into a triangle. Sarah held it up before her aunt.

"Yours?" she queried.

Julia put her needlepoint aside and reached for the scarf. She held it up, turned it over, examined the label and handed it back. "Filene's," she announced. "Rather handsome. And the label says 'all silk.' Are you sure it isn't yours?"

"Quite sure," said Sarah. "It probably arrived with the sunglasses. It looks a little used. Anyway, I don't think I'll go hopping up and down the aisle asking if someone's missing a scarf as well as glasses. I can try later."

"They may not belong to the Garden Club group at all," Julia pointed out. "And now it's my bedtime." And she reached into the canvas case at her feet and produced an eye shade which she slipped over her head, stuffed the pillow under one cheek, and folded her hands in her lap.

It was so quiet now in the cabin that Sarah could hear the whoosh of the jet moving through the night sky. The overhead lights had dimmed, some passengers, like Julia, had put on sleeping masks, others had drawn blankets around their bodies and put pillows under their heads as if to imitate normal sleeping conditions. However, the large number of tightly packed passengers did not permit the seats from going back more than a few inches so Sarah thought that the entire scene resembled nothing so much as a strange necropolis in which vertical burying was the norm. She just managed to force this image out of her brain and had wriggled her head into a sidewise position, grateful that the pill was making her pleasantly groggy when she heard Margaret Hopper turn to her sister Edith and say in a hushed voice that it wasn't entirely a bad thing that Dr. Trevino had missed the flight. "She's a little bit intimidating, all that nomenclature," said Margaret. "Besides, I heard her say the night of the dinner that she didn't believe in any side trips."

To which Edith replied, "I agree. I felt quite stupid when I asked about late-blooming phlox. She was very polite but kept talking about subspecies. Perhaps Providence prevented her from making the flight. And now we must both try and get just a little sleep. Good night, dear."

And Margaret patted her sister's hand and said, "Good night to you, too," and leaned back against her seat and closed her eyes.

And Sarah opened hers and stared wide-eyed ahead of her seeing not the seat back, but Ellen Trevino standing up at the festive dinner and speaking in her clear, low voice of the wonders of English cottage gardens. Ellen Trevino, about whose company at least two of the Midcoast Garden Club were dubious. For several minutes Sarah stayed rigid, and then the sedative overwhelmed her brain, and she drifted into an uneasy sleep in which Ellen floated above her, face obscured by sunglasses, a red and black silk scarf tied tightly over her head, while a dark and ominous cloud labeled "Deadly Nightshade" hovered over her head.

Chapter Three

NIGHTTIME OVERSEAS FLIGHTS ARE not pools of peace. Sleeping upright in the presence of a multitude of strangers, the uneasy shiftings of cramped bodies, the tread no matter how tactful of the flight attendants, the sudden cry of a baby or the snore across the aisle, all are enough to ensure a disturbed night. Of the Midcoast Garden Club tour group only those two hardheaded characters, Julia Clancy and Carter McClure, got something resembling rest. The others turned and twitched and snuffled and finally sat up to be faced with a breakfast tray at what they considered rightly to be three in the morning.

Heavy-eyed and dry-mouthed from her disturbing dream of a levitating Ellen Trevino, Sarah woke to see that the black outside the cabin windows had given away to the gray light of morning. This was a relief because she was sure that the rescue of downed passengers was certainly easier on a daylight ocean.

"Sarah," said Julia, "We'll be landing in an hour and we don't want to join the others in one of those airport hotels where you waste half a day trying to catch up on sleep."

"You don't want to go anywhere and rest?" protested Sarah. "I mean jet lag is real. Five hours difference."

"I've hired a car," said Julia, "but an old woman like me shouldn't drive in morning rush-hour traffic, so I'm letting you handle it. It's not too far away. A B&B in the country."

Sarah interrupted. "You mean a horse farm?"

"I suppose they still have horses. Dodgeson Farm has a variety of animals. A very nice place. In Dinton. I stayed there a few years ago. We'll catch up to the others tomorrow night."

"Where," demanded Sarah, "on God's earth is Dinton?"

But Julia had turned and craned her neck toward the nearest window. The 747 had begun its descent and the buckled up passengers began closing their briefcases and checking on their passports. Sarah put aside the question of Dinton and herself as a sleep-deprived driver of a strange car. What was needed again was "The Cremation of Sam McGee" recited slowly with proper attention given to its sing-song meter. Sarah closed her eyes and didn't open them until she felt the heaven-blest bumpty-bump of landing wheels touching down on tarmac. She turned to Aunt Julia and said with a sense of modest triumph, "'The flames just soared, and the furnace roared—such a blaze you seldom see; /And I burrowed a hole in the glowing coal, and I stuffed in Sam McGee.'"

Lined up for passport inspection, Sarah had no time for further argument with her aunt. The passengers of Flight 214 broke ranks and headed toward their various destinations: the Midcoast Garden Club to the Ibis Hotel to rest, Sarah and Julia to change their traveler's checks for pounds and pence and then to the Europcar rental agency.

"We're off," said Julia when she had settled into the passenger seat of a blue Ford Escort. "And the rain's about stopped. I think we'll have a pleasant drive."

Sarah looked up from the automobile map. "Pleasant drive, my foot. We're surrounded by nine million cars, and I have to get us out of Heathrow and find the M40 without having a major wreck." She blinked and yawned. "Actually, I'm the major wreck. Fasten your seat belt." And clinging to the left lane, Sarah slowly moved the Ford onto a secondary road, onto a tertiary gravel road filled with repair equipment, reversed into London bound traffic, turned, and finally eighty minutes, five villages, three road blocks, two unnecessary roundabouts, and a construction detour later, left the M40, picked up the A418, and crawled to the edge of Dinton, found an opening into a promising hedgerow, and turned into Dodgeson Farm.

Julia, who had slumbered peacefully for the last half hour, opened her eyes and looked about with satisfaction.

"Well done, Sarah. I knew you could find your way."

Sarah, whose temper had been lost for good at the last roundabout, lifted her head and snapped. "I hate hedgerows, and passing on the right; and I think British drivers are worse than Boston drivers and that's going some."

To which Julia replied by patting her niece's shoulder, then led her into the farmhouse, accepted the management's welcome on behalf of both, climbed the stairs, pointed Sarah in the direction of the designated bedroom and pushed her through the door.

The rain had indeed ceased. The air was warm, a pleasant sixty-eight degrees, and five o'clock, after a tea featuring hot scones with currant jam, found Julia and her niece wandering the byways and lanes around the farm while Sarah explored the idea that the stuffing of a silk scarf and a pair of sunglasses in her shoulder bag had something of the untoward about it.

Julia, refreshed by her tea, was tolerant. "Neither item is in any sense either strange or lethal. Just someone picking up two odd items and finding the nearest open bag to tuck them into."

"And Ellen Trevino not turning up?"

"No possible connection. Ellen will no doubt surface at the Shearing Inn tomorrow."

"You think?" asked Sarah.

"Here's what's happened. She missed her flight and now she's scrambling for a seat on another airline."

Sarah, not entirely satisfied, nodded and turned, walked to a gap in the hedgerow secured by a rail fence and a stile. For several minutes she fixed her gaze on a pasture close to the Dodgeson Farm dotted with strange black and white sheep. Sheep which, with their arching horns, reminded her of those pictured in her grandmother's illustrated Bible.

"Those are Jacob sheep, a very old breed," said Julia, joining her. She peered over at an adjoining field. "And those horses, the heavy ones. Suffolk Punch. Handsome creatures, always chestnut. Makes a good animal when you cross it with a thoroughbred. Perhaps," she added in a dreamy voice, "I could diversify."

"Aunt Julia," began Sarah.

Julia reluctantly turned away from the grazing Suffolk Punch. "Sarah, the healing atmosphere will do you no good until you get rid of this burr in your brain. It's just after noon in the States. Go and call Alex. Or the state police. The FBI. The White House. Anyone."

"No"—this as Sarah hesitated—"get it over with. I shall be right here wandering about in the lane and thinking about raising sheep and importing Suffolk Punch."

Fifteen minutes later, Sarah, after giving Alex her opinion on transatlantic air travel, unburdened herself.

And Alex, after proper expressions of love and loneliness without his spouse and complaints about her Irish Wolfhound,

Patsy, rending the sleeve of a new sweater, reluctantly agreed to move on her request. "Okay, I'll call Mike Laaka and see if he can interest the Sheriff's Department in Ellen's no-show. And I hope you're not getting into a lather about a scarf and a pair of sunglasses."

"Not a lather. Just a little worried."

"Tell you what," said Alex. "I'll call around and get back to you in about an hour. After that my office will be stacked with patients."

Sarah breathed a sigh that sounded across the ocean waves. "Thanks. Aunt Julia's about to have me locked up, so if you can learn something reassuring I'd love to know it. Even hearing Ellen's fallen down Lillian Garth's cellar steps would be a relief."

"Any other news?" demanded Alex. "Something of a familiar and domestic nature beyond the fact that you love me even more than you love Anthony Hopkins, Robin Williams, and Patsy?"

"Nothing more than Aunt Julia is seriously looking at a kind of draught horse called a Suffolk Punch and some weird spotted sheep. She's thinking of spicing up High Hope Farm."

"Good God," said Alex, and signed off.

Fifty minutes later Sarah picked up the phone. Alex reporting. "Not much at this end. Ellen Trevino's nearest neighbor—a Mrs. Epple—is taking care of Ellen's dog while she's away. Ellen left the dog off on June fifth—the day before you all left from Logan. She said something about perhaps visiting a friend and then checking with someone about something. Perhaps the trip. Mrs. Epple says Ellen was quite vague about her plans, but Mike says Mrs. Epple is on the vague side herself."

"So Ellen was driving?" asked Sarah.

"She left in her car. A gray Subaru. Two-year-old wagon. She may have meant to leave it at the Portland airport, or at Logan, or anywhere else but she didn't say. Then I called Mike at home. He said the Sheriff's Department would give one big heehaw if he started yacking about a scarf and a pair of sunglasses."

"You're saying, Drop it?"

"I'm saying, my love, you're showing the classic signs of paranoia. Mike reminded me that it's tourist time in Maine, the police are busy and they won't budge until it's clear that Ellen is really missing, not waiting around as a standby in some airport."

"Maybe someone could check flights and passenger lists."

Alex groaned. "If she doesn't turn up soon, I'll call Mike again and see about checking flights out of Maine to Boston. But I've a full day at the hospital tomorrow, Mike's up to his ears with an arson case, so don't expect any great results."

Sarah, sitting on a stiff wooden chair at the Dodgeson Farm telephone table, felt an immense weariness creep over her limbs. "Okay, Alex. Thanks. I'm probably overreacting. Flying stimulated too many apprehension genes."

"Ellen Trevino could have changed her mind about the trip," said Alex. "Maybe she decided to stay home and make whoopee. Maybe she drinks and is having a lost weekend. Had a fever or an allergic reaction and checked into an ER somewhere between here and Boston."

"You could check hospital admissions," said Sarah, and then, hearing a louder groan at the end of the line, gave it up. Let it go. There were other things to be attended to. Other things like a quiet meal followed by bed, a pillow, a quilt, and Mrs. Gaskell's *Cranford*. "Okay, Alex," she said. "Good night. And I love you."

"And I love you, too. Wildly, madly, deeply. So try and keep Julia from shipping more than twenty horses back to New England."

Unlike Sarah, Alex McKenzie was not a man overly given to imagining the untoward in the world beyond his practice. His specialty of internal medicine, together with his occasional work as one of the local medical examiners, offered enough examples of human frailty and recklessness that, left to himself, he did not feel the need to look elsewhere. As he had often remarked, why look for trouble when eighty percent of the day he was hip-deep in the stuff. When he got home from a day's work he wanted a cold beer, the news of the Boston Red Sox—or in winter of the Boston Bruins. Or, weather permitting, the freedom to go bird-watching, sailing, hiking, skiing. And at night, if not on call, to hunker down with one of the naval novels of the incomparable Patrick O'Brian.

The problem, of course, was Sarah. Since she had entered his life—literally by force of homicide—the world had started to resemble a particularly active emergency room. Sarah tried to blame this on coincidence or, more realistically, on her overgrown bump of curiosity together with an urgent wish to get to the bottom of things. But Alex had begun to feel that something alien like Fate—Fate armed with a dagger and a cup of poison—hovered over any community Sarah was part of.

But now that his wife, this beloved but aggravating woman, was an ocean away with her Aunt Julia—another female capable of attracting, in fact causing, mayhem—life in Midcoast Maine should be peacefully humming along on oiled wheels.

Except for this Ellen Trevino business. Despite his assurances that Ellen would turn up, Alex was uneasy. The day passed shadowed by all too many memories of when Sarah, sadly, had often been right. That night he couldn't settle down for a comfortable rest. The next morning couldn't read with complacency about the Red Sox annihilation of the Yankees, couldn't enjoy the soft June air as he ran Patsy down the road. Couldn't do anything without thinking about calling his old friend, Mike Laaka, Knox County Deputy Sheriff Investigator.

Which he did. Cutting Patsy's run down to twenty minutes, checking the time he was due in the hospital, he dialed Mike.

"Okay, Alex," said Mike. "I thought you'd call. Thought you—or is it Sarah—couldn't leave well enough alone. But there won't be any action unless someone files a Missing Persons. I've done what I could. Called the state police and kind of hinted at a stolen car, gave 'em the Subaru license number. So maybe in their spare time they'll take a look at cars that have been sitting around in parking areas."

"Like the ones on the Maine Turnpike," said Alex. "Ellen was supposed to be on her way to Boston one way or another."

"That leaves a hell of a lot of room, but unless something solid..."

"You mean a body?"

"Yeah, a body, a hank of hair, a bloody bra, or some relative saying Ellen was screaming help over the phone, so I'm not going to blister my butt until I have to." Here Mike paused and listened to a disapproving silence on the other end of the line.

"Listen," said Mike, "I'm up to my ears in this arson case and it looks like the owner burned down his own frigging barn first and the fire spread. I mean, Christ, what someone won't do for a few thousand lousy dollars."

"Ellen's family?" put in Alex.

"All right, all right. I did touch base with that neighbor, Mrs. Epple, who said she thought Ellen Trevino only had a stepfather somewhere in Vancouver. And"—Alex could hear a note of weary resignation in Mike's voice—"I'll do this. I'll get a photo of her from the college and pass it around. Listen, she's probably got amnesia. That's always popular. Or she's absconded with the tour funds. That's popular, too."

"Mike, shut up," said Alex, and replaced the receiver.

Mike Laaka's speculations were not unique. Julia Clancy and Sarah drove up to the Shearing Inn in the village of High Roosting in central Gloucestershire in time for tea and in time to join in the ongoing speculations about the missing Ellen Trevino.

The rain of the previous morning was a thing of the past, the sun had come out gloriously, and the temperature had stayed in the high sixties. In celebration of these favorable omens the Midcoast Garden Club had assembled on a back terrace of the inn, a pleasant place which featured tables with umbrellas, a ring of terra-cotta pots filled with a mix of petunias and geraniums. There Sarah and Julia had joined the others in the attack on a handsome spread of cakes, biscuits, sandwiches, and little tarts.

"It's flying that makes you hungry," said Barbara Baxter to her flock. She reached for a second slice of lemon sponge cake.

"Oh, yes." Doris Lermatov sighed, biting into a miniature gooseberry tart.

Margaret Hopper nodded her agreement. "It's all that anxiety about getting to the airport and worrying about the weather and having jet lag. And wondering where Ellen is."

There followed a period of relative quiet devoted to munching and sipping, then, appetites having been subdued, Margaret's last comment became the cue to return to Topic A and what in the bustle of the airport departure had just been aroused puzzlement and random comment now assumed a more anxious character.

"A bug," suggested Portia McClure. "One of those sudden stomach bugs. They can knock you absolutely flat."

"A family emergency," said Margaret Hopper. "You know, where you have to drop everything and just get there."

"Wouldn't she have called? Or faxed us here?" asked Sandi.

Barbara Baxter summed it up. "We'd have heard if anything had gone wrong. My office has our itinerary and so does Dr. Trevino. Poor thing, she's probably trapped in Berlin or Rome waiting for a flight."

This was followed by further expressions of concern and then Barbara turned to Julia and Sarah. "I wish you and Mrs. Clancy hadn't gone off the way you did. We had such a good day. After our naps, we all went in and spent the day in London. I said to the others, why just drive for hours in our bus and get to the Shearing in the middle of the night. I knew this nice little family hotel on Ebury Street, and they managed to find rooms for us. After all, it does pay to be in the travel business."

"Such fun," exclaimed Sandi. "Fred and I were so excited. We went to Westminster Abbey and Harrods and the Tower."

"And Kew Gardens," Barbara reminded her. "Because, after all, we're on a garden tour."

"Terrific food," put in Doris Lermatov. "A pub—a place called the Bulldog for lunch and a wonderful dinner."

Here her daughter looked up. Amy Lermatov, the red-haired fourteen-year-old, had been looking morosely off into space—contemplating, Sarah decided, three weeks spent in the company of her elders dragging her steps through garden after garden.

"The food," said Amy, "sucked."

"Amy liked the Tower," said her mother, giving her daughter a warning frown. "And she'll get used to the food."

"Don't bet on it," said Amy. Then, seeing the maternal eye still fixed on her, added that the Tower was okay. "You could see where they beheaded people."

At which Margaret Hopper rose to her feet. "Edith and I need a walk. All this food and sitting down. There's a church down the next lane. Some of these English village churches are fascinating and I'm told this one has a Norman tower." And the two white-haired women—twins almost in their wrinkle-proof navy skirts and white cable-stitch cardigans—set out.

Sarah also felt the need to stand upright and move her limbs. She jumped up and pulled Julia to her feet. "You, too, Aunt Julia. Your arthritis will freeze you into position if you don't move."

The two were joined by Portia McClure, who expressed a desire to look around the village, and husband, Carter McClure.

Sarah, looking him over, taking in his rumpled seersucker jacket and askew tie—donned no doubt to give a professorial appearance for the Shearing staff—saw that Carter was in a temper. It was the London visit. London hadn't been on the tour schedule. "Was this a garden trip or was it a sight-seeing expedition? Kew Gardens for only a little more than an hour? And that Barbara Baxter doesn't know a rosebush from an oak tree. Ask her a serious question about fertilizer and she comes up empty."

"She wasn't hired for her horticultural knowledge," Portia reminded him. "Lillian wanted her for the nitty-gritty tour details, reservations, timetables. That sort of thing."

"So let her stick to counting luggage," said Carter, "because I have someone up my sleeve."

"Oh?" said Sarah.

"What are you up to, Carter?" demanded Julia, who knew Carter from other days, and had tangled with him on past occasions.

Carter smiled a satisfied smile. "Since the Baxter woman is not up to snuff, I have Henry Ruggles. An old friend of ours. Lives in Moreton-in-Marsh. I'm going to call him to come and fill the gap left by Lillian."

"We've stayed at his house," Portia explained. "He has a wonderful garden. Quite a showplace."

"Right," said Carter. "He'll keep the Baxter in line. And he'll be a good foil for Ellen Trevino when she does turn up. She's much too serious and Henry's disgustingly jolly. Can charm the knickers off you."

"Hardly," put in Portia. "Henry's affections do not that way tend. But he knows his stuff. Writes articles, gives lectures, and, best of all, Henry will pay his own room and board, which is no trouble since he's simply loaded. He's like a character out of Dickens."

Julia scowled. "I'm not sure we want a character out of Dickens foisted on us. Which one did you have in mind?"

"Mr. Pickwick," said Portia. "Henry is very Pickwickian. And now I'm going off by myself to explore. Carter, you behave yourself or Julia will chop you up into liver bits."

With which Portia turned off in the direction of a small dirt path that led up a shaded hill, and Sarah, looking back over her shoulder, discovered that they were now being followed at short distance by the Massachusetts couple, Justin Rossi and Stacy Daniel. Although, thought Sarah, after a quick glance, if they are really a couple, they're certainly not working at it, the man striding ahead, the woman, falling behind.

Stacy was a tall, elegant woman, whom Sarah had privately decided was some sort of high-profile female executive trapped accidentally in a tour of garden enthusiasts. A travel agent mistake, perhaps. She had the sort of presence that spoke of expensive massage, French cosmetics, and couturier clothing. Her cheeks were high, her shoulders broad, her eyes a velvety dark blue, and her flax-colored hair swirled into a fashionable topknot. Her skin, which looked as if someone had tipped a bottle of maple syrup over it, suggested a winter spent beside pools or power walking on the beach. Sarah, watching her closely, saw that she exhibited an almost bored air that did not encourage companionship.

The reverse was true of Justin Rossi. He left Stacy behind and joined Julia and Sarah at the turn leading to the churchyard lane.

"We haven't really met," he announced. "Saw you both at that dinner and on the plane but, God, overseas flights are no places to make friends. I'm more concerned with whether the wings are holding up and if the landing gear is in working order."

"Sarah," announced Julia, "you've got a kindred spirit."

"You don't like to fly?" Justin turned to Sarah and smiled down at her. And Sarah felt a strange crawling sensation. A buzzing in her head. The pitch of Justin's voice, the angle of his chin, his dark hair, the way his shoulders swung when he walked, all of him in some uncanny way was Alex. Her husband Alex. She remembered that at the restaurant dinner there had been something familiar about him. Now, on closer inspection, this man was thinner, not quite up to Alex's six feet. The black haircut shorter. And his eyes were lighter, a pale blue gray. A lesser Alex. But the resemblance was still was unnerving.

"...not like to fly?" Justin was repeating the question.

Sarah shook herself and said something incoherent about hating to be more than eight feet above the ground. This seemed to satisfy Justin, who began a tale of an engine failure episode at Miami International.

At which juncture Carter McClure turned to Julia and began to remind her that one of his graduate assistants had broken a leg during a riding lesson at Julia's High Hope Farm and this had caused great inconvenience to the History

Department. Julia, who remembered the incident only too well, rose like a trout to a dry fly and began a condemnation of the carelessness of this same student. At which both fell into argument, raising their voices and slowing their steps.

And Sarah was left with Justin, who pointed out the little churchyard and suggested an inspection. "I don't think there's much in a botanical sense, just common roses and probably some not very interesting annuals."

"I wouldn't know an interesting annual if it bit me," Sarah admitted. "But then I don't even rank as an amateur gardener. I'm below beginner."

"Perhaps your mind is on something else. For instance, on Ellen Trevino being missing?"

"Concerned. Wondering, that's all."

"I suppose we're all concerned, particularly that very talkative Sandi Ouellette. I suppose enthusiasm has its points, but she's a bit much. As for her husband, that undertaker…"

And Sarah, much to her own surprise, found something warm inside her rising in support of Sandi. And Fred.

"Sandi's not so bad. Her heart's in the right place. And enthusiasm isn't the worst quality in the world. And Fred, well, he's just Fred. Everyone's used to Fred. He overdoes the storytelling sometimes, but he's a good citizen. I've heard he drives for Meals-on-Wheels."

Justin looked down at her quizzically. "In a hearse?"

The idea, mildly amusing, forced Sarah into a grin. "All right, maybe the Ouellettes aren't the most exciting people in the world, but that's okay by me. I've had my fill of excitement."

"I'll say you have," remarked Justin.

Sarah jerked her head up. "What's that supposed to mean?"

"I got it from your friend Sandi. She was full of some Audubon thing she went on with you. Something about a body found by the birdfeeder, and how you got in your car and chased the murderer all the way to L.L. Bean's. Sandi was a little fuzzy on the details."

"Oh, God," said Sarah.

"So I thought if you've fooled around with local Maine crime you must be mildly interested in Ellen Trevino's no-show."

Sarah took a deep breath. "I'm just sorry she's not here yet, but beyond that I haven't any ghoulish ideas." She said this, making an attempt to sound both sympathetic and totally uninterested at the same time.

"You don't think the lady is curled up in an airport locker or whirling around inside a suitcase at the luggage claim place?"

"No, I don't," snapped Sarah. "And please drop it. Ellen Trevino is an old friend of mine."

Justin grimaced. "I'm sorry. A bad joke. I didn't know."

"And I'm sorry. I didn't mean to bark. Call it jet lag."

"As good an excuse as anything," said Justin cheerfully. "Let's look at the tombstones and see if we can spot some mute inglorious Milton." And then, taking her arm he turned her toward a small wooden gate and quoted in rhythm with their steps:

"Beneath those rugged elms, that yew-tree's shade,
Where heaves the turf in many a mould'ring heap,
Each in his narrow cell for ever laid,
The rude Forefathers of the hamlet sleep."

And Sarah found herself simultaneously beguiled by someone who could recite the fourth verse of that nineteenth-century chestnut and irritated by Justin's supporting her arm. It was hardly a matter for a scene, but she firmly slid her arm free when they reached the churchyard gate and moved a step away. "I like churchyards," she said. "I think they're at least as interesting as roses."

They wandered about, peering at moss- and lichen-covered stones, finding a family called Hemstich which featured three little Eliza's, three stone lozenges on which some childish hand had laid an untidy wilting handful of primroses.

"I suppose," Sarah mused, "the second Eliza was named after the first, then she died, then came the third and she died.

Some epidemic, smallpox, diphtheria. Old graveyards are very sobering."

"*Cursor mundi*," said Justin, kneeling down and scraping grass away from an inscription. "See this. Lost at sea. Lieutenant Nichols. During action at the Nile. Was there action on the Nile?"

"I think it had something to do with Nelson," said Sarah vaguely. "Not Trafalgar but earlier." Suddenly she shivered. Partly from cold, but partly from a sense that Justin was entirely too companionable. Too familiar—not in the physical sense, he hadn't touched her again—but in a different way what with the literary references and his deep voice. And looking like Alex.

"I think I'll go back," she announced. "Regroup. Unpack. Put my feet up."

"Good idea," said Justin pleasantly. "Enough of worms and epitaphs." He waited for Sarah's reaction, but she closed her lips. "That's Richard II, isn't it? When he's feeling very very sorry for himself."

Sarah sighed. Impossible to dislike someone who came up with the proper quotation at the proper time. "Yes, Richard was rolling over and playing dead, practically handing it all over to Bolingbroke." And together they sauntered back toward the inn, pausing only for Justin to identify two chaffinches in a hedgerow and a blue tit in a tree.

Arriving in her bedroom, Sarah gave a token kick to her hated suitcase. He even birdwatches, she told herself. Maybe he's Alex's brother. Born out of wedlock and given up for adoption and now he's turned up. She considered Alex's mother, Elspeth, noted artist and loyal wife of Alex's father, and tried to picture her having some grand affair with a dark-haired stranger.

"What are you staring at," said Julia, knocking and marching into the room at the same time.

Sarah started. "Nothing. My mind is a blank."

Julia sank down in a chair and began unlacing her new walking shoes. She stretched out her feet, wiggled her toes, and then regarded her niece. "It's that Justin Rizzi or Rossini. Looks enough like Alex to be his brother. He headed straight for you."

"No," corrected Sarah, "Justin happened to be there and his name is Rossi. We hit the graveyard and he quoted Gray."

"'The ploughman homeward plows his weary way and leaves the world to darkness and to me,'" announced Julia unexpectedly. "My generation had a proper education. Forty lines each Friday. Anyway, Carter was becoming positively obnoxious about his damn student when that Stacy woman came twinkling up and joined us."

"Twinkling? She's about as twinkly as a bath towel. I think her ticket was mixed up and she's supposed to be on the Executive Woman's Tour of British Industries."

"Perfectly friendly," said Julia. "Wanted us to help identify the roses, which I couldn't, but Carter went on about grafting and hybrids and Stacy said she adored gardens. Adored—her very words. Has been looking forward to the tour, thinks Barbara Baxter is, to quote, a perfectly marvelous organizer."

"Barbara Baxter reminds me of my eighth-grade basketball coach. All she needs is a sweatshirt and a whistle around her neck. Hustling and bustling everyone around."

"Sarah, you're beginning to sound like me, and there's only room for one Julia Clancy on this trip."

Chapter Four

But BEFORE JULIA COULD elaborate on the dangers of two Julia Clancys, a knock sounded on the bedroom door and a muffled voice called, "Telephone for Sarah Deane. She can take it down in the front hall."

The Shearing Inn was one of those hostelries built in the seventeenth century and added on to thereafter in a haphazard fashion. "Down in the front hall" meant Sarah followed a short series of steps that wound up and down under low beams and ended in a small entrance space. The table holding a guest register and a telephone was midway between the front door and the Shearing pub room door, thus ensuring that a good deal of telephone conversation would consist of "What?" and "I can't hear you."

"What," said Sarah. "Alex? I can't hear you."

Alex, sounding like a seal calling from a distant harbor, repeated something and then in an interval of silence, Sarah heard, "…the car was pretty clear of stuff. No suitcases or briefcases."

"Car!" squeaked Sarah. "What car?"

"Aren't you listening?"

"I can't really hear you. The pub door is right next to the phone and everyone's in there chatting it up and…"

"Listen again." Alex raised his voice and spoke very deliberately "A car, a Buick, driven by an elderly woman."

"A Buick?"

"Listen, will you? By an elderly woman who whammed into Ellen Trevino's Subaru."

"Ellen! She's had an accident."

"Christ, Sarah. Wait up. Ellen wasn't in the car. The car was empty. At the Kennebunk exit on the Maine Turnpike. In the parking area near the end of the picnic benches. You know that exit, it's the southbound pit stop with the Burger King restaurant."

"Yes, I know," said Sarah impatiently. "But Ellen wasn't anywhere around?"

Here followed a period of noise and door openings and then Sarah exclaimed, "This is impossible." Then, "Okay, speak up."

"Ellen's car was slightly damaged. The woman in the Buick reported the accident, the police have traced the license, couldn't locate Ellen, decided it may have been stolen, and have hauled it off to give it the once-over."

"But it hasn't been reported stolen? Not by Ellen anyway."

"No, but the police are figuring Ellen doesn't know it's stolen. That maybe she took a plane from Portland to Boston and the car was taken from the airport parking garage and dumped at the Kennebunk exit."

"If she took a plane to Boston, then where is she?"

"No one has yet filed a Missing Persons on Ellen. You have to wait forty-eight hours."

Sarah drew a deep breath. "Back to square one. Shit."

"Not entirely. The police need Ellen to claim the car, so they are doing some looking around. Checking Delta and U.S.

Air flights. Commuter planes and airport limousine passenger lists for June sixth to Logan."

"Well, that's something," said Sarah. "Are you absolutely sure there was nothing left in Ellen's car?"

"Mike—he's the one who called me—got the list from the state police and told me. Jumper cables, gardening tools in the rear. A road map, car registration stuff, five or six cassettes—classical and folk music, and two paperbacks. *The Warden* and *Barchester Towers*."

"I suggested those books. Why did she leave them in the car?"

"So she forgot. You forget things like that all the time. So do I. *Homo imperfectus*."

"I'm getting a queasy feeling."

There was a pause on the line, the clinking sounds from the pub room, a burst of laughter, and then Alex again. "Mike says keep a lid on this car business. Right now it doesn't affect the tour group. Ellen may turn up tomorrow."

"All right."

"And, just for the record, says Mike, would you send him a list of the tour members with any personal bits, details of Ellen's travel plans if anyone knew about them. Nothing official. The police don't want to approach Whirlaway Tours. No point in stirring people up for no reason. Mike thinks maybe it's time to lay some groundwork in case the Missing Persons thing is filed."

"Am I supposed to mail this stuff? Or telephone?"

Behind Sarah a man in a suede jacket hovered, his gaze fixed on the telephone. "Do you mind? It's rather important. A call home," he said.

"Sarah?" said Alex. "Mike says fax it, okay?"

"Damn. Yes, I'll try."

"Thanks. And you can tell Julia—only Julia—about this because she'll screw it out of you anyway."

"Isn't faxing sort of public?" said Sarah.

"Get away from everyone. Okay? Goodbye."

"Thank you," said the man reaching for the telephone.

Sarah returned to her room—a narrow chamber connecting to Julia's slightly larger one, both rooms brave in flowered chintz, and welcoming trays supporting an electric teapot, teacups, and bags of Typhoo Tea. After washing and changing into her all-purpose blue shirtdress, she and Julia—in red paisley cotton—joined the rest for a drink in the pub room, and then dinner in the Shearing Inn dining room. This was a rectangular space dominated by heavy hewn beams and featuring uneven floors, bubble-glass windows, and, at each table, a potted geranium. Clutches of diners were already in place plying knives and forks and a soft babble of German and—was it Japanese?—rose from two tables at the darker end of the dining room. Sarah, eyeing them, thought that the elderly headwaiter—possibly a World War II veteran—may have decided that these two nationalities had something unsuitable in common and should be relegated to a space away from the light.

She took her place at an extended table with a view of the garden, and decided that the five-hour time difference combined with a strong and evil-tasting rum and Orangina had loosened her mind in a way that transformed the whole Midcoast Garden Tour. Transformed it from a benign group of persons whose interests centered on the wholesome growing of flowers to something altogether different.

It was as though each of them, Sarah and Aunt Julia included, had stepped out of their mundane personae and had been wafted onto a stage set or a movie screen. What was that movie, Sarah asked herself, as a dish called Chicken Bombay was placed in front of her—a dish she couldn't remember ordering. Oh, yes, Woody Allen. *The Purple Rose of Cairo*, where Mia Farrow had left her theater seat and had joined the screen characters on a glamorous set of the thirties: cocktail shakers, furniture made out of glass and aluminum tubes, Van Johnson in a white dinner jacket, and...

"The chutney, Sarah," said Aunt Julia. "I've asked twice. You're asleep at the switch."

Sarah shook herself. "Sorry. I was just out of it."

"You mean 'out of the loop,'" said Sandi Ouellette, who sat across the table and had dressed for this first festive occasion in a low-cut lavender outfit. She leaned across the table exposing the upper reaches of her breasts. "I just love that expression. You know when all those senators and President Bush said they were out of it."

"Sandi," said Fred Ouellette, "loves Senate hearings. Watergate, Iran-Contra. Special investigators and taking the Fifth and sexual harassment charges."

"Better than sitcoms any day," said Sandi.

There's more perhaps to Sandi's brain than had been apparent from her everyday conversation, Sarah told herself. And then she realized how little she knew about the woman. Did she work or sit all day watching Senate hearings on CNN? Then, in the minutes that followed as everyone chattered and plied fork and knife, Sarah returned to the task of assembling her cast of characters for Mike. And the movie, titled for the moment: *Ellen Is Missing*.

First, put Sandi Ouellette on hold since Sandi might reveal hidden depths that would complicate the casting process. Fred, however, seemed simplicity itself. The contented undertaker. Or mortician. Whatever they called themselves now. Sarah had heard that a new favored title was "morticle surgeon." Fred, two places down the table, was finishing one of his jokes, the plot of which seemed to involve a New York judge adrift on an ice floe. Sarah, after assigning Fred a place in the supporting cast, moved on to contemplate Doris Lermatov and her daughter, Amy.

She had neglected these two. Doris Lermatov had sat a short distance from Sarah on the British Airways flight. Doris was built on the classic lines of the old-style Coke bottle, usually wore the sort of garment known as a float, had a crown of puffed hair of ash blonde—a favorite choice for those going gray. But Sarah knew very little of her beyond the undeniable fact that she seemed upbeat and was fond of food. On the plane Sarah had seen her help herself to her daughter Amy's chocolate pudding, and now, sitting slantwise across the dinner table, she bent over her roast beef, a study in concentration.

And of Doris herself, her interests? Her job? Sarah, thinking back, remembered someone saying that Doris wrote a garden column for one of the smaller local papers.

And then there was Amy at Sarah's left elbow—a slender young person with a head of frizzy red hair, a round face, and the white skin and freckles that often goes with such hair. Right now Amy had the same sulky look Sarah had seen before. And she wasn't eating, simply pushing a heap of pasta around her plate.

Sarah, catching her eye, smiled. "Are you a garden fan? Or along for a change of scene?"

"Gardens," said Amy, "suck."

"All gardens?"

"Any I've seen. Probably the ones I haven't seen."

Sarah, hardened early by work in secondary schools before she picked up a Bowmouth College fellowship, was not put off. "I know you're Amy Lermatov and my name is Sarah," she said. "And maybe we'll hit a garden that isn't too bad. Some of them are amazing. Mazes you can get lost in. Or again we might have a chance to look at something else. Old graveyards and castles." This producing no response, Sarah asked what sort of music she liked, expecting to hear of some punk rock group with a name like "The Barf." She was not disappointed.

"Well," said Amy, her expression becoming slightly more animated, "I like a group called 'The Decomposers.' Back in Maine my Uncle Nick plays the lead guitar. But what I'm going to be is a writer. I'm keeping a journal and making notes about the trip."

"And your mother brought you along so you could do research?"

Amy looked down the table where her mother, Doris Lermatov, was lifting a second slice of Yorkshire pudding onto her plate.

"Mother," Amy said with a heavy sigh, "made me come. Like it's her turn for me this June and July. In August I'll stay with my father on Cape Cod. He's a biologist, but I think biology is an incredibly boring subject." Amy paused and then added, "Except for the DNA part. If I'm going to be a writer I have to know about things like that."

"Are you going to write about science? Or medicine?"

"I want to write novels. Not romance junk but real ones with meaning."

"With DNA as a base?"

"You're making fun of me." And Amy returned to her pasta and gave it an awkward swirl with her fork.

"No, honestly," said Sarah. "I'm just curious about how DNA fits in."

Amy looked at her suspiciously and then relaxed. "Well, for the book I'm doing about this trip I'll need some scientific information because it's going to be a mystery. That's where the psychological comes in. The murderer's going to have this weird motive. He—or maybe she, I haven't made up my mind yet—is going to be very mentally disturbed."

Sarah sat up and stared at her. "You mean you're going to use *this* Garden Club tour?"

Amy gave a slight giggle. "It's the only tour I'm on." She pushed her plate to one side. "This is lousy spaghetti," she observed. And then, "Yeah, a murder mystery. The garden tour will be raw material. I thought with Dr. Trevino missing I could use that and then figure out why someone wouldn't want her to be here."

"Dr. Trevino," Sarah began.

"Yeah, I know she might turn up by tomorrow, but I've got to start somewhere. I thought I could make notes and start working on my cast of characters." Here Amy looked up and circled a finger taking up the entire table.

"Do you know any of these people well enough to turn them into characters?" asked Sarah.

Amy regarded her with something close to contempt. "In fiction you don't have to use *real* personalities. You use your imagination. I thought you were an English teacher. Do you make your students do everything true to life? I mean I'm going to *create* people and maybe use the way they dress or talk."

Here Amy paused for breath and Sarah, feeling suitably squelched, thought if Mike were here investigating Ellen's nonappearance, he would have cat fits. Sarah *and* Amy bumbling around asking unsuitable questions.

"…your imagination," finished Amy.

Sarah, suddenly aware that Amy had been talking at some length, came to and said, "Uh, yes, the imagination."

"It's where writers aren't like other people," persisted Amy. "A lot of teachers aren't into imagination. They're grammar freaks and just about destroy you if a semicolon doesn't go where it should, and they go yacking on about proper paragraphs."

Sarah, who believed strongly in proper paragraphs, was just about to temporize in the matter when Amy shook her fuzzy head and held up a rather grubby hand.

"Let me finish about imagination. I think it's really more true than things that are supposed to be true, if you know what I mean. But I guess you only think I should use real facts about people and just pay attention to the grammar."

Sarah turned on Amy and fixed the girl with a look. "'I am certain,'" she said, "'of nothing but of the holiness of the Heart's affections and the truth of the Imagination.'"

Amy's eyes widened. "Huh?"

"'The Imagination may be compared to Adam's dream—he awoke and found it truth,'" said Sarah crisply, and she returned to her chicken curry.

Amy's face crumpled, rather as if some hand had grabbed it and squeezed. "You really are making fun of me," she said resentfully.

Sarah relented. "John Keats. One of his letters boosting the imagination. You're right, Amy. Up with imagination."

Amy looked relieved. "I like Keats. That 'Nightingale' poem and the one about a woman's head planted in a flowerpot. So what do you think about me writing a murder mystery about the tour?"

Sarah decided to derail this aspect of the idea if possible. "It doesn't have to be a murder mystery. How about a novel full of love-hate relationships. Co-dependents. People fighting over an adopted child on the tour. Then you could use your DNA material."

"You think?" said Amy doubtfully, but at this juncture a waiter's hand removed her dish of pasta and the remains of Sarah's curry and almost immediately two glass dishes supporting pyramidal lumps of crème caramel made their appearance.

Sarah, who had ordered baked apple, found that it really didn't matter. Dessert was dessert. It could have been sugared cardboard for all she cared. She was suddenly extraordinarily tired. Amy, fortunately, had lost interest in the conversation and attacked her caramel custard with the greed of a hungry adolescent, and Sarah was free to sink into a mild coma. Tomorrow would be time enough to pursue Mike's request and find out about some of the strangers in the party, their life's work, their travel routes to Logan. About Amy, she felt, she had already found out more than she wanted to know.

Julia, on Sarah's right, who had been in animated conversation with Fred Ouellette on the need to "put down" people as was properly done with ailing horses, now subsided and half-closed her eyes, so that when a general shuffling of chairs indicated that dinner was over, Julia, with Sarah close on her heels, was the first to hustle out and up the winding stairs toward room and bed.

"I'm too old to lose five hours just like that," Julia complained. "That Rossi man and Fred are going to hit the pub for a nightcap but they're in the prime of life. I'm just an old biddy and I need bed. Good night, Sarah. You look done in. As old as I feel." And with this encouraging remark, Julia pushed her key into her door, turned the knob, and disappeared.

As Julia's door snapped closed, Sarah remembered that she had intended to tell her aunt about the finding of Ellen Trevino's empty car at the Kennebunk exit. She hesitated, took a step toward Julia's closed door, and then stopped. She would tell her tomorrow when they were prowling around the tour's first scheduled garden visit, a place called Barnsley House. Large English gardens, she seemed to remember, were noted for their high hedges, little green nooks, and shaded walkways. Perfect for private exchanges. Or perfect for overheard conversations and sinister encounters. For meeting the evil suitor in the maze. Perfect for fatal trysts, for ambush. For sudden death.

Stop it, she told herself irritably. You sound like Amy. She shook herself and began to prepare for bed, grateful that Europeans install washbasins in hotel bedrooms. She could at least sponge away the travel dust. Next, deciding to do penance for untoward thoughts, she turned to a wholesome—in fact, positively symbolic, activity. Washing out her underpants, her bra. Her shirt. Her cotton socks—too long encased in rubber-soled Nikes.

She loaded these items in the sink, added soap powder from her travel supply, pumped them up and down, rinsed and draped them over the towel rack. Then she remembered. The scarf. The scarf that had turned up with those sunglasses. The one with the Filene's label. Well, if someone was going to force a scarf on her and there were no claimers, she wasn't going to refuse a freebie.

Sarah returned to her open shoulder bag and extracted the scarf with its crumpled swirls of red and black. She turned it over in her hand. Underneath the Filene label was a smaller one: "All Silk." She ran the lukewarm water into the sink—you had to be very careful about silk—added the soap powder, dunked the scarf gently, then pulled out the drain. Rather surprised, she noticed that the color had run. A muddy rusty red. Perplexed, she ran the tepid rinse water and dropped the scarf in. Less color this time, a fainter brown-red.

Well, so much for Filene's and color-fast days. But perhaps the scarf was a fake from Hong Kong or Taiwan and using the Filene label. Sarah ran a second rinse and this time was rewarded with only slightly tinged water. A last rinse, this time using only the cold tap, and now the water ran almost clear.

Enough. She could repeat the operation tomorrow and then, since it was a rather handsome object, she would probably wear it.

Sarah settled into bed, closed her eyes, and was almost immediately asleep. It wasn't until the first dawn light, which came as a pale shaft through a crack in the curtained window opening, that Sarah, with a start, sat up and reached an entirely new conclusion about the Filene scarf.

Chapter Five

SARAH PUSHED AWAY HER pillow, sat upright, and stared at the silk scarf now hanging on the towel rack over the bedroom sink. Her sensation was similar to that of someone finding a coiled cobra within striking distance.

That damn scarf. The thing appearing—along with those cheap sunglasses—in her shoulder bag. No, not "appearing," planted. Planted by some hand. A bloody hand. Then she stopped and began scolding herself. *All I can think about is Ellen missing and maybe being kidnapped from her car at the Kennebunk exit and a bloody scarf—belonging to God knows who. Aunt Julia is right. I need to wash my brain out with soap.* And with this bracing thought, Sarah swung out of bed and planted her feet squarely on the floor.

By the time Sarah had taken a shower, scrubbed herself with unnecessary vigor with a rough towel, she had made several resolutions, the first being to buy some self-help paperbacks at the nearest village bookstore. Books about getting in touch with your center, finding peace in nature's own biorhythms. The second resolution was to have earnest conversations with the most reliable tour members—the Hopper sisters, for instance—and so learn about planting her own summer garden back home in Maine. And next, above all, to avoid Ms. Amy Lermatov and all discussions of her projected mystery novel. That scarf simply ran rusty red because red is a color that runs and not because the thing is soaked in blood. Here Sarah paused and glared at herself in the bedroom mirror. "You fool," she told the face. "Look at you. A scruffy secondhand person with a head full of unfounded suspicious and abnormal inklings."

It was not a scruffy face, but there were signs of travel fatigue on Sarah's thin face. The gray eyes looked darker than usual; the dark brown hair, disordered by her shower, stood up on her skull; and her high cheekbones and chin reminded her unpleasantly of her third-grade teacher, Miss Edith Brackett.

Sarah turned from the mirror, pulled on her new travel-proof blue linen jumper and denim jacket, and, with shoulders braced and head erect, marched down the stairs and into the dining room for breakfast.

It was a fine English breakfast heavy with eggs, fried tomatoes, finnan haddie, kippers, toast, pots of Cooper's Oxford marmalade, and Fortnum & Mason's strawberry jam. Aunt Julia, busy with kippers, waved a fork in her direction and called out that she hoped Sarah had "settled down." Julia, an early riser, had been up it seemed for hours. Hair tangled, a speck of mud on her cheek, she had been regaling the table with a description of her walk to a nearby farm at which she had had a gratifying conversation on the subject of fodder with a gentleman leading a pair of Cleveland Bays—a type of horse, she kindly explained to her listeners.

Sarah moved away from her aunt and found a safe place between Portia McClure and Margaret Hopper, and listened gratefully to conversation that centered about the upcoming visit to Barnsley House, the wonders of the Laburnum Walk, the golden balm, the *Allium aflatunense*. The talk drifted pleasantly between problems of seed dormancy and methods of dealing with caterpillars.

Sarah, thus soothed, returned to her room in an uplifted frame of mind to confront the suspected scarf hanging over the towel rack. She looked at the object with disdain and then folded it—now quite dry—into a toilet paper nest and shoved it into the bottom of her suitcase. She felt that she could be entirely garden-minded if it were not for those notes about the group to be faxed to Alex in some clandestine manner yet to be devised.

Returning to the lower regions, she was met by Julia Clancy armed with a walking stick and straw hat. "I hope you've calmed down, Sarah," she said. "Looking at gardens demands a peaceful personality. As for me, I've had my horse fix and now I'm prepared to be entirely amiable and admire everything I see."

Sarah hesitated, looked over her shoulder, scanned the front hall. Then, taking a deep breath, she told Julia about Ellen Trevino's car turning up at the Kennebunk exit of the Maine Turnpike, the scarf running rusty red, and Mike's request to come up with a few remarks about the various tour members.

Julia listened, for once not interrupting, and then frowned. "That scarf was probably made in India and everything I've ever had from India ran like crazy. However," she added, "if you need any tidbits, gossip about our group, I'll be glad to help. I have a very good eye..."

"For horses," put in Sarah.

"It's the same thing. One develops an eye for the abnormal, the cowhock, the goose rump, the parrot mouth, the slew foot. The tendency to spook, to bolt. It's exactly the same with humans. I consider myself an expert in assessing humans. After all, I've been in the business of matching humans with horses for years."

"I guess so," said Sarah doubtfully.

"Trust your old Aunt Julia. Bring something to write on. Everyone will think you're taking garden notes."

"Well, I really *would* like to take garden notes," said Sarah.

"Fine," said Julia. "Mix and match. Now hurry up, we're taking off in ten minutes."

Travel by bus, Sarah decided, had certain advantages for the foreign visitor, not the least of which was the driver—an amiable Londoner named Joseph—knowing where he was going and so not taking wrong turns and spinning like a top in roundabouts.

And the bus wasn't one of those Leviathans that roared along the big motorways, but a smaller green Ford Club Car able to take the small country roads and slip from hedgerow to hedgerow without a major confrontation with some other vehicle. And it was a lovely day, the sun had come out, and from time to time shifting clouds sent long shadows across rolling meadows and pastures dotted with sheep. And always there was a small village or town, its buildings of honey-colored stone hidden away in the folds of hills or huddled on the edge of a dark copse.

Unfortunately for Sarah, who would have preferred gazing at the landscape, she had a job to do. But the small size of the bus had one disadvantage. Armed with her notebook and ballpoint, she decided that making notes was a rather public affair, particularly when seated next to Sandi Ouellette on one side and Margaret Hopper across the way.

Sandi applauded the appearance the notebook. "I should take notes, too. About everything. Even the vocabulary. All the words are so different. Did you know that your backside is a bum in England? Think of the mistakes you could make talking about bums. And I'm sure the whole Cotswold scene is absolutely going to swamp me. I mean, look at the cottages with those thatched roofs. They look like doll houses. Not real at all. And the gardens, all those Latin names. But I'm having the best time, and you know what Fred said to me this morning, he said he wants to start having an English breakfast when we get home; but I told him, Fred, you just forget that, I'm not about to cook kippers when you've been perfectly happy eating Cheerios all your life."

When Sandi stopped for breath, Margaret Hopper took over. Leaning toward Sarah, she said with approval, "You're quite right to be taking notes. I always jot down a few memories before I go to bed. We're so lucky to be going to Barnsley House. You know I wouldn't be at all surprised to find Ellen Trevino meeting us there. She's the one who insisted on the Barnsley House gardens."

But Sarah, thus reminded of her promise to Alex, found that Barnsley House had to get along without her complete attention. She clutched her notebook tightly and followed the group down a path to a bed of vivid blue iris. Here the party halted only briefly and then broke into units of twos and threes. In vain, Barbara Baxter asserted her leadership. She flourished her guide map and tried to regroup her flock in order to move everyone into an orderly progression down one garden path, up the next.

Barbara, thought Sarah, straggling in the rear, was another person about whom she knew little. What was clear, though, was that the tour leader knew next to nothing about handling garden enthusiasts because the party having been hustled down the fabled Laburnum Walk, rebelled and divided abruptly at a sundial. Sarah and Julia retreated, Carter McClure and Portia branched off announcing a desire to inspect the bronze irises, Justin Rossi sauntered in the direction of a walk featuring delphiniums and Oriental poppies, and the beautiful Stacy Daniel announced the intention of looking for a bench and getting some sun. Barbara, looking confused, found herself left with only the Hopper sisters, Doris Lermatov and daughter Amy to oversee.

Sarah, with Julia behind her, having dodged a side path, reflected that gardens aren't like museums where a brief lecture in front of a Matisse or a Rembrandt satisfies the visitor's need. Garden people have their own pet interests, their own agendas;

they like to hang fondly over certain plantings, bypass others. Perennial fans make for the perennial beds and the lovers of annuals, of herbal displays, of roses, wisteria, of pastoral prospects, go elsewhere.

Aunt Julia, never one to withhold criticism, put it bluntly. "That young woman should stop trying to herd us around." She turned to a small bench and sat down heavily.

"Barbara is trying to do Lillian Garth's *and* Ellen Trevino's job," Sarah reminded her.

Julia snorted. "Then she'd better start reading up and stop trying to organize everyone."

"Hello, Mrs. Clancy," said a voice. Amy. Amy Lermatov. "Hello, Sarah. Can I call you Sarah or should I say Mrs. McKenzie?"

Sarah shook her head. "Sarah will do fine, but I'm not Mrs. McKenzie. I use my own name. It's Sarah Deane."

"I should hope you use your own name," said Amy. "Catch me using my husband's name."

Julia gave her a look "You have a husband?"

"Are you kidding? said Amy. "But if I had I wouldn't use his name. I suppose your husband's name was Clancy because in your day women just gave up their identity."

Julia drew herself up to her full five foot three inches. "I did not give up my identity, I made a conscious choice, and I am extremely proud to have Tom Clancy's name."

"But he's dead now, isn't he?" said Amy. "So you could go back to whoever you were."

At this point Sarah, foreseeing a major storm, interrupted. Said the first thing that came out of her head. "So how's your story coming? Amy"—she explained to a purple-faced Julia—"is writing a mystery based on this trip."

Amy grinned. "I'm taking notes on everyone. I found out that Stacy Daniel used to be a fabulous model. I mean she's been in magazines and on TV, and now she works for a bank doing public relations. But I don't think she likes gardens all that much."

Sarah, having brought the subject out, tried to shut the barn door. "Where's your mother, Amy? Should you try to find her? It's easy to get lost in all these paths."

Amy assumed a look of extreme scorn. "My mother...," she began, but Julia broke in. "Why, tell me, have you chosen a mystery that features the tour group?"

"Oh, that's easy," said Amy. "Because I'm not really into gardens, so I brought a notebook. Like yours, Sarah." Amy pointed to Sarah's small spiral model. "And then when Dr. Trevino didn't show up it seemed like a great idea to write a mystery. Dr. Trevino would make a good murder victim because she's what my teacher calls an interesting character. Like Jane Eyre. Of course, it will be a real bummer if she *does* show up because I'll have to rewrite the whole thing." Amy hesitated and then brightened. "I could say she had amnesia like Agatha Christie. She'd been hit over the head on the way to Logan Airport."

Julia gave Amy the famous "Clancy eye," a look long familiar to her beginning riders. "You should not go sneaking about taking notes on people."

Amy looked offended. "I'd just take an interest in each person and find out about their life and hobbies and how everyone got to the airport. Stuff like that."

Sarah decided it was time to move Amy on. And use the girl for her own purposes. "Okay, Amy, why don't you go back to Stacy Daniel and find out why she doesn't like gardens?"

"I can tell when I'm being got rid of," said Amy. "But that's okay. I'll take notes about you both later on. Sandi Ouellette says she knows all about you, Sarah, but if I quote Sandi I'll say she's an unidentified source."

"Amy," said Julia in a grating voice. "No one wants a junior spy in the middle of a tour."

"How about a senior spy?" asked Sarah when Amy had taken herself back down the Laburnum Walk and disappeared from sight.

"One senior spy and one antiquated spy," retorted Julia. She rose stiffly from the bench and strode off in the direction of a thicker growth of evergreen.

Sarah, following, found Julia had herself produced a small spiral pad from the recesses of her denim skirt. "We need to split assignments. You take the Hoppers and Justin Rossi, because he's interested in you."

"No, he's not," said Sarah, rather too hastily.

"Don't interrupt. He looks like Alex and he may act like Alex, so you may be his type. And you're the unattached younger female."

"I'm attached and Stacy Daniel is the younger female."

"Forget Stacy. You have caught his eye. Now time is running short so we've got to mingle and be full of feigned interest and the milk of human kindness of which I have very little. Beside the Hoppers and Rossi, take the Ouellettes—you know them anyway—and I'll do Barbara Baxter and Stacy. You can have Amy and Doris Lermatov, and I'll take Carter McClure and Portia since I already know them. We'll compare notes after lunch."

"And then we'll have to find a place to fax the stuff."

"We can do it in town because I heard Barbara say we're going into Cirencester for lunch and will have an hour for looking around, for shopping—whatever—before we hit the next garden."

Sarah looked puzzled. "I checked the itinerary after breakfast and it said something about a country lunch. Near something called Lavender Cottage. Cirencester is a big town, not country."

"I heard you," said a voice behind them. Margaret Hopper and a step to the rear, Portia McClure. Margaret explained. "Sandi Ouellette and Doris were just begging to be allowed off the leash and Barbara gave in. Barbara's very accommodating."

"Well, Carter is fuming," put in Portia.

"There are interesting Roman remains in Cirencester," said Margaret. "The town was built on the ruins of Corinium, and there are sixteenth-century houses and a Woolgather's House. And many specialty shops. Sandi Ouellette is so pleased. She wants to buy a teapot. She's gone very British and talks about lorries and the bonnet and boot. Anyway, we'll eat at twelve-thirty and be on the road by two-thirty. Plenty of time to see Lavender Cottage."

"All right, all right," said Julia in a rather cross voice. "But what else is Barbara going to change? Sarah and I are driving and if the tour's changing its route it will be a great nuisance. I hope this will take care of this lust to shop, goggling at store windows. Shopping is what anyone can do back home." Julia, by no stretch of the imagination, could ever be called a shopper, unless one considered time spent in tack shops fingering blankets and turnout rugs and varieties of liniment and wormers, and all the wonderful equine merchandise so dear to the horse lover.

"Never mind about Aunt Julia," said Sarah, seeing Margaret looking slightly offended. She plucked at her aunt's sleeve. "Aunt Julia, I think Cirencester's a good idea. Remember we wanted to look for"—here Sarah hesitated because what they wanted to look for was a place from which to send a fax—"we wanted to look for gloves," she said. "The Cotswolds are famous for gloves."

"They are?" said Margaret. "I've never heard that."

"Wonderful leather," said Sarah, because after all it seemed safe to guess that leather goods could be found in large towns.

"Gloves?" said Julia. "I don't want gloves. After all, I have perfectly..." Here she paused as Sarah's toe, hidden by a garden growth marked "Bowles' Golden Grass," came into sharp contact with her ankle.

"Yarn," said Julia. "Not gloves. I need yarn for my needlepoint."

Ten minutes later, safely separated from the main body of retreating Garden Club members, Julia turned to Sarah. "You don't have to kick me. And in the Cotswolds I'm sure it's wool, but I do see that Cirencester works out for sending the fax."

"It might be easier," said Sarah peering ahead to a clump of delphiniums, and seeing Amy Lermatov with her notebook, "to fax Amy. I'll bet she knows more than we do about the group."

"Knows more dirt," said Julia darkly. "She's probably got a list of violence, molestation, drug use by our friends, and what she doesn't have, she'll make up."

"So let's go to work," said Sarah. "We'll be interested garden lovers who want to get to know everyone better."

"Like Justin Rossi? Watch your step there, Sarah."

"I can handle the likes of Justin Rossi. Most men have a healthy interest in themselves and that'll make it easy."

"As I said," Julia reminded her, "en garde." And Julia settled her straw hat firmly on her gray tufted head and marched off on a path in the direction of a small temple.

Sarah, as she had promised, "went to work" on her chosen tour members. This was made somewhat difficult by the increasing number of visitors. It was Friday, for tourists the beginning of the weekend, and Barnsley House, as one of the National Garden scheme properties, was deservedly popular.

As a result of the thickening crowds, Sarah found it almost impossible to take notes in privacy and had to start and stop a number of conversations, skipping back and forth from subjects like past interests, place of business, the trip to Logan, to exclamations of delight over the herb borders, the purple lunaria, and the fascination of a pink fuzzy asterlike growth labeled *Thalictrum aquilegiifolium*.

Feeling she had a fair grip on the Lermatov pair and already knew a lot about the Ouellettes, she concentrated on the Hopper sisters, and then caught up with Justin Rossi, who stood staring fixedly at a mix of scarlet poppies and blue delphinium.

She took a deep breath. "So, hello. Are you as good at garden quotations as you are at graveyard ones?"

Justin swiveled about and brightened. "Hey, there. I was wondering where everyone was."

"Gone every which way. Barbara Baxter's going to have her hands full if she expects us to..."

"To be led up the garden path," finished Justin.

A little too apt, Sarah decided, but she acknowledged the remark with a small smile and then launched on her program of discovery.

It was fairly easy going. After a brisk exchange of rather tired garden quotes, the identification of several common birds including the greenfinch and a yellowhammer—"I call it the yellow bunting," said Rossi—Sarah, prompted by a sense that time was slipping by, came out and asked what had prompted Mr. Rossi...

"Please. Justin."

"Justin. To decide to come on the trip?"

"You first. Why did you decide?" asked Justin looking at her with a quizzical expression.

"I adore gardens," said Sarah firmly. "I just don't know much about starting them. My husband and I"—it was time to reassert her married state—"have just settled into an old farmhouse and I've planted peach trees, but no flowers yet. Except for the stuff that comes up by itself."

"Stuff? And you call yourself a gardener? Besides, some of the best flowers are wild ones. Pearly everlasting, wild phlox, bouncing betty, marsh mallow. Lupine."

Sarah made a humble noise and submitted to a lecture on wild versus cultivated flowers. Then, when the flower stream had dried, Justin was moved to describe his life and works and egged on by encouraging murmurs from his companion, launched into biography. His college in Vermont, law school at Boston University, and finally the glory of a well-known, and most staid, solid, and conservative law firm in Boston, an outfit called Philips, Follett, Follett, Crashhow, and Rossi—Rossi being the newest star in their legal firmament. Trusts, corporate affairs, insurance suits, some criminal cases, a smattering of family law.

"I'm family law," stated Justin.

"You mean divorces, custody fights, child support, all that?"

"You've got it. Trusts, too, of course. Wills, contests, settlements. Even domestic strife, although if that gets too hot we turn it over to our criminal team."

"Well, well," said Sarah. Then, without much originality, added, "It must be fascinating."

."That's one word for it," said Justin cryptically. "There are others."

But now Barbara Baxter hove into sight and called out that it was time to leave for lunch.

Julia, however, was lingering at the end of the retreating group. She beckoned to Sarah and whispered loudly, "I've hit pay dirt."

And the two hurried forward to the car park.

Chapter Six

"How DO YOU MEAN, pay dirt," Sarah demanded as the two women hustled along the gravel path. "Is it about Barbara?"

"Keep your voice down. As an investigator you lack even the most elementary skills. Not Barbara. Stacy."

Sarah lifted her eyes in surprise.

"Yes," hissed Julia. "The beauty queen, or whatever she is, doesn't know the first thing about gardens."

"That's what Amy said." Sarah considered for a moment and then added, "Not exactly what I call 'pay dirt.' After all, I don't know the first thing about gardens myself."

"But you have a fairly intelligent interest. Stacy's like a mechanical doll. Wind her up and she'll make a few appropriate remarks about mulch or acid soil or how she just loves magnolia trees, while she's pointing at wisteria. The woman's a fraud."

"You mean," said Sarah with a grin, "a plant."

"It's no joking matter. And that child, Amy, is right. Stacy has worked as a model and now is doing PR for a Boston banking outfit. Gardens are no part in her life; she lives in an apartment. So why pretend an interest? I've spent an extremely boring twenty minutes with the woman and an equally boring time with Barbara Baxter. I've been down the Laburnum Walk five times. As for Barbara, I think it's a case of what you see is what you get. A tour leader who doesn't know squat about flowers."

"Because there was no reason for her to," said Sarah.

They had now reached the car park and Julia paused and turned on Sarah. "The only thing I am absolutely sure of is that I have sacrificed my own pleasure in the Barnsley House garden in the interests of faxing a tedious collection of gossip."

"We're doing what the powers at home have asked us to do."

"Those dim bulbs in the police department probably have Ellen Trevino locked up for a traffic violation and they don't know it."

"What's that about Ellen Trevino? Have you heard from her?"

It was Edith Hopper, scraps of her usually neat white hair poking out of its net and all flushed from her perambulations around Barnsley House.

"Oh, no," said Sarah quickly. "We were saying we missed her."

"She would have been so happy," said Edith. "Such a wonderful morning, the sun out, and the garden, absolutely incredible."

But here Barbara Baxter appeared and gestured toward the bus. "Hurry up," she called. "A new restaurant, The Grimalkin Arms in Cirencester. I looked it up in the guide and its supposed to have lots of atmosphere."

The Grimalkin Arms, once an ordinary eighteenth-century structure of the buff-colored Cotswold stone, had been transformed by its new owners, lovers of the Elizabethan look, into a gloomy space with stained-glass windows, heavy tables of dark wood, highbacked chairs, and along the wall a number of heraldic devices featuring the head of a gray cat. Waitresses in ruffs and farthingales scurried back and forth with loaded trays. Barbara Baxter, however, seemed pleased with the ambiance, and Sandi Ouellette, enchanted by what she called "a real English look," explained to all who would listen that "grimalkin" meant an old cat and had they seen the cats on those shields on the walls? The others suffered the dimly lit atmosphere in the interest of eating as soon as possible. However, when lunch proper was over and dessert had arrived—large helpings of sweetened starch in various shapes and flavors—Barbara tapped lightly on her goblet with a spoon and called for attention.

She knew that some people might be wondering why the trip plans deviated—ever so slightly—from the original schedule. But many had expressed interest in seeing more of Britain, availing themselves of the cultural opportunities. Here Barbara looked meaningfully at Sandi and Fred, Doris Lermatov and Stacy Daniel, all of whom nodded vigorously while Justin Rossi looked up and added a "Hear, hear."

"Fortunately," Barbara went on, "I found some unscheduled time in our schedule, so I've felt I could tinker a little with our itinerary."

Sarah looked over at Carter McClure. Judging from his expression he was about to reach over and strangle Barbara.

"So now," said Barbara, now well into her pep talk, "I've arranged a trip to Cambridge. We can visit some of the colleges, the chapels, the bookstores. And especially, the Cambridge Botanic Garden. I'm surprised neither Lillian Garth nor Ellen Trevino didn't include it."

"Because," growled Carter McClure, shaking off Portia's arm, "that's an institutional garden. We're doing private gardens, cottage gardens, not goddamn city university gardens."

"Oh, do hush, Carter," said Portia. "Cambridge might be fun."

Carter's opinion of Cambridge was shared by the Hopper sisters, who mentioned that cities—even ancient university ones—are often hot and crowded, a view seconded by Julia. However, the others made approving noises, and even Sarah thought it might be a nice change of pace.

And then it was time for shopping. Freedom to wander about Cirencester and then meet back at The Grimalkin Arms at two-thirty for the trip to the Lavender Cottage garden, a site which lay to the north, outside of Little Barrington.

"Free," said Sarah as she and Julia stepped off in the direction of the high street. "Free to dig up a fax machine."

"A nuisance, writing out everything," complained Julia.

"There's a stationers across the way," said Sarah. "I saw it when we came out. Paper, pens, and probably a place to sit down."

Not only paper and pens, but a fax machine, the stationers being one of those all-purpose shops that catered to many needs.

"There," said Julia when they returned to the street fifty minutes later. "We've just time to look for gloves for you and wool for me. We have to be authentic."

"You mean cover our tracks." said Sarah. And then she started. Amy. Amy Lermatov, looming just behind her shoulder.

"What tracks?" demanded Amy. "Are you on an assignment? Or is it just PI stuff?"

Julia, who had whirled around at the sight of Amy, recovered first. "PI? Whatever are you talking about?"

Amy smiled broadly, showing a large stretch of tooth hardware. "Private Investigator. Like Kinsey Millhone and V. I. Warshawsky. Because PIs are the only people who cover their tracks except for hard-core criminals or spies."

"We are looking for leather goods," said Julia. "And wool."

"For needlepoint and gloves," said Sarah.

Amy's grin grew wider. "Yeah, right. You bet."

"Why," demanded Julia, "are you floating around Cirencester by yourself?"

"Honestly, Mrs. Clancy," said Amy, "I'll be fifteen next month and I'm allowed to explore. I've been very cultural. Do you see that art gallery?" She pointed across the street. "I followed the Hopper ladies into it. To get a line on them. They didn't even see me. And I've almost finished the notes for my first chapter."

"Good grief," said Julia. "Sarah, I think I see a leather shop down that side street. Goodbye, Amy. There's nothing of cultural interest in a leather shop."

"Oh, don't mind me," said Amy. "I should visit the boring places as well as the good ones. I'll just tag along. Writers need atmosphere."

In an entirely too real atmosphere in the late afternoon, Alex McKenzie sat in the claustrophobic space that Deputy Sheriff Investigator Mike Laaka called his office. This small rectangle, more closet than workspace, crouched in the lower reaches of the Knox County Sheriff's building and accommodated one scarred metal desk, a number of gray file cabinets, three elderly wooden office chairs and a calendar featuring Cigar, recent Horse of the Year. Mike was a diehard race fan, and the fact that the State of Maine had no thoroughbred racing never deterred him from putting together Byzantine betting combinations through unidentified off-track betting establishments.

"Lot of silly garbage," announced Mike, pushing the thin sheets of fax paper to the back of his desk. "Have you read it?"

Alex shrugged. "I've stuck my neck out having the fax sent to my office. My nurse, that's Betty Bartlett, gave me a very fishy look when it came in. She knows some of those people. And, what do you expect, an FBI report? An Interpol workup? This is from two women trying to put some random information on paper without anyone knowing what they were up to."

Mike pulled a sheet toward him. "Listen. Stacy Daniel. Model, PR bank executive. Doesn't know about gardens, jogs, member of health club, done modeling. Classy dresser. Lives in

Lexington, Mass. No friends in group except maybe B. Baxter, leader pro tem.' That's signed by Julia. You see, worthless."

"Okay, so it's not very meaty," agreed Alex. "What's next?"

"Nothing we couldn't figure out about the Ouellettes or the two Hoppers. And Doris Lermatov is eating her way through Britain and loves treacle tarts, trifle, spotted dick—what in hell is that? Daughter Amy says she's writing a mystery based on the idea that Ellen Trevino didn't show up because she's been murdered."

"Christ," said Alex.

"Carter McClure is another bad-tempered academic kept on track by wife Portia. Justin Rossi looks like you, quotes poetry and knows birds. Lawyer, family law, and seems to know flowers—the common names anyway."

Alex stood up. "I'm glad Sarah's found a replacement for me. I've looked over the rest. Except the Barbara Baxter blurb."

Mike pushed the fax papers into a neat pile. "Acting leader and to quote Julia, she's 'overorganized.'"

"Not a bad quality in a tour leader," observed Alex.

Mike nodded. "Actually, the state police did a little checking for us. Last job by Baxter for Whirlaway Tours was a six-city art thing in the U.S.: Boston, Chicago, Philly, Santa Fe, L.A. Before that a southern tour: Louisiana, Mississippi, Alabama, the Carolinas. Historic houses, old plantations. Last year Hawaii."

"I suppose," said Alex, "at some point you'll have to be checking departure times. Who flew in from Maine, who drove."

"Yeah, I suppose," said Mike in a tired voice, "and that'll take..." but the telephone rang and the sentence hung in the air. Mike held up his hand to keep Alex from leaving and picked up the receiver. And then.

"Jesus H. Christ. I mean Jesus. Where? Well, sure. Yeah, I'll come right away. Sure. Okay. I mean, Christ Almighty."

"You're repeating yourself," said Alex. Then, "What's up?'

"What's up is Ellen. Ellen Trevino. Or rather she's down. Along the Maine Turnpike. Off the Scarborough exit."

Alex stared at him. "What do you mean 'along the turnpike'?"

"What I said. Along it. Off the exit ramp. In one of those sections with trees and bushes."

"You mean an accident? A hit-and-run."

Mike shook his head. "No accident. The lady was rolled up in a plastic sheet. Like a sausage. I'm on my way down now. The state police need a positive ID because there wasn't any found on the body. Dental records take too long."

"So why do they think it's Ellen?"

"We haven't got any other missing females who fit her general description. Maine isn't Chicago or L.A. with fifty women reported missing every day. So there's a fair chance it's Ellen."

"You know her well enough to identify her?"

"No, but I'm bringing you. You're not on call, are you?"

"No, not tonight."

"We'll take your car. Mine's in the shop and the cruisers are out. At least you won't have to do the medical examiner bit. She was found out of Knox County. We'll drive straight to Augusta and see the body there. They'll do the post sometime late tonight—or tomorrow morning. Johnny Cuzak will meet us. You remember Johnny, assistant state medical examiner. Nice guy, but he hates bodies turning up on weekends. Anyway, if you make a positive ID we can try to get in touch with her family."

Alex walked to the office door and held it open, Mike following. "This'll be some gruesome scene from what the dispatcher said. Lady's a mess. Jesus Christ, and to think I've been saying Dr. Trevino must have missed her plane and telling everyone to stop making a fuss."

It was Ellen Trevino. Or what was left of her. Even Alex, familiar as he was to death in various shapes and conditions, felt a wave of horror as he studied the swollen and barely recognizable features of the woman now stretched out on the autopsy table, still partially wrapped in the full-length plastic sheet in which she had been found. And unbidden in his mind rose the picture of the Ellen Trevino he had heard giving a lecture on need for stricter state environmental controls. Her voice had been low, but she brought a certain intensity to her remarks. And she had had that appealing otherworldly appearance, right out of an antique illustrated book. He also remembered Sarah saying that as a child she had been painfully shy and this fitted with the diffidence he remembered when the lecture was over and the audience had crowded about her for questions. And now this.

Johnny Cuzak, the assistant state medical examiner from Augusta, shook his head in disgust. "She was wrapped up like some goddamn piece of meat," he complained. "Killed inside that sheet maybe or lying on it. Like whoever did it wanted to keep everything tidy, didn't want to get splattered with blood. Which from his point of view is a smart move."

"Stabbed?" said Mike Laaka, pointing to a dark and sodden perforation in Ellen's blue print dress just below her sternum.

"Murderer was right on target," said Johnny. "But the guy tried to kill her twice. Maybe three times. Maybe a karate chop to knock her out. And a plastic bag over her head. Must have been a race between asphyxia and hemorrhage. If I had to lay money on it I'd go for exsanguination. But it's a guess. Temperature's been in the seventies the last few days so we've got putrefaction to deal with."

"Doesn't look like a knife wound," observed Mike.

"Nope," agreed Johnny. "Entry's too large—but we'll know more later. Now we'll have to take the photographs, with and without that damn plastic bag, with and without clothes, get an X-ray, check her for sexual assault, all the usual. I'll schedule the autopsy for tomorrow, eight o'clock. Talk about a loused-up weekend, why does it always happen?"

"How about time of death?" asked Mike.

"Don't be impatient. Stomach contents, degree of lividity, tissue dissolution, the whole picture. I keep telling you guys that we can't fix the time down to the last minute unless the victim's wearing a smashed wristwatch."

Alex, foreseeing a lecture on forensics, stepped in. "Where exactly was the body? And who found her?"

"This guy in a pickup pulled off on the Scarborough exit road to take a leak. There's a bunch of bushes and trees in there and since he was kind of modest he went way in. Found the body. Wrapped in the plastic sheet with a few old branches pulled over it. Not a real job of hiding, but I guess from a car driving out the exit you wouldn't have seen it. Forensic team is there now sifting through the place. So far the usual crap mostly along the road edge. You know, plastic cups, beer cans, cigarette butts."

"Weapon?" asked Alex.

"Nothing so far. Meanwhile we'll let the state police know we've had an ID. You two go home and get your beauty sleep while poor old Johnny Cuzak spends the night fooling around with body fluids and leaving his family alone for the nine-hundredth consecutive weekend."

"God, what a lousy scene that was," said Alex as he turned his Jeep into Route 17 out of Augusta and headed toward the coast. "That poor woman. Sarah told me Ellen Trevino was a very quiet private person."

"And now," said Mike, "she's as public as all hell."

Alex nodded. "Ironic, isn't it? Okay, what's next? Ellen's family, I suppose. Who and where?"

"The state police CID will take that on," said Mike. "I'm just a handyman. Still only that stepfather in Vancouver as far as we can tell. But I know what's next. That tour group has to be shaken up and interrogated. What they knew about Ellen, when she was last seen, and so forth. They'll have to go to some cute little English village police station and give depositions."

Alex shook his head. "I keep asking myself, For God's sake why? Why would anyone hurt such an entirely harmless woman who lectures on horticulture and specializes in English country gardens?"

"Freak accident, maybe. Wrong place at the wrong time. She got out of her car at the Kennebunk exit and then, wham. Some fucking maniac nailed her. Raped her, maybe. Robbed her, maybe, because her handbag, luggage, everything's missing. Stabbed her, wrapped up the body, and toted it out to the Scarborough exit and dumped it. And got the hell out. Okay, I suppose you want to call Sarah and the others, but don't."

"Because I'm not allowed to?"

"Our old friend George Fitts will want to do it kosher. Not let the sheriff's department or you handle anything so tricky."

This proved the case. The redoubtable Sergeant George Fitts, Maine State Police CID, human refrigerator and specialist in the analytical approach to crime, did indeed want to follow proper procedures through proper channels. And these involved communication with one Inspector Defoe of High Roosting Police Department in the County of Gloucestershire, and the setting up of the machinery for the taking of statements followed by the faxing of same. Notification of what was in store for the Midcoast Garden Club of Knox County Maine, USA, to take place the next morning, Saturday, June the tenth.

"We'll let them get their beauty sleep," said Inspector Defoe, echoing as if by transatlantic telepathy Johnny Cuzak's words.

Chapter Seven

An innkeeper does not take kindly to finding the constabulary on his doorstep. This is especially true at seven-thirty in the morning, a time when guests are coming down for breakfast or returning from early morning walks.

But at least, thought Mr. Thomas Gage, the Shearing innkeeper, he's not driving one of those great bloody white police cars with its horizontal orange stripe for all the neighborhood to gawk at. And he's not in uniform, so I suppose I should be thankful for small mercies. Thomas made an attempt to fix his face into a neutral frame and told him to come in.

Inspector Defoe stepped over the threshold. He was indeed a low-key presence. Gray suit, maroon tie, blue shirt. Polished black shoes. Quite respectable, except, of course, no one with half a glance would take him for a tourist.

"Come out of the front hall, please, and go into my office," said Thomas Gage, after he had scowled at the identity card produced by the inspector—an unnecessary gesture since High Roosting was a small village and everyone knew the man by sight, but Defoe liked to do things by the book.

"Now," said Mr. Gage, when the inspector had joined him in the tiny office off the front hall. "What's this all about? I can't have our guests upset. The inn is full. We've had no trouble since those two Albanians with the motorbikes left."

"Thomas, please," said Defoe, who knew Mr. Gage as a fellow supporter of the High Roosting Football Club. The inspector was a sturdy, gray-haired, heavy browed man with a square jaw who bore the burden of the first name of Daniel and was forever fending off cries of "Have you found Crusoe yet, Defoe?"

"There'll be no fuss," continued Daniel Defoe, helping himself to the one comfortable office chair. "You won't even know I've been here. I will tread very softly. All I want to do is talk to the American tour group. Nothing to do with the increasing crime rate of High Roosting. I'll be wanting to see the whole lot of them in your front parlor, everything quiet and private. Then their tour bus can bring them over to the station for statements."

"I still don't know what on earth you're going on about, Daniel," said Mr. Gage, becoming informal in his exasperation.

"Homicide. In the States. New England. Or Maine, to be exact. Some woman who was supposed to be with the group and missed her flight. Missed it, apparently, because she was dead. Or kidnapped and then died. Not alive, anyway."

"Why do you want statements then if it's a murder in the States?" demanded Mr. Gage.

"I don't want them. The Maine State Police CID want them. They're working through Interpol and we cooperate. It's not as if we're dealing with Iran or China. The Maine State Police want certain information and we'll supervise the statements and send the information along. And there's the end to it with not a bit of bother to you and the Shearing. Now, when do they have breakfast?"

"I expect some of them are down now," said Mr. Gage in an unhappy voice. "I heard the tour driver—he's got a room over the old stables—say they were due to leave at nine. Going to a couple of special gardens north of Chipping Camden."

"The best-laid plans," said Inspector Defoe. "Please ask each of them to step along to the parlor after breakfast."

"The parlor is open to *all* our guests," said Mr. Gage. "It's where we put the papers. The periodicals."

"And for about an hour or so this morning it won't be open to all your guests. I'll meet them there."

"Damn the police," said Mr. Gage to Mrs. Hosmer, the Shearing secretary, when Inspector Defoe was out of hearing. "If he lets on about this affair, even if it happened in the States, it may put people off."

The secretary looked up from her computer keyboard on which she was tapping out the evening's dinner menu specials. "None of our guests is going to be put off by a murder in the States. Everyone expects murder in the States. That's what they do over there. Kill each other. It's a perfectly normal everyday thing."

However, it fell to Mrs. Hosmer to speak to each member of the garden tour, urging them to come directly after breakfast to the parlor. That someone wanted to meet them. All of them. Together.

"What someone?" demanded Julia Clancy, looking up from her poached egg.

"Oh, I can't rightly say," said Mrs. Hosmer, avoiding the Clancy eye. The secretary had been instructed to keep quiet about the nature of the meeting.

"I'm sure you can rightly say," returned Carter McClure, who sat next to Julia. "So say it. Otherwise, we have no reason to go to the parlor. We all know each other, the plan for the day is set, and we're due on the bus by nine."

"And we have just time after breakfast to write postcards," said Doris Lermatov. "I haven't sent a single one and three days have gone by."

"In the parlor," said Mrs. Hosmer with greater firmness. "It's the small room leading off the front hall. The gentleman will meet you there and explain."

"Gentleman!" exclaimed Julia. "What gentleman?"

But Mrs. Hosmer was on the move, only turning at the door and calling across two tables, "His name is Defoe. Daniel Defoe."

"*Robinson Crusoe*," said Carter McClure. "How jolly. The author himself."

"*Moll Flanders, Journal of the Plague Year*," added Sarah, who had used both books in her English class the past year. She had been listening to Mrs. Hosmer's request, and now decided that this must be part of some High Roosting village affair going on in the village which needed tourist money. A church fête or a white elephant sale—what did they call it here, a jumble sale?

Sarah bent again over her thickening porridge. She had chosen oatmeal out of a sense that a day spent slogging over two of the United Kingdom's major gardens demanded serious fortification. On her right side Justin Rossi was finishing his second cup of coffee and ignoring Barbara Baxter's descriptions of the wonders of the Kiftsgate and Hidcote Manor gardens. Barbara, Sarah decided, must have spent a large portion of the previous evening boning up because she was now regurgitating what sounded like an entire guidebook of information. But if Justin Rossi appeared uninterested, then Stacy Daniel went him one better. She yawned, shifted in her seat, wondered out loud if there were any good movies around.

In fact, only Sandi and Fred Ouellette listened to Barbara with anything like attention. Portia concentrated on her muffins, Doris Lermatov sorted postcards, Carter McClure dissected his trout, while young Amy Lermatov spent the time between large bites of toast with writing in her notebook.

Sarah looked down the table, taking in the still unfinished breakfasts, the second cups of coffee and tea now being poured, and then rolled up her napkin and stood up. "Please excuse me," she said. "I need fifteen minutes of fresh air before the meeting.

I'm going out and check out the garden right here. We've been neglecting what's right on our doorstep."

The Shearing Inn garden was rich in early summer flowers, red and white valerian, hanging wisteria, and trellised roses. After rambling aimlessly about for several minutes, Sarah, hearing agitated female voices, moved away toward a grassy terrace that overlooked a pasture dotted with sheep. There she remained for some ten minutes in a sort of post-breakfast trance watching the sheep moving separately and by twos and threes, the ewes followed by their now partly grown lambs. Then, with a guilty start, she remembered the parlor meeting, turned and started back.

And came upon the Hopper sisters, whom she realized had not been at breakfast. Both were in some disrepair. Red eyes, trembling lips, Edith holding a handkerchief, Margaret swallowing hard.

Sarah hesitated. Was this a private moment of grief or did they want help? Or comfort?

She settled for comfort.

"I'm sorry, I don't mean to interrupt, but is there anything wrong? Something I can do? Have you had bad news?"

Margaret snuffled and then shook her head. "No, Sarah dear. Nothing at all. Just a little shock. Something we'd forgotten..."

"Or didn't know about," said Edith.

"About our passport, a sort of mixup," said Margaret, but with such lack of conviction even Edith looked puzzled.

"I'm sure that it can be straightened out," said Sarah, who wasn't in the least sure; she had a horror of losing documents.

"Oh, I'm sure it can," said Edith, "Only we, well, we didn't know at first. Just a mistake."

"There you are." It was Barbara Baxter standing at the garden gate. "We're wanted right now. Mrs. Hosmer sent me to find you."

"Are you sure you're both all right?" asked Sarah, "because I'm sure this Mr. Defoe will excuse you if you're ill."

"No, I mean yes," said Margaret. "Quite all right. Just an upset. Unexpected. But nothing we can't deal with."

"Never mind us, Sarah," said Edith. "We'll be right there. I just have to put my hair to rights."

Your face to rights is what you should do, thought Sarah, looking at Edith's cheeks where tears had streaked lines through the light face powder. She left the two sisters to recover from whatever calamity had overwhelmed them and climbed the stone steps to the Shearing Inn entrance. And walked into Amy Lermatov, who stood by the door with her notebook.

"I'm making a sketch of the outside," said Amy. "Setting is important, and I have to remember where the doors and windows are. Old inns are good places for mysteries because they have those twisty staircases and the high bushes outside to hide in."

"We're supposed to be meeting in the parlor," said Sarah. She had about had it with Amy as a private investigator.

"I know," said Amy. "That's where I'm having my characters meet the chief inspector. That's what they call them in England, chief inspector. My chief inspector's going to meet the group and tell them this body's been discovered..." Here Amy paused and Sarah could see that she hadn't yet decided where the body was to be found. But Amy wasn't blocked for long.

"The body was in the graveyard. That old church. Saint something or other. Under a bush, so it wasn't found right away. Maybe the body is Dr. Trevino's sister. I haven't decided."

Sarah took Amy by the elbow, and pointed the girl toward the front door. "Right now we're supposed to be in the parlor. And I think you should keep your story ideas to yourself. People like Edith and Margaret Hopper don't want to hear all the gruesome details about some dead body."

"People love gruesome details," announced Amy, but she opened the door and followed by Sarah walked into the parlor.

The room was a cheerful little space overlooking a side garden. It had comfortable chintz-covered chairs, a fireplace, a bookcase filled with a number of elderly looking novels, and low tables on which were scattered recent editions of the less strident British newspapers: *The Observer, The Times, The Daily Telegraph,* and *The Guardian.* Sarah settled herself on a window seat next to Julia who had chosen a wingchair. Amy Lermatov stationed herself on a stiff chair by the door, the better, perhaps, to study her cast of characters. Then, just as the brass mantel clock struck nine, the Hopper sisters appeared, hesitated, and then joined Sarah on the window seat. A wise choice, she thought, since the light would be at their backs and not illuminating their red-eyed, puffy faces.

There was a moment's pause after the clock had finished its nine chimes, a pause in which Carter McClure tapped his foot with impatience and Stacy Daniel gazed at the ceiling, and then Daniel Defoe appeared on the threshold, nodded to no one in particular, and took a chair directly in front of the bookcase.

He went directly to the point. "Good morning. I am Inspector Defoe of the High Roosting District Police." He paused and looked about the room, allowing this piece of information to sink in. Then he said, "I'm very sorry to be the bearer of bad news, but we've received word from the States—actually from the Maine police—that there has been an accident to one of your members."

Here Inspector Defoe paused again and then, by some sort of intuition he settled on Barbara Baxter as his focus and went on. "Dr. Ellen Trevino—I believe she was to have joined you on your tour—has died. To be accurate, the state police believe, because of the circumstances in which she was found, that her death must be considered a homicide." Another pause and Sarah felt the whole room begin to wobble and for a second put her head down, then choking back a gasp, she turned away from the inspector and so found herself staring at Amy Lermatov. Amy, with her mouth gaping, her eyes wide, had let her notebook and pen slip to the floor. Otherwise, except for small choking sounds from Margaret and Edith Hopper, and an audible gulp from Sandi Ouellette, there was silence. A general holding of breath, and then slowly, as if a large balloon had been punctured, a slow exhalation. And then, only then, exclamations.

"Ellen!"

"Not Ellen! Our Ellen?"

"Ellen Trevino? Oh, my God."

"But we thought she just missed her plane."

"What do you mean how she was found?"

"Homicide? You're saying Ellen was murdered?"

"Holy shit!" Amy Lermatov had found her voice.

"You mean someone actually killed her?" demanded Stacy Daniel, alert and awake for the first time that Sarah had seen her. Stacy shook her head back and forth. "God, is this some sort of bad joke? I mean, aren't you putting us on? One of those mystery weekends they do for tourists?"

"Be quiet all of you and listen to what Inspector Defoe has to say." This was Carter McClure in his academic mode.

Seconded by Julia. "Carter's right. Wait and see what the man wants."

Broken into by Barbara Baxter, "This is terrible, horrible news. I don't believe it. Not Ellen Trevino. Are you sure?"

"Holy shit!" repeated Amy, who seemed to be stuck on that single response. Then Doris Lermatov, suddenly awake to the fact that her daughter had been making unsuitable comments, turned and said loudly, "Amy, you be quiet and pay attention."

And now the two Hopper sisters, already upset by whatever private grief had hit them earlier, began to sob in a muffled way. And to Sarah, unbidden, rose the image of Ellen Trevino standing at the dinner table, heard her thanking the Garden Club and saying how she was looking forward to the trip, how she hoped it would be a memorable one because English gardens in June were as close to heaven as anyone was likely to get. And then Sarah heard, as if from a long way away, the voice of the twelve-year-old Ellen calling after her father, "You're killing them, you're a murderer, you're killing all the flowers." And now someone had killed Ellen.

Inspector Defoe, having allowed a small space of time for the news to sink in, gathered the reins in his hands. "I regret having to give you this sad news, but now you must all do what you can to help your police. Miss Baxter, ah yes, over there. I understand that you are in charge of the tour details? Good. What the Maine State Police want are voluntary statements from each of you. Just a few simple questions to answer, so the sooner you can arrange for your driver to bring your people down to the station to make those statements under our supervision, the sooner you can return to your tour schedule."

Here Inspector Defoe, a grave expression on his broad face, looked slowly about the room, catching those eyes that were lifted to his, and then he rose from his chair, thanked them for their attention, and strode out of the room.

Again a collective silence except for the soft moist sounds from Edith and Margaret Hopper and a sort of whistling noise from Justin Rossi. And then Barbara Baxter stood up, seemed to brace herself for something heroic, and announced that she would warn their driver, Joseph, of the change in plan, and that they must all be ready in fifteen minutes. And that she, herself, was horribly shocked, she still couldn't believe it, it was awful, but they must help the police in any way they could.

At this there was a general rising and movement toward the door, a returning to rooms for handbags and passports—there seemed to be an unspoken agreement that passports might be required—and then an anxious clustering outside of the front door.

"That poor Ellen Trevino, oh dear, oh dear," repeated Edith Hopper. This, like some sort of responsive reading was repeated in theme and variations throughout the group. Only Justin Rossi and Stacy Daniel, who after all had only met Dr. Trevino at the pre-tour dinner, seemed by their silence immune to the general sorrow.

"Look at them," said Sandi Ouellette. "Cold fish. They don't care." She peered at Julia. "And I don't think you do, either."

"Never mind me," said Julia Clancy, "but I think that if Mr. Rossi and Ms. Daniel went into paroxysms of sorrow I'd have handcuffs on them in a second."

"What?" said Sandi. "You mean you think..."

"I don't think, I know that Dr. Trevino was more or less a stranger to both of them, and so the best thing they can do is keep quiet and not make inappropriate noises."

"You," said Sandi, "are a mean old woman. There, I've said what I've thought and I'm sorry but it's true."

Julia smiled. "Correct. I'm a mean old woman, but I'm a sensible old woman, and I'm not going to loose any sleep over two of our group who aren't sprinkling ashes over their heads. As for me, everyone deals with grief in their own way. I'll deal with mine in my own way, thank you."

At which Sandi, head high, moved away, and Sarah pulled her aunt's sleeve. "Aunt Julia, ease up."

"Well, I'm extremely sorry about Ellen Trevino, it's a terrible thing, but I'm not going to start a public keening."

"You're too hard on Sandi. I think there's more to her than meets the eye. She's perfectly intelligent, but that fact gets lost in the delivery."

"All right," grumbled Julia. "I'll make it up to her."

"We certainly won't be going to Hidcote and Kiftsgate this Saturday," said Doris Lermatov, joining the two. "It wouldn't be a very nice thing to go off and look at gardens when poor Ellen Trevino is dead."

But this observation was cut short by the arrival of their tour bus, and hardly had the group settled in their seats but they found themselves decanted into the police visitors' car park, and led into a spartanly furnished room with a desk, several wooden chairs, a file cabinet, two long tables, and a framed photograph of Her Majesty, Queen Elizabeth II.

"Interrogation room," announced Amy, who seemed to have recovered something of her equilibrium. And then, looking around, saw a tall man in a dark suit standing by the file cabinet. "Are you a constable in plainclothes," she asked. "Or a sergeant? And isn't this an awfully big police station for High Roosting, because it's such a dinky little village?"

The man looked down at Amy much in the way one might examine an unexpected earwig. Not a very large one, but nevertheless an earwig. "I'm Chief Inspector Wingate," he said. "And the police station here serves more than High Roosting. We're responsible for what goes on in the surrounding area: Nether Roosting, Lower Roosting, Little Swinecote, and Swinecote. And to answer your question, young woman, we have uniformed constables and sergeants and plainclothes detectives, just as you do in the States."

Then Chief Inspector Wingate turned and addressed the now assembled group, told them that the questions were simple ones intended to fix for the Maine State Police the times and places when they had last seen or heard from Dr. Trevino. "And thank you very much for your cooperation. Sorry for the unhappy occasion. Inspector Defoe will take you one at a time in the next office."

"The questions were certainly simple-minded," remarked Julia when she, Sarah, and the tour group emerged blinking into the noonday June sun.

Sarah shook her head. "I can't believe this is happening. I can't do a thing about Ellen and I feel sick and totally useless. The trouble is that I've been worried about her since Boston."

At which point they were joined by Doris Lermatov and her daughter. Amy, still somewhat subdued by her immersion in the real world of police and homicide, was on the receiving end of a lecture. "I hope," her mother was saying, "that poor Ellen Trevino's death will put a stop to your turning our trip into some cheap mystery novel."

For a moment the girl's lip trembled and then the old Amy returned. "I wouldn't write a 'cheap' novel," she said. "I'd make it all true to life because my English teacher wants us to keep notes no matter what happens."

But then up came Sandi and Fred Ouellette and pointed out that the bus was loading. "Barbara," announced Sandi, "says there won't be time to make it all the way to see those two gardens, you know Hidcote and the other one, but she'll arrange for us to go somewhere. She says Ellen would want us to, and if we keep busy we won't have so much time to be upset."

"Being busy," said Julia sharply, "does not prevent me from being upset. I'm not that easily distracted."

And here Portia came up and defended Sandi. "It does make sense, Julia. What's the point of us staying at the inn and stewing. We can feel awful about Ellen and still look at gardens. Because, honestly, there's nothing on earth we can do. Except what we've done. Help the police at home with our statements and cross our fingers they can hurry up and nail whoever did it. So a garden might just be the thing. A garden keeps Ellen in our mind and gardens are hopeful places."

"There's nothing hopeful about Ellen being murdered," complained Julia. "But I see your point. You can go and look at gardens if Barbara Baxter has another one up her sleeve."

"I remember," said Sandi in reminiscent voice, "how after we found the body of that woman by the bird feeder, and after we'd given statements, we all went out and had dinner together. To be with each other. It helped us get through the rest of the day."

You see, Sarah wanted to tell Julia, Sandi has a perfectly normal brain. But then these kindly thoughts were interrupted by the necessity of climbing back on the bus and returning to the Shearing Inn. As the bus rolled to a stop in the car park, Barbara Baxter stood up by the driver. "I've the very place. That nice constable at the police station suggested it. A National Trust house called Snowshill Manor. It has a collection of toys, musical instruments and antiques and even a very lovely garden."

Here Carter McClure, siting in the rear of the bus, exploded. "*Even* has a garden she says. We didn't come to Gloucestershire to see antiques and toys and musical instruments. I'm extremely sorry about Ellen Trevino. A real loss to the college and everyone who cared about gardens. But the fact is that she's gone, so I have a proposal. I'm going to call my friend Henry Ruggles. He's very knowledgeable about gardens. Lectures all over the place. Henry lives in Moreton-in-Marsh. Retired. He'll probably eat up the invitation to come down and take charge."

Barbara Baxter looked aghast. "Really Dr. McClure, we can't just add people to the tour."

"Don't give it a thought," said Carter, climbing past her and pausing at the bus door. "You've done very well, I'm sure, with all the tour details so far, but we need a garden leader. Henry will fill the bill nicely. Right, Portia?"

"Carter, I think you could have waited before mentioning Henry," said Portia. "It's as if you're rushing someone into Ellen's place, which isn't tactful." She smiled at the group at large. "But Carter, for once, is right. Henry Ruggles is a real expert. And a very agreeable person."

"I don't think," began Barbara, but the others, possibly thinking of luncheon—it was past one—rose soberly from their bus seats and one by one headed for the Shearing Inn.

But just as the dining room was reached, Margaret Hopper stopped cold. "I know it's lunchtime, but I couldn't touch a bite." She looked over at her sister, who nodded vehemently. "After all, poor Ellen Trevino has been murdered," went on Margaret, her voice taking on a tinge of hysteria. "Murdered and now she's a body somewhere waiting on some table and we're about to go into the dining room, and I think that it's...it's almost obscene to sit down and enjoy lunch." Here Margaret took hold of Edith's arm, and moved her sister away from the dining room entrance.

Sarah, who was not feeling much like eating herself, watched the retreat of the two sisters with sympathy, but, as the troop stepped into the dining room, she came reluctantly to the conclusion that whatever was blighting their appetite was not entirely due to answering police questions about Ellen Trevino. Their faces still held traces of the early morning's anguish and Margaret had developed a noticeable facial twitch.

Chapter Eight

"THE HOPPERS MUST FEEL very badly about Dr. Trevino," said Sandi Ouellette, who was working her way through a substantial helping of Cotswold pie—Sandi being determined to sample all the regional dishes, her appetite not being diminished by grief.

"Edith and Margaret Hopper have always struck me as being on a very even keel," said Sarah, who sat on Sandi's left.

"But they must be super-sensitive because I heard on the plane that they hardly knew her. Only met her a few times at lectures. In fact, they said she frightened them a little because she knew so much. I know what they meant because after I'd met Dr. Trevino at that get-acquainted dinner I thought, Whoa, Sandi, better keep your lips buttoned and so had Fred. Because we are such beginners."

"Yes," said Fred. "Ellen Trevino in her quiet way could be intimidating. Some funeral directors are like that. Perfect gentlemen, but at our conventions they can make the younger directors feel, well, inadequate. Of course, in our profession there's no substitute for years of hands-on training."

"I suppose," said Sarah, beating a retreat from the embalming table, "that it isn't so much Ellen Trevino by herself—since they didn't really know her—who upset Edith and Margaret, as it was the horror of someone being murdered."

"They're probably not as used to violence as the rest of us," remarked Justin Rossi. "A sheltered life, small town, nothing more terrible happening than the minister's daughter running away with the town drunk or a teenager driving off a dock."

"Really, Mr. Rossi," said Julia Clancy, spearing a prawn, "small towns have their share of misery. Besides, I think that Edith and Margaret were upset before we heard about Ellen. They both looked as if they'd been crying when they came into the parlor."

"What I want to know," said Doris Lermatov, "is whether we're suspects? All those questions about how we got to the airport? When did we last see Ellen? Did we notice anything unusual?"

"What was unusual," said Carter, "is this tampering with our schedule. Going into London and mooning about in Westminster Abbey and Harrods. Scheduling Cambridge."

Barbara Baxter, at the end of the table, leaned forward and said in a patient and much tried voice, "I'm doing my best without Dr. Trevino's help. Several people on the tour wanted very much to see a bit of London and we did go to the Kew Gardens. And quite a few of you seem to be in favor of Cambridge. Since Dr. Trevino wasn't here I had to make some decisions. Broaden the base of the trip, so to speak." Barbara paused and looked up and down the table, and smiled, a rather wistful smile. "What do you all think? Can we live with the changes? How about you, Stacy?"

Stacy shrugged. "It's okay by me, I guess. This Snowshill place today, Cambridge later. Fine. Great. Go for it." And Stacy returned to her salad.

Justin Rossi seconded this opinion—if so offhand a response could be called support. "Sure, I'm agreeable. Someone has to run this thing, and Barbara seems to be doing a good job."

"Well, thank you," said Barbara. "And I'd like to say that no one could be sorrier about Ellen's death than I am. Such a nice person. Before we left I drove out to her house—it's at the end of nowhere, only one farm around—to go over plans. Three days before the trip. Ellen said she'd really worked on her lectures."

"There you are, Carter," said Portia, the peacemaker, "and," she added, "when, Henry Ruggles comes..."

Sandi looked up. "He's *really* coming?"

"Carter says yes. And I'm sure Henry—though never a replacement for Ellen—will fit right in and add a great deal."

"I called before lunch," said Carter complacently. "Henry's delighted. He'll be here after dinner ready to take over."

"Take over?" Barbara's voice rose.

"Don't worry," said Portia. "I've made Carter promise that he'll make it perfectly clear to Henry that you're the tour chief. He'll just do the garden lectures."

"Well," said Barbara, "then we'll do our best to welcome him."

And the group returned to the matter of lunch, breaking naturally into small conversational segments.

And Sarah, whose mind had been busy with something closer to the bone than the arrival of Henry Ruggles, turned to her aunt. "I didn't put it on my questionnaire, but I think maybe something unusual did happen at the airport. Logan, I mean. Those sunglasses and the scarf that turned up in my shoulder bag."

Julia raised her eyebrows. "I thought we had disposed of those questions. I don't think either item could qualify as a murder weapon...no, listen to me. Not that scarf. Thin cotton and hardly big enough."

"You're an expert on scarves used for throttling people?"

"I've read enough mysteries to know that you need strong material and a piece large enough to get a grip on the ends of the scarf and twist. And plastic sunglasses couldn't hurt a flea."

"And the fact that the scarf ran a sort of reddish color."

Julia regarded her niece with exasperation. "Sarah, just what do you want to do? Tote the scarf and glasses to New Scotland Yard and demand a forensic exam?"

Sarah sighed. "Relax, Aunt Julia, I'm not going to annoy the British police. But those two things bother me. Particularly after all of us being knocked down—maybe deliberately—just before boarding. So I'm going to mail the scarf to Alex, and he can turn it over to the police. I want to got rid of the thing."

"Splendid," said Julia, folding her napkin. "Now, while everyone is off to look at toys and musical instruments, I've decided to take the car—Sarah, you're welcome to come—and go for a drive in the countryside. I know of nothing so soothing after a shock than seeing fields and pastures and farms."

Sarah shook her head. "I'm going to stay local. I haven't even started to come to terms with Ellen's being dead. Killed like that. I feel as if I've swallowed a stone. I need to be alone, be quiet, and think about her, so I'll just wander around the village and the footpaths."

Johnny Cuzak peeled off his surgical gloves, untied his protective apron, and briefly ran his eye over the body of Ellen Trevino, her body now slit, probed, gutted, suctioned, hosed; her stomach contents, samples of hair, fingernails, blood, brain, other organs, fluids, tissues, extirpated, withdrawn, weighed, examined and photographed. Then he placed these items in appropriate envelopes, flasks, and tubes, sealed and dated and stored.

"So far, so bad," said Johnny. "We're fixing the time of death sometime on June sixth. For now we can't make it closer. Too bad a gun didn't do the job because we'd have ballistics to go on. Now we're stuck with a monster chest wound and whatever made it."

"Not asphyxia," said Alex, who standing behind Johnny, had watched the proceedings and, as was usual with him, trying to detach his professional observing self from the human one that had known and admired Dr. Ellen Trevino.

"That plastic bag tied over the head didn't do it. Someone trying to make double sure. Well, yeah, it would have done the trick, providing the victim stayed unconscious. That conk on the head was probably meant to keep her quiet, not to kill her."

"Which it didn't. The conk, I mean."

"Nope." Johnny pointed at the chest cavity. "Peculiar wound. Narrow at the base, wide at the entry point. Did the job though. Rupture right through the descending parts of the thoracic aorta." Johnny turned to his assistant. "Okay, take her away. I'm done. For now." He turned to Alex. "No sign of rape, no pregnancy, no long-standing pathology. Organs, tissues all look pretty healthy."

"Being healthy won't protect you from having a hole punched in your chest," said Alex. "Lab tests to follow, right?"

"Yeah. And the police can start sniffing around for the weapon. Probably something the shape of an elongated ice cream cone. One with real heft. The thing went in more or less straight with a very slight upward thrust. Suggests the victim was lying down when she got the blow. If she'd been standing face to face with the murderer the line of the entry wouldn't be so on target. Just try and direct a heavy blow like that without bouncing off the sternum, going a little down, or sideways."

"Why not up?"

"Slightly up, okay. But up would have been awkward. Try it yourself. You lose force by striking underhand and up. I'd say it was well aimed for doing what it did."

"A railroad spike?"

"Something like. But more tapered. Sharper point."

"What about that plastic tarp she was wrapped in?"

"Lab's working on it. So far only one blood type present. Ellen's. DNA testing to follow. They're going over it for fibers and hairs and other crud. But that plastic tarp looked pretty new. No evidence to show it'd been used to cover a lawn mower, or a greasy motorcycle."

"Possibly bought for the purpose," Alex said grimly. He turned and, followed by Johnny, walked out into a small office off the autopsy room.

"Tarps like that are sold everywhere," said Johnny, sitting down at a desk and switching on the monitor of his PC. "Tell Mike it's time the police came up with some family. Then we can think about releasing the body for burial."

"They're looking. Ellen's neighbor—Mrs. Epple—thinks the stepfather may be hiking somewhere out west. They're putting the park rangers on it. Her own parents are dead. No kids, no husband. No signs of a lover of either sex. Looks like Ellen Trevino was going through life solo. I gather Bowmouth College will be having some sort of memorial service for her in the chapel this week."

Johnny scowled at his monitor and moved the mouse pointer to "File," then said, "Okay, Alex, get out of here. I've got to write my report. And tell Mike and his buddies in the state police to leave me alone next weekend. Both my kids have Little League and Jennifer's pitching her first game."

"Like a heavy-duty ice cream cone," said Alex to Mike Laaka when the two met at the Mary Starbox Hospital cafeteria for dinner; Alex having just admitted a patient and Mike checking on an uncle with a broken hip. Mike, Alex thought, looked incongruously healthy in the hospital setting with his fair almost white hair and his deep summer tan. But he looked worried. "You're kidding about an ice cream cone, aren't you?"

Alex shook his head. "Sorry, I'm not."

"Okay, you're not. Well, the field lab team hasn't come up with anything close to a weapon like that. Actually, except for an area of depressed grass and pine needles where the body was, they've come up with zip. Besides the crap I told you about, they've picked up a dead groundhog, two hubcaps, and a pair of boxer shorts. There was a lot of blood on that tarp, but so far none seems to have leaked out onto the ground."

"Footprints?"

"Only after the fact—from that truck driver who found her body. She was dumped before it started raining—the earth was dry under the tarp. With the ground hard and dry like that footprints wouldn't have made much of an impression. Of course, later in the day it rained like hell. So the only marks that survived the rain were some old sharp deer hoofprints."

"Johnny says it's up to you to dig up the weapon. He's never seen a wound quite like this one, and Johnny always claim he's seen everything." And here Alex addressed himself to a slice of meatloaf while Mike worked his way through macaroni and cheese.

Then, Mike put down his fork and said, "Okay, okay. So the weapon is weird. Let's give it a rest. Don't you want to know about the questions and answers we got from the High Roosting police? God, what a name. High Roosting, Jesus."

"You like Slippery Rock or Kalamazoo or Scraggly Pond better? No, don't answer. Just tell me in three short sentences."

"Right. Nothing much to tell. The only people of the Garden Club to go by car to Boston were Sarah, Julia—driven by you—and Fred and Sandi Ouellette with the Hopper sisters, who took an airport limousine all the way. The rest drove, got a ride, or took a taxi to Portland and left from the Jetport to Logan. US Air and Delta. Different departure times. Ellen Trevino was found at Scarborough exit 4, northbound. Her car was at Kennebunk, exit 3 South."

"And her car was clean?"

"Absolutely. Her own dog's hair, her hair, plus the stuff I've told you about. The car was pretty tidy. No sign of a struggle or blood. As for prints, hers and about three other sets. Her car went in for a tune-up last week, so maybe the prints belong to the mechanics who worked on her car. The lab's working on a match."

"But no heavy ice cream cones."

"No. There was a weeder—sharp devil with a V notch at the end. And a heavy folding shovel, but no blood. Ellen's prints on those. We're guessing she left the car voluntarily. It was locked and the keys were gone. Mrs. Epple says Ellen was careful of her car, so it doesn't seem likely she'd go off on her trip and leave it in a turnpike parking lot. So maybe she went in to buy some food at the restaurant, or to use the ladies' room, and expected to come back to her car. But she ran into someone who changed her plans."

"Changed them for good," said Alex. "But isn't a rest stop a very public place in which to stab someone to death."

"Yeah. No one can figure out how Ellen could have been hit, stabbed, and had her head bagged at a pit stop that was swarming with tourists. By June first the state is alive with the buggers. But who said it was done there? Say she was kidnapped. Gun or knife in her face. 'Get in my car and don't say a word or I'll blow your head off.' Someone trying for cash. Because where is her handbag, her suitcase, all her travel gear?"

"You're betting on robbery? Homicide cum robbery?"

"Could be. Anyway, according to Barbara Baxter's deposition, she met with Ellen three days before departure to talk about the tour, and Ellen was all set for the trip but never mentioned when and how she was getting there. Sarah and the neighbor, Mrs. Epple, are the only ones who heard Ellen say she intended to drive."

Alex brought his chosen apple crisp front and center and considered the application of whipped cream. Rejected it and returned to the subject at hand. "Have you thought that Ellen meant to meet someone at the Kennebunk exit and drive to Boston with them—or him—or her? What was that Mrs. Epple said about visiting a friend and then checking with someone—possibly about the trip?"

"Aaarr," said Mike thickly, his mouth full. He was now well into pecan pie with a frosted brownie on the side. Mike had the digestion of an alligator and had inherited from his Finnish ancestors a physiology that seemed to be unaffected by food or lack of it. "Forget about Mrs. Epple. She doesn't know any more than she first told us."

"Maybe Ellen made arrangements for her car to be picked up and stored. At a friend's house. Or a garage."

"We've checked with garages in the area and come up with zip. As for seeing a friend, meeting someone? Who? When? That'll take a hell of a lot of sweat and pavement pounding to find out."

Alex pushed back his chair and threw his napkin on the table. "So if it's robbery and murder, it goes like this: Ellen with a gun at her head, gets in the other car—murderer's vehicle—is driven off to a cozy corner and is killed and her body dumped at the Scarborough exit. The murderer first heads south, then changes direction and gets off at a north-south interchange. But why? Why not keep going south, find a side road and real woods to hide the body?"

"You only turn around and head north if you have a plane to catch," said Mike, adding with a knowing look, "A plane that flies from Portland Jetport to Logan. And then on to Heathrow."

"Or you live north of Kennebunk. You kill Ellen, dump the body, and head home. Wherever home is."

"But I keep saying, where the hell's her luggage? The police all along the pike are starting to hit town dumps—not many left anymore. And trash bins, refuse containers. Landfills. Airport dumpsters. Fields and marshes by the edge of the road."

Alex stood up. "Well, keep after it. Me, I've got to be off. Serious poker tonight. A chance to lose a few bucks."

Mike grinned. "Glad someone's got leisure time. I'm supposed to meet Sergeant Tightass Fitts and reread the questionnaires the UK police sent on. George wants to correlate Sarah and Julia's profiles with those answers. Trouble is that except for Julia, and maybe Carter McClure, it's a pretty ordinary bunch of people."

"Add Sarah Douglas Deane to the oddballs. Her bumps of curiosity exceed that of the dromedary. I'm sorry I'm not there to throw safety nets over her head or pull her away from the edge of a cliff. I can only hope she sticks with the tour and doesn't try any solos while there's even the faintest chance that someone in the group may be tainted."

Sarah, being unable to read transatlantic warnings, spent, as she promised, a solitary Saturday afternoon in High Roosting. Julia, joined by Carter McClure, took off by car to check out the local farm scene, but otherwise most of the faithful climbed into the bus and went off to view the wonders of Snowshill Manor.

High Roosting was a small Cotswold settlement which in the past had boasted little more than the usual village collection of churches, a school, two pubs, a post office, a chemist, and a limited number of shops selling food. However, with the ever-burgeoning tourist trade, High Roosting had become swollen with a number of new gift shops, tea shops, a new pub, a wool shop, and several emporiums displaying antiques and works of art.

Sarah, after posting her suspect scarf airmail and wandering for several hours about the streets and paths of the village with no particular purpose other than to think and mourn the death of Ellen Trevino, heard the town hall clock strike four. The air had turned chilly and she stepped into a wool shop and purchased a raspberry-colored cardigan and then betook herself down Market Street to Mrs. Jellicoe's Tea Shoppe.

The soft warmth of the new sweater and the hot tea did much to soothe Sarah's mind. Ellen's death moved a little distance away and, in fact, the absence of chatter about homicide made her almost wish that she might never return to the Shearing Inn. Seated near a geranium-crowded window, she made an effort to imagine that she, and she alone, was on a voyage through Britain with nothing untoward having happened, no timetable, no scheduled visits, no need to do, see, or say anything to anyone.

She began to think where she might travel and then in her mind began a tour which involved owning an ancient two-seater Triumph and a large bank account. Perhaps down to Dorset and the Hardy country. Then off to Cornwall—Daphne du Maurier—swing around east to Lyme Regis—Jane Austen and *Persuasion*. Then perhaps Canterbury, Brighton, and the Pavilion. Or should she reread *Northanger Abbey* and begin with Bath? Then north to Yorkshire, Haworth, and the Brontës? Later meet Alex in Scotland and they could do the Highlands together. The Great Glen. Climb Ben Nevis. Alex had said he'd always wanted to climb Ben Nevis.

From these musings, Sarah was aroused by finding a woman of comfortable proportions—perhaps Mrs. Jellicoe herself—standing by her table and pointing reproachfully to the clock. Five-thirty and closing. "We're only a tea shoppe, miss, and we don't do dinners. There's the Shearing Inn down across the way if you're looking for something more solid."

And Sarah paid for her tea, took her departure, and walked slowly back to the inn on a winding route that took her over a curved stone bridge and past a reed-edged stream inhabited by a family of mallard ducks. Like Cranford or a hundred other fictitious villages, she told herself, still lost in a literary tour of the British Isles. And in this detached and tranquil frame of mind she arrived at her room, opened the door. And stared.

Ransacked.

Suitcase open. Bureau drawers pulled wide, clothes spilling out. Her toilet article bag on the floor, unzipped and upended. Her shoulder bag open on the bed, its contents dribbled on the counterpane.

Chapter Nine

SARAH STOOD FOR A moment absolutely still, turned to cement, her mouth open, her hands curled into fists. Then reaction. Rage. Fury. She stormed into her room, slammed the door closed behind her, and snatched at her empty suitcase and hurled it against the chintz chair. Kicked angrily at her toilet article kit, which lay disemboweled on the floor, little bottles and tubes scattered about it. Then swore loudly. A spate of serious four-letter words.

And then stopped and ordered herself to cool it. She was out of control, her rage at Ellen's death spilling out over this mess. But random hurlings and kickings would get her nowhere. But what now? She was torn in two directions.

One direction: Sarah the enraged tourist should fling herself down to the office of the Shearing Inn and raise holy hell. Drag the manager by the scruff of his neck to the room and point and exclaim and generally foam at the mouth.

Other direction: Sarah of the long nose, Sarah, whose friend Ellen had been murdered, might want to hold it. Look around. Check for missing things. See which members of the garden tour were back from their various sight-seeing toots, from Snowshill Manor and country driving. Check on those two overwrought women who had retired to their room. She walked purposefully over to the washbasin and splashed cold water over her face—her invariable remedy for an overwrought emotional state.

Drying her face, she found herself prey to the awful possibility that she had forgotten to lock her room before she went out. But, no, she had just used her key to unlock it. So perhaps one of the maids had rifled her room or had carelessly left the door unlocked when she finished her tidy-up work. Or—this was also possible—someone had come in through Aunt Julia's room since there was an unlocked door between the two rooms. And that meant that Julia may have forgotten to lock her bedroom door.

Well, she couldn't go screeching into the office if there had been free access somehow to one or both bedrooms. She was sure there would be one of those ubiquitous signs at the front desk reminding guests to not keep valuables in their room and that they were responsible for keeping their doors locked AT ALL TIMES.

But why her room? Or Aunt Julia's? Or both? Nothing about either of them suggested women of great wealth. Was it just a random hit, or had other rooms been torn apart? But even as Sarah asked herself these questions, the small, sickening seed of doubt grew, bore leaves, flowered, and resolved itself into the answer. Or one answer.

That goddamned scarf. Never mind what Julia had said. The scarf had certainly shed any claim to being an innocent piece of wearing apparel and by now had taken on the sanguinary quality of Lady Macbeth's hands. Blood, blood. The miserable scarf that all the perfumes of Arabia would not sweeten.

But, for God's sake, she had just mailed the thing. And another wave of anger swept over her and she had to keep herself from shouting. So cool down, count to ten, recite the alphabet backwards. In French. And then breath deeply and slowly.

Okay. First, check calmly and carefully through all her things to see what, if anything, was missing, then see if Aunt Julia was in her bedroom and ask about unlocked doors. Next, find out who of the Garden Club had returned. Last, see if anyone else had found his or her room in disarray. Shake these answers around and if nothing useful emerges, go to the manager and report the disturbance.

Nothing was missing in her own room. It seemed that the visiting vandal had simply rummaged about, opened and closed, pitched and tossed, and departed.

Sarah knocked on the door connecting Julia's room with her own. No answer. She knocked louder, rapped, drummed, and then opened. The room was empty. The counterpane on the bed was smooth, and everything else was in its place. Julia, though not a notable housekeeper, always kept an orderly stable: Saddles, bridles, buckets, blankets, all in place. And here, in her own "stall," shoes were lined up, toilet article bag was zipped, and suitcase closed. Certainly not the scene of a search. But her bedroom door into the hall was unlocked. Careless Aunt Julia. Or careless maid. And lucky intruder who could have slipped through Julia's room into Sarah's and exited the same way. An intruder who knew Julia was off on a pastoral adventure with Carter McClure.

Sarah opened the door into the hall and was instantly rewarded by the appearance of Sandi Ouellette, swaddled in terry cloth. "There's still hot water," said Sandi, "but you'd better hurry. Everyone will want a shower. We walked and walked. All over Snowshill Manor and then took a hike. The footpath between Nether Roosting and Little Roosting."

"How long have you been home," demanded Sarah, getting to the point.

"We had tea here at the inn, so I guess we've been home an hour. Or a little more. Does it matter? Were you looking for someone? I don't think Julia's back yet. She and Carter McClure drove off together, so maybe they've eloped."

Here Sandi giggled and then added, "At least it gives Portia a free day. She spends so much time trying to keep Carter from yelling at Barbara Baxter. And I think Barbara's been wonderful to have found Snowshill Manor. It was great. I mean we were still all terribly sad about Dr. Trevino, but Snowshill was a terrific distraction. You wouldn't believe the stuff like Japanese warrior masks mixed up with toys and doll's houses and ship's things. I mean it was the sort of place someone might go totally mad in."

"Sandi," said Sarah, breaking the flow with greater urgency, "did everyone have tea with you here? After you got back from Snowshill? Or did some go back to their rooms and not come down?"

Sandi frowned. "What's the matter? Is someone sick? One of the Hoppers, because they certainly looked awful."

"No, no. I just have a personal reason for wanting to know, something to do with my room and Aunt Julia's. I found a message but it wasn't signed," said Sarah, not entirely untruthfully.

"I'll bet it's because your room has a view of the garden and some of the others—like ours—look out on the parking lot. Maybe someone wanted to switch rooms and went in to look your room over. Anyway, it's a fact, isn't it, that you and Julia and Barbara Baxter and the McClures and the Lermatovs have the best rooms?"

"Maybe you're right," said Sarah. "I just wondered who went upstairs after your bus came back. I thought maybe the maid let someone in my room. Or Aunt Julia's."

"I think we all went upstairs to wash before tea. Change our clothes, shoes. The footpath was pretty dusty. Of course, Edith and Margaret Hopper didn't have to wash up because they stayed right in their room. But they did turn up for tea, only they hardly said a word. They just sat there looking like they'd swallowed something that tasted awful."

Sarah thanked Sandi, told her that she and Julia didn't want to trade rooms with anyone, and returned to her bedroom to regroup.

And there in the middle of the rumpled clothing and scattered shoes and toilet articles stood Amy Lermatov, notebook in hand.

"What do you think you're doing here?" Sarah almost shouted, her rage boiling up again.

"Wait, hold it. It's okay." Amy backed up stammering, looking genuinely frightened. "I just came in to ask a few questions about my book. Because you're an English teacher."

"And," said Sarah fiercely.

"I knocked and there wasn't an answer and your door was open a little so I went in to see if you hadn't heard me and then I saw all this stuff. And I didn't think even if you were as messy as I am you'd start throwing your stuff around the room unless..."

"Unless what?"

"Unless you were sick or having some sort of a seizure and then I thought you might be under the bed because of the seizure and maybe I need to call for help but then I decided..."

"Go on."

"That you probably weren't having a seizure but that someone came into your room looking for something valuable and searched it and threw the stuff around and that you'd been robbed. Or something. And then you came in," Amy finished lamely.

Sarah blew a long-winded breath through her cheeks and subsided into a chair, a chair now covered with her uprooted underwear, shirts, and jeans. "Oh damnation, Amy. What am I going to do with you?" she said in exasperation.

Amy showed her braces producing something halfway between a grimace and a grin. "You could look at my mystery story. I've put someone in it who's searching the rooms for clues."

Sarah stifled the impulse to shake Amy until the braces flew off her teeth. But no, she told herself, I can't pretend nothing happened. "Look, Amy. You're here so you certainly can see someone's been looking around. But I'd appreciate your not mentioning the incident. I'm not going to make it a secret, but I'd like to check with Aunt Julia to see if she's missing anything before I go to the office."

"How about other rooms being messed up? Our room wasn't, but maybe some other people's were?"

Sarah hesitated. How far to trust this girl. Just so far, she decided. But perhaps Amy might be given a small role to play.

"Okay, Amy. If, just if, you hear of other rooms being disturbed, being entered, well, come quietly and tell me. Don't worry, I'm planning to tell the Shearing Inn people about this."

Amy nodded. "You know in the beginning when Mom told me about this garden tour I thought, boy, how totally boring. A bunch of people going around smelling roses and yacking about compost. But after Dr. Trevino and now this, it's like I'm on the actual site of something gruesome happening."

"Amy," said Sarah in a severe tone, feeling when she spoke to the girl that she always sounded like her own grandmother. "Go on and write your story, but don't run away with the idea that you're living real-life crime just because someone came in here and threw my underwear around."

"But what about Dr. Trevino?"

"A horrible accident. Probably one of those awful random attacks. Nothing to do with this tour. So please don't consider our group just a mass of raw material. Dr. Trevino's death is much too sad and too serious." Good, thought Sarah, seeing the light die in Amy's eyes, that might just put a damper on teenage journalism for a while.

Amy turned to leave, then hesitated at the door, and Sarah was sorry to see that the girl was beginning to bounce back. "Look, I'll turn Dr. Trevino into someone else—a man maybe. But I want to keep in some of the other details like your finding those sunglasses in your bag and like the two Hopper sisters being upset. I mean one minute they're having a good time and the next they're totally unglued. But, of course, I'll change all the names. Everyone is staying at the Black Sheep Inn, which is a pretty good name, and I'm having two Asians and two African Americans in the story and also one Latino, which makes it more real. After all, Dr. Trevino was the only Hispanic person we had and she's dead, and Mrs. McClure is the only black person and that doesn't…"

"Amy," said Sarah in a dangerous voice. "Go away. Now."

"But you want me to listen around to see if anyone's room has been busted into, don't you?" said Amy in a plaintive voice.

"If," said Sarah, "you can do it without inciting a riot, accusing anyone of breaking and entering."

Amy took one step back into the room. "But someone did break and enter. Right into your room."

"OUT!" shouted Sarah. "OUT. BEGONE. SCRAM. BEAT IT."

Amy beat it and Sarah turned to find Aunt Julia, returned from her drive and coming to report. The expedition had been restful; she and Carter McClure having been shown around a large breeding facility, visited a pasture of mares and foals, and had a useful discussion with the farm owner on the management of strangles.

But Julia's contentment evaporated at the sight of Sarah's room. "You think," Sarah told her, "that I have an overheated imagination, that I look for trouble, but believe me, trouble has walked right in the door and made itself at home. And my door was locked and yours was open."

"But I always lock," began Julia and then stopped. "I came back for my jacket and I might have, well, I could have left it unlocked."

"And everything in your room is in order?"

Julia nodded. "Yes. Just as I left it. But I don't bring anything valuable with me. Did you," she began accusingly, "bring some jewelry, leave money in a drawer?"

"No, I did not," said Sarah, biting off each word. "The only item of any interest that I possessed was that blasted blood-soaked scarf someone stuffed in my shoulder bag."

"You don't know it was blood-soaked," said Julia. "Was it taken? Was anything taken?"

"I mailed the scarf this morning. And, from what I can tell nothing is missing."

"Jealousy," announced Julia. "Someone wants our rooms. I've heard rumblings. A maid or a guest with sticky fingers. Or it's a terrorist group hitting the tourist scene."

"Sure, you name it. The Mafia is busy and the Pink Panther is loose. Well, what I want to know is if mine is the only room hit."

Julia settled herself in the pink-and-green-flowered chintz chair. "I haven't heard any outcries." And then, she sat up straight. "I know. That's what's wrong with Margaret and Edith Hopper. Their rooms were entered and they've lost something valuable, some jewelry, and they're too ashamed to admit they didn't put the things in the office safe."

Sarah looked up. "Maybe you're right. There's a thief on the loose and the sisters were the first hit. Well, damn, it's time I went down to the office and made a scene. And, Aunt Julia, why not go over to Edith and Margaret's room and see if that's why they're in such a stew. But, please, be tactful."

And Sarah, fire in her eyes, strode out of the room while Julia, who, as a woman of direct and sometimes abrasive action, never liked the role of the psychologist, walked with reluctant steps down the hall and tapped on the door of Margaret and Edith Hopper.

Twenty minutes later Sarah met Julia in her still-disordered bedroom, Sarah having raised suitable Cain in the office and been appropriately reminded about unlocked doors, the propensity for crime among American citizens who made up a large number of the inn's guest population, and an offer—a lukewarm offer—to bring in the police. But this, Sarah was told, was rather pointless since she had found nothing missing. And no other guest had yet reported a similar intrusion. Innkeeper Thomas Gage and his assistant, Mrs. Hosmer, both suggested gently that Sarah ask her fellow tour members whether someone in their party had, for some personal and, they hinted, some unsavory reason, a motive for the search.

"All a bunch of bullshit," Sarah told her aunt, "but they're right. I'm not missing anything. And no one else has reported trouble. So how about Edith and Margaret?"

"I struck out. Well, in a way. Their room was a miracle of order. I told them about your room, and they said they were appalled. They always lock, they make a special point of it, and nothing was out of place. But, I'd say your little scene didn't occupy more than a fraction of their minds. What they're really upset about didn't come out. Some secret sorrow. They're past the age of menopause or I'd have thought they were both unstrung by a simultaneous hormonal breakdown. They've obviously been crying again and weren't sure about coming down to dinner."

"Not the Hoppers' room then," said Sarah, slowly sinking down on the bed among the crumpled pieces of clothing.

"No, but if you're hell-bent on mystery you might find out what's eating those two women. They're perfectly miserable and won't say why. I probed, then asked directly, but they just shook their heads. I think Barbara Baxter should talk to them. Isn't that one of her jobs? She knows little enough about gardens, so let's hope she can at least handle a little social work."

And, as if on cue, a knock on the door sounded, the knocker was admitted, and Barbara Baxter walked into the room. She took one quick look around at the debris and exclaimed. "You, too!"

Sarah jumped to her feet. "You mean the room? You've been broken into?"

Barbara nodded. "Someone came in and opened drawers and tossed my clothes around. Out of the closet. All over the place."

"Was your room unlocked?" Sarah demanded.

Barbara's freckled face took on a rueful expression. "I must not have," she said. "I'm usually so careful, but I went back to get the directions to Snowshill Manor for the driver—he's from London and not sure about driving around Gloucestershire—and I must have forgotten to lock. Wouldn't you know. Here I am a tour director and I do something stupid like that."

"Did you go to the office," Julia put in.

"I thought about it, but nothing was missing and it was all my own fault. And I thought we've already had enough of the police because of poor Dr. Trevino, so, anyway, I decided not to."

"I did," announced Sarah. "I made a fuss but it was the same with me. Julia's door was open and we have connecting inner doors. So it's on our heads if someone came in."

"Come and see my room," urged Barbara. "I'm right down at the end of the hall."

"That's not necessary," said Julia. "We'll take your word."

"But you might see if you think it's the same sort of mess. If it looks like the same person hit both rooms."

"Well, I'd certainly hate to think that there were two room destroyers at large," said Sarah. And then, "Barbara has a point. Let's take a look."

Barbara's room did indeed mirror the disorder of Sarah's. Shoes, clothes, toilet articles, drawers spilled open. Even, in Barbara's case, the bedding rumpled, the mattress askew.

"As if I'd hidden jewelry or something," said Barbara.

"As long as nothing is missing," said Julia, "you'll both just have to count it as vandalism. But I have something else on my mind. I think, Barbara, you need to find out what's eating Margaret and Edith Hopper. If some tragedy has befallen them or if one of them has come down with an incurable disease. I think it would help if they talked to someone. Or went home to deal with it. They shouldn't be dragging around all over Europe if they're utterly miserable."

Barbara nodded her agreement and seemed to square her shoulders as if to bear this new burden. "I hoped they'd get over whatever was bothering them, but apparently not. I'll go now and see them before dinner."

And Sarah and Julia watched Barbara Baxter head out down the hall ready to offer a sympathetic ear.

But before the sound of her footsteps on the creaking boards of the upper hall had faded, Amy Lermatov had taken her place.

"Amy," said Sarah sternly, "I thought I told you to get lost."

Amy grinned, her spirits obviously revived. "But it's what you told me to find out about. There weren't any more room searches. Everyone seemed okay except the Hoppers and they don't count because they're a wreck anyway. I was very subtle. I went around asking when was dinner and so I saw into all the rooms and no one was yelling about being searched."

"Except Barbara Baxter," said Julia in a low voice.

"Hey, really?" Amy looked positively pleased. "That's sort of exciting. She didn't answer when I knocked, but then I saw her come out of your room and take you both into hers."

"So," said Julia in a stern voice, "please leave us in peace and thank you for your information. And don't talk about this to anyone."

"Hey, no sweat," said Amy. "And I'll keep my eyes open. Tonight I'm watching Justin Rossi. I think he wears a wig."

"God help that girl," said Julia when Amy had departed.

"A wig," said Sarah slowly. "Do you think?" She let the question hang in the air.

"And God help you, too," snapped Julia.

Chapter Ten

BARBARA BAXTER APPARENTLY HAD counseled to some effect because the Hopper sisters made it to dinner, where it was generally felt that they seemed to have taken a turn for the better. Both had taken trouble with dress: blue silk with lace collar (Edith), red print with navy buttons (Margaret). Across each shoulder a soft white shawl, on their feet low-heeled navy pumps suitable for formal dining or gentle evening walks. They were of the generation, Sarah decided, who used proper dress as armor against the world.

Thus, as dinner progressed from soup to entrée and on to the sweet and the savory, although no one could have thought them lively, Margaret and Edith from time to time put in a small word whenever the subject matter took a horticultural turn.

As for the rest, the trip to Snowshill Manor seemed to have provided not only an escape from the dark cloud of Ellen

Trevino's death, but it also provided a common subject for discussion.

Only Carter McClure complained. An unnecessary trip. Not even a very distinguished garden. Fortunately, Henry Ruggles would be arriving that evening and a proper focus would be reestablished.

At which Portia McClure turned to her husband and pointed out that he, Carter, hadn't even visited Snowshill Manor; he had been gadding about the countryside with Julia Clancy. And if he'd been so wild to see superior gardens, why hadn't he gone and found one. There were plenty in Gloucestershire. So be quiet.

And then Stacy Daniel took up the torch for Snowshill. Sarah, looking up from her lamb chop, saw Stacy, her color heightened by the task of making a public appeal, hold forth on the attractions of Snowshill. It was almost, Sarah decided, as if she had taken notes for some class.

"Do you remember the French sedan chair?" prompted Stacy. She ticked off the items of interest: the ship models, the Japanese Samurai armor, the banners, the Sicilian cart, the old bicycles.

This recitation and the responses were good enough to carry the group all the way to the Stilton, coffee, and brandy.

And then, just as the attractions of Snowshill Manor began to fade, Justin Rossi took up the cause. His was the humorous, semi-scholarly approach. The great enjoyment to be had from viewing such a truly idiosyncratic collection, the amazing diversity of artifacts. The Indian oxcart, the Balinese and Javanese dancing masks, the mangle, the baby tether.

Justin's enthusiasm resulted in almost universal support for Barbara's choice of Snowshill Manor, even by the Hopper sisters who had not been there. As to future changes in the tour plan, they would all leave it in Barbara's capable hands. "And," declared Sandi Ouellette boldly, "we can't let this Mr. Henry Ruggles interfere with Barbara. He can stick to talks in the gardens."

"We want what everyone wants," said Margaret and Edith Hopper almost in unison, although in tremulous voices, proof that emotional recovery was not complete.

"So, okay," said Stacy Daniel, "that's settled. Barbara is chief. It's easier that way. We don't need a lot of hassle every morning about who goes where."

Sarah, who was essentially neutral in the matter, helped herself to an after-dinner mint and let it melt slowly in her mouth. She had reached two conclusions during the recent scene. First, Barbara Baxter, cheerful and energetic as she was, must have leadership qualities that she, Sarah, was as yet unable to fathom.

Her second conclusion was that Justin Rossi, despite Amy's suggestion, was surely not wearing a wig. Several times, while speaking, he had absently reached up and run his hands through his short-cropped black hair—a gesture unnervingly reminiscent of Alexander McKenzie's, although Alex wore his hair longer. And Justin's scalp and facial skin seemed natural, no signs of an artificial attachment. Of course, today they could do wonders with hairpieces. However, Sarah put the idea for the moment on the shelf and returned her attention to Barbara.

Flushed by the wave of approbation, Barbara beamed on the assembled group, and then suggested that a small contribution in Ellen Trevino's name be made to the National Trust. She had picked up a pamphlet at Snowshill Manor and began a lengthy explanation of the Trust's almost hundred years of protecting the British countryside, its historic buildings, its coastline.

Sarah, finishing her coffee, decided that the whole tenor of the table was becoming entirely too high-minded and decided to seek fresh air, so, followed by Julia, she slipped away from the table and headed for the garden.

"Really," said Julia. "Barbara Baxter is power-mad. It's not like we're an Elderhostel on the hoof or a collection of dentists and bank clerks from Terre Haute who don't mind being jerked around because they've never been in Britain before."

Sarah objected. "Barbara is organized, not power-mad. And everyone seemed to love Snowshill Manor. And I don't think the Cambridge Botanic Garden sounds like a bad idea. Besides, we're still going to all the gardens that Ellen planned. And you, Aunt Julia, are beginning to sound just like Carter yourself."

Julia plunked herself down on a stone bench overlooking a series of rosebushes in full creamy bloom and Sarah joined her. It was quite dark by now, but a lamp shone distantly from the back of the inn and the narrow paths and flowers were just visible as forms of light and dark while the scent of the roses, the bordering sweet alyssum, and the wisteria hanging on a nearby trellis was almost overpowering.

And Julia softened and became sympathetic. "Oh, I suppose Barbara means well. She's always cheerful, and she seems to be popular, not just with Sandi who would probably love Dracula, but with the others, too, even Rossi and Stacy Daniel, who seem to have minds of their own. But I do not understand the Hopper sisters chiming in like a secondhand chorus. They were quite critical of the Cambridge plan but now they're all for it. Though," she added, "I'm truly glad they're pulling themselves together. When they're cheerful they're a great asset, and we must all try to get along with each other."

"You *are* mellowing."

"It's this garden. It's taking me back. Tom and I rented a little house—Holly Cottage it was called—in the Cotswolds. It was our last trip together because Tom died the next spring." Julia gave a heavy sigh and reached for her cane. "Anyway, for at least ten minutes I'm in charity even with the likes of Stacy Daniel, whom I suspect is as hard as a rock, and Justin Rossi, who reminds me of a slightly tame pirate."

"Because he looks like Alex?"

"Yes. Both the piratical types, though naturally I prefer Alex. And it's a funny thing. I don't mind the Ouellettes as much as I did. Sandi and Fred seem genuinely devoted to each other, which is quite remarkable in a married couple. And Fred has been kind enough to tell me in detail about the funeral practices in the Congo. He's an absolute mine of mortuary information."

Julia pushed her cane into the ground and, clutching it with both hands, rose to her feet. "Before I become entirely mush-headed I'm going in and settle down with Dick Francis. A stolen horse and skullduggery at Newmarket."

And Sarah was left alone.

But not for long.

"I suppose," said a voice behind her, "you're still mad at me."

Amy.

Sarah swallowed hard, but the wisteria and the garden lit by the now rising moon had softened her as well as Julia.

"Sit down, Amy," she said. "I am not mad at you. And I will look at your story sometime. But not tonight. Okay?"

"Okay," said Amy, plunking herself down on the bench beside Sarah. "It's neat out here. The moonlight. You can just see the edges of things, the garden and the pond, and those bushes clipped into shapes. And everything smells wonderful. What is it?"

"The wisteria, the roses. And those white flowers along the borders, I forget the name. And the bushes are box. I do know that much. You can clip them into shapes—rabbits and urns and swans. Topiary. You'll see a lot of it before we're through."

"England is really different," Amy sighed. "It's so tidy with all those little cottages and villages and footpaths. Like a stage set in one of those old romance movies. Or a *Star Trek* show when the crew is blasted back into the past and everyone is wearing top hats and hoop skirts." For a moment Amy was quiet apparently considering. Then, "I suppose I could write a romance instead of a mystery but my English teacher says my strong point is realistic description. Besides," she added, "I think our garden tour group is too weird to put into a romance, don't you?"

"I think," said Sarah, lapsing reluctantly into her teacher mode, "that any group all with a particular hobby would seem a little weird. They have one interest in common and not much else."

"But that's not what I'm saying," cried Amy. "What I mean is this great interest in gardens isn't so great. Only a few people are really into it. But Stacy Daniel and Mr. Rossi and Mrs. Clancy and you aren't. Like you look at the flowers and you don't know any of the names."

Sarah wanted to interrupt and say that she and Julia were there through the accident of free tickets and lodging, not because of any horticultural passion, but suddenly it seemed of no importance. Instead she rose from the bench. "What I think is that we're wasting time on speculation and it's a beautiful night. Let's walk around the garden and then go in. It's getting late."

"Okay," said Amy agreeably. She stood up and shook her mane of hair. "I'll save weird for my novel."

And so they walked, slowly moving from one moonlit path to the next, the fragrant air, the faint night breeze, the moving shadows all acting for Sarah as an anodyne to the day's events. Even the terrible fact of Ellen Trevino's death lost some of its immediate resonance. And the attack on her bedroom faded from being a personal assault to the sort of annoyance one might expect when traveling in alien places. Certainly irritating but not overwhelming, and, after all, Barbara had had the same thing happen.

Amy walked by her side with that easy careless movement of the young, and Sarah found herself humming the "Music of the Night," which was the sort of melody once begun cannot be easily shaken loose.

"Hey," said Amy, "I know that, I played the Phantom in our eighth-grade production. We had a really creepy set. And I've been thinking, maybe I need a mysterious person or a phantom in my story. Like that woman last night who was sitting in the garden."

"Woman?" said Sarah. "Have you seen a phantom woman?"

"I don't know. It's just that last night I had to go to the bathroom in the middle of the night because of all that Orangina I drank, and my bed is next to the window, and so when I got back I looked out of it and there was this woman walking up and down out in the garden. Because of the moon I could see her pretty well. She had white hair and wore this long silvery gray dress, and I thought, What is she doing out there?"

"But not from our group?" Sarah asked, in spite of her intention to squash any more of Amy's flights into fiction.

"I don't think so. She looked pretty tall, but maybe the angle from my window made her look that way."

"Well, there's no law against walking in the garden at night. And the air is marvelous. No bugs, mosquitoes, or black flies. It was probably someone who couldn't sleep."

But Amy shook her head. "It was two in the morning. I know because my mother has one of those travel clocks that glow in the dark. And don't laugh, but when I was looking at the woman, I thought, Hey this is England, and I could be looking right out at a ghost because isn't that one of the specialties in this country? In Europe. Ghosts, I mean."

Sarah laughed. "Maybe you're right. A friendly ghost taking the night air."

"Or a vampire," said Amy. "Or are those just in Transylvania and Louisiana? Anyway, I thought maybe I could put a ghost in my story. Some woman who'd been abused or raped or strangled a hundred years ago and she walks in the garden until someone avenges her. It happened in the garden, you see. The rape or the strangling. What do you think?"

"What I think," said Sarah firmly, "is that it's after ten-thirty, which is past my bedtime. Maybe even past yours."

"Yeah. Okay, I suppose it is. Mother's probably having a fit wondering where I am. Anyhow, I'll think about putting a ghost into my mystery, though it might make it too complicated."

"Much too complicated," said Sarah. "I'd say scrap the ghost. But, you know, suddenly I feel as if I could sleep for sixty hours."

But she couldn't.

Whether it was the moonlight, or a reviving distress over Ellen's death, she couldn't settle down. Finally, as the luminous hands of her wristwatch hit eleven, she climbed out of bed, reached for her jeans and a sweatshirt, and headed back to the garden. It was one of those nights, she told herself, that are meant to send people outside. And where better to go than a sweet-smelling moonlit garden.

But Sarah was not alone in her sleeplessness. It was as if a spell had settled on the Shearing Inn—or at least on the members of the garden tour.

Julia Clancy, a light sleeper at best, put Dick Francis aside and settled herself by her bedroom window. Here, looking out but not really seeing the nighttime garden, she fell into a reverie over past times. Tom and that last visit to the Cotswolds. Tea with farm families talking over new foals and promising yearlings. A visit to the bird sanctuary in Bourton-on-Water, an overnight in a seventeenth-century hotel in Lower Slaughter, a picnic by the River Windrush. "Tom, Tom," Julia whispered aloud, "damn it, Tom, you old Irishman, I do miss you."

Barbara Baxter was awake, not from a surfeit of nostalgia, but from a lively sense that she had homework to do. Seated at a small writing desk, surrounded by pamphlets and maps of the Cotswolds, she tried to chart the next few days for the Garden Club so that the dissenters—Carter McClure in particular—would be mollified. But, although Ellen Trevino's blueprint called for almost every hour of the day to be spent at a garden of note, unlike hotels and inns, reservations for these had not been necessary, and so some shuffling was possible. And, furthermore, she, Barbara, would show them that the details of English gardens were not beyond her. To this end, she reached for a handbook on British wildflowers purchased in haste during the London expedition. Not that wildflowers would be the feature of the tour, but one had to start somewhere, and Barbara, at the outset of the trip, had not been aware that there was much difference between wildflowers and the tame ones in gardens, except that the tame ones seemed to be bigger. She opened the book and with great determination began reading the details of the *Ranunculaceae*: the buttercup family.

The two Hopper sisters were also awake. The improvement in their spirits noted during the dinner hour had not been sustained. Wearing white lawn nightgowns covered by crêpe-de-chine bedjackets, they sat, each on a twin bed and faced one another. But now instead of choked-back tears they turned to lamentation and blame. "If only you hadn't started it," said Edith to Margaret, "then I wouldn't have and none of this would have happened."

"How can you say that," said Margaret to Edith. "You went right along with me. You even thought it would be fun. You agreed it would make a difference. And it did. It really did."

Edith gave a heavy sniff. "But I'm younger than you are and I've always looked up to you from the very beginning. And so I just followed along. Your idea from the start."

"You have to admit we did it very well," said Margaret with a certain tearful complacency.

"Until Friday, we did it very well. And now, only a day later, we've lost everything."

"But I repeat, we needed to. Otherwise we might not have managed." And, Margaret went on, gathering steam, "It's always been a matter of discipline. Of self-control. And you've never had much. You get excited. And now look at us."

"Perhaps," said Edith in a hesitant voice, "it won't be quite as bad as we think. At least there's an alternative."

A long moment of silence. A sob. Then breakdown.

At last Margaret swallowed hard, reached for a tissue, blew loudly, stood up from the bed, walked to the window and put her forehead against the glass. "The end of everything," she repeated.

But Edith had recovered. She joined Margaret at the window and put her arm around her sister's waist. "We can't argue. We're together in this and we'll get out of it someday. We can live with it because what choice have we? Look out there because it's such a lovely night. You can see way across the car park. The houses and the garden gates and the beginning of the footpath. Later on I'll mix some Ovaltine. I packed a supply."

Margaret with one final gulp, one notable sigh, pressed her sister's hand, and the two women stood together at the window.

Amy Lermatov, too, was wide awake. Excited by the idea of inserting a female specter into her mystery story, she sat hunched in a chair by a standing lamp and sucked on the end of her ballpoint pen. Should the specter or ghost have unearthly powers or perhaps be simply the manifestation of some spurned or tortured highborn lady? Could ghosts be lowborn? A serving maid, a peasant? Should the ghost be headless? Or visible to only a chosen few? Or, even in the face of Sarah's objections, should the specter take the form of the late Dr. Ellen Trevino?

Amy's mother, Doris Lermatov, after halfheartedly urging her daughter to go to sleep, gave it up herself. She shouldn't have had that second helping of pudding and now she was wide awake. She turned on the bedside light, pulled out a copy of *Gourmet* and settled down to read.

Unlike the two Lermatovs, Sandi and Fred Ouellette had no literary interests to engage them. Instead, moved likewise by the moonlight and the excitement of being in a foreign place for the third night of their lives, they decided to see more of it.

"Such a beautiful night," said Sandi. "Not a bit cold or damp. Whoever said it always rains in England? Let's just walk around the village."

To which Fred agreed, adding that if time permitted he would like to visit the local undertaker. He had been eager to discuss embalming problems and techniques in the United Kingdom.

"Not tonight," protested Sandi. "It's past eleven."

"Might be the best time. I often do my best cosmetic work in the middle of the night. No distractions. I'll check the telephone book for the location of the funeral home and then if we see a light on we can make a call. Professional courtesy."

"You can call," said Sandi with unusual vigor, "but I'm going walking. I don't think they have muggers in little English towns."

"Now you just be careful," said Fred. Then he leaned over and kissed the back of Sandi's neck and together they prepared for an evening expedition.

Stacy Daniel and Justin Rossi also had nocturnal plans. Without consulting the other, each decided to check out the local pubs. Each had noted these establishments on their trips first to the police station and then on the round trip to Snowshill Manor. To the north on the same road as the Shearing Inn sat the Hound and Hare, to the west on a street off from the churchyard was the Black Badger, beyond that The Jolly Blacksmith. Stacy planned to make the rounds, but Justin hadn't made up his mind. However, for each the evening plan entailed a change of costume.

Stacy shucked her dinner outfit of gray knit trousers and long gray silk blouse to something more striking, more suitable for the night prowl. To this end she chose a tight short skirt of tangerine, black heels, and a loose black jacket over a low-cut cotton tank top. In other words, Stacy dressed up.

And Justin Rossi in the next room dressed down. He wrenched off his necktie without bothering to untie it, pulled off his trousers, his blue-striped shirt, and began searching around in his suitcase for looser and more comfortable garments. Garments that would not immediately identify him as a tourist attached to an American garden club group.

As for the others, Portia McClure, like Sarah, opted for a garden stroll, while her husband, Carter, said he'd look in at the Shearing pub for a last pint before bedtime—or take a walk, look around the village.

Portia, who had been settling a light wool jacket over her shoulders, turned toward her husband. "Please don't get into an argument with anyone because when you put your mind to it you can be an absolute monster." She shook a token fist at her husband, opened the door, and stepped into the hall. Followed by Carter.

And within the hour, Henry Ruggles, Esquire, garden lecturer designate, arrived, signed the register, received his room key, and took possession of the single room which had been reserved for the late Dr. Ellen Trevino. By eleven-thirty Henry was in bed and so became the only person connected with the garden tour who fell asleep before midnight and slept without stirring until morning.

Chapter Eleven

SARAH, WANDERING AT THE foot of the garden, found herself falling increasingly under the potent spell of the soft nocturnal breeze freighted with flower scents. And now, somewhere below her, she heard the distant rustling of something moving through the underbrush. Perhaps a fox or a weasel. Or a badger. Sarah had never come across a badger except in the pages of *The Wind and the Willows*. Walking along the extreme verge of the lower garden she found a small worn path that descended for about thirty yards into a bordering pasture. Well, why not? The sight of a badger would be worth much. And then, as if she had entered into a different kingdom, close to a low stone wall the rustling again, then a soft moaning ooo-ooo-ooo. And from a great distance a rising and falling long drawn out churrr—churr.

Birds as well as the possible badger. She needed Alex— Alex the birdwatcher. Was she hearing owls and what was that other night-flying bird? She frowned thinking of nineteenth-century poets and came up with nightjar. Not a poetic name. Back home they were called whip-poor-wills because that was what they called, over and over. And how about a nightingale? She would gladly give up the badger for a nightingale even if she hadn't the least idea what they sounded like. But she was sure the song would ravish her because it had for centuries ravished poets without number. Keats had certainly been ravished, going on about light-winged Dryad of the trees and thoughts of easeful Death.

But high-flown thoughts often end, as another poet has warned, in the muck, and Sarah's next steps through a small gap in the stone wall took her into a boggy patch of meadow and forced her into several squelching steps before she worked her way back to higher ground. There she found the length of a fallen tree and sat down, the more comfortably to contemplate the possibility of a nightingale.

What she got was a cow. Several in fact, their tan hides almost colorless in the moonlight, creatures who, as restless as the other species of the area, had wandered up close to the fence.

"Good girl," said Sarah tentatively, withdrawing her legs from a large moist breath that blew on her bare ankles.

And suddenly far behind her a human noise. It sounded—though at the distance she couldn't be sure—like a low chuckle and felt as if an icy finger had drawn itself down her back. She twisted around at first seeing nothing but low-growing bushes. But then, looking ahead some fifty yards on the footpath she made out the figure of a woman. A tall white-haired woman in a long silvery gray dress. She was standing quite still, her head turned toward Sarah. A specter? Or, to be exact, Amy Lermatov's ghost! This idea no sooner came into her head than Sarah dismissed it. Statuesque, yes, unearthly, no. Sarah could see now that the woman had tied a light shawl over her shoulders, and this suggested a very human desire to keep out the night chill. Then, just as Sarah was thinking about calling out, the woman raised her arm in greeting and continued her way up the footpath toward the village, her layered skirt billowing gently behind her.

Almost, Sarah thought, as if a Greek statue had stepped down from her pedestal for an evening's stroll. Artemis, perhaps. Wasn't she the one worshipped very early as an earth goddess who concerned herself with wildlife and growth of the field? And human birth. Later on, of course, the virgin huntress who watched over all living species. One of the more positive goddesses. But why had the woman laughed like that? That low chuckle had certainly had an eerie quality. But then, Sarah reminded herself, the sight of a lone woman beset by cows was probably mildly amusing.

From these thoughts, she was diverted by the more insistent attentions of one of the cows which began pushing against her knees, and just as she was trying to think of how to rid herself of the animal, a voice sounded behind her.

"Hello, Sarah. Beautiful night, isn't it?" Portia McClure.

"I couldn't sleep," explained Portia, "so I thought I'd take a walk. There's a footpath here that goes by the edge of the pasture and leads to the village. I walked along it yesterday. Shoo, shoo," she called to one of the cows who was now pushing its head into Sarah's lap. Apparently offended by this lack of welcome, the animal turned and with its companions made a leisurely departure.

"One of those nights," said Portia, settling down on the tree trunk beside Sarah. "Everyone's out and about. Half the people from the village. I saw the vicar on the road—still in his collar—and the two people from the cottage across the way from the inn and then met Fred and Sandi Ouellette heading out somewhere. As well as Stacy Daniel at the door. Said she was going pub crawling. Had had quite enough of gardens."

"Then why in heaven's name is she on the tour?" demanded Sarah. "It's hardly gotten off the ground and she's had enough?"

"Oh, I think she's one of those self-loving beauties who wouldn't be happy wherever she went. Or she's a special friend of Barbara Baxter's. Perhaps they're a couple. You never know why some people come together. Anyway, it's one of those nights. 'The moon shines bright. In such a night as this...

> When the sweet wind did gently kiss the trees
> And they did make no noise, in such a night
> Troilus methinks mounted the Troyan walls...
> And sighed his soul toward the Grecian tents,
> Where Cressid lay that night.'"

She broke off. "I was named for the Portia in the play. My parents made me learn great gobs of it because they thought it might turn me into a lawyer, but I fooled them."

For a moment they sat in companionable silence, and then Portia said thoughtfully, "You know, Ellen Trevino cared deeply about her gardens, her research. She wouldn't have wasted time slipping into poetry, and she certainly didn't have much patience for uninformed raptures. To her, gardens were wonderful and intricate arrangements of botanical items. They offered contrast and mass and pattern and color, and they presented problems in growth and propagation, and fertilization. Gardens were marvelous as living and manageable facts and they deserved our full and passionate attention." Here Portia paused and gave a small sigh. "I guess what I'm saying is, that if Ellen had been here, it would have behooved us all to have been entirely serious about our trip."

"You're saying," Sarah began.

"What I'm *not* saying is that I'm relieved Ellen isn't here. I admired her tremendously and am stricken by her death. But without Ellen in charge, there's a certain ease. Carter would have been a royal pain, argued with her every inch of the way, and I can't be pulling on his leash every minute. And I intend— or did intend—to enjoy myself. June in the Cotswolds is an absolute gift."

"But," Sarah protested, "if Ellen had been here, then Barbara wouldn't have made any changes. She would have stuck to the schedule and not done any freelancing."

"Maybe, maybe not. Two generals pulling two different ways. General Ellen and General Barbara."

"And Field Commander Carter McClure."

Portia laughed. "Right. Anyway, I hope Henry Ruggles will work out. Carter's very own choice, so he'll shut up. And Henry has a rather courtly way about him. He won't defer to Barbara but it will look like he does."

"That sounds hopeful."

"Carter has no idea of how annoying he can be. He does a lot of barking, but he hasn't any fangs. Those were pulled long ago."

"By you?" asked Sarah, wondering if this was too personal a question. But the night, the air, all seemed to encourage intimacy.

"Perhaps. He was a sort of enragé when I met him. I was a graduate student, and he was the wild and woolly instructor of the History Department. Our marriage was part chemistry and part a sort of in-your-face to our objecting parents. Mine called him a reactionary redneck and his thought I was out to ignite the entire Black population of New England. And I think the idea of racially mixed grandchildren made them queasy. But the grandparents have come round, our children were spoiled rotten by both sides, and the marriage has worked, heaven knows why. Carter will behave if you stand up to him. I think I'll give Sandi Ouellette a tip because she's cowed by him. She's not half as fluff-headed and ingenuous as she seems. Well, there you are. Thumbnail bio. But I don't need yours. Sandi has told all."

Sarah groaned. "Oh, God, I wish she wouldn't do that. But I'm glad you're here without Carter. And I am glad he's found Aunt Julia. They can work off their spleen on each other."

"Let's hope," said Portia. "And now I feel like a short walk down the footpath toward the village. Want to join me?"

Sarah did, and for some fifteen or so minutes they followed the path that wound around the pasture's edge, turned back on itself, offered a stile, a brook, another pasture, and then rose in an inviting way toward the village center. For a moment the two women came to a halt by a small brook and stood bathed in moonlight.

"Peace," said Sarah. "Perfect peace. All these little Cotswold towns and those names—High Roosting, Nether Roosting, Bourton-on-Water, Chipping Camden, Moreton-in-Marsh—make me expect toadstools and elves and dairy maids sweeping hearths with brooms made of twigs. And the houses—the cottages—like honeypots or illustrations for Mother Goose."

"I know what you mean," said Portia. "Not the inner city, is it? Or rural backyard America. I haven't seen any wrecked cars in front yards or tripped over disposable diapers on the path. But, cheer up, maybe inside one of these cottages something is brewing. Jack the Ripper is preparing for an evening stroll."

Sarah agreed. "You almost want to see blinking lights and hear a siren to make the whole place seem real."

At these words they were immediately rewarded with a siren. A distant siren rising and falling, coming closer, going away.

"So much," said Portia briskly, "for Mother Goose."

"The police," said Sarah, pointing up toward the village as two white cars, one after the other, whizzed past and turned toward the village center.

"Well, shall we go on to the village and gawk like tourists or go on back?" asked Portia.

Sarah hesitated. "I did want to just reach the rise and see the whole village spread out in the moonlight. We can ignore the police cars. It's probably just a rumble at one of the pubs."

They climbed the footpath and reached the juncture of the main road, which indeed offered a nighttime panorama of the village.

"And we can't even see the police cars," said Portia with satisfaction. "It's a wonderful view: church steeples, town hall, the market square, the high street, the whole bit."

"And the population going to bed," added Sarah, pointing. And indeed from several village streets emerged small clusters of persons on foot. Persons who seemed to be hastening toward some destination, not walking with the evening languor that she had noticed earlier,

"Time for the hot milk or a last brandy and soda," said Portia. "Or even a nice refreshing cup of hot water. Did you know Carter's parents—they're Scottish—have a cup of hot water every night before going to bed? They claim it cleans the bowels."

But before Sarah could say what she thought of hot water as a nightcap, she caught sight of a slender woman's figure coming at a run from a small side street. The woman plunged across the main road and was about to gallop on down the footpath when she saw Sarah and Portia and skidded to a halt.

"Sandi!" exclaimed Portia. "Whoa up."

"Oh thank goodness, people I know," panted Sandi. "I was going to run all the way to the inn, but now I can walk with you. Get my breath. Pull myself together."

And indeed Sandi seemed to need pulling together. Her clothes were in disarray, and she seemed to be clutching at her bodice to hold it together while her flowered skirt had swiveled around so that its belt hung down on one hip.

"Whoa, take it easy. Everything's all right. You're all right," said Portia in a soothing but firm voice, sounding to Sarah's ears like a sort of archetypal Everymother.

For a moment Sandi stood and trembled. Then she bobbed her head. "Yes, I am all right. I think I am, anyway. In fact, I'm not sure anything's wrong. Except my blouse. Torn or slit right down my front. I mean it's made to crisscross and then tie in back and now it's completely open unless I hold it together. I don't know if it was an accident or it's like what happened to that other woman. The police are still talking to her."

"Sandi, take it easy," commanded Sarah.

"We'll walk back down to the inn together," said Portia, "and you can tell us what happened."

"If anything really did," said Sandi. "I mean to me."

"Begin at the beginning," said Portia. "We'll take it easy and the moonlight makes the path perfectly clear."

"I know," said Sandi. "I came up that way. After I split off from Fred because he wanted to see the local undertaker, and I wasn't really up for dead bodies on a beautiful night."

"And so?" prompted Sarah.

"So I came back to the inn and picked up the footpath at the end of the garden. I said to myself, Sandi, you're in England so why not get the flavor, the feel of the place. Why just do gardens, why not make every minute count?"

"Where did you go to make every minute count?" asked Sarah, and Sandi gave a sort of giggle that had the slightest touch of hysteria at the top of it.

"All over the map, into the village, down the high street, but the shops are closed late Saturday night just like they are in little Maine towns. Not like Miami and Atlantic City and Vegas. Fred and I go to mortuary conventions and those places really move at night. Anyway, I walked up and down all the side streets and half the townspeople—or maybe they were tourists, too—were walking around. It was so bright we didn't even need the street lamps to see. And then I thought for real atmosphere I should try and see if a pub was open. I asked someone and they told me there were three pubs in town, and that I was lucky because right past the Wool Gathering Book Shop was a pub called the Hound and Hare. So I marched right in and the place was absolutely packed, but I found a seat near the wall and ordered up a pint of Guinness because that was about the only name I could think of."

"But what *happened*?" insisted Sarah impatiently.

"Wait up," said Sandi, who now seemed to be enjoying the role of narrator. "I've got to get this in sequence because maybe nothing would have happened if that football club hadn't come in and everyone got more jammed in than ever. Well, after I'd finished two drinks of this ale or stout—whatever it was, and boy was it strong—I thought I'd watch the darts or this really stupid game called shove ha'penny. You know, get all the local color. So I got up and moved over to the edge of a bunch of people watching the dart throwing and then it happened."

"WHAT HAPPENED?" demanded Portia in something like a shout, proving to Sarah that her companion was not endlessly patient.

"Don't rush me," said Sandi. "What I'm saying is that there we were, all in there like sardines and what happened was this screech. Pretty close to the pub room, although how close was kind of hard to judge because everyone was making a lot of noise, talking and calling. And the smoke, you wouldn't believe. Forget about no-smoking rules, the place was blue. Anyhow, the first thing I saw was this big hunk of a red-haired guy being almost thrown out from the place where the toilets are. You know, the restrooms. Only here they call restrooms the WC or the loo."

"I know," said Sarah through her teeth. She wondered if it would be ruled just cause if she murdered Sandi for drawn-out narration. This was as bad as the wedding guest and the Ancient Mariner. But that at least had a moral. She doubted if Sandi's tale would.

"Go on," said Portia.

"Well, this big red-haired guy landed in the middle of all the people and everyone started yelling, and then there was the woman screaming. She was standing in the doorway of the hall where the restrooms are, and her dress was slit right down the front. I mean there she was hanging out of her bra with one strap loose. Totally out in the open." Here Sandi giggled again and the hysteria was closer to the surface.

"Calm down, Sandi," said Sarah. "You're okay."

"Yeah, I know I am, but this woman—her hair was all messed up too, like she'd been in a sort of struggle—was half crying and said she'd been molested. Or groped. In the WC. By this red-haired guy, and she pointed to the man who was still sitting on the floor and the woman said that was who attacked her. And then the bartender, or whatever he's called in England, shouted and told everyone to stay where they were, and that he was calling the police. And for someone to sit on the red-haired man, and that's what happened. Except the woman—and she's sort of crying and screaming, said she'd been saved—or rescued by this woman who had been in one of the toilet stalls."

Here Sandi paused for breath. "Well, that's about it. So there we all were, packed in together, and I think everyone was kind of sweating—especially those football club guys—and a waitress took the woman with the torn blouse into the ladies' room and before you could count to ten the police turned up. Two of them. They took names and addresses and said they'd be in touch if they needed extra identification for this guy. The police were taking him off. Then one of the policemen turned to me and asked could I identify the man who did it to me. I didn't know what he was talking about. And then he looked a little embarrassed and pointed to my blouse and asked if I wanted to go into the WC, and I looked down and, shit, it was torn from top to bottom and my bra and me were there for everyone to look at. But I hadn't even noticed what with the crowd bumping into each other and no one feeling any pain. But I just pulled my blouse together and said I was fine, that I must have caught it on a nail or something."

"But you hadn't?" said Sarah as Sandi paused for breath.

"I don't know really. But I wasn't hurt. Not scratched or anything. I mean if someone had used a knife to slit my blouse he was pretty good at it. I suppose it was something sexual, you know, the man got kicks from slicing off clothes. I'm sorry about that other woman because she looked scared to death, but she was lucky. Saved in the nick of time. Anyway, one of the other policemen or constables—he was in a blue uniform—was making a circle around my name in his notebook and told me they might ask me to come down to the station for a statement. Then I beat it out of there. Enough is enough. I've had it with local color, and England isn't so different after all. Except no one shot anyone like they do in Vegas or Miami."

"Are you sure, Sandi," said Portia in measured tones, "that you are perfectly all right?"

"I guess so. Maybe I'd better get used to things like this. I've heard that women get their bottoms pinched in Italy. Just for walking down the street. Even people like Mrs. Clancy."

"Who pinches Aunt Julia's bottom does so at his peril," said Sarah.

"You know something," said Sandi, "maybe I've met up with a real English hero. Jack the Ripper. Only he ripped throats didn't he? Not blouses."

Here Portia—the mother born—took charge. She took off her jacket and put it about Sandi's shoulders. "You're shivering," she said. "Put this on and I'll get you a nice warm drink when we get back. The air is turning much cooler and you've had a little shock...no, don't interrupt. Not a big shock, a little one, and a warm drink will be just the thing."

And the trio made its way down the descending and winding path, now being joined by an increasing number of moonlight walkers, many of whom Sarah recognized as guests of the Shearing Inn. There were two from the German group who sat in the back of the dining room and several Americans from another bus tour. Then walking by herself, the same woman in a flowing silver gray dress, the one who had laughed at Sarah's encounter with the cows. Seen more closely, Sarah found her a handsome woman. In fact, as she overtook them, she looked very like Alex's redoubtable mother, Elspeth McKenzie. Tall, with the slightly beaked nose, the long thin mouth, the firm chin. The same white hair fastened in the back, as Elspeth often did—with a heavy clasp.

The resemblance was marked enough for Sarah to slow her steps, but then as the woman came abreast of Portia, Sarah saw that the eyes weren't right—Elspeth had the hooded eyes of a hawk. The woman merely nodded, smiled slightly, and in a husky voice remarked that it was such a lovely night and then walked past the three, down the path and out of sight.

And Sandi erupted again with that same high-pitched giggle. "That woman. The one in the silver dress. The one who passed us. She was in the garden last night. I think she's dead and has come back to haunt us."

"And I think," said Portia firmly. "The ale has gone to your head and you need Fred and that warm drink as soon as possible."

Chapter Twelve

THOUGHTS OF JACK THE Ripper do not make for sound repose, and after climbing into bed Sarah lay awake for the better part of an hour. She wished Portia McClure hadn't mentioned Jack preparing for an evening stroll. It was as if the simple evocation of his name had sent some man abroad to slit blouses and molest women. But at long last she fell into a jumble of dreams in which Alex tried to explain to her that his mother often wandered about the Cotswolds impersonating a ghost.

Sunday morning, coming too soon, brought a slight headache and a strong sense of reality. It might have brought Mr. Henry Ruggles, newly arrived garden expert, to the fore, if Sandi, arriving for breakfast, hadn't taken center stage with her tale of the night's molester. Or Jack the Slitter, as she called him.

"It's like this," said Sandi, putting down her toast and observing that everyone, even the moist-eyed Hopper sisters, were listening with attention. And Sandi launched into the disconnected saga of last night's event. "And," she added, "the maid on our floor knows the woman—it's her cousin's best friend, her name is Margery. They call her Marge. Anyway, she was at the pub and had to go to the ladies' room—the loo—and when she got in there she's grabbed by this red-haired man who starts tearing her blouse."

"Why did he do that?" demanded Amy Lermatov. But Amy's voice had alerted the others to the fact that a fourteen-year-old girl was hanging on every word, although Sarah, listening, reasoned that most teenagers have such a wide knowledge of the seamy side of life that the tale of a blouse demolition would seem rather dull.

Sandi must have thought the same because, after a brief pause she went on with only slight modifications, substituting front for breast. "He reached for her front," repeated Sandi, "and before anything really happened this other woman who had been in one of the toilet places came bursting out and picked the man up and tossed him into the pub room. Like she was some sort of weightlifter. Then a policeman came and told me my blouse was ripped down the front, so I was taken to the police station early this morning, but I told them I didn't know how it happened and I'd never met the red-haired man or the woman who'd saved Marge."

Sandi subsided and the wave of outcries and questions rippled up and down the breakfast table, and it wasn't until the second round of coffee that attention was directed to the presence of Henry Ruggles.

Henry, during Sandi's recitative, had remained quietly busy with his poached egg. Sarah, examining the newcomer from across the table, couldn't decide whether his focus on food was related to hunger or simple diplomacy.

One thing was certain: Henry most certainly wore a wig. She remembered Amy's speculations on wigs and decided that here was the real thing. Henry was somewhere between sixty and seventy with a round ruddy face, bristling eyebrows, and fluffy gray-rust colored sideburns which ended suddenly at the line of a mop-shaped wig of mixed hues. A tweed wig, Sarah decided. A gray-brown-heather mix. And not quite straight. But the whole effect of the ancient corduroy Norfolk jacket, the old school tie (or was it a regimental stripe?), the horn-rimmed glasses hanging from a black string around his neck, was rather fetching. Somewhat Dickensian, as Portia had suggested. Perhaps he wore spats. Or gaiters. And knickerbockers with great clumping brogues.

But, more important, was the question of his ability to get along with Barbara Baxter and her support team and at the same time take his place as the new garden arbitrator. After all, only the McClures vouched for the man; they had produced Henry without any general vote of approval. Now it was up to Henry.

No problem.

Henry proved to be a charmer. When the murmurs over Sandi's tale had died down, Henry went to work. He was seated between Portia McClure and Barbara and it was to Barbara he turned. Wisely, Sarah concluded, since Portia was already in his camp.

Barbara, at first, was restrained. Defensive about the side trips taken, the Snowshill Manor trip, the proposed visit to the Cambridge Botanic Garden, pointing out that many had been in favor of the changes. But Henry poured it on. He had sometimes a curious way of emphasizing certain words as if to give them extra weight. NEVER miss a chance to see Kew Gardens. What a happy thought. He LOVED Kew. How he wished he could have been with them. She must know those old lines of Alfred Noyes, "Go down to Kew in lilac time." Of course the lilacs would have gone by, but the ROSES! The iris, the lilies, the peonies. As for Snowshill Manor, the perfect distraction after the tragic news. That HORRIBLE accident. Will the violence never end. He'd read with such interest Dr. Trevino's pamphlet on *Pedicularis lapponica*—the Lapland lousewort, as you know, he added tactfully to Barbara.

By this time, Sarah, observing from over her teacup, felt that Barbara was actually purring. Even Julia, who usually devoted all her attention to her breakfast, had her head up and finally whispered loudly to Sarah that Henry Ruggles was really laying it on with a trowel. "But a good idea. That's the way to peace. Carter may have actually known what he was doing when he brought the man in. Now let's hope he knows a rosebush from a thistle."

Henry Ruggles wound up with stating his enthusiasm for Hidcote and Kiftsgate. "DEAR Kiftsgate, a miracle of planning, a perfect tapestry of color. The home of *Rosa filipes 'Kiftsgate.'* And even the swimming pool, which I deplored at first, does not detract." And then, only then, when Barbara was at her beaming best, did he throw a small pebble into her pool of happiness. "Perhaps not the WHOLE day in Cambridge. All those NOISY undergraduates. Perhaps a morning at the gardens and then out, out, and away."

"But I promised everyone a bit of shopping," murmured Barbara, not sounding entirely mollified. "And to see the colleges. King's College, Trinity, the Samuel Pepys Library, punting on the Cam"—Barbara obviously studied her Cambridge guide—"And, I think," she went on, "many of our group are enthusiastic about the *whole* day. You were, weren't you?" Here Barbara swept the table and found the two Hoppers, Sandi and Fred, Justin Rossi, Stacy Daniel—all of whom nodded their support.

"Bunch of trained seals," grumbled Julia Clancy a bit thickly, her mouth being full of toast. "And who wants to be trapped in a city." And returned to her toast and marmalade.

"Cambridge *would* be fun," said Sarah.

Doris Lermatov nodded agreement. "I've only been there once, years ago, and Amy should like it. The whole university scene."

"Amy," said Amy, "thinks Cambridge sounds incredibly boring. Rancid old churches, old buildings, old streets, and people bicycling around in black gowns. I've seen pictures."

"Not a bad setting for a mystery," said her mother. She turned to Sarah. "Amy is keeping a journal and is working on a mystery. It's to be set in England."

"I know," said Sarah, her spirits sinking.

"And," said Amy, "I've got a new chapter. About one of the characters being molested. Her, what do they call it, her bodice being ripped—or maybe all her clothes being pulled off so she has to run away into the woods. Totally naked."

Sarah gave up. Squashing Amy took more energy than she had available. "And which character is the bodice ripper?"

"Easy," said Amy. "This new guy. Henry Ruggles. Did you see he wears a wig? I was hoping that someone would turn up wearing one. They're so sinister, especially if they don't fit."

But before Amy could elaborate, Henry Ruggles raised his voice and looked up and down, now embracing the entire breakfast table. "Such a KIND reception. Miss Baxter so HELPFUL." How she had stepped in when needed. Later, when they all had got acquainted, the Cambridge stay could be discussed. Perhaps if a particularly fine cottage garden could be found close to Cambridge, well, Miss Baxter and the others, might yield. On the other hand, a day in an ancient university town had its attractions.

And so forth. Henry Ruggles was doing everything to ingratiate himself with all parties and keep Barbara from having her feathers ruffled.

Sarah, wearied of Henry, decided that it was a toss-up whether Barbara and company were to be charmed out of an entire day's worth of Cambridge, only half a day, or Henry was going to give in. As for Sarah herself, well, damn it, she *would* like a whole day in Cambridge. Look around, visit the bookshops, prowl around some of the colleges.

But now Henry Ruggles and Barbara Baxter were on their feet, the bus would be at the door in fifteen minutes, and then it was off to Brookside Cottage, then lunch back at the Shearing, followed by Upper Thatching Farm and Lavender Cottage in the afternoon. Tomorrow, Monday, the morning devoted to the Rococo Carden at Painswick House. In the afternoon a very special treat, Thalia Cottage, a name Henry Ruggles pronounced with modest pride. A splendid small garden tended by two old schoolmates with whom he still exchanged Christmas cards and paid an annual visit.

"So be it," Sarah said to her Aunt Julia as they made their way to the bus. "I'm up for a totally flower-oriented few days. No more blouse ripping or ghosts of my mother-in-law."

"Right," said Julia. "And I'm ready for little botanical tidbits. As you said I'm turning mellow in my old age. I keep seeing Tom around every farm fence corner. You may be haunted by Elspeth McKenzie, but I've got Tom on this trip. It's rather comforting."

Returned for lunch from Brookside Cottage gardens— an entirely peaceful visit—Sarah had barely finished her cold salmon mousse when she was called to the telephone. She made her way to the tiny front hall, thinking again how badly this space served anyone wanting to converse on the subject of murder.

It was Alex. Greetings, expressions of love were exchanged, and then Sarah described how Elspeth McKenzie's look-alike had suddenly appeared in the midnight gated and was assured by Alex that he had seen his mother in person only an hour ago. "I hope," he said severely, "that you're not beginning to see things. Now listen, because I do have news."

Sarah gripped the telephone receiver a shade tighter. "Yes?"

"Police think they've found the weapon. Something that qualifies, anyway."

"Not the ice cream cone thing?"

"Yes, but it's called a dibble. Sometimes a dibber. It's for planting bulbs. This one has a wooden handle and tapered metal shaft ending in a point. It was found in a drainage ditch about a mile from the body site. Probably thrown out of the car. It looked perfectly clean but the lab is working on it and we ought to know by tonight if any blood turns up."

"A dibble," repeated Sarah. "What a funny name."

"You wouldn't think it was funny if you could see it. It's a wonder more damage hasn't been done by dibbles. They're lethal."

"So are lots of garden tools. Weeders, scythes, pitchforks."

"The dibble is in a class by itself. Anyway that's it. I'll call again if something else breaks. Nothing yet on Ellen Trevino's stepfather. He seems to have vanished into space."

"Wait up," said Sarah suddenly, remembering. "I've airmailed you that scarf, the one I told you about that turned up with the sunglasses. I thought it might have bloodstains on it or the dye may have run. And if it is blood, well draw your own conclusions."

A pause on the line, Alex undoubtedly rolling his eyes, frowning. Then, "I'll keep an eye out for it. And, my dearest beloved, for God's sake don't go around talking about bloody scarves and lost sunglasses. Only to Julia. Okay?"

"Alex, come on. Give me some credit. You seem to think I haven't a cautionary hair on my head."

"You are correct," said Alex, and the line went dead.

Sarah returned to the luncheon table to find the garden tour members pushing back chairs. To judge from anticipatory chatter, Ellen Trevino—alive or dead—had receded further from the general mind, and thoughts were now focused on the upcoming gardens.

Sarah and Julia kept to their resolutions and became compliant—even docile—members of the garden tour. And in actuality the rest of the group—even the subdued Hopper sisters—seemed to have entered a new phase. Argument about the schedule ceased, individual tastes and interests bowed to the greater need of grappling with horticultural details presented in the procession of cottage gardens.

It was as if Ellen Trevino's death and the midnight incident at the Hound and Hare had brought a sobriety and purpose to the group. A sense of everyday reality so that there were fewer comments about the "quaintness" of the Cotswold villages and the idyllic beauty of each view. Instead, conversations now centered on how to remember the Latin names, how to identify variants of veronica, the optimal size of the peony blossom, the use of lady's mantel as a border, and problems of pruning. And even for that fan of the dinner table, Doris Lermatov, food yielded pride of place to the garden. Make that THE GARDEN, as Henry Ruggles might stress it. As he did stress it.

Henry Ruggles proved a miracle of information, guiding couples, singles, trios, the whole troop, up and down the paths, from this plot to that thicket, to the rockery, to the pond, to the marsh, from the climbing roses to the knot garden. Wearing an ancient topi, hands in constant motion, he expounded with boundless good nature and energy. Barbara Baxter, relegated to second fiddle, remained determinedly cheerful, collecting explanatory pamphlets at the entrance gates, and making notes as she trailed the others.

Amy Lermatov was the only holdout from the collective garden mania, but since she remained occupied with her pencil and notebook as garden after garden unfolded, no one took much notice of her. Only when Amy aimed her pocket Olympus not at flowers but at members of the tour did she excite any comment.

"Take that thing out of my face," commanded Julia. "I don't allow pictures. Who wants to see a close-up of a seventy-year-old woman."

"Damn it, Amy, get away," said Carter McClure, caught leaning over a planting of salvia, his shirt detached from his trousers, a layer of white dorsal skin exposed.

"Oh, please, not us. We're just not up for a photograph," pleaded Margaret Hopper.

"Maybe later," said Edith. "The whole group together." At which thought she gave a gulp and turned away.

Thus, Sunday and Monday morning passed and now it was Monday afternoon and the tour had arrived at the last garden of the day. Thalia Cottage, south of Moreton-in-Marsh, featured a cheerful, crowded garden, bright with purples, blues, and yellows and overseen by two retired theatrical gentlemen, Harold and Leslie, former schoolmates of Henry Ruggles.

Harold's special care was the perennial beds and Leslie supervised the roses, the wisteria, the clematis.

"I do the climbing things," said Leslie.

"And very well you do," said Harold. He appealed to the visitors. "Isn't the wisteria magnificent? Leslie has such a way with wisteria. It doesn't dare not do well."

"But have you seen the delphinium?" said Leslie, returning the compliment. "Harold has it bewitched. Twice as many blossoms this year."

"It's only a matter of proper composting," said Harold modestly.

It was past three and other visitors had gone, the shadows were lengthening, and only the dedicated Midcoast Garden Club members remained, frowning at species labels, puzzling over a bank of pale yellow poppies. Henry Ruggles, knowing that his party might soon encroach on the sacred hour of tea, approached his two friends with an eye to saying thank you and goodbye.

But Harold had time for old schooldays. He clapped Henry on the shoulder. "Toad," he said—"we called him Toad then," he explained to the others. "Toad, do you remember that fifth-form school play we were in together? *Julius Caesar*. I was Caesar and Leslie here was Brutus. And Toad, you played Caesar's wife, Calpurnia. Absolutely fetching in a bedsheet."

"I remember," said Henry. "My God, what a long time ago that was. You were both very good. And I was pretty awful."

"Well, you got through it, dear boy. But Leslie and I never looked back. Bitten by the theater bug. The whole business. Music halls, Birmingham Rep, the Old Vic. Carrying spears and bringing messages to the king. Then later a spate of cinema. Nothing too tremendous."

"Well, we did move up the ladder," Leslie reminded him. "Me in that flick with Wendy Hiller. And Harold did *The Charge of the Light Brigade* with Trevor, and then all those charity stunts with Larry and Hermione."

"What I remember," said Henry Ruggles, aka Toad, "was that the night of the play we lost the wooden dagger that Leslie was supposed to use to murder Caesar—you had a bag full of jam under your toga—and I came up with this absolutely lethal tool. I'd found it in the potting shed behind one of the playing fields—we used to go in there to smoke—and I ran to get it. The murder scene was a great success."

"Of course," said Leslie, "I had to be frightfully careful. It was a heavy devil. A gardening tool. I'll show you, there's one right in our greenhouse." And Leslie turned, disappeared, returned holding up an ice cream cone–shaped implement. Wooden handle, tapered metal shaft, sharp point.

Sarah felt a cold hand clench itself in the center of her stomach.

"A dibble," said Henry Ruggles with satisfaction. "Probably what pushed me into gardening."

"At least not into murder," said Leslie, laughing. He reached for it, held it in the air, raised his chin, frowned, stared into middle distance, and in a trained and anguished baritone cried out, "Is this a dibble which I see before me, the handle toward my hand? Come, let me clutch thee."

And then Toad Ruggles stepped forward. Opening his hands in a pleading gesture he called in a pathetic falsetto, "'What mean you, Caesar? Think you to walk forth? You shall not walk out of your house today.'"

Harold braced his shoulders, folded his arms, and confronted his wife.

"'How foolish do your fears seem now, Calpurnia!
I am ashamed I did yield to them.
Give me my robe, for I will go.'"

And then, rolling his eyes at Leslie, staggering backwards while clutching his chest, he whispered, "'Et tu, Brute.'"

And Sarah, overcome by a wave of nausea, turned away and stumbled toward the exit gate.

Chapter Thirteen

SARAH SAT IN THE returning bus, looking out the window and taking in nothing of the passing scene: The snug village with its church spire, the rolling meadow, the copse, the hillside. But for all she saw or cared these could have been scenes of Pittsburgh mills or the mean streets of Detroit.

The dibble. She knew it now. The tool that had been struck into Ellen Trevino's chest had become real. The heft and length, the sharp point of it. On the telephone, as described by Alex, Sarah had not been able to visualize the thing. Descriptions in newspapers of (in police jargon) "the weapon used to perpetrate the crime" were usually the familiar automatic, the Beretta, the Smith and Wesson, perhaps the knife or the hatchet. Or the ax. Sometimes a sports item: the oar, the baseball bat. Or the workman's choice: the shovel, the rope, the acetylene torch. Those agents found on household shelves: cyanide, arsenic, strychnine. From the garden, from the woodland: foxglove, monkshood, the deadly amanitas. All these Sarah had read or heard of, could imagine in use.

But she had never quite believed in the dibble. A childish name related to dribble and scribble and nibble. Described by Alex as partly resembling an ice cream cone. Another childish image.

But not anymore. The dibble had become the dibble-as-weapon. It had always seemed to her that there was something particularly horrible about using domestic objects for killing. Something designed for a benevolent purpose become lethal: the knitting needle that pierces, the stocking that strangles, the cocoa that poisons. And now the dibble. A tool for planting those lovely spring bulbs, the daffodil, the narcissus, the tulip, the hyacinth.

Had it all happened by chance? A fellow garden fan en route to Boston spots Ellen Trevino on the turnpike, sees her Subaru turn into the Kennebunk exit, and follows her to the chosen parking place. Makes friendly overtures. "What a coincidence!" Urges her to team up for the trip to Logan. "Leave your car here, we can arrange to have it picked up. No point in two cars making the trip. Here, let me help you with your luggage. Have you got your passport, your handbag? Give me your car keys and let me just check and see. It's so easy to forget something."

And in checking the Subaru the dibble comes to light. Such a suitable object sitting there saying, take me, use me! Grab it quickly and slip it under your raincoat, your jacket. Then under the driver's seat of your own car.

Or had everything been planned ahead? What had Alex told her about Ellen meeting a friend or checking on something? If it were all premeditated, the killer brings a gun ready for action. Then the dibble comes to light so the gun is canceled—guns are so easily traced. She could see it. Ellen unconscious in the killer's car—that blow on the temple—courtesy of the dibble's handle, perhaps. Ellen slumped on the plastic sheet—the sheet carefully provided so that blood, hairs, fibers, and other alien particles would not contaminate the car upholstery. But now the dibble is gripped by a gloved hand, is suspended for a moment above Ellen's chest. Then down comes the ugly metal point thrusting through the epidermis, the dermis, through subcutaneous tissue. It splinters cartilage and bone, splits blood vessels, the aorta itself. Blood wells. The heart gives up. And the dibble, its work finished, is pulled up, out. Wrenched free. Wiped, washed perhaps. A restroom at a gas station somewhere. Then thrown away.

And today a dibble is brought forth for a demonstration at Thalia Cottage. How Brutus struck down Caesar. Or how Leslie could reenact murder on his friend, Harold. And by their skill—these men were professionals—Sarah saw the murder taking place.

"Sarah, you look awful. White as cream cheese." It was Julia.

Sarah jumped in her seat as if some innerspring had been released. "What?"

"What on earth is the matter? Are you carsick? The bus driver can pull over. There's a lay-by coming up."

Sarah shook herself. "No, no. It's all right. Just something bothering me. Something I thought of."

Julia eyed her suspiciously. "Something that makes you look as if you're going to lose your lunch?"

"No, I'm all right. I can handle it."

"Now don't go morbid on me."

"It's just that something got to me. Well, if you must know it was that scene with Caesar and Brutus."

"You can't be serious. Just two old hams hamming it up."

"It wasn't the hams," said Sarah. "It was the whole scene."

"You mean *Macbeth* and *Julius Caesar*? You're such a literary purist, Shakespeare is so sacred that you can't stand a little foolishness."

"No," said Sarah crossly. "It isn't that at all. It has nothing to do with Shakespeare. I'll explain later. Back in my room. This bus isn't the place."

And Julia, for once, forbore to push the matter and the two rode in silence back to the inn.

Back in her aunt's room, Julia soaking her tired feet in a basin of warm water, Sarah told her about the dibble. "Alex described some of the forensic details and then, at that murder pantomime when Leslie held up the dibble, I could see the other dibble, too. I could picture the whole business, the thing going right into Ellen Trevino's chest and it turned my stomach."

Julia nodded soberly. "Yes, I can understand that. How awful. And a dibble is certainly a deadly object."

Sarah was silent for a minute. Then turned toward the door. "I'm not going to join the others for tea. I need space. I'll take a walk around town. It isn't quite five so if the shops are still open maybe I can buy something for Alex. A McKenzie tartan tie."

"We're not in Scotland," Julia reminded her.

"Tartan ties are everywhere," said Sarah. "Like locusts. Tourist items. Do you want to come?"

"No," said Julia firmly. "I'll stay here and soak my feet, but if you see a nice woven green tie for Patrick—he needn't know that I bought it in England—then buy it for me."

"Gladly," said Sarah. "It gives me a mission. I think Patrick certainly deserves a tie. Holding the farm and the horses together while you're tooting around here."

Her first stop at Maud's Wool and Linen Shop was entirely successful. A tie for Alex in the ancient McKenzie tartan, a silk scarf printed with entwined thistles for Elspeth, and a shamrock-green tie for Patrick. She was just puzzling over a set of linen place mats for her mother when she felt a tap on her shoulder.

"You're skipping the Mad Hatter's tea party," said an accusing voice. Justin Rossi.

"I wanted to be off by myself," said Sarah firmly.

"Far from the madding crowd," said Justin, adding before Sarah could open her mouth, "but this is the wrong country for Hardy. And I don't mean to start quoting the minute I see you. It's that literary aura you carry about you."

"The aura and I are about to take ourselves off," said Sarah.

"Don't go. I need your help. A woman's eye. If there is such a thing. Something for my mother. She's seventy-three and quite conservative in her tastes. What do you think? A scarf or a luncheon set? And something for my sister. A silk shirt perhaps. Size sixteen and she likes blue. Or perhaps a shawl."

Few people can resist a chance to spend another person's money. Sarah gave in. After all, she had nothing against Justin except for the fact that he looked like Alex. And knew birds and could come up with appropriate quotes at the drop of a hat.

Twenty-five minutes later found Sarah and Justin having tea and plum cake and cucumber sandwiches at The Tea Cozy.

"Usually I'd head for a pub, but the nearest one is the Hound and Hare and it's pretty smoke filled," said Justin. "So how do you like the gardens so far? Pretty spectacular, don't you think? But all that work, hoeing, edging, replanting. Digging up lilies, cutting down roses, dividing the iris. Makes my back ache to think of it. The trouble is that once you have a sensational garden you have to keep it up. Letting it go to seed would be a crime against the state."

Sarah, who was trying to keep cucumber slices from slipping out of her sandwich, managed a noncommittal nod.

"I think I like the little ones best. Thalia Cottage, for instance. Thalia, the muse of comedy or merry poetry. Seems appropriate. Harold and Leslie are enjoying their retirement. Especially if there's an audience. All those little references to Larry and Hermione. And doing scenes at the drop of a hat."

"Yes," said Sarah shortly. She did not want to review the dibble scene.

"But the scales have fallen from our eyes," said Justin, vigorously stirring a large quantity of sugar into his tea.

"What do you mean?"

"All the oohing and aahing over the idyllic Cotswold Village, which isn't so idyllic if women aren't safe in the ladies' loo."

"Oh, that," said Sarah. Another distasteful subject.

But Justin hadn't finished. "How on earth in that crowded pub—Sandi Ouellette said the place was a madhouse—how on earth did a man hide away in the ladies' loo when half the women probably had to pee at the same time. You'd have thought he'd have been nailed right off the bat. Anyway, Sandi, who's our greatest Anglo fan, must think that this England she's so crazy about isn't quite up to snuff."

"One incident shouldn't disillusion her for life," said Sarah. "I heard her chatting away happily today. She apparently loved Harold and Leslie."

"As did we all," said Justin. He helped himself to a third sandwich, bit down, and then looked at his watch. "Good Lord, it's getting late. Do you think there'll be any hot water left? Stacy Daniel spent a good fifty minutes in the shower yesterday. And Amy, our budding Agatha Christie, I thought she'd drowned in the tub. An hour if it was a minute."

Sarah, in her turn, suddenly yearned for a shower, a very hot shower, put down her teacup and stood up. "Right," she said. "Shall we flip to see who gets it first?"

"There are two showers," Justin reminded her. "One at the far end of the hall. We can each try to nab one."

And on these amiable terms the two paid for their tea and headed for the inn.

"So," said Julia when they met on the way down to dinner. "Did you find peace and quiet?"

"I found Justin Rossi and discovered he's as much of a gossip as the rest of the garden tribe. Wonders how a man inserted himself into the ladies' room in the middle of pub rush hour."

"It *is* a bit of a puzzle," admitted Julia. "But maybe he's envious. Wanted to be the molester himself. Vicarious enjoyment."

"What a horrid mind you have. He was perfectly civilized."

"That's what you say because he's your type."

"Wrong," said Sarah lightly. "On this trip I thought I'd look for short, fair, and stout. A complete change."

They went into the dining room together, and Sarah saw that Justin Rossi was in place expending his charm on Edith and Margaret Hopper, who sat on either side. And the Hopper sisters weren't buying it. Pale and rarely speaking, they kept their eyes down, twisted their water goblets, and moved restlessly in their chairs.

However, it was obvious during dinner that many of the garden tour were beginning to bond, to coalesce. Shared experiences, in-jokes, *sotto voce* references to "Toad" Ruggles and "Jack the Slitter," all these acted as integrating forces. The tragic fact of Ellen Trevino had moved yet another step into the background and talk was light and good-humored. Sarah, along with Carter McClure, Julia Clancy, and the Hopper sisters, remained holdouts from the general cheer, Julia choosing to attack Carter on the subject of academic tenure, the Hoppers picking at their food, and Sarah silently enduring several reenactments with a dinner knife of "Is this a dibble I see before me?"

She had reached the point of deciding that there had to be some strand of crazy logic connecting Ellen Trevino, the Kennebunk exit, Logan Airport, the scarf, the sunglasses, the search of Barbara Baxter's and her own bedroom. And the end of this strand must surely be tied to a member, or even several members of the Garden Club. A scary thought. But even more scary, there might be secondary filaments leading to Jack the Slitter, to the breakdown of the Hopper sisters, to the changes in the tour schedule. Even leading—and this was a longshot—to Carter McClure's pulling Henry "Toad" Ruggles out of his hat, as if Carter knew in advance that there would be a vacancy, And Henry himself, so available, so eager to fill Ellen's place. To volunteer his time and money. Henry in his ill-fitting wig.

Sarah, turning these things over and over in her mind, found that an apple tart had appeared as if by magic in front of her. She reached for her fork and picked up a morsel of apple, but before the first mouthful had been swallowed she returned to Henry Ruggles, who sat two seats down, across from her.

Well, the wig aside, Toad Ruggles appeared to be the genuine article. He seemed to know his stuff, his little lectures were larded with the scientific names, he identified plants without recourse to labels, and was able to come up with whether certain plants did well with sun or partial shade, acid or an alkaline soil. Of course, she, Sarah, couldn't have possibly told whether Henry was faking it, but surely some of the garden hotshots in the group would have caught him out if he hadn't known his facts.

In truth, all Henry's reviews had been favorable. Not only his knowledge but his upbeat personality. Not condescending either, because he included the garden beginners such as herself in his discussions. Of course, he was a little clumsy, stumbling hither and yon, but perhaps this was because he was so preoccupied. Which thought immediately reminded Sarah of Lillian Garth and her plunge down the darkened stairway, but fortunately all the tour excursions took place in broad daylight and a descent into a cellar seemed unlikely. Sarah firmly shoved the problem of Lillian to one side; she hadn't finished with Toad Ruggles.

Returning her attention to Henry, she found him addressing his dinner partners on the subject of the Cotswolds annexation by the powerful Hwicce tribe in early Saxon times. Henry was humorous but unrelenting in the matter of dates and places, and Sarah saw that his listeners had grown heavy-eyed and silent. After all, it had been a long day and the tour members clearly wanted to depart for their rooms.

Doris Lermatov started the exodus. She scraped her chair back, put down her napkin, and said clearly—in the middle of Henry's description of the Hwicce melding into the kingdom of Mercia—"This is all so interesting, Mr. Ruggles, but I'm behind with my postcards. I really must write at least three tonight and then it's to bed. Come on, Amy."

The word "postcards" acted as stimulus and the group rose almost as one murmuring, "Yes, postcards, a letter to finish, my travel diary, good gracious, why it's almost bedtime."

And Henry was left to an audience of Portia McClure and his sponsor, Carter McClure.

"Toad Ruggles," said Sarah to Julia as they reached the top of the staircase, "seems to be the real thing."

"Well, what did you think he was?" demanded Julia.

"I was trying to connect the oddball things that have happened, but I can't fit Henry into the picture."

"Because Henry doesn't fit into any lurid plot you're trying to hatch. He's a last-minute fill-in. If I were you I'd keep an eye on Justin Rossi. I saw him with Barbara Baxter before dinner, and she was giving him quite a piece of her mind. I couldn't hear what she said but it sounded very sharp, and I'm an expert on sharp."

"He was almost fifteen minutes late getting on the bus this morning. Enough to make any tour leader see red."

Julia shrugged. "Perhaps. He does seem rather casual. Now I have my needlepoint to attend to and a book to finish, so I'll say good night. And, if you take my advice, you'll stop—at least for tonight—worrying about, as you put it, oddball things. The only oddballs on this tour are you and I. We're the ones who have no valid reason to be on the trip. The others are probably as suspicious of us as you are of them." And Julia walked away down the hall to her bedroom door, inserted her key in the lock, opened the door and disappeared.

Chapter Fourteen

THE NEXT DAY, TUESDAY the thirteenth, garden visiting was put on hold. The skies opened, the thunder clapped, the lightning zigzagged, rain and hail spanked against the window, and Henry Ruggles, by permission from Innkeeper Thomas Gage, usurped the parlor for readings from horticultural works, including his own. These were sparsely attended, a fact that did not appear to discomfort the always ebullient Henry.

However, on Wednesday, the fourteenth of June, travel became possible. Uncomfortable but possible. The air was still moist, the sky heavy with intermittent showers and swept by sharp gusts of wind. But, grateful to be out and about, the Garden Club members, protected by mackintosh, poncho, and cape, clambered aboard their bus. And with the exception of Edith and Margaret Hopper—both with clear plastic boots over their shoes and muffled in plastic coveralls—the group seemed full of cheer and ready to appreciate—no matter how doubtful the weather—those two National Trust treasures, Hidcote Manor Garden in the morning and Kiftsgate Court Gardens in the afternoon.

The trip took them along the A424, and by the time they swung northwest good humor was so rife that song had actually broken out. In French. It had all begun because the irrepressible Henry Ruggles reminded them that they would be in France soon and they should celebrate by singing "The Marseillaise." Unfortunately, only four of the group could handle this request, Henry himself, Julia, and the other two being, to everyone's surprise, Sandi and Fred Ouellette, who ended with a triumphant *"Abreuve nos sillons."*

"I'm not completely illiterate," Sandi announced to the listeners. "Fred and I do speak French. Where do you think the name 'Ouellette' came from? Montreal, that's where."

"Chalk one up for Sandi," Sarah told her aunt after the singing had subsided.

"She may have her uses after all," replied Julia. "Five days from now we'll be in France and I haven't stuck to my homework."

"Et bien," said Sarah, pointing to the rainstreaked bus window, *"ce vent et cette pluie sont très miserables, n'est-ce pas?"* And then with no reply, she added, *"Est-ce que vous écoutez?"*

"Yes, I'm listening," said Julia, "but the wind is going down—*le vent est tombé*. We'll start tomorrow. Everything in French. Or Italian. *Quand nous arriverons à Cambridge*, because," she added, "I expect the Cambridge Botanic Garden to be rather dull. A good chance to practice."

"Pull them in, that's what I say," announced Mike Laaka. "They'll be heading for France in a few days and then, for God's sake, Italy. All over the blessed map. And where they need to be is where we can lay a finger on them. Or handcuffs." Mike thumped the desk in front of him for emphasis.

Mike, like some sort of Nordic warrior, fair hair ruffled, cheeks red, paced the narrow confines of Sergeant George Fitts's office—a gray cell in the CID annex of the Maine State Police barracks in Thomaston. Alex McKenzie, a more contained character, sat listening on one of George's folding metal chairs.

"Mike has a point," said George, who did not often concede that Mike had anything in his head beyond misbegotten froth. George was the by-the-book sort of a detective gifted with a fishy glance—this enhanced by thick rimless glasses—and a steel trap for a mouth; a man who, even if dressed in tiger skin or a clown suit, would not be mistaken for anything but a criminal investigator.

Mike pressed his advantage. "Those birds, the ones on the tour, are tied up with Ellen Trevino like no one else is. Everything she did in May had to do with getting ready for the trip. I've asked around the university, around the town, and everyone says the same thing. Not what you'd call a social or a sexy type. Everyone liked her, but no one seemed to have known her that well. She was, what's the expression, 'very respected.'"

"A real professional," Alex put in. "Lived for her job."

Mike nodded. "Yeah, that's what I'm saying. And her job this spring was all tied up with this goddamn Garden Club."

"Yes," said George. "We would like them in the flesh," a remark that made Alex think of cannibals. George tipped his chair back and put the tips of his fingers together and frowned. "But as of today we haven't any solid evidence to link anyone to the murder. Just the connection of the trip itself. I've talked to the investigating team in the Kennebunk area, and they're scrambling to come up with something tangible. The dibble, for instance. They've made a positive ID for Dr. Trevino's blood on that. Which we expected since a quick washing couldn't eliminate every blood cell. And we're working on the soap."

Alex, who had been staring at a wall calendar depicting a sunset view of the Maine State Prison, jerked his head up. "Soap?"

"The dibble," explained George patiently, "was washed. Soap and water. Not detergent, soap. So unless the murderer was carrying around a jug of water and a bar of soap, we think that he—or she—stopped off at some restroom facility. Gas station or one of the turnpike rest stops. The lab's working on identifying the soap, and when they do we've a chance of nailing down the washroom it came from. And if it's a gas station, there's a chance someone remembered a person whose clothes may have been a mess. Stained. Most stations keep their rest rooms locked up so you have to ask for the key. The killer must have wanted to wash up, maybe change his clothes, his shoes. Get rid of the works. Well, the CID down in Kennebunk will hit the entire area on and around the pike. Just as soon as the make of soap is nailed down."

"Don't count on bloodstained clothes," put in Mike. "Anyone careful enough to wrap the body in a plastic tarp may be in a coverall, a raincoat, a slicker, or a whole rainsuit."

"A rainsuit would be pretty conspicuous," said Alex.

"Remember," said Mike, "it was raining that day. You ought to know. You drove in it."

Alex shifted in his seat, frowned, trying to remember. The metal chair didn't encourage thought, and the small desk fan was only circulating warm, dusty air. "It wasn't raining the whole way," he said. "It'd been overcast earlier, but I don't think it started until around the time we hit the New Hampshire border."

"But," persisted Mike, "someone in a raincoat wouldn't look funny if it was about to rain."

Alex looked dubious. "I don't know many people—except Sarah's grandmother—who put on rain clothes in advance of the rain."

"Let it go," said George. "In the meantime"—here he looked at Alex reprovingly—"there's that head scarf that someone did wash. Too often. One washing wouldn't have been so bad. But all that sudsing and rinsing. Well, the lab hasn't found blood yet, but their people are practically unweaving the thing to try and come up with anything—fibers, hairs, dirt. Unfortunately, it was kicking around at the airport, in the plane, in Sarah's pocket or her luggage until it was mailed."

"You'd think," put in Mike, "that after all this time, all the things Sarah has been mixed up with, she'd have learned something about evidence. Not to mess with it."

Alex rose in defense of his absent wife. "She wasn't thinking about evidence when she first found it."

George looked from a series of doodles, squares and triangles he'd drawn on a file card. He pointed his pen at Alex and clicked it. "We'll wait and see what the evidence team turns up. For now ask Sarah to try to retrieve those sunglasses as soon as possible. Since they turned up with the scarf they may prove useful."

Alex nodded and decided to change the subject. "Can you tell from what you've got so far who could have gone through the whole process of trailing Ellen?—she must have been trailed. Or had set up a meeting place? Who then had the time to kill her, leave the Kennebunk exit, reverse directions, and dump the body at the Scarborough exit, find a washroom, clean the dibble, wash his hands, change clothes, and somewhere dump Ellen's luggage. God, that takes a hell of a lot of time, and if you happen to be a member of the garden tour, you have to make that British Airways flight at Logan, getting there two hours in advance for passport and baggage checking. Driving there would be dicey what with the summer traffic gridlock, construction areas, so flying to Logan is a must. From Portland, most likely, because the other airports are too far away from the body dumping site."

George held up his hand. "Think about charter planes, small airports—which we're checking."

"Back to the car," said Mike. "The killer's car. The killer didn't arrive at the Kennebunk exit on foot. Where is it? Was it a private car, a rental, or maybe stolen?"

George sighed, a small squeezed sort of sigh, the sort of exhalation that told Mike to shut up and stop pushing things.

"We're working on it. Now let's back up and look at what we're sure of."

"Like Ellen Trevino being dead," Mike put in.

George gave him a sour look. "Yes. The lab is fixing the time she was killed sometime between about nine A.M. the morning of June sixth to about two-thirty of that afternoon. For what it's worth, the stomach contents show she had breakfast but no lunch. The rain began on the southern section of the Maine pike sometime between three and three-thirty. Since the ground under the body was dry, it means Ellen Trevino was killed before it began raining."

"Okay," said Alex, "but the murderer has to dump his own car, switch to a limo or a rental or have a friend drive him to the airport. Or he—or she, I'm neglecting the possibility of a lady murderer—may have done in Ellen in a rental. Then turned in the rental minus, of course, that plastic sheet."

George turned a page on his notebook and then frowned at Alex. "Don't rush me. You're acting like Mike. Let's take the whole day of June sixth. Start with you, Alex, Sarah, and Julia Clancy."

"Some day," said Mike, "we can hope to find Sarah as the chief suspect. It'll make a nice change. But we've got some others off the hook. The Hopper sisters and the Ouellettes."

George nodded. "Right. We've got Alex making rounds at the hospital, Sarah at the English office, Julia on her farm. The Hoppers spent the morning with family members. Sandi had her hair done in the A.M., lunch with a friend; Fred spent the morning with a casket salesman, then worked preparing a body. His assistant vouches for him. The Hoppers and Ouellettes took the US Air 4:05 to Logan."

Alex stood up, stretched, looked out the window at the bumper-to-bumper Route 1 traffic into Thomaston and sat down again. "Were all the rest of the tour racing loose around Maine?"

"More or less," said George. "Here you are, one by one. Stacy Daniel had a rental Buick Century from Avis. She'd flown into Portland from Boston on Sunday for a bank branch meeting on Monday. On Tuesday the sixth she claims to have driven north from Portland to Freeport to do some last-minute shopping. Said she paid cash for a pair of walking shoes at some outlet, put them on, and threw away the box. And the receipt. Then drove the car back to the Portland Jetport, turned it in, and caught the 5:05 Delta to Logan."

"And her car?" prompted Alex.

"The next person to rent the Buick was a family of four driving to northern Quebec for a three-week tour. We're trying to trace it, but nothing so far. We've a problem with rental cars. After they're turned in, the vehicle is completely cleaned, deodorized, vacuumed, washed, which makes it hard on the lab."

"And get this," said Mike. "Justin Rossi—he lives in Concord, Mass.—gave a talk on family law to a U. Maine law school class Friday. Flew into Portland that A.M. and picked up a Hertz Ford Sable. After the lecture he spent the weekend plus Monday at the Samoset Resort in Rockland. Started south on Tuesday the sixth and turned in the car at Logan at around five-fifteen. And, wouldn't you know, the next renter was a mother with a sick kid who puked all over the seats and floor, so not only has it had the usual cleaning but it's been practically sterilized."

"What about the morning and noon hours for Rossi," said Alex impatiently. He had decided that if there had to be a villain, it might as well be Rossi, the man Sarah claimed looked like him and seemed to be so agreeably literary and companionable.

Mike looked cheered. "Some holes there. Rossi said he drove down from Rockland in the A.M. and stopped at a diner near Portsmouth for lunch—doesn't remember the name of the place—and said that he had time to kill..."

"Or Ellen Trevino to kill," said Alex.

"Yeah, or that. Anyway, after he made it to Massachusetts he left the freeway and drove around. Stopped to watch a high school girls softball game. In Amesbury, I think it was. So what I say, is that Rossi doesn't have any kids or a wife or a girlfriend…"

"As far as we know," said George.

"So maybe he likes high-school girls. Maybe Ellen Trevino reminded him of a high-school girl. She was pretty young looking." He looked about at two disapproving faces. "Well, it's just an idea," he added.

George scowled, "Mike, watch your mouth and don't go throwing those ideas around. Rossi's a lawyer and there's something called defamation of character."

"Get on with it," said Alex, always irritated by the often acrimonious Mike Laaka-George Fitts dynamics.

"The Lermatovs," said George, "Amy and the mother, spent the early morning packing—the only confirmation is for each other. Then Mrs. Lermatov's sister, Elsie, drove them to Portland. Sister got out at the Portland Museum of Art and Mrs. Lermatov borrowed her car to do—and I'm quoting—some looking around with her daughter. Picked up sister Elsie about three who drove them to the airport in time to catch the 5:05 Delta to Boston. To think that mother and daughter zipped back to the Kennebunk exit and killed Ellen is stretching it beyond belief."

"Next," said Mike, "is our eager-beaver tour director, Barbara Baxter. She spent the very early A.M. at her agency—Whirlaway Tours in Yarmouth—picked up a Budget Ford Taurus there and met a client for coffee around nine-forty-five in Brunswick—an art tour being arranged—left saying she wanted to hit Freeport. God, just try to track someone in that town knee deep in people looking for outlet bargains. Did she get there? Well, she claims she got a new big suitcase for the trip—the kind with wheels. Paid cash. Natch. Why can't we have a suspect who uses a credit card?"

"Not a suspect yet," observed George.

"Anyway," Mike went on, "Barbara claims she went from Freeport to the jetport in time to catch her late afternoon Delta flight along with the Lermatovs, Stacy Daniel, and Rossi. And no one has remarked that any of the tour group on that flight looked anxious, disheveled, or hurried as if they'd scrambled to make the flight."

"The 5:05," said Alex trying to keep the details straight in his head.

"Yeah," said Mike. "And you'll love this. Baxter's Budget rental has been rented twice since she turned it in. First was a one-day by a man with two Samoyed dogs who shed white fur all over—the Budget people went crazy cleaning it. The second rental was a man driving to New Jersey who got himself drunk and totaled the thing near Trenton. Hit a tree. A one-person accident with no personal property damage, so no legal case impending, and the car was cannibalized for parts and is being sold as junk—God knows where."

"What we have," said George, who liked neat summaries, "is the fact that the Lermatovs—who are very doubtful—Justin Rossi, Stacy Daniel, and Barbara Baxter were all loose in the area, had the time, maybe the opportunity, to pull off a late-morning or early-afternoon murder."

"Wait up," said Alex. "You've forgotten the tour grouch, Carter McClure. And his wife, Portia, who is not a grouch—though being married to Carter must be wearing her down."

George consulted his notebook. "Portia McClure seems to be in the clear. A long dentist appointment and a luncheon meeting. The History Department people remember Carter throwing his weight around in the early morning. But he left around ten. He met Portia at two in Wiscasset—driving his own car. They left the car at a garage and took an airport limousine all the way to Logan. The McClure car is being checked and so far is clean."

Mike shook his head. "Carter would have to have sprouted wings to get to Kennebunk and nail Ellen. And get back to meet Portia. But he could just have done it."

"Bad temper doesn't always add up to murder," said George. "I've uncovered a lot about Carter McClure. He's crotchety and difficult but he gives a lot of time helping students. Tutoring in the summer. Helping them with scholarship applications."

"Don't spoil it," said Mike. "I love to hate people like that. Especially the snooty Bowmouth College types."

Alex stood up. "Okay, so you'll leave the garden tour in peace unless some direct evidence from the tour members turns up. Or a clear set of strange prints turn up in Ellen's Subaru."

"Guess what," said George. He raised his eyebrows and peered at the two men through his rimless glasses.

"I'll bite," said Alex.

"Prints from Barbara Baxter. All over the Subaru window—passenger side—and the dash, and the passenger seat. Also hairs that match some we picked up at Barbara Baxter's Whirlaway Tour office."

"Whoa up," shouted Mike. "What are you doing sitting there? Bring her in. Put a net over her head. Call up the Brits and nail her down. Christ, George, all this crap about rental cars and flight times and Baxter's prints are in the Subaru. Hey, case over. Let me outta here."

"Except," said George smoothly, his expression benign, "we know that Barbara Baxter visited Ellen Trevino three days before the trip to go over the trip details. Not only that but Ellen drove Barbara out to lunch and to visit a greenhouse. In her Subaru." And George reached for the telephone and began hitting numbers.

"Jeezus, I hate that guy," said Mike as he and Alex left the office. "Boy, did I ever bite."

"And you're always saying George has no sense of humor," observed Alex. "Actually, I think he's quite funny."

Chapter Fifteen

Henry Ruggles stood in the entrance courtyard of Hidcote Manor Garden, his umbrella unfurled against the spattering rain, his voice raised against the rustle of raincoats. He was never one to shorten a lecture because of foul weather and he was now launched into a consideration of the vines that decorated the courtyard walls. He extolled the wisteria, "Such a PROFUSION of growth," lauded the scarlet Cape figwort (*Phygelius capensis*), examined the potato vine (*Solanum crispum* "Glasnevin") while all the members of the Midcoast Garden Club listened, took notes, and admired.

All the members, that is, but Julia Clancy, who made two restless tours of the courtyard, pulled her olive-drab riding slicker closer around her shoulders, and moved off impatiently in the direction of the garden and toward a great stretch of lawn. Her niece, Sarah, remained a damp physical presence on the fringe of the group. But her mind was elsewhere, fixed on the dubious party with whom she was associated. No, not associated, trapped, chained to them. Eyes only for them. I suppose, she told herself grimly, that from stewing on the edge of events, I'm focused. Completely focused on Ellen Trevino and her death by that most horrible of gardening implements, the dibble.

The morning progressed, the rain eased and then ceased altogether and a certain brightening in the sky promised future sun. Even to this favorable omen Sarah remained oblivious. Still tightly buttoned into her raincoat, she squelched along on the sodden grass and pebble paths from one splendid planting to the next, from the Pine Garden, along the Rose Borders through Camellia Corner, and down the Long Walk and back through paths and avenues and corners of banked floral color and saw nothing of the periwinkles, the day lilies, the polygonums, the poppies, the phloxes, the roses.

Instead, she considered the homicidal personality, the violent opportunist, the psychopath, the impulse killer, the revenge seeker. The gold digger, the drug-crazed. The defender of some dark and gloomy secret. The hater of Ellen Trevino.

Be impartial, she ordered herself. Everyone guilty unless proved otherwise. She wished, almost for the first time of her life, to talk to Sergeant George Fitts. He would, by now, know which persons had spent a harmless day in the company of reliable witnesses. Well, she couldn't call Alex now from the middle of a garden so she would have to rehash all those odd and unaccountable events of the last few days and see what came bubbling to the surface. So, after setting aside only Alex, Aunt Julia, and herself as innocent, she tried to fit the cloak of murderer over the shoulders of her other companions.

In many cases it was a terrible fit. Take Amy Lermatov. Sarah eyed the girl, standing, notebook in hand, ahead on the path next to a clump of ornamental grass. There she was in her worn blue jeans, her rumpled wind parka tied around her waist. And hadn't she been wearing that Decomposers rock band t-shirt for days? But as a suspect? Forget it. Scratch Amy. Scratch her mother. If the two of them made up a murder team, then she, Sarah, would jump into the nearest and thorniest rosebush.

How about Portia McClure? Sensible, kind, expert on herbal gardens and compost. Not a murdering type, but was she the protector of a hot-tempered husband? Well, you never could tell about the loyalty of wives, so put Portia on hold along with Carter.

Here her ruminations were broken by a call for her from Henry Ruggles to come and admire the topiary doves in the White Garden.

He stood in the center of his group, exactly as Portia had described him, a benevolent Pickwick—not quite wearing gaiters but with a corduroy hat which perched on top of his wig. He aimed the point of his umbrella directly at Sarah and then moved it to indicate the closely clipped green doves.

"Miss Deane, isn't it? I've been watching you because I do have eyes in the back of my head. I've had the feeling that perhaps flowers aren't the CLOSEST things to your heart. Perhaps you are a shrubbery person. You like the formality of green walls and verges. Or trees, a STRUCTURED wilderness? A creative tangle?"

Sarah, coming to with a start, told Henry that she admired the topiary and the garden walks and all the flowers, but she was such a beginner that she had no specialty.

"A generalist," said Henry. "The very BEST way to begin. Then choose. But these topiary doves are charming." He flourished his umbrella a second time at them, and Sarah decided that Henry must have concluded that she was a complete fool and must be appealed to on the simplest level: bird shapes. However, she managed a smile, and Henry, with the satisfied air of a teacher of the horticulturally challenged, returned to the campanulas and the phlox.

Left again to herself she considered Edith and/or Margaret Hopper. An *Arsenic and Old Lace* duo, but more lethal than those two old biddies because the dibble was on a different scale than poisoned elderberry wine. Certainly something was eating away at the two. From being quietly moist-eyed, they now seemed to have entered into an almost manic state, interrupting Henry Ruggles in the Poppy Garden in the middle of his explanation of *Hydrangea aspera villosa,* and giving in to sudden bursts of high-pitched laughter. Okay, say one or both had done in Ellen (whom they hardly knew) for some arcane purpose, would there have been a period of fulfillment, of disassociation, and then, whoosh, when remembrance and guilty conscience kicked in—wouldn't they have started to come apart at the seams? After all, Margaret and Edith belonged to that stern generation whose upbringing included a heavy dose of conscience.

And now Sarah, following the McClures into the Bathing Pool Garden, tilted her head to one side and assumed a thoughtful look in an effort to seem as if she were listening to Henry Ruggles. He had relaxed into his raconteur mode and was relating how pools and fountains—all bodies of water— made him TERRIBLY nervous because he had been tossed into the Severn as a child and told to swim. "I was never Frog Ruggles." He laughed.

Sarah joined in the amused response, but then sternly returned to what she thought of as top-rank suspects. Stacy Daniel, the lion woman, beautiful and bored; Barbara Baxter, dethroned tour leader; and last, the family lawyer, the Alex McKenzie look-alike, Justin Rossi.

And here Sarah stopped being objective. If it had to be someone, why not Stacy? Stacy had made only the faintest attempts to meld with the group, to chat it up, to even look interested. She could almost picture the lovely Stacy swathed in protective plastic, her hand closed around the dibble.

"Sarah, I might as well be traveling with a lamp post."

Aunt Julia. Where had she come from?

"For heaven's sake," scolded her aunt, "take that look off your face. You look as if you've been tasting vinegar."

"Vinegar? Well, something like it." Sarah looked about in confusion at surrounding walls of a courtyard. "Where are we?"

"We are leaving. This is where we came in. And the rain has stopped so you can unbutton your raincoat. We're going to have the sandwiches the inn packed for us and then go on to Kiftsgate. Too much of a good thing, I'm beginning to think."

Fortunately for Sarah's state of mind she was abandoned after lunch by Julia, who declared that today she wanted to be left alone to do the gardens by herself. She would see Kiftsgate Court in her own way. There were times when the elderly need space.

This was a relief. Today Julia reminded her niece of a yellow jacket—a lot of buzz and a nasty bite. Now she could pace unnoticed behind the group while Henry exclaimed over the *Salvia candelabra,* and *Rodgersia pinnata* "Superba"; while Doris Lermatov hung over the peonies, while Sandi Ouellette took pictures of the White Sunk Garden, its fountain, its hydrangeas; while the rest, invigorated by lunch, exclaimed and pointed.

For the first few gardens Sarah kept her brain in neutral and then returned to the hunt. And to Justin Rossi.

It was hard to accept him as the murderer. Men who looked like Alex didn't drive dibbles into women's chests. Did they? And today Justin wore a tweed cap and was good-looking enough to carry it off. The hat suggested to Sarah a rather engaging eccentricity. Not many Americans could have worn such a thing without hearing a British snicker behind their backs. But Justin could. Of course, there was no rule that said murderers couldn't be personable. Sarah remembered once flinging herself on the broad chest of one and crying out something like, "Thank heavens you're here!" Okay, so Mr. Rossi could be charming and Ellen Trevino was probably not totally immune to charm. Put Rossi on the doubtful list.

Ditto Barbara Baxter. Double that for Stacy Daniel.

Sarah came to a halt above a steep zigzag path that led down to a lower level through rockery and ground plants. She needed a moment to herself to consider Suspect Number One. Stacy Daniel fitted the new and popular type of murderer because wherever you looked—fiction, the tube, the movies—beautiful women who power walk and appear on magazine covers and work for banks seemed to be much in demand as killers. Yes, Stacy had all the requirements. Now all that was needed was to discover motive and opportunity.

"He's such a stumblebum, a real klutz," said a voice. Stacy Daniel. "He's going to be hurt and really he's quite a nice old guy."

Sarah gave a start and found her first choice for homicide standing at her side. Stacy. Looking today particularly lovely in a peach linen shirt and a fawn cotton skirt, a rust-colored rain coat open and hanging off her shoulders.

"Who's a klutz?" Sarah asked, trying to rearrange her thoughts. It was hard to banish the scenario of Stacy she was working on—Stacy standing by Ellen Trevino's Subaru, leaning into the driver's window, asking Ellen to join her for the ride to Logan.

"Henry. Toad Ruggles," explained Stacy. "He falls over his own feet, going down steps. God, he even stumbles going *uphill*. I'm glad he's not showing us the White Cliffs of Dover or we'd be scraping him off the beach."

Sarah made an effort to be responsive, which was difficult because she'd really put a lot of feeling into sticking Stacy with Ellen's death. And now here she was acting human, even sympathetic. Liking Henry and wanting to help him keep on his feet.

"Henry is a little on the clumsy side," she murmured.

"Clumsy!" exclaimed Stacy. "Why he needs a walker. Or better shoes. Something. But does he know his stuff. I mean, I guess he does, although you couldn't prove it by me, but that old crank Carter McClure shuts up when he talks and everyone else seems to be wowed by him."

"Henry Ruggles does put on quite a show," agreed Sarah. "Ellen wouldn't have been so dramatic but," she added loyally,

"I think she was the real expert. Henry may be more flash and talk."

"Well, I never thought Ellen Trevino came off as a really warm personality," said Stacy.

Look who's talking, thought Sarah. Aloud, she said, "Ellen was very, very serious and very shy."

"If you say so. But anyhow, I sort of like this old coot Toad Ruggles and I hope…"

"What do you hope?" It was Barbara Baxter, wearing a sort of waterproof running suit which, judging from her heightened color and wet brow, must have turned into a sweat box. She shook her head at the two women. "I've been looking for you both. I've just tracked Mrs. Clancy down and here you are. It's getting late and everyone wants to have tea here at the Kiftsgate tea room. But Mr. Ruggles thought we should all see the lower garden first. He particularly asked for you, Sarah, because he thinks you'd like the Scotch firs and the Mother and Child statue because you weren't really a garden person. So, if you could…"

But Barbara's sentence was drowned by a sudden cry from below. A sort of surprised yelp. A pause. And then muffled shout. "Help, help!"

Stacy and Sarah and Barbara—like some sort of relay team sprang into action, Barbara running first, then Stacy, followed by Sarah. Down the zigzag path, down along a wide flight of stone steps and to the edge of a clump of people. Sarah falling at the lower step and skinning her knee on a particularly unforgiving rock. She climbed painfully to her feet, ran ahead, and charged into a melee of people surrounding a swimming pool. Familiar people most of them. Her own tour group plus a small array of strangers all brought together by the cries and a joined sense of consternation.

Sarah grabbed Margaret Hopper by the arm. "Who? What's happened?" she shouted.

Margaret gestured frantically. "Henry Ruggles. In the pool. He fell in. They're trying to get him out. Sandi Ouellette and

Mr. Rossi. And I don't think Henry can swim. He keeps going down. Sandi's diving."

Sarah pushed past her impatiently. Three figures in the pool. No, two figures and a head. A head that kept bobbing up and down like a large smooth soccer ball. Henry? No, it couldn't be. But it was Sandi Ouellette and Justin both hanging on to a pair of arms. Sarah without thinking of what she meant to do kicked off her shoes and threw off her raincoat.

And felt a restraining hand. "It's okay. They've got him. They're swimming him in," said Doris Lermatov, appearing at Sarah's side. "We were all looking at the Ha-ha and we heard a splash."

"Henry?" said Sarah puzzled. "But that's not Henry."

"Without his wig," said Doris. "There, he's out. Good for Sandi. I'll never say another word about her. She just dove in and had hold of him before any of us made a move. Justin Rossi dove in, too, but Sandi really saved him."

Sarah, feeling useless, watched the aftermath of Henry Ruggles's immersion. He sat, wigless, on the edge of the pool, and coughed and choked and gasped but in a remarkably short time pronounced himself able to stand, to walk, and to look forward to tea. He even managed a wan smile when presented with a dripping wig, which looked for all the world like a small drowned fur-bearing animal.

In no time, towels appeared, blankets were produced, the ladies of the National Trust having enlisted the help of the Kiftsgate housekeeper. Then bundled up, the trio disappeared into the area marked toilets, reappeared somewhat drier and the Garden Club clambered on their bus, having agreed that tea back at the Shearing would be the wisest choice. Barbara, with Henry temporarily out of action, took charge of the loading, the thanking, and promising the return of the towels and blankets.

But just as the bus was about to make the turn out of the car park, Portia McClure called stop. "Has anyone seen my sunglasses? I've lost them. Somewhere by the pool. I had them before that. The ones Sarah gave me on the plane."

"No," said Barbara firmly. "We must get Mr. Ruggles back. He'll need a hot bath and we can't go looking around for the glasses. They weren't prescription, were they?"

"No," admitted Portia. "And you're quite right, Barbara. I'll pick up another pair tomorrow."

And the bus rumbled into life, turned the corner, and headed south in the direction of High Roosting.

And Sarah was left to contemplate the shambles of her murder scenario. Stacy Daniel had not pushed Henry Ruggles into the pool. Nor had Barbara Baxter. And that left who? Carter McClure, but he had sponsored Henry. Why try to drown him? No, who it really left—face it—was Justin Rossi. Justin, whose rescue efforts did not come into play until Sandi Ouellette had Henry almost in her grasp. Sarah felt almost actively ill.

Because if she had ever been sure of something, she was sure that Henry Ruggles, never too sure on his feet, had been pushed. Tipped, shoved, nudged into the Kiftsgate swimming pool. As Lillian Garth must have been pushed down the cellar steps. And Ellen had been stabbed. It was so simple. Henry had just made his fear of pools and rivers and ponds only too clear. Opportunity offered and Justin Rossi had struck.

It was a subdued group of garden fans who began the return trip to the Shearing Inn. After all, Sarah reflected, it had been a near miss with Henry. Now, in a seat ahead of Sarah and Julia, he sat, blanketed, a sodden wig on his knees, his hands clutching a thermos of tea. Next to him sat Portia McClure. Sarah, listening to her reassuring murmurs, decided that if anyone could restore Henry to his usual cheerful self it was Portia.

Across the way, also wrapped, sat Sandi Ouellette next to her Fred. Fred, beaming, was explaining to all who could listen that Sandi had a job teaching Red Cross Lifesaving at the Y and how lucky it was that Sandi was so alert. With a number of other visitors around chattering their heads off, no one heard Henry fall in. He hadn't, apparently, made much of a splash, and beyond crying out for help he hadn't struggled. Panic, Fred supposed. Well, Sandi beat them all to it, did a flat dive right into the pool—you know the kind of dive where you keep the victim in sight—they teach it in lifesaving.

Here Sandi interrupted, saying that no one wanted to know every little detail, but she was overruled. Everyone did want to hear it all again. And so Fred described the whole rescue operation and concluded with a few words on drowning victims—victims he had, most sadly, to deal with in the line of his profession.

"Cosmetic problems like you wouldn't believe. The skin tone has to be completely restored. Petechial hemorrhages, cyanosis are real challenges, and it takes a real craftsman and endless patience, but when you see the family's faces, how relieved they are when they see their loved one, well, it's worth every extra minute spent."

This sobering thought brought an end to the general desire for details and the listeners subsided.

"I think," said Julia in a low voice to Sarah, "that I'm going to have to apologize on two scores."

Sarah looked at her aunt with surprise. Apologies did not usually play a part in Julia Clancy's repertoire.

"First," said Julia, "I'm sorry that I suggested Sandi was a lightweight. She may not be an intellectual, but she went into action like a pro. She would have made a good rider."

Sarah nodded. Julia had just paid Sandi the highest of compliments. "Maybe she does ride," she said. "Anything's possible, and if we wait long enough, we'll probably find out that Sandi has won the Pulitzer Prize for history."

"My second apology," said Julia, "has to do with your suspicions about our traveling friends. They may have some merit. It's as if there's a plot to eliminate all the tour directors. Except Barbara. Leave the whole tour to her direction. Though I can't for the life of me imagine why."

Sarah shook her head. "Barbara was on the upper-level garden with me when Henry went in the water. And Stacy Daniel was there, too, talking about how clumsy he was. Stacy apparently has a sneaking fondness for Henry."

"Oh dear," said Julia. "That shoots my Barbara theory."

"And my Stacy theory. I'd just settled it in my head that she was a cold, calculating bitch with no interest in the trip or in anyone here and then she turns up and goes all warm and fuzzy."

"Which leaves…"

"I know. Justin Rossi. And he dove in when he saw Sandi in the water. Had to cover himself."

For a while both women were silent, and Sarah turned for relief to the window to view the passing scene: sheep, sheep, and more sheep, moving slowly along a rolling pasture, their woolly backs showing almost pure yellow from the light of the low sun. Sarah glared at them. She was sick of sheep. Cows, too. And she was sick of gardens. She turned back to Julia. "Of course, it's possible that Henry fell in the pool all by himself. Heaven knows he's been stumbling all over his feet since he arrived."

"Yes, I know it's possible."

"But not probable?"

"Probable if it hadn't been for Lillian. And Ellen."

Another period of silence. For Sarah another stare out the bus window. Stupid little houses with thatched roofs. Unreal. Too cute. Too clean. Altogether too perfect. She thought that today she'd rather look at the slums of Liverpool and Birmingham. Or backcountry Maine farms, ramshackle buildings, tire swings, old cars rusting under laundry lines.

Then, as the bus entered the outer layers of High Roosting, Julia clutched Sarah's knee.

"Ouch," said Sarah. "I fell on it. Talk about being clumsy. I'll be the next one to fall down something."

"Never mind your knee," said Julia with a noticeable lack of sympathy. "I think I figured out what's wrong with Margaret and Edith. It came in sort of a flash. I have these insights sometimes. Like suddenly knowing exactly why a horse has gone lame. Anyway, it's all perfectly simple and accounts for all the Hopper symptoms."

"You have my full attention," said Sarah.

"Income tax," said Julia triumphantly.

"What!"

"Income tax. They forgot to file their quarterly return. Or had word that they owed from last year. Took improper deductions. Or hid some little bit of income. Something like that. So they got a nasty call or letter from the IRS. No, wait," as Sarah began to protest. "Listen to me. The IRS can be absolutely brutal. Those two women are probably frightened to death by monsters like the IRS. And maybe they have fudged a little on their returns for years. A sort of game. And they've been caught."

Sarah looked doubtful.

"It fits," said Julia. "Think about it. They won't say why they're upset. They'd have told us if it had been a family tragedy."

"You know," said Sarah thoughtfully, "you may have a point. And they're pretty conservative, so I have another idea. Maybe some loved grandson or granddaughter has come out of the closet. Or been caught with drugs. Picked up as a hooker."

"I like the IRS idea because they seem to be recovering."

"Overdoing it I'd say. They were babbling back at Kiftsgate."

"Just listen. At first they were upset, couldn't eat, wouldn't join in. Then they pull themselves together. Realize they can't do anything right now and that they have to go on with the tour. But can't tell anyone because they're so ashamed. Sarah, those two are my generation, and, believe me, half my friends live in mortal fear of the IRS. It's the twentieth-century bogie man."

"You mean they might have been audited?"

"Exactly. And found wanting. And threatened. Picturing themselves in some minimum security prison. Poor dears. We must try and have more sympathy but not let on we've found out."

"If we have. I still think some family member may have done something unmentionable—in their eyes."

"Trust your old Aunt Julia. Now, here we are. I'll get in line for the bathrooms and save you a place while you're calling Alex to find out what's going on at home."

Sarah got up from her seat, offered her aunt a hand as she rose creakily to her feet.

"Damn arthritis," said Julia. "I feel like a rusty machine."

"Get in a hot bath," said Sarah. "I'll go and call Alex. I almost dread it. Every time I've called he's had worse news. All we need to hear right now is that we're in the middle of a giant consortium of horticultural racketeers."

Chapter Sixteen

ALEX ANSWERED ON THE second ring.

"Are you sitting next to it," said Sarah.

"I'm living next to it," said Alex. His voice came loud and clear, almost in the next room. "It's a mix of worrying about you and covering for a couple of other internists, and then being on tap for Mike whenever he feels like unloading on me."

"I want to unload on you, too," said Sarah. "I miss our intimate little pillow talks about blood types and fingerprints and those nice details about lividity."

"You're not getting yourself out on a limb, are you?" Alex sounded anxious. And with good reason. To his certain knowledge, Sarah had spent a fair amount of time out on a number of limbs.

"To make it short, I'm centered. Focused. I feel right down to my fingertips that someone in our friendly little garden tour killed Ellen. Maybe pushed Lillian Garth into the cellar."

"Have you just come to a boil or has something happened?"

"You could say that." And Sarah gave Alex a thumbnail sketch of Henry Ruggles's dip in the Kiftsgate swimming pool and ended by saying that Aunt Julia had become a believer.

"So, if you do find that Ellen was killed by some insane vagrant on the Maine Turnpike, let me know right away. Otherwise what Julia and I want to know is who's safe? Who we should sit next to in the bus. Who we should share a sandwich with."

"It's not a joke."

Sarah relented. "No, I know it isn't. But tell me, hasn't George figured out who *couldn't* have killed Ellen that day? And Alex, please hurry. I've got the front hall to myself now because everyone's scrambling for the bathrooms. But any minute I'll have someone breathing over my shoulder."

Alex became businesslike. "Okay. Here it is. Accounted for are Sandi and Fred Ouellette, Portia McClure, Margaret and Edith Hopper, and most probably the two Lermatovs."

"What about Carter McClure?"

"A very tight squeeze if he did it. He'd have had to drive well over the speed limit both ways and spend almost no time on body disposal and washing up."

For a moment Sarah was silent and then, bracing herself, she said, "Thanks. That's helpful. And now, I want to know a couple of things. Have you got a pencil?"

"I always have a pencil. Do you love me or do you just say so because I can come up with these exciting details?"

"I love you and exciting details. And I'm mad as hell about Ellen. Also I'm blessed—or is it cursed—with a nose like an aardvark when it comes to weird things like these garden tour experts being done in."

"Don't you mean a nose like an anteater? And Lillian Garth's doing well, and Henry Ruggles is okay, isn't he? He's just wet."

"Thanks to Sandi Ouellette he's just wet. Anyway, listen. First, find out, or squeeze it out of Mike, if there's anything nasty in anyone's background. Anything. Has anyone got a record, been out on parole, got caught selling pot? Had violent scenes? Run a shady business? Barbara Baxter's travel bureau, for instance?"

"You don't want much, do you?"

"And," Sarah persisted, "see if there's anything odd in Margaret or Edith Hopper's background."

"But they've been cleared for Ellen's murder."

"Yes, I know," said Sarah impatiently. "But something's going on with them. Aunt Julia thinks they're tax dodgers."

"You're not serious?"

"She is. Thinks they've had word that they're being audited. Me, I think someone in the family's done something they can't handle. Listen, I've got to go. Someone wants the phone. I'll call you tomorrow. We're going to be somewhere around Cambridge."

Alex had just time to call, "Be careful," before Sarah was confronted by the man behind her.

"Some people," said a man with a German accent who stood tapping his finger on the telephone table, "do not have any idea that they take so much time when other people wait."

"And a good evening to you," said Sarah, hanging up the receiver and heading for the stairs.

An hour later found Aunt Julia knocking on Sarah's door. Which was opened, revealing Julia dressed for dinner in her all-purpose paisley, a conspiratorial expression on her face.

"I think," said Julia, "I had the last of the hot water. The tap ran quite cold at the end."

"It ran entirely cold for me," said Sarah, who, shivering, had added a cardigan to her green silk jumper.

"Never mind. I have a plan. And I've memorized everyone's room number. So whatever I do at dinner, go along with it."

"Does it involve missing dinner?"

"Part of dinner. But the cause is just."

"If you're thinking about searching rooms..."

"Shhh. The walls have ears."

"I'm for searching, too. Especially tonight because Portia has lost those sunglasses I gave her, and I'm wondering if they've been stashed somewhere, dumped in a wastebasket. But how are we going to do it? Everyone locks his bedroom door. Particularly since Barbara's and my rooms were pulled apart."

Julia smiled and plunged a hand in her pocket and produced a brass key with a wooden tag. "Master key. I borrowed it from Mary. You know, our maid. Said I'd lost mine and my arthritis was acting up and I hated to climb all the way downstairs and would she? She said yes, as I promised to return it tomorrow morning. She was going off duty."

Sarah was incredulous. "She *gave* you the key."

"You should never neglect human relations," said Julia complacently. "Always show an interest. Mary Fiske lives on a farm outside of High Roosting and her father has a team of Shires. He uses them to plow with because he doesn't believe in mechanical things like tractors. And Mary used to do Pony Club and still rides when she's home. We've become quite good friends."

"Good God," said Sarah.

"Exactly. God helps those who help themselves. Now shall we go down? I'd hate to miss the cocktail hour."

Sarah sat through cocktails and through the soup course all the while keeping a watchful eye on her fellow diners, particularly Henry Ruggles. She wondered if he would show any sign of resentment, appropriate certainly if he thought he had been pushed into the Kiftsgate pool.

But Henry showed no such thing. In fact, he seemed to be doing his best to keep up appearances with lively chat, but a certain weariness was noticeable and from time to time his lip turned down and his eyes drooped. And his wig, now thoroughly dry, had not entirely recovered from its dunking. It looked more like a thatched roof than a hairpiece. And he had twice sloshed his consommé over the rim of his bouillon cup. Henry, she decided, being no spring chicken, needed bed.

As for the others, the early days of distress and the recovering good cheer seemed to now have subsided into low-key conversations that centered on the gardens visited. Henry's "accident" and Ellen's death were studiously avoided. As was the issue of the Cambridge Botanic Garden. But the details of that visit, Sarah decided, must somehow have been resolved since the tour was set to take off for Cambridge in the morning.

Dinner had advanced to the main course, for which Julia and Sarah had both ordered the lemon sole, when suddenly Sarah was aroused by a fork clattering on a plate. She swiveled about and saw her aunt lean forward, recover, pass a hand over her brow, and then give an audible gasp.

Sandi, sitting opposite, looked up with concern. "Aunt Julia, what's the matter? Are you all right?"

"It's nothing," said Julia. "A little faint, that's all. Too much sun today, perhaps."

"But it was raining and then mostly overcast. Not much sun at all," Sandi—always literal—reminded her.

"The humidity," said Julia. "The sun about to come out. Just a little faintness, but I'll be all right. I'm sure I will." This last sentence being accompanied by Julia's right hand nailing Sarah on her sore knee.

"Ow," squeaked Sarah. "I mean, oh. Oh, Aunt Julia. You do look pale."

"I don't think I can eat my fish," said Julia. "I'll just stay here quietly." She looked around the table with a brave smile.

Barbara Baxter pushed back her chair. "Let me take you upstairs to your room, where you can lie down quietly, and then if you don't feel any better soon I think I should call a doctor."

"Quite right," said Fred Ouellette. "You must never neglect a sudden faintness. You have no idea where it might lead. I've had loved ones on my table…"

"Oh no," said Julia with a slightly stronger voice. "I'm quite used to these little spells., A fall I had once, from my horse. An injured nerve. It sometimes comes over me. But yes, I think I will go and lie down. And Sarah—she's quite used to my little episodes—she'll take me up. Your hand, Sarah. And, all of you, please go right on with your dinner."

"I think you overdid it," said Sarah in her aunt's ear as they slowly climbed the stairs to their bedroom floor.

"Just your arm, dear," said Julia in a penetrating voice. "Whisper." She added, "Some good Samaritan may be tagging along behind us." Then louder, "Into my room so I can put my feet up."

Sarah steered her aunt into her bedroom and carefully closed the door. "Now what?"

"It's your turn. I'm the planner, you're the experienced snoop into other people's business. We don't have much time. Some of the group may skip dessert. And there'll be other guests prowling around."

"Okay," said Sarah. "Alex said the police have cleared the Ouellettes, the Hoppers, and the Lermatovs. We'll skip those rooms."

"We should do everyone," insisted Julia. "But start if you want with number one suspect, Justin Rossi. Room seventeen. I'll stand by the door and check out the hall for intruders."

"You mean legitimate owners of bedrooms."

"Right. Just whisk through and try not to make a mess."

"And if I'm caught?"

"That's negative thinking. Here's the key. I'll stand watch."

Justin Rossi's room was a miracle of order. Sarah poked about in the clothes closet, opened an empty suitcase, examined a washstand collection of toothpaste, brush, and deodorant, noted on the bureau a camera with a long lens, a birdwatcher's guide to British birds, a Penguin paperback mystery, and arrived at last to a number of packages and boxes that had been piled on a chair.

"What are those?" said Julia from her station by the door.

"He's been shopping. Actually, I was with him when he bought some of this. Things for his mother and his sister."

"Or his girlfriend."

"And for all I know his wife. Or daughter."

"What's in them?"

Sarah cautiously lifted a cardboard lid. "Blue silk blouse, stockings, a skirt or a slip. The next one, a white knitted shawl."

She slipped her hand into the third box. "Feels like a sweater. A wool one. Soft. Probably damn expensive. And the bottom, those placemats for his mother. An attentive son and brother, I'd say."

"Don't jump to conclusions. You can use stockings to strangle."

Sarah made a face at her aunt and then went over to the bureau and surveyed neatly stacked boxer shorts, polo shirts, and rolled socks. Zip," she announced. "And no sign of those sunglasses."

"So move on," commanded Julia, her voice anxious, and Sarah, glancing back saw her aunt's gray hair tousled, her face red, looking, as she did when agitated, like a worried terrier in search of a rat.

The McClure quarters only proved that Portia was orderly and Carter was not. And that Carter had a taste for police procedurals and Portia was reading an Eleanor Roosevelt paperback biography.

Barbara Baxter's room contained only a sheaf of notes to and from Whirlaway Tours, showing that Barbara had kept in touch with home base.

"Nothing but travel dates and reservation stuff," said Sarah, leafing through them. "And writing paper and stamps." She poked a finger at a little leather case that sat beside the notebook. "Expensive paper," she remarked. "Crane yet, with blue monogram and blue lined envelopes. Very posh. Barbara's a stationery snob. And that big suitcase like mine." She reached down and unzipped the cover. "Empty," she announced. "We should both dump them."

"Trivia," said Julia. "And hurry up," she added. "I think I hear someone on the stairs."

She heard correctly. Two female members of the Japanese contingent, both hurrying down the hall and arguing. "Or it sounds like arguing," Sarah said to Julia when the two had disappeared. "But since we don't know Japanese, they could be proclaiming eternal love."

"Stacy Daniel, next," Said Julia. "Put a nickel into it."

"Don't rush me," said Sarah sharply. "I'm the one sticking out my neck. You can just collapse against the wall pretending to be faint or say you're walking in your sleep."

Stacy Daniel's room was a major disappointment, and Sarah came out of it shaking her head. "An expensive-looking camera. No sunglasses, and underwear that would make Victoria's Secret blush. Beyond that, nothing."

"Sexy underwear isn't helpful?"

"You tell me. Okay, we've just time for the Hoppers."

The shared room of Edith and Margaret Hopper yielded one interesting document—or aborted document. Sarah rummaging in the wastebasket came up with a crumpled piece of Shearing Inn writing paper on which a firm called Warneke, Lewis, and Dubois, Attorneys-at-Law were addressed. Sarah smoothed the paper and brought it over for Julia to see. "It's just the beginning of a letter," she explained. "Addressed to Sam. Samuel Lewis. I've heard of him. He practices in Rockland with that firm."

"I can read," snapped Julia, whose job as door guard was beginning to take its toll. She snatched the paper and read in a low voice. "Dear Sam. To go straight to the point, Margaret and I find ourselves in a rather distressing predicament. What we need is advice, but it's awkward at this distance, and for all we know, our situation may be affected by some unsympathetic British laws, or rules that might make us decide to go home sooner than we planned. Anyway, Sam, we both wonder..."

Julia rolled the paper back into its original crumple and returned the paper to the wastebasket. "I think that supports my IRS theory."

But Sarah had tilted her head. "Someone's coming." She pushed Julia into the hall, turned and closed the door. "There's a lavatory next door. Duck in there."

Facing Sarah across the toilet bowl, the air humid and thick with a floral deodorant, Julia looked pleased. "I'm right. Margaret and Edith have gotten themselves into some financial mud." Then, listening, "Whoever it was has gone by."

Sarah looked at her watch. "We've run out of time. Skip the Ouellettes. They're safe." She opened the lavatory door and listened. "Okay, go on back to your room, Aunt Julia. I've got to go to the toilet. This is all too much for my bladder. I'll meet you in your room."

But she didn't.

Returning from the lavatory, she turned at the bend of the hall and fumbled in her skirt pocket for her own room key. And remembered she'd left her door slightly ajar in case she and Julia needed instant refuge. She withdrew her hand and shook her head at her forgetfulness.

And as she did, an alien arm bent around her neck, her head was violently jerked back, the arm clamped around her throat in a crushing chokehold. And the pressure against her throat increased so relentlessly that Sarah had no chance to duck her chin down to protect against the throttling grip. And no chance to swivel about and see her attacker. No chance to do anything but give a strangled gasp for breath and flay her arms about in a desperate effort at self-defense.

And with the first wild circle of Sarah's right arm the attacker increased the throat hold and with the other hand delivered a sharp chop to Sarah's elbow, and then cranked Sarah's left arm behind her back and gave it a sharp upward thrust.

Streaks of pain radiated from Sarah's shoulder to her pinioned arm and simultaneously knifed through her stricken elbow. She opened her mouth to scream, but could only give out with a strangled gurgle.

And then a knee thrust itself into her back and she was propelled forward, down the hall, pushed into a room—her own room she saw, her tilted head taking in blurred details of curtains and pictures. Then she was kneed to the edge of her own bed, twisted about, heard a rustling of the bedcovers, the stranglehold eased for a second, and a pillowcase was yanked over her head, and the arm tightened again about her throat.

"On the floor," said a low, hoarse voice. And with the command came a kick at the back of Sarah's knees and she toppled to the floor, her head in its bag striking first.

Her attacker released the neck hold and at the same time Sarah's right arm was again cranked around to her back and given another upward excruciating shove.

And then the hoarse voice. "What in hell do you think you're doing sticking your nose where it doesn't belong. Listen to me. Cut it out. You and that old aunt of yours." And one hand took hold of the pillowcase over Sarah's head, raised it, and then slammed it back on the floor.

"Got that? You understand?" said the voice. "Will you kindly lay the fuck off? Don't ever try going into other people's rooms again. Forget this spy business or I will blow the whistle for every fucking policeman in Britain to haul you and Julia Clancy in for breaking and entering. There are laws in this country." Here Sarah's head was lifted and given another bounce off the floor.

"So," repeated the voice, "you understand? Say it."

"I understand," Sarah managed in a strangled voice through the pillowcase cloth.

"And listen. We'll have a deal. I won't report you pulling a room search—and God help you if anything's missing. And you won't mention that I was a little rough on you, which I had every goddamn right to be. I'll be generous and pretend like the whole thing never happened. So don't move. Don't lift your head. Don't open your eyes. Don't even breathe. Stay here and count to one thousand. And then you're on your own. Understand? Answer me, you understand?"

"Okay," mumbled Sarah into the pillowcase.

"I'm watching you so stay put. When you finish counting you can go and give Julia Clancy my message. If she steps out of line, if you do, you will be in very deep shit. The kind of shit you don't get out of. Okay? Okay? Say it, okay?"

"Okay," choked Sarah.

"Better be," said the voice, and the grip on her arm released, soft footsteps retreated, and a door was slammed shut.

Chapter Seventeen

SARAH—AS INSTRUCTED—LAY PRONE, NOT moving. Her eyes closed. Her body stiff, her nose pressed into the pillowcase. But she was not counting to a thousand; her brain was otherwise occupied, whirring around, a maelstrom of rage, indignation, and self-accusation.

Shit, shit, shit, she said to herself. Sarah, you goddamn fool. Then, as the pain receded and the tension eased, she moved her head to one side. Something wet slipped down her chin and she stuck out her tongue and tasted salt. Her nose was bleeding. Her lip, too. A tooth must have cut right into it. And her head felt hollow with a sort of buzzing going on inside. Of course—her head had been slammed into the carpet. Was that how boxers felt when they'd been decked by a good left jab?

Well, what did she expect? To feel good? Happy and satisfied after a rewarding evening of sneaking into other people's rooms? Cautiously her tongue explored her swollen and bloody lip and then she took a deep and unhappy breath, and unbidden into her mind came her father's voice saying a hundred years ago about some childish scrape she'd gotten into: "You can't make an omelet without breaking eggs."

So she'd broken a whole carton of eggs. A baker's dozen at least. Oh, stupid, stupid, stupid.

Because just look at this not so brilliant idea. She and Julia hadn't even discussed the possibility of failure; they had just gone for it, never considering that the chances were very good that someone from their corridor would come up from dinner. Someone who needed a Tylenol, a sweater, an emergency visit to the toilet. A fix. Whatever. Or a someone who hadn't bought Julia's fainting act. And there they were, Sarah and Julia, ripe for the finding, two dumb females dipping in and out of bedrooms.

She pulled off the now blood-smeared pillowcase, lifted her head like a turtle emerging from its shell, then stopped and lowered it, aware that if someone was really watching from the door, she was breaking the agreement.

What agreement? Hell, she hadn't agreed to anything. She'd been slammed down on the floor and told to say okay. It was extortion or blackmail or felonious assault. At least.

But there was the other side of coin: being caught breaking and entering. How would her fellow tourists feel about that? Margaret and Edith Hopper, those two polite, gently nurtured elderly ladies? Shock and horror would be the least of it. Carter and Portia? She could almost hear Carter if he'd caught her looking through his bureau drawers. The others? No one would feel forgiving. She and Julia would be damn lucky if they were not turned over to that Inspector Daniel Defoe and shipped home.

Shit. A hundred times shit.

For a few moments she lay there on the floor feeling sick and violated, aware that her nosebleed had made the lower half of her face sticky with blood. And that the buzzing in her head had settled down into the heavy bang, bang of a major headache.

Then, cautiously, she rolled over and sat up.

Safe in her own bedroom. The bedroom with the door she herself had left so conveniently open. A smart move bringing her here because if she'd been hauled off to some other room the identity of her escort would have been blown. No, her own room was the perfect place to make sure she got the message about future behavior.

Sarah pushed herself into a sitting position, her head, feeling like an overripe squash, pulsing and thumping while the walls of the room wavered and lurched.

She squinted and then slowly, holding her head steady, looked around. She was alone. The room looked its usual cozy chintzy inviting self, her afternoon jeans and shirt hung over a chair, her copy of *Cranford* on the bedside table. But where was Aunt Julia? Her trusted co-enterer and breaker? Why wasn't she here hanging over her beloved niece with wet sponges and towels?

Or had she been nailed, too? And Julia—no matter how tough an item—was still a seventy-year-old woman and might not be able to recover easily from having her head bounced off the floor.

Sarah rose shakily to her feet, reached for the back of a chair to steady herself, and walked to the bedroom door, pushed it closed. And snapped the lock. So much for visitors. The last thing she—and Julia—needed was someone like Amy Lermatov skipping into the room all bright-eyed and filled with homicidal interest.

Next she walked, more steadily, and confronted the door connecting to Julia's. Knocked. Waited. No answer. Knocked again. No answer.

Hell. A wave of dizziness hit her and for a moment she hung onto the doorknob. Then a new and terrible fear. Aunt Julia assaulted, floored, helpless. Bones cracked or broken. Perhaps unconscious. Or worse. Oh, the poor old thing.

At that very moment, when Sarah's sympathy had reared up a mental picture of Julia trussed, bloodied, maybe dying or already deceased, the "poor old thing" was snuggled into her eiderdown, taking a short snooze after the rigors of garden visiting and room searching. Julia always slept soundly. In fact, her family and neighbors always said that once asleep the only thing that could wake her was the restlessness of a sick horse, the sound of a mare going down in the straw ready to foal, the neigh and snort of an aroused stallion. Not the mere noise of a disturbed human.

After ducking back into her room, Julia, not daring to reenter the hall, had paced her floor waiting for Sarah's return. Then excitement subsiding and fatigue getting the better of impatience, she had pushed aside the counterpane of her bed, pulled up the eiderdown in its flowered duvet cover, and, telling herself that it was just for five minutes, had drifted off. She was just floating into a dream of sunny pastures when a harsh whisper close to her ear broke the spell.

"Aunt Julia. Aunt Julia, are you all right?"

Here the comforter was tweaked back and Julia opened her eyes, frowned, and then sat up. She blinked, then focused on Sarah's still-bloodied face and swollen lip. "Sarah! Oh my God!"

"Oh my God is right," said Sarah. "I'm okay, but how about you? Are you all right?"

"I'm fine but you're not. You look horrible."

"It's been a tough fifteen minutes. Or ten minutes. I've no idea how long the whole thing lasted. It seemed like hours."

"What are you talking about," demanded Julia. "And your poor face! You didn't fall down stairs, did you?"

"I wish I had," said Sarah with feeling. "It would have been easier. Listen, and if you feel up to it, please make some tea. We're both going to need it. With a slug of your travel whiskey. Thank heavens for electric kettles in every room. I'll wash up and examine the damage and then I'll tell you what's going on—or what went on."

"But," Julia fumbled, "your face. You need a doctor. Let me call down to the office."

"No call, no doctor. In fact, don't answer the telephone or let anyone in the door. Not until I explain. Tea and then maybe we can order sandwiches from the grille room. After all, we've missed dinner. But right now I need soap, water, and a serious dose of whatever pills you have for bad heads."

Settled ten minutes later, Julia arranged herself on the edge of her bed, and Sarah sank into the armchair. She had changed her bloodied shirt, brushed her hair, and washed her face—a face disfigured by a swollen nose and an enlarged lip. Each woman clutched a cup of Typhoo tea laced with Julia's whiskey.

Sarah took a deep breath, fixed her eyes on a framed colored print featuring a woman in a straw bonnet, two children clinging to her long gingham skirts. She was welcoming a man in a smock and gaiters holding a crook and followed by a collie. The little woman had probably just taken a cottage loaf from the oven, while a mug of home brew and a Cotswold pie stood ready on their rough-hewn table. Later, after supper, little Fanny and Theobald would recite the Twenty-third Psalm to dear Papa. The simple life, Sarah told herself; we should all try it.

"For the Lord's sake," exclaimed Julia. "Don't just stand there staring. Get on with it."

Sarah dragged herself back to the world of breaking and entering. "It's like this," she began and took Julia step by step by grab and grasp and shove through the events of the last hour.

"So you see," said Sarah, finishing her tale and her second cup of tea-cum-whiskey at the same time, "you see, we've just been caught red-handed and we can't do a thing about it."

Julia nodded slowly, "All right. You can't complain about being mugged. I see that. But now we know, don't we?"

"That we've got Ellen's murderer along on the tour? I was sure before being mugged. The trouble is I'm not one hundred percent certain the person who attacked me is connected to the murder. Say he or she found us sneaking in and out of bedrooms and lost it. Blew up. What the hell do Sarah and Julia think they're doing. Well, I'll show them they can't get away with that kind of stuff. Nothing about Ellen—her being killed—was even hinted at when I was on the floor."

"But still..."

"Okay, the attack probably was connected, but that's just my gut feeling. But who in hell was it? No accent, but then no one on this trip is from the south or west or a Brit except for Henry. All from New England and they use everyday northeast American diction. Except whoever it was sounded like a tough—or someone trying to sound tough."

"Male or female?"

"I couldn't tell. A hoarse voice, the kind anyone can fake. But I was grabbed so fast—I couldn't turn with my head in that strangulation hold—and then shoved into my room and slammed into the floor. With all that going on I wasn't exactly concentrating on identifying the voice. Just on the message."

"To lay off snooping and keep your mouth shut."

"Right."

"How about the strength factor? I don't see Edith and Margaret strong-arming you."

"No," said Sarah thoughtfully, "but most of the others could handle it. The attack depended on surprise, getting that arm around my throat. Even Amy could probably beat me in arm wrestling."

Julia rose from her perch on the end of the bed. "Listen. You stay put and I'll go down and collect some sandwiches."

"You're supposed to be feeling faint."

"But now I'm better. And you're...well, you're tired out. And while I'm down I'll see if I can find out who didn't stay through dinner."

"I should have thought of that," said Sarah. "Of course, anyone who slithered away during dinner is the snake who grabbed me."

"Snakes don't grab, they wrap. Or strike," said Julia who was always factual about animals. "Besides," she added, "it may not have been a snake."

"An honest person acting from righteous anger," said Sarah. "Okay, we're the villains. But, Aunt Julia, take it easy. Don't go stomping into the dining room and ask for a head count."

"Trust me," said Julia. "An *eminence grise, c'est moi.*"

But, as it proved, there was no need for Julia to put on her diplomatic robes. A soft double knock sounded at the door, and Julia opened it a bare two inches. Then wider.

Doris Lermatov. Followed by Amy.

They had come to check on Julia. Faintness, claimed Doris, as they both stepped into the room, shouldn't be neglected. She, Doris, had been worried.

Then they saw Sarah. Sarah's nose. Sarah's lip.

"Wow!" said Amy. "What hit you?" Amy pushed her electric red hair out of her eyes and peered at Sarah.

"She slipped," said Julia quickly. "Hit the end of the bed."

"But," objected Amy, "the beds don't have bedposts on the beds. Only a headboard."

"The edge," said Julia. "The bed frame. A nasty fall."

"I'm all right, really," said Sarah, taking charge. "A nosebleed and I cut my lip. And Aunt Julia's feeling much better."

"Just fine. A tiny faint spell. I'm quite used to them. It's nothing. Absolutely nothing, But," said Julia, eyeing the open door, "but thank you so much for coming."

But Doris had settled on a straight-backed chair by the bed. "We would have come earlier, but it's been wild. Absolutely wild. We missed dessert completely."

"Mother's favorite," said Amy. "The sweet trolley. Went completely off the rail."

"It isn't on a rail," corrected Doris. "They just call it a trolley. But Amy's right. I think it got loose somehow. It was being wheeled over to that Japanese party, and I was turning around because the trolley went right by our table, and I was absolutely torn between the chocolate torte and the trifle, which is out of this world because I had it last night..."

"Mo-ther," said Amy.

"Yes. Well, the trolley was going by and then the waitress pushing it tripped—or at least I guess she tripped. Anyway, she fell into the trolley and it tipped over and the wheels must have caught on an extension cord from the sideboard because the lights went out in that part of the dining room. You know these old inns are absolute firetraps. They're probably hung together by extension cords."

"Mother," said Amy again.

"Well, the waitress is on the floor and there's chocolate torte and trifle and pudding and everything all over the place—the sponge cake—it has a lemon frosting, absolutely wonderful—ended up in Edith Hopper's lap—and then the lights went out. In the whole dining room. A short or something."

"And," giggled Amy, "one of those big German women began shouting about lights—at least I think that's what she said. '*Lichte*,' which must mean light."

"Then," said Doris, "the manager, Mr. Gage, came in with a flashlight..."

"They call it a 'torch' in England," put in Amy.

"Don't interrupt. With a flashlight and began poking around by the outlet in the wall, and then Edith Hopper stood up because she was all sticky with sponge cake, and she tripped over the sweet trolley, which was still on its side—you know Edith and Margaret have those thick glasses and neither can see very well and it was dark. Anyway, Margaret went to help her, and stepped into something—I think it was the bowl of trifle—and began crying. It was just like a Marx Brothers movie, only a lot worse."

"Or the Three Stooges," said Amy. "I couldn't stop laughing."

"Very funny," said Julia in a repressed voice.

"How long," asked Sarah, "did this whole scene go on?"

Doris smiled. "Who knows. It was a complete circus. It seemed like forever because the waiters and then the chef—

well, someone in a white jacket and a hat showed up and began trying to help."

"You see," said Amy, "like first there's this trolley mess and the two Hoppers trying help each other out of the dining room and people with flashlights or torches are trying to replug everything in and no one can really see what they're doing. I'm going to use the scene in my mystery because while everyone's falling over everything, I can have someone stabbed with a carving knife."

"Stop it, Amy," said her mother.

Sarah, in desperation, tried once more. "When the lights came on, did you see who was still in the dining room?"

Doris shook her head. "I don't really know. As soon as we saw that it was going to take a while to get the place cleaned up we left. Amy and I did, anyway. And the Hoppers left before we did. We went to the parlor and looked at magazines. Perhaps the others just went to the bar. You'd have to ask. Does it matter?"

"No," said Sarah hastily. "I just wondered."

"No you didn't," said Amy. "I'll bet you're on to something. Because that was such a neat scene for something to happen in. You didn't go and push the waitress with the trolley and turn the lights off yourself, did you?" Amy's voice was hopeful.

"No," said Sarah rather too loudly. "We were upstairs."

"I was having my little lie-down," said Julia. "Because of feeling faint. Sarah was so helpful."

"That," said Sarah, when the door had closed behind the two Lermatovs, "is that. Groucho and Harpo and Zeppo downstairs, Julia and Sarah upstairs. Not much difference."

"Window of opportunity, you think?" said Julia.

"Who knows. Scenes like that do happen."

"Or can be made to happen. If need be."

Sarah made a face. "I'm afraid so. Well, is the whole evening a total loss? What did we find out? If anything."

"No sunglasses anywhere," said Julia.

"Barbara uses Crane writing paper, Stacy has an expensive camera, Justin has a cheaper one and buys his mother and sister presents."

"Sandi Ouellette has a camera," added Julia. "And Carter McClure has binoculars. And a camera? I can't remember."

"All these people seem to be trusting that no one breaks in and steals their things. But, after Barbara's and my room were ransacked, you'd think they'd be more careful."

"That day those two doors were unlocked. Tonight every door was locked tight."

"And look how easy it is to find a key," Sarah reminded her.

"Not everyone has my skill in obtaining keys," said Julia.

Chapter Eightteen

SARAH AND JULIA SPENT the remainder of that Wednesday evening enduring a number of condolence calls. Tentative knocks at the door, anxious faces peering in. How *are* you, Julia? No, don't get up. You're doing too much. You know, Julia, at our age we must learn to take it easy. (This from Margaret Hopper.) When did you have your blood pressure checked? (from Portia). You really look like death (from Fred Ouellette, who found this coming out of his mouth before he could check it).

And for Sarah, exclamations over her damaged nose and swollen lip. Oh my goodness, look at you. You stumbled? Well, it's the floors in these old inns. So uneven. I watch *every* step. Have you tried ice/aspirin/a heating pad/called the doctor?

Julia and Sarah, each in her own way dealt with the visitors, some bearing welcome sandwiches, fruit, digestive biscuits, or in one case Pepto-Bismol and a bottle of mineral water. Together both women found the easiest way to divert attention from Julia's faintness (and recovery from) and Sarah's damaged face was to direct the conversation to another retelling of the absolutely hilarious sweet trolley incident and the amazing similarity of the scene to cinema comedy of the thirties.

This ploy was successful and Fred Ouellette claimed he had been convulsed and completely lost it groping about in the dark and ending up almost in the lap of an indignant German fraulein. The whole scene had reminded him of a funeral in which one of the pallbearers had been overcome by a fit of coughing—"a chain smoker," said Fred in a disapproving voice—and lost his grip on the coffin, lurched forward, upset the next pallbearer, and the coffin had slipped to the ground, slid down the snow-covered walkway of the Proffit Point Methodist Church. "Right out into the road," said Fred, chuckling at the memory. "Lucky for us a car wasn't coming."

"Hahaha," said Julia, giving Fred a dark look.

"Oh well," said Fred in an apologetic voice, "at the time it seemed hilarious. Even the family laughed and, after all, it was great-grandfather's funeral. He was ninety-two and a real tyrant."

"Tomorrow," said Sarah to Julia when the last comforter had departed, "we shall be clear of the lot of them. At least for a day. Our own car, right? Colleges and bookstores. Gives us time to sort things out. What to do."

Julia nodded her agreement, adding that indeed it had been a day from hell but tomorrow was another day.

"I've heard that one before," said Sarah glumly. "Okay lock all doors and take a sharp instrument to bed with you."

"I knew I should have brought my hunting crop," said Julia as she closed her bedroom door.

Breakfast, the Thursday morning of June the fifteenth, was a hasty affair. The sun was shining, a mild breeze had risen, the highway beckoned, and it was goodbye to the Shearing Inn. Luggage piled up in the tiny front hall, tips were disputed and translated from dollars to pounds, and Barbara Baxter and Henry Ruggles joined forces in harrying the Garden Club members into the bus. The length of the Cambridge visit had been resolved in Barbara's favor, and Henry was left urging everyone to "At LEAST make the best of the Botanic Garden." Sarah, however, had made it clear that she and her aunt might not be seeing the rest until they met that evening at an establishment called Hotel Fatima—a hostelry Barbara had described in the tour itinerary as being in the "heart of Cambridge."

"I suppose," said Sarah as she and Julia climbed into their Ford Escort, "it wouldn't hurt to drop in on the Cambridge Botanic Garden at some point in the day."

"From horticultural or investigative interest," asked Julia.

"Both," said Sarah. "I'm not letting some thug dictate my day."

"We could give it an hour of our time," said Julia. She refolded the driving map and smoothed the center section. "Head northwest on the A424 and pick up the A44 after Stow-in-the-Wold."

"North? Let me guess. We're going to Yorkshire and visit the Brontës. Or a side trip into Wales."

"Sunglasses. The ones Portia said she dropped. We can go back to Kiftsgate and ask. They probably have a Lost-and-Found."

"Good idea," said Sarah, "I'd like to know whether they've been picked up on some path or if they were deliberately dumped in some trash bin."

"You read my mind," said Julia.

Sarah's second guess proved correct. Fortunately, the rubbish of the day before had been bundled but not yet hauled away, and she and Julia were graciously permitted a tour through four large bags of tourist detritus. Reward in the shape of a familiar pair of sunglasses came at the top of bag three. But the glasses—although identifiable—were broken as to lens and bent as to eyepiece.

"They've been wrecked," said Sarah, holding them up and removing a clinging piece of banana peel.

"Someone stomped on the glass..."

"More than that. They're all twisted."

"Which means?"

"Which means that the glasses were wrecked past the point of anyone wanting to put them in a Lost-and-Found."

"Oh, dear me," said a voice. A stout National Trust woman wrapped in a coverall frowned at the glasses in Sarah's hand. "You'll not be wanting to keep those. They're no use at all. Even the frames. And quite filthy." She reached out a hand to relieve Sarah of the distasteful objects.

Sarah retracted her hand. "Sentimental value," she told the woman. "They were my mother's." And she and Julia beat a retreat, Sarah holding the glasses between thumb and forefinger.

"My sainted mother," said Sarah, when they had regained the safety of their car. "Mother set great store by these glasses." She turned the ignition, shoved the car in gear, and shot out into the access road. She turned to Julia. "I'm going to stick the blessed things in an envelope and leave them at the High Roosting police station with a note asking that they be forwarded to the Maine State Police. Care of George Fitts."

"Just like that. If you hand in an unmarked envelope they'll think the package is a bomb and you'll be held as a terrorist."

"Not at all," said Sarah. "I'll mix in with a group of people, walk by the station, pretend I'm admiring the building, climb the stairs, go down, and walk quietly away. The police can test it for explosives and when they do they'll find a pair of broken sunglasses. Then they'll call the U.S. police."

It fell out as Sarah planned. After purchasing a padded mailer and inking "Maine State Police CID: Sergeant George Fitts, Thomaston, Maine, USA," across its front, she parked two blocks from the station, strolled in a leisurely manner behind a family of the ever-present Japanese tourists, climbed the concrete steps leading to the station's front entrance, let the package slide to the ground, and made it back to the car in under ten minutes.

"Hit the road," said Julia as Sarah scrambled into the driver's seat. "This life of espionage is hard on my nerves."

"Not espionage," corrected Sarah. "Simple good citizenship. Now where's Cambridge?"

"The A43 north, then a choice. Scenic or dual-carriageway?"

"Scenic. Gives us time to think."

"Then head for Bedford and east on the A45. Find a place for lunch along the way."

"I told Alex I'd call him today, so I'll have him alert George about the sunglasses. And maybe there's news about the scarf. If the scarf is bloody, perhaps the glasses are messed up. Little blood cells in the hinges."

But the scarf was clean. Alex, tracked down in the hospital gave the news. "No blood—not yet anyway. Just dye that runs. But here's an update. The dibble was washed in a liquid soap commonly used in gas station restrooms. This particular soap matches that in an Irving station just south of Portland and in an Exxon station near Westbrook, and Westbrook is, as you know, just outside of Portland."

"Both near the Portland airport?"

"Near enough. And one of the Irving station attendants thinks he remembers someone in a scarf who acted like she was in a hurry. Dropped the restroom key. Then used the ladies' room. Wore a scarf. Slacks or dark trousers. Also wore a plastic sort of raincoat. Dark red slicker."

"*She*, you said!"

"Or he. Don't jump to conclusions. Slickers can be worn by both sexes. And a scarf makes a good disguise."

"Was she—or he—wearing glasses?"

"As a matter of fact, yes. The attendant thought the person looked like Jackie Kennedy Onassis—you know, the scarf and glasses look. Only a little heavier set. But get this. The Jackie look-alike drove off with the restroom key. Taking the key made the person stick in his mind."

"That's a real lead then."

"Could be. But two Exxon attendants at the other station each say they think they remember several people in head scarves and dark glasses, all with several kids in tow. But no one can remember exactly when."

"Great. Terrific," said Sarah in a tired voice.

"You sound a little ragged. Is Julia getting on your nerves?"

"I think," said Sarah regretfully, "that I'm getting on my own nerves. I want to do something about Ellen and at last count I was sure that at least four of our fellow garden lovers was pretty guilty. Guilty of something, anyway."

"If you feel there's any chance of trouble, I hope you and Julia will get the hell out…"

Sarah broke in. "No. It's okay. We'll take precautions. And stay out of trouble." She crossed two sets of fingers and forcing her voice to sound light and carefree, she added, "A few more days and we'll meet you in Italy and hit the pasta. Tonight we'll be at the Hotel Fatima somewhere in Cambridge. Then down to Sissinghurst, and over to France."

"I know when the subject's being changed. You haven't gone sneaking around where you shouldn't have?"

"What," said Sarah, "makes you ask such a stupid question? Listen, I've got to go. Lunchtime. The Barnacle Goose Inn. Ploughman's lunch ordered and a pint of the best. Not to worry." And Sarah replaced the receiver.

"I'm living a life of total deceit," she announced to Julia as she sat down at their table. They sat on a small brick-paved side terrace under a red and green striped umbrella which offered a fine view of a solicitor's office across the street. "Anyway, that scarf may be a bust because so far the lab hasn't picked up any blood, only dye."

Julia nodded. "Wait and see. Now, let's park somewhere in the center of Cambridge and do the sight-seeing thing. The others will be busy doing the Botanic Garden—Henry said it covers almost forty acres."

"So," Sarah concluded, "all we have to do is avoid the garden until almost closing time. That way we can relax and not have to keep looking over our shoulders to make sure we won't be jumped."

Not for the first time had the two miscalculated. The members of the Garden Club Sarah and Julia had pictured treading the paths of the Botanic Garden turned up instead at every street corner, gazing at the colleges, infesting shops, lingering by the Cam, or in single numbers, in pairs, or in clumps, wandering uncertainly down Drummer Street, pausing on St. John's Street, reversing on Hobson Street, halting on Market Street.

Sandi Ouellette they discovered issuing from a stationer's shop holding a cloth-covered journal. She looked hot, her red cotton skirt was rumpled, and her fair hair tangled.

"I'm so mixed up," exclaimed Sandi. "I've lost Fred and I've been spinning around in circles. I tried to go into some of the colleges, King's and Trinity and Gaius, and some others. I can't remember all their names. But I couldn't. Get in, I mean. Something's going on. Like maybe it's graduation or the end of exams and everyone's going to have some sort of ceremony. Anyway, you can't get into any of the colleges or the gardens. Or the chapels. Barriers all over the place. And besides half the town—the students I mean—are drunk as skunks." Sandi added this last piece of information with some resentment. Drunken undergraduates not being part of her picture of Cambridge.

Sarah made sympathetic noises. She and Julia had both realized long before they had trudged over the Magdalene Bridge that sight-seeing would have to take a back seat to University goings on.

"You could look around," said Julia. "The architecture is interesting and there's a twelfth-century round church and…"

But Sandi brushed architecture aside. "I wanted to get inside the colleges and the chapels," she insisted. "Get the feel."

During the short pause when Sandi stopped for breath, Julia said in a dismissive voice, "We'll be seeing you at dinner, Sandi. Don't give up on Cambridge. How about a graveyard? Graveyards in old cities are very informative."

But Sandi—who was quite possibly feeling a little lonely in her wanderings about town—wasn't ready to give up on familiar company. She held up her journal. "I'm keeping a record," she said. "For a book. I'm going to write a guide for dingbats like me. Like those computer-for-dummies books. But this will be for traveling dummies. No culture hints, just vocabulary and how not to alienate everyone in sight. You know how I said I got in trouble saying 'bum'? Well, there's 'bugger you' and 'sod you,' which aren't nice things to say. And 'pecker.' Did you know that the people actually go around saying 'keep your pecker up?' Try that in the States and you'll get your bum pinched or worse."

"How about the Botanic Garden, Sandi?" suggested Sarah. "Isn't everyone supposed to be there?"

Sandi shrugged. "Well, I've seen everyone all over town—taking pictures, going into shops. Like it's almost as if they're escaping gardens. Maybe it's burnout. I think only Henry Ruggles and Portia and Carter went right there, but if I have the strength I'll hike over later. I have a map."

"Good idea," said Julia firmly. "You can take a bus. Trumpington Road goes right past the garden. Come on, Sarah, we don't want to be late." And Julia plucked Sarah's shirt and propelled her into forward motion.

"That," said Sarah when they had left Sandi standing some hundred yards to the rear, "was a bit brutal. I think Sandi wanted to hang around."

"She's a grown woman. She can handle being on her own. But you know what I was thinking. It's Fred. I know you say he's cleared but he has one advantage that none of the rest do."

"Which is?"

"A perfect knowledge of anatomy. Where to strike a sharp tool so that it would kill. Maybe you could check back with Alex and see if Fred got loose for just an hour or so on June sixth."

This idea created a heavy silence and the two women strode along without much caring in which direction they went, and it wasn't until they found themselves facing Queens College on the far side of the Cam that Sarah grabbed Julia's elbow and brought her to a halt.

"I think I see another buddy. Or two buddies. Margaret and Edith. Over there. Sitting on the bench. Shall we…"

"No," interrupted Julia, "Leave them be. They've probably been hiking all over town and need a rest."

Sarah studied the two sisters for a moment, saw Edith twist around, looking to the left, then the right, and then almost completely about, and meeting Sarah's eyes, gave a visible jump. Then she swiveled back front and center and nudged Margaret.

And Julia watching, nudged Sarah at almost exactly the same moment. "Edith is acting as if she's meeting an illegal bookmaker."

"Shhh," said Sarah. "They'll hear you. And they know we're here. We can't ignore them. Come on." And she walked over to where Edith and Margaret Hopper sat upright on their bench, facing toward the river, exactly, Sarah thought, like a couple of elderly dolls that someone has forgotten to wind up.

Confronted by Julia and Sarah, both sisters gave an entirely unconvincing start.

"Goodness," exclaimed Edith. "Where did you two come from?"

"My," said Margaret. "It's Julia and Sarah. I thought everyone would be going over to the Botanic Garden."

"We thought so, too," said Sarah. "But they aren't."

Edith regrouping, shook her head. "But the whole purpose of the visit was to see the Botanic Garden. Henry said it has a great many specimen trees and shrubs."

"Then," said Julia, "why aren't you there?"

Margaret and Edith spoke at the same time and what came out was jumble about too much walking, fatigue, the excitement of visiting Cambridge, the need to rest on the bench by the Cam and watch the people go by, coupled with the desire to take pictures of the colleges, the churches, the bridges, the river. The whole, in Sarah's opinion, sounding packaged and very poorly rehearsed.

Margaret, as if to emphasize their photographic interest, held up a black compact camera.

"It's an Olympus. With a zoom lens," said Margaret, turning the object over in her hand. "I've never had a zoom lens."

"We hadn't brought our cameras," said Edith. "Because they're only ancient Kodaks. But then we thought we should take some pictures—a sort of record of our trip. And Barbara—she knows a great deal about cameras—helped pick these out. Such a useful size and so easy to use. Mine is a Nikon." And Edith lifted up a black strap that circled her neck and exhibited her camera. "We thought we'd take pictures of the general scene," she added, waving an indecisive hand at the path in front of the bench.

"You won't get any decent pictures here," said Julia. "Much too shady, all these trees. What you need to do," she added, who never took pictures and did not own a camera, "is find an interesting angle with a good light. Any of the colleges or along the river. The punts taken from a bridge would make a good shot." Here she paused seeing no reaction from the two sisters.

"I think," said Edith, fumbling with her camera case, "that this is quite a nice spot and Barbara said the lens would adjust for lack of light."

"Yes," said Margaret. "This is a good place to start. All the children in their school uniforms. So English." She pointed at three small girls in cotton frocks and straw hats who were just then tearing toward a footbridge.

"Here," said Sarah with sudden inspiration. "Give me your cameras. I'll take a picture of you both. Sitting on the bench together in Cambridge. For your family."

"No," said Edith and Margaret in a single voice. And, in an almost single action they clutched their cameras to their respective bosoms and shrank away from Sarah's outstretched hand.

Sarah, surprised, a little affronted, dropped her hand. "Sorry. I thought it was a nice idea."

"Oh it was," cried Edith, recovering. "But we, well we hate having our picture taken. Just what we told Amy. All the wrinkles. I know we're being vain, but we're just two old biddies."

And Sarah and Julia beat a retreat.

"Well," exploded Julia when they were out of ear shot, "what in God's name is going on with those two? They're acting as if they're in an Alfred Hitchcock movie."

"Or have bombs in their cameras," said Sarah. "But it is just possible that they hate having their pictures taken. I know my mother makes a great fuss and talks about looking awful."

"All right," said Julia. "I feel the same way. But this sudden interest in taking pictures under trees of passing schoolchildren. I say, Pooh."

Sarah grinned. "Strong language, Auntie. Do you think we should crouch behind a bush and see if Margaret and Edith are part of a drug drop."

"No," said Julia crossly. "Something's out of kilter, but I don't picture either of the Hoppers with a dibble, and besides you told me Alex said they were cleared for the time of Ellen's death. If they're involved with something funny, I think it's a whole different ballgame. Something to do with that nervous breakdown. Or a so-called nervous breakdown. Or," Julia added, "do you think one of those dear ladies caught us snooping and mugged you last night?"

Sarah shook her head. "Remember we ruled them out. Even both working together I don't think they could have managed it. And, besides, I was only mugged by one person. Margaret and Edith may be a little on the sly side but as lady wrestlers, well, forget it."

Julia looked at her watch. "Past three-thirty. Let's hike back and pick up our car. I think the only place we won't find any of our friends will be the Botanic Garden."

Chapter Nineteen

THE RETURN WALK TO their car brought Sarah and Julia sightings of more defectors. Stacy Daniel was espied by the door of the Cambridge University Press, looking particularly lovely in a lemon-colored safari jacket, her figure nicely set off by the white walls of the building. And like Margaret and Edith, she, too, seemed to have been bitten by the photographic bug. Stacy held her large camera to her nose and was aiming it at a confused street scene of automobiles, pedestrians, and bicycles.

Sarah suddenly found this interest in preserving the passing scene contagious. Her own camera was locked in Julia's car, and up to now she had not taken a single picture—her mind being weighted with other things. Well, why not? It might be good to have some memento of the visit; everything mustn't give way to murder and intimidation.

"Let's ask Stacy where to buy film," she suggested to Julia, as they waited for a gap in traffic to let them cross the street.

"I can't stand the woman," said Julia. "Hollow, no center to her at all. Forget Stacy, you can get film at Boots. There's a Boots somewhere along the way. I feel a little, what's the word Bertie Wooster uses, 'peckish.' Well, I feel a little peckish. All this walking. We can pick up a snack and film at Boots. They have everything."

"Boots?" said Sarah puzzled.

"You know. Big shopping chain. They're all over Britain and have everything from aspirin to shopping bags to sandwiches."

The word "snack" had had its effect, so after a brief consultation with a passerby, the two women found themselves at the entrance to Boots. And found Amy Lermatov kneeling at the entrance, camera in hand.

"Amy," exclaimed Sarah. "What are you doing?"

"It's the angle," said Amy, twisting around and looking up at Sarah with no particular surprise at seeing a familiar face. "I'm going to have a chase through Cambridge and I need different angles. Not just the stupid pictures of the colleges."

"What chase," demanded Julia. "Have we missed something?"

"My chase," explained Amy. She stood up and slid the cover back on her lens. "I thought Cambridge was going to be a total bore, mother dragging me through the colleges and going on about tradition and the classics and tutors. But we lucked out. Everything's roped off so we've just been walking around and I've been figuring out a chase scene. My murderer will be dodging some people in his group..."

"Your murderer is a man?" asked Sarah.

"Or a woman. I haven't decided. Anyway, I'll have him try to escape through the crowds and jump into one of those punts in the river and the detective will jump into another punt and it will make a terrific scene because of all the students in punts and rowboats. I don't know whether or not I'll have anyone drowned or not. Maybe just get pushed in like Henry."

"You don't know that Mr. Ruggles was pushed in," said Julia in her frostiest voice. She had never cared for the way the young referred to their elders by a first name.

"It doesn't matter," said Amy, unabashed by correction. "I'm doing fiction and I need local color. Are you going in this place? Mother's in there getting a snack for both of us because they have a million sandwiches. Weird stuff like scampi and scallions and watercress and mushrooms."

"I'd like a weird sandwich," said Sarah, and she and Julia advanced on the front door as Amy sank to her knees and pointed her camera at several arriving customers.

Doris Lermatov was indeed discovered puzzling over the sandwich collection arrayed in a stretch of glass-fronted cases.

"Think of it," she said. "Such a choice. Not just BLT and egg salad and tuna fish." She reached in and selected a roast beef and chutney number and then added a scampi and cucumber. Pleased, she smiled at the two women. "Did you see Amy out there? She's back on her fiction kick."

"You haven't been to the Botanic Garden?" asked Sarah. This appeared to be the single interesting question of the day. The important horticultural detour promoted by Barbara Baxter had turned into just another tourist visit.

Doris shifted her collection of sandwiches to the market basket at her feet and ran a hand through her hair—her ash brown hair looking like churned up waves on a windy day. "I know," she said. "It's funny. Everyone thought it was a great idea when Barbara first talked it up—even Henry Ruggles didn't fight it too hard—it was spending the whole day he didn't like. But when the bus pulled up at the entrance only Henry and the McClures got out. The rest all said they wanted to see something of Cambridge first."

"Like Aunt Julia and me," said Sarah.

Doris nodded. "You see, I had this crazy idea that some of the cultural ambiance would rub off on Amy. But, wouldn't you know, half the students are cavorting around, drinking up a storm. Not exactly your higher education role models, though

Amy's having a great time with cinema verité. Anyway, as soon as we bolt the sandwiches, I guess we'll head for the gardens."

"We'll give you a lift," Julia offered. "We're going there ourselves."

"What I don't understand," persisted Sarah, as the three made for the checkout counter, "is this rage to photograph. I mean, come on, Stacy Daniel taking street scene shots, the Hoppers sitting in the shade with new cameras. Of course, now I want to get in the act so I've picked up some film."

"Not the only people," added Doris when they all had settled on a concrete wall in a cul-de-sac made up of a gravel drive and a few bushes beyond the Boots entrance, "but Justin Rossi's got his camera out."

"I started it all," said Amy. "In the gardens. Taking those people shots for my book."

"No," said Doris thoughtfully. "Stacy and Justin were taking pictures in London. Westminster Abbey, the Tower of London, Houses of Parliament. And Kew Gardens, of course."

"Wrong," said Amy. "I don't think anyone took pictures at Kew Gardens. They just went on about the roses and the greenhouses."

"It's funny about Justin," said Doris. "He said he lived in London for a few years. Why take pictures of Westminster Abbey?"

Julia crumpled up her paper napkin and rose to her feet. "I think this is a lot of babble about nothing. My diagnosis is that everyone is secretly a little sick of the flowers and wanted a change of pace. Now let's get a move on if we're to make the garden by closing time."

"When does it close?" asked Doris.

"I asked Barbara," said Julia, "and she said not until six."

"Well," said Doris, "I don't want to spend too much waking time at our hotel. Have you seen it? Hotel Fatima. It's a sort of seraglio run by these people from—judging from their accents—New Jersey. Some woman from Hoboken married this Middle East type and went into the hotel business. The whole place is filled with brass gongs and pillows with tassels and reeks of incense. What I want to know is where did Barbara find the place? I can't think it's on Whirlaway Tours' list of Triple A hotels."

"It's only for one night," said Sarah, "and because someone's from the Mideast doesn't mean they've set up a harem."

"Pink satin sheets and dripping faucets," said Doris. "Anyway, after one look in we all left our luggage on the bus, hoping it would turn out to be a mistake." She shrugged. "Okay, let's hit the Botanic Garden. Amy and I accept the lift with pleasure. As the saying goes, my feet are killing me."

Oddly enough the party of four, after entering at the Bateman Street Gate and working their way to an artificial lake and water garden, ran almost immediately into the garden loyalists. But Carter McClure, Portia, and Henry Ruggles were not engaged in botanical discourse; instead, they faced each other on the path talking loudly. On catching sight of their fellow tour members they broke off and uttered glad cries.

Portia stretched out both hands in welcome. "Well, thank heavens. Henry has been having cat fits, and we've been trying to calm him down. A garden tour and everyone's off pounding the pavement in town. Poor Henry, he's worked so hard getting his lecture ready."

"Poor Henry" stepped to the fore. His wig had been completely refurbished from its Kiftsgate swim and appeared safely settled, but it must have added heat to the top of his head because his round face was red and moisture had accumulated on his brow, necessitating a continuous mopping with a large green silk handkerchief. He greeted the arrivals with a flip of a hand.

"Well, well," he said, in a peevish voice. "At least here are some of you. But it's almost five, and I ask you what IS the point of a SERIOUS garden tour if everyone spends the ENTIRE day goggling at buildings and sodden students. We could have done the Botanic Garden and then visited at least ONE cottage garden late this afternoon. I had counted on Edith and

Margaret Hopper at least. As for Barbara Baxter, it was her idea and where is she?"

This appeared to be a rhetorical question for Henry, pausing to mop his brow again, went on. Barbara had moved the entire tour to Cambridge. And for WHAT? So everyone could do the sordid tourist thing. And that dreadful hotel probably run ENTIRELY by terrorists. He, Henry, had given into the scheme because of course the Cambridge University Botanic Garden—Henry, his voice rising, rolled out the full name—did offer the visitor MANY plantings of merit. The Tulipa species collection, the hybrid display, the cedars, the maples, the scented garden.

"However," Henry concluded grumpily, "since you ARE here we might just as well look around since I have indeed prepared a FEW small notes."

Here Amy rolled her eyes heavenward and Henry pounced on her. "You, young lady, might have the absolutely unique experience of learning something by listening to an older person who has a SMALL store of information he is willing to impart."

"Amy," said Doris Lermatov in a dangerous voice. "Pay attention."

With the Lermatovs in tow, Sarah and Julia behind, the McClures to the rear, Henry led them forth, expounding, indicating with a flourish of a hand which signs to read, which plants to admire, which to hurry past.

And Sarah, following along, as had so frequently happened of late, heard hardly a word. Fortunately, Henry, having found Doris in a docile mood and Amy silenced, concentrated on those two with an occasional nod toward Portia and Carter for confirmation.

Returning to the entry gate, they ran directly into an entering cluster made up of Barbara, Justin, Edith and Margaret Hopper. The last three still wearing a camera around the neck or slung over the shoulder.

"Too late, too late," called out Henry, sounding to Sarah exactly like Alice's White Rabbit.

"Oh dear," said Edith Hopper. "I hope not. We just got carried away. Our new cameras. All the Cambridge sights."

"Oh the garden's still open," said Henry in a sour voice, "but I'm COMPLETELY done in. You're on your own. Entirely. I'm sorry, but that's the way it is. Fortunately, some of your group have seen fit to take advantage of a GUIDED tour."

Justin Rossi smiled down on Henry. "We've been a little thoughtless and I hope you'll forgive us. I suppose the sightseeing pull was too much and we all lost track of the time."

And Barbara, in a most conciliatory tone, took up the plea. "Mr. Ruggles, we do appreciate everything you've been doing for us. We got carried away. Such an interesting city."

"Even with the colleges closed off," put in Margaret. "So many—what do they say—so many photo opportunities."

"And," added Barbara, "we can't wait to get to Sissinghurst and hear what you have to say."

And so Henry, partly mollified, took his departure with his more loyal followers, and left Barbara and company hoisting their cameras and talking about closeup shots.

The tour bus stood at the gate, Joseph, the driver, in a slumbering posture at the wheel. The McClures, the two Lermatovs, and Henry boarded, and Sarah and Julia made for their parked car.

"Why," demanded Sarah, as she pulled out into traffic, "haven't these camera fiends taken pictures at the other gardens. Barnsley House, Hidcote, and Kiftsgate all had spectacular flowers. The Botanic Garden is a little on the dull side."

"Come on," said Julia. "You wanted to buy film, too."

"And I forgot to take any photos, so I suppose it wasn't really a priority."

"Because your priority is other people's business," said Julia. She sounded cross and her face was lined with fatigue, her steel wool gray hair looking more than usually like a bird's nest.

Sarah took a deep breath. "You know why I'm minding other people's business. For a while I put Ellen aside, but now I'm back minding Ellen's business, and anything that seems out of whack, at least deserves a little thought."

"Frankly, I'd drop this camera kick you're on. Cameras are standard tourist attire. As for me, well, as long as the cameras aren't loaded with gunpowder, I'd say skip it. Now let's hit this Hotel Fatima and see if they can rustle up something to drink." And Julia sighed, closed her eyes, and leaned back against the car seat.

Sarah focused on her driving, keeping to the left, dodging bicycles, inebriated youth, and aged residents who rushed out from behind parked cars and then stood bemused in the middle of the road. This intense concentration prevented her from seeing in advance that the entry from the Lensfield Road into the small street that harbored the Hotel Fatima was entirely blocked.

Blocked by fire engines, police cars, knots of people on the walks, long hoses snaking across the street, hurrying figures in helmets and protective coats, the whole scene fouled by clouds of dark smoke puffing out of a building. Out of the Hotel Fatima.

Sarah slammed on the brake.

Julia opened her eyes and took in the scene. "It's a bomb. Didn't Doris Lermatov say the Middle East?"

"Or New Jersey," said Sarah. "But I'll see what I can find out. Stay here and hold the fort."

She returned almost immediately. "Someone left a burner on and the kitchen went up. And so has half the hotel. They just hope they can keep it from spreading." She climbed back into the driver's seat. "I suppose we should head back to the Botanic Garden and warn the others. No rest tonight for the weary."

"Not at the Hotel Fatima anyway," said Julia grimly. "It's lucky no luggage was left off. And I've been dreaming of a hot bath."

It was Toad Ruggles who saved the day. Or to be accurate, the night. A crisis seemed to be just what Henry's injured ego needed. A chance to regain control, to flaunt his knowledge of the countryside, his possession of friends who could come to the rescue. A telephone call to an old classmate, now holding some sort of post at Trinity, produced the name of a farmhouse bed-and-breakfast at the edge of Grantchester.

"Not many rooms, we may have to double up," said Henry cheerfully. "But it's a pillow for the night and breakfast in the morning. And we can find a pub for dinner. Shake the dust of Cambridge from our feet."

And, with Julia and Sarah following, the garden tour drove to Grantchester. Henry, uplifted by a wave of gratitude, sat by Joseph and dictated the route, all the while extolling the pleasure of being in Grantchester instead of Cambridge, promising a morning sneak look at a cottage garden, calling upon the passengers to remember Rupert Brooke and his poem praising Grantchester.

"Who?" said Amy.

But even Amy could not dampen Henry's spirits. As if presenting a jewel of great price, he turned to her with a knowing smile and recited:

"And of that district I prefer
The lovely hamlet Grantchester.
For Cambridge people rarely smile,
Being urban, squat, and packed with guile."

Margaret and Edith nodded together. Rupert Brooke was a known quantity, close to their generation, and Edith murmured, "If I should die, think only this of me," and Margaret said something about "ye distant spires, ye antique towers," to which Edith said, "Dear, that's Eton College, not Grantchester."

Which remark brought out a number of ill-remembered quotations having to do with towers and spires and spring coming or not coming and then the talk died and the bus rumbled on its way.

Sarah and Julia, driving behind, were also silent. Julia perhaps from fatigue, Sarah, in the early dusk, needing to keep alert for sudden turn-offs and approaching roundabouts. Only once did Julia rouse herself to say plaintively that she thought

Newmarket was close to Cambridge and the wholesome sight of horses might be a real tonic. But, receiving no answer from her niece, she subsided, folded her hands in her lap, and dozed.

It was well after ten o'clock of that evening when Sarah, lying on a folding cot crammed in next to Julia's bed in a tiny single room, said that she hadn't called Alex about the change of hotel, and here they were in the wilds of Grantchester with the only farm telephone off limits at night except for an emergency.

"Of course, it isn't an emergency," she said, "and besides I hate to bother him at the hospital." She sighed. "I do miss him, you know. You get so used to someone being there, being close, and it leaves this hollow place."

"And I miss Tom," said Julia, "The hollow place fills in a little after a while, but it's still there."

And Sarah sat up and reached over to her aunt and kissed her cheek lightly.

Julia roused herself. "Now don't get sentimental on me or I shall start acting like Margaret and Edith and go to pieces. Maybe I need a new camera. New cameras seem to have bucked them up."

"Taking stupid pictures under shade trees," said Sarah sleepily.

But Julia had other things on her mind. "You don't suppose, do you, that Henry set fire to the Hotel Fatima? He's happy as a clam to be out of Cambridge, taking charge, with Barbara practically licking his boots."

But Sarah had turned over to face the wall and closed her eyes against the unpleasant image of Barbara Baxter's tongue lapping at Henry Ruggles's shoes.

Alex, whom Sarah had pictured busy with his patients, was actually hanging up the telephone in another fruitless attempt to trace the registered guests of the Hotel Fatima. The Cambridge police had wanted to be helpful, but the hotel had been reduced to ashes, the records had gone up in smoke, and the fire department had declared the whole place off-limits.

"Was anyone hurt? Anyone caught inside?" Alex had asked urgently.

"No," said the constable. "Just smoke inhalation—two firemen. The hotel's a total loss," he added helpfully.

With this Alex had to be satisfied, but it made for a restless evening and a night not soothed by Sarah's Irish wolfhound, Patsy, who at three A.M., having intimations of raccoons moving past the bedroom window, rose to bark his head off until Alex collared him and shoved him into the bathroom.

Morning came all too soon and with it Mike Laaka. With news.

"Been in touch," said Mike. "Meet me for breakfast. I'll fill you in. George is mad. He doesn't want anything to slip out of his control. It's bad enough that the Kennebunk police are handling one end of the murder, but add the British police into the stew and George isn't a happy camper. He doesn't like to share."

"What's all that supposed to mean?"

"Details at breakfast. Thomaston Café. Seven-thirty."

At seven-forty Alex demanded details, Mike having taken in the requisite amount of juice and coffee that would allow for coherence. Despite his job, Mike was basically an evening animal and mornings took their toll. Today, his heavy-lidded eyes, his almost white hair newly wetted down and brushed, reminded Alex of an overgrown schoolboy rousted betimes from bed.

Alex sunk his fork into a thick slice of French toast, carried a triangle dripping with syrup to his mouth, chewed, swallowed, put down his fork, and eyed Mike. "Details," he demanded.

Mike blew through his cheeks. "It'd sure be easy if we could wrap the damn thing up Stateside, but looks like we can't."

"Because," prodded Alex.

"Because a pair of smashed sunglasses turned up at the High Roosting police station with a note about sending the things to George Fitts of the Maine State Police CID."

"*The* sunglasses? The ones Sarah found in her bag along with the scarf?"

"What other sunglasses would anyone want sent to George?"

"Sarah brought them to the station?"

"Who knows. The package wasn't signed. No little message like 'wish you were here, love Sarah.'"

Alex frowned. "Sarah told me she'd given the glasses away. To Portia McClure, I think. I told her to try and find them."

"If Sarah didn't, maybe Portia McClure stamped on them and then decided to dump them at the police station care of George. Does Portia McClure even know George Fitts?"

"I have no idea," said Alex. He signaled the waitress for a coffee refill and for a moment both men concentrated on breakfast.

"Seems like Sarah's work," said Mike finally. "Her touch. But why not leave her name? Why not do it in person? Why sneak up on the police station and do a drop with an unmarked package? For Chrissake, it makes her seem like a member of the Iranian secret police."

"You can't be sure it's Sarah," said Alex without conviction.

"Aaah," said Mike. "If you want to bet I think you'll lose."

"So who has the glasses now?"

"Convenience won out. Much against George's better judgment—he hates to leave evidence in any hands but those of his own forensic buddies—he's asked the High Roosting police to send the glasses to their own labs. Which they did. And they have a prelim on them."

"Okay. And they're clean? Like the scarf?"

"Not like the scarf. Blood. Traces in the hinges of the eyepieces."

Alex looked grim. "Go on. I can see you want to lay out one more little item to cheer up our breakfast."

Mike nodded. "Blood. Type B. Rh-negative. Not the most common type, as you know. And they haven't done a DNA job yet."

"But?"

"Ellen Trevino was B-negative."

Chapter Twenty

ALEX TOOK A LONG gulp of coffee. Then he put down his cup and confronted Mike.

"B-negatives aren't that rare, but I'm not going to argue it's coincidence. I think it's time to grab this travel group, pack it up, and ship it home. And sit the whole damn lot of them down on a particularly nasty hot seat. I think Sarah's holding out on me. Something about her voice on that last call. I'm not getting the whole story. And, God knows, Julia can be as devious as hell."

"What are they holding back? If Sarah had those sunglasses she was being a good citizen by turning them in."

"Okay, but Sarah and Julia aside, what really matters is that those glasses may be the first hard evidence you've got that Ellen's killer may be on the garden tour."

Mike laid a slab of butter on a cinnamon bagel, considered, scraped off the butter, and took a bite. "My girlfriend's been going on about cholesterol. I told her I'd more likely be killed by some asshole drunk driver than by high cholesterol." Then seeing Alex glaring at him, he shrugged. "So, okay. Ellen's murderer probably flew out of Boston that Tuesday night."

Alex corrected him. "And not any old flight. That scarf and the glasses were shoved into Sarah's shoulder bag when the passengers for her flight piled up during the loading."

"Yeah, but even if the murderer's on that flight, he might not be part of the garden tour. Look, he wants out of the country. Kills Ellen—for reasons unknown, dumps the body, dumps his car, cleans up, and gets himself to Logan. Buys a ticket—or already has one—maybe he planned ahead so he's got his passport. Ends up on the garden tour flight, lands at Heathrow but keeps going. Any direction. Frankfurt, Rome. Calcutta, Beijing."

"Your point?"

"George's point. Nothing has happened on this tour. Not that we know of anyway. No threats, no strangers sneaking around."

"The only people sneaking around," said Alex grimly, "are probably Julia and Sarah. But what do you want, Mike? Another body before you jump in?"

"Well, the glasses with the B-negative blood are making George sit up."

Alex reached for the check. "Here's how I see it. The murderer—who might just be an honored member of the Garden Club—gets queasy about the scarf and the glasses being loose. Can't find the scarf—Sarah's mailed it—but knows Portia McClure now has the glasses so sneaks them away from Portia, smashes them. Someone—Sarah we guess—finds them and drops them at the police station."

Mike stood up, walked with Alex to the door, opened it and said over his shoulder, "Okay, I'll try again and see if George can pull a few wires and drag the whole crew home where they belong."

"You do that," shouted Alex after Mike, the sheriff's deputy, disappeared around the corner of the building.

Twenty minutes later at his office in the Mary Starbox Memorial Hospital, Alex hung up his telephone in exasperation. A call to Whirlaway Tours had netted him nothing more than the information that due to a fire at Hotel Fatima alternative lodging for the tour had been arranged. But Thursday night the schedule called for the group to be bedded down in Kent. "The Hagglestone Arms. Near Cranbrook. Very select. Yes, we have the telephone number." Here followed an audible rustling of papers, the number, and the request for him to "have a great day."

"Hagglestone Arms," announced Julia, who had busied herself with the tour itinerary and the road map. "It's by Cranbrook, which is near Sissinghurst. A couple of miles more and you can head south, and scoot right around London on the M25. Piece of cake."

"No one 'scoots' around London," complained Sarah. "You're goosed around by a million lorries and families in caravans and wild men in Jags. You have no idea how I hate being honked and hooted at if I let the speed slip below ninety."

Julia looked at Sarah with reproach. "You're allowing yourself to get tense. If my riders get that way I tell them to forget about having a sixteen-hand, fifteen-hundred-pound horse under them, and simply relax into the saddle, sit properly, keep their heels down, look ahead, and everything else falls in place."

"'Falls' is right," said Sarah grimly. She leaned forward, and told herself that at least she was not on top of a horse. In celebration she depressed the accelerator more firmly and shot around a startled Volvo. For fifteen or so minutes aunt and niece were silent and then Sarah picked up the familiar thread.

"I've been juggling the pieces in my head and that business about my being roughed up, and I'd say we—or I—just got caught in the crossfire and the tour leaders are really the ones on the endangered species list. First, Lillian; next, Ellen. Then

Henry. I'm sure Ellen didn't keep her travel plans a secret. And Henry certainly told everyone that he was mortally afraid of water. Maybe we're in the middle of a tour takeover and Barbara is next."

"I'd say Barbara can take care of herself," said Julia dryly. "She looks as if she could wrestle pythons."

"Barbara," Sarah reminded her, "is already the victim of a room search and she was standing next to me when Henry went into the pool. As for those tour change ideas of hers—London, Cirencester, Cambridge—what if she's afraid of keeping to the schedule? She suspects something and is trying to make it not happen."

"You are reaching."

"Someone has to," said Sarah. "Okay, check the map out for a place to have lunch and then I'll try to call Alex again."

But Alex was out of his hospital office when Sarah called from a small pub in Swanley. "Alex seems worried about you," said his secretary. "Are you okay?"

Sarah replied that yes, she and Julia were fine, and she rejoined her aunt. "Alex and I are just chasing each other by phone all around Robin Hood's barn...or the Mulberry Bush." She picked up her ploughman's sandwich—it had become a favorite luncheon choice—this one a slab of bread, ditto of double Gloucester cheese, ham, pickle, onion—and weighed it in her hand. "I suppose I should go out and plough something after eating this?"

"You'll get your exercise at Sissinghurst," said Julia. "And, remember, we keep together and look behind us."

Sarah nodded. "And picture Lady Sackville and Vita and Nigel and Violet Trefusis and Virginia Woolf and Leonard all tripping through the roses."

Sarah's idea of conjuring up the former owners and their friends on the paths of Sissinghurst proved a feat beyond her admittedly overheated powers of imagination. The parking area was jammed with cars and tour buses. The Front Courtyard was thick with visitors, a line extended around the corner waiting to climb the Tower stairs, the Long Library was stuffed, and the garden paths were thronged.

Sarah and Julia struggled through several knots of people to the Lime Walk, where the spring flowers had faded, a fact that accounted for the scarcity of visitors. Here in the comparative peace large terra-cotta pots of red impatiens offered the only note of color.

The peace was a short one. Sarah, looking down the length of the Lime Walk, saw fluttering hands, and members of the Midcoast Garden Club bustled forward, Henry Ruggles leading the way.

It didn't take more than a few minutes for Sarah and Julia to discover that Henry had taken command. He positively bounced. He joked, he gesticulated, he enthused.

With the exception of Carter, to whom smiling was always a chore, the members were all glad deference. Toad Ruggles—early on a rather suspect addition to the tour—was now chief. Barbara Baxter, for one, seemed to have yielded completely to Henry's superior botanical knowledge and, strange as it seemed, to Henry's charm. As they strolled the length of the Lime Walk she listened attentively to his explanations of the proper way to prune lime trees, and when they emerged into the shade of the grove of nut trees she apologized for Cambridge.

"I shouldn't have pushed it," she said to the assembled group. "Henry was right. A few cottage gardens would have been much more rewarding. Cambridge was a mistake. The colleges closed to visitors and then the Hotel Fatima burning."

Henry, today a dapper presence in white flannels and a straw hat, was gracious. "The Cambridge Botanic Garden certainly has merit. Unfortunate," he added with lifted eyebrows, "that so few took advantage of it."

"Oh, and we should have," said Barbara, the olive branch extended even farther.

"Mush, mush," said a voice in Sarah's ear. Sarah was standing a little to the rear of the group.

It was Amy. Amy, still in her black Decomposers T-shirt—or Sarah wondered, did the girl have a suitcase full of them.

"I think Barbara's afraid of being kicked off the team," said Amy. "But the really neat part of Sissinghurst isn't the flowers. It's those guys who lived here and the ones who visited. I got hold of mother's book, *Portrait of a Marriage*. She bought it in Cambridge."

"You mean you read it?" interrupted Julia.

"Actually, I just sort of skimmed. Talk about open marriages. Lovers all over the place. And kinky, you wouldn't believe."

At which point they were joined by Sandi Ouellette. "I read the book, too. Back home when I found out we were going to Sissinghurst, and I said to Fred that the whole scene made me think. I mean a lot of what they were doing, chasing each other around Europe and staying for ages at each others houses, took an awful lot of money and time, but it began to make Fred and me look like a couple of old drones. You know just getting up and going to bed with the same old person."

"I know what you mean," said Amy.

"You do not," said her mother, materializing at her side.

"Anyway," said Sandi, "I think the whole book is very romantic. Harold and Vita really loved each other no matter what."

"People, people." It was Henry. He clapped his hands. "It's almost a quarter of four, and I think we should return to the garden. The crowds will be going into the restaurant for tea, and we'll have a chance to see more. And take pictures," he added looking at Edith and Margaret. "You do have your cameras?" he said.

"Oh, dear," said Edith. She fumbled at the neck and shoulders of her pastel blue cardigan as if to see if she was carrying her new camera. She was not.

"I think," she said apologetically, "I've left it on the bus."

"So have I," said Margaret. "Dear me. It's just that we're not used to having cameras. Taking pictures. What a shame."

"I believe," said Edith, "that we used up all our film in Cambridge."

Henry looked at his group. "Did no one bring a camera? These are some of the most beautiful gardens anywhere. The Rose Garden alone. And with SUCH wonderful literary associations."

Amy held up a small camera. "I brought mine. I can take a group picture and I won't charge much for a copy."

"Amy," said her mother to the others, "will not charge for any pictures you may want."

This exchange gave Sarah the opportunity to check out the day's camera-bearing persons. The Hoppers and Justin Rossi, zero. Doris Lermatov, zero. Stacy Daniel, zero. The McClures, zero. Barbara, zero. Sandi, one (but only a single exposure left), Amy, one. Julia and Sarah, zero—although Sarah regretted she had again left hers in the car. Score: Shutterbugs, 2; non-shutterbugs, 10.

Henry congratulated Amy on her foresight, hoped that a group picture could be arranged, perhaps above that flight of stairs leading to the Moat Walk. They could group themselves around the garden bench designed by Edwin Lutyens. And after that he, Henry, intended to lead them along the Moat Walk. "I do not propose," he said in a jovial voice, "to fall in the Moat. I shall be EXTREMELY careful. One unexpected bath is quite enough, thank you."

Henry moving ahead to the flagstones of the Cottage Garden, now identified the overhanging white roses on the cottage wall as *Madame Alfred Carrière*, and, somehow, without actually saying it, Henry let it be known that this was hardly a first visit to Sissinghurst. He had seen the White Garden at night. Something not to be missed.

Sarah joined the party for the group photo and then followed the tour for the walk along the moat—Henry daringly stepping along the water's edge and peering in. Henry was right, she decided. The crowds had thinned and it was possible to examine portions of the gardens, clouds of roses, some just beginning to bud: pinks, reds, magentas, crimsons, all without the distraction of families circling, and chattering, and taking pictures.

And with that thought—they were now rounding a clipped hedge and making their way to the Tower Lawn—Sarah returned to the conundrum of the cameras. Cameras only carried and used in cities or large towns. Cameras left on the bus during visits to distinguished gardens where photo opportunities abounded. Where photographs could give pleasure of remembered warmth and beauty on cold winter nights with the photo album spread out on the lap.

As the group paused, preparing to line up for the visit to the tower and Vita Sackville-West's special room, Sarah grabbed Julia by the sleeve. "Hold it."

Julia turned around and scowled. "Now what?"

"The cameras. Only in cities. Not in gardens. This is supposed to be a garden tour, remember. So listen."

"How can I help it."

"I'm going to try something with Margaret and Edith. I think they're the most vulnerable."

"You sound as if you're going to suck their blood. Do you think they're working for the CIA? Taking pictures of Cambridge suspects? Why not say the cameras are filled with heroin or cocaine. Or uncut emeralds. Edith and Margaret are really Mafia agents and they go into cities to buy—or sell."

Sarah held up a cautionary hand. "Here they come. Down from the tower. Now just go along with me on this."

"I will just for the great pleasure of seeing egg all over your face."

Sarah waved a hand at the two sisters, who walked slowly over, breathing rather hard.

"It was a climb," said Edith. "But worth the effort."

"Imagine," said Margaret. "Vita's own desk with pictures of the Brontë sisters and Virginia Woolf on it. And all Vita's books and the whole room filled with flowers."

Sarah moved in. "Aren't the flowers wonderful? You know I forgot my camera, too. Left it in our car and I'm going to get it. It's a shame not to take a few pictures. And while I'm at it I can pick up yours. And some film at the little gift shop. Thirty-five-millimeter, right?"

Margaret looked at Edith. Edith looked at Margaret. Dismay. Consternation. Then Margaret.

"Oh, no dear. Too much trouble. We're just fine. And you know our hands wobble a bit. We haven't quite got the hang of the new way of taking pictures. All those settings. The lens opening."

"But you said they were automatic."

"Well, yes, but the distance. The light. And there's a bit of a breeze. The flowers will come out all blurry."

"Never mind," said Sarah cheerfully. "You point out what flowers you want pictures of and I'll shoot them for you. Or set them up so all you have to do is hit the button."

"No," said Edith vehemently. "No. We don't want... I mean it's awfully nice of you, but we'd rather not. Really. Quite tired. Up those tower stairs. It's a climb for people our age."

"A nice cup of tea," said Margaret. "That's what we need. And to sit down. And look at the shop afterwards. Postcards. Much better photographs on postcards. Professional photographers." And Margaret gripped Edith's arm, turned, and the two sisters literally scuttled away down the path.

Sarah turned to Julia who had stood entirely silent during the exchange. "Well?"

"Well yourself. Some older people can't handle technology."

"You're older. Can't you handle a simple push-button camera?"

"Yes, but if I were exhausted I might not want to go leaping around the garden doing it."

"Who said anything about leaping. I said I'd help. Come on, auntie. Those cameras are sending up—what did Big Daddy say in *Cat on a Hot Tin Roof*—a powerful odor of mendacity. I'd like to get my hands on one of those new cameras."

"What a wonderful idea. Perhaps we can search bedrooms tonight when everyone's asleep. Sarah, has experience taught you nothing?"

"It's taught me to be just a tad more careful in the future. Now let me see if Justin Rossi or Stacy will take some pictures of the Rose Garden because my camera's broken."

"It is?"

"It will be. You see the Rose Garden has absolutely ravished me, and I'm going to die unless I have some really wonderful pictures taken. For my memory book."

"Die," said Julia with a grimace, "is probably the operative word."

Chapter Twenty-One

SARAH'S ENTREATIES TO HAVE either Stacy Daniel or Justin Rossi take just a few pictures—her own camera being jammed—fell on deaf ears. Stacy shrugged, Justin smiled. Their cameras were put away, back in their cases. Perhaps tomorrow. Right now, some coffee and then hit the gift shop (this from Stacy) or some good brown ale—Hey, join me, Sarah? (from Justin). Sarah put on a disappointed face, which prompted Justin to add that some time he'd take a look at her camera. He was good with cameras. Perhaps she needed a new battery.

And then Amy moved in. "Look, Sarah. Use mine. I just loaded new film. You can pay me by reading what I've written so far." With that Amy thrust the camera into Sarah's hands.

And so Sarah found herself backtracking into the gardens with Amy's camera and taking at random a number of shots of the most colorful displays. "Just to keep it honest," she told Julia who followed shaking her head.

"The word 'honest,'" said Julia, "has no relation to what you're doing."

It was at tea—held at the restaurant next to the National Trust shop—that Henry unveiled his surprise. The White Garden by night. Special permission. He'd made a few phone calls, pulled a few strings, and now they'd all been invited—along with a garden club from Scotland, a delegation from Lyon, and a few specially anointed friends of Nigel Nicolson's family.

"Connections should not be despised," said Henry complacently. "I've never been a snob, but sometimes it pays to have moved in certain circles—even on the fringe of the circles." He spread a thick layer of strawberry jam on a crumpet and took a large bite, and nodded to the assembled party with satisfaction.

This announcement caused a happy ripple through the assembled party, and Sarah, looking about, saw no further opportunity to detach one member for a debate on the subject of photography.

That evening was notable (from Sarah's point of view) for several untoward events.

The first was the locking up of the cameras. The group arrived post-teatime at the Hagglestone Arms, sought their rooms, freshened for their evening meal, and met in the lower hall. At which Margaret and Edith Hopper, Sandi Ouellette, Justin Rossi, and Stacy Daniel all handed over their cameras to Barbara, who marched the collection to the office for safe keeping.

"What's the matter with keeping cameras locked in your room?" demanded Sarah, who saw her investigative plans for the evening going down the drain.

"Sarah, if you have a camera," said Barbara, "I think you should leave it in the office. Or any other valuables. Jewelry, binoculars. The manager said there have been recent incidents."

"I'm not giving up my camera," said Amy. "It's always with me because you can never tell when something will happen."

"That settles that," grumbled Sarah to Julia as they confronted their first course—beef bouillon.

"I should hope so," returned Julia. "I can hardly come up with another master key."

"I was only planning a few social visits to our friends."

"We're doing the White Garden this evening and then everyone will be going to bed because of the early start for France. No one would have welcomed your little social calls."

Across the table Justin was explaining to Stacy that he was going to skip the evening visit. "I've seen pretty much all I want," he explained, "so I don't need the magic of the evening. You can have the romance; I like to see flowers in daylight."

Stacy concurred. "Me, I want to see more of the area. We're right off the main village road. I think I'll go for a walk."

"You mean a pub crawl," said Justin.

"Another chance to soak up local color," Stacy said smoothly. Tonight she was looking particularly toothsome in a lime and yellow number that clung lovingly to every curve of her body.

"I guess you'll have to count me out, too," said Barbara. She had dressed in her usual plum-colored suit. Odd, Sarah thought, here's Stacy with an endless supply of clothes, and Barbara absolutely lives in that depressing cotton number.

"I'm going to read up on Monet," Barbara went on. "Giverny. I don't want Henry to be ashamed of me." Here Barbara gave Henry a dazzling smile, saying, "You added so much to today's visit that I'm absolutely inspired."

"You'd be more inspired if you come with us tonight," said Henry, detaching himself from a conversation with Fred and Sandi.

"No," said Barbara. "I'm going to do penance for the detour to Cambridge. I want to know all the flowers Monet planted and coordinate the paintings with the ponds, all those lilies."

So it was that an abbreviated tour group returned by evening to Sissinghurst—Sarah and Julia joining the others in the bus. It was, Sarah thought, Henry's finest hour. They were met at the gate by the head under gardener—he introduced himself as Phillips, Arthur Phillips—with orders to indulge the visitors with moonlight views of several of the larger gardens as well as the White Garden. Henry was particularly singled out as a "friend of the family."

Yes, Sarah thought, there was something special about Sissinghurst at night. Even with the others, an animated group from France, the ladies from Scotland, and a few singles and couples from somewhere, there was no feeling of the trampling herd. The cool of the evening, the mist rising out of the shadowy ground—still moist from the recent rain, the muted colors, the heavy scent from the borders of massed flowers, all these combined to convey a sense of the unearthly. A sense that was reinforced by the return of the ghost. Amy Lermatov's ghost.

Amy announced her presence to Julia and Sarah, who, by protective design, had placed themselves in the rear.

"She's back," said Amy in a satisfied voice.

"Who's back?" demanded Julia.

"The ghost. Or my vampire. Suck thy blood?" Amy grinned, her face pale in the rising moonlight, her teeth with the line of silver braces looking positively dangerous.

"Amy," said Sarah, "explain yourself. And make it short. Henry wants to talk about the White Garden. *In* the White Garden. Not hear about vampires."

"You know, the ghost woman. I saw her from my window sitting on a stone wall. At our inn. The Shearing."

And Sarah remembered. The white-haired woman in gray. With the shawl. The one who looked like Alex's mother who walked back from the village after the bodice snatching. Or ripping. She frowned at Amy. "The same woman's here?"

"I saw her over by that hedge. She's with that bunch from Scotland. You can tell they're from Scotland by the way they talk. All those brrrr's and rrrr's and 'weel ye no come back again, Kathleen.'"

"That's Irish," said Julia.

"Whatever," said Amy. "But the ghost is with them. Chatting it up. But she doesn't sound Scotch."

"It's always happening," said Sarah. "You see a person in one place and then they turn up all over the map. She's probably going to Giverny to see Monet's garden."

"I like the ghost idea," said Amy. She bent her head and said in a conspiratorial whisper, "Don't look now, but she's coming this way. Right toward us."

Sarah looked up. There she was. Elspeth McKenzie. White hair, the thin mouth, high cheekbones, a knitted shawl around her shoulders. Like a white-haired Katharine Hepburn who happened to be the one woman to whom Elspeth McKenzie was often compared. In short, a handsome presence.

"We meet again," said the woman. She was tall, almost six feet, and she smiled down at the three. "You were all at the Shearing Inn," she went on. "Such a nice place. Quiet, not completely overrun with American tourists." She had a soft throaty voice that put Sarah immediately in mind of Lauren Bacall doing her thing with Humphrey Bogart.

"You mean American tourists like us?" demanded Julia, never one to gloss over a possible irritation.

"Exactly," said the woman. "After all, the point of traveling isn't to bump into clusters from Kansas and Missouri."

"Maine," said Julia shortly.

"New England," amended Sarah who thought that her aunt was being unusually rude. To make up she extended her hand. "Sarah Deane. And this is Amy Lermatov and my aunt, Julia Clancy."

"Mrs. Thomas Clancy," said Julia, who was not prepared to melt into a state of acceptable civility.

"Jessica," announced the woman. "Jessica Roundtree. I'm from Boston, and really, Mrs. Clancy, I have nothing against people from Kansas and Missouri. My father was born in Kansas and voted for Alf Landon."

"How jolly," said Julia.

"Bleeding Kansas," announced Amy. "We do it in school. Free states or slave states."

"Good," said Jessica, "I'm glad some history has trickled into the schools." She paused. "What a wonderful garden. I'm glad I found a way to see it at night. Joined up with that group from Scotland. One of the women in their party wasn't well and decided to take it easy, so there was room for me in their bus."

"Perhaps," said Julia crisply, "they're looking for you. They may have a timetable and you wouldn't want to miss your bus."

Sarah stifled the urge to throttle her aunt on the spot. Okay, Julia didn't take to strangers butting into her life, but really. "Would you like to see the garden with us?" she asked Jessica.

"I'd love to," said Jessica. She smiled at Julia. "I remember, Mrs. Clancy, you used a cane at the Shearing, so wouldn't you like my arm? Just to be companionable." And before Julia could step back, Jessica had tucked Julia's arm under her own and extended the other to Sarah. "Three musketeers afoot in the Garden of Eden," she announced, and moved forward before Julia regrouped or Sarah could protest.

It is always difficult to detach a portion of one's body from the helpful grasp of another without making a scene or giving the gesture more weight than it deserved. Of course, this Jessica was a total stranger, but she seemed a well-meaning one, so Sarah allowed two circuits of the White Garden before she disengaged herself.

As for Julia, after the initial attempt to shake lose, she permitted Jessica's arm. Not because she had changed her opinion of intruders, but because evening weariness combined with increasing stiffness of joints prompted her to accept the support. Julia, when all was said and done, was practical. Of course, what had really irritated her from the first appearance of this woman was the fact that Jessica, as Sarah had noticed, really did resemble Alex's mother, Elspeth McKenzie. And Elspeth was a woman as opinionated as Julia herself and someone with whom Julia had clashed when the two had met on boards and committees in their roles as elders in a small community.

But Jessica Roundtree, oblivious of the burden of another identity, was going on about the white rosebush.

"Of course," she said, "that central rose—*Rosa longicuspis*—won't come into its own until mid-July."

"Some of the roses are out," said Sarah. "And the other flowers are lovely."

"The *Crambe cordifoli*? So effective against the hostas."

"I like those daisies," said Sarah pointing to a corner. Daisies surely were safe.

Jessica ignored the daisies. "The glory is that central rose. Did you know the family used to plan weddings around its peak blooming. The second Saturday in July."

But Julia had now revived. She removed her arm, braced her feet squarely on the path, and in a firm voice said thank you and that she and Sarah must now join their own party.

Jessica smiled, reached over and patted Julia's withdrawing arm, and said she, too, must rejoin her friends. But it had been fun. Perhaps they would meet again. Another garden.

And Jessica swept her long shawl about her body and floated off into the night.

Sarah turned to her aunt. "If you'd just waited, I was going to ask her if she had any relatives named McKenzie."

"And if she turned out to be a long-lost cousin, what did you plan to do with her?" demanded Julia. "Ask her to share our car?"

"I only want to be civil," Sarah retorted.

"I'm sorry," said Julia. "I just didn't want to be saddled with anyone else and she seemed ready to move in. And don't go on about friendless women who might want a bit of companionship. I grant your point. Anyway, as you said, without any effort on our part we'll probably find her sneaking around Monet's pond."

Knowing her aunt and that this was probably as close to an apology as she was going to come, Sarah herself took Julia's arm and both wandered about the paths of the White Garden until they came upon two middle-aged women, the taller of whom was describing to the other in a scandalized voice one of the more arcane events in the life of Vita Sackville-West.

"I think," said the speaker who spoke in a lowland Scot's accent, "that gardening—all this talk of propagating and fertilizing, do they not bring out the base impulses in very unsteady natures. It's easy to see that in certain of humankind man is truly fallen. Or in some cases, woman. This Jessica Roundbottom or Roundtree is a case in point."

Sarah moved closer.

"You'll be saying she's a wee bit familiar, will you not, Jenny?" said the shorter and stouter of the two.

"Just too forward for my taste, that's all."

Sarah moved in, bringing Julia forcibly with her.

"Hello," she said in her most cordial tone. "Such a lovely night. We've just been talking with Jessica Roundtree, too, and I heard you mention her name. Is she with your group?"

The taller woman—Jenny—shook her head—Sarah could see the movement but not the features of the woman. But there was no mistaking the disapproving voice. "Not at all. We had thought she was with you—the American garden tour."

"But you think there's something, well, odd, about her?" persisted Sarah.

"And why do you ask that?" said the shorter woman.

"We wondered ourselves," said Sarah. "My aunt and I were rather surprised when she joined us. A stranger, and my aunt never encourages strangers. Strangers make her extremely nervous." Here Sarah gave Julia's arm a warning squeeze. "You see Miss Roundtree isn't one of our group at all, although we did see her back in High Roosting."

"The woman seemed perfectly harmless and has given us nothing to complain about," said the short one.

"Now, Maggie," said the other, "you know we were a bit put off." Sarah could now hear a warmer tone. This one, Jenny, wanted to unload.

"It's just that one of our friends, one of our group, Mrs. Sinclair—she's from Peebles—actually we're all from Peebles. Well, Mrs. Sinclair, took a nasty fall. Slipped on the wet grass and this Miss Roundtree picked her up."

"And?" encouraged Sarah.

"And Jessica Roundtree picked Mrs. Sinclair right up, right off the ground, and Mrs. Sinclair is a very large woman, almost fourteen stone."

"What my friend is saying," put in Maggie, "is that she's afraid that this Jessica is one of those women."

"A lesbian," said Jenny. "Not that I'm prejudiced, but I don't hold with close physical contact between women."

"Not even in helping someone off the ground?" said Sarah.

"Mrs. Sinclair was trying to rise by herself. Of course, I've been reading about Sissinghurst, and you cannot deny that some very strange things went on here," said Jenny, her voice becoming rather shrill. "Perhaps there's something in the air…"

"I think," said Maggie in a repressive voice, "that Jenny here is making something out of nothing. A mountain out of a molehill. I certainly don't think that Miss Roundtree was about to drag one of us off into the bushes."

"How very interesting," said Julia, shaking off Sarah's arm. She had been silent during the exchange. "And now my niece and I must join our friends. We've enjoyed meeting you both." And Julia wheeled and set off down past a darkened row of box hedges.

Neither Julia nor Sarah spoke until they had reached the entrance and Sarah had settled Julia and herself on a bench to await the arrival of the others.

"Really," said Julia. "That Jenny. Dour old biddy. John Knox has a lot to answer for. I didn't expect to feel kindly about Jessica, but for heaven's sake, you'd think that someone had been raped and drawn and quartered."

"Leave it," said Sarah in a tired voice. "That Jenny is way off base. My lesbian friends would never dream of accosting strangers."

"Unless the strangers welcomed them with open arms."

"My friends," said Sarah firmly, "are extremely fussy about whose open arms they step into."

At which point they were joined again by Amy Lermatov. Obviously bored, scuffing her feet in the gravel. "I've just about had it with gardens, except," she said, "I did get some details for my story. I've decided to use poison. Get even with garden lovers. I'll poison them all. There's foxglove, which is something called digitalis, and henbane and water hemlock and even lilies of the valley are poison and so are azaleas, and then there's some sort of nightshade. I asked that ghost who has a real name. It's Jessica Round-something. She was really nice and told me all about poisons. She knows a lot about dangerous plants."

"How useful," snapped Julia.

Sarah looked over at her aunt with concern. Under the dim light over the bench she could see Julia's face looking pinched and lined. Time to go home and hit the hay. Tomorrow would be demanding, what with crossing the channel, hiring the new car, driving like mad to Giverny, and probably having language problems. They had not practiced as they had promised themselves.

"Home," said Julia echoing her thoughts. "I'm rather used up."

"Here they all come," said Amy. "I've got to start deciding who I'm going to poison first. Have die in convulsions of agony."

Julia roused herself. "You could," she said, "start with a fourteen-year-old American visitor with red hair."

That night Julia lay in her bed, comforter pulled to her chin because the evening had turned chilly. Beside her lay Sarah, on a mattress dragged in from the adjoining room. Aunt and niece had had an argument on the subject of security, of the need for both to stay together. "You can never be too careful," Julia had said. So now a straight chair was tipped against the outside bedroom door and another such against the communicating door. Julia's cane lay ready at hand by Sarah's pillow.

"You've gone and stirred everyone up about cameras," said Julia. "You may not think you're a target, but I feel a hot spot between my shoulder blades, and I keep looking over my shoulder. You know the saying: Forewarned is forearmed."

"But we're forearmed without the forewarning."

"Honestly, Sarah. What do you want? A knife at your throat or a letter with the Black Spot on it?"

And Sarah subsided and for a moment both lay in the dark. Brains at work. Brains apparently, for once, on the same wave.

"Sarah," said Julia from her bed.

"Aunt Julia," said Sarah from the floor. And then, "You go first. I defer to age and wisdom."

"As you should," said Julia. "I'm thinking about Jessica Roundtree. When we saw her at High Roosting we both thought there was something a bit strange about her. Not just because of looking like Elspeth McKenzie. Or because of Amy Lermatov and her ghost."

"Correct," said Sarah. "My thoughts exactly."

"That report from Sandi Ouellette about the bodice ripper and the woman who heaved the molester out of the WC."

"Right."

"And that perhaps our Scottish friends despite their highly unenlightened and objectionable views of lesbian women…"

"May not have been entirely off base when they thought Jessica was unnatural," finished Sarah.

Silence.

Then Julia.

"The whole thing is highly irritating. I think I shall scrub my mind out with soap."

"Good idea," returned Sarah. "Harsh yellow laundry soap." Then after a sigh, "Good night, Aunt Julia."

A long pause, an answering sigh from the bed. Then, *"Bonne nuit, ma chèrie."*

Chapter Twenty-Two

JULIA IN FRANCE WAS hardly more amiable than she had been the last few days in England. The last-minute packing, the rushed breakfast, her arthritis, the dash to the ferry, the choppy channel crossing threatening mal-de-mer had already darkened her view of the world when she hit the tourist office at Calais. There followed the discovery that the female at the tourist office did not—or would not—speak English, the taxi driver had never heard of Europcar rental, that when this office was discovered, the entirely charming lady in charge spoke only French.

Sarah and Julia finally managed to patch together their rental agreement for the offered Renault, and at last they were on their way, Julia with maps and the automobile's instruction booklet.

"The whole thing is in French," announced Julia as Sarah twisted their way out of Calais and set the Renault's nose in the general direction of Rouen, the city closest to Monsieur Monet's noted pond and garden. She flipped over several pages and frowned. *"Avons-nous plein d'essence?"* she asked.

Sarah peered at the gas gauge. "*Il y a encore* in the tank, I think. At least the little arrow isn't at the bottom. Thank heaven for icons. But we'll have to keep an eye on it."

Julia leaned her head back on the car seat rest and began reviewing those annoying verbs which took the verb *être*—to be—as their auxiliaries. Also it would be useful if she could remember a few telling phrases. *Taisez-vous* and *allez-vous en*—"be quiet" and "go away"—ought to come in handy.

Sarah, however, was not wrestling with language but with scenery. She was puzzled by the rural character of the roads. Didn't they have superhighways in France? Of course, the woods, the fields blanketed with poppies, the cows meandering down to small streams, hawks soaring in a cloudless blue sky, all these were charming, but they weren't making very good time. In particular, Julia was routing them through endless small villages whose speed was set at a snail's pace and Sarah had been warned about exceeding the limit. The French police loved to nail feckless American tourists. "What," she demanded of her aunt, "does your map say about main roads? We won't be in Vernon until midnight at this rate."

Julia bent over her map, traced a line with her finger and said that all seemed to be well. "It's a good map. Little bits of French history printed on the side. For instance did you know that *pour perfectionner le français le cardinal Richelieu…*"

"Give me that map," said Sarah, reaching over and snatching it from Julia. Driving with her left hand she frowned at it and then exploded. "*Merde!* By which I mean 'shit!' Your map is at least twenty years old. My God. When you said you had French and Italian maps I thought you had something printed after the invention of the automobile."

Julia contrived to look apologetic. "I was saving money. I have all these maps left over from old trips. Tom and I had a wonderful time driving across France back in the seventies. Or was it the sixties? After the war, anyway. Through the Loire Valley and then into Italy. Venice, Florence, and on to Lake Lugano."

"Damnation," said Sarah. "We're creeping along reading a map probably used by General Eisenhower. Let's stop and find something printed in the nineties. We can get gas then or *essence* and you can be very humble for the next hundred miles."

They reached Vernon at twilight unfortified by not much more than a couple of croissants at a highway pit stop. The waitress, annoyed at their arrival just as the luncheon period ended had slammed down their plates with a surly *"bon appétit."*

Sarah and Julia found their party gathered around two tables on a little paved area in the front courtyard of the Hôtel Fontaine. Everyone seemed to be in fine fettle raising glasses of wine, or in Amy's case, the always available Orangina. The bus trip, Sarah reflected, had allowed them all to sit back and be whizzed—via superhighways—to Vernon stopping en route at a restaurant with two Michelin stars for their *déjeuner*. Really, there was a great deal to be said for bus tour travel; she and Julia were hot, dusty, and hungry.

The spirits of Margaret and Edith seemed to have revived, so that they were able to dip into their memory book and talk of a walk taken along the Seine, of a picnic taken on a ridge above Giverny, of a memorable visit to the Château de Bizy. Carter McClure, unusually amiable—he had slept for most of the bus trip—described to anyone who would listen the details of a remarkable *civet de lapin*. Sandi and Fred Ouellette were in a flourishing state, speaking French at every opportunity, Fred announcing that he was very anxious to meet with a local undertaker—*le entrepreneur de pomps funèbres*. Perhaps he and Sandi could pay a visit after dinner. As for the rest, Doris Lermatov and Portia were deep into a discussion of Monet—haystacks versus lily ponds—while Justin Rossi and Stacy Daniel argued about wines and vintages. Wines of the Loire and the Médoc. The virtues of a *vin de la maison* compared to the high price of a *vin de cru*.

Sarah looking around at the familiar faces decided that a change had come over them all. It was as if the arrival on French soil had altered not only their spirits but their whole appearance. Everyone looked, well, smarter. Stylish. In some cases, positively chic. In England, attention had been paid to comfort. To serviceable clothes and sturdy shoes. Only Stacy Daniel had maintained a fashion profile, the others settling for being simply decent, and in Carter McClure's case, what with his rumpled jackets and cowboy boots, raffish. Now only Amy Lermatov in her jeans and T-shirt looked the same.

Here sat the Hoppers, who had added long scarves tossed dashingly over the shoulder to their usual navy blue dinner attire. Doris Lermatov wore a black float with drippy silver earrings, Carter McClure sported a white linen jacket and had a Panama hat on his knees; Justin Rossi, handsome in a blazer and an open-collared shirt, now raised his glass to Portia McClure, clad in a rust-and-black-striped caftan. Sandi, in heavy-duty eye make-up, wore an above-the-knee black number, and husband Fred had dressed up his olive sport jacket with a purple and yellow flowered tie.

But Henry Ruggles had outdone them all. A beret encased his wig, he wore a pinstriped suit with a boutonnière in his buttonhole, and the whole effect was such that Sarah would not have been surprised to have him leap to his feet and start singing, "Thank heaven, thank heaven for little girls." All in all, she thought, the group had managed to reduce Aunt Julia and herself to a pair of sordid, dirt-splotched interlopers.

Only Barbara Baxter in her cotton travel suit seemed untouched by the festive atmosphere. Preoccupied, she looked at her watch and frowned as each new car arrived at the hotel and pulled to a stop.

This behavior did not pass unnoticed.

"Looking for someone, Barbara," demanded Carter McClure. "You have a secret rendezvous?"

"Aha," said Fred. "A Claude or Jean-Philippe or André?"

"Who is *très charmant* and twirls his mustache," put in Sandi.

"Or a spy who is carrying a secret message for NATO which must be delivered by a woman at midnight at the entrance to the Louvre," said Henry.

Amy grinned. "You're meeting a representative from Colombia. A drug lord. He has the cocaine trade in his control and he wants to make a big buy. Lots of kilos hidden in gift paper which you had wrapped up in England."

Barbara gave Amy a hard look. "My brother. Greg. Short for Gregory. He's going to be in Paris on business and we set this up as a meeting place. To have dinner. I don't see him very often. He lives in South Carolina and travels a lot." She looked around at the interested faces. "I thought this would be a good time because it won't interfere with the gardens and the trip. Tonight everyone will be going out for dinner. Won't you? I mean…"

"Relax," said Carter. "You can meet your brother."

Julia smiled—it was an expression Sarah knew well. "No explanations necessary." And to Sarah in *sotto voce*—they sat at a distance from Barbara—"too many explanations."

"Don't pay attention to my evil-minded daughter," said Doris to Barbara. "Enjoy yourself. It's too bad you can't go off to Paris with him for a whole day."

"I would never do that," said Barbara. "No, this is just a quickie. To catch up on family news."

"Well, family is always important. What does your brother do?" asked Portia. Portia usually managed to restore equilibrium, but Barbara had now pulled herself together. "I don't want anyone to think I'm taking off in the middle of the trip. I didn't mention my brother turning up because, well, I like to be professional and not mix my personal life with my business life."

"Well," said Sandi good-naturedly, "we're all friends by now. Tell your brother to join us for a drink."

"We never mind," said Julia, "hearing about each others' private lives. Their special interests. Hobbies. For instance, I had no idea so many of you were interested in photography. I think knowing these things about each other makes us all seem a little more human." Julia looked up and bestowed a benevolent gaze on the gathering.

"Oh, yes," said Sandi. "Although," she added, "I'm not sure you want to hear all the details of what Fred does. I mean his life simply revolves around dead bodies."

"My brother," said Barbara, "is a sales representative. Southern crafts. He goes around the southern U.S. looking for handmade things to sell all over the world. Especially in Europe. That's why he's in Paris." She paused and then looked directly at Amy. "Sorry to disappoint you, Amy, but Greg and I are not about to pass kilos of cocaine back and forth."

Amy blinked. And then revived. "You couldn't," she said. "They have dogs now who sniff out the drugs and you get nailed at the airport. Even if you've got drugs sewed into your underwear. Or into your body. Did you know that some people take little packages filled with drugs like cocaine and shove them right up..."

"Quiet, Amy," said her mother. "And Barbara, we hope you have a lovely evening. The temperature is perfect. Your first night in France."

"Actually," said Barbara, "I've been in France before. But never right here. I've never been to see Monet's place."

"She makes it sound like a bar," sniffed Julia to Sarah.

Sarah turned on her aunt and positively hissed. "Shhhh. Behave yourself." She raised her voice. "Where are you going for dinner? Have you any recommendations? I've never been to Vernon either."

Barbara gave her a grateful look. "The hotel made lists for us. Five or six places—all quite simple and not far away and not too expensive. You can walk to all but one of them."

At that there was a scraping back of chairs, a reaching for the restaurant lists, a buzz of discussion, and then the group fragmented, some to make further preparations, some to take off and explore. Barbara to wait for her brother at the entrance. Julia to wash and change.

But Sarah lingered at the table.

Julia stopped at the hotel threshold. "Sarah? You coming?"

"Go along. I'll catch up in a minute. There's something I need to check. My passport. Some traveler's checks."

Julia returned and faced her. "Out here, on the terrace?"

"Not exactly," said Sarah. "Please, Aunt Julia. Go on up to your room. Trust me. I'm not doing anything I shouldn't. Just a little bit of evening air. I'm safely surrounded by at least twenty other hotel guests." She gestured toward a phalanx of tables.

And Julia retreated. Passing Barbara she wished her "*bonsoir*," a message Barbara graciously received and wished her the same.

Sarah in her turn retreated. Quickly, with a sort of step, jump, she sidled into the shade of a series of clipped hedges that marked the border between table area and a small front garden. Here she found a bench upon which she knelt, finding that she could just see over the hedge and so had an excellent view of arriving and departing vehicles.

Not long to wait. Some seven or eight minutes later a gray Peugeot glided into place and came to rest under the street lamp. Barbara, who had been lingering by the front door, walked swiftly down the walk to the curb, pulled open the passenger door, climbed in, the car accelerated, took a sharp left and was gone.

And Sarah, watching, did not think in the lamp-illuminated moment that she saw anything like a brotherly-sisterly embrace. But was that significant? There were times when she, herself, felt more like kicking her own brother, Tony, than kissing him.

In Julia's room she found her aunt dressed and fortifying herself with a few inches of scotch in the hotel glass. "What," demanded Julia, "were you doing down there? I thought we were going to keep an eye on each other."

"We are," said Sarah. "Until the end of time, or at least until Alex meets us in Bologna and then we can be a threesome. And don't say 'how jolly' again. Alex has a protective streak a yard wide. I'll be ready in minute. Just let me wash up and change."

"I've been looking over the restaurant list," called Julia to Sarah now splashing vigorously in their shared bathroom. "There's one called L'Auberge du Dragon only a few blocks away. It's marked 'charming and quiet'. And on the same street, Le Petit Monarque with a walled garden and marked 'budget.'"

Sarah put her head around the door. "I have something else in mind, but we'll have to drive around to find it."

"Why on earth? We've been driving all day."

"Trust me."

"If you say that again I'll scream and call for *La Sûreté*—or *les gendarmes.*"

Sarah rejoined her aunt clad soberly in a dark gray shirt and a black skirt. Her dark hair was wet and neatly brushed back from her face.

"You look a bit funereal," remarked Julia, eyeing her.

"Being inconspicuous is my game and yours, Aunt Julia. Take off that yellow chiffon scarf thing. We're going to eat with—no, not with—but near Barbara Baxter and her brother, Gregory." Sarah held up a warning hand. "Not a word. We haven't that much time. We want to get to the restaurant right after they've been settled in so as not to miss too much. We can slip in and take a seat and if we're lucky they won't notice us immediately. When they do it will be too awkward for them to leave. We'll make it clear we don't want to join them, that we just wanted to be away from the others. We've already established that you're something of a crank…"

"Thank you."

"And cranks like to eat alone. Or with long-suffering nieces. All right, I'm ready."

"I suppose," said Julia in a resigned voice as she climbed into the passenger seat of the Renault, "this all has to do with the fact that the lady hath protested too much."

Sarah busy with starting the car didn't answer immediately, but after she had maneuvered the Renault out of the precinct of Hôtel Fontaine, she nodded. "I have this feeling. Barbara wasn't happy about having us know about Greg. Why? It's perfectly natural to want to have dinner with your brother, but I don't buy that bit about it not being professional to mention it. So keep your eye out for a gray Peugeot. I'll swing round the block." And Sarah slowed the Renault by the awning of L'Auberge du Chat Noir. "Why," demanded Julia, "do we want a gray Peugeot?"

"It's the key to our dinner," said Sarah. "But I don't see it at the Black Cat. Look, I'm going to take a guess. What's the name of the restaurant not in walking distance from our hotel?"

Julia drew her finger down the list. "L'Auberge sur le Pont, so I suppose it just might be on a bridge. Or near one. Turn here, then take a right on rue Ambroise Bully, and a block after the traffic circle, a left to a bridge crossing the Seine. And while you drive I'll try and figure out why we're going to be hanging around Barbara Baxter's dinner with her brother."

"Nothing ventured, nothing gained," said Sarah.

The dinner scenario worked out as she had predicted. The Peugeot was discovered in the parking lot, the two women entered, saw Barbara and brother Gregory at a far table heads bent in conversation. The two women slid into a table in the general vicinity, nodded and smiled when they were discovered. Sarah thought that Barbara had handled their appearance rather well, waving a cheerful hello and then returning to her conversation. No attempt was made, however, to introduce the brother.

"It's just a matter of our pretending to talk," said Sarah. "There aren't many people in here and after a while Barbara will forget we're here and we can pick up little pieces of conversation."

"To make a quilt," said Julia who seemed to be backsliding into her crank mode.

"Mesdames?"

It was the waiter and after a certain amount of dithering, Sarah went for the *magret de canard* and Julia opted for a *feuilleté de foie et de poulet*, both to be washed down with a recommended *graves*.

And then industrious and silent eating—the food was splendid. Finally, when Sarah was beginning to have qualms in view of the fact that the prices noted on their list were marked "high"—small scraps of talk began to become audible. Nothing made much sense and Julia's analogy to the quilt seemed rather apt.

First, Sarah heard Barbara make a reference to Hawaii. The prices there. Nothing unusual about that, since she was, after all, in the travel business. Then Gregory responded and Sarah caught the words "steam service" and then "Liliuokalani" and the date "1891." The two seemed to be caught up in Hawaiian nineteenth-century history. Perhaps Gregory sold U.S. southern crafts to Hawaii and Barbara arranged tours there. If she had it would be incumbent on her to be knowledgeable about the islands.

Then for a space of time lowered voices and then Gregory came out loud and clear: "Two million. Can you believe it. Jesus." And Barbara's lower, "Well, you thought it might." And then mumble, mumble, the words "ten percent buyer's commission," followed by a talk of cancelation and a museum offer.

"I think selling southern crafts must be good business," whispered Julia during the rattle of coffee cups being placed on the table. Julia had the hearing, when she wished, of a nosy teenager.

"Nothing to do with cameras," said Sarah.

"Two million spells jewelry to me," said Julia. "Or uranium."

"Be quiet," whispered Sarah.

But nothing more than a few random and absolutely incomprehensible words followed. A reference to the "rotary" or "a rotary," something about a "black inverted center," and several remarks about polypro film and an upcoming Canadian auction.

Further information came, in fact was delivered by Gregory Baxter, a tall fair-haired man with the impressive shoulders of a linebacker, a cleft chin, rather startling brown eyes, emphasized by his wire-rimmed glasses. Brother and sister had risen, walked over to Julia and Sarah's table, and Barbara had introduced her brother.

"We've been talking over old times," said Barbara.

"All those trips to Hawaii," added Greg. "When we were kids. Our mother was born in Honolulu."

Sarah saw no reason to lose the opportunity to ferret out more information. "Barbara said you market crafts. Things from the south. How interesting. What sort of things? I mean if you have buyers in France you must have to know what French dealers want."

"And British and Italian and Scandinavian dealers. Greek dealers. Spanish dealers and ones in Bombay and Yokohama. Jakarta, Bangkok. All over the whole blessed world, in fact. I travel a lot and, of course, Barbara, here, can eyeball possibilities when she's on one of her tours."

"That's enough, Greg," said Barbara. "They don't want to hear all that. Besides it's getting late. We've had a long day. Haven't we?" This last addressed to Julia and Sarah.

"Yes," said Sarah quickly, "but I love to know what other people do. Teaching English is really boring. Static. And I never travel. What kind of crafts do you sell?"

"I don't actually 'sell.' I work with agents and dealers. As for crafts—I don't know what Barbara told you, but not things like salt and pepper shakers made out of walnuts or hand-carved salad forks. Unless they're old. Our things are what you'd call 'folk craft.' Dolls, drawings, small toys. Hand-made religious items."

"Jewelry," said Julia in a hopeful voice.

"Simple jewelry made from seashells, nutshells, stuff like that. Pictures, too. Sketches. Small paintings—done with herbal dyes, tempera, ink. And we do a lot with paper artifacts. In as mint condition as possible. Perfect condition counts for a lot. From the south. And Hawaii. Those are our special areas."

"You mean antiques?" demanded Julia picking up on the "old."

"You could say that," said Greg. "I don't use that description but some of our things are pre-Civil War. Or made during the Confederacy. Believe it or not there are galleries and agents and auction houses who have customers panting for the stuff. Baxter Enterprises aims to please. And provide."

Barbara pulled at Greg's sleeve. "Greg, I'm tired even if Sarah and Julia aren't. And the waiter's over there with our check."

Greg stepped over to the waiter, took a slip of paper from the small tray, frowned, fished for his wallet, and began slowly to count out franc notes.

"I hope you don't mind Greg," said Barbara. "He gets wound up about his job. All the details you never want to hear."

"But I love details," said Sarah. "They make everything seem more real. I tell my students, go for it, pile on those details."

"Pirates," said Greg, returning to the group. "But I never argue about food prices. Anyway, to finish up, I'm over here—Paris, then Amsterdam. To deal personally. Trouble is we used to mail our things but the damn U.S. Postal Service won't insure registered mail to Europe, so we've had to use Lloyd's."

"Of London?" asked Sarah

"Is there another Lloyd's? You see a really valuable shipment on the way to Germany was heisted and so now even Lloyd's won't insure our mailings anymore." He grinned, looking from Sarah to Julia. "You can't trust anyone anymore."

"I suppose," said Julia when they reached their car, "that they knew we'd been trying to overhear what they said during dinner, so Gregory decided to bring it all out in the open." She fastened her seatbelt and sighed. "A lot of trouble over nothing."

"Not so," said Sarah. "We've got a whole bag of odd references, and later Barbara didn't want Greg to go rattling on and when he mentioned not trusting anyone she stepped on his foot."

"I'd hate to take that into a court of law," said Julia.

"I'm beginning to think about Hawaiian gemstones being hidden in a bunch of old carved southern crafts," said Sarah. "But what kind of crafts do you suppose?"

"Crafts shrunk down to fit into cameras," said Julia.

"And sold in English and French gardens?"

"Or in Cambridge and Cirencester and London. Those little side trips. With support from the Hoppers and the rest. Now I think we'd better scratch this particular line."

"I do not believe in scratching," said Sarah in a firm voice. "Tonight, or tomorrow at the very latest, I'm going to get my hooks on a camera or two. Preferably belonging to Margaret and Edith. By stealth or by outright bullying. I think they can be bullied."

"As I said, Sarah, you're beginning to sound a lot like me. It's in the blood. Now there's the train station. Take the next left and we're almost back."

"I don't think," said Sarah thoughtfully, "that you'd better talk to Alex about this genetic compatibility. He's already detected signs of it and it makes him extremely irritable. Remember, that my dearest Alex is an ordinary mortal who only wants to get his excitement from the Celtics and the Red Sox."

As if conjured by the reference to his name, there was on their return to the hotel a fax waiting for Sarah. From Alex. It was short and to the point: "Cut loose and get out. I've changed plans and am flying Alitalia to Milan. I'll meet you there in two days. The train station between noon and three. Love, Alex."

"I think," said Julia dryly when Sarah showed her the sheet, "that Alex has more on his mind than the Celtics and the Red Sox."

Chapter Twenty-Three

SARAH DID NOT MAKE a preemptive strike on the Midcoast Garden Club's cameras for the simple reason that Madame at the desk—a black-browed Madame Defarge character busily knitting between guest arrivals and departures—informed Sarah that all such were under the hotel lock and key for reasons of security.

"*Toujours,*" said Madame, holding up a needle, "*prenez garde.*"

"I'm going to have to trap the Hoppers at Giverny," Sarah reported. "And forcibly snatch one of the damn things." She and Julia were preparing for bed after having activated their own security system of locks, bolts, and tipped chairs.

"Giverny!" exclaimed Julia. "We're heading for Milan. I've been looking over the map. Drive to Lyon, turn in the car, take the train for Turin, change for Milan. As we planned to do, only quicker. No stops for a château."

"*After* Giverny," said Sarah, who was kneeling on the floor wrestling with the strap on the hated wheeled suitcase. She had meant to dump it long ago.

"Of course," said Julia, "it's a pity to miss Monet's garden. I've never been there."

"We aren't going to miss it," said Sarah, standing up.

"What?"

"Not—going—to—miss—it. We'll go to Giverny in our car, park safely with thousands of others, and see what develops. 'Develop'—as in film in a camera. Or no film but a little cache of something. Tiny handcrafted items made by Hawaiian missionaries or Creole children or loyal Confederate women back on the old plantation."

"But Sarah...," began Julia.

"But me no buts. I'm absolutely determined to follow this one to the end. All we have to do is exercise sensible caution."

Julia shook her head. "Alex must have had good reason to scrap his own plans. That Lyme Disease Conference. Why don't you call him and see what's up?"

"I'm sure he expects me to call and protest, and then he'll give me fifty reasons for leaving the group and we'll end up wrangling, which will do nothing to cement our marriage. Because I'll say no."

"Alex probably wants a live wife. Even a live Julia Clancy."

"Alex knew what I was like before we got married."

"He probably knew he was marrying an independently-minded English teacher but not a candidate for the morgue."

"No more talk. It's bedtime. Keep the door open between us and think about lilies floating under a bridge."

Julia did not stop to reply but retreated to her own bed, pulled up the pink cotton blanket to her chin, turned over and gazed fixedly at the wall. Unfortunately the wallpaper featured a pattern of morning glories twined about a lattice. I can't get away from gardens and I've lost my grip on Sarah, she told herself. I've met my match. My own flesh and blood. She reached over and turned off the light but her brain, though sluggish, was still circling.

If only, she told herself sleepily, we had some sort of weapon. A pocketknife. A folding bread knife. Did they make folding bread knives? Or better, just an automatic revolver. A tiny automatic revolver. Travel size. Or a stiletto. An icepick. And for a time a parade of desirable weapons floated across Julia's inner eye, and then reaching for the handle of a miniature dibble, she fell into a troubled sleep.

Sarah, on the other hand, closed her eyes in five minutes' time and slept the sleep of the virtuous person who has not hesitated nor been swayed by wiser heads and sane counsel.

The next day, June the nineteenth, in the midcoast area of Maine, Alex reviewed again the fifty urgent reasons for Sarah and Julia to remove themselves immediately from the garden club's tour and to hit the road. Because as surely as night followed day, Sarah would call and he, Alex, would have to persuade. She would resist but he, with logic and sense on his side, would prevail. And if this approach failed, he was prepared to play the fear-and-love card: I love you and remember what happened to Ellen Trevino.

After all, things were ratcheting up. The Maine State Police in the person of George Fitts had called Alex the day before and said that at last the DA's office had okayed a plan to try and reel in the Garden Club. A message was to go out to the tour's next planned stop—they were booked for the night in a Paris hotel before they flew out the next morning to Italy. The message would be delivered courtesy of the Parisian police and would inform the garden lovers that they were all urgently wanted back in Maine for questioning in matters pertaining to the death of Ellen Trevino.

"We can't force them," Mike Laaka told Alex early that morning at their common meeting place: the hospital cafeteria. "Practically our club," Mike said, as the two men settled down over cups of coffee and cinnamon doughnuts. "I mean," he went on, "we'd have to go through the whole legal song and dance—show just cause—pull in the French police and Interpol to manage the extradition. But we can't and so they wouldn't. But what we can do, George thinks, is put the fear of God—or the fear of the Maine CID—into them. Suggest ever so delicately that delay in returning might be construed as an obstruction of justice or a withholding of evidence or some such garbage."

"I've put a firecracker under Sarah and Julia," Alex told him. "Sent a fax telling them to hit the road and meet me in Milan."

Mike dumped a second plastic cup of cream into his coffee and shook his head. "You're sure Sarah will jump when you whistle."

"I'm just making a reasonable request," said Alex crossly.

"I don't think reason figures in," said Mike. "Besides, Sarah's traveling with an unreasonable person called Julia."

Alex shook his fist at Mike. "You're a troublemaker. Sarah will listen and I know Julia. Her bark is worse than her bite."

"We're not talking about bites, we're talking about a woman who once decided to steal three horses on Christmas Eve. Assisted by Sarah."

"Goodbye, Mike."

Mike held up a restraining hand. "Relax. I've got other news. We've run bios and work profiles on the whole tour group."

"And?"

"About Stacy Daniel—only that isn't her name."

"You said she's done modeling. Maybe her own name wasn't very fashionable."

"Previous name was Sherri Norton."

"Which wasn't real either?"

"Apparently not. We're looking and so far have come up with a stepmother in a nursing home called Janice Hirschenburgh. Not much help there, she has Alzheimer's."

"Dead end?"

"Not yet. We'll keep trying. And something funny has turned up about Margaret and Edith Hopper, but we bumped into a stonewall when we tried to run it through the system. Sealed documents or case dropped, that sort of thing. Intervention by judge. George is trying to get the DA's office to do some digging."

"If Edith and Margaret Hopper are candidates for anything other than sainthood, then I'm a monkey's uncle."

Mike grinned. "I'll try to hurry that part of the investigation."

"No other stupid red herrings?"

"More sealed briefs because he was a minor at the time. But it looks like our legal eagle Justin Rossi was arrested one Halloween in Cambridge. Sixteen at the time."

"You can break into those records?"

"If we can show justification, the need to gather evidence—but evidence of what? Hell, half the teenagers in New England have probably been in police trouble on Halloween."

"I was picked up for throwing raw eggs," Alex admitted. "I hit the dean of the medical school in the back of the neck."

"You see," said Mike. "And the law has protected your youthful reputation by sealing the record."

"Actually," said Alex, "I wasn't that youthful. I was a first-year med student at the time."

That June morning in Vernon was again clear, sun-filled, with balmy currents rustling the roadside poplars and featuring a kindly temperature in the mid-seventies. It was the sort of day, Sarah thought, that said "Get thee to a garden." Sniff the roses, wander down paths, and linger in bowers. It was not the sort of day, she told Julia as they walked down the stairs for breakfast, to be cowed by forebodings, or the apprehensions of an absent husband. Giverny and Claude Monet beckoned.

These sentiments seemed to be shared by Aunt Julia, who had awakened in good humor. "I'm with you," she announced. "Loaded for bear."

Arriving at the breakfast for the shared *petit déjeuner*, they found that the group's good humor of the previous night had blossomed into a tangible excitement. There at a long round table set with a snowy cloth and carafes of coffee and silver pots of chocolate, with baskets of hot croissants, apricot and blackberry confiture on the side, they rehearsed the pleasures of the day to come. Presiding over the whole was Henry Ruggles. Monet was apparently his "thing," if an eminent artist can be so styled. Henry, Sarah thought, spoke of Giverny as if he personally had helped the artist buy the place, arranged the placement of the Japanese bridge, and laid out the flowerbeds. Henry, a croissant in hand, waxed eloquent on the subject of color expanding in the air to vanquish figurative form, the dialectic harmony between still water surfaces and the embedded water lilies, the decomposition of substance, the triumph of sensation over visual fact.

"I don't quite get it," Sandi Ouellette whispered to Julia. "Maybe we should buy a guide when we get there. I read up on Monet before we came, but I didn't know he vanquished figurative forms."

"Don't fight it," advised Fred. "And don't get hung up with art criticism. Enjoy."

"You might want to read Kandinsky," put in Justin Rossi in a kindly tone. "He's quite good on Monet." Justin, too, seemed infected by the general atmosphere of pleasantness, along with the usually aloof Stacy Daniel, who was making an effort at conversation with Margaret and Edith Hopper, asking them details of Monet's life, a subject on which they seemed quite knowledgeable.

Sarah, who was sitting next to Barbara Baxter at a far remove from Henry's sphere of influence, decided that Monet and Giverny could, for the moment, take a back seat, inquired after her brother, Gregory.

"He should have joined us for breakfast," said Sarah. "I'd have loved to hear more about those craft objects. For instance, I never imagined that so many people in the Confederate States, in the middle of a horrible war, were busily carving or painting miniature pictures."

"Life did go on," said Barbara. "On the southern home front it wasn't all war and burying the silver and making clothes out of curtains and worrying about escaping slaves. And a lot of Gregory's objects were actually made on plantations. Items that are very collectible, very marketable, you know."

"So were the enslaved," said Portia McClure, giving Barbara a steely look. "My great-great-grandmother was collected and marketed."

Barbara paused, put her hand to her mouth. "I didn't mean…"

"I don't suppose you did," said Portia crisply.

Amy broke in. "That's sort of exciting. Having a great-great-grandmother as a slave. Have you written a book about her?"

Portia eyed the girl. "Not everyone is a subject for fiction, and I doubt if my great-great-grandmother found being in bondage on a plantation exactly exciting."

Amy flushed and looked chastened. "I'm sorry," she said in a low voice.

Sarah, turning back to Barbara with the hope of grilling her further on the subject of Gregory's business interests, found her now deep into conversation with Justin Rossi. Never mind, she told herself, there are the cameras. She looked around the table noting the empty bread baskets, the drained coffee cups. "I suppose, we're about ready to take off," she announced to the party in general. "I'm all packed because Aunt Julia and I will be leaving from Giverny in our own car. So why don't I get all your cameras out of the safe. Save you all one more step."

The Hopper sisters rose in their seats like a pair of scalded cats. Both with an emphatic and high-pitched "No!"

And Justin Rossi turned and gave a little shake of the head. "Thanks, but I'll pick mine up on the way out."

Here Barbara intervened. "Actually, I have the receipts for the cameras. Except yours, Sarah," she added reproachfully. "So I'm the one to retrieve them. But thanks anyway."

"Well, you struck out again," said Julia as she and Sarah mounted the stairs on their way to pick up their luggage.

"Never mind. I'll snatch one of those cameras by force if I have to."

"Knock the Hoppers into the pond, hurl them into the rosebushes."

"Something like that," admitted Sarah.

"I can hardly wait," said Julia. "And when you are hauled off by the local police I will say that *vous êtes une femme que je n'ai jamais vue* in my whole life."

The single fact to register on every member of the Midcoast tour when they arrived at the car park at Giverny was that the entire population of the known world had decided on that day to pay their respects to the artistry and the home of Claude Monet. Even after crossing the road leading to the farm house and studio, the group found that a long line had formed by the ticket door.

"*Merde,*" said Julia with feeling. "This is going to be worse than Sissinghurst. We'll be lucky if we even see a garden path let alone a garden. Or be able to hear Henry."

At which Henry bustled forward, his arms outspread as if to embrace the whole group. "Now everyone, you don't want to hear ME nattering away for the whole day. I suggest that I do what you Americans call a show and tell at the house, the gardens, across to the ponds. Then lunch and you're on your own to take in Giverny for yourself. To IMAGINE yourself with a canvas. Try to see and feel the colors, the light. The provocative magnificent light. You by the pond. You are MOTIONLESS but the breeze moves, the water breathes, images wave under the surface of the water. The light changes. Or as Monet said, 'The light that fades and is reborn.'"

For a moment the group remained respectfully silent, and then Carter McClure, always impatient, said, "Well put, Henry. Now let's get on with it. There's another bus pulling in and we want to get ahead of the stampede."

But Henry was not finished. "I've talked to our good driver, Joseph. He'll have the bus ready at four. I have a little idea that deviates just a trifle from the master plan. I know we're are all going to fly from Paris tomorrow. Straight to Milan. And then off north to Lake Como and WONDERFUL Bellagio and two or three last MARVELOUS gardens. Now, I'm proposing that we take a later flight—I've called the airport and there's room on Air France—and come back here at dawn. We can walk along the hills with a view of the Seine, we can sit quietly by the little Epte River that feeds the ponds. We can be closer to the SPIRIT of Monet than we will with these crowds. Barbara, will you go along with this? You are our faithful tour director."

Sarah looked quickly over at Barbara, but her face had set into a listening smile. And then she shrugged and turned to the others. "What do you all think? It means getting to Milan later, but…"

"Sounds like a fine idea," said Fred. "I like getting the feel of a place. And I'm always up for a morning hike."

Barbara nodded. "All right, but I'll have to see if there's room at the Fontaine for another night."

"There isn't," said Henry, "but the Fontaine has found us rooms in the area. A little pension."

"I'll tell Henry no rooms for us," said Julia to Sarah, as the queue shuffled forward and Barbara began the negotiations for the entrance tickets.

"Well," said Sarah, doubtfully. "Maybe we should hang in…"

"Sarah, do not push it. Alex is meeting us in Milan."

"Okay, but only if I can get hold of a camera."

And so, along with the throngs of tourists and garden lovers and art appreciators, Henry and Barbara's charges moved ahead to enter the world of Monet, Henry flushed with excitement, a man in love with every word he spoke.

And Sarah half listened to Henry—he was going on about aesthetic principles as they applied to the plantings of columbine, foxglove, nasturtiums, gentians, sweet peas—how their colors rioted and quieted, how they persuaded, transformed, and retreated. The other half of Sarah's attention centered on the cameras. The very sight of them hanging from Edith's and Margaret's shoulders acted like a magnet. She dogged their footsteps, exclaimed over the flowers at which they lingered and again offered to take pictures of the two on a bench, by the bridge, but to no avail. Nor were the suggestions that one or the other take pictures of Sarah herself at some memorable spot since her own camera was still ailing. "I thought," said Sarah in a pensive voice, "that Alex—and my mother and father—might like a shot of me at Giverny."

It was a suggestion that cut no ice; Margaret fidgeted, and Edith finally told Sarah irritably that she was making them very nervous and please go away.

Sarah retreated.

"And you're making me nervous, too," said Julia who had been tagging along several steps behind Sarah.

"Okay, so it's time to get physical. A little push and shove can accomplish wonders."

"Like a broken hip."

"As Madame at the desk said, I will take care."

But opportunities for upending either of the Hopper sisters were nonexistent. Henry kept a tight hold on the flock and the streams of visitors up and down the paths, lining up to get into the farmhouse, crowding into the kitchen, the yellow dining room, the bedrooms, circling the studio, thronging the tunnel to the ponds—all these confounded assault on the Hopper equilibrium.

At the café outside the farmhouse, Sarah turned to Julia and shook her head. "It's harder than I expected."

"What is?"

It was the ubiquitous Amy holding a basin of stew. Amy, who was possessed with the sensitivity of radar. "I know," she said. "You're investigating. Is it about Barbara's brother?"

"What!" exclaimed Julia and Sarah in one voice.

"I'll whisper," whispered Amy. "I'll bet you've found out about something about her brother, Gregory. Do you know that this morning he stopped by to say goodbye and she gave him her big suitcase and told him to get rid of it. It was too big. She said you should get rid of yours, too. And I think Gregory's a sinister name. It's Russian, isn't it? Grigori. We did Russia in Social Studies this year and there were a lot of them. That crazy man, Rasputin, his first name was Grigori."

"Amy," said Sarah in a voice usually reserved for freshman who are handing in late term papers. "You can join us at our table if you'll stop pretending we're all on the Orient Express with a corpse hidden in the lower berth."

"Or hidden in Barbara's and your suitcases," giggled Amy. "But how about the cameras?"

"Cameras!" said Sarah, a little too loudly. "What do you mean cameras?"

"Sarah, you can't be as dense as you pretend. Those two Hoppers don't know one end of their cameras from another. I saw Margaret trying to take a picture with the shutter closed. And Stacy Daniel. She just aims at anything. People's feet, the tops of trees, the backsides of buildings."

Julia put down her fork. "Amy, have you looked carefully at Monet's collection of Japanese engravings? The pearl divers, for instance. Naked from the waist up. By Chikanobu Yōshu. Very distinctive. And the woman breastfeeding her baby. By Utamaro Kitagawa. Late eighteenth century, I think. You might be able to find copies at the gift shop. Souvenirs of the trip. You could take them to school next year. For your homeroom bulletin board."

Amy showed her braces. *"D'accord. Mais oui.* Mrs. Clancy, I know you're trying to distract me but it's kind of a neat idea. And I've had it with this stew thing." Here Amy looked disdainfully at her bowl of now congealed meat and vegetables. "What I'm really dying for is what the French people call a 'ahm-boor-gaire.' I want one with fries and catsup and relish and mustard. I have withdrawal symptoms."

"Hurry up to the gift shop before all the Japanese engraving copies are sold out," said Julia putting spur to the moment.

And Amy departed.

Sarah was admiring. "Brilliant. But how in God's name did you know the names of the Japanese artists?"

"Simple, my dear Watson. Tom had a collection of Japanese engravings—many rather graphic. We sold them at auction and bought a Hanoverian stallion with the money." Julia put down her napkin. "And now I suppose we're ready to wander about and discover Monet each in our own way."

"Discover the Hoppers," said Sarah. "Preferably alone by a large thicket of lilacs. But I don't want you to get too tired traipsing after me."

Julia squared her shoulders, almost, Sarah thought, flexing her biceps. "I am an old workhorse. If Claude Monet could ramble around the place in his eighties, a New England woman of seventy should be able to handle it. We said we'd keep an eye on each other, so I'm going to dog your every footstep."

But she couldn't. A restless night had taken its toll, and after a short time, Sarah left her on a bench under a willow at some distance from the stream of visitors.

And now where were Margaret and Edith Hopper? Sarah fell in behind a group of visitors and followed them around the ponds, through the tunnel to the farmhouse, the studio, back to the café. Then back to the lily ponds. Only Stacy Daniel (taking the sun in a clearing) and Doris Lermatov with Portia McClure (on the Japanese bridge) had been encountered. Sarah, feeling cheated of her prey, decided to linger by the far margins of the pond where the less populated areas might lure purists like the Hoppers. She remembered that Edith had remarked rather tartly that the true spirit of Monet and the understanding of his vision certainly couldn't be found in a crowd.

After walking back and forth for a time, she decided to work her way toward the water that fed the ponds—the little River Epte. Here, too, she drew a blank, and just when her watch told her it was time to give it up, pick up Julia and leave, perhaps grabbing at Stacy Daniel's camera as she rushed out— an unlikely scenario at best—Margaret and Edith, one after the other, stepped cautiously across a moist patch of ground and coming out of the shadows, paused blinking in a patch of sunlight.

Sarah, shrinking back behind a heavy growth of vines, took a deep breath. It was all very well to talk briskly about giving a hearty push, seizing a camera, and speeding off into the underbrush, but now faced with the two elderly women—two people who had always seemed the epitome of gentleness and kindness—well, it wasn't so easy.

She was saved the trouble.

There was a distant splash, a gurgling noise and sort of yelp. Thrashing. Another cry. A choking noise. Running footsteps. A long pause. Then another splash. Another pause. Then a series of heavy sodden thuds.

And Sarah was in motion. But the sounds apparently came from off the beaten path, and, desperately, she had to double back, begin a short climb, come down and then found herself at the edge of the stream.

On the banks of which knelt Barbara Baxter, soaked to the waist, giving CPR to a body.

Chapter Twenty-Four

SARAH PLUNGED DOWN the bank and stopped. The body, soaked, the eyes closed, the bald head. Sarah saw it all again even as she knelt beside Barbara. The sodden lumpish body being hauled out of the Kiftsgate swimming pool. The wig afloat. Henry. Henry Ruggles.

Barbara, without stopping her efforts, jerked her head to the side, saw Sarah and shouted, "Get help. Anyone. See if there's a doctor. Call an ambulance."

Sarah rose to her feet and found she had been joined. Margaret and Edith Hopper and two men and a woman all hastening forward. And then a troop pushing through the brush. A man in a striped shirt and shorts shoving people aside.

"Je suis médicin," he announced. *"Alors. Permittez-moi?"*

Barbara yielded and, without missing a stroke, the doctor took over, Barbara sitting back on her heels, quite red in the face and breathing hard from her exertions.

And now, summoned by the cries, the splashing, a swarm of visitors, what appeared to be the entire complement of the Garden Club, another physician, and a woman who announced in a Texan accent that she was an emergency technician.

For what seemed an interminable period the doctor continued his exertions, and then suddenly Henry opened his eyes and struggled to sit up. And was gently forced down. And over on to his side. At which he coughed, vomited, coughed again, sighed deeply. And closed his eyes.

And then Portia McClure pushed through the crowd and sank to her knees on the damp ground beside the doctor. "Henry. Henry," she repeated. "What have you done?"

Henry opened his eyes. "I'm shhick," he said in a slurred voice.

The doctor shook his head. *"Eh bien, monsieur. Restez tranquille. Içi. Sur la terre. Vous comprenez?"* He reached for Henry's wrist, felt for the pulse, shook his head again. *"Un peu rapide. Et vous avez froid."* He looked up at the assembled crowd. *"Un couverture, un manteau? Vous, monsieur?"* pointing at Carter McClure, who had stepped forward and was now bending over the top half of Henry.

Carter stripped off a light cotton sweater and several others followed so that soon Henry was covered with a colorful array of jackets, cardigans, pullovers.

"He's English," Carter told the doctor. "Do you want me to translate for you?"

"Eh? No. I speak English. Not so good, but a little." The doctor addressed Henry, speaking directly into his ear. "Stay quiet. Okay? You will feel better soon, I think."

"Better now," said Henry in the same thick voice. "Want to go home. Soon as possible."

"But no. We will check you in my hospital, your vital signs," said the doctor. "You will go on—what is the word—a litter, a stretcher. *D'accord?* Not *à pied*, not walking. Then, if everything is how you say 'go,' okay, you may leave. To England, is it?"

"We'll come with you," announced Portia. She looked at her husband. "Won't we, Carter?"

And Carter—who looked, Sarah thought, genuinely shaken—nodded vigorously. *"Nous sommes les amis de Monsieur Ruggles,"* he said. "We will take care of him."

"An ambulance has been called," said a voice from the crowd.

"Bien," said the doctor. He looked up and around at the throng. "Okay, give him air. The two friends may stay. The rest, all of you, go away. *Allez-vous en. Abgehen Sie, bitte.*"

A faint smile crossed Henry's gray face. *"Merci. Dankeshön. Gracias."*

"Ah, you see, Monsieur Ruggles," said the doctor, smiling down on him. *"Vous n'êtes pas mort. C'est bon."*

Henry managed a weak grimace. "Not yet. *Pas encore.*"

"Come on, Sarah." It was Aunt Julia plucking at her sleeve.

"But Henry."

"Henry is in good hands. The doctor. And Carter and Portia. There's nothing we can do."

"But we can't just leave him here."

"They're taking Henry to the hospital. Then he'll go home. Or stay if he wants. But we have to get out, get to Milan. If I thought we could be of any use here, we'd stay."

And now Sarah and Julia, fully caught up with the retreating crowd, found themselves pushed away from the riverbank, back toward the ponds, and there, by the side of the beaten down path, spied two most sought after objects.

Two cameras.

Sarah with a quick glance left and right, scooped the two up, thrust one down her shirt where it sank to waist level creating an awkward midriff lump. The other she shoved at Julia who for once didn't stop to argue but stuffed it into her large handbag.

"Hurry up," said Sarah. "Margaret and Edith must be behind us. They were around just before Henry went into the water."

"How do you know these cameras belong to the Hoppers?"

"An informed guess. Here's the bridge. Hurry, we can beat them to the exit."

"And if the cameras belong to the Japanese ambassador or the German High Command?"

"I'll mail 'em back here with an apologetic anonymous note."

Sarah looked anxiously behind her. Margaret and Edith might any second raise the cry. She could hear it now: Thief, stop thief. There she is. She's been after our cameras for days. "Come on," she said, "let's get out of here." And she grabbed Julia's arm, dragged her to the exit, across the road, and then pushed her into the Renault. And then, over her shoulder, she saw them. An ambulance, lights blinking, slowed by the entrance and a police car, siren yelping, roared down the road.

"Give me the camera," demanded Sarah. She seized Julia's handbag, emptied it, unearthed the other camera from her shirt and threw both onto the back seat and covered them with a jacket. Then started the car and with the greatest decorum, brought the Renault out of the car park and turned its nose in the general direction of Italy.

"What I think," said Sarah, "is that Margaret and Edith dropped the cameras when they heard Henry go into the water."

"You mean when Henry was pushed into the water."

"Of course. You can't tell me that two dunkings of a man that everyone knew couldn't swim a stroke are anything but homicidal."

"Not an efficient push. After all he's not dead yet."

"It was close. The water in that river may not have been over his head, but he panics in water. So he was damn lucky."

"Or unlucky. Depending how you look at it."

Sarah slowed the car. "The way I'm looking at it is we're a couple of rats deserting a sinking ship."

Julia made a face. "Change that around. We're a couple of ships deserting the rats. Because as sure as my name is Clancy there are rats we've left back there."

"I still feel guilty."

"And I have the cure. Where are those cameras?"

"I threw them in the back. Under my jacket."

Julia hit her seat-belt button, swiveled about, and returned, a camera in each hand. She laid them carefully on her lap and rebuckled her belt. "One Olympus and one Nikon."

"Be careful. They may have film in them."

Julia peered at the camera, pushed the slide to "On" and shook her head. "The battery sign is blinking and there's no film number. So I can open. Presto." There was a long pause and Julia said in a disappointed voice. "Nothing. The thing is empty."

"You mean out of film. You already knew that."

"No, it's completely empty." Julia looked over at her niece. "I suppose you expected diamonds or white powder packets?"

"Something at least," Sarah admitted. "Try the other one."

Julia turned the second camera over in her hand and examined it. And frowned. "Empty."

Sarah, looking ahead, spied a gravel indentation that led down an embankment to a widening river. "I'm going to pull in over there. If these cameras are innocent, then we're a couple of thieves..."

"One thief. You."

"You're an accessory. And poor Margaret and Edith have lost their new cameras. And the fuss they made about my borrowing them might have been perfectly natural. They didn't want me fooling with their new toys. So if these are on the level, I'm driving back and return them."

She turned the car and pulled it under a sheltering oak. "Okay, let's have a look." Sarah opened the two cameras, compared one with the other, and slid her fingers around the interior of both instruments. Then, turning to Julia, she said, "These little buggers are about as innocent as an empty syringe."

"But I said they were empty."

"They're empty all right, but they're hollow. There's no place for film and no spool to wind the film on. The only difference is a piece of loose plastic at the bottom of the Nikon. But, the things are dummies. They may have started life as cameras but now they're containers."

"Containers for what?"

"God knows. Certainly not little Hawaiian and Confederate handcrafts. Even miniatures. We've got to think very small."

"Diamonds. Or emeralds. I thought so all along. Or drugs."

Sarah turned on the ignition. "Wait and see. Okay, we're off." And they drove, on through the countryside, farmhouses, cows, more poppy fields, the Seine, mist rising, on their right hand, distant villages, the Loire Valley speeding by. Once Julia pointed to a distant spire. "Café, tea?" she said plaintively.

Sarah accelerated. "No time. Let's get this trip over with. I've got a nasty feeling that we're being followed. There's a car that's stayed behind me for the last hour. I keep asking why it hasn't passed me. No French driver stays behind anyone."

"Of course not. It's national pride," said Julia. "It's called èlan. But do you recognize the car? It's not that gray Peugeot?"

"Barbara's brother? God, wouldn't that be interesting. But I can't tell the make. There's a ground fog coming up. It's just a gut reaction I'm having."

Julia turned an anxious face toward her niece. "So move it."

"Okay, hold your hat. And when it gets dark we'll try and find a B&B off the beaten track. A place to crash tonight."

"Don't use the word 'crash.'"

"Listen, Aunt Julia. You check behind us and keep an eye out for the police at the same time. I'll drive like fury and try not to think what I'm going to do to certain lousy no-good people belonging to the Midcoast Garden Club Tour."

"Tough Ms. Deane."

"Angry Ms. Deane."

Sarah, as promised, drove like fury. They shot past villages, sped around astonished drivers, and then when the fog had thickened and the shadows had lengthened over the Loire Valley, Sarah, with one hasty glance in the back mirror, wrenched the wheel around and plunged down a gravel road, took a left, a right, and by some sort of Gallic miracle pulled screeching into the outskirts of the tiny town of La Verdière, and after two rights and a left stopped before an iron gate in a small street, Rue St-Simon. On the gate, written in curling gold letters, "Hostellerie: La Maison de Celeste." Julia took a long breath and unfastened her seat belt. "My Lord, Sarah, you deserve the Croix de Guerre."

Sarah let her body slump. "We've lost it. The car. I haven't seen hide nor hair of it since we turned off."

"I think," said Julia slowly, "that we should find a church and light a candle. For heavenly favors received. It's enough to make me turn Catholic."

What Julia referred to as the "mystery car" did not reappear, and the remainder of the trip took on the aspect of a bad comic movie. Or as Sarah remarked as they spun in and around Lyon, down one ramp, reversing, and up another it was more like a daytime nightmare. The most positive thing that could be said about the hit-and-run visit to one of France's most bustling cities is that after the Renault had been turned in, Sarah, encased in a vault-like room high up in the Pullman Part Dieu Hotel made the heroic decision to scuttle her oversized suitcase by shoving it under her bed, and then deliver half of her wardrobe to the tender mercies of the French postal system for mailing to Maine.

"If Barbara could do it, I can too," Sarah remarked as, clutching only a shoulder bag, she pushed her way with Julia through the station crowds into a second-class coach bound for Turin. "You know," she added, "for a while I considered that Barbara's big suitcase was something sinister. But when we searched her room the thing was completely empty."

But Julia was not listening. She was wearing her half-glasses and held up a small volume. "I'm studying up. Learning to ask for tickets for Milan when we hit Turin. *'Due biglietti per Turin. Seconda class, per favore.'*"

"You say *Milano*," Sarah corrected her. "And Florence is *Firenze*."

"We're not going to Florence," said Julia. "But what a lovely language. It has a real swing." She held the book up to the light. *"A che ora parte il primo autobus per Villa Adriana?"*

"What!"

"What time is the first bus to Hadrian's Villa? You never know when you'll want to say something like that. And how do you like, *'Da dove parte l'aliscafo per Lugano?'* which means, 'From where does the hydrofoil for Lugano leave?'"

Sarah sighed. "Lugano sounds peaceful. Away from our group and if we were lucky there wouldn't be a garden in sight."

Turin proved another scramble, fumbling for passports and puzzling over the Italian lira numbered in millions, the only refreshment being the view of a long stretch of the distant Alps seen through a smutty train window. But at last, Milan. Or Milano.

And Alex. Looking a little disordered, dark hair rumpled, shirt wrinkled, jacket slung over his shoulder.

He kissed Sarah soundly and embraced Julia.

And then he took a second hard look at Sarah. Saw her face, the bruises on her forehead and cheekbones now an interesting mix of yellow and fading purple.

"Sarah! In God's name what happened? Are you all right? Why didn't you tell me?" He stopped and ran a professional and concerned eye over her face. "Your nose seems okay. But you cut your lip, didn't you? Sarah, love of my life, what in hell have you been up to?"

Sarah lifted her face. "I'm okay. Really. A minor accident. A little miscalculation at the Shearing Inn. The floors are very uneven and I wasn't watching where I was going." Or who was following me, she added to herself. Avoiding Alex's direct gaze, she said, "It happened days ago. I'm fine now. Not to worry. But you look tired. That long flight."

Alex shook his head with resignation. "You're changing the subject, my beloved. I know you're lying through your teeth. But I won't torment you about it. Not yet. Meanwhile, let's get out of here." He looked at his watch. "Not bad timing. You made it with an hour to spare."

Sarah grinned at him. "And thank God for someone who isn't carrying an empty camera or sunglasses and doesn't know a dibble from a donkey."

Alex made a rueful face. "I know more than I want about dibbles. So let's get out of here. The airport, right?"

Sarah put a hand over his mouth. "Not now. Let's find a lunch place, dig into some pasta, and talk about the next phase."

Alex removed her hand. "The next phase is called airport. I've got our reservations. Milan to Heathrow to Logan. And home."

Sarah scowled. "Reservations can be cancelled because Julia and I have other ideas. We can't talk here." She waved a hand at the waiting room packed to the gills with people—students, children, pilgrims, the clergy, the aged, the tour groups, the cacophony sounding like opening day at Fenway Park.

Alex ran his eyes over Sarah again, took in not only her bruises but the shadows of fatigue under her eyes, her hands gripping the strap of her shoulder bag, saw Julia drooping, and decided that Sarah was right about one thing: the airport discussion should take place after the intake by all travelers of a quantity of protein topped by some friendly carbohydrates.

Alex led the two women to a white rental Fiat, and after the three had settled themselves, brought the two women up to date.

"George is going to call the rest of the group at their hotel tonight in Paris. Hit them with a lot of ambiguous legal language and hope they'll pack up and come home and cooperate with the forces of law and order. Skip the Italian leg of the trip."

"I have news for George," said Sarah. "Henry Ruggles made other hotel arrangements, but then Henry almost drowned at Giverny, so God only knows where they all are."

Alex stared at her. "Whoa, back up. What do you mean, Henry Ruggles almost drowned? Do I know about Henry Ruggles?"

"I told you. I'm sure I did. The little man with the wig."

"If I knew, the name has gone. Blame it on sitting up all night with a crying baby in the seat behind me. Bring me up to speed."

"Sarah did tell you about our ghost, didn't she?" demanded Julia. "Or about Edith and Margaret's new cameras. Sarah had to steal them. And guess what? Completely hollow."

Alex visibly braced himself and took a long breath. "I'm going to drive out of town in the general direction of the airport, and you will both speak very slowly and enunciate clearly and tell me what the hell is going on. Me, I've just been in Maine worrying about Ellen Trevino and bloodstained sunglasses while you've obviously been consorting with the powers of darkness."

"It's like this," Sarah began, and launched into a not-entirely-sequential description of events, a narration addled by remarks from Julia on the personalities involved, her opinion of fourteen-year-old mystery writers, and of dubious women who roam gardens at night.

"Actually," said Sarah, "Jessica Roundtree—that's her name—was impersonating your mother, Alex. Just like her, the hawk look, you know. But not Elspeth's hooded eyes."

"Shall I let Mother know you've been thinking of her?"

"I'm serious. Do you have any stray relatives slinking about gardens this month?"

"That much of a resemblance, was it?"

"Striking in a way," put in Julia. "But there was another McKenzie look-alike. Justin Rossi. Looks like you. Sarah was quite taken."

Sarah made a face. "Honestly, Aunt Julia. Justin has his points, but he's a poor replica of the original."

"This Jessica turned up twice, you say," Alex persisted. They were now fairly well out of the city, and Alex turned off the multilane highway and swung the Fiat in the direction of a small group of stores: a *farmacia, a trattoria,* and a *gelateria.* "Have you considered," he added, "that this resemblance—not just to the McKenzie clan—might be legitimate. That Justin Rossi and this Jessica might be related. Mother and son. Or aunt."

"You mean," said Sarah, "some relative who's following Justin around England for some nefarious reason."

Alex pulled into the parking lot of the tiny *trattoria* with a red-striped awning that sat between a small settlement of houses. "This looks okay. Let's hope it's open." He twisted about to face Sarah and Julia. "This tour group of yours. It's as if there are partners. Two by two. Noah's Ark."

Sarah looked puzzled. "I don't get it. You mean people like Sandi and Fred Ouellette."

"Those two are natural partners. I mean if there's something odd going on, there seem to be teams. Carter McClure and this Henry Ruggles. Barbara and brother Gregory. The Hopper sisters acting like two spies in an old movie. And now this Justin Rossi and his look-alike mother—or whoever." Alex cut the engine and opened the car door. "My theory," he said, "is still in the planning stage."

It is amazing what food can do—especially simple food well spiced and pleasantly served by cheerful people. The little restaurant was off the beaten tourist track, and Maria, Carlo, and daughter, Flora, owners of the Caffé Allegro, had apparently not grown hardened to travelers from foreign parts, and the meal was attended with a good deal of jollity in the matter of selecting and ordering a variety of fish and fowl with pasta on the side.

Alcohol and coffee also did their part. Julia, finishing her second glass of *vino bianco*, declared her arthritis in remission, Alex relaxed with draught beer (*birra alla spina*) and listened to Sarah's plan, while Sarah, warmed by *cappuccino*, gave her arguments for staying in Italy in a reasonable manner—when before lunch she had been planning to browbeat Alex into submission.

"You see," said Sarah, putting down her coffee cup, "it's not just Ellen's murder—the police are dealing with that, the evidence, the forensics angle. I want to tie together all the things that have happened on our trip. And if it means seeing Margaret and Edith Hopper behind bars and Justin Rossi and Barbara Baxter and Stacy Daniel hanging by their thumbs, well, so be it. To me it seems obvious that there's been this ongoing crazy plan to get rid of tour leaders."

"Barbara's still going strong, isn't she?" asked Alex.

"Maybe she's next. Or maybe she's behind it, but I don't think so. Her room was searched when mine was and she didn't push Henry in the pool at Kiftsgate. And, from what I saw, she probably saved his life at Giverny. We've really drawn a blank on what's going on. Lots of theories. No conclusions."

"And poor Sarah," said Julia, "her searching of everyone's room only ended in her being mugged." Julia always enjoyed stirring up the waters, but in this case Alex was only too ready to jump into the subject; it had been with great difficulty that for the past hour he had stopped himself from pressing Sarah on the subject. Now he pointed accusingly at her face.

Well, it was time to come clean since Alex was now imitating some sort of animal glowering at the mouth of its den. Sarah grimaced and admitted to breaking, entering, and being caught in the act. "Not a big deal, really. It could have been much worse. Though I do wish I'd spent more time learning self-defense." Then, she added that she hoped it was all settled. They would not go to the airport but would join the tour group—as planned—at the hotel in Bellagio and see what developed. They would exercise extreme caution, stay together.

Alex hesitated, frowning.

"We'll regret it if we don't."

"I'm afraid we'll regret it if we do."

It was Julia who put the objections to rest. "We must stay and find out about those hollow cameras. Besides, I have another job. Margaret and Edith. Please, leave them to me. Those two are my generation. I will take them aside—away from all of you because you'll only make them more nervous than they already are, and I will talk to them. Gently. Firmly. It's like horses, you know. Be calm. Be kind but don't give in, don't allow for distractions, and after a while the animal comes around. Knows there's no choice."

Alex grinned a resigned grin. "When you put it that way, Julia, it's absolutely irresistible. Did you bring your saddle?"

Chapter Twenty-Five

THEY DROVE NORTH ON a large highway, Alex assuring the two women that he wanted to drive and would not fall asleep at the wheel. Why didn't they talk to him? For instance, why was everyone going to Bellagio anyway? Weren't there gardens enough in France?

"I think," said Sarah, "the idea was to give us a taste of three countries. Bellagio is supposed to be the grand finale. Lake Como, cobbled streets, ancient ambiance, plus super gardens. The hotel—Albergo Nuovo—has a swimming pool..."

"The better to push someone into...," observed Julia dryly.

"And shopping might even be allowed. Especially since Portia and Carter McClure—he fought shopping all the way—are taking Henry back to England. Anyway, Alex, I'll buy you an Italian silk tie. A tie to kill for."

"See," said Julia, "that's all she can think of. Crime on the brain. Well, I'm going to bring a little culture into your lives. I've got the Bellagio guide." Julia leaned forward from the backseat and informed them that Bellagio was already a going concern between the seventh and fifth centuries B.C., that Celts and Gauls, assorted Teutons, sundry Roman consuls, and a bunch of Germanic tribes had been at each others' throats over the centuries.

"Goths, Visigoths, Ostrogoths," said Alex.

"Then those city-states," said Sarah. "The Guelphs and the Ghibellines. Dante was mixed up in all those wars. Aunt Julia, we should read Dante while we're here."

"I have several circles in hell ready and waiting," said Julia, turning the pages of the guide. "Now let's see, we have the Sforzas and Viscontis. And the Medici. They were a tricky bunch and Gina Giacomo Medici seems to have caused a lot of trouble."

Alex turned to Sarah. "Can you possibly believe that Edith and Margaret Hopper are involved in a criminal conspiracy?"

"Well, why were they waltzing around Cambridge pretending to take pictures with fake cameras?"

"Where did they get the cameras?"

"In Cambridge," said Sarah. "It was Barbara Baxter's idea."

"Bellagio, along with the rest of Lombardy, became subject to Spanish rule in 1519," announced Julia.

"So Barbara Baxter is behind the camera buying," said Alex. "That should make you think. Unless—and this is reaching—some sleazy camera dealer in Cambridge was trying to unload a couple of dummies. Cameras they use in display cases. And along came these stupid Americans. Perfect dupes."

"Maximilian of Austria in 1493 went along Lake Como, leaving destruction and death behind him," read Julia.

"If Edith and Margaret found their cameras were dummies they'd have made a fuss," said Sarah. "I have the feeling money's pretty tight. I think they're a working part of some scheme—or scam."

"Connected to Barbara? Her brother Gregory? Who?"

"Shall I skip to Garibaldi?" asked Julia. "Or how about Liszt? He sneaked off with someone's wife—her name was Marie—and they holed up in Bellagio."

"I can't think," Alex went on, "that Barbara Baxter—who from all accounts is a practical female—would actually choose Edith and Margaret Hopper to help pull off some scam."

"But," objected Sarah, "if the Hoppers don't fit the bill, who've you got left? Justin Rossi and Stacy Daniel."

"Of course," said Julia, "there's no mention in the pamphlet of Mussolini. I suppose he's an embarrassment. The pamphlet just goes on about fishing and gardens and churches. And all sorts of boutiques and *pasticceria* and *gelaterie*. And bars."

"*Gelaterie*," exclaimed Sarah. "I feel like ice cream. Let's find a place, okay?" She consulted the map. "We'll be turning off the big road and heading for Lake Como in a few miles."

Fifty minutes later Alex and Julia and Sarah, each armed with the ice cream cone of their choice, stood at the edge of the Via Pescallo. Each felt for that brief span of time that an Italian lake in June was the proper place to be. The sun shone but not too hotly, the breeze blew but not too fiercely, some unidentified bird chirped and fluttered in a nearby unidentified bush, and even Alex, serious birdwatcher, did not reach for his binoculars, but was content just to sit on the edge of a boulder and work his way slowly through a ginger cone. Sarah by his side ran her tongue around a pyramidal lump of strawberry, and Julia, leaning against what might or might not have been an oak tree took satisfying bites of her vanilla.

And then it was on to Bellagio, that ancient little jewel of a town that raised its turtle-shaped head between the misty waters of Lago di Como and the Lago di Lecco.

The Albergo Nuovo proved a recently constructed complex that sat to one side of the Via Roncati well above the tangle of narrow cobblestone streets and buildings, and piazzas that made up that part of Bellagio called the Borgo. The hotel itself boasted a small garden and a most welcome swimming pool; an item that had much refreshed the rather frazzled automobile party of Julia, Alex, and Sarah. Each had spent a reviving hour in the pool; even Julia, wearing an ancient full-skirted navy blue bathing costume—Sarah told Alex there was no other term for the outfit—had spent a placid period doing a stately breaststroke up and down the length of the pool.

And now at six o'clock on the evening of Wednesday, June the twenty-first, the members of the Midcoast Garden Club had gathered on the patio that overlooked the terraced garden and the pool. Even with the welcome news that Henry Ruggles, although fragile, was now safely back in England, the group in Sarah's opinion was sadly fragmented. Each person seemed somehow detached from the others as if the threads that in Gloucestershire had made for cohesiveness had been severed—severed when Henry lay on the bank of the River Epte gasping for breath. Perhaps that was it; the enthusiastic Henry, the peppery Carter McClure, the soothing Portia—had taken with them some of the glue that had held the group together.

Sandi Ouellette, usually bubbling about a new visit, remarked only that she missed Henry, he added so much. And then fell silent, bent over a list of museums to be found in the village. Justin Rossi sat somewhat apart, nursing a carafe of red wine and jotting in a notebook. "A case coming up when I get back," he explained. Doris Lermatov and Amy argued about a book report that Amy had due when she returned to school in the fall, and Stacy Daniel, as beautifully draped as usual, oblivious of anyone around her, occupied herself with making a list of the dress shops in the town.

As for the Hoppers, Sarah saw them with increasing concern. They seemed to have shrunk inside their navy travel dresses and their white cardigans. Their faces were lined and pale, Edith's hair had lost its careful wave, Margaret's hairnet was torn, and they had both abandoned the modest efforts at make-up employed at the beginning of the trip. Sarah looked over at Julia and saw her aunt studying the sisters, planning no doubt the attack on what was left of the Hopper peace of mind.

Only Barbara Baxter and Fred Ouellette presented façades of good cheer. Fred—apparently impervious to emotional undertones—had cornered Alex and launched into an enthusiastic plan for visiting the remains of a necropolis discovered in the area. Burial vaults and cemeteries, Fred told Alex. "I thought," he said, "that Bellagio would just be more gardens. But I've lucked out."

As for Barbara, she seemed determined to make a success of the Italian phase of the trip. To this end she had studied the Bellagio guides and now spoke glowingly of the famous gardens. Should they try Villa Serbelloni first with its hedges of yew and box, its cypresses, its bay trees? What did everyone think?

The question hung unanswered until Barbara, ignoring community apathy, switched gardens and began a confused description of the wonders of the Villa Melzi. Grottos, goldfish, camellias, a cedar of Lebanon, a cedar of the Himalayans, a sequoia, a chapel—all these Barbara brandished before the group.

Then, as she was running out of steam, Justin Rossi picked up the thread and admitted if you liked villas and gardens and goldfish, well the Villa Melzi might be as good a place as any to see them. Seconded by a nod from Stacy Daniel.

But Barbara, as if possessed by some Spirit of Tourism, got her second wind. Churches and museums opened their doors to evening visitors, as did the many specialty shops. And a ride on the lake, a walk along the shore would be fun.

"And," added Barbara, "I think Margaret and Edith might find a store selling new cameras." She turned to Alex and Julia and Sarah. "They've been so depressed. It's as if you can't trust anyone. Their new cameras were stolen at Giverny. Of all places. You'd think a famous garden like that would be safe."

Alex looked over at Margaret and Edith. It might be a good idea to find out exactly what the two sisters thought about the disappearance of cameras. "Were they snatched?" he asked. "Were you held up?"

"Oh no," faltered Margaret. "We were so careless. When we heard the shouting—it was Henry when he'd gone into the river—we just dropped our cameras…"

"And I dropped my purse," said Edith.

"And we ran. To help if we could, but, of course, Barbara had already pulled Henry out, and with all the excitement we forgot the cameras, what with Henry being so terribly sick."

"We left," said Edith, "because the doctor didn't want us crowding around, and then I remembered the cameras and my purse. But when we went back…"

"Only Edith's purse," said Margaret. "The cameras were gone."

"How dreadful," said Sarah, feeling it was time to join the chorus. "And you'd only had them a day or so. But, then," she added, "you didn't seem to want to use them."

"Nonsense," said Barbara stoutly. "Everyone wants to take pictures of the places they've been. And I feel very sorry that it all happened on—what's the term—my watch. So Margaret and Edith, Whirlaway Tours is going to buy you two new cameras. Right here in Bellagio. There's bound to be a photography shop. We'll use my VISA. Go down into town and look. Even if the ones you find are a little more expensive, I want you to buy them."

"We're to choose them?" faltered Margaret.

"Of course. I only helped find the others because you weren't sure about new models. Whirlaway Tours wants you both to have two nice cameras. Let's say about two hundred each for replacements." Barbara's confident smile gathered everyone to her. "Face it. It's good PR for us, too. We can't have Margaret and Edith going home and saying Whirlaway runs a loose ship."

"I think," said Julia, later that evening after dinner, "that Whirlaway—or Barbara—runs a very tight ship indeed."

Julia, with Alex and Sarah, was on her way down one of the steep, narrow cobblestone streets that snaked its way down to Piazza Mazzini and the waterfront.

Alex paused in front of a crowded pizzeria. "I stopped Margaret and Edith after drinks—and I may say both seem like candidates for Prozac—and ferreted out the information that yes, Barbara produced two compact cameras from some store in Cambridge. An Olympus and a Nikon."

"Name of store, name of street?" demanded Sarah.

"They can't remember. And no sales slips."

"Just like that Barbara turns up with hollow cameras from a legitimate store."

"So," said Julia, "the store may front a smuggling operation run by a camera store and they dumped the cameras on Barbara. Anyway, tomorrow will reveal all. I told you I have a plan. The Hoppers are my babies."

"As long as your plan involves no strong-arm business and is done in broad daylight surrounded by two loved ones," said Alex.

Julia nodded and the three set off again and the rest of the evening was spent ducking in and out of small stores, the purchasing of a striped shirt and checkered tie for Alex, a journal covered with handmade paper by Sarah, and a carved letter opener by Julia. "In case I need a personal weapon," she explained with a sidelong glance at Alex.

Their tour of the town proved to be refreshingly clear of members of the Garden Club, although Sarah admitted to missing Henry. "He really enjoyed what he was doing and when he'd been pulled out of the river he looked so forlorn, like an old doll that had lost its hair."

They stood at the waterfront looking into the mist that hung over the lake, each silent with his or her own thoughts. And then, just as Sarah was rejoicing in the absolute tranquility, Amy appeared. A somewhat subdued Amy.

"It's the whole place," admitted Amy. "I couldn't have imagined it. Lake Como, all it needs is the Loch Ness monster. And the winding stairs and the narrow streets. And people sticking their heads out of overhead windows and all the niches in those high walls where you can leave messages or poison or something." Amy stopped and shook her head. She sounded, Sarah thought, for the first time on the trip, genuinely awed by her surroundings.

But then Doris Lermatov loomed and, taking Amy by the arm, drew her away, saying that she wasn't to go around by herself because some Italian men—just some—find redheaded girls particularly interesting.

"You mean sex objects," said Amy, at which her mother suggested a gelato and the two went their way.

Julia had just said she was going to start climbing back up the stairs to their hotel when Sarah jabbed her elbow into her aunt's side. "Look over there. Alex, there she is. Our ghost. The one like your mother. Down by the entrance to the Hotel du Lac. Quick, or you'll miss her."

There indeed she was. The gray draperies, the shawl, the abundant white hair. She walked along slowly, stopping to look into store windows, and then she disappeared into a dress shop bordering the hotel.

"Your mother?" asked Julia of Alex.

"Something like," said Alex. "There's sort of an aura."

Sarah didn't answer. In fact couldn't because two images—no four images—had begun to mass in her brain, joining, separating, rejoining, reforming. But she couldn't quite make the final fusion.

Alex was also thinking. His mind was busy rebutting the idea that this Jessica Roundtree was pursuing them for some unknown purpose. "I think you have to credit coincidence. People on trips do keep bumping into the same people."

"Yes, they do," said Sarah, "but I don't think this is any coincidence. And I'm not one hundred percent sure but I may have the answer to this particular puzzle."

"You're going to let me participate in your brainstorm?"

"You can even help. I need basic research. Now let's float up these stairs and think beautiful Italian thoughts. Listen, it's a wonderful language. *Da dove parte l'aliscafo per Lugano?*"

"Which means?"

"Translation ruins it. But if you must know, it means, 'From where does the hydrofoil for Lugano leave?'"

"I think you can forget Lugano. Bellagio is enough of a challenge."

And the two caught up with Julia, who was just starting the long climb to the top of the stairs. Alex offered his arm and Julia without protest gratefully accepted.

They reached their hotel floor and were about to part for the night, when Julia stopped Alex. "I need your car keys. I've left my needlepoint in the Fiat and I've been neglecting it terribly."

"Let me get it for you," Sarah offered.

"Nonsense," said Julia. "I'm feeling quite brisk again."

"I'll go with you," said Sarah. "Remember we're going to keep an eye on each other."

"Certainly not," said Julia. "No one has the slightest idea where anyone is. Besides the parking lot is lighted and there's an attendant standing right there by the lamp post. So stay put and I'll see you in the morning."

Morning came and when Alex opened the bedroom door he found a folded sheet of hotel stationery on the threshold. He confronted Sarah, who was pulling on her shorts, ready for a morning run.

"Julia has written us," he said grimly.

"She has what!"

"She says she's very sorry about taking the car keys but she needs them to start the car. Make her apologies to the group and tell them she had a wonderful chance to visit a private garden with two old friends. And for us not to worry because everything will work out and she'll be in touch."

"That's it?"

"That's it. Wait here a minute." And Alex flung the door open, sprinted down the hall and out. And returned almost immediately. "She's right. No car," he said.

Sarah stood in the middle of the room, red-faced and looking as if she wanted to bite someone. "What old friends," she demanded. "Let me see the note."

"She doesn't say," said Alex as he handed over the note.

"Well, I have a damn good idea," said Sarah. "She's gone and kidnapped Margaret and Edith Hopper."

"In our car," added Alex ruefully.

Sarah pulled a T-shirt over her head. "Okay, before I start spitting nails and throwing furniture, let's run a check on the two old friends."

Twenty minutes later, after a joint check of the grounds of Albergo Nuovo, they gave it up.

"Now what," demanded Sarah. "Any bright ideas?"

"Yes," said Alex. "It's a beautiful day, so let's run a mile or so and then have a swim. To hell with Julia. At least for the next half hour."

"And then?"

"We will telephone Signore Hertz or Signore Avis or Signore Budget and find a car and then consider whether we can speak Italian well enough to call on the Carabinieri or the polizia."

"I think I can handle that. More or less. *Mi scusi, per favore. Mia zia mi ha rubato mia macchina.*"

"Which means?"

"Excuse me please. My aunt has stolen my car."

Chapter Twenty-Six

AT HOME IN MAINE, when alone in her car Julia Clancy drove with abandon; however, with passengers—often these were horses tethered in a trailer behind her truck—she exercised the greatest care. Today she kept a conservative foot on the accelerator.

It was four A.M. and Julia didn't like driving before it was light. But really, there was no help for it. Her plans had been laid with care and they depended on a predawn departure. All the way on the still dark road that had led from Bellagio to Como and then turned north, she had kept up, for her passengers, a soothing stream of comment on the beauties of the Italian hills and the magical quality of the Italian lakes.

These passengers, unfortunately, remained resistant to comfort. They had been aroused by telephone in the small hours of the morning, told to pack up, bring their passports, and by stealth to join Julia in the parking lot because it was a matter of life and death. Now, almost two hours later with the town of Como well behind them both Margaret Hopper, in the front passenger seat, and Edith in the rear, teetered on the edge of collapse.

Julia regretted using the threat of "life and death," but had felt that no other phrase would move the two. Now she kept up her efforts to calm her passengers. No need—as yet—to pounce. Finesse, though never Julia's strong point—was the way to go.

"Not quite life and death," she told the sisters. "But almost. You were in real danger. And I had to try and do something. Please just sit back and rest. Take deep breaths." She indicated a faint lightening of the sky. "It's going to be a beautiful day, we'll be able to see for miles. Like a Bellini painting."

Margaret Hopper coughed. "I don't think Bellini painted around here; he was a Venetian. And Julia, you are making a terrible mistake. We should have stayed in Bellagio. With our friends."

Margaret seemed to be rallying, so Julia decided to skip the finesse. "Stuff and nonsense. What friends? I'm your friend and I and no one else understands about your situation. And the danger."

Margaret turned a frowning face. "You keep saying danger, Julia, but I don't know what you mean. And by what possible right are you forcing us…"

"Not forcing," said Julia with some irritation. "It's called—what's the expression—crisis intervention." She slowed the car, pulled to the right, and allowed an irate Maserati—coming out of nowhere—to gun past. Returning to the road, she checked a sign announcing Capolago, and nodded with satisfaction. "I did some research at the hotel desk yesterday and they came up with a nice quiet little *penzione*." Here Julia accelerated and swung past a road sign announcing *Curva Pericolosa*.

"That sign says 'Dangerous Curve,'" said Edith sharply, and Julia was pleased to hear a measure of energy in her voice.

Both women were recovering. It was time for the medicine. At least a small dose. She took a deep breath.

"You two ladies are not spy material and you're in danger because you're trying to pull off an act for which you are very ill-equipped. You're completely out of your depth."

"What are you talking about," demanded Margaret with a brave show of anger,

Julia waved her into silence. "Please. Hear me out. In the first place neither of you has any notion of how to conceal your feelings. You've been in terrible state since High Roosting and everyone has noticed it. Sooner or later you were going to be seen as a pair of god-awful liabilities. And suffer the consequences."

"What do you mean, 'consequences'," said Edith. "We haven't done anything except cooperate with everyone." It was a poor effort at best and Julia ignored it.

"Margaret and Edith, we all go back a long ways. School, summer camp. You were always older and wiser, always on the honor roll. You went in for education, and I was the ragtail tomboy who lived in a horse barn. But now, all of us, we're part of the old guard. So I want to help you and you have to let me."

"We have always taken care of ourselves," began Edith.

"Let me finish," said Julia, trying to keep her voice from its usual sharpness. "If you go back to Bellagio you may end up like Henry Ruggles, only there may be no one around to pull you out of the lake. Or if you survive Bellagio, you'll go home to sizzle on Sergeant George Fitts's hot seat, and it will be very public and very nasty. I think I can make it easier for you. Now here's the turn-off I'm looking for. South of Lanzo. It's a nice family place, quiet and peaceful. La Pensione Vittoria."

Julia drove carefully the last few miles, peering at signs and then pulled in front of a small tiled-roof stucco building snugged into the hillside. The Pensione Vittoria was indeed small and peaceful, and the sun coming up gave a sparkle to its small casement windows. All in all, Julia decided, it was exactly what the doctor had ordered. One night in a new place can make all the difference.

They were greeted by the son of the establishment, a wiry youth called Roberto, who seized the Hopper suitcases and led them up the stairs. Julia, prodding the reluctant Hoppers, saw them into their room. It was a cheerful chamber with whitewashed walls, and beds, chairs, and bureaus all painted a bright blue. She gave the sisters—who had ceased to resist—orders for an hour's rest to be followed by a meeting outside. Lunch with a view of Lake Lugano and the mountains.

Seventy minutes later Julia ushered her reluctant guests to a table on a paved terrace. The table faced a tiny garden set about with pieces of statuary, including a donkey and cart, a cherub with a broken arm, and a pair of griffins, all looked over by a solemn St. Francis holding a birdbath and a Virgin Mary in a blue coat, her arms outspread. An ideal setting, Julia decided, for the telling of truth and the unburdening of the soul.

The setting was completed by the table on which several white roses stuck out of an earthenware pot and a bottle of *vino bianco* sat next to a serving platter of *cannelloni al forno*. Edith Hopper had asked wistfully for tea—but Julia had voted this down. Courage—even if it came in a bottle—was the order of the day.

"Now," said Julia, when the first glasses of wine had gone down the Hopper throats, "tell me what has been going on?" And Julia reached for a pack of tissues—she had come prepared—and put it in front of the sisters. There was a long pause, and then:

"It started," said Margaret in a shaky voice, "a long time ago. Edith was nine and I was almost eleven."

"About a week before your birthday," said Edith.

"Are we going to try and trace Aunt Julia?" demanded Sarah. "Get the police into the act. Or just hope for the best?"

She and Alex, after a demanding run and serious lapwork in the pool, were now settled at eight o'clock at a tiled table having breakfast. Sarah wore her tourist jumper of blue denim.

Alex buttered a chunky piece of toast, dribbled honey across its surface, and took a bite. He was, Sarah thought, looking less haggard than he had on arrival. The run had given him color and his new green and red striped shirt gave him a rakish look—a look at variance to Alex's ironic and usually realistic approach to life.

"You fit in," said Sarah approvingly. "Almost Italian. You can go out on the town after breakfast and mix with the natives. Anyway, I'd say let Julia get on with what she's doing, which I suppose is pumping the poor Hoppers. I just hope she doesn't scare them into a total breakdown."

"Come on. Julia won't hit them with rubber hoses and put lighted matches under their fingernails. I say hold it for now."

"Agreed. Now, as I've said, I have a research job for you."

"You mean as your back-up? I ride shotgun and you head for the border?"

"No, listen. It's research worthy of your talents. The Garden Club is supposed to do the Melzi Gardens this morning. The bus loads up at ten, so you've got about two hours. You'll have to table-hop during breakfast or lurk on the terrace. You're the new face and everyone will probably chat it up."

"This is a worthy cause? It ties in directly with Ellen?"

"No," admitted Sarah. "This is peripheral. But it may lead to Ellen. What did the man say, by indirections find directions out. Well, I'm going the long way round because I need to be very sure about someone. And something."

"You want to share?"

"I don't want to taint your objectivity. As follows. Please cozy up to Sandi Ouellette, which ought to be easy because she's friendly—and a gossip. Ask if she can give you any new details about the woman who bounced the molester out of the Hound and Hare pub back at High Roosting. All we know so far is that the woman was tall and that she must have been strong to pull off the bouncing act. And here on deck we've got two tall strong women and one shorter strong woman, and we need to do some weeding out."

"Okay, I'll work on Sandi. I rather take to her. She says what she thinks and doesn't bother about impressing people."

"You're right. I'm growing very fond of Sandi. Okay, next job. Take a notebook because you're doing research on pubs."

"I'm what?"

"On pubs. English pubs. French and Italian pubs. It's a long-standing interest of yours. Throw in some medical angle if you want, like the therapeutic value of draught beer. Whatever. You're writing a monograph. No, make it a guidebook. And you've missed out on some of the Cotswold pubs. Particularly High Roosting area pubs. Move in on Stacy Daniel and ask some questions."

"She's a pub expert?"

"Pub crawler. Everyone says that at night she takes off. Never hangs around with any of the rest of the group. Justin Rossi doesn't either, but I'm leaving him until later."

"Good," said Alex. "I'm not crazy about doppelgangers."

"You said things were happening by twos," Sarah reminded him. "Anyway, find out if Stacy's ever been to the Hound and Hare in High Roosting. Say you need a critique of the place. And ask about the other town pubs just to be legitimate. One's called the Black Badger and I can't remember the name of the other one."

"There's no such thing as a black badger."

"For God's sake, Alex, it doesn't matter. Some fool in the sixteenth century thought there was and named the place."

"This is important?"

Sarah reached for a last roll and spread it with apricot jam and faced her husband. "You can bet your life—or mine—it's important. And one last thing. When you finish covering the breakfast scene, look over this list." Sarah fished in her pocket. "This has the items mentioned by Gregory Baxter and sister Barbara when Julia and I had dinner next to them."

"Dinner, as in eavesdropping."

"That was the point of being there."

Alex examined the list. "Something rings a bell. But I don't know if any of it ties into those hollow cameras. And, by the way, where are they?"

Sarah made a face. "They're in the Fiat. Julia may be sticking them in Edith and Margaret's faces as we speak. But the only thing I found was that piece of clear plastic in one of them."

Alex put down his napkin and stood up. "All right. I'll hit the breakfast crowd. You stay put in our bedroom until bus time. Door locked, okay?"

Sarah nodded and then added, "A tip. Stacy Daniel, as you may have noticed, is absolutely gorgeous. She reminds me of a lioness stalking through the veldt. I never can picture her locked up in a bank job. So let her know you're taken with her."

Alex grinned. "No problem."

Exactly one hour and fifty minutes later, Alex escorted Sarah to the meeting place for the tour bus.

"I've worked on my notes. For my guide to pubs of the world."

"And?"

"Sandi remembers nothing new about the lady bouncer except she didn't think she was young, but Stacy was crazy about the Black Badger because you can meet people there and have a great evening—whatever that means, although I can guess. Stacy said she wouldn't be caught dead at the Hound and Hare. She'd heard the place was a mob scene and some football club practically lived in it. And," Alex added, "she's glad she's met me and perhaps we can hit the local pubs some night. La Grotta, or better Il Tiglio, which is a pub and restaurant. She was sure you wouldn't want to come because, and I quote, 'Sarah is the home type.'"

Before Sarah could express her feelings on that score, Alex held up his hand. "Here come the others. Does my report make the whole mess a little clearer now? To you anyway?"

"Some clear parts, some clear like mud," said Sarah.

"Can't you skip this Melzi Garden visit?"

"No. It just might clear some of the mud."

"Don't get yourself off in a corner with anyone even if it's Mother Teresa. Buddy up with Sandi and Fred. Or Doris Lermatov. I'll see you here at the hotel when you get back."

But Alex didn't find Sarah at the hotel, and, in fact, by noon of that Thursday, the twenty-second of June, the Midcoast Garden Club had ceased to function as a tour group.

It resembled—this last trip to the gardens of the Villa Melzi, the last trip to any garden—other trips taken by the club. Because, even in its sadly diminished form, some small degree of excitement remained. Here was all the usual paraphernalia: the notebooks, the Bellagio guides, the flower identification books, and, in the case of Amy and Sandi, cameras (genuine ones, Sarah hoped). Stacy wore her straw hat with the wide brim and the flame-colored ribbon, Doris and Sandi had canvas hats of the boating variety, Amy wore a genuine Pittsburgh Pirates baseball cap pulled over her eyes, and Barbara sported a tennis visor. Sarah had explained to everyone that Julia had taken Margaret and Edith Hopper for a drive into the hills, and this was accepted without much comment. Julia, often an irascible presence, would not be much missed and the Hoppers had become mere traveling shadows.

Of all the gardens Sarah had visited, those of the Villa Melzi had the distinction of receiving her full attention. Actually, she had little choice; no opportunity offered for private talk, and there was no Julia with whom to argue or plot. The diminished group—only eight of the original fourteen—clung together, and leader Barbara, relentless in the pursuit of the advertised specialties of the garden, was alert for stragglers. The moment anyone slowed their steps on a path or lingered too long over a planting, she halted the group and waited until he or she caught up.

"If we'd all stayed together at Giverny," Barbara explained, "poor Henry would be with us today."

"Maybe, but staying together wouldn't have helped Margaret and Edith," said Sandi. "I just don't think we cared enough about what was wrong with them." She turned to Sarah almost accusingly. "And now your Aunt Julia has driven off with them. I'll bet she's trying to browbeat them into telling some awful family secret when it's none of her business."

This was so close to the actual truth that Sarah for a moment had to scramble for an answer. She was only able to come up with the feeble remark that Julia was concerned for their happiness. To which Sandi gave an unbelieving, "Sure. Right."

But Barbara had held up her hands again. It was as if she was possessed of the wish to be the most informed, the most attentive, the most energetic tour leader in all Italy.

"She's trying to win Camp Spirit," whispered Sandi to Fred.

"Sandi," said Barbara. "Did you know Napoleon visited the Villa? And had his portrait painted? And Liszt came here. And the gardens have wonderful ponds and vistas and a grotto. Some really interesting tropical plants." Here Barbara glanced down at her guidebook. "It says here that these grounds were the very first example of English gardens in the whole area."

"Then why," demanded Stacy Daniel, "are we here? We've already done English gardens."

But Barbara didn't blink. "These are Italian gardens with an English flavor," she said. "There's all the difference. Now let's walk around the pond. You can see the goldfish from the bridge."

But Fred rebelled. The Grotto—the one by the gate—well, he'd read that it held a cinerary urn brought from the tomb of the Scipioni family in Rome. He wondered if it was visible. On display. Perhaps there was special information to be had at the ticket office about Roman habits of ash disposal. And Fred marched off in the direction of the gate.

Barbara, torn in two directions, hesitated. And then decided to chase the stray sheep. "Stay right here. Please," she ordered and took off after Fred.

"She needs a Border Collie," observed Justin to Sarah. Both had climbed onto the little bridge while the others gathered at the bank.

Sarah gazed down into the pond, spiked by reeds and an occasional floating lily pad, and saw—as advertised—a number of large goldfish lazily circling in and out of the shadows. A large, deeper-hued one was making persistent runs at two smaller fish. Then these two wriggled themselves into pursuit of even smaller, less brilliantly colored ones. Just like the English Department, she thought.

Justin, too, was looking down into the pond. "Poor old Henry," he said. "This is only a few feet deep, but even that would be too much for him if he went in. He'd have panicked, sunk to the bottom, and just lain there until someone fished him out again."

Sarah looked at him quizzically. "Are you saying Henry has gone through life falling into ponds and being rescued?"

But before Justin could answer, Doris Lermatov, waiting on the bank, called out in an anxious voice, "Amy. Has anyone seen Amy?"

Everyone turned to everyone else, Barbara came bustling up with an apologetic Fred in tow, and, after a certain amount of circling and calling it became clear that Amy had departed.

"Or," said Doris, her voice rising, "she's been taken."

"Don't be silly," said Barbara. "Amy's done it on purpose. To drive us all crazy. She's never enjoyed the gardens."

"Which is putting it mildly," said Justin to Sarah. He raised his voice. "Look, Doris, I'm finished with the Melzi Gardens. I'm going back to the hotel so I'll keep an eye out for her. Don't worry, Amy is a smart girl. She just has had it with the tour scene." And, with long strides and without looking back, Justin stepped off the bridge and headed for the gate.

"Well, I'm going to start looking," said Doris. "I think she'd go into the town. I'll head that way."

"Wait," said Sandi. "We might as well be systematic. No point in everyone looking in the same place. I'll take the lake side and the cafés and Doris can do the stores and hotels facing the waterfront." She pulled out her guide. "It's called the Piazza Mazzini."

Here we have, thought Sarah, a person who teaches life-saving. She stepped down from the bridge and went up to Doris. "Amy was with us just a few minutes ago, so she can't have gotten far."

"I'm sure," said Fred, "she's just gone off to look at the shops. She said at breakfast she wanted to explore the whole town."

"She didn't tell me that," said Doris in an injured voice.

"Because," Sandi pointed out, "you wouldn't have let her go."

"I think we need to organize," said Barbara belatedly.

"Sandi already has," said Fred. "She's good at it."

It was decided. They would go back along the promenade to the town center and then split. Sandi and Doris as assigned, Sarah, Fred, and Barbara checking the narrow shop-lined roads and the steep little stairways that led to the upper levels. Stacy Daniel would explore the full range of the Villa Melzi gardens and then head for the main road and the hotel.

"I think we're overreacting," said Fred, as five members of the search party hustled along the promenade. "Teenagers never stay put. It's a wonder she didn't get loose sooner."

"I know," puffed Doris, who was having a hard time keeping up with Fred's long striding walk. "I know she's been bored, and I usually don't go into a fit over something like this. It's only that it's a strange place and a strange country and with everything that's happened...well, I feel better trying to track her down."

Amen, thought Sarah. She was entertaining a familiar sinking sensation. Amy loose on the town. Amy with her notebook asking all those questions about ghosts and murder mysteries. Amy might have been asking for it. It? Oh hell, Sarah told herself and quickened her stride.

Then, as the group approached the Piazza Mazzini, she asked herself a crucial question. Should she sound an alert, point a finger? But at whom? She knew Barbara Baxter was probably dealing in hollow cameras but to what end? And yesterday she and Julia may—or may not—have been pursued by the gray Peugeot. Or an unknown car. But none of this seemed directly life-threatening. She didn't know who tipped Henry into the Kiftsgate pool and later into the river. And, damnation, she didn't know who had killed Ellen Trevino.

Biting her lip, Sarah walked on without speaking. And following Sandi's direction, she began climbing the nearest stairs leading toward the top of the town, while Barbara and Fred split and each set off on other routes.

But spotting Amy among the throngs that pushed in and out of the *pizzerie, ristoranti, gelaterie,* the grills, bars, clothing stores, and trinket shops was just about hopeless. Sarah dodged in and out, shop after shop, up the stairs, down again, up again. More and more anxious. Spotting a frizzy redhead here, there, in a doorway. On a stair. But never the right redhead.

It was now long past noon, almost one o'clock, and the sun was burning hot, but there was a heaviness to the air and some thick looking clouds hanging low over the mountains that promised a later storm. Panting, holding her side, Sarah had stopped on the upper reaches of one of the narrow steep stairways—a *salita* it was called, she remembered. I've got to get my breath, she told herself. If I pass out it won't help find Amy. And they should have arranged for a meeting place. Or a signal if she were found. Now they all might be doomed to spend the day scrabbling around Bellagio while Amy would be taking her ease with a gelato on some distant park bench.

At least this particular stairway was not a popular tourist route and no one was in sight. There were other, easier climbs. Sarah leaned gratefully against a rough stone wall and wiped her forehead with her sleeve. She'd take five minutes' rest and then start hunting again. And, wouldn't you know, Amy hadn't worn her distinctive black Decomposers T-shirt today, a shirt Sarah might have spotted in a crowd. No, she was in a plain white number with an Italian flag on its back. Just like millions of others. "Damn," she said aloud.

"Damn is right," said a woman's voice above her, behind the curve of the wall. Sarah whipped around.

"You're alone," said the voice. "Good. So, okay, where are those cameras?"

Sarah found her voice. It felt thick in her throat. "What cameras?" she managed.

"Don't give me that shit. Margaret and Edith Hopper may think they're stolen—the dear old things would never think ill of a friend. I know better. You've been after them for days. So, where are they?"

Sarah braced her back against the wall, only too aware that the two of them were completely alone. "I don't have," she said slowly, "any cameras." String this out, she told herself. Someone's bound to come.

The woman inched closer and now stood on the step above her. "I've had it with you. You've pushed it too far. You'd think that after everything that's happened, you'd get the idea. Kept your nose clean. Now listen, someone will be along any minute so I can't fool around. Where are the cameras?"

Keep stalling, Sarah ordered herself. "What have cameras to do with this tour?" she asked in what she hoped was a calm and reasonable voice.

"Bloody hell. For the last time tell me where you've put those fucking cameras or I'll blow your head off. And, no one in this fucking town will think a thing about it. It happens all the time in this country. Just like home."

"Oh, come on," said Sarah. "You're not making sense. You haven't got a gun. Let's go on down and work this out." Sarah lifted her head and ran an eye over the woman. Her face was almost raspberry from anger—or exertion. Her shirt was sweat-stained and she was hanging over Sarah as if she meant any moment to hurl herself into Sarah's midriff. But no telltale revolver-like bulge showed in her skirt pockets.

"I'm going to count," said the woman, and Sarah knew from the lower register of her voice that she'd heard it before. Heard it in the hallway of the Shearing Inn.

"Hey, wait, hold it." And Sarah took one step down the stairs and moved toward the center of the stairs. The idea of being rammed into the wall was not appealing. But neither was falling hundreds of feet into the piazza. "How about meeting back at the hotel?" she said softly. "See if we can figure out where those cameras have gone." She tilted her head slightly. Footsteps. Heels. High heels. Someone coming down the stairs. Thank God. Only another minute to hang on.

But her companion had ears, too. And she didn't have another minute. She reared back, lowered her head like a bull about to charge, put both fists in front of her body and rose on her toes and launched herself at Sarah.

And Sarah had only time to dodge aside one step and then she found herself grabbed and flung violently back against the wall.

And saw the woman in her full-attack posture become airborne, and hands still clenched, plunge through the space where Sarah had just been. And then down. Down.

Down the steep, cobbled steps. Head-first she plummeted. Step after steep step, one after the other. And now the whole body bunched itself and curled into a grotesque somersault, head bent, it turned over, banged against the wall, hit the next step, thudded into the next one, and rolled heavily to rest at a small paved landing some fifty feet below. And like the sack of laundry clothes it so now much resembled, it did not move.

Sarah turned away gasping. And looked straight into the face of the person whose arm had flung her aside. Whose arm had saved her from the fall she had just watched.

The face and the arm of Jessica Roundtree.

Chapter Twenty-Seven

ALEX HAD NO SOONER seen Sarah climb aboard the bus bound for the Villa Melzi Gardens than qualms set in. He tried to settle to the study of European birds in his field guide, but time passed slowly. Even in the face of Sarah's assurances that she would cling like a limpet to the certified "safe" tour members he felt his qualms deserved more attention than he was giving them. At last he stood up and unfolded the map of Bellagio. Where were these gardens, anyway? Why not just stroll down in that direction?

This moment of indecision was broken by the desk clerk arriving at his table. A call for S. Deane or A. McKenzie.

Alex took the phone in the hall just off the main lobby.

"Hello, Sarah? Alex?" croaked an electronic voice. "This is a terrible telephone. I think it belonged to Marconi. Or do I mean Alexander Graham Bell?"

"Julia! Is that you? If it is, get back here. With Margaret and Edith in one piece. And the car."

"You sound like Mussolini. It must be the Italian male thing. Testosterone in the air. Listen, Alex. Be grateful. Edith and Margaret have explained the whole affair. A lot of tears but now they're feeling better. And they'll fly home tomorrow."

Alex resisted the impulse to pull the telephone out by its roots. Between clenched teeth, he said, "From what airport?"

"I won't say because you and Sarah will come charging down like a couple of bulls in a china shop and upset things. It's all arranged and I've talked to their families."

"For Christ's sake, Julia."

"Don't swear. They'll be met in Boston and driven straight home. I've got to go now. And you should have that Fiat checked. The frame shudders and it's leaking oil."

Alex tried again. "What did Margaret and Edith tell you? It's important, for God's sake."

"I'll tell you when I see you. The poor dears were in her clutches. Blackmail. Goodbye, Alex. You and Sarah be careful."

"Julia!" But the line was dead.

Alex, in a high state of exasperation, returned to his table, drained his cold cup of coffee and picked up his Bellagio map. To hell with being circumspect. He'd just march down and join that blasted tour. Perhaps even announce that Margaret and Edith had confessed everything—since they were safely out of reach—and watch reactions. Let chips fall where they may.

But these heady thoughts were throttled by the entirely too familiar voice calling out *"Buon giorno."* And then, in guidebook Italian, *"Come sta?"*

And next like an apparition from another planet, complete with flowered shirt, navy shorts, gleaming white new Nikes, the broad-shouldered Nordic presence of Mike Laaka.

Alex stared, unbelieving.

Mike, an enormous smile spread over his face, sat down at Alex's table. *"Buon giorno, Alessandro. L'Italia e molto bella."*

Alex confronted the still grinning Mike. "What the hell! You here? Who let you loose? Not George, I'll bet. And make it fast. I want to track down Sarah."

"You haven't let her off by herself, have you?"

"She's with the garden group. She thinks she's got an answer to one of the puzzles and wants to check it out."

"With a Beretta in her hand?"

"It's a safe scenario, believe me. But even so I'd like to be around. Now explain yourself while we head for the tour group." And Alex stood up and headed for the road leading to the town center. Followed by Mike, who was shaking his head.

"No word of welcome for old Mike? Okay, why am I here? Answer, Ellen Trevino's stepfather finally surfaced. Big timber man, lots of cash. We put him in the picture and met with some of the other tour families. The upshot is I've been sent to persuade the whole bunch to move it and then escort them home."

"The sheriff's department has paid your way to Italy?"

"God, no. They wouldn't pay me to go ten miles. Nor would the state police. It's Kevin Webster—Ellen Trevino's stepfather. He didn't see much of Ellen, but apparently was crazy about her. He's in a rage about her being killed. He paid for my ticket after George flunked the job of trying to haul the tour back from France. So here I am. How do you like the outfit? Do I look Italian?"

"You look like an American tourist who got lost on the way to Hawaii. Listen, a lot's been happening. The tour group has shrunk, one of the leaders almost drowned, and Julia's been putting the squeeze on two Hoppers, with the result that they're flying to the States tomorrow. Come on, Mike, step on it." This as Mike stopped to admire the display of baked goods in a *pasticceria*.

And Alex began a downhill jog followed by Mike, both ducking around clumps of slow-moving tourists, dodging the occasional motor scooter, and reaching the shopping mecca of the Piazza Mazzini.

And running smack into Amy Lermatov.

Or to be accurate Amy ran into them. From a dead run she stopped almost under Alex's chin. Her hair, wilder than usual, her face bright red, her eyes wide and scared.

"Dr. McKenzie. Dr. McKenzie. You've got to come."

"Take it easy, Amy. What's the matter?"

"Down the stairs. The whole way. Or almost. And she's dead. Or she looks dead. And there's blood all over the place and her teeth are sticking through her lip, and her legs are bent in a funny way." And suddenly Amy—Amy the tough junior writer of murder mysteries—burst into tears and became a frightened fourteen-year-old girl.

"WHO!" Alex and Mike shouted together.

Amy lifted a tear stained face. "They're all there. Sarah and the ghost woman, Jessica, and Barbara."

Alex grabbed Amy's shoulders with both hands. "WHO FELL DOWN THE STAIRS?"

"Barbara Baxter. She fell almost the whole way. I was down here by myself looking at the shops because I couldn't stand any more gardens. Then I started to climb the steps to go back to the hotel and she almost landed at my feet. And she looked dead, and Sarah and this Jessica came running down, so I thought I'd better tell someone. And get help."

"Show us where," commanded Mike, as Alex broke into a run heading for a sizable crowd at the foot of one of the narrow stairways.

Barbara Baxter was not dead. But she was injured. Badly. And in shock. Sarah had not left the crumpled body. Still in horrified astonishment at the attack, her rescue, and Barbara's fall, she could think of nothing more to do than to grab Jessica Roundtree's shawl, cover Barbara, call out for a doctor and then sit holding one bloody broken hand between her own two hands.

Jessica Roundtree, her long skirts torn, her white hair unraveled, knelt down on the other side of Barbara, checking her pulse, listening to gurgled respirations, but with the arrival of a vacationing Swiss doctor, a Swedish dentist, then Alex, Jessica stood up, stepped to one side, and disappeared into the crowd.

Alex did not immediately reappear at the Albergo Nuovo; he and Mike had followed—in Mike's blue rental Fiat—the ambulance to the hospital in nearby Lecco. Sarah had joined the remnants of the garden tour in an entirely silent lunch. And then everyone had risen and scattered to their rooms. Or went to sit on the terrace and stare at a sky weighted with cumulus clouds and at flashes of lightning that burst over the darkened mountains.

Sarah moved by herself to a cluster of chairs placed under an olive tree. She was certain she would be followed.

She was.

Justin Rossi, in immaculate khaki shorts and a blue tennis shirt. Freshly shaved, a look of resignation on his face. He took a seat beside her. "How long have you known?"

"I'm not sure," Sarah said slowly. "I think it started with Amy. Going on about the ghost in the garden. Before that she said you looked suspicious. Thought you wore a wig. But I looked you over and decided you didn't."

"We all make mistakes," said Justin. "And I think Amy Lermatov should have been at summer camp learning how to pitch a tent."

"Amy's just had a nasty close-up look at the real world. She's quite subdued. But I think it's the McKenzie look-alike business that really got to me. Jessica Roundtree looked so like my mother-in-law, Elspeth, that it sent shivers up my back."

"Mothers-in-law often have that effect," Justin observed.

Sarah ignored this. "Of course, you look like Alex, and Alex looks like his mother, and it seemed unlikely that two McKenzie types would turn up at the Shearing Inn, and then at Sissinghurst giving nervous fits to those ladies from Scotland."

"Go on."

"And then turning up in Bellagio last night in the piazza."

"Three appearances by Elspeth McKenzie."

"Yes, and, of course, Aunt Julia and I were worried because of Ellen being killed, and the Hoppers falling apart and Henry being pushed into pools. We wondered which of you was behind all of it. But I found out Jessica Roundtree was safe. And so was Justin Rossi."

"Detective Inspector Deane?"

"It didn't take much detecting. A tall strong-armed older woman had tossed that Jack the Slitter into the pub room of the Hound and Hare. Stacy Daniel is strong—all that power walking and aerobics—but she never went near that pub. Preferred the Black Badger. And Barbara Baxter isn't what you call tall. But Justin Rossi had been to the Hound and Hare because he mentioned the smoke-filled air. Anyway, Jessica fit the strong older woman description. And today she did another good deed or I'd have probably been in that ambulance on it's way to Lecco. If I happened to be so lucky. End of story, I guess. Except"—Sarah turned to Justin who turned his head slightly away from her—"I do thank you." She touched his hand lightly and smiled.

For a moment both were quiet and then Justin indicated the sky. "We're going to have one hell of a storm tonight."

"Why did you go out in the daytime? Take a chance?"

"I'd seen enough of the Melzi Gardens, and all at once I'd about had enough of Barbara and her thumbscrews. I was going out in the daytime and to hell with it. I wanted to show her that I just didn't give a damn anymore, and if it meant I couldn't practice law—at least not in that stuffed shirt law firm, or maybe in any law firm, well, so be it."

"So she caught you dressed and blackmailed you into carrying hollow cameras around Europe. And the Hoppers. And Stacy Daniel."

"Me, she did. I don't have a clue about what she had on Margaret or Edith. Or on Stacy—unless it was that Stacy can be such a bitch."

"Except Stacy liked Henry—a redeeming quality. But who pushed Henry into the Kiftsgate pool? Into the Epte River at Giverny? Not Barbara. Not Stacy. Did you?"

"God, no. I wouldn't do that. I liked old Toad Ruggles."

"And the real question. Who killed Ellen Trevino?"

Justin ran his fingers through his short black hair—the Alex gesture that had unnerved Sarah. "I did not. And I don't have the least idea who did. Barbara never told me exactly what she was up to. Just be in certain towns and certain places and hand over the camera to some designated person. Who would take something out of it. Believe me I never looked into the camera. I didn't want to know what I was passing around. Just hoped to hell it wasn't drugs. Call me an ostrich. Or a bloody coward."

Sarah thought of the mugging scene. Had Stacy been involved, perhaps keeping watch in the hall? "Did Stacy work with Barbara?"

"Could be. I just don't know. I'd say ask her, but I'm not sure it's safe to mess with Stacy."

Sarah nodded. She listened to another rumble of thunder and saw another streak of lightning knife across the mountain tops. Then she returned to Justin. "I've got two more questions. Do you have a mother and a sister? And do you buy clothes for them?"

"A devoted mother. No sister. I buy clothes for Jessica. Not Mother. She's only a size eight."

Sarah smiled over at him. "And are you by any wild chance related to any McKenzie?"

Justin gave her an answering smile. A wry one. "We're all related, aren't we? Down from Adam. Or," he added, "from Eve."

It was late afternoon and the sky had gone from being slightly threatening to distinctly ominous. Mike and Alex, having grabbed a quick lunch after leaving Barbara Baxter in an intensive care unit at the hospital in Lecco, were now headed back to Bellagio to tie up the last loose ends.

"Too many loose ends," complained Mike.

"I think she'll make it," said Alex. "Internal bleeding is under control. In fact, after they stabilize her, set the fractures, she should be able to travel in a few weeks."

"With a serious escort," said Mike. "George will probably try to have her extradited."

"On a charge of murder?"

"For assault—to begin with. But Barbara qualifies—time and opportunity—for the murder. And the police have finally tracked down the car Barbara rented—the one that was wrecked and sold for parts. The lab's found fiber and hair matches on the upholstery."

"But motive? Did she attack the other tour leaders—Ellen and Henry, and possibly Lillian Garth—in order to change the tour schedule to hit designated cities and sell some mystery contraband in hollow cameras? With the help of brother Gregory?"

"Gregory's got to be the key. You said you had a list of things Sarah and Julia overheard at that dinner and some of it rang a bell. Run through it for me. Maybe a bell will ring for me."

Alex reached into his pocket and pulled out the sheet of paper. "I swear I associate some of this with an old uncle of mine and a magnifying glass sitting at a desk. But he died when I was five or six and it's just one of those shadow memories."

"Read it," urged Mike.

And Alex read. Hawaii, handcrafts, Confederate States, auction. Big bucks, no postal insurance. Lloyd's canceled. Theft. Rotary, black inverted center, perfect condition, polypro film..."

"Hold it," yelled Mike. "Did you say inverted center, rotary? Hey, buddy, I've got it. Hear that? I've got it. What stupid shitheads we are. Or you and Sarah are. And Julia. Jesus, isn't that a cute little operation. Big bucks is right. Hey, Alex, I've gone and beat you on this one. You just didn't have a proper boyhood. And I did. I got a Boy Scout badge for it."

"Okay, okay, spit it out. And does my uncle's magnifying glass fit in?"

"Does it ever." Mike stamped on the gas, whirled into the road for Bellagio and chortled. "Stamps, you idiot. Itty-bitty stamps that are so valuable, so easy to hide, and so easily swiped that even registered mail isn't safe. Lloyd's paid up once too often and doesn't want to insure the stuff anymore. Stamps are great big bucks. A Hawaiian envelope with two U.S. stamps and two Hawaiian Missionary stamps went for over two million. An auction in New York at the Robert A. Siegel Galleries. Besides, I get this stamp magazine, *Linn's Stamp News* and you should read about the stealing that goes on. Listen, I still collect stamps. Nothing very valuable, mostly U.S. stuff, but I've some nice old stamps from Finland."

"And I thought horse racing was your thing."

"That's my outdoor love. I do stamps on cold winter nights with the snow raging outside my window. I'm versatile. Everyone has these secret things. Julia plays the piano and Sarah snoops and you chase after birds." Suddenly Mike twisted his head around as a rather battered limousine with the inscription AEROPORTO writ large on its flank, slowed and crowded the blue Fiat.

"Bugger," said Mike turning his car toward the road's edge.

"Not bugger," said Alex peering at the faces behind the glass. "Stacy Daniel. I think. Beautiful woman, one of a kind."

"Hey," shouted Mike, slowing the car, "we want her."

"I don't think you can do a thing about her now. Just get to the hotel, call, and try to block her at the airport."

Mike sighed. "I don't have any authority for that. And I doubt George can crank up the international machinery in time."

The telephone call, as Mike predicted, produced nothing of substance. George Fitts, a man not given to four-letter words, used several to no avail.

Mike did not return immediately to Alex, who was left prowling about the lobby. But when he did he wore a wide smile that radiated satisfaction. "Good news and bad news," he announced.

Alex gave him a sour look. "I can only imagine bad news and bad news."

"Come on out on the terrace," commanded Mike. "Away from flapping ears."

Settled in a far corner of the terrace surrounded only by empty chairs and a trellis laden with small yellow roses, Mike unburdened himself. "Bad news. We can't nail Stacy Daniel. Not yet. She can't be charged with anything so far and even George back in the States can't pull off one of those airport scenes you see in the movies."

"You can find out what flight, where it's going, can't you?"

"We can and we will. Now, you want the good news? Stamps is it. What I said."

"How do you know? You've just been guessing."

"Listen to Detective Laaka. He's been working hard. While we were at the hospital and you were playing doctor, I took a look at Barbara's clothes. They were dumped in a heap on a chair outside the ER. Found a key in her skirt pocket and, since it had a number and the hotel name on it, I decided to keep it. Not that I don't trust the Italian police but this is a hometown matter."

"Go on," growled Alex. "So you went up to her room just now."

"Making sure the management had its head turned. And you guessed it, I found stamps."

"In a camera!" exclaimed Alex.

"Keep your voice down," said Mike. "Not in a camera, fitted into Barbara's writing case. Tucked into lined envelopes—between the lining and the outer paper. A nice selection of Confederate States issues. Nashville and New Orleans. And a couple of cuties from Hawaii and Guam, plus a couple of beautiful mint-condition Colombian issues. Something for every budget. And we're talking budgets well over a thousand bucks."

"God, what did you do with them? The stamps, I mean?"

"Put 'em in the hotel safe. Under my name. Soon to be flown home and handed over to George Fitts and his merry men." Mike rose from his chair and stretched. And yawned. "Busy day," he remarked. "Okay, is Sarah joining us? A night on the town before I gather up the garden lovers and take them home."

"Under lock and key?"

"If only. But when we make it home the DA is going to hit at least two of them—no, add the Hoppers, that makes four—with being accessories to fraud, robbery, and God knows what else."

"Accessory to murder?" Alex asked, quietly.

Mike shrugged. "We'll see, but I'm sorry Stacy's off into the wild blue yonder. She's got quite a background. Did I tell you?"

"Tell him what?" It was Sarah. As if prepared for a party: dark hair brushed smoothly, small gold shell-shaped earrings in her ears, wearing her green silk dress.

Alex eyed her. "New?"

Sarah touched her ears. "A prescription for depression. I feel like the weather—about to blow up. Or come down. Spending a little money seemed to help. After I'd talked to Justin I decided to walk around town, look into shops. See Bellagio as a place to visit, not the scene of a crime. Also I bought these." Sarah reached into her handbag, produced a narrow white box and drew out a chain made from twisted strands of gold.

"It's for your mother," she told Alex. "Somehow I feel I owe her something, although I can't exactly say why."

"Nice," said Alex. "But don't ever try and explain it to her."

"So, okay," said Mike. "Tell us about this guy, Justin. What has the Legal Eagle been up to? Is he part of the camera scam? I only know the Hoppers were in on it and so was Stacy."

"At dinner," said Sarah. "At some little *ristorante* with a large menu and a view of the lake. Let's go before the storm hits. And I've had a call from Aunt Julia. She's not coming back here and wants to meet us in Milan tomorrow. I'm to pack her things. But she did squeeze it out about the Hoppers." She shook her head. "It's quite sad, but I'm hoping that someone—the Maine police or some kindly old judge—will have a little mercy."

"So what is it?" demanded Alex. "Julia wouldn't tell me."

"Give," said Mike.

"Over the antipasto, I will," said Sarah and headed for the door.

Chapter Twenty-Eight

THE RISTORANTE ANGELICA, standing two-thirds of the way down the winding stone stairs of the Salita Serbelloni, was an establishment whose best feature was a roofed terrace giving a wide view of Lake Como. And because a rising wind had ruffled the now gray lake into whitecaps and thunder growled at the very gates of the town, the terrace was almost deserted.

"Privacy," announced Sarah. She indicated the roof overhung by a profusion of red flowers. "And we won't get entirely wet."

"Only struck by lightning," said Mike, unfolding his napkin.

There followed the serious business of ordering in a mixture of confused Italian, shreds of French with a base of English: Mike chose the *lasagne verdi* because the name was familiar; Alex, crab with cheese; and Sarah, chicken with asparagus tips. All begun with antipasti and the recommended table wine—*vino da tavola*. "At least," Sarah had said, "I guess the waiter's recommending it. He keeps sticking that carafe in our faces."

"His brother probably owns the vineyard," said Mike. "That's the way it works back home. Family backscratching."

After early hunger had been satisfied, and the storm had for the moment settled into a low snarling, Sarah put down her fork and returned to the subject of Stacy Daniel—for her, the least loved member of the tour party—Barbara Baxter excepted.

"Stacy," said Mike, "wasn't Stacy. That was about name number five. George worked through a heap of names, jobs, identities. Had to go out of state and dig around."

"And," prompted Sarah.

"Stacy was a sort of child crime prodigy. Drugs, rehab, kid hooker, junior pimp for a teenage prostitution ring. But she was pretty sharp at getting out of things. Youth home, couple of suspended sentences, assault charges dropped because not enough evidence. Name changes when necessary. But then, about six years ago, when she was about twenty-two, she pulls up her socks and enrolls in a community college."

"She found God?" queried Alex. "Or a good man?"

"Or a good woman?" put in Sarah. "Never underestimate the influence of a good woman."

"Actually, a good job," said Mike. "Modeling. She is, as you've noticed, quite a dish. Well, she pulled herself together, picked up a few contracts for sports ads and women's catalogues. Then hit the magazine covers. Made enough money to fund college tuition. Business major—accounting and personnel management. Honors degree. Then a year of grad school. A few years go by, and bingo, there's Stacy Daniel, publicity director for Back Bay City Bank, which has a bunch of branches in and around Boston."

Sarah put down her empty wineglass and Mike reached over and filled it. "And Barbara knew all this about Stacy?" she asked.

"That's Barbara's specialty," said Mike. "To know things about people. Dig dirty secrets out of the woodwork."

Alex nodded. "This is one case that doesn't make sense if you try to start with Ellen's murder."

"Yeah," Mike agreed. "Usually you begin with the homicide and branch out from there. But poor Ellen Trevino was just one obstacle—another wrench in the works. Barbara's works."

"What works, for heaven's sake," demanded Sarah.

"First," said Mike, "you tell us about Justin Rossi—Alex's rival—and about the Hoppers. Then I'll put it together for you. Though you did it yourself when you and Julia listened in on the Gregory-Barbara dinner scene. No, wait"—this as Sarah seemed about to explode—"George isn't here to force us to be logical, so I'm taking his place. I feel very George-like. So what did Barbara have on Rossi?"

"She caught him dressed up."

"Dressed up? Like for a party? You mean undressed?"

"Dressed. In a dress. He cross-dresses. It's what he does. His quirk, his hobby. What makes him feel good. He brought some women's clothes in store boxes and added to the wardrobe in High Roosting. In fact, I helped him buy some of the things. For his sister, he said. Only he hasn't got one. But Barbara found out a few years ago. He went on one of her art tours to Hawaii—the tours are legitimate, but I suppose they're also apart of Barbara's operation—the operation you're going to tell me about. Anyway, she caught him in drag—maybe in a grass skirt for all I know. Well, he was a great target for blackmail. A lawyer who's a member of a super-conservative Boston law firm, a lawyer whose specialty is family law. He swears he didn't know, didn't want to know what he was passing around in those cameras. And he says he had nothing to do with killing Ellen or dunking Henry. I really believe him. He's the woman who took care of Jack-the-Slitter at the Hound and Hare back in High Roosting—judging from the description of her. Besides, he saved my life—or my bones today," said Sarah. She grinned at her husband. "And anyone who looks like Alex must have redeeming qualities, even if he's been dealing in hollow cameras."

"Thank you," said Alex. "Saying nice things like that is what warms a marriage. Now the Hoppers. I could have wrung Julia's neck for not telling me."

"Julia took Edith and Margaret off to this little B&B overlooking Lake Lugano and calmed them down. I give her full credit for once in her life not acting like a Tyrannosaurus."

"Does this tie in with the information the police dug up about some sealed records pertaining to the Hoppers?" asked Mike.

Sarah nodded. "The first thing to know is that the Hoppers have never had much money. Their parents struggled and times were tough. So one day before Margaret's eleventh birthday when their parents had told her not to expect much in the way of presents, they went shopping. And Margaret came home with a new watch. And that began it. The sisters worked as a team and every now and then simply lifted little tidbits. Gloves, junk jewelry, handbags, perfume, cosmetics—they adore Lancôme products. They didn't do it too often, never at the same store twice in a row."

"Kleptomaniacs?" asked Mike.

"No. Not compulsion. They liked nice things and didn't have the money to buy them. They only got caught once, but the judge was friendly, the evidence wasn't clear—they'd dumped the stuff—and they were such upstanding members of the community that the charges evaporated and the records were ordered sealed. That's it. Until Barbara Baxter—who has the eye of a raptor—saw Margaret lifting a pair of gloves in Cirencester. And added the Hoppers to the camera distribution team."

"Something I'll bet Barbara regretted," said Mike.

"Two worse operators I can't imagine," said Sarah. "Just because they were good at shoplifting didn't mean they were ready for the big time. And they were so humiliated at being caught and so afraid of it all coming out and so nervous about pretending to take pictures and meeting agents that they simply went to pieces."

"They're well over seventy," said Alex. "What's their future?"

Mike shrugged. "Depends on a lot of things. Good defense lawyer, mitigating circumstances, willingness to cooperate with the DA's office and testify about Barbara. If it comes to trial those two ladies would look pretty pathetic on a witness stand. They'd have the jury in tears. I'll bet they end up with some sort of suspended sentence. Rossi might not fare so well, but then he's a lawyer himself. He may find a loophole."

The waiter arrived with three little dishes of strawberries covered with cream and looked meaningfully at the waterfront. *"Tempesta,"* he announced.

Sarah following his glance saw that the lake surface had gone from gray to dark slate. "Five more minutes and then I think we'll have to evacuate. Or find an ark. So, go on, Mike. You're driving me crazy. What *was* in those cameras? I've thought of everything from cocaine to radioactive diamonds. Or miniature folk art made entirely of eighteen-caret gold."

"None of you had the proper childhood hobbies," said Mike. "It was stamps. Valuable rare stamps. The sort that are impossible to find unless you're a millionaire or you steal 'em."

"Stamps?" repeated Sarah stupidly.

"Alex told me Gregory dealt in southern crafts. That was his cover. Baxter Enterprises. But he was dealing in stamps. Moving them out of the country, passing them to agents all over the map, I suppose. Confederate stamps are very desirable if they're in good condition. And if he'd got his mitts on a collection of Hawaiian missionary stamps, well, the prices for those have gone through the ceiling. As have the prices for early U.S. issues. We're talking thousands and thousands of bucks. As soon as Alex said 'off center' and 'polypro film'—that's the stuff used to protect them—I was pretty sure what Gregory and sister Barbara were up to."

Sarah's eyes widened. Suddenly she remembered Gregory after dinner. Talking about his business. Smiling his smooth, deep voice explaining, "We do a lot with paper artifacts. In as mint condition as possible. Perfect condition counts for a lot. From the south. And Hawaii." And that those were his special areas.

"What a slime!" exclaimed Sarah. "He told us right to our faces." She looked up into Mike's face. "You've got proof?" she asked.

"Genuine proof. Made a little visit to Barbara's hotel room a while ago and looked in her writing case. Beautiful stamps tucked into the lining of the envelopes. Made my eyes bulge."

"Her Crane writing paper!" exclaimed Sarah. "And I only thought she liked to write expensive letters."

"The rest of her so-called helpers used cameras," said Mike. "You don't need a lot of space for stamps. Just a safe container. Gregory or Barbara probably picked up cheap or used cameras and gutted them."

Sarah speared a strawberry with an angry thrust. "I never guessed. And old cameras are everywhere. The Good Will shops. Yard sales. Everyone wants new models and they dump the old ones."

"Harmless-looking tourist types traveling with a camera," said Mike, "aren't questioned by airlines. Put those cameras through X-ray, let 'em be sniffed by dogs and they're clean. Tourists *without* cameras are conspicuous. As for the others on the trip, Barbara probably recruited them to carry the stuff. Help with the distribution."

"Not just to carry stamps in cameras," put in Sarah. "Those assistants acted as a back-up chorus. All those tour changes Barbara suggested—London, Cirencester, Cambridge—her assistants, Stacy, Justin, and later the Hoppers supported her. Of course, Sandi and Fred helped out innocently because they were always up for a side trip. Both Ouellettes are more tourists than garden lovers. But some of those assistants were less than ideal help. Justin floated around at night in drag—Julia said Barbara chewed him out once, so maybe she caught him as Jessica Roundtree. Then there were Margaret and Edith red-eyed and trembling like leaves."

Mike grinned. "You just can't get proper help these days."

"Of course," Sarah added, "I noticed that Justin and Stacy didn't take pictures in the gardens. Only in the cities, where I suppose they met their assigned contact. And, of course, Margaret and Edith were hopeless. That scene on the bench in Cambridge, pretending to take pictures of trees. Really. But the Hopper cameras were new, weren't they? Not old yard-sale models."

"Barbara just said the cameras were new. Margaret and Edith wouldn't know what a state-of-the-art camera looked like. They'd been using twenty-year-old Kodaks," said Mike. "The cameras probably all looked okay."

"Margaret and Edith," repeated Sarah. "The poor dears."

"Those poor dears," said Mike with a noticeable lack of sympathy, "have apparently been operating on the wrong side of the law for years." He raised his wineglass. "Now, let's skip the rest of the crap and have a good time. Here's to a terrific dinner."

"No, wait," said Sarah. "What about Ellen? And Henry?"

"Come on," said Mike, "you can figure that one out."

But before Sarah could answer lightning split the skies, the thunder crashed, the wind swept down on the town, on the streets, the houses, the shops, the restaurants, café umbrellas down along the piazza folded, the rain spattered on the terrace roof and blew through the open sides over the dinner table. The candles flickered and expired and for a moment time stood still.

Sarah, Alex, and Mike moved back against the far wall and watched the storm work its will. Watched tree branches thrash, vines tremble, and, most wonderful of all, saw lightning in double and triple streaks play across the mountains, strike into the lake, zigzag back over the rooftops, and skewer a distant clump of trees.

And then, grumbling, muttering as if in high dudgeon at being recalled, the storm retired again behind the mountains. The rain shrank to a small patter and the wind softened and turned away.

And somehow, the storm had not only cleansed the heavy air, it had cleared away the patches of fog in Sarah's brain.

The three found the waiter, paid the bill—"millions and millions of lira," marveled Mike—and began the climb up the wet cobblestones of the Salita Serbelloni toward their hotel.

"It's all coming together," said Sarah. "Poor Ellen was killed because garden tours aren't like ordinary tourist tours. The kind Barbara had been leading. The kind where she was the boss. She could do what she wanted with her own groups."

"That's right," said Mike. "Up to this Midcoast Garden Club thing, she handled all tour details. Set the convenient—convenient to her—itinerary, changed reservations en route if she had to, and no one argued with her about where to stay, when to leave. She knew enough about art galleries and museums, the southern states, about Hawaii—she was born there—to give satisfaction. Knew her way around South America. So the tours must have worked on two levels: legitimate sight-seeing and undercover to move stolen stamps to agents and dealers who had clients salivating for certain issues. Gregory was chief, Barbara his field commander."

"And then," said Sarah, "Barbara comes smack against a tough co-leader, Lillian Garth, who adds another strong-minded expert—Ellen Trevino. Later, of course, Carter fills the gap with another expert, Henry Ruggles."

"So," said Alex, "Barbara pushes Lillian down the cellar stairs—by turning off the light—if she did. You may never prove it because Lillian doesn't remember. Typical for head traumas."

"But next," said Mike, "there's Ellen. Barbara saw her three days before the trip and Barbara undoubtedly found that Ellen had a mind of her own."

"Yes," said Sarah. "Barbara would find out fast what Ellen told me. The trip was entirely serious and there weren't going to be any tourist deviations. No fancy restaurants, no shopping excursions, no daytime pub visiting. The schedule was sacred."

"Remember," Mike pointed out, "Ellen mentioned to Mrs. Epple, her neighbor, about a meeting, seeing a friend, going to check on something. Well, it looks like Barbara was ready for her. Either by prearrangement, or she trailed Ellen into a turnpike rest stop. Came prepared to kill and covered the rental car seats with a plastic tarp. Maybe brought a gun but then found the dibble among Ellen's gardening tools. Wore a slicker to protect against blood spattering and put on that head scarf and the dark glasses so no passing tourist will get a good look at her."

"So," said Alex, "since Ellen is a trusting soul, Barbara, at some point, talks her into sharing the ride to Logan. Maybe Barbara goes to a phone booth to make a fake call and then tells Ellen she's arranged to have her car picked up and so they can travel in her rental."

"So," put in Mike, "Barbara loads Ellen's luggage into her car. But we haven't found the car or the luggage."

"Wait up," shouted Sarah. She came to a halt in front of a shop announcing "La Lanterna—Snack Bar." A great light had suddenly broken. "Barbara brought that big suitcase. She tells us to travel light, then there she is at the Logan with this monster. Like mine. I thought hers must be filled with her tour stuff, guidebooks, and garden folders. But then she dumps it in Vernon and has the gall to say I should dump mine, too. But I did notice that even with a big suitcase she only seemed to have a few changes of clothes. Always in that plum cotton thing. Because—"

"Because," broke in Alex, "her suitcase didn't hold clothes, it held Ellen Trevino's luggage. Ellen probably did travel light. A carry-on and a briefcase. And Barbara could just fit them in a big suitcase along with a few of her own personal things and the suitcase flies to Heathrow on Barbara's ticket."

"If I were pulling this off," said Mike, "I'd empty out Ellen's stuff as soon as possible. Put it in storage. Or deep-six it. In London, maybe? Barbara wouldn't want to take the chance of someone opening her big suitcase. Someone like Sarah."

"Who went snooping into everyone's room at the Shearing Inn," said Alex in a disapproving voice.

"The big suitcase was in her room," said Sarah. "I unzipped it and it was empty. And Barbara's clothes were in her bureau."

"Okay, she must have dumped Ellen's things by then," said Mike. "George can ask the Metropolitan Police in London to check out storage units. The hotel the group stayed at. Bus stations, train stations. Heathrow."

"Or the Thames," added Sarah. She resumed the walk and then, as they reached the glistening wet pavement of the Via Garibaldi, stopped a second time and faced the two men. "Some other things don't make sense. Why was Barbara's room ransacked at the same time mine was? And who pushed Henry in the Kiftsgate swimming pool? Not Barbara. Or even Stacy. And last, why did Barbara give Henry CPR at Giverny when he was one of the tour people she was trying to get rid of?"

"Think. Both of you," said Alex.

"Well, I don't get that part at all," admitted Mike.

But Sarah was remembering. She returned to her ravaged bedroom at the Shearing. Listened again to Barbara's voice saying, "You, too." Then heard Barbara insisting that Sarah and Julia inspect her own room. That perhaps the same person had ransacked both.

"We were set up, she wrecked her own room," said Sarah, shaking her head. She walked ahead a few steps, turning her thoughts to Henry. Excitable, talkative Henry. Never looking where he was going. Who stumbled. Tripped over his own feet. "I suppose," she said, reluctantly, "that Henry simply fell in the Kiftsgate pool. A genuine, honest-to-goodness accident."

"Which gave Barbara the idea," said Mike.

"But," protested Sarah, "what about resuscitating Henry? There she was giving him CPR, really working him over."

"How hard do you suppose she would have worked if you hadn't shown up and then the French doctor?" said Alex. "And it's possible that she didn't have to drown him, just waterlog him, damage him. See that he quit the group. Which is just what happened."

They had reached the gate of the terraced garden of Albergo Nuovo. And, as if by agreement, the three friends walked down to the lower level and stood facing the lake—

now a dim wrinkled expanse set under the dark outlines of the mountains.

"My first night in Italy," said Mike. "And my last night, too. So much for foreign travel. Well, it hasn't been dull."

"I suppose," said Sarah, "I'll look back on some of the trip as not being entirely awful. There were moments."

"Like tonight," Alex reminded her. "The storm."

"And some of the gardens, the roses, the wisteria, the red valerian, Sissinghurst at night. Monet's farmhouse and the lily pond. The drive to Bellagio. I'd like to come back."

"So let's," said Alex.

Mike yawned. "What do they call it when you go through a lot of time zones? I feel a little groggy."

"You'll feel worse back home tomorrow night," said Alex cheerfully. "It's called double jet lag."

"Hey," said a voice. A remembered voice, one noted for breaking into moments of quietness and peace.

"It's me, Amy," said Amy materializing from behind a clipped hedge. "Mother said I could stay up late because it's my last night here. As long as I stayed here in the garden. And, Sarah, I have this new idea for a book. Not a modern murder mystery. Those are gross. This is going to be an Italian romance thing. Here in Bellagio back in the sixteenth century with poisoned wine, and someone being killed because he owes moneylenders, and lovers hanging over balconies, and families having feuds and duels and ghosts of dead fathers haunting their sons."

Alex walked over to Amy, took her by the shoulder and pointed her toward the hotel terrace. "Good night, Amy. *Arrivederci. Ciao.* Go to bed. Your story has already been written. It's called *Romeo, the Merchant of Hamlet.*"

Afterword

ENGLISH TEACHERS WHO ARE both mystery novel addicts and fans of the nineteenth-century novel appreciate an ending. Or closure, as it is popularly called. Sarah Deane was no exception, so five days after the evening of the Bellagio storm, she and Julia Clancy and Alex, forces joined, sat together on a soft June evening on several lawn chairs overlooking a distant pasture. The pasture belonged to the Dodgeson Farm, the very place where the Clancy-Deane English experience had begun. Where Julia had considered adding Suffolk Punch to her stable. Where Sarah had become agitated about an alien scarf and a pair of sunglasses. And where Julia today had chosen as a place for the three to decompress before they had to take up everyday life.

The three, however, had been busy communicating with the world at large and with the police world in particular.

Barbara Baxter, Alex informed them, would be ready to be flown home under guard and, although she had not admitted to murder, she had talked at length about the business of transporting stamps in innocent-looking containers. She had balked at first, but it had been pointed out that her best interests lay on the side of the truth. Further, her cooperation was motivated by her fury when she found out that brother Gregory had taken off from Bellagio and...

"Hold it," said Sarah. "How did he get to Bellagio? And how did he know Barbara had been hurt?"

"Gregory," said Alex, "along with Barbara, got the wind up when you and Julia turned up to sit in on their restaurant dinner in Vernon. He decided to trail you to Giverny and follow you across France. See if he could ditch you or, worse, get rid of you."

Sarah turned pale. "The gray Peugeot."

"Since he didn't catch you, you must have been driving like fiends from hell." Alex looked at the two women with lifted eyebrows. "Then," he went on, "Gregory made for Bellagio to check on Barbara, found she was in the hospital, and took off for points unknown, leaving her—in gang talk—to take the rap. Barbara claims that Gregory planned everything, including the elimination of strong-minded tour leaders. She blames him for Ellen's murder and said he masterminded the disposal of Ellen Trevino's body at the Biddeford Maine Turnpike exit. That she, Barbara, was horrified, and was just along for the ride."

Sarah shook her head, her expression grim. "There was no Gregory around when Lillian Garth fell down the cellar stairs or when Henry went into the river at Giverny. And judging from her expression when she came at me on the steps at Bellagio, she was more than capable of driving a dibble into poor Ellen Trevino."

"Barbara's trying to sing. Or squeal. Isn't that what gangsters do?" asked Julia. She had returned to her equestrian scene needlepoint with renewed vigor and was engaged in driving her needle back and forth through the knee of a rider.

"They don't sing anymore," said Sarah. "That's passé. Now I think they rat on each other. In this case I think we have two large rats and some lesser ones."

But Julia had other news. "I talked to Portia McClure. The McClures are back home, but they left Toad Ruggles doing well. He had a touch of pneumonia but he's better and is staying with Leslie and Harold to recuperate. Remember Thalia Cottage, Sarah?"

"How could I forget? Calpurnia and Julius Caesar."

"Portia reports that Leslie and Harold are being very attentive, and she hopes Henry doesn't drive them crazy making suggestions about their garden."

"How about Margaret and Edith?" asked Sarah, turning to Alex, who had just finished a long call to Maine.

"In good hands. A family lawyer and plea bargains in the works. They may be able to keep their past activities fairly quiet because Ellen's murder and the Baxter Enterprise scam are really the attention getters."

Julia looked up from her needlepoint. "What about that unpleasant Stacy Daniel? You and Mike saw her heading out in an airport limo?"

Alex nodded. "She beat it out of Italy, flew to Lisbon, and jumped on a flight to Amsterdam, where she was met by the local police. Which, in due course, is what will happen to Gregory. He's said to be holed up in Switzerland. And Ellen's luggage has finally turned up. Her passport, her wallet, and any other I.D. had been dumped somewhere, but the duffel and briefcase came to light in a utility closet in that hotel on Ebury Street—you know, where the group stayed the first night in London."

"But why the delay?" demanded Sarah. "Why didn't the hotel people call the police right away when they found the luggage?"

"Because," said Alex, "when she got to London Barbara made out new luggage tags for Ellen's bags, and since Ellen's briefcase had the initials E.T. stamped on it, she had to come up with a matching name."

"Are you going to tell me the hotel people thought they were entertaining an extraterrestrial visitor?" asked Julia.

Alex grinned and shook his head. "You won't believe this but Barbara came up with one name that stopped the hotel cold."

"I'll bite," said Julia, pulling her wool too tight and bunching the stitches on a rider's head.

"Elizabeth Taylor," said Alex with satisfaction. "When the luggage was found, the hotel people had a sort of collective seizure, but because no one had reported Miss Taylor missing, the manager decided she'd been staying incognito at the hotel and wouldn't be pleased to have the police called."

This information was sufficient to bring about total silence, and for a few moments the three sat quietly watching the pasture scene. Sarah saw that the two chestnut horses—the Suffolk Punch—were moving toward the gate. It must be feeding time. She and Julia had really come full circle. Tomorrow they'd have to drive to Heathrow and fly home. Full circle was right. The airborne panic, sweaty palms, and having to recite "Sam McGee."

"Alex," she said. "Don't you have a real knock-out pill? So I'm completely out of it until we're back on the ground."

Julia smiled her all-knowing smile. "Sarah, calm yourself. I have solved your flying problem. You may rest easy tonight."

Sarah looked at her aunt doubtfully. "You have?"

"Yes. I have talked to the DA's office and we've a period of grace for our depositions. And Alex had already cleared the rest of this week and his back-up agrees to cover for a few more days."

"Aunt Julia, you're not making sense."

"Don't interrupt. You and I and Alex will not be going to Heathrow. I'm giving myself a seventy-first birthday present ahead of time. We will drive to Southampton and there climb aboard *The Queen Victoria*—that new Cunard cruise ship. Sister to the *QEII*. On it we will cross the Atlantic, not fly over it."

"You mean we're going by boat?"

"Or a ship. Ship is the preferred word."

Sarah got up and threw her arms around her aunt's neck. "Hallelujah. We don't have to take off and look down from thirty thousand feet and then circle over Boston for hours. You've made me very happy."

"And," added Julia, with a sidelong glance at her niece, "only a few icebergs have been reported on our route."